EQUILIBRIUM

EQUILIBRIUM

Darin Miller

DARIN MILLER
WRITES

This is for those who like it
a little darker.

The little boy who
hid behind the living room sofa to
watch Night Owl Theater
is alive and well…

TABLE OF CONTENTS

Since the dawn of time, the world has remained in a fragile state of equilibrium. Forces of good seek to vanquish the tyranny of evil on global stages both big and small. It is a war that is hard fought on many simultaneous fronts, each side racking up its wins and losses in a constant struggle to remain in this pendulous state.

For without one, the other ceases to have any real meaning.

What you are about to read is but one such story, set in the not-too-distant past.

The year was 2000, and the world was only just beginning to believe that Y2K wasn't the actual End of Days. Rest assured, when that dark day inevitably arrives, it will be without warning…

PART ONE

AWAKENINGS

CHAPTER ONE

I

Lisa Mitchell was tired. Months of selfless servitude had brought her to this half-existence. She worked long shifts at Morgan Township Hospital five days, sometimes six per week, sponge-bathing, feeding, and monitoring the bedfast before heading home to put in another several hours caring for Nanna Grace. Exhausted was a distant memory, replaced by something far closer to zombified.

If only Nanna Grace would just die.

The guilt flooded Lisa's cheeks crimson, and tears stung at the corners of her eyes. Nanna Grace had always been so good to her. Nanna deserved more than a death wish from an ungrateful orphan who had been fortunate enough to find shelter with the kindly woman when no one else wanted her. If Nanna were to die now, it would be Lisa's fault. The thought shouldn't have even been creeping around in her mind, and yet there it was, occasionally surfacing of its own accord. It didn't matter how many hours Lisa had to clock; she owed the old lady at least that much. Consciously, she knew this, but the subconscious is a tricky little bastard, giving voice to thoughts both awful and inappropriate.

Lisa put the last of the dinner dishes in the drainer and wiped her hands on the red-and-white checkered towel lying on the knife-scarred countertop. Perspiration matted her honey-blonde hair, trickling through her ponytail to dampen her neck. It was nearly ten o'clock on this sweltering summer evening, and the only rest that Lisa had taken all day was done sitting behind the wheel of her fifteen-year-old Toyota, driving to and from work. She allowed herself a moment to sit at the rickety card table in the center of the kitchen, close her eyes, and think about absolutely nothing.

Thump! Thump! Thump!

Nanna Grace didn't have the strength to walk—she didn't have the strength to do much of anything—but she was still able to wield her hand-carved mahogany cane with brute force. The sound reverberated through the floorboards, making the overhead lighting fixture dance on its cheap chain.

"LISA!"

There wasn't anything wrong with her lungs, either.

Lisa clenched her eyes and prayed for strength. She didn't want Nanna Grace to see her at her worst. It wouldn't be fair to take her frustrations out on the old woman. Nanna might even have a heart attack.

For an instant, Lisa smiled.

Thump! Thump! Thump!

3

"I'm coming, Nanna!" Lisa called from the bottom of the stairs. She went back to the counter and poured a cup of tea. Nanna Grace functioned like clockwork. It was teatime, and tea would now be served. Lisa returned the teapot to the stovetop and turned off the flame. Nanna never wanted more than one cup of tea, and Lisa couldn't stand the stuff herself.

Thump! Thump! Thump!

The persistence of the cane distracted Lisa, causing her to shift her gaze to the stairs when she should have been watching what she was doing. Her right hand swept the cup of tea from the counter, down to the floor where it exploded into a million tiny ceramic fragments. The scalding brew spattered across Lisa's left foot and ankle, and she screamed out loud from the pain.

"*LISA!* What's goin' on down there?"

Lisa shook her burnt little bird leg like a cat who stepped in something undesirable, willing the pain into something more manageable before she began cleaning the mess. Nanna would be furious. The cup had been one of her mother's, handed down from generation to generation. Its pieces were small and scattered; the cup was beyond repair.

Lisa felt tears stinging the corners of her eyes, but she bit her bottom lip and forced them back from where they came. She collected the cup fragments and deposited them in the wastebasket beside the ancient refrigerator. She poured another cup of tea and tiptoed toward the stairs, keeping the cup level, its contents contained.

"I'm on my way, Nanna," Lisa called, hoping to avert another angry outburst from the walking stick.

She reached the top of the narrow little staircase and paused. Her bedroom, small and pink, was through the door to the left. Lisa wanted to put the teacup down and sneak into her room, lock the door and slip into her comfortable twin bed. *Let Nanna bathe herself.*

Lisa was immediately mortified by her own thoughts. Nanna hadn't been able to do such seemingly simple tasks in a very long while. Her bones had become brittle, her arms thin and undependable. Where there had once been a robust woman, hearty and hale, all that remained was a rapidly withering shell, betraying its host at every conceivable opportunity. Lisa found it almost physically painful to watch. Nonetheless, she turned right instead of left and paused only long enough to take a deep breath before entering Nanna Grace's room.

A single forty-watt bulb strained vainly to push back the shadows from the attic bedroom. The room was small, its ceiling low at each end. Nanna Grace's bed was centered under the roof's apex. The old woman couldn't weigh more than eighty pounds, unable to make even a substantial dent in her pillow. Her snow-white hair, once coiled and coiffed, now leapt from her head in angry defiance of the laws of gravity. She rested under a heavy, mustard-yellow comforter, her back propped upright by pillows. The air reeked of incontinence, something which Nanna Grace insisted did not afflict her.

"'Bout time," Nanna muttered, reaching a spindly claw for the steaming teacup.

"Sorry," Lisa said, looking down at her feet. "I had to get your tea ready."

"You had to break one of my damn cups."

"No," said Lisa. "I just made—"

"Don't tell me fibs," the old woman snapped. "I heard it go—*WHAM!*—to the floor. Why you wanna make it worse by tellin' fibs?"

Lisa's bottom lip trembled. "I'm sorry, Nanna. I didn't know what to do. I was afraid—"

"'*I was afraid*,'" mimicked Nanna, fixing Lisa in one of her patented death glares. "Child, you've spent the better part of your time on this planet bein' afraid. *Truth*. That is the only liberator."

Lisa was chewing on her lip subconsciously. "I'm sorry, Nanna," she said, her voice but a whisper.

"That was my mama's china," Nanna reminded.

"Yes, Nanna."

"It *meant* something to me."

"Yes, Nanna."

"You wouldn't know nothin' 'bout nothin' like that, though, wouldja, child? You don't have no little keepsakes, do ya? Remind me about that later, will ya girl? I want to give you something to remember me by when I'm gone. But 'til then, let's get my bath."

"Yes, Nanna," said Lisa, shuddering. She slid a hand behind the frail woman's jaggedly bony shoulders and another underneath her beanpole legs. With no measurable degree of effort, Lisa hoisted Nanna Grace from her bed and carried her to a recliner in a corner of the room. The recliner was upholstered in a tacky but washable plastic, ideal for sponge bathing without spoilage. Dr. Fenkel, Nanna's doctor, recommended a shower chair, but there was no showering facility on the premises. Nanna Grace didn't indulge in such extravagances. No air conditioning, internet, or answering machine. According to Nanna, it was all electronic evil.

Lisa performed her nightly ritual, washing the fragile woman with a soft washcloth and a pan of warm, sudsy water. She never made contact with Nanna's eyes during the process, choosing instead to watch her own hands. Lisa hoped to never reach this stage of personal disrepair. Better to be hit by a bus at thirty than to live to one hundred as an incompetent, incontinent shadow from the past.

Lisa's pale skin shined with perspiration as she lifted Nanna back into her deathbed. "How are you feeling tonight, Nanna?" she asked.

"I'm dying. How do you think I feel?"

Lisa's eyes darted around the room, fiercely determined to avoid Nanna's piercing, ice blue stare. "I'm sorry. I just wondered if you were comfortable."

The old woman snorted, sipping her cold tea. "How can I be comfortable? There's so much dust floatin' in the air, I feel like I'm buried already."

"I just dusted yesterday," Lisa said.

"Well, girl, you didn't do a very good job. You can't just hit surfaces. You have to *move* things. Are you going to shortcut everything in life?"

"No, Nanna."

"See that you don't! I want you to spend the next two evenings giving this house a thorough cleaning."

"Yes, Nanna."

"Change the filter in the furnace, too. Probably ain't been done for a while, has it, child?"

"No, Nanna." Lisa's voice was the whisper of a mouse.

"Stop dawdling."

"Yes, Nanna."

Lisa backed toward the door, grateful to be on her way. Nearly out, nearly clear...

"Girl!" Nanna barked.

Lisa jumped visibly. "Yes, Nanna?"

Nanna set her tea down on her nightstand and pulled open the drawer where she kept her cotton handkerchiefs. Her twisted, arthritic hand extracted another ceramic teacup and offered it to Lisa. "Go on, girl. Take it. Be more careful next time. It's my mama's good china, you know."

Lisa reached for the cup, her timid hand shaking. "I'm sorry, Nanna," she whispered. "I didn't realize that I left a dirty cup in your room."

"Quit fussin'. You got plenty to do, and I need my sleep."

"Yes, Nanna."

Lisa backed out of the room and closed the door behind her. She descended the stairs with the china cup held carefully in her hands. The teacup puzzled her. Lisa's was a routine carved in stone, and every morning, she collected the empty cup from the previous evening's teatime before leaving for work. She didn't recall any deviation from this routine.

Once in the small kitchen, she pulled open the cupboard door and began counting the cups. Nanna Grace's treasured china collection was comprised of twelve full place settings—dinner plates, soup bowls, saucers, teacups as well as a gravy boat and various other presentation pieces. There were nine cups on the shelf. The dish drainer held one, and Lisa had broken one. Including the one in her hand, there were twelve cups.

But Nanna still had one at her bedside, making the count thirteen.

Lisa peered into the trashcan by the fridge. Food waste, old newspapers, and junk mail. The remnants of the cup were gone.

6

ll

The pretty, dark-haired girl's face went from confusion to shock as she dove for cover behind the elegant sofa. The bundle of bound pages that had been thrown at her flapped like a demented bird across the set before crashing into the backdrop, damaging the drywall.

"That little bitch is stepping on my lines!" shrieked Crystal, her picture-perfect features tinted angry red.

The dark-haired girl, an sixteen-year-old contest winner named Paula, peered over the back of the couch. "I didn't mean—"

Crystal stormed across the set, an exquisitely manicured fingernail threatening the integrity of the young girl's eyes. "I *know* what you were doing, you little wannabe! Let's get something straight. *I'm* the actress. *I'm* the one trained for this job. *You're* the one who is literate enough to have completed an enrollment form. *You're* the one who was lucky enough to have your name drawn from the proverbial hat!"

Marshall Dawson inserted himself between the two women. "Crystal, darling, Ms. Haversham is only in this one scene. She's not trying to steal your thunder—"

"The hell she isn't! She wants to be the next Crystal Bright!"

"Honey," Marshall said soothingly. "There's only one Crystal Bright, and that's *you*."

Someone in the darkness behind the cameras muttered, "Thank God."

Crystal's eyes glowed like coals. She stood at the edge of the set, peering into the void. *"Who in the hell said that?* I want a *name*. Was it you, Howard? Monty? *Rick?* When I find out, you'll wish you never met me."

"We already do." Another nondescript voice floated in.

Crystal shrieked and kicked over an end table, its Tiffany lamp exploding into tiny, multi-colored fragments on the floor. She stormed off the set and down the hall to her dressing room. People scattered as if Godzilla was bearing down on them, no one brave or stupid enough to get in Crystal's way.

Paula Haversham was still squatting on the floor behind the couch, sobbing uncontrollably at having provoked her idol's rage. Marshall sighed and massaged his temples. Crystal was becoming more and more of a problem. *Benny and the Girl* had been a summer replacement series two-and-a-half years ago. Good writing and charismatic performances had built an audience slowly—but not too slowly, thank God. The networks barely gave fledgling shows a chance anymore. If a program didn't immediately draw ratings, it would soon find itself in a different time slot every week. Often enough, viewers who might have enjoyed the show grow weary of the mad scavenger hunt and tune out. Fortunately, this had not been a problem for *Benny and the Girl*.

The show was Marshall Dawson's baby. He had created it with his life partner, Sam Novak, and had been allowed creative control in regard to casting. He had insisted upon two unknowns for the leads. Blake Jagger had been cast as Benny, a hard-working, good-looking trash man. It was not too far from the truth. Blake, whose real name was Bill Josten, had been working as a mail carrier when Marshall spotted him playing basketball on the court with a group of buddies. Shirtless and in shorts, the dark-haired mailman had riveted Marshall's attention, hypnotizing him as he sank a handful of impossible shots and blocked countless others. Marshall had no lascivious intentions when approaching Bill—he had Sam at home. But he couldn't deny the powerful attraction that this man exuded. He knew immediately that the hot young stud had the right look for the part, if only he could *act*. As it turned out, the gods had been very kind to Marshall in that regard, as well.

The female lead had been much more difficult to cast. Marshall had seen countless preening bimbos parade through his offices, pushing their tits across his desk, futile though it was, while he evaluated their résumés. Crystal Bright— formerly Crystal Williams of Lucasville, Ohio—was discovered at a Bloomingdales in North Hollywood, peddling women's shoes. Marshall was picking up a suit he had left for alterations and had been drawn by an animated conversation Crystal was having with a fellow employee. Her face was flawless, her figure perfection, her voice tinkling music. She effortlessly commanded the attention of everyone in her presence, and Marshall noticed how most passersby paused to see the source of the upbeat chatter and laughter. Her magnetism was almost a tangible thing. She was undoubtedly the center of attention everywhere she went.

What had differentiated Crystal from a zillion other aspiring actresses was the genuineness of her beauty, and the heartfelt laughter which was like improvisational music. Her chestnut hair accented her startling blue eyes, eyes which twinkled with mischief. She was undeniably The Girl for Benny. She had been auditioning for various roles since arriving in California six months prior, but short of being cast as an extra in a Grade Z schlockfest—and inevitably ending up on the cutting room floor—Crystal hadn't worked in her desired profession to date. Change was in the air on that fateful and fortuitous afternoon.

The name changes were a necessary part of the business. Williams and Josten simply didn't pack the punch of the new surnames, and in show business, presentation is *absolutely everything*.

Blake Jagger was a wonderful surprise, absorbing stage direction and dialogue like a thirsty sponge. If he was aware of his extreme good looks, he was neither conceited nor apologetic. He seemed to instantly grasp the concept that fame is a fleeting thing and should be savored while it lasts. With the success of *Benny and The Girl,* now in its third season, Blake's bank accounts had grown proportionally, but the young man was far too frugal to squander his money. He hired a reputable accountant and kept a careful eye on him as well, never comfortable with leaving his entire financial status in the hands of a third party.

Crystal Bright started her career on the right foot. The show had begun filming in early summer that first year, all members of the cast and crew feeling the magical chemistry that had been building during readings and dress rehearsals. Crystal and Blake had an instant personal rapport, but not a romantic one. The aftermath of such a relationship could tear a show apart before it even found its legs—Marshall had seen it happen more times than he would care to admit during his twenty years in the biz. Crystal was not only punctual but always early for rehearsals and tapings, helping other cast members with lines and blocking.

Sadly, within the last year, Crystal's attitude had derailed like that of an overly precocious three-year-old. It started with *People* magazine's assertion that she was The Sexiest Woman Alive. Movie offers began rolling in, staggering sums of money offered for her mere presence in truly awful celluloid nightmares. Her agent, Billy Ball, was exceptionally greedy and had talked her into appearing in what was supposed to be 'a trendy little horror flick.' The movie was to be filmed during a hiatus from *Benny and the Girl.* The critics had howled, mercilessly ripping her to shreds in their cruel reviews. It was the first real taste of Hollywood ferocity that Crystal had ever experienced. In short order, she fired her agent and replaced him with a high-powered shark named Vinnie Corona. Vinnie's client roster was very impressive, and Crystal was destined to be the jewel in his crown.

Star power is an incredibly addictive thing, and only a select few working actors seem able to avoid the common pitfalls associated with it. Marshall had always worked behind the scenes, never experiencing this glory for himself. He had, however, seen countless people evolve from hard-working, well-mannered individuals into self-important, egomaniacal monsters. A true superstar can strike a balance between the two, offering a public persona that is both interesting and scandalous, while treating this persona as if it were just another role that must be played. Actors who actually *believe* their press clippings have a propensity to become unmanageable.

Crystal's subsequent on-set tantrums were constant fodder for the national gossip rags, and she had already driven two regulars to quit the show. Fortunately, they had been insubstantial supporting characters who could easily be recast. Marshall feared the day when Crystal decided that Blake wasn't good enough to work with her—and he was certain that that day would inevitably arrive.

In Marshall's opinion, Crystal had tainted her unique beauty by bleaching her beautiful brunette hair a ghastly shade of pale blonde. Fortunately, he *had* been able to intercept her before her breasts and lips had been enhanced by one of Hollywood's countless plastic surgeons. As with most entertainment contracts,

Crystal's agreement stated that she must clear any dramatic changes to her physical appearance with Marshall before she could proceed. The hair had been an act of defiance, the breasts and lips more a sign of the times. In any case, Marshall hadn't been in the least amused. He had warned her that he would slap her with a breach of contract suit if she proceeded, and for a frightening couple of days, he was certain that she would do so if only to irritate him. Fortunately, good common sense, good legal counsel, or some combination of the two had prevented her reconstruction. Marshall felt that it was her natural beauty which had made her so right for the role of Chloe (The Girl), and so accessible to women in that all-important age demographic. There was no doubt that Crystal was impossibly beautiful, but she wasn't another cookie-cutter Barbie, and Marshall was certain that a large part of her appeal was due to this.

Marshall noted with despair that Crystal was entering a new phase in her tumultuous career, The Jealous Stage. Crystal was barely twenty-two, but she already felt the pressure to stay young and beautiful. Adolescent, nubile guest stars were often perceived as threats, but today's envious rampage was completely off the charts. Paula Haversham had won an inconsequential walk-on role by entering a network sweepstakes. The coveted prize included a single line of dialogue delivered during a less than critical moment of the episode. Crystal's extreme reaction had been paranoid and delusional. She had *no reason* to fear this shy Midwestern girl.

Marshall sighed again and returned his attention to his idle crew. "We're going to go ahead and call it a day." The weary crew began to grumble and disperse— anything to get away from the all-too-frequent histrionics of Crystal Bright.

Paula dried her pretty eyes and tentatively approached Marshall. "I'm very sorry, Mr. Dawson. I didn't mean to wreck the filming."

Marshall's smile was warm and gracious. "Ms. Haversham, you did nothing of the sort. Sometimes Ms. Bright is—sometimes Ms. Bright can be—" He couldn't find the words to apologize for Crystal.

"Oh, it's okay," Paula said, her warm puppy eyes round and completely starstruck. "She's the *star* of the show. I'm just blessed to be in the same *room* with her." She smiled and retreated, leaving Marshall alone with his thoughts as the stage lights were extinguished one by one.

CHAPTER TWO

I

"Paging Lisa Mitchell, paging Lisa Mitchell. Extension 403, please."

The receptionist's voice on the intercom was like warm, liquid butter, unobtrusively floating from one corner of the hospital to the other.

Lisa was on her hands and knees in a woman's lavatory on the second floor, scrubbing rust stains from the basin of a toilet. Her perspiration-soaked brow knitted with concern as the page registered in her brain.

Maybe Nanna Grace died.

It was always the first thought that came to Lisa's mind whenever she heard her name ringing from the hospital's intercom. More likely, a patient had gotten ill and soiled his bed sheets.

Lisa washed her hands and exited the bathroom, stopping at a wall phone mounted several feet to her left along the sterile white corridor. She pecked out the extension and held the phone to her ear, praying for the blessed news that Nanna had finally seen fit to depart from her withered and diseased old frame.

"Ms. Kelsey's office," the saccharine voiced receptionist cooed.

"Um, hi. This is Lisa Mitchell. I was paged?" Lisa cringed at the sound of her own voice, high-pitched and timid, audibly quavering.

"Ms. Kelsey would like to see you immediately."

Lisa grunted in response and replaced the receiver. What could Ms. Kelsey want? The hospital administrator was renowned for her icy demeanor and the purposeful distance she kept from her employees. She was difficult to satisfy, impossible to ingratiate and blessed with a wicked temper to boot. No employee wanted to be called into her office. It was never good news.

Lisa traversed the busy corridor slowly, one foot in front of the other, counting her footsteps and willing time to stop. Patients were wheeled by, bathrobe-clad sickies on their way for another battery of humiliating tests. An old man in an aqua-green hospital gown hobbled down the hall with the assistance of a walker, oblivious to the fact that his gown was flapping open in the back, his bare white ass exposed for all the world to see. Lisa elected to concentrate on her feet, glancing up only occasionally, so as not to knock anyone down.

Maybe Nanna Grace died.

The thought persisted. Hard-ass or not, Ms. Kelsey surely wouldn't render such tragic news over the telephone. It was a glimmer of hope, shining brilliantly in the gloom that was her life. Resultantly, her pace quickened. Not much. Just a little. Dead Nanna Grace or not, no one in their right mind would be in a hurry to see Ms. Kelsey.

It wasn't that Lisa *hated* Nanna Grace. Heavens, no. The woman had raised Lisa as if she were her own daughter, taking her into her home when she was only a child. Lisa couldn't remember a time before Nanna Grace, even though she was seven when Nanna had taken her in. Blank spaces caused by empty days. She didn't know who her birth parents were and had never been inclined to pursue the issue. She didn't think Nanna was a blood relative, but she couldn't be sure. They were nothing alike, neither physically, temperamentally, nor spiritually. Nanna was stoic and direct, God fearing and minimalistic. Lisa had these qualities thrust upon her, unable to go to high school dances or even watch television like all her friends—well, not so much friends as classmates. Forced to attend church three times a week. Lisa wasn't permitted to be a social butterfly. She hadn't even been permitted to be a social *housefly*. Oh, but how she had wanted those things—and still did. Despite the enormous guilt accompanying the thought, Lisa knew that liberation was one dead Nanna away.

She reached the end of the corridor and stopped abruptly. The administrative offices were to the left and just around the corner. Was it too much to hope this might be the reason Ms. Kelsey had summoned her? Lisa reflected for a moment. Was there any reason she should fear speaking with Ms. Kelsey? Not that she could think of. Lisa was punctual and her work output, while maybe not the fastest, was above reproach in terms of quality. Surely Nanna must be dead.

Lisa took a deep breath and rounded the corner. She entered the gray carpeted reception area and closed the heavy wooden door behind her. Roxanne Carson, icy cool receptionist for Ms. Kelsey, languidly perused a document on her desk, never bothering to lift her gaze or acknowledge Lisa's presence. If anything, her pace slowed, a perfectly manicured fingertip tracing lines of text as she followed along. Lisa stood at the corner of the desk like a withering dandelion, waiting for the first good breeze to blow her away. She waited for Roxanne, afraid to disrupt the receptionist's concentration.

Roxanne's sigh was long and slow, bored and bothered. Her brown eyes flicked disapprovingly up at Lisa and one sculpted eyebrow arched exaggeratedly. "Can I help you?"

Lisa opened her mouth and squeaked like a little titmouse. Her left hand flew up to stop the sound from making an encore. Her eyes widened like she had eaten a bug, and she felt embarrassed heat pulsing through her face with each heartbeat.

Roxanne sighed again. "You are?"

"Lisa. Lisa Mitchell." The voice of a little girl.

"Oh," said Roxanne, reaching for her telephone.

It was only one word, but the inflection with which it was delivered left no room for doubt—whatever the purpose of this summons, it was bad news.

12

"You can go in," said Roxanne, cradling the receiver. Her attention had already returned to her desktop project.

Involuntarily, Lisa straightened her uniform and checked her hair, making sure that no crazy strands had escaped the bun in which it had been securely pinned. She took a deep breath and strode purposefully toward Ms. Kelsey's door, determined to get this whole thing over with.

Please let it just be that Nanna is dead.

She rapped lightly on the door before twisting the handle and stepping inside. Ms. Kelsey sat like royalty behind an enormous cherry desk, her patrician features fixed in a permanent scowl, her long, bony fingers interlocked on the desk pad in front of her. She had short, salt and pepper hair, very tidy and kempt. It reminded Lisa of her high school gym teacher, Ms. Dixon. The girls had affectionately referred to her as Ms. Dykeson. Lisa wondered if Ms. Kelsey liked girls.

"Ms. Mitchell," Ms. Kelsey said, her voice flat and wooden. "Please have a seat."

Lisa perched on the edge of one of the two guest chairs which were positioned in front of Her Majesty's throne. The chairs were cheap and uncomfortable, in sharp contrast to Ms. Kelsey's plush red leather butt rest.

"Is there a problem?" Lisa asked, her voice still foreign and out of key.

The corners of Ms. Kelsey's mouth moved back in what may have been intended as a smile, but instead reminded Lisa of a wolf baring its fangs. "Mr. Sexton will be down in just a moment. We'll talk then. Would you like some coffee?"

Mr. Sexton was the head of Human Resources at the hospital. Lisa shared twenty minutes per year with the man, sitting across from him while he dispensed yet another impersonal critique of her job performance before handing out an insignificant raise and sending her on her way. Lisa was pretty sure the man wouldn't be able to recall her name without the aid of her personnel file in front of him.

Why would Mr. Sexton be coming to tell Lisa that Nanna Grace had died?

Lisa realized that Ms. Kelsey was still waiting for a response to the question about coffee. She didn't trust her voice not to crack, so she opted to nod her head instead. Ms. Kelsey picked up the telephone on her desk and asked Roxanne to bring in two cups of coffee. She covered the mouthpiece and asked Lisa, "Cream? Sugar?"

Lisa shook her head. "Cream and sugar are gluttonous."

Ms. Kelsey gave her a funny look before returning to the phone. "Yes, Roxanne, I'll need one cup black for Ms. Mitchell, and mine as usual—" Her eyes locked onto Lisa's. "—with cream and sugar."

Lisa could feel herself blushing again, this time the heat radiating to the tips of her ears. "I didn't mean—"

"It's all right, Ms. Mitchell," said Ms. Kelsey, but her tone indicated her observation had been noted.

Lisa decided it would be best to keep quiet until Mr. Sexton arrived. If she didn't speak, she wouldn't be able to put her foot in her mouth. Fortunately, she didn't have long to wait. The door opened and the silver-haired administrator entered the room, followed by a graceful, coffee-dispensing Roxanne.

"Would you like some coffee, Mr. Sexton?" Roxanne asked, batting her eyelashes and cooing at the senior executive.

"No, thank you." His speech was clipped and businesslike. He wouldn't be staying long enough to drink coffee—how long does it take to tell you your Nanna is dead?

Roxanne gave Lisa a knowing, pitiful look before backing out of the room. *She feels sorry for me*, Lisa thought. *She knows about Nanna*.

Mr. Sexton crossed the room and stepped behind Ms. Kelsey, resting his administrative bottom on the cherry credenza behind the desk.

Lisa, who could not tolerate another second of the uncomfortable silence, said, "Is it Nanna?"

Ms. Kelsey exchanged a puzzled look with Mr. Sexton then pulled a file folder from a stack on the corner of her desk and positioned it in the center of her blotter. "Nanna? Would that be a patient?"

Lisa sighed, disappointed and slightly exasperated. "No. My Nanna is very ill. I thought—" Lisa's voice trailed off as Ms. Kelsey made a note in the file. "What's that?" she asked, indicating the folder.

Ms. Kelsey cleared her throat and refocused her attention on Lisa, ignoring the girl's question. "Ms. Mitchell, you are familiar with a patient of ours in Room 315, a—" She consulted the file. "—Mrs. Baylock?"

Lisa nodded her head. "I change her linen. Wash her up. She's very sick, you know. I don't expect she'll live much longer."

Ms. Kelsey made another scribble in the file. "Why would you say that?"

"She's very old."

"Seventy isn't what I would call old."

Lisa sighed again, frustrated that she couldn't find the appropriate way to convey what she meant. "Look at her. That's all you have to do."

"I don't think I understand."

"The spirit's gone out of her eyes. She doesn't *want* to live any longer."

Ms. Kelsey's pen was active again, and Lisa felt tension rippling up her spine and spreading down to her clenched fists. Mr. Sexton remained silent, observing the conversation unobtrusively.

"You know that it's not up to us to determine," Ms. Kelsey advised.

"Oh! Of course not! I'm not saying that *I* think she should—I just mean that *she* thinks—" Lisa said.

"How would you know what Mrs. Baylock thinks?"

14

"We talk. I talk to everyone I work with. Some of them don't even have families."

"Still, did Mrs. Baylock ever indicate that she was ready to pass on?"

Lisa was confused. What was the purpose of this interrogation? Mrs. Baylock was one of several patients who had been hospitalized for an extended stay. She was a good patient, too, complying with direction so Lisa could get her job done most effectively. Some of the dirty old bats who were brought in thought that Morgan Township Hospital was some kind of resort, with employees like Lisa available to fulfill their very specialized needs. Why all the focus on Mrs. Baylock?

"Well, not in so many words, I don't suppose," Lisa answered, then added, "But you can see it. In her eyes. *Look*."

Ms. Kelsey shook her head and regarded Lisa with pity. "Ms. Mitchell, I'm going to get to the point. We've been having complaints about you."

"Me?" Lisa's eyes widened with disbelief.

"Several of our patients have complained about your obsession with death and the unsettling comments that you seem to always make—well, like now, when you told me that you didn't think that Mrs. Baylock would live much longer. No one wishes to be reminded of their mortality, Ms. Mitchell," said Ms. Kelsey. "Especially during a lengthy hospital stay."

"Obsession with death? Me?" Lisa reflected over her various conversations with patients. She couldn't swear that the topic had never come up, but it wasn't as if that was the only thing she ever talked about. Ms. Kelsey was making her sound unbalanced.

"That in itself would be troubling," Ms. Kelsey continued. "But combined with Mrs. Baylock's injuries—"

"Injuries?" Lisa was a mockingbird, selectively latching onto points of Ms. Kelsey's commentary.

"Mrs. Baylock says that you are very rough when you bathe her."

"Rough? No, not rough. Thorough, maybe, but *never* rough."

Ms. Kelsey's eyes narrowed. "That isn't what she says."

"Well, then she's lying!" Lisa said, surprised at the strength in her own voice. "She's very old, you know. She might be senile."

"She's not senile."

"How do you know? When was the last time *you* saw Mrs. Baylock?" Lisa countered, able for the first time to meet Ms. Kelsey's cold steel gaze.

"She's got bruises."

Lisa fell silent. What was Ms. Kelsey implying? "I don't understand," she said.

"Ms. Mitchell, the patients are afraid of you. They are afraid to be left in your care."

"I don't understand."

15

Ms. Kelsey closed the file folder and folded her arms across it. "Let me be blunt, Ms. Mitchell. Mrs. Baylock was prepared to file suit against the hospital as well as report your actions to the police."

"The *police?* That's ridiculous! I didn't do anything!" Lisa protested.

"That's not how Mrs. Baylock sees it. She didn't have anything more concrete than bruises, but I think a jury would find her sympathetic."

Lisa was beginning to understand. Mr. Sexton was acting as a witness on behalf of Ms. Kelsey, protecting the hospital's legal rights should this conversation need to be repeated in the context of a courtroom setting.

"What are you saying?" Lisa asked.

"The hospital has no choice but to consider you an extreme liability. We are asking for your resignation."

"You can't! I need my job!" Lisa cried. "I won't do it. You can't make me, and neither can that lying old woman!"

"Either you resign, or we'll be forced to let you go. If you choose the latter, you should be aware that Mrs. Baylock will press charges against you."

"But *why?* I didn't do anything *wrong!*"

"I've seen the bruises myself, Ms. Mitchell. What you've done is reprehensible," said Ms. Kelsey, her disgust evident.

"I didn't *do* anything!"

"The best I could do was strike a deal with Mrs. Baylock. She says that she will not press charges if you voluntarily leave your position. The choice is yours, but either way, you'll not be caring for any more patients at our hospital."

Mr. Sexton remained perched on the credenza, expressionless, observing. Lisa's eyes searched his face for any trace of compassion, but he was no ally. Spineless bureaucrat.

"What am I going to do?" Lisa asked.

"Again, let me be blunt," said Ms. Kelsey. "If it were up to me, charges would be filed against you, the police would arrest you, your face would be all over the evening news, and you'd never work in healthcare again. Unfortunately, there's no way to do that without publicly exposing the hospital's liability. Lawyers would beat a path to Mrs. Baylock's door if they thought she might retain them to represent her. As it happens, Mrs. Baylock is a very kindly woman and doesn't wish to cause any trouble. She's afraid of you and wants you out of here. If we honor her wishes, she'll release the hospital from any future litigation concerning the matter."

Lisa was dumbstruck, her jaw hanging open like a defective gate. Ms. Kelsey spoke with such intensely personal hatred, yet she barely knew Lisa. She assumed the old gasbag was telling the truth without ever offering Lisa an opportunity to defend herself. "I didn't do anything," she said, meekly.

Mr. Sexton finally broke his silence, rising to his feet. "If you'll please collect your things, Ms. Mitchell, I will escort you from the premises."

16

Lisa let herself be led from the room by her elbow, hot tears streaming from her eyes. Why, oh, why couldn't Ms. Kelsey have simply told her that Nanna Grace had died?

II

"Where are we going?" Crystal asked, her body angled away from Marshall to peer at the dilapidated city buildings passing by the passenger window.

"There's someone that I'd like you to meet," said Marshall, turning his SUV left at the next traffic light.

"You've *got* to be kidding me, Marsh," said Crystal exasperatedly. "I wouldn't let my dog walk through this neighborhood. I hope to goodness we aren't stopping anywhere around *here*."

"Hey, you're just along for the ride, right?"

Crystal brooded. "We should have security."

"Oh, for heaven's sake, Crystal. Would you relax? You're with me."

"Big comfort."

"Thanks."

Crystal sighed, looking at Marshall. She really did owe so much to the man. She would never forget everything he had done for her. But he didn't understand the pressures of superstardom. He didn't understand the constant public scrutiny, flashbulbs bursting out of nowhere to capture every intimate moment, every moment that appeared intimate, and every moment that could be Photoshopped to look intimate. Hair had to be perfect. One strand out of place, and Joan Rivers would be all over her on her nasty little fashion show. Clothing and style were vital, as well. Crystal was a trendsetter. Every move had to be strategically orchestrated for maximum effect. Friends and long-lost family members came out of the woodwork like bloodthirsty carnivores, ready to tear anyone apart who came between them and their dear, sweet, rich and famous Crystal.

"I'm sorry," she said quietly.

Marshall grinned sideways at her. "S'okay."

"So, where are we going?"

"I want you to meet a former client of mine from my days as an agent," he said. "Well, I guess she still sort of *is* a client of mine. I keep her on mostly out of sympathy. She's not in very much demand anymore."

"Some friend who wants an episode of *The Girl?*" Crystal asked, immediately suspicious. She had begun referring to her television series as *The Girl*, poor *Benny* unmentioned and irrelevant.

"Not at all."

17

"What then? You can't tell me that you dragged me out to this Godforsaken hellhole just for my company," she said. "Good Lord! What if the tabloids were to get photos of me down–*here?* I'd never be able to hold my head up again."

"I'm sure you'd find a way," Marshall said dryly.

The buildings bore graffiti and fluorescent gang symbols sprayed onto their grimy red brick façades. Teens in enormously baggy pants worked the streets, scoring and selling, hanging with their homeboys. The Hispanic population was high, as was that of the underprivileged elderly, people of different nationalities, heritages, and ages mixing uneasily along cracked city sidewalks. Crystal regarded the whole scene as if she had smelled something foul.

Marshall didn't even seem remotely affected. Of course, he was over six feet tall and in better condition at forty-two than he had ever been in all the years before. He didn't appear to be an easy target, and maybe that discouraged muggers and other thugs—Crystal didn't know. She herself was a petite and fragile flower, guarded almost around the clock by a hired entourage who could make the Secret Service look like amateurs. Rarely did she dismiss her security force, but she trusted Marshall implicitly—or at least she did until this afternoon.

Marshall parked at the curb of a brownstone tenement. Teens littered the stairs leading to the lobby door, rap music blaring from bass enhanced portable stereos. Their attention was immediately riveted to Marshall's maroon Lincoln Navigator, eager eyes wondering what part of the vehicle might be easiest to remove.

"What in the hell are you *doing?*" Crystal demanded. "Don't stop here!"

"We have to stop here," Marshall said. "This is our destination."

"Well, *I'm* not getting out of the car," said Crystal, crossing her arms and settling back defiantly into her seat.

"Fine," said Marshall, switching off the ignition and releasing his seat belt. "Stay out here. I'm sure you'll be safe."

Crystal's head whipped around, her eyes widening with fright. She reached out and grabbed Marshall's arm. "You can't just *leave* me here!"

"Well, then I suggest you come along." And he was out of the vehicle, shutting the door behind him. He crossed around the front of the hood and opened the passenger door. "Are you coming?"

Crystal mulled her options for a moment, not liking any of them. Reluctantly, she descended from the relative safety of the passenger compartment and clutched Marshall's arm with white knuckles. "We're never going to get out of here alive," she muttered.

"MARSH! My man!" A teenaged wannabe strutted up to Marshall, ghetto clothes hanging from his bony frame. "How you been, Jack? Ain't seen my boy in a long, long time."

"Stu," said Marshall, smiling at the youth. "Checking in with the old lady. You keeping an eye on her?"

"That bitch is *crazy*," Stu said. "She keep comin' down and makin' a fuss, and she gonna get herself popped."

"That's why I need you to keep an eye on her."

"Yeah, bro, right. I do what I can."

Marshall smiled. "Thanks, Stu. See what you can do about keeping my Lincoln in one piece, huh?"

"Yeah, yeah," said Stu, waving Marshall away.

Marshall led Crystal up the narrow stairs to the building's entrance and held the door open for her. The foyer smelled of booze and urine in equal parts. Hung from the ceiling were gloomy, low wattage bulbs encased in globes which revealed a graveyard of flies through their translucent surfaces. Crystal pulled tight against Marshall's side, trying to disappear entirely into his shadow.

"He didn't even recognize me," she muttered.

"What?" Marshall asked, leading her to the stairway on the left side of the foyer.

"I said, 'He didn't even recognize me.' How can that be possible? I'm ranked highest in demographics with teenage boys."

"Some teenage boys don't watch TV."

"Oh."

They passed the landing of the second floor and went on to the third. The once regal burgundy and gold carpeting had worn over time, giving the interior the look of a faded photograph. Crystal pressed so close against Marshall that she almost caused him to trip.

"For heaven's sake, Crystal," he said. "Are you trying to kill me?"

"I could ask the same of you," she countered. "So, who is this client of yours?"

"Vida Leon."

Crystal searched her memory but came up with nothing. "Should I know her?"

"Probably not," he said. "She was a big star in the late forties, early fifties."

"Well, she couldn't have been *that* big of a star. I've never even heard of her."

"Oh, there was a time when you would have. Long before I was her agent, of course."

"So why do you keep her on?"

Marshall shrugged and knocked on the door of Apartment 3K. Music from *Oklahoma* was playing too loudly from the other side. Marshall knocked again, more sharply this time. The music abruptly halted, and footfalls approached.

"Whozit?" The voice was broken glass and barbed wire.

"It's Marshall, Vida."

"Oh! *Marsh!*"

Tumblers began turning as deadbolts retracted and soon the door swung inward. The woman who answered the door was not at all what Crystal had expected. She was in her late sixties but looked ninety, overweight and obscured by layers of heavy and inappropriate makeup. Judging from her demeanor and aroma, she was also drunk as a monkey. The frizz that was left of her hair had been bleached the color of straw, pink scalp showing clearly through the locks. Her smile revealed unsettlingly perfect dentures, bright red lipstick smeared across the two front teeth like a skid mark.

"Vida," Marshall said, taking the old woman's extended claw. "You look well today. I've brought someone I'd like you to meet."

"Oh, certainly, certainly," she said, stepping back to allow entrance to the apartment. They crossed the threshold, Crystal still wary and sticking close to Marshall's side.

"This is Crystal Bright," said Marshall, indicating Crystal. "She's the female lead in the series that Sam and I developed, *Benny and the Girl.*"

"Mmm?" Vida said. "You'll have to speak up, dear. The hearing's gone, you know." She turned her gaze toward Crystal and recognition lit her features. "Oh! You're that pretty girl on Marshall's show! Aren't you sweet! Look a little thin, but I know how that camera can add a pound or two. You wouldn't *believe* how I look onscreen, darling. Oh!"

Crystal smiled politely then looked expectantly toward Marshall.

"Uh, well, Vida," said Marshall. "I did need to discuss some business with you—if you're up for it."

"Business! *Oh!*" Vida's eyes sparkled. "Did the Purina ad come through? *Oh!* How about the grandma? Am I the grandma? *Oh!* Tell me, Marshall! Tell me!"

"No, Vida, I'm sorry, it's not good news."

"Mmm? It's not?"

"No, I'm afraid not," Marshall said. "Dryzies pulled out."

"What?"

"I'm afraid that Dryzies has elected not to renew your contract." Dryzies was an adult diaper, designed to protect clothing for the bladder impaired.

Vida's eyes misted over, and she walked unsteadily to a small yet well stocked wet bar. Once there, she helped herself to a large tumbler of straight bourbon. "Why?" she croaked. "Didn't I *pee* good enough?"

"No, Vida, nothing like that," said Marshall. His voice was soft and gentle, trying to deliver bad news with grace. "They were able to sign Rita Malloy—"

"*What?*" Vida said, sloshing her drink as she suddenly turned to face Marshall. "*Rita Malloy?* Will I *never* be rid of that damned harpy?"

Marshall turned to Crystal. "Rita is an old rival of Vida's. They've been competing for parts longer than you've been alive."

"Well, then, *what?* What am I supposed to do, Marshall?" Vida asked, lighting a cigarette and taking a deep drag with a shaky hand.

"Well," said Marshall, "there's still the grandma part. It hasn't been cast yet."

"What about Purina?"

Marshall looked away.

"Oh, *great!*" said Vida, slamming her glass back on the counter. "What the hell?"

"They just went in a different direction is all," said Marshall. "But I did bring your Actor's Union subsidy for this month. That should tide you over for a while." He withdrew an envelope from his inside jacket pocket and offered it to Vida. Her mouth was frozen open, her words cut off by the desire for the check inside the envelope. She snatched it from Marshall's hand and ripped it open.

"Oh! This will be fine," she said, approving of the dollar amount. She then returned her attention to Marshall. "But don't you let them give that grandma part to Angela Lansbury. *Do you hear me?* I'll run her down in my car, I swear to God—"

"You'll do nothing of the sort," said Marshall. "I'll let you know if I hear something. In the meanwhile, I'll keep my eyes open for other possibilities for you."

Vida smiled, revealing her unsettlingly perfect teeth. "You're such a dear, Marsh. You stop in again. Oh! And *you!*" She tugged at Crystal's sleeve as Crystal looked completely taken aback. "You stop by anytime. Maybe you can work me into your show. Does your character have a mother? I'd make a great mother. Or if you need something older, I could be the grandma. Dammit, I *want* to be the grandma. Obviously, I would have to wear a lot of makeup—"

"I assure you," Crystal said icily. "*No one* would believe that you and I were related."

"Oh," said Vida, disappointment creeping into her voice. "Well, if you think of anything, you know where I am."

"*Mmmm,*" said Crystal, following Marshall out of the apartment.

Once the door was closed and they had begun walking down the dingy hallway, Marshall said, "You didn't have to be rude."

"The hell I didn't! You said this old bat wouldn't be panhandling for a role, but she was, wasn't she?"

"I didn't know she was going to do that," said Marshall.

"Right."

"*Really.* I had no idea. Vida's very unpredictable."

"So why did you bring me here? Why was it so important that I meet her?"

They had reached the ground floor and fell silent until they were outside. Stu was leaning against the hood of the Lincoln SUV, projecting the attitude that the vehicle was his own.

"She's just as you left her," Stu said, easing himself away from the Lincoln.

"Thanks, buddy," said Marshall, transferring an undisclosed sum of cash into the youth's hand. "I'll catch you next time, right?"

"You bet."

"Keep an eye on Vida, will you?" asked Marshall.

Stu sighed and shook his head. "I got no real choice, do I?"

Marshall smiled and shook his head.

"Dirty old bat."

Marshall held the passenger door open and helped his fuming starlet into the cabin. As he crossed around in front of the hood, he mentally braced for the long ride home. He hadn't yet told Crystal why he had brought her to meet Vida, and he was pretty sure that it was going to be ugly when he did.

III

Chad Collins cried out as he erupted from a dream. His lanky teenaged body was sweat soaked, bed sheets sticking to his legs and chest. Air pumped in and out of his lungs as if he had been running a marathon. His eyes slowly acclimated to the darkness of his bedroom, narrow bands of moonlight slipping in through the slats of vertical blinds. Chad looked at his bedside clock. Eleven-twenty. His mother wasn't home to console him; she wouldn't even leave Hayes Safety Equipment until midnight.

Naomi Collins confirmed all of the data uploads from the regional sales managers and processed nightly sales figures after all of the uploads were in. Peter Collins, Chad's father, had staunchly objected to his ex-wife's choice of employment, citing the dangers of working alone and making the nightly trek through the parking lot by herself. Naomi was obstinate; the pay was good, and as a single parent, she needed every advantage she could get. Nevertheless, Peter never failed to recount stories of horrible violence, perpetrated by insane night stalkers against helpless citizens who were merely trying to get through another day. Perhaps that was what had inspired the dream.

It had been a horrific nightmare, unfolding from within the eyes of a monster. Chad could see his mother, her arms laden with boxes—of what he did not know. She wobbled uncomfortably in high heels across the large dark parking lot toward her ancient Chevy Cavalier wagon. She fumbled with the boxes while attempting to unlock her door. The keys slipped from her fingers and landed without a sound on the pavement below. As she stooped to pick up the keys, Chad's perception altered, like a camera moving in for a close up.

Suddenly, a butcher knife glinted from the right side of Chad's peripheral vision. Oddly, it was almost like he was holding the knife.

He wanted to cry out, warn his mother, tell her to run. But in the dream, he had no voice, heard no sound. Naomi hadn't been aware of anyone approaching and was still stooped over, having dropped one of the parcels as she scooped up the keys.

When she had finally collected everything, Naomi started to stand, and that was when the knife went in, piercing her side and slipping between her ribs. All of the parcels fell, scattering sheets of paper haphazardly.

The knife found its target again, this time in Naomi's back. She turned, terror and pain twisting her familiar features. Her eyes widened as if in recognition, then the knife thrust forward again, puncturing rather than slicing her throat. She collapsed amongst her fallen cargo into an ever-widening pool of Technicolor blood.

It was at that point Chad had awakened, gasping for breath and stuck to his bed sheets.

Chad threw back his covers and stood in his underwear beside his bed, digging at his eyes to remove the crust of sleep that had collected in the corners. He felt like he had been asleep for hours, yet he had gone to bed less than an hour ago. A large poster of Crystal Bright, clad in a form-fitting bathing suit and frolicking on the beach, hung on the wall at the foot of Chad's bed. He wished desperately that he could join her there. The small, two-bedroom cottage that he and his mother rented was so quiet, so empty.

Chad missed his father. Peter's presence alone would have chased away the boogies that now threatened to work Chad into a full-fledged panic. He had never been a latch-key kid until his parents had divorced. Naomi was so determined to sever ties with Peter that she refused his financial assistance, even when she and Chad desperately needed relief. Her position at Hayes was the best-paying job she could find with her limited experience. Peter's insistence that she quit the night shift only made her more determined to stay on, stating that Pridemore was statistically a very safe Indiana town. The tales of true crime which Peter felt necessary to relay were a byproduct of his watching too much reality television.

Chad felt stupid for letting his dream get to him. He was seventeen years old, for heaven's sake. If Ricky or Bill or Davy ever got wind of this, they would tease him until graduation.

But the dream had been *so real.*

Chad exited his bedroom and went down to the kitchen. The summer humidity was like a hot, moist, blanket. The rental house didn't have air conditioning and even in just his underwear, the boy was burning up.

He pulled a plastic jug of orange juice from the top shelf of the refrigerator and took a healthy drink, overflow running from the corners of his mouth. He looked at the digital clock on the stove. Eleven-thirty.

Maybe I should call Mom and warn her, he thought.

Warn her of what? A nightmare? Yeah, right. Next thing he knew, Chad would end up with a babysitter. *Then* what would Ricky or Bill or Davy say?

Chad hated the little cracker box rental house, preferring the upper middle-class comfort of his father's two-story *air-conditioned* Colonial. In an age when marriage only lasted until something better came along, Chad had hoped his family would defy statistics. They *belonged* together. It had taken him completely by surprise when Peter and Naomi had called him in for a family meeting ten months ago, announcing their plans to separate. Sure, they had occasional disagreements, but Chad never had any concept that the deceitful façade they presented would someday crumble at his feet. His memories, although scant in his early years, were full of family events and laughter. He had never seen his parents have a knock-down, drag-out fight. Maybe that was the problem. Maybe they just stopped caring about each other. In any case, their ability to put on happy faces ended as abruptly as their marriage. Naomi could barely keep her contempt for Peter below the surface, seizing upon every opportunity to berate him in every imaginable way. Peter was only moderately better, grilling Chad for details about Naomi's new life. Was she seeing anyone? As a matter of fact, no she wasn't, but Peter never looked as though he believed it.

Chad had been stuck firmly in the middle, pulled this way and that until his arms felt like they were twenty feet long.

Maybe I should call.

Chad picked up the receiver of the wall phone and hesitated only a second before dialing. He would ask his mother to bring home some milk, and oh, by the way, *be careful in the parking lot.*

The phone rang. Three times. Four. Five. Eight.

Chad replaced the receiver, anxious caterpillars evolving into butterflies in his stomach. "There's no reason to panic, dickhead," Chad said aloud to himself. "If she's in the back, she can't even *hear* the phone."

That said, he began to scour the pantry for snacks, finding a bag of barbecue corn chips on the bottom shelf. He sat at the table and gobbled a few handfuls. He needed to get back to bed. He and Ricky were going across the state line tomorrow, into Ohio and on to King's Island amusement park. Shelley and Julie would be going, and if everything went well, they might just stop at a motel on the way home. Ricky and Shelley had been going together for two years, but Julie was almost like a blind date for Chad. They had gone to school together for years, but he didn't really know her, hadn't really taken notice of her. What had finally gotten his attention was the rapid expansion of her breasts over the last six months. He dreamed about her often, running his tongue in lazy circles around what were most assuredly the finest nipples in the entire junior class. He usually woke so stiff he couldn't cross the hallway to the bathroom for fear that his mother might be standing there and would see his pride, erect and straining against the fabric of his undershorts.

They were much nicer dreams than this one of brutal violence.

Chad glanced at the circular clock above the sink. Eleven-forty.

He tossed the corn chips back into the pantry and picked up the phone, dialing again. One ring turned into ten. He replaced the receiver, his hand lingering for a moment on the handset.

The dream had been *so real.*

Chad went to his room and pulled on a pair of sweatpants and an old Hoosiers t-shirt. Hayes Safety Equipment was a few miles away, easily accessible by bicycle. Naomi would think that Chad was overreacting, but he couldn't push the imagery of the nightmare from his mind. He had never given any consideration to the possibility of clairvoyance or any other sort of precognition, nor had he ever experienced anything like it, but his internal processes were standing on point, warning him that he needed to verify his mother's safety. He couldn't call the police. What would he say? *I had a nightmare where...* Yeah, that should bring the cavalry a-runnin'.

He considered phoning his father, but that would be the absolute *last* thing that the fiercely independent Naomi would want. No, it was up to Chad to calm his own paranoid nerves.

He was nearly out the door when he realized he had no weapon, nothing to use against a possible assailant. If his dream had somehow transmitted knowledge of events to come, then the brutal killer would surely think nothing of filleting Chad, as well.

Naomi didn't allow guns in the house, not even a BB gun. Chad considered taking one of his baseball bats from his bedroom closet but decided it would be too cumbersome on the bicycle, as well as too awkward to use effectively should he have to square off against a knife-wielding assailant.

He went back into the kitchen and selected a butcher knife from the block. An eye for an eye, so to speak. He glanced at the clock. Eleven forty-five. He had to *go.*

The evening's nightfall had brought little relief from the intense summer heat. Night bugs sang in choruses to each other from the shelter of trees and weeds. Chad straddled his ten-speed and began peddling through the city blocks, pumping his legs as fast as they would go, clutching the large knife in his right hand against the handlebar while praying for his mother's safety.

CHAPTER THREE

I

Nanna Grace lay in her bed staring at the ceiling. It was the middle of the afternoon, but time had lost all meaning. Morning, noon, or evening—she was nearing the end of the line, no matter what time of day it was. She knew it—had known it for quite some time.

She had been reading her Bible, but it now lay beside her, upside down and open, its spine cracked from frequent perusal. Her arms had grown too weary to hold the book upright. With more and more frequency, her energy bottomed out like this. Normally she found solace in the Good Book, but not the same way others did. Historically relevant, thematically urgent, manipulatively misleading—overall, she found it to be amusing.

She wasn't afraid of death. She couldn't recall ever having been afraid of death. It was merely a transition to another state of being. Heaven, reincarnation, worm food—they were all variations of the same thing, a transference of energy. In her eighty-eight years on the planet, Nanna Grace had learned many simple truths, and this was one of them. Billions had gone quietly into the dark night before her, and billions would go after. How bad could it really be?

What concerned her was Lisa. The girl was devoid of ambition and unable to make up her own mind. Who would keep watch over her? Nanna had been able to keep her in check for the past fifteen years—she had taken Lisa in when the girl was only seven. Lisa didn't seem to remember anything from her early childhood, and Nanna had always considered it a blessing.

The girl had evil flowing through her veins, of this Nanna was certain.

Nanna stared at the backs of her eyelids for a while. She could feel the pressure building within, the next inevitable course of action waiting to unfurl. Of course, she would be no part of it. She would be dead.

Tonight. She must speak with Lisa tonight—before it was too late. Make her understand that the demon within her would lead to grave misfortune for many others.

The thought made Nanna laugh out loud. Lisa could never understand the negative energy from which she had come. In fact, trying to reason with Lisa might lead to a realization of her dark power, initiating the entire chain of events Nanna was certain would transpire with or without her intervention.

She should have killed the girl when she was just a helpless child. There would be no more reason for reflection, no more need to carry this awful burden. Filthy devil-child.

Nanna didn't have the raw strength necessary to kill Lisa now. Maybe she could find a way to mentally undo the girl. She had never allowed modern conveniences in the house, not only because they were gluttonous (which they *were*) but also because Nanna feared too much exposure to the outside world might inadvertently set the girl off. She hadn't wanted Lisa to go to work at the hospital, but there wasn't any money coming in and Nanna was too weak to work. *Someone* had to provide income, and that someone was Lisa.

Nanna drifted off, knowing for her the end was near.

She had the dream again. Although still very abstract, with each occurrence the events of the dream became more tangible and three-dimensional. A silver-headed man on a mountain of Pez candy, fire and smoke—death and destruction. Nanna always woke with her heart racing, blood pressure soaring.

This time, Nanna Grace didn't wake at all.

II

The Lincoln Navigator rejoined the freeway, taking Marshall and Crystal away from the rundown neighborhood of Vida Leon. Crystal hadn't said a single word to Marshall, her cheeks tinted blotchy red.

Marshall, in turn, had been making small talk about everything from the weather to the shit they play on the radio these days, but had thus far elicited no response from his young star. Her brooding fury was making the inevitable conversation all the more daunting.

"What was that bullshit about an Actor's Union subsidy?" Crystal finally asked. "There's no such thing."

"I know. Vida doesn't work much these days. She's a proud woman and doesn't take charity easily. I try to make sure that she's got a roof over her head and food."

"And *booze*."

"Hey, that's Vida's choice. I can't babysit her twenty-four hours a day."

"What about the Dryzies commercial? I don't recall ever seeing her onscreen before," said Crystal.

"That's because she never really was the spokesperson for Dryzies. I had the commercial put together by my own crew and ran a videotape to show her. Dryzies never used to advertise on television, and I never in a million years thought that they would get a celebrity endorsement, much less Vida's old showbiz rival. If Vida saw Rita Malloy doing the television ads, she would probably call Dryzies corporate headquarters raising three kinds of hell. I didn't want her to get hurt."

"Is the Purina ad real or did you make that up, too?" Crystal asked. "How about the grandma?"

"Oh, they're real alright, but Vida won't get them. No one in Hollywood is interested anymore."

"So, why did you think that I would be?" Crystal demanded.

"I needed you to see her," said Marshall, deciding that he may as well get this over with.

"Why?" demanded Crystal, twisting in her seat to burn a hole through him with her beautiful blue eyes. "What in the world would make you think I would be interested in meeting some old has-been? You've wasted my entire afternoon, Marshall. My time is *way* too valuable for this bullshit."

"We're friends, right?" asked Marshall.

"Looking less and less likely if you ever do *this* to me again."

Marshall took a deep breath. "We need to talk."

"We could've talked over lunch in Beverly Hills."

"This isn't easy, but I'm just going to say what I have to."

"Fine."

"There is no doubt that you are a young star on the rise. Teenage boys count on you to get them through puberty, old men want you to sit on their laps, women identify with you without feeling threatened—" Marshall hesitated, metering out his words carefully. "You've got a lot going for you."

Crystal listened in silence, her demeanor impassive.

Marshall cleared his throat. "You're going to lose it all if you're not careful."

"Excuse me?"

"Nobody wants to work with you anymore, babe. Your reputation has gone beyond that of a diva. And it's not just tabloid fiction, it's the truth. You treat everyone around you like shit. That contest winner, what's-her-name, she sold the story of your script-throwing assault to the *National Enquirer* and is going to make a pretty penny for doing so. The stagehands seem to come through a revolving door, staying only long enough to get your teeth marks in their backsides before moving on. We were in negotiations for *ten months* with Molly Nichols to do a guest spot on *Benny and The Girl*. Do you know what kind of publicity a movie star like Molly Nichols would have brought to our show? Well, trust me, it would have been a real casting coup, but she walked away after observing your on-set behavior from the green room. Even Blake is requesting limited contact with you. Now how can that be? He's *Benny*. You're *The Girl*."

"And how does that old bat figure into your berating of me?" snapped Crystal, her tone ice cold.

"Vida Leon was the star of a short-lived sitcom in the late fifties. *Daisy Does*. I doubt if you remember it. It was only on for a season-and-a-half—there weren't enough episodes for syndication. Hollywood's discovery of Vida Leon was very similar to its discovery of you—fast and fortuitous. For about a minute-and-a-half, no one in the business mentioned Lucille Ball without also giving a nod to Vida. Things definitely looked up for her. But then the whole shebang went to her head. Vida began to see herself as a sort of intermediary step between mere mortals and gods. Her co-star, Paul Padrone, walked away from the series. The show was canceled almost immediately. After that, Vida drank herself into obscurity. She had some truly embarrassing moments in the tabloids, including the birth of an illegitimate child, and her career was over. Simple as that."

Crystal absorbed the story in silence, but her face reflected her mounting fury. "So, this is some sort of *intervention?*" she asked, her disdain for the term evident.

"Sort of."

Crystal cleared her throat. "Pull over," she said, her voice barely a whisper.

"Excuse me?"

"I said pull over!" she demanded. "I can't be near you right now."

"Crystal, I'm trying to help. I've been in this business longer than you, and—"

"And *nothing!* That's right, Marshall, you've been in this business longer than me. And until you *found* me, your career was like so many others, nondescript and spectacularly unsuccessful. *I am your meal ticket, you bastard!* When you speak to me, you will do it with respect! Without me, there *is* no *Benny and The Girl*, and you'd damn well better remember it!" She slammed an open palm against the dashboard for emphasis. "How *dare* you compare me with that withered old crow. Do you have any *idea* the sheer volume of fan mail that I receive on a *daily* basis? I don't believe I've heard of the Marshall Dawson Fan Club? Is there one? *Of course not!*"

Marshall absorbed the verbal assault in silence. When Crystal paused, he said quietly, "I'm telling you this because I thought we were friends. I don't want to see your career go off track."

"And you thought that introducing me to some nut job who used to be an actress—and probably not a very *good* one—would make me see the 'errors of my ways?'" Crystal laughed bitterly.

"I want you to consider the way that Vida lives," said Marshall. "Try stepping into her shoes for a moment. Try to imagine—"

"Oh, for God's sake, Marshall!" she snapped. "Would you stop playing amateur psychiatrist on me? You have some nerve. I could have you fired, did you know that?"

Marshall chortled. "It's *my* show, dear. You'd be hard pressed to convince me to fire myself."

"Let me out of the car."

"We're on the freeway."

"Well, then you'd better take the next exit. I'm not riding another mile with you. If you don't stop, I swear to God, I'll jump right out the door."

"Oh, that's good," said Marshall. "Right into oncoming traffic? I don't think so."

"You *don't?*"

Marshall mentally kicked himself. He should have known better than to say that. Now, he had more or less challenged Crystal to prove her point. She grabbed the handle of the passenger door and flung it open, smacking the side of a minivan in the next lane. It veered off to the right, horn blazing, its angry driver flying the bird wildly. The Lincoln's door bounced back and closed.

"What in the hell are you doing?" Marshall demanded. In the rearview mirror, he saw the minivan driver pulling close enough to get his license plate number before zipping around him, flipping him off one last time. It didn't surprise Marshall that the driver hadn't elected to stop; anyone crazy enough to throw open a car door in the middle of highway traffic must be a carjacker or kidnapper or murderer. Nonetheless, he pulled over to the side of the road and stopped the car. Crystal's self-satisfied smirk brought his blood to a boil. "This is a brand-new Lincoln," he said, his voice steady even if his nerves were shot.

"Big deal!" Crystal shrieked.

"Get out," Marshall said. "You wanted out, *now get out!*"

Crystal's eyes narrowed and she clenched her jaw tightly. *"Fuck you, Marshall!* Fuck you and that whole damn show of yours! You can't treat me this way!"

Marshall stretched across the cabin, reaching for the door handle on the passenger side. Crystal squealed, showering Marshall's arms and face with blow after blow. Finally, he managed to pull the handle and push the door open. One last firm shove, and Crystal was forcibly ejected from the SUV, landing roughly on her side on the tarmac. She screamed with fury, struggling to regain her footing almost as soon as she hit the ground.

Marshall put the SUV back into gear and stomped on the accelerator pedal, the forward momentum causing the passenger door to close. He saw Crystal receding in his rearview, flailing her arms and throwing her shoes uselessly at his escaping vehicle.

His head throbbed with red-hot rage. This time, she had simply pushed him too far. Now, he was going to have to take his brand-new car in for bodywork. *Fucking bitch!*

III

By the time Chad actually arrived at Hayes Safety Equipment, he felt downright stupid. His mother's station wagon occupied its normal slot towards the back of the poorly illuminated square of blacktop. The building itself was an industrial, corrugated metal structure, housing both administrative and manufacturing areas. The main entrance was at the leftmost corner of the building, framed by large plate glass windows which looked into the receptionist's area. Lights blazed from one of these windows, the office in which Naomi Collins performed her nightly duties.

It was eleven fifty-eight. No boogeymen or banditos. Just Chad, feeling childish and ridiculous. Still straddling his bicycle, he walked it to the far-left corner by the main entrance and propped it behind an enormous row of hedges which bordered the lot. He didn't want his mother to know he had worked himself into a case of the willies. She didn't need to worry that Chad wasn't capable of staying by himself—never mind the fact that he was seventeen years old, and if his friends got hold of this little piece of info, he'd *never* hear the end of it.

Chad dropped down to his knees beside the bicycle. Although he didn't want his mother to see him, he still wanted to make sure she made it to her car safely. After all, he had come all this way, and she should be out in just a minute or so. Once he saw that she was all right, he'd hurry back to the house and sneak back into his room via the rose trellis which conveniently scaled the wall just outside his window.

Chad realized he was still clutching the knife with white knuckles and forced himself to put it down. He hadn't seen another soul for the last several blocks. Hayes Safety Equipment was tucked away at the edge of a residential neighborhood in the quiet town of Pridemore. At this hour, traffic had all but evaporated. The nighttime silence was broken only by the chirp of crickets and the hum of a faltering overhead light in the parking lot. Chad was sure that he would hear if anyone were to approach.

This whole thing was so stupid. *Mom shouldn't be working at all*, Chad thought. *Mom should be* home, *Dad should be* home, *I should be* home.

He didn't understand what had gone so terribly wrong between his parents. In fact, he thought that it was a little selfish of them to terminate their marriage so close to his graduation. He almost had to switch school districts when his mother suggested they move into some shithole on Third Street. He didn't understand why she hadn't kept the two-story Colonial and sent his father on his way. Wasn't that the way it was usually done?

Maybe this whole divorce had been his mother's fault. Peter was always giving his son the inquisition as to what Naomi was doing and with whom she was doing it. Could it be possible?

Naomi wasn't an overly doting mother. She had expected Chad to be independent early on, freeing as much of her own time as possible. Was this because she didn't relish the role of wife and mother?

Chad didn't know what to make of any of it. When his parents had announced their intention to divorce, it had turned his world upside down. Simple facts taken for granted were now hauled back out for reexamination, and Chad had little confidence in his own ability to separate truth from well-structured fiction.

One thing for certain, Chad never blamed himself for his parents' marital rupture. He *knew* that he hadn't done anything. He was quiet, studious, and generally helpful around the house, considering his age. No one in the family participated in easy discourse, but Chad had shared a quiet mutual bond with his father. They often read for hours in silence on the back porch of the Colonial, enjoying each other's company without contributing a single comment. Chad knew that Peter was a very important person in his life. Chad knew that he needed Peter.

Naomi was quite different. Her features were sharp, reflecting her constant desire to GET THINGS DONE. Everything was set to schedule, a time for everything and nothing done out of sequence. One disruption of this routine could spell apocalypse for neighboring villages as the she-beast he referred to as Mothra disintegrated into a whining, shrieking shrew. She was not abusive, by any means. She just screamed a lot. It was rare to see a smile flit across Naomi's face; if one did, odds were good it was actually a wince.

Chad noticed that the crickets had stopped chirping, adding a layer of cottony stillness to the evening. The dim overhead light continued to buzz. Naomi wobbled past the front glass, still unsteady on her new high heels.

High heels.

What was *that* all about? Naomi had always subscribed to the theory of happy feet, happy soul. This meant loafers, moccasins, tennis shoes, flats, sandals—not these stiletto spikes she had begun wearing lately. She was of average height, but with the heels on, she was statuesque, her soft calves instantly toned by the slant of the shoe.

There had to be someone else, thought Chad bitterly. *If it wasn't for her, we'd all still be together.*

The streetlight above suddenly increased its output, the level of luminosity swelling steadily before culminating in a telltale *zzz-zz-z-t!* like a bug caught in a zapper. The parking lot fell into both darkness and suffocating silence.

A light in the corridor beyond the main entrance flicked on as the light in the reception area switched off. Naomi must be wrapping up. Chad rarely heard her arrive at home after work. He wasn't much of a night owl—he'd usually been asleep for about an hour by the time she would get home. *How do you even know she was coming straight home, dickhead?*

The thought crept in unbidden from the dark recesses of Chad's mind. The dark recesses frequently referred to him as dickhead.

She could be meeting some stud with a fifteen-inch dick.

And, in fact, she could be. Chad had never once heard her come home. He assumed that she arrived around twelve-fifteen, twelve-thirty, but it could just as easily be four or five in the morning. Who was to say? There was no instant replay option.

32

The pieces were all coming together. Naomi must be living some sort of secret life. She slept all damn morning, getting up only a few hours before she had to head off to work. Sure, it was summer now, but once school started, Naomi would have another whole block of time in which she could bring her new boyfriends home. Chad shuddered to think what would happen next.

Naomi was at the main entrance, struggling with several boxes. She was propping the door open with her butt as she carefully maneuvered the boxes through the doorframe. She locked the door and turned toward her car, pausing to frown at the burnt-out overhead lamp. Then she continued across, her high heels clicking like a woodpecker, her legs shapely but unsteady, her boxes barely balanced and teetering.

Chad watched her pass his vantage point and said nothing, shaking his head in disgust as he watched her hips sway first left, then right, then left, then right. She was like a goddamned bitch in heat.

He stepped quietly out from behind the shrub and watched her continue. The image in his nightmare had fused with the reality of the moment, and Chad smiled savagely.

Unconsciously, he had already begun to move forward, quietly, *quietly*. The only sound in Chad's ears was the persistent pecking from those damned shoes. *Oops!* Down went the car keys, then one of the parcels.

It was uncanny how accurately the dream had captured the angles and vantage points.

He didn't remember picking it up, but there it was, glinting in the moonlight, clutched in his right hand.

Into the side, between the ribs.

Just like cutting chicken.

Papers scattered, absorbing blood like towels.

Whoop! Into the back! Just as quick as that!

Naomi turned, her terrified eyes visibly jolted by recognition as she stared into her son's face. Her lips moved, but there were no words, just burbling, wheezing exhaust.

Stop making that sound, Chad thought angrily. *STOP MAKING THAT SOUND!*

He thrust the knife forward, jamming the point deep into Naomi's throat. She was silent *now*.

Chad stepped back and examined the carnage before him. Several of the wounds he had inflicted were arterial, thick spurts of blood shining like oil on the tarmac in an outward radiating pattern. Drops and drizzles had spattered the car, as well.

Chad brought the knife to his mouth and carefully removed the blood from the cold steel. Delightfully coppery. He returned to the shrub to collect his bicycle and head home. Halfway across the lot, he noticed that his clothes were impossibly clean, completely free of blood and gore.

IV

The sun dipped into the rolling hills. It was warm as Kentucky summers usually are, but the humidity was low, and the evening was prime for relaxing on the porch, which was exactly what Lucas—Luke, to his few friends—Leighton had decided to do with the rest of the night. The twilight sky was tinted various shades of blue, light to dark, as the sun continued taking its leave. Luke was propped along the wooden rail that bordered the porch, his back pressed against the wall of the house, his long legs sprawled out in front of him.

Old Paulie had been in bed for hours, now, and it seemed that with each passing season, the man was signing off earlier and earlier. He had been called Old Paulie for so long that no one really remembered when it began—he was just so damned old! On his next birthday, he would be ninety. He had occupied the property on which this modest dwelling stood since he had inherited it decades before from family he barely knew. It was a family plot and was meant to stay that way. Luke supposed that one day, Paulie would be forced to will it to him, although he knew how disappointed the old man must be.

Although married three times, Paulie had never been blessed with children. He laughed it off, claiming that it didn't really matter, always blaming it on his 'faulty kickstand,' but Luke knew better. Paulie had wanted his own brood with whom he could share his family's legacy.

On Old Paulie's eightieth birthday, he had happened upon twelve-year-old Luke pounding the shit out of one of the abandoned outbuildings on his property. Luke was one of Jasper's delinquent orphans. Okay, he was Jasper's *only* delinquent orphan. With a population of just over five hundred, Jasper wasn't apt to have more than one of anything. Old Paulie had offered the boy odd jobs around the farm, replacing broken rails in the property's fencing, planting or harvesting vegetables (depending on the season), repainting sun-bleached walls of the farmhouse—whatever he could think of. In return, Luke could smoke his cigarettes right out in the open (something Sister Margaret from the orphanage would never allow), stay overnight with the approval of the Sister, and once he was fourteen, occasionally partake in an evening of moonshine and poker with Old Paulie and his crony friends. On Luke's fifteenth birthday, Old Paulie had done the necessary paperwork to assume legal responsibility for the lad, something no one else had ever been willing to do, even going the extra mile to change the boy's last name to Leighton. While hanging out with a group of cantankerous old men had never been Luke's idea of a good time, it was infinitely better than his tenure at the orphanage—Sister Margaret's two-room guilt shack. If it brought a smile to man's face, then it was undoubtedly sinful, she was known to say. Her presence in the town was as a representative of the Catholic church, and although Baptists and Methodists were predominant, they were more than willing to let the Sister tend to the upbringing of the town's only orphan. Had she not been in town, Luke would have likely been shipped off to Lexington where he would have been placed in foster care or with a state-operated orphanage.

Luke was a loner by nature. Although he had friends, none of them were particularly close, and rarely did he have a boy's night out with them. At twenty-one, he had only been on three dates—all with hungry-eyed farmers' daughters who knew a whole lot less about chastity and piety than the good Sister had led him to believe a good woman should. There was a lot of giggling and blushing, but when push came to shove, they had always been the aggressors. Luke was unlike most guys his age; he had no interest in casual sex. He wanted to know a woman mentally and spiritually before he contemplated the physicality—this may be residual programming from Sister Margaret, but he didn't think so. He knew the perfect woman was out there for him somewhere, just not in Jasper.

Luke admired the healthy landscape sprawling before him. The wraparound porch offered a panoramic view, a large garden sprawling at the rear of the property, a flat, well-maintained lawn toward the front. At the outer edge of the lawn, just beyond the split-rail fence, the hillside rolled gently down to a valley below, trees and long grass crawling up from its depths. The landscape dropped away similarly on the opposite side of the house, and the view from Old Paulie's property was a breathtaking display of the surrounding scenery. If it weren't for the power and phone lines overhead, it would be easy to forget about civilization altogether.

Luke lit a cigarette and took a long, slow drag. Paulie's frequent naps weren't the only difference in the old man these days. He seemed to be suffering from moments of delirium, as well. For as long as Luke could remember, Old Paulie had sworn off modern medicine, citing the Lord God as his primary caregiver. Luke often wondered how much longer he should wait before dragging Paulie in to see Dr. Ricart in the village, but he knew how vehemently opposed Paulie would be. Paulie could be very stubborn when he applied himself.

All this talk about something lurking in the back field. It was downright *eerie*. Paulie's eyes shone with fleeting determination as he babbled about good, evil, and all the things in between. Teacups and crystal balls. Then sweet lucidity would return, and Paulie had already forgotten what he'd just said.

Whenever Paulie eventually passed away, Luke wasn't sure he could stay in Jasper. His friends were merely acquaintances, and he couldn't help but feel that life had more in store for him than this.

Darin Miller

A sudden burst of noise from the house, and Luke knew that Old Paulie was awake again. Paulie always had a love for music of all types, and although frugal in many ways, when it came to audio equipment, he always went all out. The glass in his bedroom windows rattled in their panes, the Bose speakers within thumping out a steady beat.

> *Do you remember a long time ago?*
> *There was a man called Cotton-Eyed Joe*
> *I could-a been married a long time ago*
> *If it hadn'ta been for Cotton-Eyed Joe*
> *Where did you come from? Where did you go?*
> *Where did you come from, Cotton-Eyed Joe?*

Luke smiled and flicked his cigarette down into the flower bed at the side of the porch. It drove Old Paulie nuts when he did that, but he just couldn't seem to help it—it was habit. He swung his stockinged feet down to the porch and boosted himself upright. He stretched lazily, his spine cracking like a half-shell, and ambled toward the door. Paulie was always talkative after his naps. That's when the most far out, ridiculous stories came to him, apparently. Luke wondered what tonight's tale would be. It would surely be more entertaining than anything on TV.

CHAPTER FOUR

I

Odd.

The day had at long last arrived, and Lisa didn't know how to feel.

Happy? Gruesome.

Relieved? Completely.

That horrible afternoon at the hospital, only a few short days ago.

Lisa had driven home at a snail's pace, deliberating what she could tell Nanna Grace, why it was that she was no longer needed at the hospital. It didn't matter. Nanna Grace would know. She always knew when Lisa was being anything less than forthright. "I can see your soul," she had often said, her inflection flat and without emotion. Lisa shivered at the thought.

The gloomy gray sky hung like dirty cotton, drizzling down on the burial service. Lisa was dressed appropriately in black, her detached expression obscured by the lacy veil of her hat. She stared at the coffin in front of her, aware of the minister reciting passages, but nothing really registered. Her mind was a blank page, stripped of the past and ready to begin again, clean and fresh.

The funeral procession was appallingly small. Only three other people were in attendance, two elderly women Lisa recognized from Nanna's church, and a scraggly, middle-aged fellow whom Lisa didn't know at all. He was making a fool of himself, crying and carrying on like he had lost his very soul mate. He was making a fool of her as well, acting as though Nanna had meant more to him than she ever had to Lisa. The man hadn't shaved in days, and rough stubble coated the lower quadrant of his face.

"—Amen."

Lisa's attention refocused. The minister was closing his Bible and smiling sympathetically at the small group of mourners. The two women stood, each taking a turn patting Lisa's arm and offering sincere-sounding apologies before waddling off, huddled together under an umbrella, already discussing where they might stop for a quick nibble of lunch.

Out of her peripheral vision, Lisa realized that the strange man was now on his hands and knees, crawling toward the coffin, his beige trench coat tangling in his legs as he pressed forward. He sobbed shamelessly, his face twisted with grief, rain and tears intermingling and flowing freely down his cheeks.

Who in the hell *was* this clown?

Lisa stood, smoothed her black dress, and approached the grave. She bowed her head for what she hoped would be an appropriate length of time before turning away and heading for her own car. She didn't speak to the minister as she passed. She really didn't like him very much. He didn't seem to be interested in memorializing Nanna so much as preaching a Sunday School sermon. Lisa thought it was in very poor taste.

Most importantly, Lisa wanted to get away from the strange man, writhing in the mud around Nanna's grave. Who could he be? Nanna didn't have visitors at the house. Even the two ladies who had come were acting only as representatives of the church. Nanna had been a member, even if she hadn't actually been able to attend for many years—*someone* from the church had to put in an appearance. Nanna didn't have any living relatives that Lisa knew of.

Lisa opened the door of her rust-infested blue Toyota. The hinges screeched in protest. She hadn't brought an umbrella, and her dress was fairly well soaked through. She had fastened her blonde hair into a matronly bun at the nape of her neck, and it now felt as heavy as a bowling ball, full of water weight.

As she started to ease herself down into the car, she suddenly felt steely fingers clutching her shoulder. She gasped involuntarily and whirled around. It was the lunatic in the trench coat, breathing toxic fumes just inches from her face. His eyes were widened in urgency, his yellow teeth clenched together.

"What do you want?" she asked, her voice little more than a squeaky whisper.

"I—can see—YOUR SOUL!" he cried, tossing his head back and laughing hysterically.

Lisa froze. Nanna had said that so many times. Who *was* this man?

"Do I know you?" she managed to ask.

"I CAN SEE YOUR SOUL!"

Lisa wrenched free from the man's clawlike grasp and hurried into the car, pulling the door closed and locking it. The man pressed his face to the glass, laughing and pounding his open palm against the windshield. Lisa fumbled for her keys, finally finding the right one and inserting it into the ignition. For a second, she feared this was like some bad horror movie, she would turn the key, and the car wouldn't start, but the Toyota had always been dependable, and the engine turned over immediately. As she reached between the seats to release the brake and put the car into gear, she became aware of a different sound, something clinking against her windshield. Her eyes followed the noise, focusing on an object the man was now rapping against the glass.

It was a china teacup. The pattern was unmistakable. It was one of Nanna Grace's china teacups.

Lisa dropped the gearshift into drive and lurched forward, leaving the crazed man dancing in the rearview mirror, his image growing smaller and smaller until he was swallowed up in the distance.

Lisa parked in the driveway and hurried into the house, shutting out the rainy day and anything else that might be lurking. She twisted the deadbolt and secured the door chain as well. That creep must have gotten into the house at some point, stealing one of Nanna's prized cups.

How had he known what Nanna always said to her?

Lisa shivered, suddenly aware of every shadow in the old house. She began a methodical sweep, checking to see that every window was latched and all the doors were locked. Only afterward was she able to breathe easier. She didn't want to look up and suddenly find that whacko standing in her living room.

Her living room. Ah.

She had barely taken the time to absorb what Nanna's death meant for her. It was *liberation*. No more antiquated rules, no more Bible stories, no more sponge baths.

Lisa sank into a straight-backed Victorian chair and surveyed the room. The decor was cherry and mauve, uncomfortable antique furniture crowding the small space. The air was old and uncirculated, a cross between spilled perfume and old lady bathroom. Lisa got back on her feet and crossed to the window which overlooked the front yard. She tentatively pulled the blind up, allowing the first daylight in years to spill into the room. The natural light, gloomy due to the rain, made the room seem somehow stuffier and even more intolerable.

Lisa went to the kitchen to pour herself a glass of water. She paused at the cupboard where Nanna Grace's teacups were stored. She opened the cabinet door and gasped. All twelve of the teacups were neatly lined up in rows of three. None were missing.

Lisa had had enough. She reached into the cupboard, and in one clean sweep sent the cups crashing to the floor. "So much for your mama's good china," said Lisa aloud, giggling when she realized she was talking to herself. She then proceeded to stomp the fragments, rendering the pieces into dust. When she felt the cups had been appropriately demolished, she leaned against the counter, staring at the mess she'd made. She hadn't realized the fury with which she had taken the cups to task, but her ragged breathing and sweaty brow were testaments to the energy she had exuded. Seeing the cups laying broken beyond repair made her positively giddy with delight. She bounded up the stairs to her room and began stripping out of the shapeless black dress she had worn to the funeral. She had a lot of work to do, and she would be so much more comfortable in blue jeans and a t-shirt.

Lisa started at the root of the problem, going into Nanna Grace's room and surveying. It was an easy decision—everything must go. Lisa sang hymns to herself as she started at the far corner of the room, stripping the walls of everything, tossing it all into an ever-widening pile on the floor. When the pile grew too large, Lisa kicked it out of the room and down the stairs. After the walls were bare, she made a clean sweep of all surfaces, tossing knick-knacks and bric-a-brac and eventually furniture itself down the stairwell.

The rain had stopped, and night had descended, but Lisa was too busy to notice. She wouldn't be satisfied until Nanna Grace's bedroom was down to its bare walls and floor. The last piece to go was the blasted recliner, encased in plastic and reserved for cleansing the old woman. There was really no way to fully describe the awkwardness of bathing an invalid. There was no way to preserve dignity, and dignity had always been so very important to Nanna Grace.

Exhausted, Lisa went down the stairs, climbing over the large pile of ruined furniture that lay at the bottom. It had been a good day, overall. A few more days like today, and all vestiges of Nanna Grace would be gone.

Lisa washed her hands in the kitchen sink and splashed cool water on her face. Afterward, she went back to the base of the stairs and stared at all of Nanna's possessions, busted and broken. A gold-plated handheld mirror lay outside the general radius of the wreckage, its shattered glass in menacing shards spread around the floor. Lisa winced as she caught her reflection in the glass. Dark circles framed Lisa's droopy eyes, and her skin was white like paper. Her blonde hair was saturated with perspiration and stuck to her head like a skullcap, her ponytail heavy and damp. Dark roots were showing, and Lisa absently raised a hand to touch the sweaty strands. She giggled spontaneously. Time to touch up the roots. As a child, Lisa's hair had always been blonde, but puberty had begun to take a dark crayon to it. She had bleached her hair ever since, and it was one of the few things she had managed to do without Nanna Grace noticing. Nanna had disapproved of hair coloring, makeup, and form-fitting attire—all of the things which differentiated the cool girls from the rejects back in high school. Lisa had been a reject. She had never allowed her roots to grow in this much, fearful that Nanna would force her to shave her head or something equally extreme. She had no idea what the true color of her hair might actually be. She didn't really care either. All of the truly gorgeous models and Hollywood actresses were blonde, and blonde Lisa would continue to be. She didn't know what to do about her homeliness, though. She had never had a mother or even a best girlfriend in high school to teach her how to make the most of what she had. Nanna was certainly no help. Vanity was a sin. Period. Lisa hated the face that peered back at her from the mirror fragment on the floor, and she stomped the piece into smaller fragments with the heel of her shoe.

Although completely exhausted, Lisa decided she would take a quick bath and go to Morton's Supermarket to pick up hair coloring and cosmetics. Without a job, she had all the time in the world to experiment with the face paint, designing a new look for her new life. She had a little money saved up.

Her new life. More spontaneous giggling, then she was up the stairs like a rowdy teenager, feet pounding on each step like thunder rolling uphill.

II

Crystal lay naked in her bedroom underneath a thick, pink comforter. Her head pounded from too much vodka the night before, and her stomach performed acrobatic maneuvers trying to coax her back into dry heaves.

She couldn't believe so much could happen in only a month.

She had been one of Hollywood's hottest new commodities. She was *People*'s Sexiest Woman Alive, for Christ's sake! Since that afternoon with Marshall, the one in which she had been forcibly ejected from his vehicle, she had watched her career crumble piece by piece, like dominos dropping.

Obviously, she had declined to participate in the production of *Benny and the Girl* the next week, calling in sick each day. She had decided she wouldn't speak with Marshall when he called, not until she had made him suffer a little. The network would be all over him to make his star happy and get her back on set. She had enjoyed knowing the pressure Marshall would be under.

But Marshall hadn't called.

The National Enquirer ran a horrific piece on Crystal the following weekend. SPOILED STAR EATS PAVEMENT AND DITCHES SHOW! The headline screamed from above a photo of Crystal running along the berm of the interstate, hurtling her shoes at Marshall's Lincoln. She looked positively rabid in the photo, actual spittle spraying from her lips and frozen for all eternity by a high-speed shutter. How in the world did the tabloids always manage to have a camera in just the right place at just the right time? It was uncanny.

The day the paper hit the streets, Crystal's agent, Vinnie Corona had called.

"Need to know what's up, babe," he said in his usual salesman voice. "I'm sitting here looking at this paper—"

"What a bunch of bullshit!" said Crystal. "You know the tabloids. They'll make up anything."

"That photo sure don't look airbrushed to me," said Vinnie.

"Well—"

"You haven't been on the set in a week. Sounds to me like there might be some truth to this little scoop."

"Marshall and I got into a fight. He's such an ass. He took it upon himself to try and tell *me* that I was getting too big for my britches."

Silence. Crystal expected Vinnie to hop right in and assure her that she was the star. The show needed its star. Marshall was crawling—*anything*. Instead, silence.

"What, you think he's *right?*" she demanded.

"Babe, you gotta understand something about Hollywood," Vinnie said, using his most diplomatic tone. "It's all just a great big game. It doesn't matter what kind of talent you have. It's how you look and how you sell yourself. You got the looks. Hell, you even got some talent. But you're too new to be throwing your weight around like you are. Remember what happened to Shannen Doherty after that *Beverly Hills* show? She didn't work for quite a while, and she was very popular at the time she got axed."

Crystal was furious and speechless. "I can't believe this shit," she finally said.

"Yeah, well, you better believe it. The studio has contacted me. They're prepared to sue you for breach of contract."

"*What?*" Crystal demanded. "They think that's going to make me come back? Well, I'll show them. I'll stay right here for a couple more weeks, then they'll be *begging* me to come back."

Vinnie was silent for a moment. "They don't want you back."

Crystal was stunned. "Impossible. The show is *huge*. My fans will—"

"Hey, all I can tell you is they've already been screening replacements."

"*Replacements?* Impossible."

Vinnie sighed. "You need to get your ass in there, talk to the producers, work this thing out before it's too late."

"You have got to be kidding me! I'm not the one who—"

"Look, have I ever lied to you? I'm telling you this is serious. Blake Jagger said he might not be interested in renewing his contract next year if the studio doesn't replace you. He's fed up, Crystal. A lot of people are fed up."

"This is ridiculous," said Crystal. *"Benny and the Girl* is making big money. It would be suicidal to try and recast my part."

"I think they want to kill you off."

Crystal laughed from deep within her throat. "Oh, that's *rich*. The ultimate revenge, hunh?"

"Something like that."

"Well, you can just tell them I said to kiss my ass. I'm not jumping through hoops for them. They *need* me. They'll be back." Crystal slammed the phone down and spent the rest of the evening pouting.

She was served with the lawsuit the next day. A tall, thin, freckle-faced kid told her to have a nice day as he placed the documents in her hands. For the first time, she felt a real jolt of fear. Maybe she *was* in over her head. Maybe she *was* cutting her nose off to spite her face. She called Alvin Lowenstein, her attorney, and he made a special trip over to retrieve and review the summons.

The show didn't want her back, that much was plain. They were seeking damages in the millions, money that Crystal didn't have. Lowenstein seemed very disturbed by what he read and seemed to only go through the motions of offering encouragement about the outcome.

Then the studio hired Britney Bramblett. She would not be taking over the role of Chloe but would instead play a college friend of Chloe's visiting town to pay her respects at Chloe's funeral. *The National Enquirer* continued to have a field day with all the backstage shenanigans, and Crystal was prominently featured on the cover of consecutive editions of the tabloid, her picture always unflattering and furious.

And just like that, Britney was in, Crystal was out.

Viewers don't like change. It's statistically proven. With but a few exceptions, most recasts don't survive their first season. The recasting of a principal character is an even trickier business. Crystal took great satisfaction in her firm belief that the show would falter and die the minute Britney appeared on screen. There might even be angry fans in the studio audience who would jeer her off the soundstage. Crystal closed her eyes and allowed the daydream to last a few minutes, savoring that vision of ultimate victory. She couldn't believe Marshall hadn't even had the common decency to talk to her. Oh, sure, he tried to act like her father or something that day in the car, but not a word since. She thought they were friends.

Crystal was unpleasantly surprised when other offers failed to materialize, now that her schedule had cleared. She checked in with Vinnie every day only to be told, "Nothing yet."

After several days of this, Crystal said, "I get the feeling you aren't trying very hard on my behalf, Mr. Corona."

"Truth is, no one will touch you right now. I've tried to throw your name in the hat for several projects, both television and the big screen, but because of your pending litigation, nobody will provide a completion bond if your name is attached. Television is an incestual market. People at ABC have worked with people at NBC who have eaten dinner with people from CBS who have slept with people at FOX. You get my drift? If the poison is strong enough, all the networks get a taste. You're the poison right now, sweetheart."

"What are you saying, Vinnie?"

"It would be awfully trite to say, 'Don't call us—,' so I won't. But I'll let you know if I come across anything, 'kay? Bye-bye." And the connection was severed.

A couple weeks later, Vinnie dropped Crystal as a client. Re-enter Billy Ball, former agent and general sleazebag.

"So's you need my help, hunh?" He leered at her from behind his little metal desk in his little metal office. Thick smoke hung like a hovercraft in the center of the room. Billy's thick black hair was reminiscent of the late Roy Orbison's famous 'do—big and in one piece. Crystal figured that it hung on his bedpost at night.

"Don't be an ass, Billy," she snapped. "Can you help me, or not?"

"That depends," he said, leaning back in his chair and studying her with his beady little rodent eyes. He tried to look cool and desirable, but instead looked paunchy and lecherous.

Crystal sighed and stood, preparing to leave.

"Wait!" Billy said, sitting upright and gesturing for her to sit back down. "I might be able to find you something."

"I just don't get it," Crystal mused aloud, sitting back in the chair. "It's like I've been washed up overnight."

"Blackballed," supplied Billy.

"Blackballed? Really? I didn't think that sort of thing happened much since the old studio days."

Billy tossed his head back in a genuine laugh. "Boy, you *are* naive, honey. Marshall Dawson is an up-and-comer in this biz. He's been involved in some of the biggest hits of the past few television seasons. Him and his boyfriend are about to go big time this winter with their first attempt on the silver screen. It's some sentimental schlop about a girl who thinks she has a disease falling in love with a roughneck with a heart of gold. Sounds like shit on paper, but Julia Roberts and Kevin Bacon are in it, and all the buzz around Hollywood is very positive."

"What's that got to do with the price of tea in China?" Crystal cut in.

"Marshall Dawson is behind this whole vendetta against you. He's still sore over the *Benny and the Girl* thing."

"He started this whole mess."

"Whatever. Point is, he's got the influence to make it very hard for you to work right now. Tell me, have you ever considered porn? Soft core wouldn't be bad, but you'd get more money—"

Crystal's face contorted with revulsion. *"Unh!* Stop!" she said, holding up a hand to deflect his words. "No way would I do porn. You should know better than that."

Billy shook his hands in concession. "Fine. It's just going to be tough. We might be able to work you into another horror flick. A lot of them are filmed in Canada, and we might be able to bypass the little network Marshall has established against you. I wouldn't think it would be hard to find someone who will pay bucks to kill you off." He smiled smugly, then added, "Onscreen, of course."

Crystal sighed and looked out the grimy window of Billy's office. There was nothing to see, just the backside of the building next door. "See what you can do. I'm having to pay my lawyers some big bucks because of that lawsuit. I need to be making money, not sitting on my ass."

"Maybe things will loosen up in a week or two," said Billy, absently scratching a note on his desk calendar.

"Why's that?"

"The first new episodes of *Benny and the Girl* are supposed to air. If public reaction is strong, then Marshall might lighten up on you. Otherwise, you're dead meat," said Billy, leaning back in his chair.

"Well, then, I'm dead meat," said Crystal, standing again. "Shows that recast principal characters always fail. Especially one like mine."

"*Cheers* didn't seem to have much difficulty," said Billy.

"Okay," conceded Crystal. "But that's like a one in a million shot. *Cheers* is the exception, not the rule."

"I hear this Britney is very good, very engaging."

Crystal stared at him in disbelief. "Do you want to come over here and slap me around a little while you're at it, Billy? That bitch took my job. I don't want to hear about how wonderful and sweet and good she is!"

"I didn't say anything about her being sweet," said Billy, smiling.

Crystal was dumbfounded. This short round bastard was enjoying watching her squirm. She turned and headed for the door, calling back over her shoulder, "Call me as soon as you find something suitable."

"You sure you won't do porn?"

Crystal froze with her hand on the doorknob, her back straight as a board. Standing there, she felt dirty and ashamed, like she had sneaked back to a drug dealer for a quick fix. She paused for only a second before continuing out of Billy's office, slamming the door behind her.

She didn't see Billy's amused smile.

The next few days brought even worse news. Her accountant, Marty Crabtree, had apparently been keeping two sets of books, one to keep Crystal happy and one to bleed her dry. His affinity for weekend trips to Vegas had prompted him to take what was left of Crystal's money before the studio won it all in the lawsuit. The police were efficient in taking the report, but the priority for arresting Crabtree was pretty low, and it was obvious. Crystal felt beaten down, unable to summon any more outrage. Unable to afford her rent. Unable to get a job.

The tabloids were waiting outside the precinct, in Crystal's face as she left the station, flashbulbs flaring and reporters' questions swirling. It didn't matter what she said—they'd make up their own truths later, so she opted to say nothing.

The only stop that Crystal made on her way home was to a liquor store in Brentwood, where behind sunglasses, she purchased large quantities of vodka, whiskey, and tequila. It would likely be the last trip in her BMW before it was repoed, anyway.

Crystal didn't remember much beyond that; the evening had been very liquid. Now, as she lay enveloped in her pink comforter, the urge to dry heave became insurmountable, and she hoisted herself to her feet and ran-stumbled to the bathroom. She barely reached her target when her stomach contracted, and she vomited loudly. Whaddaya know? It wasn't dry heaves after all.

Crystal rested her forehead against the rim of the toilet bowl, appreciating the coolness of its surface. Her head pulsed with the hangover, but after a moment, the nausea settled, and the headache faded to a dull throb. Crystal stood and crossed to the sink, where she splashed cool water on her face.

Her face.

She looked in the mirror and almost broke out into tears. Her hair was tangled and knotted, her eyes dark and puffy, and a mystery bruise had appeared on her cheek. She had probably fallen over something when she was drunk, but she didn't remember. This wasn't the face of a star.

After a few more moments, Crystal steadied on her feet and ambled out into the large apartment. The living room afforded a magnificent view of the San Fernando Valley, but the blinds were pulled shut, and Crystal had no intention of raising them. It was too depressing. The monthly expenses associated with this place were astronomical. With next to no money to her name, Crystal would be out of here in no time flat, no doubt involved in another lawsuit for breaking the lease.

Crystal went to the entry, unlocking and opening the door, its chain still fastened securely in place. She stooped down and reached through the crack, retrieving her *L.A. Times* from the hallway. She closed the door and slid the deadbolt back into place, heading for the kitchen as she scanned the headlines.

She tossed the paper onto the dining room table while she went into the massive, stainless-steel kitchen and put coffee in the pot to brew. She popped a couple of blueberry bagels into the toaster, repulsive as they sounded, because she thought some food might settle her stomach.

Steaming and buttered, she brought the bagels to the table along with a large mug of black coffee. Crystal hadn't noticed that it was a *Benny and the Girl* mug until she had seated herself. She turned the mug sideways so she wouldn't have to look at the smarmy picture of Blake Jagger and herself. She picked up the newspaper and scanned articles while she nibbled at her breakfast.

She was about to toss the paper aside when she saw it. A short piece in the obituaries, near the lower right corner of the page. It read:

VIDA LEON, ACTRESS, FOUND DEAD IN APARTMENT

Vida Leon, popular 1950s sitcom actress, was found dead in her apartment Tuesday evening by her son, Hollywood powerhouse, Marshall Dawson. The cause of death has not been determined, but police have not ruled out foul play.

Ms. Leon, best known as Daisy in the 1958 sitcom *Daisy Does*, had been retired for many years. Her son is the creator of the popular ABC series, *Benny and the Girl*.

Arrangements for Ms. Leon's funeral are being handled by Dukakis Funeral Home in Brentwood. A private service will be held for friends and family.

Crystal put the paper down slowly. Marshall hadn't mentioned that Vida was his mother. He had sat right there while Crystal had called her a dirty old bat. No wonder he had taken her tantrum so hard.

And now the old woman was dead—did the story implicate foul play? Crystal scanned the paper. It hadn't been ruled out. What had happened?

Crystal felt awful. Marshall had been a dear friend. He had helped her get her career on track. No matter how unreasonable he had become in the end, she certainly hadn't wished for this kind of personal tragedy to befall him. It had been very brave of him to use his own mother as an example for Crystal, no matter how far off base he might have been.

She folded the newspaper with the article facing up and placed it on the dining room table. She crossed the room and fished out the bulky Yellow Pages, flipping through to the funeral homes. After locating the entry for Dukakis Funeral Home, she snapped up the handset of her cordless phone and pecked out the number.

Crystal Bright would be attending this funeral.

III

Chad had the dream every night without fail and would wake up thrashing and tangled in his green army blanket. The metal bed was hard and unyielding, and the sounds of snoring pervaded the acoustically unappealing chamber.

"Shut the fuck up, Collins!"

It was Norton Jones, a big, black oversized son-of-a-bitch who ruled the roost. His parents had used him regularly as a punching bag, so he wasn't afraid of much, certainly not Chad Collins.

"Sorry, Norton," Chad whispered, straightening his blanket, and hunkering back down into the thin mattress.

A little grumbling, then silence.

Chad thought about the dream, the vivid reenactment of that night only one month ago. His mother's horrified expression, the blood, the *rush*.

It had been exhilarating, like an orgasm to the hundredth power.

Afterward, he had guided his bicycle back out onto the street and pedaled toward home. He hadn't gotten two blocks when he spotted a very familiar vehicle coming in his direction. Conservative yet expensive, Peter Collins' maroon Volvo was heading toward Hayes Safety Equipment. Chad had instinctively dropped between two parked cars, staying out of sight.

This was too good to be true. His father deserved the satisfaction of finding that two-timing slut cut to ribbons in the parking lot. On the downside, Chad needed to get his ass home and back in bed, like *pronto*. He still didn't understand how he had avoided getting splattered with his mother's blood, but he was more than happy to consider himself extraordinarily lucky.

As soon as Peter had passed, Chad straightened his bike and pedaled like his life depended on it. He was far too young to spend it locked away. Especially when he had done the world a great big, gigantic favor. Naomi Collins had never been good for anything more than a fuck for strangers and the occasional peanut butter sandwich. Something simply had to be done.

Chad was completely winded when he reached his house. He hadn't seen anyone other than Peter, and he hoped that no one had seen him. He let himself in and crawled back into bed, listening to the crickets chirp and the wind scuttle the leaves. Waiting for the sound of cars, cars full of policemen, here to tell him that there had been a horrible accident.

Chad thought he would be anxious, laying in a pool of his own sweat until the officers arrived. He feared that his own anxiety would betray his guilt to them. He feared that he might giggle uncontrollably.

What he didn't expect was to fall asleep, which was exactly what he had done. It was a deep, peaceful, dreamless sleep—the only one he would get for quite some time. He was awakened the next morning at nine by a rhythmic rapping at the front door. Two somber looking police officers and a hard-faced woman in a business suit stood on the front stoop, the officers shifting back and forth on their flat feet while the woman consulted a file folder clutched in her heavily veined hands.

Chad had opened the door rubbing sleep from his eyes. *"Mmm?"* he mumbled.

"Charles Collins?" the woman asked, her voice sharp and no-nonsense.

Chad nodded dumbly.

"May we come in?" one of the officers asked. He was a wide-shouldered Black man with big brown eyes brimming over with sympathy. He flashed his police identification as if it were a hall pass. Officer Thomas Drake.

Don't giggle.

Chad stepped back, allowing the trio to enter the living room.

"Am I in some kind of trouble?" asked Chad, self-consciously tugging his t-shirt down to cover as much of his boxers as possible.

"No, son, no," said the other officer, a middle-aged and paunchy white man. His identification read Officer Herman Kaut. "I'm afraid we're here with some bad news."

Chad had managed a blank look and a half-smile. "Bad news?"

"I'm afraid so," said Officer Drake. "Yesterday evening, your mother was— in an accident as she was leaving work."

"An accident?" Chad hoped his voice sounded innocent and confused. He sank down onto the floral print couch and stared with big open eyes at the officers.

"Not exactly an accident, son," said Officer Kaut. "Your mother was attacked as she left work. I'm afraid she's gone."

"Gone?" *Oh, God,* please *don't giggle.*

The stern-looking woman stepped forward and offered a bony hand. Chad shook it absently, trying to remain dazed and confused. "I'm Donna Mulligan," she had said, her voice hard and superficially sympathetic. "I'm with Children's Services."

Chad gave her a perplexed look. "Where's my dad?"

The officers exchanged a silent glance. "I'm sorry, son. He's been taken into custody. He was at the scene when the police arrived."

The urge to giggle was almost painful. They thought *Peter* had done it. What was the appropriate response? Chad decided on righteous indignation. "You're *crazy!* My dad would *never* hurt anyone, much less Mom."

"It's up to the courts now, son," said Officer Kaut.

"Your father tells us you don't have any other relatives," said Ms. Mulligan. "I've come to take you to Children's Services."

Chad stared stupidly ahead. Both his parents had been only children, and his grandparents had passed away before he was ever born.

"Charles?" Ms. Mulligan leaned in close to peer at Chad's gaping face. "Charles? Are you alright?"

"Chad," he whispered.

"Hmm?"

"Chad. Everyone calls me Chad," he said dully, carefully draining all of the emotion from his voice.

"Oh. All right, then. If you would like to get some things, we can be on our way."

Chad heard the sound of another car in the drive, then a door slammed while the engine continued running. Ricky Whalen stuck his pimple-pocked face through the open front door, his black hair still wet from his morning shower. "Chad—?"

Chad looked up at him but said nothing. The policemen were already escorting Ricky back out onto the porch.

"A friend?" asked Ms. Mulligan.

"Uh-huh," said Chad. "Ricky Whalen. Him and me and Shelley and Julie were goin' to King's Island. I should tell them I can't go." He had risen to his feet.

"It's okay," said Ms. Mulligan, easing him toward the rear of the house. "You go on and get your things. Officer Kaut and Officer Drake will make your apologies for you."

Chad meandered back to his little bedroom, hoping he looked like he was in shock. He quickly filled a duffel bag with a few changes of clothes and underwear. He had started to leave when he paused, placing the duffel bag on his bed. He removed the poster of Crystal Bright from the wall at the foot of his bed, carefully peeling the tape away from the edges before rolling it up and tucking it under his arm.

The next several days were a whirlwind of activity. Chad asserted that he was at his house the entire evening in question, and the police weren't inclined to look much further. No one had come forward to dispute his statement. Peter Collins' fingerprints had been found all over the knife handle. Peter had claimed he picked it up without thinking, but isn't that what they all say?

After about a week, Chad was allowed to see Peter in jail. Bail had been denied, and Peter looked like a fish out of water behind the reinforced safety glass that separated the inmates from their visitors. He had lost about ten pounds and grown a shaggy, unflattering beard. His bloodshot eyes were tired behind wire-rimmed glasses, as if he hadn't slept since the arrest. His sandy hair wasn't brushed, and his teeth looked like they hadn't been either.

Peter and Chad picked up the handsets to the phones which were mounted to the wall on each side of the safety glass.

"Chad, oh God, Chad," said Peter, tears welling in his eyes. "What have they done with you? Are they taking good care of you?"

"I'm fine, Dad," he had said simply, staring coolly at his father.

"They won't let me out to take care of you—"

"Did you do it?" Chad asked, enjoying the expression of revulsion that crossed Peter's face.

"Of course not! How could you even ask such a thing? I loved your mother!"

"Then why were you getting a divorce?"

"That was her idea, not mine. I really think we could have worked everything out in time. As a matter of fact, that's why I was going over that night. I was hoping she might grab a cup of coffee with me."

"*Mmm,*" said Chad noncommittally.

"What were *you* doing out there? I saw you when I passed, you know," whispered Peter.

This came as a surprise to Chad. He had been certain that Peter hadn't spotted him. Wouldn't he have said something before this? "I don't know what you're talking about. I was in bed," said Chad, hoping the surprise on his face had passed as quickly as it had come.

Peter studied him dubiously. "I didn't mention anything to the police. I wanted to keep you out of it. Did you see something? Did you see who did it?"

Chad almost laughed out loud. Peter's stubborn refusal to consider Chad as a suspect was most delightful. This new game was far more entertaining than all the evenings they had spent together at home, reading on the porch. "Really, Dad, I don't know what you're talking about. I went to bed about eleven that night. Didn't wake up until the police came by the next morning."

Peter stared at Chad for a long, silent moment. "Alright, if you say so," he eventually said. "Have you been okay? I heard they transferred you to Children's Services. I hope it's not too horrible."

Chad shrugged. "Some of the kids are really messed up. I just keep to myself. It's okay."

"I swear, I'll be out soon," said Peter. "Then I'll get you out of that place, I promise."

They had talked about this and that for the next few minutes before a sour-faced guard told them their time was nearly over, and they had one minute to wrap things up.

"Hang in there, champ," Peter had said. "And I won't say anything about seeing you that night, okay? Maybe we can talk about it later."

"Dad, I told you I wasn't—"

Peter waved the words away, hanging up his receiver and turning back to the guard.

This isn't good, Chad had thought. Peter could place him at the scene at approximately the time of the murder. The police were so cocksure that Peter was the bad guy, they hadn't bothered to analyze Chad's alibi. He didn't think there were any other vulnerabilities in his story, but he hadn't thought Peter had seen him, either.

Officer Drake stopped by a few days later, checking in on this newest ward of the State of Indiana. "How ya doin', fella?" he asked, smiling with big white teeth. They were in the courtyard, designed for outdoor recreation, but with the telltale reminder of a tall chain link fence bordering the yard. Other adolescent rejects laughed and grouped together in the yard. Chad sat by himself at a weatherworn picnic table, picking at a bologna sandwich.

"Okay, I guess," Chad said.

"Good!" said the officer, a little too enthusiastically. "I was hoping I might be able to ask you some questions about your folks. You feel up to it?"

Chad shrugged as Drake placed a yellow legal pad on the picnic table. "S'pose."

"I'll try to keep it brief, or Ms. Mulligan will be all over me. She's a real tight-ass," said Drake, still smiling.

"I'll say," agreed Chad. Donna Mulligan had missed her calling entirely. Her discipline was military, and she gave zero latitude. Life at Children's Services was

51

much smoother if you adhered to her rules. Many of the charges had figured this out; a few of the slower ones had not.

"So how were things between your folks? I understand they had recently filed for divorce."

"Uh-huh. It came as a real surprise to me. I thought they got along real good."

"Any idea what it was all about? A couple of your mother's former co-workers say she was seeing someone new, but none of them knew his name. You ever meet him?"

That bitch! Chad had been right all along! His mother *had* been seeing someone after hours. He had never been certain until this moment, so he was being truthful when he said, "I didn't know she was dating anyone."

The officer nodded. "She probably didn't want to hurt your feelings. She told people at work that the divorce was really messing with you."

Chad nodded slowly. "It seemed like it was kind of out of the blue. Did my dad really kill her?"

Drake's smile faded. "It doesn't look good," he said. "Did they fight much?"

"Toward the end it was pretty bad. After they actually separated, Dad always wanted to know what Mom was doing, you know? I think he was jealous. I thought it was ridiculous, but then again, I didn't know she had started seeing someone else."

"Was your dad ever violent with your mom?"

Chad squirmed on the picnic table bench. Peter had never laid a hand on his mother. Never. However, what he said was, "Umm, well...do I have to answer if it hurts my dad?"

Chad saw the look of victory in the officer's big brown eyes. "It's alright, Chad. Did he ever hit you?"

Chad wasn't sure how to proceed from here, so he decided to break down and cry, pushing his sandwich aside and burying his face in the crook of his arms.

Drake left him shortly afterward, and soon Ms. Mulligan was escorting him to a counselor's office where he might be able to unburden his soul. So much of this was giggle-worthy, but Chad worked it like he was after an Oscar.

Now, he lay awake in the pre-dawn hour, listening to Norton saw mammoth logs on the bunk above him. He had been at Children's Services for three weeks. The only reminder of home was the poster of Crystal Bright, peering down at him where he had taped it to the bottom of Norton's bunk. It was like having an angel overhead, floating like a personal guardian.

There were fifteen male wards of the state bunked military style in the gunmetal gray barracks. Everything was made of metal and painted dark green, further contributing to the overall gloom of the quarters. The girls were housed in a similar facility across the grounds, although their facility was mustard yellow.

Chad had elected to stay out of everyone's way. He was almost eighteen, at which time he could bid the institution farewell, leaving all these losers behind.

Norton Jones, aforementioned king of the hill, was destined to spend his short life behind bars of one sort or another before he eventually drank or drugged himself to death. Most of the kids here were like that, dealt an uneven hand from the start. Whoever said, 'When life hands you lemons, make lemonade!' should be beaten soundly about the head and shoulders. These kids were learning how to survive on the street. Some had more experience than others and were quite willing to share what they knew about being a juvenile delinquent. Chad wasn't interested in learning from amateurs. None of them had killed their mother.

From the end of the darkened room, the door opened a crack, spilling a narrow band of light into the room. Chad raised his head from his pillow and focused on the dark form standing there. He could tell from the visitor's shape that she was female, long hair and full breasts outlined in shadow.

"*Pssst!* Chad!" The voice was urgent and mischievous. "C'mere!"

Chad raised a finger to silence the girl, then swung his legs out from underneath his blanket. Norton was still buzzing overhead, unaware of the girl's presence. What was she doing here? Ms. Mulligan would have a stroke on the spot!

Chad pulled on a pair of gray sweatpants and a threadbare white t-shirt. He didn't bother with shoes. He padded across the cold concrete floor toward his waiting visitor. When he could almost see her, she stepped back and let the door swing shut.

Sighing, Chad hurried out the door just in time to see the girl's gown trailing around the corner at the far end of the hall. Lonnie Akerman, resident security guard and halfwit, was asleep at his little desk by the door, oblivious to everything around him. He snored like he had a nasal blockage, wet and loud. Chad eased down the hallway, following the apparition with increasing urgency.

He rounded the corner and stopped. He didn't see anyone waiting for him. He cast a glance over his shoulder, but the hall was empty in that direction, too. This section of the building had been unused for some time, with empty room after empty room ready to provide shelter to unwanted or orphaned children. The light grew dimmer as Chad progressed, leaving the civilized part of the building behind.

He had traveled nearly three-quarters of the way down the hall when he was suddenly seized from the right and pulled into a dark room. It was the girl he had seen framed in his doorway. Her smile was full of purpose, as were her hands, which slid effortlessly under the waistband of Chad's sweatpants and deeper still into his underwear.

Her mouth was on his like a magnet, her tongue sliding in, teasing. She pulled her gown off and pressed her full breasts against him, leaning him against the wall. She had his pants off without him realizing how, her hands fondling, groping. They slid down the wall as one, and soon they were, Chad bucking, and the mysterious stranger riding him like a moaning bronco.

IV

Old Paulie was up, dancing like a little North Pole elf, waving his arms and kicking his knobby little legs in rhythm with the music. Luke leaned against the doorframe of the old man's room, an amused smile hidden behind one hand. He hadn't seen Paulie this active in years. His old bones usually ached with arthritis so severe he did little more than hobble from one place to the next. Many lesser men would have succumbed to the affliction entirely, planting their asses in easy chairs for the rest of their lives, but not Paulie. Sure, it slowed him down, but eventually he got where he was going.

Tonight, either his pain receptors had completely shut down or he had discovered the Fountain of Youth. In any case, he was stomping and whooping and flailing his arms with an energy exhausting to watch.

The song faded out, and Luke cleared his throat. Old Paulie turned, smiling a big gummy smile. He had apparently put the CD in before he had gotten around to his teeth. Luke crossed the room and stopped the CD before it launched into the next hoedown.

"Hey, old man," Luke said, smiling crookedly at Paulie.

"Mmmm," said Paulie, chomping on his own lips. He held a finger up and waddled over to his nightstand where his teeth lay at the bottom of a mason jar. He popped them in upside down, then flipped them over and tried again.

"Feelin' a little frisky, huh?" asked Luke, still grinning.

"Wipe that shit-eatin' grin off yorn face, young'un. I got the spirit, and when you get the spirit, you just gotta go with it." Paulie didn't even appear to be winded.

"So, how you feelin' tonight?" asked Luke, sitting on the edge of Paulie's antique wrought iron bed. It had been painted with white house paint years before, hiding the intricate ironwork etchings which adorned the frame.

"Howzit look like I'm feelin'? Damn fine, my boy! *Damn* fine," said Paulie, grinning from one side of his face to the other. He pulled up a footstool from beside his bed and perched on it like a low barstool. Luke didn't see how Paulie would ever be able to get back up.

The attic bedroom had low ceilings where the rafters descended from the peak of the roof to meet the eave below. The room was musty and hadn't been thoroughly cleaned in decades. The only sign of modern amenities was the magnificent Pioneer sound system on a black stereo stand in the corner of the room. Four large speakers were aimed at the center of the room where Old Paulie's bed was. Ancient three-shelf bookcases, built in the backyard by Paulie himself, lined the southern wall, loaded with Louis L'Amour and Zane Gray paperbacks and an eclectic collection of other authors. Westerns, war epics, mysteries, science fiction—Old Paulie was a voracious reader.

"You best simmer down before you give yourself a fit," said Luke.

"Pffft." Paulie waved the comment away. "I'm glad ya stopped. Been meanin' to talk to you for years."

"I been right here for the past six years or so," said Luke.

Paulie shot him an annoyed glance. "I *know* you been here for six years—*or so.* Ya think I'm senile? Course you been here for six years—" His words dissolved into discontented grumbling.

"You hungry?" Luke asked.

"No time for that, boy. You and me need to talk."

Oh boy, here it comes, thought Luke. What would it be? The creature in the back field? The town counsel infiltrated by Middle Eastern oil barons with deadly biological contaminants hidden in vials in their pockets? Aliens who had taken over network television, sending subliminal messages embedded in their broadcasts? Luke spotted a science fiction anthology that was open and face-down on Paulie's nightstand. He mentally placed his marker on the alien theory.

"Tonight's the night," Paulie said, grinning even bigger than before.

"Hmm?"

"I put my time in, punched the clock and am goin' home."

"What are you talkin' 'bout, Paulie?"

"When I turn out the lights tonight, that'll be it."

Luke's bemused grin faltered then fell. "Don't talk like that."

"Oh, don't be a pantywaist, boy! You're born, you live, you die. Happened a million times before me, and it'll happen a million times after I'm tomb dust."

"Most people can't predict exactly *when*, you know, Paulie. Unless they're planning suicide."

Paulie looked shocked. *"Suicide?* What's the matter with you boy? Are you thinkin' of killin' yourself? That's *crazy!* God don't take kindly to people disrespectin' themselves. You'll fry like bacon in hell."

"Not me, I meant—oh, never mind what I meant," said Luke. He had to remember that Paulie was just rambling. Granted, this was a new and disturbing direction, but probably as harmless as his frequent stories of alien invasion. But still... "You don't still keep a gun in here, do you?"

"Course I do! I always have. Ain't gonna let some punk thief steal me blind while I sleep, no sir! Ya know, you're askin' the dumbest questions tonight."

"Sorry."

"It's okay. But keep your mouth shut for half a minute and let's see if I can tell you something important, okay?"

Luke nodded and smiled, pressing his lips together firmly.

"As you well know," continued Paulie, "tain't got no children on account of—"

"Your faulty kickstand."

"—my faulty—boy, you gonna let me tell the story?"

"Sorry."

"Anyways, because I ain't never had no kids, I'm leaving this place and all its yardage to you. I went to see Morty King last week to make sure I had crossed my t's and dotted all my i's." Morty King was the grandson of Paulie's original lawyer who had died so many years before.

Luke squirmed uncomfortably on the edge of the bed. "Why you talkin' like this, Paulie?"

Paulie sighed impatiently. "Because I'm going to sit with Jesus in the Kingdom of the Lord. Ain't no use fussin' about it. I'm happy."

"Do we have to talk about this?"

"Yes, we do," said Paulie, his tone firm and unyielding. "You don't get to just bury me and then prop your feet up on the couch. You get to keep the house on condition."

"On condition?"

Paulie's head bobbed in confirmation. "That's right."

Luke smiled in amusement. This should be good. The last time that Paulie had granted something to Luke conditionally, it had been the opportunity to live at the farmhouse. The condition was that Luke would do whatever odd jobs Paulie fed to him in exchange for food and shelter. It had been an equitable arrangement for both.

"Not that I'm in any hurry to see you go, old man, but what are these conditions? You aren't going to make me play that *Cotton-Eyed Joe* song full blast every mornin', are you?"

"This is serious, boy. Stop crackin' wise."

"Sorry."

"You get the house if and only if you get out of town."

Luke's eyebrows twisted upward in confusion. "Hunh? That don't make sense, Paulie."

"Sure, it does. You been in Jasper your whole life, ain't ya?"

"Well, yeah, but—"

"No buts, boy. Either ya have or ya hain't, an' since I know you have, quit your arguin'. Anyways, what was I sayin'?" Paulie's eyes grew glassy and distant as they often did when he tried to convey a story of any real length. Most times, when his eyes swam back into focus, he was on to a different, unrelated thread. Not this time.

"Oh, yes! One year. You need to go and find out about yourself, boy. You been on pause for your whole life. I don't know what you're waitin' for, but I'm gonna force you to go out and take a taste of the world. I been through wars and hard times and good times, too. You been through nothin', and it's time for you to stop pissin' your life away. The house, the property, and a wad of cash you don't know nothin' 'bout are waiting for you after the year is up, but not a minute before. If Morty King sees you on the property, he'll call the sheriff."

Luke was silent for a moment, wondering if this was truth or fiction. He would place a call to Morty in the morning to confirm. Assuming it was true, it was still generous, even considering the unusual stipulation. "While I thank you, you're talking gruesome, Paulie. Cut it out."

"I will not. I'm tellin' you, tonight's the night. If I don't talk to ya now, what am I s'posed to do, haunt ya? I don't want to stick around for that."

"What am I supposed to do?" Luke asked.

"Any damn thing you want, you just have to get out there and *do* it! You're a good boy, Lucas. I knowed it when the townsfolk were callin' you Satan hisself. I know you got more to ya than just growing old on some podunk farm."

"Where'm I supposed to go?"

"The teacups never lie." Aha! Again, with the teacups. Apparently, Paulie had maintained lucidity as long as possible, but his tale was about to self-destruct into nonsense and gibberish. This usually signified that he was ready to go back to sleep.

"I don't know what that means. Teacups don't talk, how could they lie?" asked Luke.

"*Everything* talks, boy. You just gotta *listen.*"

"Thanks for clearing that up for me, Paulie," said Luke sarcastically.

"Anytime, boy. There's a young miss just waiting for you out there."

"Underneath a teacup?"

"Maybe."

Luke stood and helped Paulie to his feet from his position on the footstool. His earlier surplus of energy had vanished as quickly as it had come. Paulie felt brittle and shaky, and Luke carefully guided him back to his bed.

"You want some music?" Luke asked.

"Something soft. Enya."

"In my what?"

"E-N-Y-A. Enya."

"Oh." Luke flipped through Paulie's stack of CD's. His collection was marvelously eclectic, with Madonna, Stone Temple Pilots and KISS sharing shelf space with Frank Sinatra, Billie Holliday and Loretta Lynn. He eventually found the disc he was looking for and put it in the machine, adjusting the volume before hitting play. Chords flowed like water from the speakers, as soothing as a full-body massage.

"Luke?"

"Yes, Paulie?"

"I love you, boy. You'll make me right proud o' you, I know it."

"I love you, too, Paulie, but you're creeping me out." Luke stood beside Paulie's bed as the old man stuck his spindly legs underneath the covers. Paulie

57

had never seemed so vulnerable, in stark contrast to the dancing scarecrow he had just been. At this moment, he looked every minute of his age.

Paulie smiled. "There's no reason to be creeped. I'm happy. I'm leavin' you my CDs. You should be happy, too."

"I am, Paulie, I am. Nothing makes me happier than to know that you are, too." Luke turned off the lamp beside Paulie's bed, plunging the room into darkness. "I'll see you in the morning."

"So, you will, but I won't see you. Goodbye, son."

"Quit it."

"Okay, whatever."

Luke backed out of the room and closed the door. Enya sang softly on the other side, and Luke stood for a minute, listening to the house around him. Soon, he heard Paulie's snoring, loud intakes of air through nostrils exhaled seconds later in a high-pitched whistle.

Luke went down the stairs into the sparsely furnished living room and stretched out on the tattered sofa. Paulie had bought the furniture when he had been married to his third wife, Geneva. She had died of cervical cancer the year before Paulie had adopted Luke. *It must've been rough on Old Paulie, outliving three wives*, thought Luke. Paulie had rarely spoken of them, but Luke knew that he kept their memories near and dear. Little mementos of each decorated the house.

Paulie's post-nap ramblings had never been so cohesive, nor had they been so ominous. If Paulie were to die, what would Luke do for a year? Hitchhike around the country? Maybe. Attend college in Lexington? Definitely not. Luke was sure that Paulie was right about one thing, though. A special young lady was out there waiting for him somewhere. It wasn't optimistic dreaming; he *felt* her presence, pulling at him like the moon on the tide. He had no predetermined mental image of his soul mate but knew that he would recognize her when he saw her. He knew that she wasn't in Jasper and may never be.

As Luke drifted off to sleep on the couch, he said a quick prayer for Paulie's health. He didn't want to admit it, not even to himself, but Luke was afraid to start this mysterious journey which Paulie had outlined. Paulie seemed so certain that he would be cashing in his chips that night, and Luke wanted nothing more than a twenty-year postponement on the inevitable.

You can't always get what you want.

CHAPTER FIVE

I

Streetlights passed overhead in a surreal blur. Lisa guided her Toyota through the city streets, her mind a million miles away. She had been to Morton's a thousand times and autopilot had kicked in.

She thought she might get a dog in the morning—a big, loud dog. She would keep it inside with her to stand guard against the wino from the funeral. She shuddered at the memory of the delusional man, speaking the words Nanna Grace had spoken so many times before.

I can see your soul.

It wasn't a threat; it was a fact. The old woman haunted Lisa long before she had ever died. Lisa wondered if it might stop now—if she might be able to have some normalcy in her life.

What was normalcy, anyway?

The Carpenters were crooning on the radio, and Lisa hummed along off-key. Tiny droplets began to fall from the sky, the day's rainfall not yet finished. Lisa flicked her windshield wipers on, and they began their steady and hypnotic *tick-tock.*

Lisa was exhausted. She had no idea of the time, her watch at home on her dresser and her dashboard clock frozen for the past five years at three forty-one. She had lifted and tugged and hauled furniture for the past—eight? ten? twelve?—hours. She had scrubbed away the fumes of incontinence imbedded in Nanna Grace's walls and flooring. She had wrenched her back getting that damned recliner down the stairs.

Once, when it had gotten very still, Lisa could have sworn she heard Nanna Grace laughing. It was fleeting, then gone.

Lisa had made a clean sweep of the walls, raking down golden crucifixes and porcelain praying hands. She would not be intimidated by the old woman any longer. The house was hers. The belongings in the house were hers. If she wanted to break them, she would damn well break them.

The rain fell harder, causing Lisa to squint her eyes against the oncoming traffic. It couldn't be too awfully late. There were too many cars on the road. Morton's was only a few blocks away.

Lisa giggled suddenly, filling the cabin of the car with girlish delight. She might decide on a different hair color. She had used the same white-blonde since her hair first started to darken when she was thirteen. Looking in the rearview mirror, she realized the color did not suit her features at all. Her hair was thick and bone-straight, grown long because righteous women didn't cut their hair. They didn't color it, either, but what Nanna Grace didn't know wouldn't hurt her. The color was more like the absence of color, and her pasty complexion blended with it in uniform blandness. She looked anemic. Her eyebrows were dark and bushy—because righteous women didn't pluck—and her pores were engorged with large blackheads from years of poor facial hygiene. She wondered if she could paint a pretty picture on this substandard canvas. The task would be daunting, but Lisa didn't feel depressed, as she would have only yesterday. She considered it an interesting challenge. Nothing could be worse than what stared back at her from the rearview mirror.

Lisa decided she would get a TV. Nanna Grace hadn't allowed television, calling it the lazy reader. *It drains the imagination*, she said, and perhaps it did. Perhaps it broadcast subliminal messages telling Americans to stock up on Cheese Whiz. Lisa didn't care to speculate. She wanted to see the programs people talked about. Since her days at St. Ann's School for Girls, she had listened to her classmates chatter about their favorite programs, their favorite actors, and their favorite music videos. Later, it was coworkers theorizing about their evening serials. Lisa never had anything to contribute. When people found out that she didn't own a television, they thought she was from Mars, and Lisa felt like she was. No more. The TV had moved to the top of the shopping list, even ahead of the big, loud dog. Lisa doubted that she could afford a new set, but she saw second-hand models at yard sales all the time. She didn't care if it was large or small, just so long as it was functional.

So many problems solved with the cessation of one bitter heartbeat. Lisa smiled and turned the Carpenters up.

She wished she could subscribe to cable, but with her current employment status, a monthly financial commitment didn't seem particularly prudent. She had heard about the sex. She wanted to see the sex. Ultimately, she wanted to *have* the sex, but one thing at a time. There was a custodian at the hospital named Leonard Barnes. Most of the women found him repugnant, but Lisa's eyes had always been drawn like magnets to the cleft of his buttocks, the swell of his crotch. It didn't matter that he was at least thirty years her senior, and his teeth were corrupted and missing in a few places. It didn't matter that he bathed infrequently. In some ways, that made it more exciting, more perverse. Now that she had been fired, she doubted she would see Leonard again. Shame.

Lisa's eyes were heavier as she pulled into Morton's parking lot. A handful of cars still occupied it, but only a number befitting this time of night, whatever time that might be. Lisa took a spot near the entrance and parked.

Once inside, Lisa picked up a bright blue plastic hand basket and plodded along toward the health and beauty section, counting the yellowed tiles beneath her feet as she went. Nanna Grace had always told her that it was impolite to stare. She passed faceless people, identifiable only by their feet, and pressed on to the proper aisle. She had shopped Morton's for so long that she could find just about anything, even blindfolded. She felt like a ghost, wafting from aisle to aisle, shoulders hunched over, eyes downturned. No one ever said anything to her, allowing her to pass like an insignificant cloud. A fat, red-headed baby in a shopping cart stared long and hard, drool stringing down from its bulbous bottom lip. Lisa hated babies. Well, "hate" may be too strong a word. She didn't understand babies. Eyes of innocence? Lisa didn't think so. Unfettered by the bonds of structured language, babies seemed to possess incomprehensible wisdom in their gigantic, round eyes. As soon as complete sentences could be formed, that mystical light seemed to flicker and fade until only a simple-headed child was left behind. Even a child prodigy seemed to lose the connection to the all-seeing, all-knowing power. Lisa's gaze skipped over the child's face as soon as she recognized it for what it was, and she hurried to the rear of the store, her ultimate destination.

Half of the aisle was devoted to hair coloring products, manufactured by many and a color for every crayon in the box. Lisa imagined herself with jet black hair, cut in a pageboy framing her face. *Eech*. Red? Big, tall curls piled high and teased into a tangled tower. *Better*. Blonde? Lisa had been blonde for so many years now. It was time for something different. Brunette? Hmmm. *Distinct possibility*. A mane of chestnut hair cascading around her shoulders.

Lisa smiled and selected a tint called "Acorn."

As she placed the box of colorant into her hand basket, her eyes skimmed across something familiar in the next aisle over. She leaned forward, pressing her face nearly flat against the second shelf and peering over the tops of the boxes which lined it.

Ms. Kelsey was there. Her back was to Lisa, oblivious to her presence. She was examining the various options for controlling foot fungus, absurdly spraying a sample of each on her arm and smelling. Lisa's eyes narrowed, and her contempt for this woman came alive, crawling underneath her skin like a sandworm. How dare Ms. Kelsey question Lisa's professionalism? Lisa had provided nothing but top-notch care for Mrs. Baylock. What had possessed the old woman to betray Lisa? What had caused her to make such baseless allegations? Or had Ms. Kelsey made the whole thing up just to rid herself of Lisa?

Ms. Kelsey eventually decided on one of the products and tossed it disinterestedly into her shopping cart. She wore a blue and purple nylon running suit, and Lisa could barely suppress the giggle playing at her lips. She had never seen Ms. Kelsey in anything but her administrative suit, professionally styled from head to toe. Tonight, her short, graying hair was damp with perspiration over her ears and above her collar, and her running suit was pit-stained and rumpled. Although she never wore much makeup, the total absence of it was unflattering, adding years to the woman's stern countenance. Such grim determination reminded Lisa of Nanna Grace.

Lisa eased away from the shelf and waited to see which direction Ms. Kelsey would go. She thought momentarily about confronting the hospital administrator, telling her exactly what she thought of her, but then realized she hadn't a coherent thing to say. Her words always turned to mush in her mouth when she was forced to deal with Ms. Kelsey, even on issues that were insignificant. Lisa wouldn't allow the woman the satisfaction of winning a verbal duel in the middle of Morton's Supermarket. Ms. Kelsey turned right, so Lisa went left, heading as quickly as possible to the checkout lanes at the front of the store.

Only one lane was open, and ten impatient customers stood between Lisa and the exit.

Just put it in your pocket, a voice whispered hypnotically in her ear.

No. She wouldn't allow Ms. Kelsey the satisfaction of seeing her arrested in the parking lot should she be caught. Lisa had never shoplifted anything, and now was not the time to test her potential.

Only six customers now. Lisa glanced around furtively, hoping that she would clear the bottleneck before Ms. Kelsey rounded the corner.

Don't be stupid, girl. She doesn't even remember your name.

Lisa jumped with the thought, the voice in her head undeniably that of Nanna Grace. She returned her gaze to the floor, staring at her shabby brown loafers, cracked across the tops and stained after years of daily wear.

Three customers now. Lisa still didn't see Ms. Kelsey anywhere near the front of the store. She was probably back in sporting goods buying a protective cup. Lisa giggled and the woman in front of her gave her a quizzical look.

Finally at the counter, Lisa surrendered $6.80 and then hurried out into the parking lot, still watching her feet. The sky still dribbled down, and a dense fog had crawled into the parking lot, shrouding it in cotton batting. Lisa settled into the driver's seat of her Toyota and started the car. All of the windows responded the same, frosting and obscuring Lisa's visibility. The car was not equipped with the luxury of air conditioning which would have defrosted the windows in no time, so Lisa sat, letting the engine warm and the ventilated air do its slow work.

After a few moments, Lisa adjusted her seatbelt and flipped on the windshield wipers and headlights. The rain had intensified, pounding on the thin metal roof like nails falling from above. The noise was so loud that Lisa couldn't even hear the sound of her own engine running. The fog obscured everything in the parking lot, leaching the color away and bathing everything silvery-gray. The overhead vapor lights fought a losing battle, unable to pierce more than a few feet of darkness in any direction.

Silver glinted brightly in Lisa's headlights.

Lisa squinted her eyes together and leaned over the steering wheel toward the windshield, trying to discern the flash which had caught her eye. As if taking a stage, Ms. Kelsey pushed her twinkling cart forward, into the path of the headlights. Her head was bowed down, tucked under a pocketbook held above in a futile attempt to keep dry. Ms. Kelsey was oblivious to everything else, focused solely on reaching her car, a shiny black Lexus parked at the far end of the lot nearest the street entrance.

Lisa had no recollection of shifting the car into gear, but the Toyota began a gradual glide out of its parking slot, easing up the lane behind Ms. Kelsey. The rain fell and the fog thickened, and the beam of the headlights seemed to literally bend around the scurrying administrator. She gave no indication that she saw Lisa's car at all.

Lisa's hands clutched the steering wheel tightly, easing forward. Ms. Kelsey— did she even *have* a first name?—was nearing the Lexus, her handbag still in place overtop her head. Suddenly, she stopped dead in her tracks, as if a sense of foreboding tickled at the short hairs of her neck. Lisa stopped the car, her gaze locked straight ahead. She was less than twenty feet away from Ms. Kelsey now.

Slowly, Ms. Kelsey turned, sensing the presence behind her. Her eyes squinted against the glare of the headlights, screwing her stern features into jagged lines. Her scowling mouth twitched with annoyance, incredulity—and fear. The fear was mostly buried beneath the other reactions, but it was undeniable, creeping up to taint the hard gaze of her eyes.

The sound that spilled from Lisa's mouth was foreign to her own ears, a pitiful, wounded caterwaul which reverberated inside the car's cabin.

She stomped on the accelerator.

The front of the car lifted slightly as the tires spun on the wet tarmac. Ms. Kelsey's face registered sheer horror, and Lisa's eyes saw it all in tunnel vision. Then came recognition—sweet, glorious recognition. It wouldn't be nearly as satisfying if Ms. Kelsey didn't know who, didn't know why.

Oh, she knew all right.

The Toyota's front bumper made contact before Ms. Kelsey could run, pinning her to her own cart from the sheer velocity of the maneuver. Only thirty feet separated Lisa's car from the street at the end of the parking lot's entrance, but she kept her foot pressed firmly down. Ms. Kelsey remained securely pinned between the hood and the cart, as it rolled faster on its wheels than it had ever been designed to do. It was as if invisible hands were holding her up, keeping her from sliding down beneath the grill and under the tires.

Her expression, borne of pain, confusion, and terror, was delicious.

Lisa stomped the brake pedal reflexively, and the car came to a screeching, sudden stop. Ms. Kelsey, however, was propelled by inertia into the street, her cart flipping forward and bucking as if it were a belligerent young bronco, sending Ms. Kelsey headlong over its top.

Later, the driver would blame himself. *If only I had seen her in time,* he would say. But there was no way of avoiding the projectile; it was upon him before he even had the chance to blink.

Darin Miller

Lisa watched from the mouth of the parking lot as Ms. Kelsey dissolved into a pulpy goo on the front of the large yellow sanitation truck, the metal cart twisting and mangling under its wheels. The truck's brakes slammed on, casting a sickening red glow over the bits of carnage that spewed from its backside. There were no other cars in the vicinity, no other shoppers in the parking lot.

No witnesses.

The truck driver was instantly obsessed with washing Ms. Kelsey's face from his windshield, frantically using his wipers and frequent spurts of blue windshield cleaner. His foot tangled in the pedals and the truck jumped up on the curb, clipping a parked car before coming to rest with its nose imbedded in an oak tree.

As quickly as that, it was over. Lisa's heart pounded furiously in her chest, and warm perspiration coated her underarms.

What had just happened? The aftermath lay all around. Lisa jerked her steering wheel hard to the left and fled the parking lot with all the power the Toyota could muster.

The bitch got what was coming to her.

The obscene thought rang clear as crystal against the pounding rain, ticking windshield wipers, and throttling engine. Lisa realized that she had said the words aloud. It had been her own voice giving utterance to these inappropriate words. A voice cold and unfeeling—but true. The bitch *had* deserved it. Her superior car; her superior job; her superior everything. Based on the deluded ramblings of one senile old bat, Ms. Kelsey had summarily judged and dismissed Lisa. She couldn't be allowed to simply get away with it.

Lisa's hands began to cramp on the steering wheel, and she realized that she was still clutching it with ferocity. She consciously forced herself to relax, and when she did, she began to giggle. Giggles grew into laughter. Laughter climaxed in guffaws.

Didja see the look on her face? POW!

Tears streamed down Lisa's cheeks—wonderful, jubilant tears. She had done the unthinkable, and yet it had seemed so natural, so liberating. The years of enduring Ms. Kelsey's constant haranguing washed away clean, and Lisa felt reborn. She had actually taken a stand, quite possibly for the first time in her entire life.

Had anyone seen?

Lisa glanced into her rearview mirror, scanning for police lights or a Good Samaritan following from Morton's. There was nothing but darkness and the spray of rainwater dancing off the trunk.

Surely there was evidence on the hood of the car. Lisa's eyes followed the thought, and for a brief instant, she thought she saw a teacup, sitting on the edge like a hood ornament. She blinked the hallucination away, realizing belatedly that she had just run a red light.

A decades-old Pontiac thundered into the intersection, and the cars collided in a sickening crunch of shearing metal. Lisa's persistent giggling caught in her throat as bones broke and blood spattered the windshield.

II

"I'm very sorry, ma'am, but you're not on the list."

Crystal glared at the blue-suited man, biting back the impulse to rip his head off. This was a somber occasion, after all, and not the place to make a huge scene. The man was one of several hired to provide security to the high-profile funeral, all of them interconnected with earplugs and walkie-talkies. You'd think the President was being interred.

Crystal forced a smile. She was an actress, for God's sake; she would act. "Marshall Dawson is a dear friend of mine. I'm sure there must be some mistake."

"No, ma'am, I'm sorry." He smiled with perfectly capped, pearly white teeth. There was no hostility in his voice, but there was no budging him, either. He was almost robotic, standing there with his sandy hair slicked back, shoulders squared, feet planted.

"Could you at least check with him?" Crystal asked.

"Mr. Dawson left explicit instructions that he was not to be bothered. The list is written in stone. I really am sorry," the man said. He added, "I enjoyed your work in *Benny and the Girl* very much."

Crystal exhaled a frustrated sigh. "Thanks."

She turned and worked her way through the crowd at the front of Dukakis Funeral Home. Industry types were everywhere, eyebrows arching inquisitively as they noted Crystal's attendance, but no one stepped forward to actually speak. Many of the cast and crew members from *Benny and the Girl* had come, avoiding Crystal like the plague. Britney Bramblett stood amongst them, the new *Girl* for *Benny*, her eyes drifting over for frequent glimpses of her predecessor. At one point, Britney had actually begun to approach Crystal, but she was intercepted by Blake Jagger and led in the opposite direction. Blake had looked back over his shoulder at Crystal, his gaze contemptuous and full of disgust.

Attempts had been made to keep the press at bay, but with their typical regard for celebrity privacy, helicopters had hovered over the area all morning, high-powered lenses picking out tomorrow's headline from the tragic event below.

Crystal hadn't actually seen Marshall. He was most likely in the building, waiting for the funeral to begin. All that she wanted was to tell him how sorry she was. As ugly as things had gotten on a professional level, Crystal needed Marshall to know that she was still a friend.

Maybe he will forgive me, and I'll start getting offers again.

Crystal winced at the thought, mortified that it had even taken shape inside her head. This wasn't about *her*. It was about her friend.

Limousines continued to arrive, depositing celebrities and other Hollywood players, past and present. The crowd began to slowly drift inside the building, security checking identification and confirming invitations. Crystal had already approached three of the well-dressed guards, testing the waters, seeing if her former celebrity status still carried any weight. It didn't.

Just as she was about to give up and leave, a commotion broke at the front of the crowd. The nondescript security guards were conversing urgently back and forth on their walkie-talkies, and one by one, they drifted from their posts, keeping a tentative eye on their stations while assessing the disturbance. Apparently, an overzealous photographer had gate-crashed, driving his Geo Metro right up onto the sidewalk.

An opportunity presented itself as the guard nearest Crystal wandered a few yards from his post. Crystal wasted no time slipping through and into the funeral home, hoping that there wouldn't be a second layer of security just inside. All she needed was another tabloid photo, this one of her being forcibly ejected from the proceedings.

Somber chords spilled from the organ, filling the cherry-paneled foyer with gloom and despair. Crystal had worn a tidy black suit with a dark hat and veil, and she pulled the veil down to conceal her instantly recognizable features as much as possible. Although there had been no further security, most of the people in the room would surely know who she was, and the threat of the tabloid photo was still very real.

Twenty rows of heavy wooden pews led to the pulpit where Vida Leon's rosewood casket was centered. The casket was closed, which made Crystal wonder what kind of shape Vida had been in when she was found. A publicity photo from Vida's days in television had been enlarged and placed on an easel near the casket. Crystal could hardly believe that it was the same woman whom she had visited with Marshall. In the photo, she was young, vibrant, beautiful. A mischievous smile played at the corner of her lips and her eyes twinkled with vivacity. Her hair had been its natural brunette, curled under and accentuating the porcelain of her skin.

Marshall was standing near the casket while his partner, Sam Novak, offered support. They were like Mutt and Jeff; Marshall was tall with salt-and-pepper hair and a slightly rounded midsection concealed within his immaculately tailored Armani suit. Sam was shorter, blond and tanned, muscular and extraordinarily handsome. Marshall's expression conveyed his emotions better than any actor ever could, grieving for the mother who had one day been a real star but lately had barely been a memory. Crystal realized how deeply Marshall must have cared for her by trying to sustain some illusion of stardom for her.

The people in the room were friends and business associates of Marshall's, not Vida's. Most of them probably didn't even know her. Soft conversation murmured about the room like a lazy wave, lapping at Crystal's eardrums.

Murdered. Stabbed. Her own living room. What's the world coming to?

Broken phrases told the story in summary, and Crystal realized that Vida's life had come to a brutal end. She thought of her own Aunt Maude, the woman who had raised her back in Lucasville, Ohio. At eighty-eight, the old girl was as lively as ever. Crystal hadn't been home in over a year, and she was suddenly awash in a sea of guilt. She had lived with Aunt Maude since she was five, when her parents had been killed in an automobile accident. She had no recollection of them whatsoever, just Aunt Maude. Crystal spoke with her over the phone occasionally, but not with any regularity. Crystal wasn't a very good surrogate daughter. Oh, there was a time when she had been. She had been a good student and was popular throughout high school. She had helped Aunt Maude with cooking and cleaning and chores around the house. She had volunteered for charity food drives at the church and had even driven the church van, picking up members of the congregation who had no way to get back and forth.

What had happened to that girl? Crystal Williams had been killed by a vicious bitch named Crystal Bright. Aunt Maude would be so ashamed.

From across the room, Marshall's eyes suddenly settled on Crystal, and he was in motion instantly, storming up the aisle with Sam chasing along after him. His eyes burned with fury, his cheekbones tinted red.

"What in the hell are you doing here?" Marshall demanded, his face inches from Crystal's. She shrunk back from the heat of his attack.

"I just—" stammered Crystal.

"GET OUT!" Conversation dwindled, and even the organist hesitated before continuing her dirge.

Sam positioned himself between the two. "Marshall, please. Let me handle this, okay? You're too upset."

Crystal was confused. "Handle what? I just—"

"Get her out of here, Sam, or I swear to God, I will bust her in the mouth," warned Marshall.

"I'll handle it," said Sam. "Go on back up front. I think Julia Roberts was trying to find you earlier."

Marshall's gaze was cold steel, his lips clenched together in a tight line. Reluctantly, he turned and went back to the casket, mourners offering condolences the whole way.

Sam watched Marshall until he was out of earshot and then turned to Crystal. "Why are you here?"

Crystal's eyes filled with tears. "I just wanted to tell Marsh how sorry I was."

"Yeah, right."

Crystal was dumbfounded. "You think I'm *happy* that his mother is dead?"

"I don't think you care one way or the other. I think you saw an opportunity to try and smooth things over with Marshall."

"You've got to be kidding me!" protested Crystal. "I would *never* do that!"

"I've seen you at work, Crystal. I wouldn't put anything past you. You're history, and that's where you're going to stay. You have no right to be here," said Sam.

Tears spilled down Crystal's cheeks. "I can't believe you have such a low opinion of me."

"I don't know why it should surprise you. You did your level best to destroy our show. I'm happy to report that the first numbers are in since Britney joined the cast. They're good. Very good."

"I don't care about the numbers! I just—"

"This isn't the time or place for this. I don't know how you even got in here. We specifically told security to keep you out. Just go away," said Sam, turning his back and returning to his partner.

Several of the other guests stared openly, waiting for Crystal's reaction. She wanted to hold her head high, turn and leave the room unfazed. It didn't matter what she wanted. Tears flowed and sobbing had started from deep inside her throat. She nearly knocked over an elderly woman trying to flee the room.

⚬————◇————⚬

A stop at the liquor store, then home.

Crystal had cried for fifteen minutes before her vision cleared enough to drive. Onlookers had stared, and the damned tabloids had gotten their pictures after all. Crystal didn't care. Nothing mattered anymore.

Her rent was due the next day, and Crystal couldn't afford to pay. The police hadn't had any luck locating Marty Crabtree or any of the money he had pilfered from Crystal's accounts.

The answering machine's message light blinked rapidly, and Crystal said a silent prayer before setting it to playback. She prayed that one of the messages would be offering a role. *Any* role. She needed the money desperately.

The first call was from her attorney's office.

"Um, Ms. Bright? This is Sylvia Turnbull in accounts receivable at Alvin Lowenstein's. Could you please call me at your earliest opportunity? There's been a problem with the expense draft you sent in. The number is—"

Crystal skipped to the next message. Of course, there was a problem with the expense draft. There wasn't any money in Crystal's accounts to cover it.

"Hey, babe, it's Billy. Want to run something by you. Got an offer for a part. It's a jungle flick, really hot, lots of action. The money's good, too. I know you said you wouldn't do porn, but—"

68

Crystal skipped to the next message. There was a long silence, almost enough to cause the machine to cut off, but then a tremulous female voice began, thick with country twang.

"Crystal? This is Kathy Duncan. Remember me? I used to live next to Maude? Honey, I hate to be the one to break this to you, but your aunt passed away last night. She went in her sleep, real easy. I didn't know who else to call—"

Crystal didn't hear the rest. As surely as glass shatters when dropped to the ground, Crystal's world disintegrated. She hadn't spoken to Maude in months. The last time she had seen her was shortly after *Benny and the Girl* was picked up for renewal. Crystal shuddered at the memory, mortified by her own behavior. She had made the trip to Lucasville for the sole purpose of showing her old friends what a big shot she had become. She had barely spent any time with Maude while she was there. After all that Maude had done for her, this was how she had repaid her.

She hadn't told Maude how much she loved her, and now she never could.

It was like the tip of an iceberg that stretched for miles below the surface, one embarrassment piling on top of the next. For the first time, Crystal was actually able to detach from herself and view her actions from an outside perspective. She *had* been atrocious to her co-workers. She *had* taken her fame and wealth for granted. She *had* assumed that she was more famous than Jesus Christ himself.

And now she had nothing. Everything, then nothing. Like a light switch flipped in the wrong direction. Nothing was ever good enough for Crystal Bright, and now Crystal Bright wasn't good enough for anything. Except porn.

Crystal Bright. What the hell kind of name was that anyway? She sounded like a floor cleaner.

Aunt Maude was gone. There was no way for Crystal to go back and undo what she had done wrong. There was no way to repair her fractured relationship with Marshall Dawson. There was no way to tell Aunt Maude goodbye. Crystal couldn't even afford an airline ticket to fly back to Ohio for the funeral.

After what felt like gallons of tears, Crystal's ducts ran dry, and she pulled herself together, snuffling the whole while. She half-walked, half-stumbled to the bathroom, looking at herself through stinging eyes. Her reflection was an abomination, a wretched hag from an alternate universe, peering through the mirror with pinched eyes and swollen features. She couldn't look at herself for long before turning away.

The medicine cabinet contained a veritable cornucopia of pharmaceuticals; everything from cold medicines and laxatives to sleeping aids. Crystal was indiscriminate in her selection, retrieving whatever would fit in her hands. She went back into the kitchen and opened a bottle of whiskey.

"It's okay, Aunt Maude," she whispered. "We'll talk real soon."

She swallowed mouthfuls of pills, chased with shots of whiskey straight from the bottle.

After a little while, the room felt warm, and Crystal was barely able to keep her eyes open. She walked partway to the living room before collapsing in a heap on the floor, her ragged breathing slowing with each sweep of the second hand on her kitchen clock.

III

Chad pulled his t-shirt and pants back on and lay on the floor, looking at the corkboard ceiling above. His nighttime angel lay naked on her side, dark hair spilling over creamy white shoulders, a satisfied smile playing on her lips. She stared at Chad as if he were the whole universe.

"What's your name?" Chad finally asked.

"Suzette," the girl said impishly. "You can call me Suze."

"Okay, *Suze*," said Chad, his voice cold and mocking. "What's the deal?"

"What's what deal?"

"Is this the way you greet all the new guys?"

Suze threw her head back and laughed from deep within her throat. "Yeah, and I do the social workers, too. They give me free cigarettes."

"Really?"

Suze sighed exaggeratedly and smacked Chad's arm. "No, dipshit. I'm not a nympho."

"What are you then?"

"Look, dick," Suze said, sitting up and pulling her gown over her head. "I just thought you had a nice ass, that's all. I don't need this shit—"

Chad grabbed her arm. "Then what shit do you need?"

Suze turned her head slowly, her dark eyes boring into Chad's. "I need you."

Chad laughed cruelly. "Are you some kind of fucking stalker?"

Suze's arm flashed out, and her hand rapped sharply across Chad's groin. Chad doubled over and squirmed on the floor, grunting and wheezing, cupping his genitals.

It only took a few seconds before he had the horrible sensation under control, and the pain was replaced with anger. Chad rolled over and grabbed Suze by the throat, forcing her backward and cracking her head against the hard floor. She opened her mouth to scream, but Chad was squeezing too tightly for anything to escape.

"Let's get one thing straight, bitch," Chad hissed as he straddled her, keeping his hand locked tightly around her throat. "You don't *ever* hit me again. Do you understand? *Do you understand?*"

Suze's eyes shone with excitement. She wasn't scared; she was turned on. "You wanna hit me?"

70

Chad was disgusted. He rolled off of the girl and got to his feet. "You're sick."

Suze grinned and folded her legs into a lotus position. "Don't like it rough? I'll bet you do."

Truthfully, Chad suspected he did, as well. He wanted to bash the girl's face in, render her featureless, then fuck her again. He was slightly aroused just thinking about it.

"What do you want?" he asked again, his voice cool and even.

"We're gonna get out of this place," she said, her eyes glittering in the relative darkness.

"What, tonight?"

"Whenever you're ready, sugar. I got things to show you."

Chad scoffed and turned around. "I thought I already seen your things."

"Don't be a dick," Suze snapped. "You've got a higher purpose than screwin' around in some state-run orphanage. Can't you feel it? *I* can feel it, that's for sure. In some way, I'm supposed to help you—I can feel that, too."

"Help me? What in the hell are you talking about?" Chad was irritated. Why wouldn't she just go away? He was done with her now.

Suze sighed and stood, placing her hands on her hips. "This would go so much easier if you wouldn't be a dick. We need to just take things one step at a time. I don't know all the answers just yet."

"One thing at a time, hunh? But you do know *some* of the answers?"

Suze nodded her head slowly, sexily.

"Answers to what?" Chad asked.

"How it's supposed to go, dick. They come to me in dreams."

"Oh, good Lord," Chad said, turning and heading for the door.

"I know you killed your mother."

Chad froze, his hand on the doorknob. There was no way this girl could know that. The only person who had even seen him in the area was his own father, Peter. And he hadn't even admitted to Peter that he had been there that night. She must be bluffing.

He turned and laughed, a sound that was slightly off-key. "You're so full of shit. My father killed my mother. That's what the police are saying."

"Yeah, well, the police are wrong," she countered. "You know it, and so do I. But, hey, don't freak out about it. It's not like I want to call 911 on you or anything."

Chad stared at her blankly, unsure how much this bitch knew. It sounded as if she knew enough to be dangerous.

"Yes, I could be very dangerous, dick," she said, as if reading his thoughts. "But I prefer that you think of me as empathic. Do you see it yet?"

Chad continued to stare. "Empathic?" he finally said. "You read minds?"

"Not really *read* them," she said. "It's more like little snapshots. And let me tell you, baby doll, you've been starring in the last several dozen. How did you manage to stab her that many times and walk away without any blood on you? That really slays me. *Oh!* I made a little joke!" She laughed from the depths of her soul, warm and meaty, and just a little venomous.

Chad didn't know how to respond. He felt like running away as quickly as he could, but he knew this girl would find him again. "What do you want?" he asked again.

"First things first, we gotta get out of here," she said.

"It wouldn't make sense for me to suddenly run off," said Chad. "I might look guilty."

"You won't," said Suze. "You'll look scared and confused by all the shit that's gone down in your life lately. I mean for God's sake, your mother's been murdered by your father, right?"

Chad shook his head. "It's all a moot point anyway. I turn eighteen next week. I can walk out of here the minute I do."

"You'll still need me," said Suze.

Chad smiled, faking self-confidence that he didn't feel. "I'm going back to bed. It's been interesting." He walked out of the room and hurried back to his quarters.

This girl was dangerous. She knew too much for Chad to feel entirely comfortable. But if she knew that Chad had killed his mother, why hadn't she already spoken with the police? Maybe she didn't intend to cause Chad any trouble.

She had been a hell of a good fuck.

Chad smiled as he eased back under his blanket. Norton Jones lay overhead on his bunk, one meaty Black leg swinging freely over the side. He snored like thunderclaps, but Chad had no trouble drifting off.

Peter looked even more haggard than the last time Chad had seen him. He was making no attempts to groom himself, and his face had hollowed and sunken in. His orange prison wear seemed clean enough, but that was surely due to the regimented laundry process of the facility.

"Chad," Peter said, smiling half-heartedly. "I wanted to see you on your birthday. Thanks for coming, son."

Chad nodded his head almost imperceptibly.

"Is everything alright?" Peter asked, concern twisting at his features.

"What do you mean is everything all right?" Chad demanded. "My father is in prison for killing my mother. No, everything is *not* all right."

"My lawyer is working on a new strategy."

"And he will be every day until the jury finds you guilty. And they *will* find you guilty, Dad," said Chad.

Peter winced at the words. "I didn't do it, son. I promise you that. I didn't kill your mother."

Chad lowered his head to the table, feigning upset while actually hiding an uncontrollable grin. He kept the receiver of the telephone as far away from his head as he inconspicuously could just in case he giggled.

When he regained control of himself, Chad looked back up at his father through the security glass. "I'm leaving Children's Services this afternoon."

"You can use my house if you—"

"I'm not sticking around," said Chad.

Peter's eyes registered surprise. "Not sticking around? Where are you going?"

"I don't know. I'm just going."

"Chad, that doesn't make sense. What will you do for food? What will you do for money?"

"I'll figure it out."

"Chad, this whole mess will be over soon. Then we can get on with our lives, okay? You can get your plans back on track for college, you know? Move forward with your life."

Chad grinned tightly. "I'm not going to college, Dad. That was your plan, not mine. I'm going to travel a while, see what's out there, you know? And you and I both know that you're not getting out of this."

Peter looked as though he had been struck. "You really think I killed her, don't you?"

Chad laughed, unable to help himself. He leaned very close to the glass, close enough for his breath to frost the pane. "This is the last I'll say on the matter. If you didn't kill her, Dad, then who did? Who did?"

Chad smiled as he hung up the receiver, turned and walked away. It didn't matter if his father pieced it all together. The evidence against him was overwhelming. Would the district attorney be interested in a wild story offered by a condemned man desperate to free himself? Hardly.

<hr />

Chad packed his few belongings back into the duffel bag he had brought with him when he had moved into Children's Services. He wouldn't miss this place at all, not even if he had to sleep out in the rain. Norton Jones watched him casually, as if ensuring that Chad wouldn't steal any of his belongings when he packed.

Ms. Mulligan had tried to discourage Chad from leaving, but he had his mind set and was now of legal age, so there was little she could do to stop him. She merely requested that Chad stop by the counselor's office before he left.

"Ms. Snyder will have some helpful pointers on how to get started on your own, Charles," she said.

"I don't need any help," he replied.

"Humor me, okay? It's a big step going out on your own. Ms. Snyder may be able to advise you about government assistance, as well."

Free money? Hell, yes! Chad had decided that he would, indeed, humor the social worker.

He stopped outside the counselor's office and rapped on the door, his duffel tossed back over his shoulder. "Come in!" called a female voice from within. He opened the door, his best cursory smile firmly in place—until he saw the young woman seated behind the desk.

It was Suze.

Her dark eyes glittered knowingly, and she gestured to the chair across from her desk. "Hey, Chad. I've been expecting you all afternoon," she said.

Chad had assumed the girl was one of the 'inmates,' so to speak. She looked so youthful that night, barefoot and clad in only her nightgown, her dark hair tumbling around her naked shoulders. He hadn't seen her at all in the week since their rendezvous, and he had assumed that she had gone to stay with relatives, or perhaps her parents had come for her. Today, she wore a smart, navy-blue business suit, and her hair was fastened in a tidy chignon. It added several years to her appearance.

"You're the *counselor?*" Chad couldn't help but ask.

"*Mmm-hmm,*" she purred. "Surprised?"

Chad looked at her vacantly.

"I see you're keeping to your word," she said.

"How so?"

"I believe it's your eighteenth birthday, no?"

Chad nodded his head.

"And you're out of here. Good for you! What's your plan?" she asked.

He eyed her suspiciously. "Why do you want to know?"

"Because I want to know where I'm going," she said simply.

Chad laughed. "What makes you think I'll tell you?"

Suze sighed. "I wish you'd stop being such a dick. Really. All I want to do is help you. It's my mission in life, if you will."

"You're pretty creepy with all this double-talk," Chad said.

"I've got cash. I've got a feeling that you know you need me. Deep down inside, under all that false machismo, you need a little bit of guidance."

"Guidance from a psycho like you?" Chad retorted.

"Absolutely," she said, not a note of anger in her voice. "Bonnie and Clyde, Starkweather and Fugate—they'll have nothing on us, baby."

"So, we're just going to hit the road, carving a path as we go? That's real brilliant, Suze. We should last about three days before we're arrested and hauled in."

"Ah! Interesting. I notice that the problem you have is with the possibility of getting caught, not with doing the deed," she said, smiling triumphantly.

"Listen, you crazy bitch," Chad hissed. "You are not going to sit across from me psychoanalyzing. You're twisting my words all around. Who do you work for, anyway? The police?"

Suze laughed. "Oh, my God, no!" She shuddered at the thought. "The problem as I see it is that you don't trust me. I thought surely you would after I offered myself to you last week, but I guess that wasn't good enough."

"*Trust* you?" Chad repeated. "I don't have any idea who you are or why you're bugging me. Everything you've said has been a bunch of mumbo jumbo."

Suze sighed again, staring at Chad with mischievous eyes. "Okay, tell you what. Howzabout I prove myself to you? Show you that I'm on your side. How would that be?"

"Prove yourself? What do you mean?"

Suze smiled. "Meet me at eleven o'clock tonight at the corner of Frontier and High Streets. Do you know where that is?"

Chad nodded but remained noncommittal. "I might be there."

"You'd better be. Your future depends on it. I'm telling you—"

A series of rapid-fire knocks sounded against the door, and Ms. Mulligan stuck her head in. "Almost ready to go?" she asked.

Chad turned and nodded, smiling meekly. "I think so."

"I wish you wouldn't be in such a hurry. You're under a tremendous strain."

"I'm fine," said Chad. "I need to get on my own two feet."

"Has Ms. Snyder been helpful?"

"Oh, yes," Chad said. "What she's had to offer has been very interesting."

"I'm so glad," said Ms. Mulligan, offering a practiced smile. "Today is Ms. Snyder's last day. We haven't found a replacement yet, so if you had waited a single day longer, we wouldn't have had anyone on premises for you to speak with."

"Last day?" Chad repeated, shifting his gaze to Suze.

"Mmm-hmm," Suze said, her face remaining impassive.

"Listen, Suzette," said Ms. Mulligan. "I hate to interrupt your session with Charles, but I'm leaving for the day, and I wanted to wish you the best of luck. It's been a real pleasure working with you."

"Thanks, Donna," said Suze. "I've enjoyed it, too."

"If you get things straightened around at home, please come back and talk with me. I'm sure we could have your position reinstated. You've done top-notch work with these kids."

"Thank you, but I doubt I'll be back anytime soon," Suze said. "My father is very ill, and my mother is too old to manage by herself."

"So, you've said. I'm sorry. I guess I'm being selfish. It isn't every day we have someone who is so good with the kids. I hate it that we didn't have time to throw you a proper goodbye party. Seems like the least we could have done, but—"

"Please, Donna," interrupted Suze. "Let yourself off the hook. This has all come about so quickly. It should be *me* apologizing for giving you less than adequate notice."

"Don't you fret over it," said Ms. Mulligan, backing out of the room and closing the door behind her.

Chad studied Suze in silence for a moment, and she studied him right back, her eyes sparkling with secret knowledge. "You already knew you were leaving?" he finally asked.

"Mmm-hmm," she said. "From the first moment I saw you, I knew."

"So, there's nothing wrong with dear old dad?"

Suze laughed. "Other than being a crusty old asshole, not a thing."

Chad collected his things and headed for the door, mulling over the possibilities of what Suze was saying and doing. Although he had no idea about her motivation, he was inclined to believe that she was on the up-and-up.

"Don't forget," she called after him. "Eleven o'clock tonight. Frontier and High."

"Maybe I will, and maybe I won't," he said.

"I suggest you do," she said. "It'll be well worth your while."

Chad closed the door behind him as he stepped out into the hallway. Lost souls meandered through the corridor, hollow eyes staring out from faces devoid of hope. Chad felt nauseated by their resignation to their lives. If they wanted something different, they had to rise up, seize control, make a difference. No one would do it for them.

He took a deep breath of fresh air as he stepped outside the facility. For the first time, he was accountable only to himself, and it was wonderful.

Still yet, he wondered what Suzette Snyder had in store for him tonight. His loins began a familiar throb reflecting on their brief encounter in the abandoned wing of the building. Perhaps sex.

Probably something more.

IV

Paulie's funeral was an odd event. He had outlived most everyone he had ever been close to. Still yet, plenty of townsfolk turned out for the event, offering sincere condolences to Luke, as well as dinner invitations which would keep Luke fed for the next few years. Paulie was well-respected and well-liked. Luke was accepted by association.

Morty King had approached him at the funeral, confirming the details of Paulie's unusual bequest. Morty was an odd-looking man, in his mid-fifties with thinning dark hair and a roll of flab around his midsection. His face was elfin, with round, wire-rimmed glasses perched on the tip of his nose.

"Did Paulie discuss the terms of his will with you?" Morty asked after expressing his sympathy.

Luke nodded.

"Odd request, I have to say, but the terms are legal—unless you're thinking of challenging the will."

"Challenging it?" Luke asked. "Why would I do a thing like that?"

"It might be suggested that Paulie couldn't have been in his right mind to have made such a request."

Luke laughed. "Paulie was a little loopy, but I don't think that he was crazy."

"So, you intend to follow his wishes?"

Luke thought carefully before slowly nodding his head. "S'pose I am."

Morty smiled, nodding his own. "That would make Paulie very proud, my boy."

Now, Luke stood in the room that he had called his own for most of his life. He could still remember where his posters had hung, supermodels guiding him through puberty. He could still remember laying on his bed reading on a cool summer evening, the smell of Paulie's famous fried chicken wafting in from the kitchen.

Where would he go?

He had no idea. He would simply put his head down and move forward, taking one step at a time. The first step was to pack. He could only carry so much. Paulie had stipulated that Luke couldn't use the truck, either, and that seemed rather cruel. Luke didn't know if the coming year would teach him all of the things that Paulie had hoped for, but he knew the old man's intentions were good, maybe even righteous.

Paulie had set aside a fund from which Morty King would maintain the property in Luke's absence, as well as collect a modest salary for his trouble, so Luke had very few ends to tie up before he left. Still, he wandered the house for hours, checking and rechecking things.

Paulie had allowed Luke three days after the funeral to get himself on the road, and it was the last night before he was to head out. Luke was exhausted, and he really didn't know why. He hadn't really done anything substantial since the funeral, just a lot of pacing and reminiscing. He had intended to develop some sort of game plan, but so far, his plan consisted of walking to US 68 on the east side of town and putting his thumb in the air. He didn't have very much money, but that didn't really concern him. He could find odd jobs as he traveled.

He *had* always wanted to see the Grand Canyon, but somehow, he didn't believe it was Paulie's intention for him to take a vacation.

Luke fell asleep almost instantly. He hadn't slept well since Paulie had died. How had the old man known that he would die that night? It was eerie and unsettling and had kept Luke awake most nights.

At first, his sleep was deep and dreamless, but at around four in the morning, Luke had awakened with a start, the traces of a dream tickling at his memory.

The dream had been nonsensical. Luke remembered a large gravel parking lot with a half-dozen semi-trucks parked toward the rear. He could hear the distant rumble of their idling engines, sounding very far away. The sky had been dark, but an unseen electric pink light blinked on and off, casting an intermittent glow on everything. In the front corner of the lot, an old-fashioned phone booth stood isolated from everything else. It had its own inner eerie luminescence, cast from an overhead lighting fixture.

In the dream, Luke had entered the phone booth and picked up the Yellow Pages which dangled on a rusted chain. He flipped through them—to what end he didn't know—and found a crisp, new twenty-dollar bill tucked in the binding. The portrait of Jackson had been replaced by one of Paulie, grinning wickedly without his teeth in place. Then one of the semis in the back row flipped on its headlights, momentarily blinding Luke. The sound of its engine became a roar, closing in.

That was when Luke had awakened, twitching and jerking his bed sheets onto the floor. He checked the time on his clock radio and was surprised to see that it was only four. It felt much later than that.

Luke sat upright and lit a cigarette, hoping the warm rush of nicotine might calm his nerves. In the dark room, the embers glowed orange and the faint crackling of burning tobacco sounded disproportionately loud.

It was a long time before Luke again found sleep.

Morty King met him at the front door at seven o'clock. "Morning, Luke," he said. He looked as he always did, dressed in a crisp navy suit, briefcase tucked under one arm.

Luke had stumbled down the stairs in a half-daze, barefooted and in jeans, his chest and stomach lined from the seams of his bed sheets. He looked like he hadn't slept at all. His sandy hair was tousled and twisted into clumps. "Mmm," he growled, rubbing his eyes, and standing aside so Morty could enter.

"You look like hell, boy," Morty said, setting his briefcase on the coffee table. "You having second thoughts?"

Luke shook his head. "No, I didn't sleep very well. I'd just as soon get on my way."

"Old Paulie also stipulated that I usher you from the premises on your day of departure at promptly eight o'clock. I guess I forgot to mention that."

"Really, it's okay. I'm normally up at six, but I just couldn't get goin'."

"Listen up, Luke. I'm not real sure how Paulie would've felt about this, but I want you to call me from time to time—collect, of course. I don't know any more than you as to why he's sending you on this wild goose chase, but it's killing me to think that you're going to be out there on the road by yourself for a whole year, no one to talk to, no one to reach out to if you need something."

"Thanks, Morty," said Luke, taking the business card from the lawyer's hand. "I'll do that."

Luke invited Morty to stay for breakfast, and they sat down to scrambled eggs and bacon.

It was the last time Luke would cook for a long while.

<hr />

The sun was high in the noon sky, temperatures soaring well above ninety. Luke had been walking for three hours, winding through back roads that weren't on the map, surfacing on US-68 several miles north of a little town called Paris. Now that he was on the highway, he hoped to catch a ride with someone who would take him the rest of the way to Lexington. He figured he would find someplace to crash for the night and look for work in the morning. He didn't intend to stay long, just long enough to make some traveling money.

Traffic was unusually light this day, and none of the passersby showed any interest in offering a stranger a ride. Luke could hardly blame them. He would have been reluctant to pick up a hitchhiker, too. All of the crazy stories on the news and in the papers—the world was becoming more dangerous every day. People living in filth and disease, stealing to feed babies or drug habits, counterbalanced by others who idolized celebrities and treated them like pagan gods. To be rich, young, and beautiful was everything. In reality, the beautiful people were far outnumbered by the average, yet as a society, we ran like mindless cattle, giving this elite group their choice of everything and thanking them as they take it from us. And we never have enough to give—nothing is *ever* enough. Luke had just recently read a *People* magazine article about the ugly behavior of a popular sitcom star that had ultimately led to her dismissal from the show. She had apparently been the epitome of a temperamental star, throwing temper tantrums on set and generally driving her coworkers crazy. Luke found it especially disappointing because the starlet in question had come from very humble beginnings in a small Ohio town not so awfully far from Jasper. It's amazing how fame corrupts.

At long last, a semi-truck eased over onto the narrow berm, its driver firing the horn in a couple rapid bursts to hurry Luke in. Luke ran up to the passenger door and opened it, tossing his duffel bag in before hoisting himself up onto the seat.

"How far ya goin'?" the driver asked. He was a meatloaf of a man, barrel-chested with thick arms and legs. Tattoos of naughty vixens winked from his biceps.

"I dunno," said Luke. After seeing how difficult it had been to get a ride, he thought that Lexington may be too close to ditch this one. "Which way you headed?"

"Louisville."

"Well, then Louisville it is," said Luke.

"Bert Parnell," barked the man, offering a big hand.

"Luke Leighton," said Luke, giving the man's hand a solid pump. "Thanks."

"No problem. I hate making these drives alone. Get sleepy as hell. Let's get one thing straight, though," he said warily. "I'm not into any of that kinky pretty boy stuff, so if that's what you got in mind, you should go ahead and move on. I got a wife and kids."

It took a moment for the man's meaning to sink in, and when it did, Luke's face flushed. "I'm just looking for a ride, that's all."

"Well, all right then," said Bert, releasing the clutch and coaxing the big rig back onto the highway. "You workin' your way back home?"

"Not really," said Luke. "I'm sort of taking a year off, seeing the country."

"Hmm. I guess there's no wife or kids?"

"Nope. My father just passed away, and his last wish was for me to get out and see the world, so that's what I'm doing." Luke had never referred to Old Paulie as his father, but in retrospect, that is exactly who he was. Besides, it was a far easier explanation than the truth.

"What do you do for a living?" asked Bert.

"We own a farm. It's being taken care of by an old family friend while I'm gone."

"That's nice for you. That's why I drive a rig, you know? I get to see the whole country and get paid for it, too. It's a pretty good deal. Greta—she's my wife—is real strong-headed, and we probably would've killed each other by now if we were together every single day. I do miss my girls, though. I got three of 'em. Betty is eighteen and graduates this year, Laurie is two years behind her, and Little Tater is just four." Bert smiled and flipped down his sun visor, revealing pictures of his aforementioned clan.

"Nice looking group," Luke commented. "Did you say the little one's name is Tater?"

"Oh, not really. That's just what we call her. I call her Monkey Butt, too, but her real name's Virginia, after my mother. She's ornery as a chimp. Neither me nor Greta care for 'Ginny' or 'Virgie.' The other girls call her Little VeeVee. Try and tell me that child isn't gonna need therapy by the time she hits kindergarten! Soon enough, she'll answer to anything aimed in her direction." He laughed and absently touched a small Polaroid of the sticky-faced child in question. His devotion to his family was proudly worn like a badge on his sleeve. "Have any brothers or sisters?"

Luke shook his head. "Un-unh. Just me. No grandparents, aunts, or uncles, either."

Bert whistled. "Well, I guess that's total freedom, ain't it? If I didn't have any ties, I suppose I might ride the wind, too."

Conversation was amicable and easy, and the miles passed quickly. Luke learned about Bert's no-good brother-in-law, Ted (aka Weasel Ass), who was currently serving a fifteen-year sentence for armed robbery. Aunt Ruth (the one with the foot held on by screws), had gone around the bend during the last year or so, adopting sixty-some cats and eating cat food herself. But it was the stories about his immediate family that were the best, even when they involved silly arguments that the girls had or disagreements between him and his wife.

In Lexington, Bert had to stop at a parts distributor to drop one load in exchange for a different one before moving on to Louisville. He was strictly freelance, taking assignments that would take him where he wanted to go and get him back in the time frame that suited him best. Luke helped unload the boxes and reload the new ones, and after two hours of hard work, the men decided to break for food. It was nearly six o'clock by the time the big rig was on US-64 heading west.

About halfway there, traffic ground to a complete halt. Stopped cars stretched to the horizon, hazy heat rising from the surface of their hoods. Bert instigated a quick exchange on his CB radio.

"Big pile up just outside Frankfurt," came a detached voice through the speaker. "Gasoline truck. Wiped out a few cars before turning over and exploding. It's gonna be awhile."

"Ten-four," said Bert, holstering his microphone.

Bert was a conversationalist and Luke was a born listener. The time, although indeed lengthy, passed quickly enough. Traffic stood still for quite some time before finally creeping forward, but even when it did, the next ten miles took two hours to cover. The summer sun had long since set by the time Bert and Luke neared Louisville.

"I don't know about you, boy, but I'm right near starved," said Bert.

Luke flicked a cigarette butt out the window. "It has been awhile. No place real expensive, okay?"

"I'm not taking you to the Chateau Lé-Foo-Foo. What are you thinking?"

"Sorry. I just don't have much cash on me," said Luke, thumbing through his wallet.

"It's alright. Dinner's on me."

Luke shook his head vehemently, realizing that what he had said earlier might have been interpreted as fishing for charity. "No, Bert. Thanks, but I can manage."

Bert laughed. "Well, you're not going to manage for very long if you don't wise up."

"What do you mean?"

"It's not like you're a welfare case. You helped me out with unloading earlier, and I would think I owe you at least this much."

Luke hesitated, still uncomfortable with taking the other man's money. Reluctantly, he finally said, "Well, I suppose that it would be alright."

"Done!" said Bert triumphantly, blowing his horn like a madman.

Within fifteen minutes, they were pulling into a stereotypical truck stop called Fat Louie's BBQ. The country music was loud, the crowd was rowdy, and the food was saturated in grease. For Luke, it was ideal. Between him and Bert, they polished off six pork barbecue sandwiches and a family order of deep-fried onion rings, using an entire dispenser of napkins to sop the shine off of their faces and arms.

Bert stretched back on his red vinyl booth seat and loosened his belt a notch. "Oh, my Lord! That was good!"

Luke nodded in agreement, lighting a cigarette. "The best tasting food is the worst for you."

"Amen. Would you look at the time? Unbelievable!"

Luke glanced at the neon clock above the counter. It was almost midnight.

"Burton Industries doesn't accept deliveries between midnight and six," said Bert. *"Shit!* That puts me behind schedule for tomorrow before tomorrow even gets here. *Shit!"*

"We could park there overnight and be waiting first thing," suggested Luke.

"Or we could grab a room at a motel and catch a few hours' shut eye somewhere comfortable. My truck only sleeps one, and I have to admit, my back's been killing me since this afternoon," said Bert.

Luke shook his head. "I can't pay for a room, not even half. If you want to, that's up to you, but I'll sleep in the truck."

"That's ridiculous," said Bert. "I'm gettin' the room either way. You may as well use the other bed. I gotta take a shit. Why don't you see if you can find a motel near here in the phonebook. Look for one with specials. I ain't made of money, either."

With that, Bert hoisted himself out from behind the table and swaggered off to the bathroom. Luke smoked his cigarette and leaned back in the booth. If any other trucker had suggested that they get a room, Luke might have been suspicious, but Bert was a good man, and Luke knew it intuitively. Actually, he wasn't all that different from Old Paulie, only younger. Luke found it odd that a man who was so obviously devoted to his family would choose to spend so much time away from them, but he didn't presume to judge Bert for his choices. Everybody had their own unique motivation as singular as a fingerprint.

Luke stood and crossed to the glass-lined pie counter which also served as the checkout. An anorexic bleached blonde waitress named Joni leaned across the counter and popped a pink bubble between her crimson lips. "Hey, darlin'. Didja get your fill, or would you like to try somethin' else?" Her teeth were large and crooked, and her breasts were leaving sweat prints on the glass of the counter. Luke felt his cheeks brighten involuntarily.

"You got a phonebook?" he asked, avoiding her probing gaze.

"Payphone outside," she said, managing to use her tongue inventively with just two words. Luke's ears burst into flames.

"Thanks," he mumbled, heading for the door. Although very handsome, Luke was completely oblivious to this fact, and despite several girlfriends in Jasper, his experience with the opposite sex was fairly limited. His previous relationships had been lightweights. Luke still found himself tongue-tied and mush-mouthed when women showed interest. He didn't care for particularly forward women like the waitress, but his IQ plummeted nonetheless when faced with their blatantly open desire.

The large parking lot was gravel, and Luke could see the phone booth, an old-fashioned style free-standing unit, positioned in the far corner under a dim streetlamp.

The déjà vu was instantaneous.

Luke's pace slowed to a crawl as he crossed the lot, taking in the details. A row of semis lined the back of the lot, engines growling in a mechanical snore. The neon sign over the restaurant threw its pinkish glow out over the lot in lazy winks.

As Luke neared the booth and saw the phonebook dangling on its rusted chain, he forgot why he was going to the payphone in the first place. His purpose had been replaced by the overwhelming need to see the twenty-dollar bill which he knew would be tucked in the binding.

Five steps.

Four.

Three.

Two.

One.

Inside the booth, Luke thumbed through the book, knowing that the crisp bill would surely be there. In the section that listed Hotels, Motels and Motor Lodges, Luke found what he was looking for, the only difference being that Andrew Jackson occupied the space in the center of the bill instead of Old Paulie.

The deep resonance from a short burst of throttle drew Luke's attention to the line of semis parked in the back of the lot. Headlights flared on and one of the trucks sprang forward, crossing the lot and heading in his direction. For a moment, Luke felt like a helpless deer, caught in the blinding glare, rooted to the spot and unable to call his limbs into action. The truck cut to the left as it pulled up beside the booth, brakes groaning in a high-pitched wail of reluctant compliance.

The passenger door was opened from the inside, and Bert leaned out from the cabin of the truck. "Didja find us someplace cheap?"

Luke stared at the man dumbly, the twenty-dollar bill clutched firmly in one hand. The phonebook slipped from his other, clattering against the wall of the booth as the rusty chain pulled taut.

PART TWO

ALLIANCES

CHAPTER SIX

I

Detached voices floated through the hazy gray, whispering gibberish before fading off into the distance. Lisa felt as though she were suspended by unseen wires, hanging in the empty air. Maybe she was falling, hurtling toward the ground below at an alarming rate. In either case, her eyes didn't appear to be working. Everything was the same flat gray. The voices she heard sounded far away, echoing from the depths of a fathomless corridor.

Is this death?

Surely not. Lisa felt a stinging in her side, not really pain—just discomfort. She remembered Ms. Kelsey's final graceless pirouette into the path of the yellow sanitation truck. The memory made her want to laugh, but her body would not cooperate.

There had been a horrible accident afterward. A large, heavy car had slammed into the front passenger side of hers, sending it skidding off to the left and into a large oak which had marked that particular corner for the better part of a century.

Lisa knew she must have been hurt badly. The impact had been colossal. She remembered the crunching of bone, the coppery taste of blood in her mouth.

Cracked ribs.

Punctured lung.

Two disconnected fragments of sentences which floated amidst other nonsensical sounds. Neither injury should be life-threatening. Why wouldn't her eyes work? Time was somewhat meaningless, but the periods in which Lisa experienced sensory input seemed to lengthen with each occurrence. Fragments grew into whole sentences.

"—patient has suffered head trauma, as well as assorted minor fractures—"

"—unable to determine a reason for her current comatose state—"

"—neurology exams are completed with no discernible—"

"The patient was an employee of the hospital for some time."

"She was released from her position by Ms. Kelsey almost a week ago."

"Did you hear what happened to Ms. Kelsey?"

Lisa waited for the inevitable. Surely, they would piece two and two together, placing her at the supermarket at the same time Ms. Kelsey had been murdered. Surely, there was surveillance video from the store showing that both women had been shopping that night. Surely, the police were waiting for Lisa to regain consciousness so that they could arrest her.

She dreamt often, and almost every dream ended with Ms. Kelsey ramping out into traffic. The vehicle which struck her was always different, sometimes larger, sometimes smaller—one time, a riding lawn mower. But each time, Ms. Kelsey ended up pureed on the pavement. Only once did Lisa dream of anything else. In that dream, she floated up the hospital corridor like a detached spirit, looking down at the tops of the heads of passersby in the hallway. She passed through walls indiscriminately, and for a fleeting moment, she thought she really must have died.

After passing through yet another wall, she found herself looking down at a sleeping old woman, lit from above by an ethereal blue glow. The woman looked like a stereotypical, cookie-baking grandmother; chubby, rosy cheeks fluttering with the sounds of sleep, snow white hair spilling across her head in short curls.

It was Mrs. Baylock, the woman who had caused Lisa to lose her job in the first place. She looked positively cherubic, whistling softly as she slept. Why had the old bat told Ms. Kelsey that Lisa had mistreated her? Lisa had only been doing her job. Mrs. Baylock was perpetually incontinent, and Lisa had only been thoroughly cleaning the mess. That *was* her job, wasn't it?

Lisa floated down, descending from her position near the ceiling to sit squarely on the old woman's face, cutting the whistling noise off completely.

And then she awoke.

The gray matter was gone, replaced by brilliant, blinding white light. Piece by piece, the room came into focus, Lisa's pupils adjusting to the sunlight pouring through the window. The pain in her side was a steady throb, reminding her of her injuries. This was no dream. Lisa had found her way back.

A heavyset duty nurse wandered in and did a double take when she saw that Lisa's eyes were open. "Sleeping Beauty wakes," she said, crossing the room and angling the blinds down to cut back on some of the glare.

Lisa recognized her as Helen Martin, a head nurse on the hospital's second floor. No doubt, Helen had no idea who Lisa was beyond the notes on her chart—she was too far down the food chain to be noticed by an upper-level employee.

Lisa tried to speak, but her throat was thick with mucus, and only a dry rasping sound escaped.

"Now, now, dear," said Helen. "You just lie still. I'll get Dr. Devereaux to take a look at you. If he says it's okay, I'll bring you some ice chips for that cottonmouth."

Within minutes, a distracted-looking man in green hospital garb returned with Nurse Martin and took Lisa's chart from the foot of her bed. "I'm Dr. Devereaux," he said, looking directly at the clipboard. "Can you tell me your name?"

Lisa's throat was still thick, but she managed to wheeze, "Lisa Mitchell."

"Very good," he said, making a note on the chart. His fingers were long and thin, almost skeletal. "Do you remember what happened, Lisa?"

"Can I have something to drink?"

"Oh, certainly! Nurse Martin, can you—"

"I have it right here," the nurse said, feeding Lisa ice chips from a paper cup. After a moment, the fire in Lisa's throat diminished to a smoldering ember, and she found her voice more easily. "I was in a car accident," she said.

"That's right," said Dr. Devereaux, running a hand distractedly through his thinning hair. "You were crossing Maple Street when another car ran a red light. You fared pretty well, all things considered."

Lisa was momentarily perplexed. She had no missing links in her memory, yet she was certain she had been the one who ran the red light, not the other party. Ultimately, she decided there was no use in arguing fault. The end result was the same.

"You cracked a couple of ribs," continued Dr. Devereaux. "You also sprained your right arm and hit your head on the steering wheel. It must've been a pretty good impact. You've been unconscious for six days."

"Six days? That doesn't seem possible!" Lisa said.

"Truthfully, we were getting pretty worried about you," said the doctor. "We couldn't find any physical reason for you to remain comatose. We'll want to run some tests, of course, but I suspect the worst is over for you."

Lisa smiled weakly and nodded her head. Dr. Devereaux made a few more notes on the chart before heading back to the hall. Helen stayed behind, fluffing pillows and feeding Lisa a few more ice chips.

"Pretty soon you'll graduate to the real thing," Helen said.

"Mmm?"

"Water. A glass of water instead of these blasted ice chips. Won't that be nice?" Helen's smile was genuine, and Lisa felt a sense of respect for the professionalism and personality of the woman. She smiled and nodded in response.

"I haven't seen any family members stop by. Do you want me to call anyone?" asked Helen.

"There's not anyone to call," said Lisa. "My nanna died last week. She was my only family."

"Oh, I'm sorry to hear that." Helen's face reflected concern that seemed genuine, although Lisa knew that it must be a reflex from all her years of nursing. All of the sickness, disease, and death taught one quickly how to feign sympathy. The notion did not upset Lisa. She admired the woman's ability to project feelings that were insincere. If Lisa had been better at doing it, she might not have lost her job.

"I understand you used to work at the hospital," continued Helen.

Lisa nodded her head but said nothing. She didn't want to elaborate on anything even remotely connected to Ms. Kelsey. She still didn't understand why there wasn't a police officer waiting at the corner of her bed to arrest her the moment she woke up.

"I'll check back with you in a bit," said Helen, heading toward the door. "Get some rest. I know that sounds stupid since you've been out for six days, but rest is the only way to make the body heal."

Lisa managed another smile, realizing that she was completely exhausted. She drifted off to sleep before the nurse had even pulled the door closed.

⋄

"Well, I see no reason to keep you any longer," said Dr. Devereaux, glancing up from Lisa's clipboard to study her. It had been four days since Lisa had first awakened from her coma. She had been eating as if she hadn't in weeks, and her strength had returned rapidly. Helen Martin kept a watchful eye, making sure that Lisa didn't overdo it, but Lisa knew there was nothing to worry about. Her moment of crisis had passed.

"I feel fine," Lisa said, tying her shoelaces.

"Will you be okay?" Helen asked.

"Yes, thanks." Lisa wore jeans and a t-shirt that Helen had bought for her. The clothes she had worn the night of the accident had been bloodstained and torn. "I've got my nanna's house."

"If you experience any unusual symptoms like lightheadedness or nausea, please come back to the ER immediately," advised the doctor.

"I will. Thank you both." Lisa just wanted to be out of there. Every moment of every day was anticipatory, waiting for the time when the police would arrive to escort her to prison for killing Nola Kelsey. She had finally determined the woman's first name after reading an account of the hit-and-run in the local paper. Nola. She had sort of looked like a Nola, Lisa supposed—before the truck had hit her, of course. Afterward, she had looked no different from the roadkill left behind by any other animal stupid enough to wander out into traffic.

On the second day, a police officer stopped by, and Lisa's breath caught in her throat. He was completing an accident report in regard to Lisa's own traffic mishap, however, and didn't mention Nola Kelsey once. Lisa couldn't imagine a force so inefficient that it wouldn't investigate someone with an obvious motive, especially considering that same person was also involved in a high-speed accident moments later while fleeing the scene of the crime.

Dr. Devereaux's comment floated back to Lisa. *You were crossing Maple Street when another car ran a red light.*

Maple Street was on the wrong side of town.

Darin Miller

Morton's Supermarket was on the east side, and Maple Street was on the west, a fifteen-minute drive.

That simply isn't possible, Lisa thought. Then again, the doctor had also indicated that the other driver had run the red light, and she knew *that* wasn't accurate. She had seen the red neon glow just before impact. She didn't pay much attention to the questions the policeman asked her, answering them perfunctorily while he took notes. The only thing she remembered was the enormous relief she had experienced when she realized she wasn't about to be hauled away in cuffs. Later, she would examine the copy of the police report which he left with her for her insurance company.

Lisa glanced around the hospital room. She felt as if she was leaving something behind, but she knew that was impossible. All she had was the clothes on her back and a bag that Helen had bought for her. She pressed her lips into a tight grin and walked out into the hallway.

It seemed odd to be on this side of the fence. Until now, whenever Lisa had traveled the corridors of Morgan Township Hospital, it had been with a mop bucket in tow, stooped over like a gnome, doing the menial labor that everyone else was too good to do. Today, her back was straight, and her head was held high. She recognized former coworkers, but none of them even acknowledged her. It was as if she hadn't spent the last several years toiling elbow to elbow with them.

Lisa realized as she looked at the empty faces that she truly had been done a great service by Ms. Nola Kelsey. Her coworkers looked soulless, plodding around their stations, shuffling their paperwork, hauling their laundry carts. A blessing in disguise, Nanna Grace would have said, and Lisa grinned.

Nearing the far end of the corridor, Lisa slowed as she spotted the first policeman. He was walking up the hall toward her, his expression vacant. He was very tall, well over six foot, his long, muscular arms swinging like pendulums in time with his footsteps. Lisa's heartbeat accelerated, and she found that her legs were suddenly very heavy. He was still fifty yards away but closing in when Lisa was startled by a hand on her arm.

It was Helen Martin. "Lisa, dear, I can hardly stand to see you just disappear out the door like this. I know that you *say* everything is all right, but I would certainly feel better if I could check in with you in a couple of days. You know, make sure you're settling in," she said.

Lisa was glad for the distraction. It meant she didn't have to stare guiltily at the police officer as he passed by. "Really, I'm fine," she said. "But if it would make you feel better, it's fine with me."

Helen smiled, satisfaction showing in her eyes. "Oh, good! I can get your information from your patient file, if you don't mind—address, phone number, that kind of thing. Now don't you worry, I won't be a nuisance. I'll call before I stop by."

90

Lisa returned the smile, although she was certain that hers didn't convey the warmth of the nurse's. "You're very kind. Do you get this personally involved with all of your patients?"

Helen laughed. "No, it actually isn't a very good idea in my line of work. But the days you spent in a coma—well, I can't really explain it. You looked like a helpless little girl. Reminded me of my daughter, in fact."

Lisa hadn't noticed that the first police officer had passed by until the second one had too, trailing behind by several yards. She turned her gaze to follow the men as they continued down the corridor. "What's with all the police?" she asked.

Helen grimaced and shook her head. "We're not entirely sure at this point. Several days ago, we had a patient pass away on the third floor. She was quite elderly and not in the best of health, but then again, she wasn't my patient, so I probably shouldn't speak out of school. Still, the woman's daughter has been making an awful fuss, insisting that her mother was killed in her sleep—suffocated."

"Wasn't there anything to suggest cause of death?" asked Lisa, but she already knew that there wouldn't be.

"No, nothing that the police are admitting, anyway. I think they're merely trying to placate the daughter. Her name is Genevieve Maddox—the same Maddoxes who funded the construction of the hospital's new pediatric wing. Most folks would just as soon keep her happy," said Helen.

Lisa already knew the answer to her next question, but it was something that she needed to hear aloud. She paused, wanting to phrase the question just right. She didn't want Helen to be suspicious of her. "Um, as you know, I used to work at the hospital. I knew many of the patients. May I ask who died?"

Helen smiled sadly. "Of course, dear. It was Alma Baylock. Did you know her?"

II

"So, that's how you think it's done?"

Crystal thought her eyes were open, but all she saw was pitch blackness. The voice, old and sharp, penetrated the dark abyss and reverberated against things Crystal could not see.

"Answer me, Chrissy."

Crystal's mind swirled. The voice was *so* familiar, but without a face to see, comprehension lay just beyond her grasp. "Hello?" she called. Her voice sounded the same as always.

"What has happened to you?"

A bright light switched on overhead, casting blinding illumination down to carve a column out of the pitch blackness. Crystal couldn't see herself—she was just outside the spotlight—but once her eyes began to adjust, she was able to discern a rocking chair positioned center stage, an elderly woman swaying gently while stringing beans.

"Aunt Maude?" Crystal asked, her voice trembling.

The woman sighed and rested her hands in her lap. "I'm very disappointed in you, Chrissy," she said.

Crystal's face was dampened with tears that came from nowhere. "I'm *so* sorry, Aunt Maude—"

"I know, sweetheart, I know. But shut your mouth and listen a spell. Killing yourself is the coward's way, and I didn't raise no cowards. Things are surely bad, but step back. Get your head together, child. It's not as bad as you think."

"But—"

"*Listen,* child," Maude said. "Half the trouble is, you never *really* learned how to *listen.* The world is full of light and shadow. Life has more meaning than just how much stuff you have. You already know this, but you've forgotten. Soon there will be people coming. Some of them want to help you, some want to hurt you. You need to be ready—and you need to be able to tell the difference."

"How—"

"I don't know how. That's up to you."

"So, I'm not—"

"Dead? Oh no, Chrissy. Today's not your day."

"Aunt Maude?" Crystal said in a small voice.

"Yes?"

"I'm so sorry—"

"Sorry for what, child? Sorry for not throwing your future away and spending your days in a trailer in my backyard? Sorry for not calling so often—you know, it wouldn't have killed you. Sorry for not being at the funeral? Let yourself off the hook, sweetheart. I was always proud of you—still am. I know you love me, just as you know I love you. That's why I am so disappointed about what's happening now. You've been tricked. Don't let them fool you again," said Maude.

The light was gone, and Crystal was immersed in total darkness once more. Not *total* darkness—Aunt Maude's guest appearance had left a residual trace of warmth and lightness in Crystal's heart. It had been good to converse with the old woman again, even if only in a brief, delirious dream. Crystal's instincts told her that it wasn't *just* a dream, though. The message seemed somehow apocalyptic. Who was coming to help her? Who was coming to hurt her? Why would anyone care one way or the other?

The next time Crystal saw light it was the real thing. Her eyes were crusty slits, struggling to open. Her mouth was thick and dry, and her tongue felt like it was swollen to three times its normal size. Her limbs were leaden and non-responsive.

She hadn't been awake but a minute when a chubby though industrious nurse bustled into the room and started poking and prodding. The nurse's demeanor was cold and disinterested as she went about her duties, noting various comments on the clipboard at the foot of Crystal's bed. Crystal watched the nurse's sausage fingers manipulate her cheap ballpoint across the page. She removed several of the wires which were monitoring Crystal's vital signs. Then, as quickly as she had come, the nurse headed back for the door.

"The doctor will be in to see you shortly, Ms. Bright," the nurse said. Her odd emphasis on Crystal's name belied her disapproval. Another show business type, overdosing and creating headlines—and more responsibility for an already overextended hospital staff.

As the door closed behind the nurse's ample derriere, Crystal realized that she wasn't alone in the room. A dark-haired girl sat in a chair tucked nearly out of sight in the corner of the room. She looked vaguely familiar, but Crystal couldn't place her.

Presently, the girl stood and crossed the room, her eyes lit with urgency. "Come on, we have to hurry." She was carrying a duffel bag in her right hand and placed it beside Crystal on the bed.

Crystal tried to move her mouth, but she was still very weak. The girl lifted Crystal's shoulders from the bed and worked her platinum mane of hair into a clumsy knot at the nape of her neck. She then reached into the duffel and retrieved a jet-black wig, nearly identical to her own hairstyle, and plunked it down on Crystal's head.

"What's going on?" Crystal managed weakly as the wig was adjusted.

"You need to pull yourself together, Crystal, and I mean fast. Pretty soon, the doctors will be in here, and you've got to be gone by then. Do you understand?" The girl's voice was insistent.

Crystal shook her head. "Are you kidnapping me?"

The girl chuckled. "More or less. But believe me, it's better than what will happen if you stay."

Crystal didn't resist the girl's efforts to get her dressed. Soon, she was wearing blue jeans and an Ohio State University sweatshirt, identical to the girl's own outfit. The girl stepped back to see the results, shrugged and tucked Crystal's hospital gown into the duffel. By then, Crystal felt a little stronger, and her head had somewhat cleared.

"Why do I have to be gone when the doctors get here?" asked Crystal.

The girl was tugging at Crystal's arm, maneuvering her into an upright position. "Because if you don't get out of here, it's off to the psych ward with you."

"What?" Crystal asked. "The *psych* ward?"

"You tried to kill yourself. You've been automatically enrolled. Come *on*, we don't have much time," said the girl. "Now listen carefully. There's a silver Honda Civic on Level 3 of the parking garage. It has big, pink fuzzy dice around the mirror. Here are the keys. Let yourself in and wait for me. You *have* to act normal, so test your feet out, see if you can walk."

Crystal slid off the bed and stood, her knees surprisingly shaky. After a few tentative steps, enough strength had returned that she could maintain the illusion of sure footing. "Is this okay?" she asked.

The girl nodded. "Just *go*. I'll be there as soon as the coast is clear."

Crystal hesitated at the doorknob. "Why—"

"Later," insisted the girl. *"Go."*

Crystal opened the door and stepped out into the hallway. She half-expected an armed guard to seize her by the elbow and lead her away to her own private padded room, but there was no one there, only patients and hospital employees, traversing the halls with varying purposes. Crystal cast her eyes downward, avoiding making contact with anyone else. She was certain she would be recognized, although she hadn't seen herself in a mirror since being disguised.

Soon there will be people coming. Some of them want to help you, some want to hurt you. You need to be ready—and you need to be able to tell the difference.

Aunt Maude's words came back to Crystal. Was this mysterious girl here to help? Crystal's instincts told her that she was. The only thing she knew for certain was that she didn't want to go to the psych ward. Talk about scandalous headlines!

Crystal instinctively avoided the elevators and entered the stairwell. According to the signage by the door, she was currently on the fifth floor of the facility. Not entirely trusting her legs to support her, she started down the stairs tentatively, gaining speed and surety with each step. When she reached the landing at the third floor, she noticed a small china teacup centered in the doorframe—what it was doing there, she had no idea. She opened the heavy door and entered the third-floor hall, leaving the cup where it was. The aftereffect of her narcotic cocktail might well produce pink elephants around the next corner.

As on the fifth floor, the corridor bustled with activity. Stretchers were wheeled by and doctors, deep in thought, passed quickly on either side. No one seemed to recognize Crystal or question her presence. Why should they? She could be visiting a sick relative for all they knew. Nonetheless, Crystal didn't waste any time. She checked a directory that was conveniently mounted to the wall near the elevators, finding the most direct route to the parking garage. Her nervous hand was sweaty against the cold metal of the car keys. She wanted to be out of this place desperately. She wanted to go home—not to her luxurious apartment, but rather to Aunt Maude's house in Ohio. To hell with the whole Hollywood scene.

Crystal found the little Honda with no difficulty and let herself in the passenger side. She crouched down so as not to be seen. She was suddenly exhausted, the short journey from her room to the parking garage feeling as though it had been miles long. She supposed it was a residual reaction from her overdose. It wasn't long before she was sleeping soundly, curled into a ball in the passenger floorboard.

The pecking on the window was insistent, and Crystal grudgingly lifted her head. Her brain felt like it was packed in cotton. The urgent expression on the girl's face seemed exaggerated and surreal. Why did she look so familiar?

Ah, yes. The girl from the hospital room. She wants inside the car. *Let her in.*

Crystal struggled across the center console, nearly impaling herself on the four-speed gearshift before reaching the lock on the driver's door. With what little energy she could muster, she flipped the switch and then slumped back into the floorboard on the passenger side.

The girl had the door open and was behind the wheel in one fluid movement. "The keys," she said, sticking a quivering hand palm up in Crystal's direction. "I need the keys."

Crystal's brows furrowed. What keys?

"Oh, *dammit!*" the girl cried. "I need the goddamned *keys!*" She started thrusting her hands into Crystal's pockets, stopping when she realized that Crystal was lazily dangling them in front of her.

"What's going on?" Crystal asked. She was in a strange state; neither anxious nor interested in her current situation. It was as if it were a huge bother to lie curled up like a snail in the floorboard, contributing nothing whatsoever to this unknown heroine's effort.

"We're getting you out of here, that's what," the girl said, turning the key in the ignition. The little engine hummed, and the girl put the car in reverse, twisting to peer through the back glass as she maneuvered the car out of its slot. She flipped the headlights on and shifted into drive. "Now, listen. I don't really know what we're going to run into up ahead. The doctor came back to the room before you had been gone too long. They know you're gone. I'm sure they've alerted security, but I don't know how widespread that alarm might have sounded. They may be checking cars as they leave the parking garage."

"Well, that's some plan you've got!" barked Crystal, suddenly infuriated at the girl's amateurish attempt. "Why did you even bother at all? They're bound to see me down here."

The girl's head swiveled sharply, fresh tears burning in the corners of her eyes. "I'm doing the best I can, okay? I've got an old blanket in the back. Let me—" She reached into the back seat and produced a rose-colored wool blanket, the kind pink-cheeked little girls sleep under. She awkwardly arranged it around Crystal, but the resultant heap was so obviously a person hiding under a blanket that the girl's frustration broke into a sob. "I'm doing the best I can!"

"The longer we fuss, the more likely security will be at the door," said Crystal from underneath the blanket. "Let's just go."

"Okay," the girl dried her eyes with a wadded handkerchief that she produced from above her sun visor.

Crystal could feel the car slowly rolling forward, gradually declining as it wound around the parking structure. "Why did you stay?" she asked.

"Huh?" The girl's voice sounded yards away, obscured by the thick layer of pink wool.

"Why did you stay in the room?" Crystal asked.

"I don't know. I thought I could buy you some extra time to get away. I've come to the hospital every day since—They thought I was your cousin from Lucasville," the girl said. "I figured I'd tell them that you went to the bathroom, you know, give you a little more of a jump start, but I didn't think about them trying to detain *me*."

"Why would they detain you?" Crystal asked.

"I thought the whole plan was so great," the girl snorted. "Yeah, *right*—great. Big town like Hollywood sees this kind of shit all the time, I guess. They figured I was trying to help you get out. I guess they've been watching me almost as closely as they've been watching you."

"Who are you?" Crystal asked, as if the question hadn't even entered her mind until this moment.

"Paula," the girl said. "I'm a fan."

Crystal laughed to herself, laughter which devolved into tears. She had nearly killed herself, and only one goddamned fan cared enough to be there for her. After all she had given of herself—

Chrissy!

"Well, Paula, what can I say?" Crystal finally said. "Thanks?"

"Shhh!" Paula whispered urgently. *"Shit!* The exit is blocked! *Shit!* Shit-shit-shit!"* There was no way to better disguise Crystal. They were busted, and there was little doubt about it. Still, Crystal hunkered down into the smallest, most-compact bundle she could become and held her breath.

A light rapping on the window. Crystal could hear Paula fiddling with the crank.

Paula squinted up into the flashlight shining directly into her face. "Hey, what's going on?" she said, raising an arm to shield her eyes.

"Hospital security, ma'am," a detached male voice announced, deep and authoritative. "Please keep your hands where I can see them. Are you traveling by yourself this evening?" He began circling the vehicle, waving the flashlight around to examine the inside of the car.

Paula cleared her throat. "Uh-huh," she said, nodding her head. She could see another member of the security team across the lane, observing the situation with keen interest. Both men were burly, thick-necked ex-football types with cold eyes and large knuckles.

Once the guard had completed his circuit around the car, he paused again at Paula's window. He reached inside his uniform jacket and retrieved a black-and-white photograph of Crystal Bright, smiling dazzlingly from the cover of *TV Guide*—back when she was still *The Girl.* "Have you seen this woman?" he asked.

"Well, sure," Paula said, taking the picture from the guard and examining it carefully. She metered her words out carefully. "That's Crystal Bright. I'm just about her biggest fan in the whole wide world."

The guard's stern countenance cracked for a grin. "I *know* that. I mean, have you seen her here *tonight,* you know, live and in person."

Paula's eyes widened, and she laughed a nervous giggle. "Crystal Bright is *here? Tonight?*"

The guard interrupted, "Don't be getting all excited. She won't be seeing fans. Can I take that as a 'no' then?"

"Um, I guess," Paula said, looking perplexed.

The guard from across the lane called out, "Anything, Thomas?"

Thomas retracted his flashlight, stepping back from the Honda. "Nothing here, man. This chick ain't seen shit."

Crystal slowly exhaled from underneath the blanket. How could they have possibly overlooked her? Either the security guard was completely inept, or—

"Can I go now?" Paula asked, batting her eyelashes at Thomas.

"Yes, ma'am. Sorry to trouble you," he said, bowing slightly and stepping back.

Crystal felt the car move slowly forward, clearing the exit and turning left before accelerating into the flow of traffic.

"All right," said Paula, tapping the blanket lightly under which Crystal's head lay. "Coast is clear."

Crystal had been in that position for so long that her muscles didn't want to cooperate at first. Then slowly, the blood started to recirculate through those ignored parts, first tingling then burning. After what seemed an eternally long time, Crystal had finally unfolded herself and found the passenger seat.

"That was close, huh?" asked Paula, grinning crookedly at Crystal. "I had a feeling we'd be okay, though."

97

"A feeling, huh?" asked Crystal. "I don't see how that guy could've missed seeing me."

"I don't either," said Paula, laughing. "What a goofturd!"

"Yeah," said Crystal, smiling. "A goofturd, all right." She studied the girl's face as she drove, and she was again struck by the sensation that she had seen her somewhere before. "Do I know you?" she asked.

Paula hesitated, the victorious look on her face faltering. "No, not really, I don't suppose."

"What the hell kind of answer is that?" Crystal snapped.

The girl looked as though she had been slapped. "I mean, it isn't like someone like you would be expected to remember someone like me," she said.

"Remember you from where?"

"Benny and The Girl," Paula said. "I was the contest winner. Paula Haversham. I won a walk-on part."

"I threw a script at your head," Crystal said, suddenly overcome with laughter. "I threw a fucking script at your head!"

Tears had begun to roll down Paula's cheeks, and she nodded furtively.

"Well, Paula Haversham," said Crystal, relaxing just a bit. "It's pretty safe to say that I won't be throwing anything at you tonight. See?" She held out both of her hands. "I don't have hold of anything." She laughed again.

Paula laughed too, although uneasily. "So where do we go, now?" she asked.

"Up to you," said Crystal, stretching and easing the passenger seat of the Civic back. "I'm just the hostage."

Within seconds, she was snoring softly, purring like a kitten. Paula's eyes returned to the road and steeled. As if by unspoken direction, she turned the car to the east.

III

Chad lay on his back, staring at the off-white tiles which adorned the ceiling. He hadn't intended to return to his father's house, but he really didn't have anything to do until he was to meet Suze at eleven. He was in the room that had been his when Peter and Naomi were married and still living together. Even though the room had remained his after the divorce, it had never felt the same. It was more like a hotel room to him now.

It was when he dozed that he thought of the girl. He didn't know anything about her, the shoeless little creature with straggly black curls and mud on her backside, but he sensed the urgency surrounding the wide-eyed waif. Although he had never before laid eyes on the child, he knew that she was as real as he was. Her expression was unreadable, her eyes were windows to nothing. She stood in a yard that was equal parts mud and grass, her arms clasped behind her back, her dirty toes drawing lines in the squishy brown below. Behind her was a plastic table, the type all little girls her age had, set for an imaginary tea party with her stuffed animals and baby dolls.

Momma's gonna bust your ass when she's sees you've got the good china, Chad thought as he examined the table. He said as much in the dream, but the girl didn't hear or didn't care—just the same vacant expression.

Chad woke feeling more tired than when he had fallen asleep. It was only eight o'clock, which still gave him plenty of time to inspect the house for items which might prove useful before he had to meet Suze. He had hoped to find some sort of weaponry, but either Peter didn't own any or the police had seized it when they had searched the premises. It didn't really matter. He *did* find a spare set of keys to his father's Volvo, and if Chad needed weapons—and he invariably *would*—he would do a smash-and-grab in some neighboring po-dunk town.

Chad had awakened at seventeen, or at least that was his current perception of the changes which had taken place in his mind. He had always been a good boy, had gotten decent grades, made decent friends, said *yes, no, thank you,* and *excuse me* at all the appropriate times—but he had not even been *alive* back then. He couldn't identify the catalyst, but there had definitely been one, and he was now operating on intuition gleaned from a higher power.

Still, Chad was not a fool. He knew that he couldn't run around stealing and killing without any consideration whatsoever. He would need cash to continue on his journey, and in that regard, he was flat busted. Suzette Snyder may claim to have plenty of money, but Chad had no way of verifying that and wasn't at all sure he was willing to pay Suze's inevitable fee. Peter Collins was a budgeteer by design, and despite his respectable salary and many wise and profitable investments, he had always subscribed to what he called a 'safety net theorem.' It was the rough equivalent to jars of cash buried in the backyard for a rainy day. Peter always took 6.285% of his salary and hid it in envelopes around the house. How he had arrived at that peculiar percentage was of the stuff that only accountants understood, but by God, he knew where each and every dollar of that money was hidden. Naomi hadn't been privy to this information and neither had Chad—although he suspected a 'treasure map' was attached to Peter's will.

Chad wandered down the hall in his stocking feet, feeling like an intruder in his own father's house. He padded down the beige-carpeted stairs and across the highly polished wood floor of the hallway. Peter's spacious study was tucked into the back corner of the house, beyond a set of French doors. Out of habit, Chad knocked before he opened them. He caught himself and laughed out loud.

The room was an exercise in neutrality. Everything was brown or some shade of brown, from the curtains to the wallpaper to the overstuffed furniture. Peter's desk was centered in front of a large bay window which afforded a serene view of the Collins' large backyard and the woods which bordered it. Now, the fading light of day cast long shadows as if the woods were slowly gobbling up the lawn. A royal red leather chair sat behind the desk, looking like the throne of a king who had long since abdicated. Chad had rarely been allowed in this room. It was his father's private space.

Only private space I ever got was by locking the bathroom door, thought Chad.

He took the room in slowly. Heavy-handed artwork featuring dogs and hunters in frosty looking landscapes was proudly displayed on each wall. Peter had left the pictures of Naomi where they had always been—he wasn't the one who wanted the divorce in the first place. Chad saw the boy he had been, giggling hysterically as a multi-colored clown handed him a balloon. His eyes shimmered red from the flash of the camera. There were others of him at various ages, smiling and laughing, looking like everyone's dream child. There was no evidence whatsoever of the murky stain which had spread across his soul. These early memories were there, but with no emotional undercurrent to accompany them.

Chad sat in the leather chair, feeling the contours created by years of use by Peter. The surface of the desk was a textbook example of orderliness with not so much as a paperclip out of place. Chad felt compelled to rumple some of the junk mail that was tidily stacked on the corner and scatter it across the desktop.

Enough dawdling. Chad systematically began searching the desk drawers, pulling the contents out haphazardly and tossing them on the floor. Bank statements, utility bills, receipts—*whoops!* Envelope of cash! $75.00—healthcare information, instruction manuals; all these things had been filed neatly in hanging folders, labeled in Peter's familiar penmanship. Chad plodded forward until he had emptied all of the drawers, accumulating $435.00 for his trouble.

Chad swiveled the chair and tugged at the drawers of the lateral file behind the desk. Locked. The two-drawer cabinet was made of heavy cherry, the locking mechanism more durable than the usual plunger lock found on less expensive furniture.

After a quick and fruitless perusal of the desk's center drawer—Chad didn't discount the possibility that the key might be hidden in there; he didn't credit Peter with having much in the way of imagination or common sense—Chad wrapped his fingers around the handle of a long, silver bladed letter opener that Peter kept in his pencil caddy. Chad could feel his heart beat faster as he touched the metal and ran his finger along the sharp edge. It was like a sleeker version of the butcher knife with which he had killed his mother, not the same but not entirely different either. The potential for murder was within this desk accessory, and the rush of adrenaline that Chad received was jolting. Sliding his fingers along the shank, Chad realized how turned on he was. His teenaged cock, always eager to show its interest in *anything*, was so hard it actually *hurt*. Murder, violence, agony—who knew they could be so erotic? If Suze were here *right now*, he would have plunged the shiny dagger into her breastplate—without question. Afterward, he would have fucked her—also without question.

Instead, Chad plunged the letter opener deep into the recesses of the lock, twisting and turning as he ground the point inward.

The lock held fast.

As metal shavings sprinkled to the ground, Chad emitted a frustrated grunt and flung the letter opener aside. The point had chipped off in the lock, and the shank had bent to the left. Chad balled his fists, clenching and unclenching, his cheeks blossoming a fierce red. With animalistic enthusiasm, he wailed like a creature of nature and assaulted the lateral file, kicking the front repeatedly, rocking the heavy piece of furniture on its base, scratching and marring the flawless cherry surface. It was the final burst of fury, as Chad used his body weight for leverage, that proved most fruitful. The cabinet toppled forward, the back panel splitting from the stress, and exposing the rear of the drawers which slept within.

Jackpot.

Chad knelt over the pulverized furniture and used the bent letter opener to pry the splintered back panel completely away. Once inside, he was able to wrestle the drawers out. They were very heavy, laden with file folders and paperwork, but Chad's accelerated adrenaline made the effort seem minimal. He carried them to the middle of the room, awkwardly kicking his father's glass and wood coffee table out of the way. It contributed its own remnants to the growing pile of wreckage in a room that had only moments ago been pristine.

No wonder Dad never wanted me to come in here, thought Chad, and he giggled. If he had found $435.00 in the desk, he was *bound* to hit the mother lode in this junior Fort Knox.

The first drawer contained hanging file folders, stretched like a wide grin across a wire frame. Chad thumbed through the thick files quickly, not absorbing their contents but merely scanning for more of those magical little money packets. There were none to be found, and as Chad finished with each folder, he tossed it carelessly over his shoulder into yet another growing heap on the floor.

The second drawer was instantly disappointing; it contained nothing but a leather-bound family album. It wasn't even particularly thick. Chad turned the plastic-coated pages quickly, half-heartedly treasure seeking, although he suspected it was useless. There was no money tucked away in the album, just old family pictures; Naomi with tall and frizzy 80s hair, holding toddler Chad up to face the camera; Peter grinning crookedly from the wooden deck which extended off the rear of the house, dressed in Don Johnson pastels and whites, also circa 1980; friends, maybe family members, huddled close to Naomi and Peter as they collectively fussed and cooed at toddler Chad. Chad could have been no more than four years old when these photos were taken, yet he could almost hear the silly women babbling nonsense over his head, the men busily plotting Chad's future, first as an all-star athlete, then as a doctor or scientist or some other humanitarian bullshit—providing the pay was good. Chad closed his eyes and breathed deeply, smelling charcoal and mesquite blending with succulent steak. It was almost as if the pictures were individual movies. The subjects appeared ready to self-animate, eager to tell their stories. Chad snapped the album shut, not willing to listen to what they had to say. The Collins had been useful, but now they were just history.

Chad was ready to dismiss the lateral file's contents when his eye skittered over his own name typed neatly on one of the folders he had tossed aside. He stooped down and picked it up, coaxing papers that had slid through the top back into the jacket. It was neither thick nor thin, but natural curiosity required its examination, and Chad sat down again in Peter's leather chair, sweeping the contents off the desktop and onto the floor, all except for the green-shaded banker's lamp, which Chad turned on by pulling its delicate gold chain.

The contents of the file were mostly correspondence, but the item at the back was jolting. It was a certificate of adoption, legally binding Chad to Peter and Naomi Collins.

I'm adopted.

Chad was dumbfounded. Neither Peter or Naomi had ever given any indication that Chad was anything but their own flesh and blood. Countless times he had heard how he had his father's eyes, his mother's hair—apparently through the arbitrary whims of fate other than a real, biological connection.

After the initial shock passed, Chad turned his attention to the correspondence. Most of it was on notebook paper, written in unfamiliar penmanship.

May 3, 1982

Dear Pete,

How are you, old buddy? Jessie and I are doing well, all things considered. The job sucks and the plant keeps laying people off, but so far, I've been safe. How're things at Fisher's? Investments must be slow what with the economy.

Jessie's due in July, and I can't wait until she has the baby. She hasn't been herself for months. It's kind of scary to watch. Someday you'll know what I mean, buddy, when Naomi tells you she's expecting. The hormone thing is crazy.

We should be in Pridemore in June, if Jessie's up to it. She really misses Naomi. We'll see you then.

Buster

The first few letters were derivations of the first, *Hi, how are ya? See ya real soon.* It was the letters from late June that proved more interesting.

June 23, 1982

Pete,

Things are such a fucking mess. Jessie's going into depressions so fast and out of the blue that I don't even remember what she used to be like. The doctor keeps telling me that it's extreme but normal, but I know better. Pete, I think she's lost her mind. I don't know if it's the hormones or the nightmares or the constant nausea. I just don't know. It was great to see you guys last weekend. Naomi seems to be the only one who halfway calms Jessie down. God, I can't apologize enough for Saturday night, though. She was way over the top. I mean, for Christ's sake, it was <u>Yahtzee</u>. But that's how she's been—well, not entirely accurate. She's been much worse.

I think she hates the baby. I don't know what's going to happen once it's born. She took a little tumble down the stairs on Wednesday, and I swear to God, I think she was trying to kill it. I can hardly believe I'm putting this on paper. Jessie always wanted kids, but something's changed. I'll call you soon.

Buster

The names were unfamiliar to Chad. Throughout the years, he had met countless business and social acquaintances of the lying bastards who had called themselves his parents. The names 'Buster' and 'Jessie' meant absolutely nothing to him. Without any tangible reasoning, Chad intuitively knew that Buster and Jessie were the people in the photos with Toddler Chad, Naomi, and Peter.

The last letter in the file was dated more than three years later than the previous one.

October 28, 1985

Pete,

I'll keep it brief. I know you and Naomi just want us to go away, and as much as that hurts me, I understand.

I can't sign off until I tell you how much this means to me. The baby wouldn't have ever been safe with us. God help me, I've never been so ashamed in my life. First, I thought it was all Jessie, but now I know it wasn't. It wasn't! I don't feel like I can trust myself anymore.

Thank you for everything, buddy. I doubt we'll see each other again. If some day you do see me, be careful. I doubt if I'll be able to control myself.

Buster

Chad was enthralled, realizing that these letters were from his biological father. Chad's dad—Buster. Buster was sort of a cool name. The anxiety which dripped from the letters intrigued Chad. What was wrong with Jessie? What had Buster been so ashamed of? Obviously, they thought that it was in Chad's best interest to be transferred to the Collinses. But who were Peter and Naomi to these people? Friends? Family? Chad wondered if he had Buster's eyes and Jessie's hair. He wondered why Jessie had wanted to terminate her own pregnancy. He wondered if she would try to kill him if she were standing in front of him today. He wondered what type of man Buster was. He stretched across the floor and retrieved the photo album, flipping it open to the pictures which he knew were of his birth parents. Now that he had read the letters, Chad could see the mental disturbance playing in Jessie's head through the windows of her eyes. Her haggard face was weary and taut, her smile forced and pinched, her eyes dark of inconceivable thought. Chad smiled slightly as he realized the woman had given him something far more valuable than a shiny head of hair. His rage was from inside this woman—on that he would have bet his life. Buster was much harder to read. He didn't look anguished as he had sounded in the letters. He looked like the neighbor next door, plain-featured and ordinary, waggling a hand at you as he pushed the lawnmower by every Saturday. In some ways, that made him more intriguing to Chad. The man was obviously disturbed by what was happening in his own home, yet the mask he wore for photographs was perfection. His eyes said absolutely nothing about the pain he was hiding, the things which brought him shame because although he knew they were wrong, he just couldn't help himself. Chad wanted to meet these people. He wanted to know the darkness that tore at Buster. He wanted to know if Jessie still wanted to kill him.

Unfortunately, that could never happen. Taped to the back of the folder was an aged newspaper clipping from *The Columbus Dispatch*. It was an obituary for the late Bernard Lybrook, loser in a game of highway tag with a semi on I-70, just west of Dayton, Ohio. The picture accompanying the article was clearly of the man who called himself Buster. He had been residing in the Columbus suburb of Reynoldsburg at the time of his death. There was no mention of Jessie at all, but the obituary said he had no surviving family.

Well, that's not entirely true, Chad thought grimly.

He felt entirely robbed. He had never been given the opportunity to know the people who had brought him into this world, and there was no way to correct that now. He wished that he could kill Naomi all over again—once just simply wasn't enough. It had seemed like delicious irony to see Peter go to jail for the very crime which Chad had committed, but now Chad longed for the opportunity to kill Peter, too. These people had misrepresented *everything* to him. Chad could feel the rage building, rising like bile in the back of his throat. The urge to break things tickled his ribs and raised his blood pressure.

Ten-thirty.

Chad had lost track of the time, and it was nearly time to meet Suze. It was with considerable effort that he forced the beast inside to return to its cage. Suze was his only real connection to the world, absurd as it seemed. Peter was dead to him now, and if he had half a chance, Chad would render Peter dead to the rest of the world as well. Suze was playing games with him, and Chad didn't care for that. That implied that she thought he was less intelligent than her, and that really pissed him off. Still, he needed her for now. He didn't know exactly *why* he needed her, but again, intuition whispered her necessity into his ear.

Frontier and High Street intersected in the center of downtown Pridemore. The town was a small province in a small county, close enough to the Ohio border for daytrips to Cincinnati, yet far enough away to seem detached from the rest of the world. Still, the town's citizens enjoyed themselves like any other typical American citizens on any given night of the week, drinking, dancing, fucking. The town's most active nightspots were located near this intersection, and pedestrian traffic, although much lighter than it would have been under the noonday sun, was still straggling from one bar to the next in small groups.

Chad parked his father's maroon Volvo in one of the metered slots along High Street. He ignored the meter; parking was free in Pridemore after sundown. He stood near the corner, his hands tucked deep into his jeans pockets, his nervous eyes dancing from side to side. He didn't see Suze anywhere. He glanced at his watch and saw that it was eleven fifteen.

What in the hell are you up to? he thought.

A hand on his shoulder.

Chad jumped and spun around. Suze grinned mischievously as she tucked her hands behind her back and shifted from foot to foot. "Hey," she said.

"You're late."

Suze rolled her eyes. "Are you *always* this much fun?"

"I have no idea what you want with me. Who are you? What's your game?" Chad asked.

Suze laughed. "That's rich. You sound like TV. My name is Suzette Snyder, I prefer to be called Suze, I like cotton candy, and beans and weenies, and I'm your new best friend. You and me have some work to do."

Chad raised an eyebrow. "Work?"

"Oh, you know," said Suze, walking around Chad in a lazy circle, forcing him to turn with her, his eyes fixed on her grinning face. "Maybe a little killing to do."

Chad laughed. "Killing? You don't know anything about killing. You're full of shit. I'll bet you get off on studying serial killers and shit like that. I'll bet it really pisses your daddy off."

Suze stopped and cocked her head to the right. Her eyes should've been angry, should've reflected *something* in response to what Chad had said. Instead, she looked highly amused. The expression chilled Chad to his bones. *He* was the killer. *He* was the one people should fear. Suze should be afraid of him, too. He could kill her as easy as snapping his fingers.

And that's what sent a cold finger down Chad's spine—deep down inside, he knew he wouldn't kill Suze—couldn't. It gave her an ultimate advantage over him that he found hard to accept but impossible to refute.

"Point," Suze said, her unblinking eyes challenging Chad, taunting him.

"What?"

"Point," she repeated. "Waggle your little finger at the first person that strikes your fancy. Think about it or don't, just *do* it. Then I suggest you head for your car and get it started."

"Why?"

Suze only smiled in response, again challenging Chad, challenging his manhood. Chad's patience was running thin. With a low grumble, Chad diverted his attention to the trickle of people strolling along the sidewalks. There were at least three elderly couples walking in various directions, and this surprised Chad. He assumed that these people would be in bed by this time of night. A boisterous group of six friends laughed their way from McDougal's on High to McTavish's on Frontier—Irish pubs were popular in Pridemore. A fortyish woman with tall, ice-white hair and heavy makeup staggered out of McTavish's as the group entered, smiling lewdly at one of the guys despite his girlfriend.

Chad brought his arm up and pointed at the woman as she continued west on Frontier. Suze smiled with satisfaction, and quick as a cat she moved away from Chad and toward the inebriated ice princess.

Chad stood transfixed, the keys to the Volvo dangling between his fingers. Suze's gait never faltered, and she purposefully strode across Frontier to intercept the woman. Chad saw the woman's face twist in a perplexed smile as Suze neared, trying to determine if she knew her before realizing that she did not.

It all happened so fast.

Suze's arms reached out as if she were offering the woman an embrace, the dear old friend that she hadn't seen in years. The woman smiled uncertainly and began to pull back, but it was too late. In one swift motion, Suze grabbed the woman's head and twisted it sharply to the right.

The pop that issued from her neck carried across Frontier as clearly as the peal of a church bell. The woman dropped like a stone at Suze's feet, and from somewhere farther down the street, another woman screamed in terror.

Before Chad fully realized what had just happened, Suze was running back across the street, the hard soles of her sandals slapping against the pavement. "Go! *Go! GO!*" she screamed, flailing her arms like a windmill.

Chad snapped from his reverie and ran for the Volvo, unlocking the doors with the remote on the key chain. He and Suze slipped into the front seats and Chad nervously flipped through the keys until he finally worked one into the ignition. The Volvo's engine turned, and Chad pulled out onto Frontier, narrowly avoiding a Ford Explorer which had been about to pass. Horns blared and fingers flew, but there was no impact.

Chad could feel his heart thudding in his chest, his inner rage feasting on the adrenaline of the moment. Still, the reckless abandon with which Suze had displayed her ferocity was jolting. Witnesses were *everywhere*.

Suze laughed so hard that tears streamed down her cheeks.

"What in the hell *was* that?" Chad demanded.

"You didn't believe I have what it takes," said Suze between guffaws.

Chad turned sharply to the right and headed for the county road which would take him most quickly away from Pridemore. He accelerated to seventy-five.

"That was *stupid*," Chad said. "A million people saw you do it. We should be in jail in time for breakfast tomorrow morning."

"*Pfft*," said Suze, waving Chad's worries away. "If we get caught for anything, it's going to be the way you're driving. Christ, can't you stay on this side of the sound barrier?"

"We need to get the hell away from here. You just killed someone, you crazy bitch. People saw my car, probably got the license number. *Shit!* I should've *known* better than to come here tonight."

"Relax, Chaddie boy," said Suze, reclining her seat a bit. "Nobody saw anything. Well, anything that could hurt us. They sure as hell saw that woman kiss her ass goodbye, though."

"How could they have not seen—*Hey!* Put that shit down!"

Suze had leaned into the back seat and retrieved Chad's duffel bag. She was up to her elbows in his belongings, nosing around shamelessly. She pulled out the rolled-up poster of Crystal Bright that Chad had been toting around with him. "What's this?" she asked.

Chad was suddenly embarrassed, his ears burning red. Somehow, it seemed incredibly uncool to have the poster. It made him feel like a teenager who was more likely to read *Tiger Beat* than to kill his mother. And the killing was far more erotic than Crystal Bright on a beach had ever been.

Suze had unrolled the poster now and laughed as she saw what it was. "Oh, you've *got* to be kidding me."

"Shut up," said Chad, reaching over and snatching the poster away. It tore as Suze held on to the corners. "Just shut up."

"What?" asked Suze, her eyebrows raising innocently.

"I don't like it when people make fun of me."

"I'm not making fun of you."

"Yeah?" challenged Chad. "Then what *were* you going to say?"

"I was going to say how fascinating it is," said Suze, dropping the torn corners of the poster back into the duffel. "How long have you been attracted to Crystal Bright?"

"I mean it," said Chad. "Quit making fun of me." Much to his surprise, they had cleared the Pridemore's corporation limit without being intercepted by the city police. The county road stretched out to the west as dark pavement was swallowed by the black night. Chad flipped on the Volvo's brights.

"No, *really*," said Suze, shifting in her seat to face Chad. Her expression was serious. "How long?"

Chad sighed. "I don't know. I guess since *Benny and the Girl* came on TV. She's hot."

"As hot as me?"

"Christ!"

"Sorry, had to ask," said Suze, her expression still serious. "You know that you're going to meet her, don't you?"

Chad looked at Suze inquisitively. "How would I meet her?"

"I don't know. I just know that you will. And I'll tell you something else," added Suze. "When you do, you better kill her. Kill her before she kills you."

IV

Luke ran through the cornfields with his heart thumping in his chest. The rows were thick and unyielding, snapping back at the exposed skin of his arms and face as soon as he released his grip. The corn was unnaturally tall, obscuring Luke's view of anything but the brilliant blue sky above.

Where is she?

He could hear equipment roaring in the distance, the unmistakable sound of Old Paulie's thrasher crawling through the field. It wasn't the right time of year to be harvesting...

The sound was deafening, the thrasher's voice intensifying as it neared. Suddenly, the horrified scream of a terrified girl pierced the mechanical thrum, sailing easily through the densely packed corn and setting Luke's nerves on edge.

Where is she?

He pushed stalk after stalk aside, hoping to catch a glimpse, hoping that he wasn't too late...

Luke awakened with a jolt, sitting upright in the motel bed. His body was covered in sweat, and the rhythm of his heart was keeping pace with the rhythm of the dream.

Where am I?

The room was dark, and the childlike scream still rang in his ears. Luke's eyes flitted anxiously from right to left, desperately searching for something familiar, something to guide him back to reality.

Familiarity came in the form of a naughty vixen, winking knowingly from the bicep of the large man sleeping in the room's other double bed.

Luke was in the U Stay Here Motel just outside of Louisville. Bert Parnell snored noisily through his swollen adenoids, liquid rasps wheezing out before being abruptly pulled back in. The room was simple and utilitarian—two beds, one lamp, a small card table with two metal chairs, and a closet-sized bathroom which was primarily decorated with rust stains. The room's color scheme was directly from the 1970s, complete with orange bedclothes and green shag carpeting.

Luke felt his blood pressure ebbing as the memory of the dream began to lose its vividness. He lay back down on the bed and tucked his hands behind his head, staring at the ceiling with wide, sleepless eyes.

What's happening to me?

Luke had never been plagued by dreams before, and he had experienced two very unusual ones in as many days. The first had involved the phone booth at Fat Louie's BBQ, and sure enough, the eerie dream had come to pass. Did that mean that over the next day or so, Luke would find himself trying to save a faceless girl who was lost in an unfamiliar cornfield from a derelict thrasher? Surely, he was reading too much into the dream, allowing one freakish occurrence to open his mind perhaps a little too widely. Precognition and divination belonged to palm readers, not simple farm boys.

The girl's scream had been filled with terror. He didn't know what it would take to elicit such a scream, but he hoped to never find out.

For the second night in a row, Luke found himself staring at the ceiling, unable to find any restful comfort in sleep.

⚬ ⎯⎯⎯ ◆ ⎯⎯⎯ ⚬

"Up and at 'em, Leighton," said Bert, roughly shaking Luke by his shoulder.

Luke had managed to fall into a fitful sleep around dawn. It was only seven-thirty, which meant he had racked up a grand total of two-and-a-half hours for the entire night. *"Mmm,"* he growled.

The water pressure in the dingy shower was almost non-existent, and Luke stood for what seemed like hours under the dismal stream, trying to coax the cheap motel shampoo out of his hair. Afterward, he felt admittedly better, but realized that sooner or later he was going to have to actually get some quality rest.

"Let's grab some breakfast," suggested Bert, sitting on the edge of his bed, and stooping to tie his boots.

"I thought you were behind schedule," said Luke, toweling his hair into a mad scientist's coif.

"I am, but I'll be damned if I'm going to lose a meal over it," said Bert, patting his ample midsection. "Greta likes me this way, and it's up to me to keep up my shape. Says it gives her something to hold onto."

Luke winced at the unrequested mental image. "I could use some coffee," he admitted, running a brush through his wild sandy hair.

The men gathered their belongings and tossed them in the big rig which was parked at the far end of the motel lot. A small diner called Horton's was across the county road, bustling with early morning patrons, most of whom were also truckers. Luke and Bert walked over, taking the last available table near the back of the restaurant.

The diner was perhaps the most stereotypical one ever constructed and still in operation. Thick grease residue coated every square inch of every single surface, from the tabletops to the menus to the sticky floors underfoot. Loud chatter floated nonsensically throughout the air, sounding like the world's least synchronized orchestra playing twenty tunes simultaneously. Thick cigarette smoke hung in the center of the room like a fog bank, ready to descend on the lot of them at any given moment.

A nearly toothless old bird named Nettie took their orders—a double stack of pancakes and bacon for Bert and black coffee for Luke—before she sidled off to tend to her other stations.

"Just the coffee?" asked Bert.

"Yep," said Luke. "I'm still full from last night."

"Not me. I could eat a double-wide horse," said Bert, patting his midsection.

Luke laughed and lit a cigarette, contributing his own exhaust to the swirling bank overhead.

"So, we're nearly in Louisville," said Bert, taking a drink from the dubiously spotted glass of water Nettie had placed before him. "What are your plans, son?"

Luke shrugged. "Don't know exactly. I figured I'd stick around and try to find a job."

"What kind of job?"

"I don't know."

"You're real big on planning, aren't you?"

Luke shrugged again. "Can't say that I've ever had a regular job. I always worked with Paulie on the farm."

"Paulie?"

Luke remembered that he had earlier referred to Paulie as his father. "My dad," he added, offering no further explanation. For all intents and purposes, Paulie had *been* his father.

"Hmm," said Bert, setting his glass back on the table. "So basically, you've got no idea what you're doing."

Shrugging seemed to be Luke's favorite form of communication this morning. "I guess not."

Nettie wandered back with Luke's coffee and an enormous plate piled high with pancakes and bacon for Bert. Bert liberally doused the pancakes with maple syrup which pooled like a moat around them at the bottom of his plate. He forked in a mouthful, and his eyes rolled heavenward in ecstasy.

"I can feel this shit lodging in my arteries, but if I have to go someday, this would be my first choice of how," he said through half-chewed hunks of food. Luke grinned and sipped his coffee, which was also pretty damn good.

Bert swallowed, then said, "I have to drop off this load at Burton Industries and haul another across the river to Terre Haute. You're welcome to go with me if you want."

Luke wondered if Bert would be so generous if he knew about the odd déjà vu which Luke had experienced in the parking lot of Fat Louie's BBQ the prior evening. Maybe he would think Luke was a circus freak and jettison him as quickly as if he were a leper. Luke left nothing to chance and had kept the odd experience to himself.

"I don't want to impose," said Luke.

Bert snorted and shoved another forkful into his mouth. "You're not imposing. I'm inviting," he said, adding, "If you want."

Luke considered the option for a moment, realizing that he really didn't want to be out on his own just yet. The thought made him feel weak, and he was disappointed in himself for that. Back in Jasper, he had always considered himself

111

the ultimate loner, no family, few friends, no one depending on him but himself. Now, he realized that he wasn't entirely comfortable with that, not entirely sure of himself, not ready to trust his own instincts.

God, I miss you, Paulie, thought Luke, vacantly stirring his steaming coffee.

"Tell you what," Luke finally said. "I'll go, but only if you let me do all the heavy lifting. That way I'll feel like I'm paying something for my ride."

"No argument here," said Bert. "My back is throbbing like a son-of-a-bitch. I'm gettin' too old for this shit. After Terre Haute, I'm heading back home to Borden—that's in Ohio. You're welcome to go there, too, provided you keep your hands off my daughters."

Luke grinned in response, and the men got down to the more serious business of finishing their breakfasts.

They were met at the dock by a red-faced receiving manager named Timmonds. It was nine o'clock, and Timmonds wasn't happy about the delay.

"I had extra help last night," he whined, shaking his shiny bald head. "This morning's unacceptable, just unacceptable."

Luke stayed in the background and kept his mouth shut. Bert didn't seem bothered by Timmonds' distress, unlocking the back of the trailer and hoisting the metal door up. Timmonds was like a gnat hovering around the big man's head.

"Hey!" screeched Timmonds, unwisely inserting himself between Bert and the dock. "I'm *talking* to you!"

Bert stopped and looked down at the man, his expression never faltering. "Mr. Timmonds, there was a huge accident just outside of town last night—you can verify that in the morning newspaper, I'm sure. I'm sorry to hear about your scheduling difficulties. I have a worker with me, and we'll pitch in as best we can to help out. That's really the best I can offer, and you can bet your sweet ass it's more than any other driver would do. So, either we do it my way, or I'll pull forward and drop your cargo in the bottom of the dock—your choice." His voice was polite but firm, and Luke had no doubt that if Timmonds didn't fly away, the pallets would go exactly where Bert said they would.

Grudgingly, Timmonds nodded his head and stalked off, leaving Bert and Luke to begin unloading the freight.

Four hours later, they were driving north on I-65, heading toward Indianapolis. For lunch, they opted for economy, buying dirt-cheap mystery meat from a roadside gas station, nuked to near blistering intensity.

"Are you always so laid back?" Luke asked between desperate gulps for cool air as he attempted to chew a bite from his sandwich.

"Come again?" Bert asked, shifting his food from cheek to cheek to avoid being scalded.

Luke swallowed and took a healthy drink from his Coke. "Shit's like lava! *Whew!* Like you said, ain't no other trucker that would've pitched in like that. Aren't you way off schedule now?"

Bert shrugged and shook his head. "Not really, son. I'm on my *own* schedule. Well, okay, not *entirely* my own schedule, but pretty damn close. Dearborn Labs receives until seven. We'll have plenty of time."

"You'll be late gettin' home," said Luke.

"Yeah, I know. Guess I was feelin' a little like a Good Samaritan." Bert squinted and pulled his sunglasses down over his eyes, craning for a look in his side mirror before changing lanes and passing a shriveled old man pedaling a Dodge Dart down the interstate.

Luke fell silent, continuing to eat his sandwich now that it had cooled down. Bert Parnell was a good man, his innate congeniality radiating from him in great waves. Of all the things Luke had imagined when trying to picture how this adventure might play out, he hadn't expected to meet someone so naturally honest and likeable right off the bat. Quite the opposite, in fact. He hadn't spent any time to speak of outside Jasper. The city limits were like an invisible but impenetrable wall that held the rest of the world at bay. Luke didn't know what to expect of outsiders, but his natural instinct was to stay quiet and observant, trusting only those who proved trustworthy. As Bert let loose with a whopper of a belch followed by a powerful exclamation point from his colon, Luke suddenly felt ridiculous for having been so concerned. People were people—it didn't matter where they were from.

"You just wait 'til you get a taste of Greta's chicken and noodles. I won't be able to get rid of you, boy," said Bert with a grin.

Luke smiled. Somehow, Bert was instinctively finding the emptiness inside Luke, the space so recently created when Paulie had finally gone home to God. His paternal effect was hypnotic, and Luke found himself eager to meet the rest of the Parnells. It felt like it was the reunion of a family to which he now suddenly belonged.

As if reading Luke's thoughts, Bert added, "But I'm serious—you better keep your damn hands off my daughters." He raised his sunglasses and winked before dropping them back into place.

The last stop had gone without a hitch. Dearborn Labs actually had a crew to unload the truck, running back and forth like ants, synchronized in a master plan that only they could hear. Luke wondered fleetingly if these were experimental humans, created in the deep recesses of the lab's basement to be worker drones, then realized he had no idea what type of lab Dearborn was, anyway. They could make contact lenses for all he knew.

By five-thirty, they were back on the road, headed back toward Indianapolis. Luke was exhausted from too little sleep and the strenuous workout of the morning. Bert wasn't in a talkative mood, and the roar of the diesel engine acted like a potent sleeping pill, dragging Luke down into a deep slumber moments after Bert had leveled out at highway speed.

The corn was taller than corn should be. A slow breeze wafted by, lifting Luke's sandy hair with invisible fingertips. He squinted his eyes against the sun's blazing glare, trying to get his bearings.

In every direction, corn. Tall corn.

The nightmare from before came crashing back, and in Luke's memory, he heard the terrified shriek of the faceless girl and the roar of the encroaching thrasher.

Today, there was only silence. No birds, no bees—nothing.

It was almost as disquieting as the horrific screams.

Luke began to slowly push his way forward, shoving stalk after stalk aside. The corn was too densely planted—it was too tall. The effort was enormous, but Luke plodded on. He tried to determine his direction by watching the sun, but each time he looked up, it never seemed to be where he expected it. Any moment, he expected to hear the ignition of the thrasher, pulling the engine to life, laying its vicious teeth into the field, and searching for the little girl that Luke knew was out there somewhere.

He wished he knew what she looked like. He didn't know if he could save her if he didn't know what she looked like. He was afraid he would know too late, only as he looked down at her dead, mangled body. Helplessness washed over him, but still he pushed forward.

The sun's heat poured down, and perspiration beaded on Luke's shoulders and forehead, dribbling down and stinging his eyes. Luke wiped it away, only to add salt from his arm to the mix.

Suddenly, the sun was gone.

Dark clouds rolled overhead, appearing as if from nowhere. The temperature began to fall rapidly, and the dark clouds became black before taking a yellowish cast. The silence of the day was broken by a sudden whispering, as the wind found footing out of nowhere and swept its angry hand across the tall, thick corn. Luke shielded his eyes from the thrashing cornstalks, watching the sky swirl overhead, funnel clouds hovering and threatening to drop their bottoms on the field below.

Luke leaned forward and continued to push on, straining his ears for any sound above the howling of the storm, sure the little girl was in tremendous danger. There was no way to locate her by sound though, as thunder echoed across the landscape. Rain began to fall in torrential sheets, saturating Luke instantly. His clothes became heavy with water, and his arms had to work harder to forge a path through the corn. His heart pounded in his chest, an inner alarm sounding in a deafening peal. The child wasn't safe. She wasn't safe.

Suddenly falling forward, Luke was clear of the cornfield, clear of the storm, clear of everything. Silence filled his head with cotton, nearly making him scream from the sensory deprivation. He was on his knees, his hands pressed to his ears, his mouth hanging open.

The rain was gone, and so was the daylight. A full moon watched from above, shining like a magnificent gemstone against a midnight blue backdrop, tiny diamonds sprinkled liberally all around.

Luke lowered his hands slowly, his eyes wide with astonishment. His clothes were dry and so was his hair. Luke examined his hands to make sure they were his own—they were.

Slowly, Luke stood, brushing the dirt off of his t-shirt and jeans. He stood at the edge of a narrow blacktop road, ink black in the night with reflectors catching moonlight and winking off into the distance. It wasn't quiet here; the night was alive with the sounds of crickets and other nocturnal creatures. Luke turned and looked back in the direction from which he had come. The cornfield stretched back to the horizon.

But it wasn't the same cornfield. The corn was just regular corn. Not tall, not seeded to grow into a tangled forest.

Just corn.

Luke turned back to face the road and squinted from the harsh light waiting to greet him. *Dammit!* His eyes wouldn't adjust. Where seconds ago had only been dark countryside, there was now a large, bright structure almost immediately across the street from where Luke stood.

How could he have missed it? He couldn't have. He would've had to have been blind—which he nearly was. His eyes watered as he took a few tentative steps toward the light before stopping to try and rub his eyes back into focus. It appeared to be a business, but Luke couldn't tell what it was.

Then a male voice, high-pitched and low-pitched intermittently, announced, *"Baby Bonnie, she's gonna BLOW!"*

Just as Luke thought his sight might clear, a fireball roared to life in the center of his field of vision. It rolled upward before spewing out in all directions, sending waves of heat to announce its impending arrival. The building— whatever it was—was no more. Several smaller explosions sent bricks which had formerly comprised the structure in all directions.

Luke shielded his eyes and watched the flames race toward him. A chunk of mortar glanced off of his forehead, knocking him down on his knees. Below his dazed face was a square of paper. It looked like a photograph, lying face down on the ground.

It was the little girl. Luke knew it.

If he could just reach the snapshot and flip it over...

Luke lurched forward in his seat and gasped as his seatbelt took hold. Bert jumped from the sudden motion, wavering slightly in his lane. Daylight was dwindling, but the sun still hung stubbornly over the western sky, bleeding red into the western horizon.

"You alright, boy?" Bert asked, shifting his eyes over worriedly.

Luke struggled against the seatbelt. His breathing was ragged and heavy, and his eyes bulged in their sockets. "She's not safe!" he shouted, his voice booming in the cab of the truck.

"Who's not safe?" Bert asked, unconsciously slowing the truck.

"I—I—" Luke's head shifted from side to side, drinking in his surroundings. Slowly, his breathing eased, and the wild look in his eyes began to recede. "I don't know. I guess I was dreaming."

"What about?" Bert asked.

Luke shuddered, not wanting to remember. "It doesn't matter. It was just a dream," he said.

Bert watched him for a moment longer before refocusing his attention on the road. They had just passed through Indianapolis and were on I-70 east, heading for Ohio.

Luke lit a cigarette with jittery fingers. The dream had evaporated, leaving behind a sticky residue of perspiration on Luke's brow. He rolled his window completely down and let the passing wind cool him off.

"You okay?" asked Bert.

"Yeah, man, thanks," said Luke, taking a long, slow drag from his cigarette.

It was only a dream, Luke told himself.

Like Fat Louie's BBQ had been a dream?

CHAPTER SEVEN

I

It hadn't been a dream after all. The feeling of floating down and silencing the old woman's breathing had somehow actually transpired.

Lisa stared vacantly at Helen Martin, the color draining from her cheeks. "Mrs. Baylock?" she repeated. "Who would kill Mrs. Baylock?"

Concern knitted Helen's eyebrows. "Oh, dear. She must have been in your wing. Did you know her very well?"

Lisa shook her head absently. "Not really. Who would kill her, though?"

"I doubt if anyone did," said Helen, guiding Lisa over to a bank of chairs and easing her into one. "Like I said, I'm sure the police are just trying to settle Mrs. Baylock's daughter. Are you alright? You're white as a ghost."

React, you stupid shit, Lisa thought to herself. *You're sitting here like the cat who ate the canary.*

"I'm okay," said Lisa, smiling weakly.

"Dizzy?" asked Helen.

"Uh-unh. What you said—it just took me by surprise. It's creepy to think that someone may have been *killed* here."

"I'm sure there's nothing to it," said Helen. "Genevieve Maddox just can't get her mind around the fact that death doesn't offer the wealthy preferential treatment. The woman's a shameful mess. She barely spoke with her mother anymore. God forgive me for saying it, but I swear I think that woman is only playing this up for high drama. If there's one thing Genevieve likes, it's attention. There, now. That's not very Christian of me, is it?"

"It's okay," said Lisa. "I understand."

"Tell you what," said Helen. "How about it if I drive you home?"

Lisa shook her head. "Oh, no, Nurse Martin, you shouldn't. What would the hospital think if you suddenly took off?"

"First of all, my name's Helen. Secondly, I've been off the clock for a half an hour—the hospital couldn't give two shakes about what I do on my own time. Most importantly, I would feel so much better if I were to see you safely home. I don't want to impose, but you looked like you were about to faint a moment ago, and I would appreciate it if you would humor an old woman, even if only for her own peace of mind."

Reluctantly, Lisa nodded. "If you're sure—"

"Positive." Helen offered a hand to help Lisa back to her feet, and soon the two women were passing through the double glass doors and into the sunlight of the afternoon.

Lisa gave Helen her street address and slightly reclined the passenger seat of the dark green Buick Regal. She had just begun to relax when Helen asked, "How long did you work at the hospital?"

Lisa's back involuntarily stiffened. "A year or so," she said.

"Why did you leave?" Helen asked, slowing to turn left on Brice Avenue.

Was it possible she didn't know? Rather than catch herself up in a lie that Helen might see straight through, Lisa simply shrugged. "Time to move on," she said.

"Hmm," said Helen, slowing at a traffic light. "My daughter thought she wanted to work at the hospital, too. Her name was Evie. I think she fantasized that it was exciting like on TV. Cleaning bedpans was a rude awakening."

"I never watch TV," said Lisa.

"Never?" asked Helen incredulously. "Are you from this planet?"

"Nanna Grace didn't approve of television. She said it rotted the soul," said Lisa.

"I don't know that I disagree with her entirely. I haven't watched a sitcom in *years*. They're truly insipid. But I have to admit, I'd be lost without my afternoon soaps. I tape them on my VCR every day."

"You said your daughter's name *was* Evie," said Lisa. "Is she—?"

"Dead? Yes, for seven years now," said Helen, her voice disconcerting in its nonchalance. "Drunk driver. She never stood a chance."

"I'm sorry," said Lisa.

"There's nothing that can be done about it now," said Helen, smiling tightly. "After that drunk bastard hit my daughter, he crossed the median and found himself in the path of a semi. He died before Evie did. Evie held out as long as she could—three days—but the injuries were too severe. I just hope she didn't feel anything."

"That's horrible," said Lisa. "I'm so sorry."

"So, tell me about yourself, Lisa Mitchell. Have you lived in Morgan your entire life?" asked Helen, abruptly changing topics.

Lisa shrugged. "As long as I can remember."

Helen laughed. "As long as you can remember? Are you an amnesiac?"

"No, it's just that—I was raised by my Nanna Grace. I never knew my real parents. Nanna told me they never wanted me."

"That's a horrible thing to say!" gasped Helen. "How could someone not want a baby? It's absurd! Some of us would give a limb to have a child."

"Was Evie an only child?" asked Lisa, steering the conversation back toward Helen.

Helen nodded briskly, her eyes tinged with melancholy. "I didn't have an easy time delivering," she said. "They almost lost me on the table, and when I finally pulled through, they had to perform an emergency hysterectomy just to get the bleeding under control. Bryce and I weren't meant to have more children."

"Is Bryce your husband?"

"He was. He's been gone for five years now. I don't think he ever recovered from Evie's death—what a thought! Like any parent ever *could*. No, what I meant to say is that Bryce was never able to deal with the aftermath. It's really strange, you know? Once someone decides he has nothing else to live for, the body just seems to start shutting down. Bryce aged years overnight. It really didn't surprise me when they found the tumors in his lung."

"Oh, Helen. That's so much to have to deal with at one time. How did you ever manage?" asked Lisa.

"Didn't really have any choice, did I? Helen Martin is no quitter. I have a staff and patients who rely on me at the hospital. I figure that God knows his own plan, and these—*things* are just lessons I'm supposed to learn."

"I don't know how you can do it. With Nanna Grace gone—I really don't know what to do next," said Lisa. What she meant was, *With Nanna Grace gone— I'm free to do whatever I want next.* Somehow, that didn't seem entirely appropriate.

"So, tell me about Nanna Grace," said Helen, seeking once again to change the subject.

"She passed just days before I was in the accident," said Lisa.

"Was she ill?"

"Old. Really, really old. You could say that I anticipated it."

"We've all got to go sometime, dear," said Helen, smiling with pity. "I hope she wasn't in pain. Was she your grandmother on your mother's or father's side?"

"Neither."

Helen gave her a surprised look. "Oh! I just assumed—"

Lisa shook her head. "She took me in when I was very young. I don't even remember my real parents."

"Sounds like she was a wonderful person."

"She was what you might call old school. She was pretty strict. She didn't trust anything that was a modern convenience."

"There's something to be said for that," said Helen. "Today's kids are so caught up in television and computers and video games. Sometimes I think the world would be a better place without all that crap, too. But then again, I would surely hate to give up my afternoon soaps."

Lisa fell silent as she realized where they were. In several more blocks, Morton's Supermarket would loom on the right, and they would cross the very pavement where Nola Kelsey had died. Lisa's eyes began searching for the corner of Greenbriar and Main, knowing it was that intersection at which she had wrecked her Toyota, despite what the accident report had cited.

119

For a moment she was disoriented, only slowly realizing why the intersection wasn't immediately familiar. The old tree was gone—completely. It had stood on that corner long before there had ever been streets. "What happened to the old tree?" she asked.

"Hmm?"

"The old tree," repeated Lisa, indicating the empty corner.

"Oh, yes. What a pity! Someone smashed into it. It was the weirdest thing, too. There was so much damage to the tree that the city had to cut it down, yet whoever hit it was apparently able to drive away. That tree was a landmark," said Helen.

And I was found on Maple Street, thought Lisa. *Am I losing my mind?*

Helen's head turned slowly to the right, observing something but saying nothing. Lisa knew instinctively that they must be passing Morton's. As she turned her head to look, she suddenly gasped and grabbed for the steering wheel. *"WATCH OUT!"* she shrieked.

Helen stomped on the brake pedal, and the Buick skidded to a stop, its nose veering off to the right. Fortunately, there was no car behind them; it wouldn't have had sufficient time to stop.

"What? What's wrong?" Helen asked, her heart pounding. "Are you alright?"

Lisa unfastened her seatbelt and got out of the car, hurrying around to the front. She looked at the road dazedly, then got down on her hands and knees and peered under the front of the car. "Where did she—?"

Helen put the car in park and joined Lisa. "Who? Who are you talking about?"

Lisa's face contorted, panic and confusion becoming one. "Didn't you see her?" she asked.

"See who?"

"The little girl!"

Helen looked at Lisa vacantly. "Little girl? I didn't see a little girl."

"She was standing right there!" insisted Lisa, pointing toward the front of the car. "I wasn't looking because of that damn tree, then—she was standing *right there!* She had dark curly hair—you *have* to have seen her!"

Helen slowly shook her head. "I was watching the road the whole time, Lisa. I didn't see anybody in the street."

"So, you think I just made it up?" demanded Lisa.

Helen tried to put a comforting arm around Lisa, but she shook it off immediately. "No, dear. That's not what I meant at all. Just relax a minute, Lisa. It was probably some sort of optical illusion. What's important is that everyone's okay."

Lisa looked at her doubtfully. "I could've *sworn* she was standing right *there.*"

"Maybe we should go back and see Dr. Devereaux," Helen suggested.

Lisa shook her head immediately. "No. I don't think that's necessary." She forced another weak smile. "If I can just get my heart to slow down, I'm sure everything will be fine."

Lisa wanted to be away from this place. She was standing in the approximate area of Nola Kelsey's demise. To her right, Morton's Supermarket thrived with customers, a few of whom had stopped to gawk at the scene in the street. She allowed Helen to guide her back to the car.

"If you're sure you're okay," said Helen.

"I am," assured Lisa. "I'm sorry. I don't know what I was thinking. It just seemed so *real*." She settled back into the passenger seat.

Helen walked around the front of the car and resumed her position behind the wheel. "There's nothing to apologize for, dear. I'd much rather be safe than sorry, wouldn't you?"

Lisa nodded, retreating into the depths of her mind. She couldn't let Helen know the truth. She couldn't let Helen know she had tried to steer the car toward the girl. She couldn't let her know the kind of monster she was becoming—or maybe had always been.

Nanna's two-story house looked more foreboding than ever, its black shuttered windows staring like soulless eyes from ivy-covered walls. Helen eased her car to a stop along the curb at the front.

Lisa suddenly remembered what she had been doing just before her accident. She had been disposing of all of the house's furnishings. The rooms were in shambles—and Helen was bound to find that unusual.

"Well, here we are," Helen was saying.

"Thank you, Helen," said Lisa, getting out of the car. "I don't want to take up any more of your time."

"Oh, *pish*," said Helen, waving a hand at her and getting out of the car. "I don't mind at all." She looked at Lisa expectantly, waiting for her to lead the way.

"You don't have to come in," said Lisa, stopping on the sidewalk. "I'm alright now."

"It's no bother at all, dear. I've taken you this far. I won't rest until I've seen that you made it safely inside." Helen smiled congenially, but her eyes suggested that she wouldn't take no for an answer.

Lisa shifted uncomfortably. "Oh, gosh, Helen—I don't really know how to say this without being rude, and you've been so kind to me—but the house is a mess, and I really would hate for you to see it for the first time like this."

Helen chuckled. "I'm sure I've seen worse—" She stopped when she saw the look in Lisa's eyes. She couldn't decide if it was pleading or alarm. Either way, it was now Lisa who wouldn't take no for an answer. Helen decided to let it go. She didn't want to seem too intrusive. She had grown rather fond of Lisa during her brief stay in the hospital. Lisa's delicate features reminded Helen so much of Evie—but Evie had never been so timid. Plain as she was now, Helen didn't doubt that Lisa could be quite pretty. All she needed to do was get some color in her skin, some style in her wardrobe. Of course, it's easy to offer advice on how someone else should spend her money—if she even *had* any money. Lisa had been fairly evasive when Helen had asked her why she had left her job at the hospital. She hadn't mentioned any specific plans for the future, either.

"Please," said Lisa, her voice softly begging. "When you come back next time, I'll have everything all fixed up."

Helen put her hands on her ample hips and sighed. "Well, if you're *sure*."

"Oh yes, Helen, I'm sure. Maybe you can come by for lunch in a day or two. I'm fairly competent in the kitchen," said Lisa, a tentative smile flickering across her face.

"All right, then," Helen said, lowering herself back behind the steering wheel. "I'll call."

Lisa nodded and waved as Helen pulled the Buick back into traffic. She watched the car disappear down the street, her smile fading in time with the taillights. She turned and entered through the gate of the peeling picket fence which surrounded the postage stamp yard. It was choked with weeds and hadn't been mowed in some time. Mr. Parker who lived across the street was probably about to have a stroke—he was the unofficial homeowners' association, and nothing riled him more than an unkempt lot.

Lisa collected the mail from the wrought iron mailbox which was mounted on a brick column of the porch. Enough junk mail had accumulated during Lisa's stay to prop the rusty mailbox lid open. It was odd to see the driveway empty; her Toyota had been hauled away to the auto graveyard to be recycled into whatever it could be recycled into.

Lisa used her key to let herself in. The house was just as she had left it, in utter devastation. As much furniture as she had hauled out through the back door, debris was still scattered from one end of the first floor to the other. Helen would have known something was terribly off-kilter with Lisa had she seen the wreckage.

Lisa closed the door and twisted the deadbolt. She surveyed the room solemnly, then moved purposefully to the far corner and began cleaning. She had a lot of work to do before Helen decided to drop by again.

The sun had gone down hours ago. Lisa had the oddest feeling of déjà vu; the last evening she had spent in the house had been much like this one. Soaked in perspiration, her back and side aching—especially from where she had cracked a rib, Lisa straightened and ran her forearm across her brow. Her hair hung in damp tendrils down her neck.

She had dragged the garbage from the house into the back yard. It was about three times larger than the front, enclosed in chain link fencing and enshrouded by tall pines at its far borders. Nanna Grace had always kept a burn barrel near the back of the yard—nearly all of the other neighbors did, as well. It never hurt to have a place to quickly dispose of leaves or excess newspapers or even spent furniture, provided it wasn't *too* big.

Lisa kept the barrel red hot all evening long. She had been spared the curious stares of passersby from the cover afforded by the pine trees. She had broken Nanna Grace's belongings down into pieces small enough to burn and then fed the gaping red mouth of the barrel all it would take. She had soon discovered that some things burned faster than others, and some things burned incredibly slowly.

This could take days.

Helen Martin surely wouldn't stay away that long. Besides that, the next problem would be the unusual emptiness of the house. Helen would have to question that, too. Yet Lisa couldn't stand the thought of hauling any of the furniture back in. Most of it had been smashed beyond repair anyway.

Lisa ran her fingers through her wet, matted hair before twisting them together nervously. Helen Martin might become a problem. Lisa had a gut feeling that the nurse would be following up on her. Hell, she had asked Lisa if it was okay, and Lisa had said *yes!* Lisa was disappointed in herself. She truly didn't wish any ill will toward Helen, but if she proved to be constantly underfoot—well, Lisa wasn't sure what might happen.

One thing at a time, thought Lisa, going into the kitchen, and closing the door behind her. *You told Helen to call first. Just put her off for a few days. The old stuff will be gone, and you can hit yard sales to buy new.*

The air in the house was suffocating. Lisa hadn't opened the windows since she had been home. She crossed from the kitchen into the dark, empty living room. Lisa hadn't given it much thought when she had thrown out the lamps, but now she regretted it. Except for the kitchen, which had overhead lighting, the house was nestled in deep shadows.

As she neared the window, Lisa heard something creak behind her. She gasped and whirled, her eyes searching the gloom.

At first, she didn't see anything. Then, she noticed the door that led to the basement slowly swinging open.

Lisa's heartbeat thrummed in her ears. She was frozen to the spot, staring into the dark abyss which lay beyond the slowly opening door. Lisa's first thought was that Nola Kelsey had come back for her revenge. She *knew* that Ms. Kelsey was dead, had *seen* the truck hit her. Still, Lisa was fairly certain that it was the spirit of the hospital administrator, lurking in the basement, waiting for Lisa to come home.

A dark shape emerged from the doorway. It stood erect, slowly obscuring the light which shone in from the kitchen behind it. For a moment, Lisa thought it would continue to grow, taller and taller until it had to stoop forward to keep from hitting its head on the ceiling.

But surely that was an illusion of the light.

"Wh-who are you?" Lisa asked, repulsed by the weakness in her own voice.

Silence, save for her own heartbeat. The shape stood completely motionless, and as Lisa's vision adjusted slightly to the darkness, she thought she could perceive its glistening eyes.

"Who are you?" Lisa repeated, trying but failing to sound more forceful than before.

The dark figure took one step forward, and Lisa countered by taking a step back. Finally, it spoke, its voice little more than a whisper.

"I can see your soul."

II

Crystal awakened to the sound of Paula warbling off-key with an epic Celine Dion tune. She rubbed her eyes against the harsh morning light, squinting and stretching.

"For God's sake, Paula! You're hurting my ears!" Crystal groused, covering the aforementioned ears with her hands.

Paula's voice froze instantly in mid-croon. She flushed hot pink and turned wounded eyes in Crystal's direction. "Do you always have to be so nasty?"

Crystal sighed and straightened herself in the passenger seat. "I'm crabby in the morning. I always have been. I didn't mean anything by it."

Paula returned her attention to the highway, but the sting stayed in her eyes, playing at the corners.

Crystal focused on the flat landscape that whisked by on either side of the narrow two-lane blacktop they were speeding along. There was little to no vegetation, and the soil looked like dry powder. "Where are we?" she asked.

"Nevada."

"Where are we going?"

Paula turned and looked expectantly at Crystal. "Ohio, I thought," she said.

"Did I tell you that I wanted to go to Ohio?"

Paula's eyes flickered nervously. "N-no, not really. I just thought—"

Crystal smiled questioningly at the girl. "No, really, it's good. I just didn't remember mentioning it. If you're a fan, you must know that I'm from there."

"That's right," said Paula, smiling. "From Lucasville, a small town just a little north of Portsmouth. You used to work at the Speedway on Route 23—until you earned enough money for your bus ticket to California, that is—"

Crystal stared in amazement as Paula summarized the highlights of her short life to date. The girl was a walking, talking fanzine. It was also apparent that she was afraid of displeasing Crystal.

It was unsettling.

"Whoa, whoa!" said Crystal, interjecting. "I already know all about me. Why don't you tell me something about *you?*"

Paula sucked in on her bottom lip, her eyes dancing furtively from side to side. Her steady stream of fan facts trickled off as she struggled for something to say. "There's nothing really to talk about," she finally said.

"Oh, come on," said Crystal, shifting in her seat to face Paula. "You won a contest to be on the show. That's some pretty exciting stuff. Lots of people enter those contests and get nowhere. You were the one big winner out of how many?"

Paula smiled and her cheeks tinted again. "Yeah, I have to admit, that was very cool. It was the break I needed."

Crystal's eyes narrowed slightly. "I *knew* you were trying to make a break in the business."

"No, really I wasn't," Paula said quickly. "I was really looking forward to meeting you, of course, but—" Her voice trailed off.

"But what?"

"That's all," Paula said. "I have just always looked up to you."

"You're not some weird psychopath, are you?" Crystal asked. If nothing else, she believed in being direct.

Paula flinched and pulled the car off the road, slamming on the brakes and sliding in the loose dirt. Once the car had stopped, she shifted the car into neutral and turned to face Crystal, her eyes sparkling with a surprising amount of anger.

"I admit," she said, her voice daring Crystal to challenge her. "I may seem a little over the top to you, but I have been a Crystal Bright fan for three years, ever since I was thirteen. It's more than a little weird for me to be sitting in a car with you right now. But I'm not entirely naive, either. You screamed at me when I was on the set of your show, do you remember? I couldn't believe it. You were so different from the image that I held in my head for so long. And you know what else? I'm really pissed at myself because I can't seem to let that image go. I keep expecting you to suddenly be this person I had in my head, and you're just never going to be her, are you? No matter how badly you treated me, I still came back and got you out of that hospital—why I don't know. I could've gotten into a lot of trouble lying to that security guard, too. Right about now, you should be locked in a padded room, but you're not, and that's because of *me*. Does it really matter if I'm a psychopath or not?"

Crystal stared at her for a long minute, jolted by Paula's sudden change in demeanor. "A simple 'no' would do," she said, easing the tension that had suddenly erupted between them. "Chill."

Paula steered the car back onto the highway and returned to cruising speed. "I'm sorry," she said.

"Don't be," said Crystal. "You're right. I really do appreciate all that you've done, and I have a pretty shitty way of showing my gratitude."

The remaining tension drained out of Paula's face, and she smiled. "You're welcome."

———◇———

"So, why Ohio?" Crystal asked, breaking the silence which had fallen over the two women during the last hour. They had driven in silence through the lights and glitter of Las Vegas, staying on I-15 north. Moments ago, they had driven across the Utah border under a cloudless night sky littered with stars.

Paula looked at her and raised an eyebrow. "Huh?"

"I mean, why did you decide that we should go to Ohio instead of, say, to your hometown?"

Paula shook her head instantly, wrinkling her nose. "I won't go back there."

Crystal cast an inquisitive glance. "Why not?"

Paula shook her head again, her features tightening. "Let's just say that I won't, okay?"

"Fine," said Crystal breezily. "I just thought I might make some conversation."

"Conversate away, but let's stay away from that one, 'kay?"

"Fine," repeated Crystal. "What time is it?"

"It's right on the dash," said Paula with mild exasperation. "Half past midnight."

"What are we doing for food? I'm starving."

Paula looked at her expectantly. "Me too, but I don't have much cash."

"How much is not much?" Crystal asked.

"Fourteen dollars."

"Fourteen dollars? We'll run out of gas *long* before we see the Midwest, and that's without bothering to eat!" roared Crystal.

Paula looked astounded. "Don't *you* have any money?" she asked. "For heaven's sake, you're a *star!*"

"Was a star, Paula, *was."* Crystal buried her face in her hands and groaned. "Oh, God! This is a fucking *nightmare!*"

"You've *got* to be kidding me! You don't have *any* money whatsoever?" Paula couldn't believe her ears. Weren't Hollywood stars rich?

When Crystal raised her face, she was laughing uncontrollably. "My accountant robbed me blind. I *might* be able to squeeze about a hundred bucks off a credit card, but we better haul ass to a bank machine. My accountant may not be done fucking me over just yet."

"We're in the middle of nowhere!" wailed Paula. "God*damn* it! If I'd said something earlier—we've passed about a billion bank machines since we left Los Angeles!"

"There's no sense worrying about it now," said Crystal.

"What do you mean?" Paula shrieked. "When *would* be the best time to worry about it? *God!* I'm so *stupid!"* She began to strike her forehead with her open right hand, leaving an angry red print behind.

"Hey! *Hey!"* Crystal leaned over and stopped Paula's arm in mid-swat. "We'll be fine! What are you so upset about?"

"I never do anything right!" said Paula, her voice breaking and tears rolling down her face. "I-I-I—"

Crystal watched the girl begin to dissolve. She wondered again if her psychopathic question had been a valid one. Wherever Paula Haversham had come from, it hadn't been a good place. She teetered back and forth between timid and outspoken, her emotions leaving stress lines on her young face. She was like a powder keg ready to blow, but Crystal had no idea why. Without Paula's assistance, she would've never gotten out the hospital. Maybe now Crystal owed it to the girl to try and find out what was causing her so much pain.

"You're doing plenty right," Crystal said gently. "You had no way of knowing I didn't have any money."

"I *should've* planned for the possibility, though," Paula insisted. "Joel would've—" She stopped abruptly.

"Joel would've what?"

Again, with the stiff and jerky head shaking.

"Who's Joel?" Crystal persisted.

The pain in Paula's eyes was palpable. "No," she said, her voice barely more than a whisper.

"Your father?"

"I WON'T TALK ABOUT IT!"

Crystal recoiled in her seat. "I'm sorry," she said. "I didn't mean to pry. I thought—well, it doesn't matter what I thought. I'm sorry."

Paula nodded, still on the verge of sobbing.

Jeez! thought Crystal. Inside, she was torn. She didn't really know *how* to help Paula, and Paula very obviously needed help. Crystal had her own problems. She had adapted very easily to the glamorous Hollywood lifestyle, only to have it wrenched away from her, along with all of her worldly possessions. Her name was now poison amongst her colleagues. She really had no friends to speak of. The woman who had raised her, acted as her mother during all her formative years, had died, and Crystal had been too late to see her one last time. She truthfully didn't know if she was even capable of helping Paula.

The silence was awkward. Eventually, Crystal said, "Next town we come to, let's try and find an ATM. If I can get some money, we'll find a place to sleep for tonight and get something to eat. Okay?"

Paula nodded her head. "What if you can't get any money?"

"We'll cross that bridge if we come to it."

"Okay," said Paula. She looked across at Crystal, unable to meet her eyes. "I'm sorry about yelling earlier."

"It's okay," said Crystal. "And just for the record—and then I won't ever bring it up again—if you want to talk, all you have to do is start talking. If you don't, that's okay too."

"Thank you."

The tension in the car again began to ease, and Crystal noticed lights on the horizon. Hopefully, they would soon be feeling much better about their situation.

Crystal would have liked to claim that she had never seen a motel so seedy and rundown as Bob's Motel, but it was just like the type she and her high school friends had rented for parties back in Lucasville and its more populated southern neighbor, Portsmouth. Threadbare green carpeting barely covered the floor, stretching from one grimy wall to the next. The bedclothes were dubiously clean, and the bathroom was a science experiment gone horribly astray.

Fortunately, she had been able to pull $375 from the ATM in Cedar City. Apparently, her accountant, Marty Crabtree, hadn't gotten *everything*. They had stopped at a roadside diner and eaten greasy hamburgers and even greasier fries. Both Crystal and Paula had been ravenous, and they polished the food off like wild beasts feeding from a trough. Afterward, they had found the motel room and immediately gotten ready for bed.

Crystal stared at the ceiling long after Paula had begun to snore rhythmically in the next bed. Recalling the weekend motel parties she and her friends from high school used to attend had made Crystal melancholy. Dusty Turner, Sheila Boynton, Dana Hemphill—it had been years since she had really spoken with any of them. They had been inseparable in high school, comprising four-fifths of the varsity cheerleading squad. The last time Crystal had visited her Aunt Maude, she made of point of seeing them, but it wasn't with any real interest in learning about their lives. *Benny and the Girl* had started gaining popularity. Crystal was a hot new commodity in Hollywood. She wanted to make sure that all of her friends knew it.

Crystal couldn't remember when her mind had begun processing things in such a way. She was never the type to grind her good fortune in the faces of her friends—at least not before the show had broken into the Nielsen top twenty. Suddenly, she had friends coming out of the woodwork, gushing praise, and treating her like royalty. It hadn't taken long before Crystal began to believe her own press.

At the time, Dusty was pregnant and afraid that her father was going to kill her.

Crystal had no idea how the situation had resolved.

Sheila had gotten married to Tommy Gulley immediately after high school. That hadn't surprised anyone—they had been making eyes at each other all through school. Toward the end of their senior year, Tommy had shown an alarming propensity to overindulge in alcohol, turning him mean and sometimes physically abusive. Sheila had taken the brunt of his wrath on more than one occasion, and there was a time when Crystal had worried for her safety.

Crystal had no idea if Sheila was even still alive.

Dana had gone to college at Ohio State. During her sophomore year, she had been raped and beaten, left to die beside a dumpster behind a campus bar. Although she made a miraculous physical recovery, Dana was never the same mentally.

Crystal hadn't spoken with her once since the assault. She hadn't sent cards, lent support, or availed herself in any other way.

Crystal nested deeper into her blanket, disgusted by what she was seeing in herself. She hadn't always been that way, had she? *Had she?* She was suddenly unsure, half-convinced that what she had perceived as friendship back in high school had only been instances of the other girls complying with Crystal's demands.

No. It hadn't always been that way. Crystal had to hold on to that, because if she were wrong, if she had been this manipulative and compassionless from the start, then she wouldn't be able to see anything worth salvaging in herself. She might have to find an all-night pharmacy, and to hell with Aunt Maude's opinion on suicide.

Crystal turned her head and focused her eyes on Paula, sleeping on her back in the other bed. She almost looked like a child, the soft contours of her face illuminated by moonlight that streamed in through the window.

Yes, Crystal thought. *I'll help her. I don't know how, but I will. I'll find out who Joel was and what he's done to make Paula so afraid of him.*

Aunt Maude would've been proud.

III

Chad's mouth gaped open as he turned to look at Suze. "What planet are you *from?*" he demanded. "Crystal Bright is about as likely to kill me—or meet me— as I am to having a twenty-two-foot cock."

"*Mmm,*" Suze purred.

"Knock it off!" Chad said, batting her hand away from his crotch. "I have to pay attention to the road. I swear to God, any minute now, and we're going to hit a roadblock."

"I'm not kidding, you should just slow down," said Suze. "Other than the fact that you're driving *way* too fast, we're all good."

Chad eased up on the accelerator, and the Volvo slowly found its way back to the speed limit. The two-lane blacktop stretched out through the countryside, surreal under the moonlight. A cloudless sky stretched overhead, stars winking from their celestial positions.

"You wanna tell me what's going on?" Chad asked.

Suze looked at him unblinkingly. "What do you mean?"

"Tell me about this so-called empathy of yours," he said.

Suze smiled. "I knew we'd come back to that sooner or later."

"It's not every day you meet someone who reads minds," said Chad.

"I told you, I don't read minds! Don't you pay attention?" snapped Suze, who then sighed dramatically. "Let me think, let me think...let me think of a way I can explain this to you so you can get your mind around it."

Chad bristled at what he interpreted as a shot at his intelligence.

"Do you believe in God?" Suze asked abruptly.

"Like Sunday School and stuff?" asked Chad, and Suze nodded. "Not so much."

"Do you believe in fate?" she asked.

"You mean like predestination?" asked Chad, and again, Suze nodded. "I don't know—what's with all the weird questions? I don't believe in Scientology either, if that's what you were going to ask next."

"A-*ha!*" said Suze, a forefinger raised to punctuate the exclamation. "That's *exactly* what I mean. Okay, you and I are right here at this specific point in time, riding in this oh-so-yuppie Volvo, right? Sitting here talking about some real deep shit, right? Okay. We are coming up on a county road that cuts across the highway we're on. See it? Wa-a-a-y up on the horizon."

Chad squinted ahead, then nodded.

"When we get to that road, you have three options. One, you turn left. Two, you go straight. Three, you turn right. Any one of those choices forever changes the course of our little road trip here. There could be a massive roadblock waiting for us, or maybe even little green men that popped down from Mars for a quick Whopper and fries at Burger King. At this point, we don't know what's going on down there. But once we decide which way to go, we have interjected ourselves into the things that will happen while we're there. Do you see?"

Chad's eyebrows furrowed. He hated it when she talked like this. It was like he was too stupid to understand some ridiculous and vacuous concept. The problem was, he *didn't* understand it and didn't want to let her know.

"You're nuts," Chad said.

Suze sighed again, her exasperation evident. "It ain't brain surgery. See if you can follow. We have three choices up ahead. Depending on which road we take, we will commit ourselves to our future along that path. But until then, until we pass through that intersection, our future is undetermined. One of my talents is the ability to occasionally tell which one of the three roads is the one we want to take."

"*One* of your talents?"

"Then there's the empathy. I explained that to you before. It's like I see things in snapshots. That's how I knew about your mother."

"That's not empathy," scoffed Chad. "Some sort of telepathy, maybe—"

"Oh, no. It's empathy," said Suze. "I *feel*."

"You feel? You feel what?"

Suze cocked her head toward Chad and smiled coyly. "When you slid that big sharp knife into your mother, I felt the heat, the anger, the arousal—I felt everything that coursed through you at that moment." She paused. "It was delicious."

Chad sat in silence, trying to decide how much of this freak show he wanted to see. The intersection which they had been debating was quickly approaching. They were alone on the highway, no other headlights piercing the darkness.

"I think we should go right at the intersection," Suze said, her words casual and nearly inaudible.

"Why would we want to do that?" asked Chad. Suze shot him a glare that dared him to ignore her. He wanted to so badly. She thought she knew everything, but she knew nothing. She had no real inner rage and was simply feeding off of Chad's like some kind of parasite. Admittedly, Chad lacked direction. He knew he had crossed a threshold and that he was destined to do great things, but he had no idea what they were. His anger and fury bubbled under the surface, ready to seize control and empower him, but to what end? Suze's talents may serve him well. She had seen what happened between Chad and his mother. So far, she had been correct in that they would be safe from the police as they had fled town. It did take a certain amount of chutzpah to dart across the street, twist some old crone's head until her neck popped, then run away as easily as if she had just egged some poor sap's house.

He slowed the Volvo and turned right at the intersection, winding northwest along a barely maintained tar and gravel road.

"If you know so much, then how about filling me in on the plan?" Chad asked.

"So, you're gonna trust me?" asked Suze, smiling.

"I don't have much choice."

"Good enough," she said. "I don't know."

"You don't know what?"

"I don't know what the plan is," she said, the smile faltering.

"Oh, for Christ's sake!" Chad muttered.

"Would you shut up, please?" Suze asked, her voice remaining calm. "I'm starting to get a headache, and you're not helping. Listen, it doesn't work like some movie I can just tune into and watch. It comes a piece at a time."

"So, you have no idea what it is that we're doing?"

"Of course, I do. I just told you to turn right back there, didn't I?"

"Then where are we going?" Chad asked.

"I don't know."

Chad sighed with frustration. "How will you know when it's time to turn off of this road?"

"I'll just know."

"How?"

"I can't explain it," Suze said. "Do you remember what it was like to be little? You might have gone shopping somewhere with your folks. You're walking along and walking along, and suddenly, you realize your mother's attention has fixed on something, and she's not paying one bit of attention to what you're doing. Do you know what I mean?"

Chad nodded.

"So, you look around, taking in all of the things around you, and suddenly, you see the snack bar over to the side. You can tell it's the snack bar because of the gigantic red and blue plastic ICEE that stands taller than any of the cashier stands. Your mom still isn't watching, so off you go. It's a compulsion you can't resist. You couldn't stop yourself if you tried. Do you know what I mean?"

Chad nodded again.

"Well, this is like the same thing, only it's probably magnified by ten. I absolutely *have* to follow."

"What happens if you don't?" Chad asked.

Suze shuddered. "There've only been a handful of times. Each time I got a migraine that lasted for about a week. Each time, the migraine was worse than the time before. It's been years since I ignored it. There doesn't seem to be any point. It's never led me astray. Besides, it takes a while to pick it back up if I screw up and don't follow. I think I'll always find it again, no matter what, but the last time, it was almost three months before I felt it again. It's like losing one of your senses. I truly felt handicapped."

Chad drove in silence for a few minutes. The road was degenerating rapidly into a mostly dirt path. "So, we just drive along and wait for you to quiver?"

"Pretty much," said Suze.

"Great."

"In the meanwhile, would you like to hear what I *do* know?"

"You said you didn't know anything!" Chad said.

"I said I didn't have a plan. There's a big difference."

"Would you quit splitting hairs and just talk?"

"I think it has something to do with a little girl," Suze said.

"A little girl?"

"Yeah, I'm pretty sure. I've been having these dreams the last several nights. The girl's always there. She looks so innocent with her little rings of black hair and that rag doll she always totes around with her. But she's dangerous. Very dangerous."

Chad was taken aback. His dream had featured a little dark-haired girl, hosting a tea party for her stuffed animals and baby dolls. They couldn't have been dreaming about the same little girl, could they?

"What?" Suze asked.

"Nothing," said Chad.

"Nothing my ass. What?"

"I had a dream, too. The little girl was in it."

"Really?" Suze could barely contain her excitement. "What happened in the dream? What did she do? Could you see where she was?"

"No, nothing like that. She was just having some dumb old tea party for—"

"Oh! The teacups! Did you see the teacups?" Suze was talking animatedly now, her hands gesturing wildly. "That's why I think she's part of it!"

"What do you mean?"

"Sometimes, there's a teacup. Like the turn in the road back there. I saw a teacup sitting in the intersection as we passed."

"How in the hell could you see a teacup sitting in the middle of the road?" Chad challenged.

"I *did!* I've seen it several times. I saw it when I first saw you."

"So, you see a teacup when you have these compulsions," said Chad.

"Not every time. Not even most times. I just think that it's the common thread. Like every time I see one, I'm one step closer to finding the little girl."

"You think that's what this is all about? Finding some little girl?" Chad couldn't believe his ears. He thought they'd be robbing banks or stalking victims in the park. A little girl? Ridiculous.

Suze nodded. "It has to be. Now that I know you've dreamed about her too, it seems so clear."

"Clear, huh? And just what do you plan to do if you find this girl?"

"Not if, when," Suze said firmly.

"Fine. What do you plan to do *when* you find this girl?"

Suze didn't even hesitate. "Kill her."

Chad had no idea where they were. Suze had indicated a turn to the left several miles back, giggling with delight as she spotted another of her phantom teacups. Chad followed her direction, deciding to trust in her for the moment, anyway. He didn't have a better plan.

This road was much better than the one from which they had come. Its two-lane pavement was relatively unbroken and here, they weren't the only other car on the road. Traffic was far from thick. It merely served as a reminder that they weren't alone on the planet. So far, there had been no law enforcement to evade. Apparently, Suze had been correct in her belief that they would be safe.

Chad looked at the digital clock on the dashboard and was amazed to see that it was only twelve-fifteen. It had only been about an hour since Suze had performed her self-prescribed rite of initiation. It felt like it had been days.

"I've really got to pee," Suze said suddenly, breaking the silence.

"You want me to pull over here?" asked Chad. They were in between two slices of nowhere, bushes and trees bordering the road. A classic Mustang whipped around them from behind, using the southbound lane to pass with a roar.

"I don't have to pee that bad," said Suze. "Next time you see a gas station, pull in. You could use some coffee."

Chad cringed. "I don't drink coffee."

"You need something to help you stay awake. We might be driving for a while."

"I've got money. We could stop at a motel."

Suze leered at him. "Now, that's my frisky boy. And I might be up for that, too. But not until I say so."

"Let's get something straight," said Chad. "You're along for the ride. You have some things to contribute—fine. But *I'm* the one who makes the plans. *I'm* the one who decides what we do."

Suze looked at him evenly. "Without me, you'll fuck it all up. Without me, you'll never realize your potential. Without me, there is no you."

Chad laughed. "You're overestimating your importance."

"I don't think so."

"So, why's Crystal Bright supposed to kill me?" asked Chad, changing the subject.

"I don't know."

"That seems to be your favorite answer."

"I won't lie to you, Chad," said Suze. "I won't make up shit just to try and impress you. But I'll let you know when I see something important. I had one of my snapshots. In it, Crystal Bright is bearing down on you in a car."

Chad laughed again. "Oh, that's good! She's going run me over?"

"Lord knows I feel like it right about now. Hey, *hey!*" Suze suddenly pointed to a dim light on the horizon. "Yes, Virginia, there *is* a Santa Claus! A gas station! My bladder's about to blow."

The woods had given way to farmland, corn racing along the passenger side while acres of empty dirt stretched out along the driver's. They had traveled miles without seeing so much as a single house. People apparently lived in the hollows that cut back and away from the main road. The gas station loomed quickly, seeming almost out-of-time as well as out-of-place. Its sign declared *Friendly's*, and it featured four banks of state-of-the-art pay-at-the-pumps. A small trailer sat behind the station, probably belonging to the owner of the franchise. A clothesline laden with forgotten bed sheets twisted lazily in the wind. Chad wondered if the owner had actually seen this highway's flow of traffic before planning the establishment. There was a seventies model Chevelle parked near the back of the building—undoubtedly belonging to the poor sap who operated the counter. Off to the far side, the underground tanks were feeding through a huge hose from a gasoline tanker like a child suckling on a teat. There were no actual customers in sight.

Chad parked the Volvo at the far corner of the lot, outside the glare of the overhead canopy lights and parallel to the tanker. Suze grumbled as she fumbled with the door latch. "Could you have parked any further? I gotta *pee!*"

As if *pee* was the magic word, Chad suddenly became aware of his own bladder, full and straining. He loosened his seatbelt and joined Suze in her mad dash across the parking lot, under the canopy and to the automatic door of the station, already whooshing open from the motion of their approach.

A red-headed woman somewhere in her fifties stood behind the counter, barely lifting her eyes to acknowledge them. She was short and stout, her ample midsection filling the space behind the counter. She held a copy of *People* in her hands, thumbing through the glossy pages before stopping for a quick perusal. Britney Bramblett, the raven-haired beauty who had taken over for Crystal Bright on *Benny and the Girl*, smiled suggestively from the cover under a headline that read, "Crystal Who?"

"Restrooms?" Suze asked, hopping from foot-to-foot in the universally recognized pee-pee dance. The woman behind the counter lifted a meaty arm and pointed toward the rear of the building. Emblazoned in bright blue paint on the wall were outlines of faceless, shapeless stick people, the woman standing out because of the lines of her skirt and the flips at the bottom of her hair.

Chad and Suze headed toward their respective facilities, Suze nearly running while Chad tried to look less desperate. No doubt about it, though. He really had to go, too.

He pushed open the door to the men's room and heard water running in the sink. An enormous man stood at the wash basin, washing his hands and forearms and splashing cold water against his face. Unlike the frumpy attendant of the service station, this man was raw muscle, barrel-chested and ham-fisted with thick, salt and pepper hair covering his arms and hands and the entire lower half of his face. He looked up as Chad entered and shot him a hostile glance.

Chad nodded slightly and turned to stand at one of the urinals. He lowered his zipper and brought himself out, waiting for the familiar relief as his bladder emptied its contents into the porcelain bowl.

Instead, there was silence. His urine had frozen in place, unwilling to flow. Chad glanced nervously over his shoulder and saw that the man at the sink was watching him in the mirror, his eyes narrow slits.

"What're you staring at?" the man asked, his voice dark and gravelly.

Chad averted his attention to the task at hand. Dammit, his piss was still locked up. His situation worsened when the man shut off the sink's faucet. The hollow silence was deafening.

"I asked you a question," the man said, turning away from the sink and facing Chad's backside.

Chad's mind raced. He had no weapons of any sort on him, and he was no physical match for the other man. "Nothing," he finally said. He was astonished at the sound of his voice, all high and quivery. He felt the familiar rumblings of anger eating at the corners of his periphery and felt completely powerless to express it.

"You tryin' to get a look at my *package*, son?" the man leered, grabbing his crotch and squeezing. "You runnin' around lookin' to knock cocks with some sleazebag in a public restroom?"

"No."

"Bull*shit*. I've seen you pretty boy types before. Fucked one of 'em up real good over in Dayton. You should've heard the fucker scream when I stuck my big yang up his ass."

If there had ever been any hope of peeing before, it was gone now. Chad tucked himself back into his jeans and stepped away from the urinal, keeping his eyes carefully averted from the man at the sink.

"Where you goin' boy?" the man asked, his voice sneering. "You gonna be a bad boy and run from daddy?"

Chad fumbled with the hinged door, trying to push when he needed to pull, finally managing to find his way back out into the food mart. Suze was still in the other bathroom, leaving just him and the red-haired clerk, who had traded *People* for *Soap Opera Digest*.

And the big man from the bathroom who just then stepped out into the store. The man's gaze was fixed on Chad, eyeing him openly. The corner of his mouth was drawn up, smiling suggestively. His hands never strayed far from his blue-jeaned crotch, which he occasionally gave an affectionate squeeze. He blew soft kisses anytime Chad looked in his direction.

Where the fuck are you, Suze? Chad thought, moving over toward the entrance to the women's facilities. *You said you had to pee. How the hell long does it take?*

Just then, the door opened, and Suze emerged. "Whew! I didn't think I was going to make it!" she said, smiling.

"C'mon, let's go," said Chad, his voice little more than a whisper.

"What's your hurry?" Suze asked. "I'm hungry. I'm grabbin' some chips."

Chad turned his head and saw that the chips were on display just behind the big, leering man. As his eyes skirted by, the man blew him another kiss, but Suze's attention was riveted to the bin of snack cakes in front of her.

"We can get chips somewhere else," said Chad. "C'mon."

"Christ! Fine! I'd rather have these snack cakes anyway," she said, scooping six packages of brownies into her arms.

"Well, then get 'em and pay for 'em. *C'mon*," Chad urged, guiding Suze by the arm up to the counter.

"What the hell's the matter with you?" Suze demanded. "I *told* you we were safe—"

"Just shut up, pay for the fucking food, and let's get the hell out of here," Chad hissed through gritted teeth.

The clerk looked up from her magazine and sighed as she was forced to put it aside. "Any gas?" she asked in a voice marked by years of heavy smoking.

Chad shook his head. "Just these."

Suddenly, the large man was standing behind Chad, pressing himself against his back. "You better throw these in, too," he said, tossing a box of condoms on the counter.

The woman behind the counter scowled and put her hands on her hips. *"Earl!* How many times do I have to tell you to leave the customers alone?"

"But Loretta! Lookit how pretty," said Earl, running a rough forefinger along Chad's jaw line.

"Never mind Earl," Loretta said to Chad. "He's ornery as the dickens. He likes to make people squirm."

Chad looked up at her uncertainly. Earl hadn't budged. From the corner of his eye, he could see that Suze had taken a step back and was observing. The note of amusement that played across her face was unmistakable. Apparently, she enjoyed seeing Chad squirm almost as much as Earl did.

Loretta could see the look of wild helplessness building in Chad's eyes. "Go on, Earl! I mean it! If you don't back off, I'm calling home office. Work's hard to come by out here, and there's plenty of half-wits willing to deliver all the gas I want to buy. Now *shoo!"*

Earl backed off, his leering smile still present. When he thought he was out of earshot, he began to grumble, "Fatass cranky old PMS'n—"

"Knock it off, buddy, or I'll tell your mother, too," said Loretta, pointing a red-tipped fingernail in his direction. "And you *know* I'll do it." Earl fell silent and wandered to the back of the store to ruminate over the selection of alcoholic beverages in the standing cooler. The glass door slid open, and another burly trucker came in, heading toward the restroom.

Good, thought Chad. *Earl's got a new girlfriend.*

"$6.45," said Loretta, turning her hand palm up and resting her elbow on the counter. "Sorry 'bout that. Earl's a real ass. Has nothin' to do while the tanks fill, so he amuses himself like this. You should see him when he's been drinkin'."

"Yeah, well, I'll take a pass on that," said Chad, clumsily placing the money in Loretta's plump hand. After making change, Loretta dumped the snack cakes into a brown paper bag and nudged them across the counter.

"Thanks. You-uns stop in again." The statement was automatic and insincere, and Loretta had her nose back in her magazine before Chad had even picked up the sack.

Chad could feel Suze's eyes burning into his back as he walked out of the store, and he couldn't keep the embarrassment from tinting his cheeks bright red. "Stop staring at me," he hissed.

"Got yourself a boyfriend?" Suze teased.

He stopped abruptly and turned. "I don't want to hear another word about it. Do you understand me?" Suze tried to maintain a poker face but couldn't quite keep the corners of her mouth down. Chad thrust the paper bag of snack cakes into Suze's arms and turned away, crossing the lot toward the Volvo.

"C'mon, Chad," Suze called after him. "It was funny!" She giggled and trailed after him.

Chad walked around the front of the Volvo and continued on, passing between the oil tanker and the freighter which had carried Friendly's latest customer in. Hard, packed dirt lay beyond the tarmac, and clouds of dust kicked up as Chad passed through.

"Hey!" said Suze, stopping to put the bag on the hood of the car. "Where are you going?"

Chad didn't say anything. He continued to the front yard of the trailer which was nestled behind the service station. The little structure was nearly obscured by the shadows cast from the canopy lights. The clothesline twirled in a sudden gust of wind, its white bedsheet flapping as Chad approached.

Striking like a venomous cobra, Chad snatched the sheet from the line and wrapped it loosely around his arm. He turned and stalked back toward the gas station parking lot.

"C'mon, Chad!" said Suze. "We've got better things to do than steal someone's laundry!"

"Shut up," he hissed as he crossed back between the parked semis. He turned left and walked to the rear of the gasoline truck.

Suze watched Chad, trying to see what he was up to. As he knelt near the plate where the tanker was linked, she trotted up behind him. "What are you doing?"

"Shut up," he repeated.

"Buddy, you better stop telling me to shut up. I don't like that," she said.

Chad stood and scratched his ass as he studied the linkage. He traced the hose back to the tanker and found the mechanism to cut the flow of gas. He deftly turned it off and turned to stoop again over the linkage. He worked it loose, exposing the mouth of the underground tank.

"What are you doing?" Suze asked again, peering over his shoulder. "Oh, *shit!* Are you doing what I think you're doing?"

"I suggest you get in the car. Get it started."

"What are you *thinking?* This is nuts! There's bound to be video cameras taping the whole outside of this place!" Suze's eyes were wide, her expression conveying complete disbelief.

"That bastard made a fool of me," Chad said, feeding the twisted end of the sheet down the mouth of the tank. He stood and grabbed Suze roughly by the shoulders. "Take a note, Suze. *No one* makes a fool out of me. Do you understand? Now get in the car and get it started. When I come, you better be ready to go. Do you understand?"

Suze nodded dumbly and caught the keys as Chad tossed them to her. She returned to the Volvo, fumbling for the ignition key. She snatched the bag of snacks off of the hood and tossed them into the passenger seat, starting to lower herself into the driver's seat. She paused, squinting at the other truck.

She straightened and turned to Chad. "Hey! Wait a minute!"

IV

Bert slowed the rig and eased into the rest area. It was the third stop they had made in the last two hours. The prepackaged dinner he had eaten was wreaking havoc in his stomach and lower intestine.

"I'm sorry, son," he said, grimacing. "But when you've got to go—"

Luke laughed and lit a cigarette. "Believe me, I'd much rather you do it in there than in here."

Bert waddled off toward the facilities, and Luke reclined in his seat. There were only a couple of other travelers making use of the rest area, a man reading a newspaper behind his steering wheel and a pretty young woman holding a baby, walking around the grassy lawn to stretch her legs.

These pit stops had slowed them down even more. It was nearing eleven o'clock and they still hadn't crossed into Ohio. They were close, though. The last time Bert had felt the compulsion, he had been in the stall for over half an hour. Luke was starting to worry about food poisoning. They hadn't chosen the same variety of mysterious foodstuff, and Luke felt fine, although the sandwich *had* stained his breath.

Luke looked at his surroundings. Corn. Great. It was just normal-sized corn, but so was the corn toward the end of his dream. Of course, between here and Ohio, there would be no shortage of cornfields. He'd better get used to it.

The hairs on the back of Luke's neck bristled.

He took the last cigarette from his pack and lit it, taking a long, slow drag of warm smoke. He didn't know why he was staying with Bert. He doubted that this was Paulie's idea of independence. Still, he was seeing parts of the country that he hadn't seen before, even if they weren't too far from Jasper.

After about twenty minutes, Bert ambled back and hoisted himself behind the big rig's wheel. His complexion was clammy, and a thin sheen of perspiration glistened on his brow.

"You okay?" Luke asked.

"Better," said Bert with a slight groan. He started the truck and pulled back onto the highway. "That's the last time I trust that microwave shit. I've lost about forty pounds."

"You don't look so good."

"Well, thanks for the update, buddy. If it was *your* innards tryin' to find their way out, tell me how *you'd* feel."

"No, I mean, *really*," said Luke. "Your color's all off."

"I'll be fine. It isn't the first time I got hold of something bad," said Bert, settling in at sixty-five miles per hour. "I'm hopin' that was the end of it."

"That's what you said *last* time."

Bert grinned half-heartedly and clicked on his bright lights. Traffic was nearly non-existent in these parts. Just the occasional farmhouse tucked back from the road, wooded sections which ran parallel before giving way to fields of tall grass, and of course—corn.

"So, you worked the fields back home?" asked Bert, breaking the easy silence.

"Uh-huh," said Luke, exhaling a stream of blue-gray smoke. "Paulie was a very old man. Sharp as a tack, but *old*."

"How old?"

"He would've been ninety on his next birthday."

Bert glanced over at Luke, grinning. "Ninety? That's old, but I've seen older. Still, he must've been a frisky old fella. You can't be more than twenty-five or so yourself. How old was your mother?"

140

Luke smiled at the thought of Old Paulie cruising Jeb's, Jasper's only drinking establishment, for hot young chicks to marry and impregnate. "I'm twenty-one," he said. "I don't know anything about my mother. Paulie adopted me when I was a teenager. He's the only family I've ever had."

"Wow! I didn't know they let someone so, um, old adopt a child."

"In my case, they made an exception. I was the only orphan in town, and Paulie was willing to take me off the county's hands. Besides, Paulie was from old Jasper stock. He was almost a landmark himself. They knew he'd take good care of me."

"Still," said Bert. "You'd think the state would cart you off. Aren't they pretty strict about stuff like that?"

Luke shrugged. "I don't know. I never really *examined* the process. Things aren't always done in small towns the way they ought to be. No one makes a fuss if everything is overall pretty much okay."

"What happened to your parents?" asked Bert.

"I don't know," said Luke.

"How can you not know?"

"They abandoned me."

"Oh," said Bert. "Sorry. I just thought—"

Luke waved his hand and flicked his cigarette out the window. "Really, it's okay. It's just that when your own folks don't even want you, you find it real hard to care about who in the hell they were, you know? Paulie was my family from the time I was twelve."

"Don't you remember the time before that?" asked Bert.

"Well, sure," said Luke. "I was at Sister Margaret's before I went to live with Paulie. I was there for a little while."

"What about before that?"

Luke searched his memory. Oddly, he couldn't find anything before his tenure in the two-room orphanage which had also doubled as accommodations for the Sister. Clearly, he could remember her stern admonitions for his ungodly ways. He had been a young boy, acting as young boys do. Energetic, curious, ingenuous, inscrutable and just downright mean sometimes. No matter how he behaved, it wasn't good enough for the Sister. Paulie had saved him from a nun. What an odd thought.

Before that, nothing. Did most people forget their first six or seven years? That didn't seem feasible.

"Hmm," he replied, tired of talking about himself. He decided to divert the conversation. "So how long have you and Greta been married?"

Bert shot Luke an odd look but allowed their banter to shift gears. "It'll be thirty years this September."

Luke raised his eyebrows appreciatively and whistled. "Thirty years is good. I can't do math in my head, but if I'm thinkin' right, you got started pretty late on your family yourself."

"That's right," said Bert. "I'll be fifty-five in November, and Greta turns fifty in December. She's gone crazy over that. I never thought the woman would give a good goddamn one way or the other. She never seemed to care about stuff like that. Well, now that's coming out all wrong. Greta's a fine-looking woman."

Luke grinned. "I've seen her picture. I know."

Bert blushed slightly. It was good to see color back in his face. "Oh, yeah. But she never seemed to get hung up on getting older. Forty was a snap. Forty-six, she had a baby. Didn't see that one coming. She was thrilled, though. Said it kept her young. That was the first time she had ever even mentioned aging. Fifty's looking like it's going to be a really rough one."

"Eventually everyone has to face his own mortality. I can't imagine it's going to be a real good time for any of us."

"I just hate to see her upset. Betty—she's my oldest—is losing sleep over it. She's a worrier. Completely selfless. Fiercely protective. She doesn't take a notion to trust people much, though. Too much TV, I think. Sure, there's lots of bad types in the world, but there's just as many good, don't you think?" asked Bert.

"Most of the people I know seem okay to me," said Luke.

"TV really plays that shit up. Crazies runnin' the streets. I'm not stupid enough to think it isn't true in some places. Thank God Borden seems to keep its small-town ways," said Bert.

"I never wanted to live in a big city," said Luke. "I think it's best to keep life simple."

"Amen. Now, Laurie's a whole different story. She turned sixteen a few months back, but if you saw her, you'd swear she was eighteen or nineteen. Filled out in all the right places. Knows how to use it, you know, to tease guys, get them to do what she wants. Worries me a little. I only hope she doesn't figure out screwin' feels so damn good. I may be fifty-five, but I'm not ready to be a grandpa yet," said Bert. "All that girl talks about is gettin' out of Borden just as soon as she's old enough."

Luke fumbled in his duffel for a fresh pack of cigarettes. He noticed that it was his last pack as he pulled it out and ripped away the cellophane. He'd have to pick some up at the next stop.

"That Little Tater is going to be the death of me, though," continued Bert. "She's ornery and gets her way every damn time." His face cracked in a wide grin.

"You feelin' better? You look better."

"Yeah. I think three times was a charm," said Bert. "If I'm still feelin' okay by the time we hit 18, I'm gonna cut off on it. There's next to no cops, and we can cut the distance home by a bit."

"You're the boss," said Luke, slumping back into his seat and taking lazy drags from his cigarette.

Route 18 was a narrow two-lane blacktop, like so many others in rural areas, but was relatively well-maintained and straight. There weren't many houses, just more grassy fields, and of course, corn.

Bert and Luke fell into an easy silence as the big rig hummed along, its big nose sniffing out Borden, Ohio.

* * *

A warm, summer afternoon.

No humidity to speak of, just a gentle breeze that riffled through his hair.

Luke stood at the edge of a bright green grassy meadow. To his left was a gravel road, barely wider than a sidewalk, stretching from one end of the horizon to the other. To his right and off in the distance was an enormous Colonial farmhouse, white with black shutters. It was surrounded by tall, ancient trees, well-trimmed shrubbery and deftly arranged flower beds. A red picnic table was positioned under the shade of a mighty elm. There were people around the table, but they were too far away to be distinguishable. Three women who were relatively the same size and a little girl, busy chasing butterflies.

"C'mon, son."

Bert was standing beside him.

"What are you hangin' back for?" asked Bert. "Hot dogs don't stay warm for too long."

Luke grinned and followed Bert across the field. As they approached the table, Bert called out, "Honey, I'd like you to meet Luke Leighton. I told you about him on the phone."

"Oh, that's right," she said. She was working at the grill with her back to the men. Now she turned.

Her face had no features.

Luke shot a glance at Bert, but Bert seemed to be fine. He looked back at Bert's wife.

Still no face.

"Glad to m-meet you," Luke stammered, tentatively offering his hand. He expected her hand to be a single piece of flesh, uninterrupted by the usual flow of digits.

It looked normal. He looked back up. Still no face.

"Grab ya a plate," she said. She turned and called, "Tater!"

Luke turned to face the table. The girls turned to look at him.

No faces.

143

The little girl, giggling hysterically, had just reached the table and was shrieking for a hot dog.

No face.

Luke felt dizzy, panic crawling into his throat. The air that had seemed so nice just moments ago had become thick and difficult to breathe. The paper plate in his hand slipped from his fingers and wafted lazily back and forth as it began its slow-motion descent toward the ground.

His knees buckled and he felt himself sliding down...

———◇———

Luke's head snapped up and his eyes opened.

The truck was slowing and turning left into a gas station. The bright lights from the overhead canopy momentarily blinded Luke as Bert maneuvered the truck to the rear of the lot.

It had been another dream. Luke wondered if he was ever going to get another moment's peaceful rest.

"What's up?" Luke asked.

Bert groaned and farted. "I guess it ain't over 'til it's over." The truck came to a stop with a mighty whoosh. "Sorry, son. We'll get there sooner or later." He threw open his door and stepped down onto the tarmac, hurriedly waddling off toward the gaily decorated food store. Four rows of empty gasoline pumps were between the truck and the road, shiny metal gleaming under the light of the canopy. The station looked like it had just come new out of the box.

Luke rubbed gritty sleep from the corners of his eyes and tried to will them to adjust to the light. He reached into his duffel bag for his pack of cigarettes and then remembered that it was his last pack.

Luke unfastened his seatbelt and opened the door, lowering himself to the ground. He had been seated in the same position for far too long. Whole portions of him were asleep, unwilling to cooperate with his conscious mind. He stooped and then stretched, squatting several times to revitalize his legs.

As his eyes adjusted to the light, he caught a flicker of movement across the road. The pumps were blocking the way, so he took a few steps right and tried to focus again.

Corn. Great.

But even as the wind made the plants dance, Luke saw there was something else. Actually, *someone*. If he had looked just a second later, he would've missed it. As it was, all he saw was the backside of a tiny white dress disappearing into the corn.

His cigarette forgotten, Luke crossed the lot underneath the canopy, staring intently at the swaying row of corn that lay beyond the highway. There was no more evidence of the girl.

Luke wondered if he had imagined it, still half asleep and immersed in the weird, faceless dream. He didn't think so. Frankly, he had never considered himself one to have much in the way of imagination.

He stood between two pumps in the front row which ran parallel to the street. The corn waved gently as if in greeting. Luke listened to the whisper of the plants wrestling with each other. He didn't hear anything that sounded like someone pushing through the corn. Of course, the girl had looked very small. Her progress would probably be virtually soundless.

But wouldn't she be afraid? Wouldn't she be calling for her mother or father? It didn't seem like a natural reaction. It was nighttime.

Clouds passed overhead, allowing the moon to cast its silvery glow on the scene. Luke's eye caught a small glimmer from where he had seen the girl enter the cornfield. It was very low to the ground, maybe a shoe.

Luke looked both ways along the highway. The reflectors gleamed in different colors as they crossed to each horizon. The night was quiet, no cars on the roadway. He slowly crossed the street, his eyes fixed on the shiny object.

A shoe?

He reached the far side of the road and stepped off onto the dirt berm. This was not his imagination. There was definitely something there.

He kneeled and parted the tall grass which surrounded it. Not a shoe.

A teacup.

Luke picked the delicate china up and examined it under the moonlight, squinting to decipher the pattern. He didn't know one damn thing about fine china, but it looked and felt authentic. Off-white with a distinctive rose border. Despite its odd placement, it was still in one piece, albeit a very dirty one.

Luke placed the cup back where he found it. It wasn't his. He stood and stretched his aching legs. He needed some quality rest, and *soon*.

He turned back around and took a step back toward the food mart.

Luke's peripheral vision suddenly closed in on him, and he found it very hard to breathe. His legs wobbled fiercely at the knees.

Wha—?

The thought barely registered before Luke's legs turned into putty and he fell face forward into the hard dirt, gasping desperately for air.

145

CHAPTER EIGHT

I

"I can see your soul."

The voice was so low that Lisa had to strain to hear it. A cold chill crawled down her spine.

"Nanna?" she asked, her voice quavering.

The dark shadow took another step away from the basement door. It was too tall to be Nanna Grace. Too thick.

Standing still.

Eyes glistening.

Lisa's vision adjusted slowly to the dark, and she could discern the same straggly beige trench coat she recognized from Nanna Grace's funeral.

It was the crazed man who had accosted her as she went to her car.

"I can see your soul."

"What do you want?" asked Lisa, taking a slow sideways step to the right, trying to inch her way to the front door.

The man moved like lightning, suddenly blocking her escape. She could smell his fetid body odor hanging in the air. "I can't let you hurt that li'l girl," he said, his haggard, unshaven face looking curiously remorseful.

Lisa took a step backward. "What are you talking about? I don't want to hurt anyone."

The man laughed, a jagged chord restricted to flat notes. "Like you didn't want to hurt that lady from the hospital?"

Lisa froze. "What lady?"

Again, with the laugh. *"You know* the one."

"You're crazy."

"Like you didn't want to kill my mother?"

Lisa stared at him in silence. Who was his mother? Had this been Nola Kelsey's son? No, she had seen him before Ms. Kelsey had died, at Nanna Grace's funeral, bawling like an overgrown baby. He certainly wasn't Nanna Grace's son. She had no children. Besides, Lisa hadn't killed Nanna Grace. Mrs. Baylock? Could this be *her* son?

"Who are you?" asked Lisa.

"I am my mother's avenger."

Lisa could see the man's arms trembling at his sides. His hands were tucked into the pockets of his tatty trench coat. Oily strands of dark hair adhered to his sweaty forehead. He needed a haircut badly. He was nervous as hell.

"How can you possibly be your mother's avenger when you're not even brave enough to give a name?" asked Lisa, her voice steadying. This was better. She felt more in control of the situation.

"You know who I am!" he spat.

"Baylock?" she asked, weary of the game.

His laugh echoed through the empty room, dissolving into anguished sobs. He slumped to the floor. He nodded his head weakly. "Chris Baylock," he managed to say.

"I don't understand," said Lisa. Her anxiety was draining away. This man was a shambles. Whatever plan he had in mind had long been forgotten. He curled up like a whimpering child, rocking on his heels while he tucked himself against his knees.

"No, it's *me* who doesn't understand," sobbed Chris. "Why did you kill my mother?"

"Why would I kill your mother?" asked Lisa, studying the man curiously.

His face pivoted and stared at her as if astonished she would try such a tactic. He knew she had killed his mother. He *knew*.

"I know what you did to her in the hospital," he said. "She told me how you—*washed* her. She told me how you—*cared* for her. I didn't believe her at first." He stood up, his knees creaking as he straightened. His hands were still tucked into the coat's big pockets. His eyes were agony.

"Ginny—my sister—believed her right away. I go to Ginny with business ideas, and she laughs me off. Mama pops off with a crazy story like this, and she drinks every word right up. She filed papers with the hospital. You lost your job. I felt real bad about that," he continued.

"Why would you feel bad about that?"

"I still didn't believe them. I saw you at the hospital. I saw you in the halls. You looked so innocent—kind of like an angel. I think I might have had a crush on you." He was talking like a love-struck teenager instead of an unshaven and filthy forty-year-old man. His breath reeked of alcohol.

He went on. "Before Ginny filed the papers, back when Mama was beginning to grumble, I followed you home one evening. I wanted to see if what Mama said could possibly be true. More like I wanted to prove to her that it *couldn't* be true, you know? I thought that once it was all cleared up, I might ask you out to dinner, a movie." He grinned wistfully.

"The next day," he continued. "I came back to the house after you had gone to work. I don't know why. I wanted to prowl around, see the things you saw every day. I didn't intend to go inside the house, but as I stood on the porch, I heard her calling my name. 'Chris! Chris!'"

"Nanna was calling you?" asked Lisa.

He nodded his head. "It scared the hell out of me. It sounded just like one of those voices like in the B-thrillers, you know?"

147

Lisa shook her head. She had never seen a B-thriller.

"She told me to come in, that the door was unlocked. She said she wanted company and couldn't get out of her bed. I went upstairs and stood just inside the door to her room. I was still half scared. I had never met her before. I had no idea how she knew my name. She told me that she knew I had come to find out about you. She told me all sorts of things," Chris said.

Lisa's eyes narrowed. "Nanna Grace called you into this house? That's impossible. How would she have known you were even here? Her bed wasn't anywhere near the window upstairs. She couldn't get out of bed. Her legs were too weak. Impossible."

Chris shook his head. "I'm telling you what happened. She knew my *name*, too. That's why I came in. That's why I had to hear what she wanted to say."

Lisa folded her arms across her chest and sighed. "What did she have to say?"

Chris lowered his head, but his haunted eyes remained fixed on Lisa's. "She told me that you were evil. She told me that I should kill you."

Lisa laughed. "Again, impossible. Nanna Grace wouldn't say such a thing. I cared for her. I was her connection to the outside world."

"It's what she said," Chris said with a note of childish belligerence. "And I don't mind telling you that I was ready to cut and run right then. It's not every day that someone tells you to kill someone else. I came hoping to find out how very wrong Mama was about you. Instead, I have this old woman I assume is related to you telling me you are evil incarnate. I was about to turn and leave when she called me over to the bed. I didn't know what she wanted, but I didn't want to go. Before I knew it, I was right beside her anyway. She reached out her arms, and—and—"

"What?" asked Lisa, arching an eyebrow. "What did Nanna Grace do to you?"

"I don't know!" he shrieked, sobs pouring forth again. He pulled his hands from his pockets, the right one holding a compact gun. Light from the kitchen glinted on its black surface as he lifted it.

Lisa felt panic begin to swell in the pit of her stomach. She thought she had the situation in hand. She thought Chris had lost his nerve. She hadn't counted on him finding it again.

"She—she—touched me, and then—Oh, *God!*—and then—it *happened!*" Chris was hysterical, his swollen eyes shiny with tears.

"What happened?" asked Lisa, stalling for time, hoping to reassess the situation. The room was completely bare. She didn't even have a broom handle to joust him with.

The gun quivered in tremulous hands. Chris could inadvertently pull the trigger at any second.

"It—it—*transferred?*" Chris's tone was abruptly quizzical. "Is that what I'm looking for? Yes. She touched me, and I knew, and I haven't been the same since."

"Talk to me, Chris," said Lisa, her eyes locked on the fidgeting gun. *"What did you know? What's so bad about me?* You know, we could still have that dinner—"

"SHUT UP!"

Lisa covered her face with her hands, expecting the gun to discharge. It didn't. When she looked back at Chris, his hands had steadied. The gun still targeted her—sure and steady now. Chris's angry and malevolent eyes glistened from beneath bushy black eyebrows.

"I know you did it because I saw. I saw what you did to your old boss— Kelsey, wasn't it? I saw what you did to my mother. I see what you're going to do next. Nanna Grace wished she had been strong enough to kill you when you were a child. She could see all these things, too. She knew she was dying. She gave me the gift—or curse. I have to be strong enough. I *have* to."

"Why's that, Chris?" asked Lisa, her voice trembling slightly. She was going to have to act quickly.

"Because—I can see your soul."

"Tell me one more thing, Chris," said Lisa, her muscles tightening. He cocked his head quizzically and waited.

Lisa dropped low and rolled to the right, narrowly avoiding the gun's first shot. Intuition superseded conscious thought, and Lisa went on autopilot, rolling toward Chris instead of away from him. She stood and found herself tucked under Chris's arm, which was holding the gun. She grabbed it by the wrist and pulled it down over her shoulder until she heard the satisfying pop of his shoulder dislocating. The gun fell to the floor. Lisa stooped to pick it up while Chris staggered back against the wall, shock from the injury registering across his slack-jawed face.

Lisa crossed the room in two easy strides and thrust the gun into Chris's mouth. "Did you see *this* coming?" She pulled the trigger, and Chris's head exploded backward, painting the wall with bloody bits of brain and bone.

<hr />

Lisa was completely exhausted. Her side throbbed insistently, telling her it was time to knock off for the evening. She couldn't quit yet. There was a mess to clean up. She found an old metal bucket in the garage, filled it with hot, soapy water and was sponging the remainder of Chris's head from the rungs of the banister.

She tucked Chris Baylock's body into the basement. The burn barrel was still full, and Lisa was hesitant to attempt to dispose of the body in that manner. She was afraid it would smell like roasting meat, wafting freely through the neighborhood, and drawing the attention of hungry neighbors.

She would have to dispose of the body soon, though. The smell of its decomposition would permeate the house and betray its presence. Lisa wondered if Genevieve Maddox—Ginny—would immediately think to look for her brother here. It seemed odd that Genevieve was so well bred and affluent— obviously wealthy, yet her brother seemed almost like a street person. It was evident from the man's breath that he had a drinking problem. He must have been the black sheep of the Baylock family. Maybe Ginny would be glad to be rid of him.

The blood and particulate matter had managed to collect in unimaginable places, and Lisa meticulously scrubbed the woodwork and flooring to remove any residual trace. She stopped occasionally to straighten her back and mop her forehead. This day would never end.

What had Chris meant when he said he saw what Lisa was going to do next? *She* certainly had no idea what she was going to do next. Something inside her was awake and aware, planning and plotting, committing her to courses of action of which she had no conscious knowledge. If what Chris said was to be believed, then Nanna Grace had been working against her from the moment they had met. It was an interesting revelation. Lisa wandered through the corridors of her memory, applying this knowledge to her history with Nanna.

Nanna Grace had been staunchly authoritarian, God-fearing and law abiding. She had believed in rules and consequences. Lisa had thought Nanna was trying to protect her and give her guidance. Now, it seemed as though Nanna had merely been feeding Lisa and keeping a roof over her head, sort of like a family pet. Nanna hadn't wanted Lisa to attend public schools, but the State of Indiana had insisted the child receive some form of formal education. In the end, Nanna had been forced to comply and had enrolled Lisa at St. Ann's School for Girls. But she had been very insistent—no extracurricular activities and no socializing with the other girls. When Lisa had taken the job at the hospital, Nanna had been furious. Lisa had seen it as her only course of action. Nanna's medications were growing in number, and the expense had become more than Nanna's meager subsidies could afford. Lisa couldn't figure out why Nanna had been so unreasonable and had attributed it to old age or senility. Lisa had taken the job because she saw no other choice. It was as if Nanna was trying to keep Lisa away from the entire world.

Upon returning from hauling Chris's lifeless corpse to the basement, Lisa found another teacup at the head of the stairs, sitting innocuously on the floor, centered in the doorframe. Lisa picked it up and examined it carefully. It was one of Nanna Grace's.

Impossible!

Lisa had ground the china cups into rubble and thrown them away. But in her hand, unblemished by chips or cracks, was one perfectly good cup.

"Am I losing my mind?" Lisa said aloud as she absently crossed into the kitchen and returned the cup to the cupboard. She expected the other eleven place settings to be waiting in the dark recesses of the cabinet, but it remained empty.

A sharp knock sounded on the front door.

Lisa froze, her hand still on the cupboard. Was it the police, sent over at the direction of Genevieve Maddox to retrieve her drunken brother? Neither Lisa nor Nanna Grace had ever socialized with any of the neighbors. She knew some of their names, but not many. In the twenty years that Lisa had lived with Nanna, she could count on one hand the number of times someone had wandered up to the door and knocked. An unfortunate Avon lady who was promptly told that makeup was for whores and jezebels—Nanna Grace hadn't been confined to her bed back then. A Jehovah's Witness who had been re-enlightened before being sent on his way by the doggedly Christian Nanna. No young boys calling on Lisa, though. They knew better than to try. Even the children of the neighborhood knew to stay away on Trick-or-Treat. Nanna Grace was scarier than any old Halloween witch.

The knock came again. Sharper. More insistent.

Lisa peered around the corner of the cabinet, trying to discern who might be standing at the door through its frosty pane of glass. Lisa had left the shade up, trying to catch whatever light she could from the waning sunlight. Now, the figure at the door stood ominously in place, its outline drawn by the streetlight behind it.

Rather short. Thick.

Lisa stepped around the corner and crossed the room. As she neared the door, she realized that her nighttime visitor was none other than the good nurse Helen Martin. She had pushed her pudgy face up against the glass and was craning and squinting to get a glance of the house's interior.

Lisa sighed and pulled back the chain, twisted the deadbolt and opened the door. As an afterthought, she hoped she didn't have any of Chris Baylock's blood on her.

"Helen?" asked Lisa. She was perspiring heavily and didn't fail to notice Helen's once over of her appearance. "What are you doing here?"

Helen hesitated only an instant before smiling, the big warm smile of an old friend. She wore a beige, ankle length coat—utilitarian, not fancy—and kneaded her hands together nervously in front of her pot belly. She carried a matching beige handbag that looked more like carryon luggage. "I'm so sorry to barge in," she said. "I know this will seem silly, but I tried to call earlier to make sure you were settling in okay, and the phone just rang and rang. I was worried. I hope you'll forgive me. It's such a relief to see that you're—all right. You *are* okay, aren't you Lisa?" The smile was displaced by a look of concern.

"I'm fine, Helen. Just fine. I was just getting ready for bed," said Lisa.

Helen glanced at her nervously. "You seem a little flushed. If you don't mind me saying, dearie, you're a tad damp too."

"I've been moving some things around," said Lisa.

Helen tutted and tsked. "You're overdoing it! You need to *relax*, take it easy. You just got out of the hospital!"

"Really," said Lisa. "I was going to take a bath then go to bed. I just had a few things to do first, and when I get a notion in my head—" Lisa smiled thinly, watching the nurse intently. This wasn't good. She hadn't even been home a whole day and Helen had already made her first uninvited appearance.

Helen laughed. "Oh, say no more, dear! I'm stubborn as a mule once I get hold of something. But you need to take it easy."

Lisa nodded her head and started to ease the door closed. "I will."

"You might want to check the ringer on your phone, too," said Helen.

Lisa paused, the door still open the width of her body. "Ringer? What do you mean?" she asked.

Helen arched an eyebrow and said, "You know. The *ringer*. It might have accidentally gotten turned off. I called about a dozen times earlier. Let it ring and ring—" Nice going. If Lisa actually *had* been resting, the shrilling phone would have surely put an end to that. "—but you didn't answer."

"Oh," said Lisa absently. "We don't have that kind of phone. It's an old-fashioned sort. Its ringer is always on."

"Well, then you better call the phone company. They might have to come out and fix your lines."

Lisa stepped back from the door, scratching at the base of her neck. When was the last time she had used the telephone? Definitely during the arrangements for Nanna Grace's funeral. At least three times that week. The phone had worked fine. She turned and retreated slowly into the dark recesses of the living room, crossing into the lit kitchen to stand in front of the claw-handled black wall phone that hung by the back door. She picked it up and tapped the metal claw which extended like an upturned arm on the side of the rotary device.

No dial tone.

Lisa turned and realized belatedly that Helen had followed her into the house and was standing in the middle of the empty living room. Her confusion was evident.

Lisa scrambled for a reason. "I had just sent the furniture out to be cleaned after Nanna died. I haven't had a chance to pick it back up yet."

All of it? thought Helen. *Even the end tables? Gad! I didn't realize this girl was so destitute!* She smiled weakly and looked around the empty room. The ceiling was littered with cracks, the paint on the walls peeling. The hardwood floors were nice, though. Well-polished, too. Especially that place near the stairs—

Helen turned back toward Lisa, reinforcing her smile. "As old as that phone is, it might have pooped out on you."

"Hmm," said Lisa, still pondering the mystery of the telephone. She had paid the bill. She *always* paid the bill. The phone wasn't used much. She couldn't imagine it simply ceasing to operate. She doubted that it was the phone itself. That meant that it must be something in the line. That meant a service call to the phone company. That meant another stranger lurking about Lisa's property. She scowled and ran a hand through her matted and damp hair.

"—I can check it for you, so you'll know what to expect," Helen was saying.

Lisa's eyes widened and her heart kicked into overdrive. Helen had opened the basement door and was at the head of the stairs, slowly lowering herself down to the first step.

II

It had been a long day.

Paula had taken I-70 east just before Cove Fort and driven straight through into Colorado. They had crossed the Rockies, the little Honda performing admirably in the vast mountainous expanse. The white snowcaps seemed curiously out of place in the middle of July. Crystal had never seen Colorado before. She had taken planes when she needed to travel from coast-to-coast. It was breathtaking.

Through Denver and on to the east, still following I-70, they passed through Burlington and into Kansas, the flat geography in stark contrast to the mountains from which they had come. Tall fields of lazily swaying prairie grass bordered the road between the towns. The effect was hypnotic.

Once they passed Fort Hays, the weather took a severe turn for the worse. Low hanging black clouds rolled across the prairies, suggesting tornadoes but guaranteeing lightning and rain. Wind gathered at an alarming rate, rocking the Honda from side to side. It was not yet sundown, but Paula had to turn her headlights on. It was dark as night.

"This isn't good," said Crystal, fidgeting with the tuner of the radio.

"—warning is in effect for the following counties: Osborne, Mitchell, Russell, Ellsworth, Saline and McPherson. A warning means that tornadoes have been sighted in the area. You should immediately take cover—"

"I don't like this one bit," said Crystal, eyeing the swirling clouds overhead. "Let's find a place to bunk for the night."

Paula had become fidgety and nervous. Each bolt of lightning made her jump as if it had made direct contact. The car swerved slightly with each thunderclap.

"Where should we stop?" Paula asked. "We're in the middle of nowhere."

Lightning flared and thunder boomed in violent concerto. Rain began falling in torrential sheets.

"Anywhere, anywhere!" said Crystal. "We've got to get out of this!"

Visibility was near zero. The beams from Paula's headlights were refracted and thrown back at them in the cascading drops of rain. Hail dropped from the sky like golf balls, pounding at the car's metal roof like gunfire. Paula had slowed to thirty miles per hour, unable to safely navigate at any greater speed.

A mailbox appeared on the right.

"Turn! *Turn!*" Crystal flailed her arms madly toward the right, and Paula found the narrow dirt driveway with her headlights. The house that loomed before them was dark and foreboding. Broken glass dangled from panes which had once been windows. The front door had been kicked in and was swinging in the wind by its bottom hinge. The rotten wood of the porch sagged, pulling at the porch rails like a funhouse mirror.

"Oh! *OH!*" said Paula, slamming her foot on the brake. "We can't stay here! Look at this place! It'll fall down around us!"

Crystal couldn't agree more. Much more urging from Mother Nature would pull this heap to the ground. Crystal could actually see a funnel cloud out in the distance, swirling lazily in the forceful wind. It had a yellowish hew that made it look nasty—malevolent.

"We can't stay in the car. It's not safe either," said Crystal, scanning the unkempt yard which sprawled around the leaning structure. "Don't most people out here have storm cellars or something?"

"They did in *The Wizard of Oz*," said Paula.

"We're in *Kansas*, for God's sake!" said Crystal, loosening her seatbelt and fumbling with her door handle. "I'll bet there's a storm cellar somewhere around the property. Let's go!"

Paula didn't want to move. She had seen severe weather before, but nothing like this. The wind growled with ferocity, a wild beast about to pounce, but from which direction?

More lightning, followed by ground-rattling thunder.

Crystal exited the car and crossed around to the driver's side. She was instantly soaked by the downpour, her white cotton blouse and jeans sticking to her like a second skin. She fumbled with the door handle and pounded on the glass when she found it was locked.

"C'mon, Paula! I think it's a fucking TORNADO! We have to GO!"

Paula snapped out of her reverie and opened the door. The wind seized the flimsy metal and pulled it out of Paula's grasp, stretching the hinge to the limits of its endurance. Paula stumbled out of the car, a high-pitched gasp involuntarily flying from her mouth as the cold rain doused her. The wind was like a hand, pushing her against the Honda's open door and pinning her there.

Crystal reached for Paula's arm and pried her away from the door. The wind abruptly shifted positions and slammed it shut. Crystal and Paula clung together as they made a quick sweep of the weedy front yard. Then they moved to the side. It was in the back that they found what they were looking for.

Jutting up from the ground was the mouth of an underground storm cellar. The wooden doors which covered the opening were still fairly sturdy and seemed to be on solid hinges. Crystal and Paula ran against the rain and wind, dodging hail as best they could and fumbled their way down into the inner recesses of the dark hole, pulling the doors shut behind them. It was pitch black.

"I think I felt a spider!" shrieked Paula.

"You'll have to live with it," said Crystal. "At least we're not out in *that* anymore."

"I can't take dark places! I *can't!* You have to get me out of here! You have to—" Paula was hysterical. Crystal could feel the girl fidgeting and pacing in the darkness. She was headed back to the door, on her way back out into the storm.

"Paula! *Stop!*" Crystal said, summoning the most authoritative voice she could find. "I've got matches. Maybe we can—"

"I CAN'T STAND THE DARK! *PLEASE!*"

"Okay! Okay! Just stand right there. Look up. You can see the lightning through the slats in the door. Try not to get too close but look at it. Stay focused on it. Give me just a minute—" Crystal was fumbling in her pockets for her matches. She had taken them from the end table at Bob's Motel just before they had checked out. She didn't know why. She didn't smoke. It was just a compulsion. She found the book and struck one of the matches.

The room filled with eerie shadows as the light from the match danced along the dank surfaces. Shelving had been constructed along the far wall. It was mostly empty, save for a small box on the middle shelf. A crude wooden bench had been fashioned along the wall to the right.

The match burned down to Crystal's fingertips, and she shook it out involuntarily. Paula began to whimper softly.

"Hang in there, Paula. Let me see what we've got over here," said Crystal, fumbling with the matchbook and lighting another.

Miracle of miracles, the box contained candles. They were previously used, but that was fine. There was a dozen of them, and it would have to storm for days before they would use the last. Crystal lit two candles and placed them on the top shelf of the storage space. Paula calmed immediately as the shadows were chased away, and her eyes began to adjust.

Soon, they were seated side by side on the crude bench, dripping water in expanding puddles. The wind roared outside, and Crystal guessed that the Honda had arrived in Ohio by now—airborne. She kept the thought to herself. She didn't want to give Paula another reason to fall apart.

"Don't like the dark much, huh?" Crystal asked.

Paula's exhalation was slow and shaky. "Uh-unh."

"How come?"

Paula shook her head stiffly, sending water droplets spraying.

Crystal sighed. Getting information out of this girl was like extracting teeth from a piranha. Lightning flared, casting brilliant beams of illumination in through the slats of the door. Tucked away in the far corner, underneath the bottom shelves, the lightning was reflected.

Oh God. Not rats.

Crystal refused to become panicked. It would be contagious, and soon Paula would be uncontrollable. Trying to act casually, Crystal stood and plucked another half-spent candle from the box and lit it from one of the two they already had burning. As she lowered herself back to the seat, she allowed the candle to wave in a wide arc in front of her, taking it as close to the floor as possible without risking suspicion.

The light glinted again from underneath the shelves, still in the exact position in which Crystal had first seen it. Too big to be eyes. About the size of a softball. Shiny along its entire circumference.

A bottle.

Crystal leaned forward and reached under the shelf, extracting a vintage bottle of gin from underneath the shelving unit. It was dated 1973, a leftover from the previous tenants. Its seal was still intact. Its best quality was its massive quantity.

"Ha!" exclaimed Crystal, holding the large bottle up for Paula to see.

"What?"

"Here," said Crystal, working its screw top loose and breaching the seal. She handed the bottle to Paula, who sat very still and stared at the bottle.

"What?" she said again.

"Drink," said Crystal. "Doctor's orders."

"You're not a doctor," said Paula.

"But I play one on TV," said Crystal, grinning. The joke was obviously lost on Paula, who continued to stare with confusion. "Seriously, I think you'd feel better if you had a bit. It'll calm your nerves."

Paula hesitated only briefly before taking the bottle from Crystal and upending it in her mouth.

"Whoa! Slow! That shit'll burn!" laughed Crystal. "And it ain't like we've got chasers down here."

"S'okay," Paula said with a gasp. "I'm used to it. Joel—" Her words froze, and she wiped her mouth.

Crystal looked at Paula expectantly, but she said nothing else. She handed the bottle back to Crystal. "You," she said.

Crystal tossed her head back and took a long swallow. It burned all the way down to the tips of her toes. The last time she had drank something so cheap, she was still a country girl in Lucasville. She grimaced and started to replace the cap, but Paula took the bottle from her, taking another healthy drink.

As she handed the bottle back again, Crystal asked, "Better?"

Paula nodded her head and reached for the bottle again.

Crystal pulled it back slightly. "Do you really think that's a good idea?"

Paula nodded again and snatched the bottle away from Crystal. She took a sloppy drink, dropped the cap on the ground and slumped back against the wall, all her agitation spent. Crystal grabbed the bottle before it tumbled out of Paula's hand. She cautiously took another drink herself before setting the bottle out of reach.

"Is this some shit or what," said Paula. "This was supposed to be my big break, my chance to get my shit together and move on. What a fucking disaster."

Inexplicably, Crystal craved nicotine. Although not a smoker, she did partake occasionally in smoking a cigarette or two while she drank. Neither she nor Paula had cigarettes. Shit.

"What do you mean?" Crystal asked.

Paula's face twisted suddenly, and silent tears streamed from the corners. "I don't know where else to go, and I can't go home. I don't have any money, and—I can't go home."

Crystal retrieved the gin and took another pull from the bottle. She offered it to Paula who took another half-hearted sip. "Paula, I'm going to tell you something about me. It's something you won't find in magazine articles—well, maybe the tabloids. I left home when I was eighteen. I left my Aunt Maude by herself and decided to see the country. I felt invincible. I wanted to see what there was to see. I saved up enough to fly to Los Angeles, figuring I would work my way back across the States. You hear about students backpacking through Europe? I thought it might be nice to start at home first."

"I thought you said you were telling me something new," said Paula, her words slightly slurring. "I've read all this stuff. *Seventeen* and *YM* and—"

Crystal motioned for her to stop. "Yeah, okay, *that* stuff you know. But that isn't my point—" Her words had begun to slur a bit, too. "I never went anywhere else at all. I stayed in California because I met Marshall Dawson, and he made me a star. You know that part, too. What you don't know is what all this has done to me. I'm not the person I used to be. I don't care about anyone but myself. I'm the *last* person in the world who you would ever want to tell anything to because I wouldn't be paying attention anyway."

"You're rambling."

Crystal sighed. "What I'm trying to tell you is, you've got no reason in the world to tell me anything. But if it would make you feel better, I'm listening."

Crystal licked her lips and waited. A little devious, perhaps. She had purposefully gotten Paula a little more drunk than she had previously intended. She wanted the girl to take the bait. She wanted to know about Joel. She wanted to know what made Paula such a mess.

Their eyes locked. Crystal could almost hear the deliberations going on inside Paula's head.

"I was six years old the first time he—did it," Paula began, her voice detached and weak, dampened by the hard-packed dirt walls of the storm cellar. "He—did it to my sister, too. You always knew the nights he was coming. He unplugged the night light. I used to lay awake and stare at the ceiling and—and—"

"Who was he?" Crystal asked gently.

Paula's vacant gaze shifted away. "The man my mama married. He ran the candy store on Briardown. All the children—it was a dream job."

"Joel?"

Paula nodded her head slowly. "Angel was so smart. She had a plan."

"Who's Angel?"

"My sister. She's about four years older. Right after she turned eighteen, she had enough of Joel's shit. She batted her eyes at Roy, the boy down the street who'd been crazy about her since the beginning of time. Got him to marry her. Off she went, from city to city. Roy was in the Army. He got transferred a lot. She went to school. Got out of all the shit. Just as soon as she graduated, she divorced Roy and moved on. She never really loved him. She just needed out." Paula's eyes were still away, looking at things that had transpired years before.

"How'd you get out?" asked Crystal.

Paula laughed. "That goddamned contest. Would you believe it? There hasn't been five days I can count that Joel hasn't opened every piece of damn mail that came through that door for me. He was paranoid as shit. He thought I'd tell Children's Services or something. It isn't like the thought never crossed my mind.

"Joel had a doctor's appointment or something and Mama was out when the mail ran that afternoon. He'd have been mad if he knew I got it. But it had been weeks since I had entered the contest, and I started thinking he wouldn't give me the mail even if it did happen to come. I didn't think I'd win. I mean, what were the odds? But there it was. A number to call and confirm. I had my bag packed and was out of there before they ever got home."

"What did you think you'd do once you got to California?" asked Crystal.

Paula shrugged. "Did it even matter? I'd be *there*. I mean, the contest included a hotel stay the entire time I was out there, and round-trip airfare. Joel would never let me work back home, you know? I couldn't even put together bus fare. I figured by the time the shoot was over, I could find some little job, some little apartment. I started waitressing at Bob's Big Boy, bought the Honda from a U-Pay-Here, got me a little shithole apartment in a neighborhood that kept me awake most nights."

"Why would you stay there?" asked Crystal.

"It was *still* better," she replied. "I figured that in this neighborhood, at least I stood a *chance* of not being raped. At home, I knew what I was in for."

Crystal and Paula sat in silence. The storm had quieted down, only gentle rain falling on the storm cellar door. Candlelight flickered across the dark hole, barely keeping the shadows at bay.

"I'm sorry," whispered Crystal.

Paula nodded. "Me, too. I hope you're not in a real hurry to unload me. I'm not quite ready to go anywhere yet."

Crystal smiled. She had broken through, and it felt good. Paula's anxiety level had dropped, whether from the alcohol or the true confessions, Crystal didn't know. It didn't matter. Her gut instinct told her that it had been cathartic for Paula, even if the girl didn't realize it yet. You can't undo the past, only come to terms with it. It was a step in the right direction.

They were asleep in a matter of minutes.

III

Suze straightened and squinted harder.

The semi parked in front of the gasoline tanker had something on the ground, something by its driver side door.

"Really, Chad!" she called out. "Hang on!"

He didn't respond, and she took a few steps around the driver's door of the Volvo.

It was a teacup. Another teacup.

Why would there be a teacup by the door to the truck? It made no sense.

Suze turned and looked back toward Chad, expecting him to be just behind her, coming to see what was going on.

Instead, he knelt by the exposed length of bed sheet, fumbling with his lighter.

"You wanted to be Bonnie and Clyde, didn't ya babe?" he said softly, then stood as the sheet began to burn.

Suze froze in a second of indecision. The teacup was right there—

But the sheet was on fire, and there was no undoing that. She returned to the car and fired up the Volvo's engine as Chad came running.

Chad was shrieking now. "Well, *BABY BONNIE, SHE'S GONNA BLOW!*"

———◆———

Luke coughed and gasped for air. Dirt from the ground sputtered from his lips with each rough exhalation. He had landed on his face. His eyes watered, and his vision blurred.

Oh, God.

It was the dream.

Luke knew it instantly. The service station in the background, unidentifiable through Luke's watering eyes. The moon overhead. The sounds of the night.

It was the dream.

Luke struggled to find his footing, but his legs were still jelly, making the process nearly impossible. He had managed to raise up from his hands, but he was still on his knees when he heard the words, sailing across the clear night sky.

"*—SHE'S GONNA BLOW!*"

Luke saw movement as someone ran from the gasoline truck toward the only other car parked in the lot. His eyes were still watering, and he couldn't discern any details. It could've been a man, it could've been a woman.

Oh, God. Bert.

◦————◇————◦

Suze had the car in gear before Chad was completely inside. She flew around the banks of pumps and cut sharply to the right, guiding the car back onto the highway.

They had just cleared the parking lot when the underground tank exploded. Chunks of concrete from the lot flew through the air, riding the ballooning wave of fire. Seconds later, the gasoline tanker itself exploded, contributing its own angry fireball to the nightscape.

Chad twisted in his seat to watch through the back glass, laughing uncontrollably. "*That'll* teach that son-of-a-bitch!" he repeated between hysterical seizures.

Another explosion, more forceful than the first two, ripped through the air. Both Chad and Suze ducked instinctively, and when Chad looked again, he saw that the food mart itself had blown apart. Apparently, the underground explosion had compromised the natural gas lines leading to the building. The chain reaction was complete when, almost as an afterthought, the other semi-truck detonated from the flames licking at it from all directions.

Chad turned and relaxed in his seat, still chuckling. He looked across at Suze, whose attention was firmly riveted to the road. She was driving like a bat out of hell, the Volvo wobbling left and right as she tried to maintain a steady course. Her eyes were narrowed, her face angry.

"What the hell's the matter with you?" asked Chad, his laughter trickling off.

"*You fucking asshole!*" shouted Suze. "You may have just ruined *everything!*"

◦————◇————◦

Luke knew he could do nothing about it but watch. His vision had cleared some, and he saw that the passenger car was square and maroon. He couldn't see the faces of its occupants, only that there were two of them. As the car entered

160

the roadway, the first explosion rocked the ground, followed a few seconds later by the gasoline tanker detonating. Chunks of concrete and twisted machinery sailed high into the air before returning like unholy rain. Luke felt himself being pelted by fragments of the lot and the truck, not realizing how lucky he was that no substantial bits fell on his unprotected head.

Maybe that's it. Please God, let that be it. Bert's okay. He's inside the—

The building exploded abruptly, storefront glass shattering and spraying outward in a wide arc. More debris. More fire.

Bert was dead. There was no doubt.

Bert's truck joined the circus in progress, as if saying, "Oh, what the hell?" before wrenching itself apart in its own thunderous fireball.

Luke was on his feet now, debris falling all around him. How could this be? What good is a precognitive dream if there isn't enough time to react? He mewed like a wounded animal, unaware of the sounds issuing from his own throat. His face was hot and wet, tears and salty perspiration mingling and stinging his eyes.

Abruptly, a chunk of concrete the size of a quarter hit Luke right between the eyes, knocking him back down. His head reeled, and his vision blurred, but he held onto consciousness and forced himself back to his senses.

He was on his hands and knees again, fragments of the service station and semi-trucks scattered around him. A rectangle of paper lay on the ground just below his face. He could see "Kodak Paper" stamped on it and realized he was looking at the backside of a photograph.

The little girl.

He remembered waking from his nightmare before he could flip the photograph over, but he had known then that it was the little girl, the one who had screamed so horrifically in a previous dream, running through the cornfield from the unseen thrasher. She was in terrible danger.

His fingers trembling, he reached for the photo, its curled corners rippling in the wind. The heat from the raging inferno rolled across the blacktop in blistering waves, and dark smoke poured into the sky, blotting out the moonlight.

He lifted the photo gingerly by its corner and turned it over.

Little Tater smiled mischievously back at him from the glossy print.

CHAPTER NINE

I

"Where are you going?" asked Lisa, her voice louder than expected—higher-pitched, too.

Helen turned and looked back into the kitchen, her smile faltering. "Weren't you listening to a word I said?"

Lisa's eyes narrowed as she strained to recall. She had no idea what the nurse was talking about.

Helen sighed and took a step away from the basement stairs. "The *phone*, dearie, the *phone*. I told you I brought over a spare." She reached down into the large beige purse she had draped over one shoulder and extracted a cheap one-piece telephone, its cord coiled around the unit. "See? I can go downstairs and hook it directly to the main jack. If the line to the house is good, it'll get a dial tone. That way you'll know if it's your phone that's bad."

Lisa laughed nervously. "Helen, you're a nurse, not a telephone repairman. I don't know that you ought to be rewiring my phone line."

Helen looked at her curiously. "What are you talking about?"

"Well, don't you have to wire that thing in somehow?"

Helen laughed. "Oh, heavens no! There should be a jack downstairs where I can just plug this in. See?" She dangled the modular end of the phone's cord in front of her.

"Oh, well, that's no good," said Lisa, trying to look disappointed.

"Why is that, dearie?"

"Well, take a look at my own phone," Lisa said, indicating the vintage black rotary contraption hanging on the kitchen wall. "It's the only one in the house, and it's hardwired to the wall. Nanna Grace never had the phone lines upgraded. There's nowhere to plug that one in."

Helen's face registered disappointment, and she tucked the phone back into her purse. "Well, rats. I thought I was being helpful."

Lisa inserted herself between Helen and the basement door and eased it shut. She hoped that Helen hadn't noticed the traces of Chris Baylock's blood on the wooden stairs. Helen had been a nurse for a very long time. She would recognize blood when she saw it.

"It was a good thought," said Lisa, putting an arm around Helen and guiding her back toward the front door. "It's just that Nanna never saw the need to update something that worked just fine. Truthfully, I guess I never did either."

"You'll have to call the phone company then. Oh!" Helen laughed and clapped a hand up to her mouth. "And just how can you call them when you're phone isn't working? Silly me. I'll call for you in the morning."

"Don't do that," said Lisa, a little too quickly.

"It's really no trouble at all," said Helen.

"I have to be out tomorrow anyway. I'll call while I'm in town," said Lisa. Spontaneous lies were new to her, but she found it easy enough. "I need to make sure I'm here in case they need to get inside the house."

"Well, if you're sure," said Helen.

Lisa nodded. "And as you can see, I'm alive and well, so—"

"Of course," said Helen, allowing herself to be led across the threshold to the porch. "You need to get your rest. I'm sorry again about barging over. I was just—I was just afraid you weren't well."

"It's okay, Helen," lied Lisa. "It was very thoughtful of you. After I take a nice bath, I'm going straight to bed."

"Sleep in," instructed Helen.

"I won't even set an alarm."

Lisa closed the door, twisted the deadbolt, and secured the chain. She leaned back against the door and sighed. Helen Martin was going to be a problem. But a problem for another day.

Lisa crossed the dark, empty living room and went down into the basement, carrying her pail of soapy water. She pulled the chain of the low wattage bulb which was mounted overhead at the bottom of the stairs and began a methodical sweep of the bloodstains which trailed down the steps. When she was finished, she descended again, this time to stare curiously at her handiwork. Chris Baylock was piled in a dark corner like a marionette freed of its strings, arms and legs splayed absurdly, the remnants of his face frozen in grotesque surprise. Lisa took slow steps toward him, stopping within inches of the soles of his shoes. This man had ceased to be alive because of her. She had taken whatever life force flowed through his veins and snuffed it out as easily as flame from a candle.

She felt nothing.

Perhaps curiosity, much like a scientist. In the last couple of weeks, Lisa had killed not one, but *three* people, yet she felt no remorse for her actions—none whatsoever. None of her crimes had been premeditated—hell, she had killed Alma Baylock while she had been *asleep*—and Chris Baylock would still be alive if he hadn't caused Lisa to defend herself. Lisa's attack on Nola Kelsey had been spontaneous and exhilarating, and the only instance in which she had truly felt the venomous pull of retribution. For the most part, she didn't feel much of anything. The unexpected visceral sensation of rage had been both enlightening and alluring. Lisa had no doubt that she would someday feel it again.

She studied Chris Baylock's corpse a moment longer before turning and going upstairs, squelching the light as she passed under it. Chris's empty eyes watched her long after she was gone.

———◆———

Lisa woke with the morning sunlight finding her eyes. She got out of bed and stretched languidly, her injured side feeling almost normal. She knew that she was healing faster than she should. The enormous amount of physical work she had done the previous day should have set her back completely. Instead, she felt stronger, perhaps even stronger than she had been before the accident.

She brushed her long, blonde hair over the bathroom sink, staring at her reflection in the vanity as she carefully parted her hair down the middle. The dark circles beneath her eyes had disappeared, but her skin was pale from a fundamental lack of sunshine. Lisa placed the hairbrush on the sink and grimaced as she realized that her dark roots were even more visible than they had been before the accident. She hadn't gotten the opportunity to color her hair, as she had set out to do on that fateful evening. Something for tonight. She might even take scissors to it.

Lisa had more important things to attend to first. She pulled her hair back in a twist and fastened it at the nape of her neck. She selected a sundress of which Nanna Grace would have surely disapproved—it showed too much cleavage—and a pair of her black Sunday heels. It was quite makeshift, but the effect was startling to Lisa. In her reflection from the standing mirror, she could see that her legs were shapely and toned, her abdomen flat, her chest desirable to men, enviable to women. The twist made her hair presentable, but nothing more. She would definitely have to do something about it.

Still, she looked infinitely different from the mouse who had crept through the halls at Morgan Township Hospital so few weeks ago. The transformation in Lisa was now beginning to extend to her exterior, and the thought excited her. She had spent her whole life trying to fade into the background, avoiding notice, avoiding participation. Now she wanted someone to recognize the curve of her legs, the fullness of her lips, the swell of her breasts. Nanna Grace couldn't overwhelm her ever again with the atrocities of sin or command bitter restitution which must be repaid.

As the sun flowed brilliantly through windows which had been blinded for as many years as she could remember, Lisa felt completely free.

Lisa walked down the street with her head held high. Children ran and laughed in the summer sun. Retired men tended to their lawns, mowing and edging. Women knelt in flowerbeds, pruning and watering. Birds soared overhead. Lisa noticed these simple things with wonder, having never dared to look before.

Nanna Grace had instilled in her a deep sense of fear for the outside world. It seemed so ridiculous now.

As she continued down the street, Lisa felt the gazes of her neighbors, pausing from their chores if only for a second to look. They sensed the change in her from the confidence of her stride, the way she held her head. She knew that the old men were looking at her legs, so shapely in the low heels, and it made her smile.

Morgan Township First National Bank had a neighborhood branch five blocks from Lisa's house. Nanna Grace had always done what modest banking she needed to do with them, and once Lisa had gotten a job, she had opened an account of her own, squirreling away little bits here and there into a savings fund. Her account book showed the balance at just under three thousand dollars. This morning, she would need to make a substantial withdrawal.

Mrs. Gulker, a spindly and slight gray-haired teller, did a double take when Lisa stepped up to the counter. "Why, Miss Mitchell! I almost didn't recognize you!"

Lisa smiled and laid her account book on the marbled ledge. "Thank you, Mrs. Gulker. I need to make a withdrawal."

"Certainly, certainly," she said, lifting her glasses into place from where they were suspended around her neck on a gold chain. "How much will you need today?"

"One thousand dollars," said Lisa. "I may be back for more."

"My," observed Mrs. Gulker. "That's a lot of money for a young woman to be carrying around. Wouldn't you prefer traveler's checks or perhaps a debit card?"

Lisa shook her head. "No, I'm going shopping."

Mrs. Gulker arched an eyebrow but set about the business of making the withdrawal. "Quite a lot of shopping you can do with that," she said, after she had counted the money and slid it across the counter to Lisa.

"I intend to," said Lisa, oblivious to Mrs. Gulker's disapproval.

Still, customers are always right, and Mrs. Gulker was in the business of customer service. "I just can't get over the change in you," she said. "You look like you could be on the TV."

Lisa's smile widened. "Thank you, Mrs. Gulker. Have a nice day." She tucked the money into her handbag and turned from the teller's window, her heels clicking against the tiled floor as she exited the bank.

She bought a copy of *The Gazette* from the vending machine outside Norville's Donuts and went in to eat two chocolate éclairs while she pored over the classifieds. Garage sales were common occurrences in Morgan. Free advertising space was given in the newspaper for these neighborhood events, and Lisa made note of the ones within walking distance. Since her Toyota had been totaled, she found herself trapped relatively close to home. Without a job, it would be impossible to finance another vehicle. For the moment, that was fine. She wanted time to discover who it was she was becoming. She might discover that she didn't want to live in Morgan any longer. Like Mrs. Gulker said, maybe she should go out to California and get herself 'on the TV.' It was an interesting daydream. Lisa revisited a mental note, remembering a television was high on her list of furniture that she needed to acquire.

Lisa had hoped to have at least a few days to refurnish the house, but it seemed painfully obvious that Helen Martin was going to be somewhat of a nuisance. She remembered telling Helen she had sent the furniture out to be cleaned and knew that the nurse hadn't believed her. She didn't even know if people *did* that sort of thing. Nanna Grace would have considered it to be supremely gluttonous, paying someone to do things Lisa could do herself. Nonetheless, unless she wanted to be the endless recipient of the good-natured nurse's charity, Lisa had to rectify the emptiness of her house.

Lisa had no intention of calling the telephone company. She hadn't figured out how to dispose of Chris Baylock's body yet, and that would most certainly have to happen first. It would have to be tonight. Lisa knew that she would find the odor of the decomposing body intolerable. She wasn't a complete monster, after all. In the meanwhile, the phone would have to stay out of order. Helen would surely notice, but Lisa would tell her that she was unable to make an immediate appointment which suited both hers and the phone company's needs. That should buy her at least a few days.

Near the end of the garage sale listings, Lisa found what she was looking for. It was an entire estate sale, just a few blocks over. She took the last bite of éclair, washed it down with black coffee, then tucked the newspaper under her arm and headed back into the sunny morning. As she crossed the street, she heard the appreciative whistle of a passing motorist, and pride swelled in her breast. She had never given any consideration to her own appearance before, and was surprised that, given a few modifications, it was now so completely palatable.

Lisa found the cottage on Deerport without any difficulty. It was a small white cinderblock house with a low roof and black shutters. Its tiny yard was choked with overgrown shrubbery and weeds. A rusting black wrought iron lamppost stood near the drive, its globe yellowed with age. A wooden sign hung from the post by a rusty chain and *'165, The Lovells'* was burned into its weathered surface. There was a matching detached single-car garage, its door open and tables lining its interior. A sandy-haired man in his early thirties sat behind one of the tables, looking vacantly out into the neighborhood, his legs crossed lazily in front of him. He had no other customers at the time. He wore loose khaki shorts and a sleeveless white shirt, showing unremarkable shoulders and arms, nearly as white as the shirt itself.

Lisa crossed the driveway. "Hi," she called.

"Hi, yourself," said the man, unfurling his legs and standing. "Come to take a look?"

Lisa nodded and scanned the tables. It was mostly small items—kitchen appliances, jewelry, home decor. None of the things she was looking for.

The disappointment must have shown on her face because the man asked, "Something wrong?"

"Well," said Lisa, turning to face him. "I was actually looking for larger pieces. I thought this was an estate sale. Am I too late?"

The man extended a hand. "I'm Jack Lovell. This was my mother's house. She died last month."

Lisa took his hand and smiled. "I'm Lisa Mitchell. I'm sorry about your mother. My Nanna just died, too."

"Something in common," he grinned. "Mother was sick a very long time before she died. We'd all been expecting it for years. It was probably best in the long run. No more pain, you know? Anyway, there are some larger pieces left, it's just that they're in the house. I didn't see any point to moving them from where they were. Quite a few have already been sold, but you might want to come in and see what I've got left."

He led the way into the little house, and Lisa wandered around. Quite a few pieces had indeed been sold. Even considering its size, the house seemed bare. The kitchen had been stripped down, as well as the bedroom. But the living room still had its contemporary sectional and matching walnut end tables with speckled clay lamps atop them. A small television sat on a metal cart. It was everything Lisa needed.

"How much for these things?" Lisa asked, indicating the pieces.

"Oh, I don't know," Jack said, rubbing his chin. "Six hundred dollars?"

"I'll take it," said Lisa, opening her pocketbook and rifling through its contents.

Jack laughed. "Wow! I guess when you make your mind up—"

"Yes," said Lisa, smiling as she handed the money to Jack. "I make my mind up very quickly. This is perfect."

"Well, good!" he said, pocketing the cash. "That's pretty much the last of the big items. I should be able to go back home soon."

"Home?"

Jack nodded. "I live in Cleveland. I took some vacation time to come down and sort these things out. Janice couldn't get away, so I came by myself. It was okay. Gave me a chance to think about Mom."

"Janice?"

"She's my wife," said Jack. Nonetheless, his gaze lingered on Lisa's breasts before returning to her eyes.

Jack cleared his throat and turned, walking toward the front door. "So, when did you want to pick the stuff up?" he asked.

167

Darin Miller

"Pick it up?" asked Lisa. "Hadn't thought about that. I suppose I could rent a U-Haul or something."

Jack turned and smiled. "No need. Since you've been so kind as to relieve me of the bulk of my merchandise, the least I could do is deliver it to you. I've got a truck."

Lisa wetted her lips. "Are you sure? That'd be very nice of you."

"I'll need some help getting the sectional into the truck bed. It's pretty heavy. Do you know anyone who could help lift?" he asked.

"I can," Lisa said without hesitation.

He smiled sympathetically at her, and for an angry second, she wanted to tear the flesh off his face. "It's pretty heavy."

"I can handle it," she said coolly.

"If you say so."

"I say so."

Lisa's smile returned, and she winked at Jack. He shuffled his feet and felt his ears burn crimson.

"I have another errand to run while I'm out this way," said Lisa. "Can I come back in a couple of hours? I want to change clothes before hauling furniture, anyway."

"Sure, sure," said Jack. "I was just going to sit around and read. See if anyone wanders over to take a look at the junk on the tables out there."

"Are you sure this isn't too much trouble?" she asked.

"Not at all," he said. "But I should probably warn you, it's probably going to take about three trips."

Lisa looked at him with round, innocent eyes. "It's okay with me. But I'm going to have to think of some way to thank you. I'll be working on that."

She turned and walked down the drive, turning right when she reached the sidewalk. She felt his eyes on her the entire time.

It was all coming together. Now Lisa knew how to get rid of the body. The only possible flaw with the plan was the potential for Helen Martin to make another unannounced visit. She took a quick left at the next intersection. It seemed she was spending as much time at Morgan Township Hospital now as when she had actually worked there.

II

Sunlight streamed through the slats of the storm cellar door. The candles had melted overnight, leaving waxy globs behind. Crystal's head shrieked in protest from the cheap booze, throbbing at the temples with every beat of her heart. Her stomach was tied in knots, as if she had been beaten. Paula seemed unaffected, hurrying up the wooden stairs and throwing open the door.

The sky was brilliant blue with only traces of frosty white clouds drifting overhead. Birds chirped amongst themselves and traversed a network of treetops, lighting for just a moment before flying to the next. It was as if the violent weather of the previous night had only been a dream. The ramshackle farmhouse still looked structurally unsafe, but no more so than when they had arrived. Crystal had expected the yard to be littered with branches wrenched from the trees, but it was no less tidy than it had been when they had descended into the cellar. The Honda was still in the driveway, still on all four wheels, none the worse for wear. If anything, it was as if the storm had given it a thorough washing, its silver surface gleaming in the ample sunlight.

They returned to I-70 in uncomfortable silence. Crystal had learned some of what she wanted to know about Paula's past but felt unable to say anything about it now. Paula acted somewhat remorseful, as is if she regretted the honesty prompted by gin. Crystal hoped she hadn't permanently damaged the lines of communication between them. Other than necessary exchanges, they remained quiet.

They refueled in Abilene and continued eastward on the interstate. Paula grabbed a quick bite of lunch in Topeka. Crystal passed, as her stomach was still unsettled. They took I-470 around Kansas City and emerged in Missouri. By the time they reached St. Louis, Crystal's appetite had come around, and they stopped at a roadside diner for supper.

The air was thick with smoke, but the mouth-watering smell from the kitchen met them at the door. A thin waitress named Lottie led them to a booth with cracking red vinyl seats. The table wobbled unevenly on its pedestal, but it was clean and that was good enough for them. After placing their orders, Paula finally broke the interminable silence.

"I wish I hadn't told you all that stuff," she said, her voice so low that Crystal could barely hear her.

"Why would you wish that? Do you think I'll tell people?"

"No," said Paula. "But you haven't hardly said two words to me all day. I hoped it wouldn't make a difference, but I can see that it has."

"I didn't think that you wanted to talk about it," said Crystal. "I didn't want to bring it up because it's painful for you."

"Well, we didn't have to talk about *that*," said Paula. "We could talk about anything."

"Okay," said Crystal. "Go ahead."

"Have you ever been in love?" asked Paula.

Crystal sat back in her seat. "Where'd that come from?"

"None of the articles I've read about you have ever talked about a boyfriend. I mean sure, *The Tattler* reported that you were secretly dating Marshall Dawson about two minutes before *The Enquirer* reported that Marshall was gay. He wasn't even *hiding* the fact that he was gay, but *The Tattler* didn't bother to check their sources. Basically, you can't rely on those things for information. They're chock full of bullshit," said Paula.

Crystal smiled. "If only the rest of America felt that way. I've seen myself portrayed in every imaginable way in those things. After a while, I just stopped reading. To be honest, though, sometimes they get things more right than I would care to admit."

Paula raised her eyebrows. "You *were* dating Marshall Dawson?"

"*No!*" Crystal exclaimed. "He's been with Sam Novak for over fifteen years. No, I just mean that when the media is watching you so closely, sometimes they catch you with your pants down. I saw a lovely picture of myself chasing Marshall down the highway, hurling my shoes at his truck."

"Oh," said Paula, nodding. "So?"

"So what?"

"Have you ever been in love?"

"Oh," said Crystal, leaning her elbows against the table. "No, I guess not. I mean, I had a couple of boyfriends in high school, but nothing serious. We went to the school dances and things together."

"No boyfriend in California?"

"I was too busy for that," said Crystal. "You would be amazed at how much time goes into maintaining a public persona. You're contractually obligated to do this or appear there—it gets crazy."

"Weren't you ever tempted with Blake Jagger?"

Crystal shook her head. "He's gorgeous and built like a brick shithouse, but we both knew that to become romantically involved would jeopardize the show. We thought that was *all* we had to worry about."

"What do you mean?"

Lottie returned with their food—pork chops and mashed potatoes, smothered in dark gravy for Crystal and fried chicken and green beans for Paula—and Crystal took a moment to savor the first bite. "It all started with the goddamned fan letters."

"How?"

Crystal shrugged. "This isn't a good story to tell. I don't come out looking so good."

"So?"

"I started keeping track of the fan letters, you know, how many each of us got. It was easy enough to do, because they were mailed in care of the studio and the network. I swear, I think people had bets going for a while. Some weeks I'd get more than him, and some weeks he'd get more than me. Big deal, right? Well, for me it became a big deal. Midway through the season, my popularity just went right through the roof. My face was everywhere. It was weird and exhilarating, and my quantity of fan mail tripled. There were internet sites springing up left and right. Some were fan clubs, others promised nude pictures of me," said Crystal.

"Nude pictures?" Paula was stunned. She had never heard of Crystal posing for anything like that. Of course, at home, she had never enjoyed the luxury of the internet. Joel would never allow for such wasteful things.

"It's amazing what you can do with a computer and a good graphics program," said Crystal. "I never posed for anything. That's beside the point. It wasn't long before I stopped thinking of Blake as my equal, and I was too busy for anyone else."

"I've never had a boyfriend either," said Paula. "It might be nice. But after what Joel—I just have a hard time trusting men."

"You flirted with that security guard back at the hospital," said Crystal.

"Men are dumb. It doesn't take much to get what you want out of them," said Paula.

"True enough."

"So, what was growing up like?" asked Paula.

Crystal shrugged and took a bite of mashed potatoes. "It was good."

"It must've been hard to lose both of your parents when you were so young."

"To tell you the truth, I barely remember my parents. I was only five years old when they died," said Crystal. "Aunt Maude was my mother's aunt, and she took me in. She never married or had any children of her own. I was the only family my Aunt Maude had. She taught me to be strong and self-reliant because we didn't have anyone but ourselves to depend on."

"Did she want you to go to California?" asked Paula.

Crystal nodded then reconsidered. "I don't suppose she *wanted* me to go as much as she wanted to be supportive of my choice. She couldn't very well raise me to be independent and then balk when I took my first step, you know? So, I went and really made a mess of things. Now, Aunt Maude's gone, and I can't even make it up to her."

"I'm sure she knows," assured Paula.

"Your turn. What about Joel?" asked Crystal.

The fork froze in front of Paula's mouth as she stiffened. "What about him?"

"Haven't you ever thought of calling the police?" asked Crystal.

Paula shook her head. "I've got a bit of a record in town for running away. It's not like I did anything bad, but Joel has told the police everything you can imagine about what kind of delinquent I am. Once, he told them that I attacked him with a kitchen knife. Can you believe that? He cut his own damn arm and told the police that I did it to him."

"Why would he do a thing like that?" asked Crystal.

"So, the police won't believe me if I tell them what he does. His brother is on the goddamned force. Small towns have a fucked-up sense of justice."

171

"Have you told your mother?" asked Crystal.

Paula rolled her eyes. "Angel did. She got into the biggest fight with Mama, and by the end of it, Mama kicked her out. It was only for a few days, but it scared the hell out of me. If she kicked Angel out, she wouldn't think twice about doing it to me. She had accused Angel, her own daughter, of trying to steal her husband. It made it real clear where the lines were drawn."

Crystal ate for a moment in silence. She didn't know what she could contribute. Paula had grown up in an inescapable environment. The fact that she was relatively well adjusted was a miracle. Crystal couldn't imagine having to deal with that kind of oppression day in, day out. She would've probably killed the bastard.

⌒────────◇────────⌒

Conversation was easier as the evening progressed. They drove through Illinois talking about superficial nonsense as if they were old girlfriends. The sun dipped down as they crossed into Indiana and Terre Haute. Paula's responses were becoming logy and slurred, and Crystal knew she would soon be asleep.

Crystal looked at the clock in the dashboard. It was only a little after ten o'clock. She didn't feel the least bit tired herself. She decided to press on before finding a place to stop for the night. She knew that if she drove nonstop, she could be in Lucasville in the wee hours of morning, but she doubted she would feel as alert then as she did now.

They crossed the state in silence, with Paula snoring quietly in the passenger seat. She stopped in New Lisbon, where she refueled the car and got a tall cup of black coffee. As an afterthought, she bought two road maps, one of Indiana and one of Ohio. She knew that she didn't want to stay on I-70 for much longer. It crossed Ohio at its midsection, taking her nearly 100 miles north of where she wanted to be. Besides, the monotony of the interstate was hypnotic, and Crystal's eyes were becoming leaden. She considered taking a motel room here but decided to try and push herself an hour longer.

Crystal spread the maps over the hood of the car, trying to choose an alternate path that would take her to the southern part of Ohio. She saw that Route 1 went south and intersected with I-74. It would take her to I-275, which circled Cincinnati. From there, she could intercept Route 32, which would take her much more directly to Route 23, about twenty miles north of home.

It was a plan. Crystal folded the maps and stashed them in the back seat of the Honda, then got behind the steering wheel. She took a long sip of the nearly scalding coffee and eased the car back onto the interstate.

The coffee was completely ineffectual. Within moments of being back on the road, Crystal's eyelids began to droop. She wanted to turn on the radio, wake herself up with some music, but she didn't want to disturb Paula. Instead, she opted to crack her window, letting the humid night air blow across her face.

Route 1 appeared more quickly than Crystal expected, and the Honda's tires screeched as she made the turn at the last moment. She was halfway to Fort Wayne when she realized her mistake. She had turned north on Route 1 instead of south.

"Shit!" Crystal said, pounding her hands on the steering wheel.

"Wha—?" Paula lifted her head and looked at Crystal vacantly.

"I'm finding us a place to stop for the night. Go back to sleep," Crystal said, turning east on Route 18. She was too tired to work out her coordinates tonight. With her entire soul, she wished for the familiar emerald letters of Holiday Inn.

Darkness stretched to the horizon. Endless miles of tall corn whipped by on the passenger side of the car. Houses were sprinkled few and far between, brief reminders that civilization was still out there. Paula had fallen back asleep, her head bobbing in time with the dips and ruts in the road. The radio crackled and fizzed as reception fell apart. Crystal adjusted the tuner, finding only a country and western station with decent signal strength. That was okay. It felt like home.

It was when her eyes returned to the roadway from the radio that she saw the girl. She knelt in the darkened street, retrieving a stuffed rabbit from the center line. Her tiny body was white in the glare of the headlights, her face obscured by dark curls which spilled around her shoulders.

Crystal cried out and slammed on the brakes, pulling the steering wheel sharply to the right. The Honda skittered off the pavement and into the rutted dirt which skirted it before jumping nose first into the corn. The car stopped abruptly, the momentum snapping Paula forward against her seatbelt. She let out a strangled cry and then was wide awake.

"What happened?" asked Paula, her eyes darting around. They were surrounded on three sides by corn, the dark roadway visible through the hatchback. The Honda hissed its disapproval, billowy white steam rising from its front grille.

Crystal struggled against her seatbelt, finally working it loose, then tried to open the driver's door. The thick corn provided resistance, but she inched her way through.

"Where are you going?" asked Paula, fumbling with her own seatbelt.

Crystal said nothing, forcing her way through the corn. She reached the berm of the road and stopped, scanning the long, empty blacktop in both directions. There were no other cars in sight, no streetlights to provide illumination. The pale moon hung overhead, partially obscured by a bank of rolling clouds.

The girl was nowhere to be seen.

Paula appeared behind her. "What's going on?" she asked.

"I thought I saw something," said Crystal, scratching her head.

"Something? What?"

"Nothing. It's stupid," said Crystal, turning to smile weakly at Paula. "I should have stopped at a motel a while back. I'm too tired to be driving."

Paula cast a glance over her shoulder at the Honda, which was nearly buried in the row of corn. It sat far enough off the road that it wouldn't necessarily attract the attention of cars passing by. Not that there were any cars passing by. It continued to hiss and spit, like a coiled snake hidden in the corn.

"I think the car's fucked," said Paula.

Crystal nodded slowly. "I'm sorry. I should have stopped earlier."

"What are we going to do?"

"It may not be anything too serious," said Crystal.

"Are we supposed to call a tow truck? Besides the fact that we can't afford it, we're in the middle of nowhere," said Paula.

"I said I was sorry."

"Dammit!" Paula was pacing.

"Will your insurance cover it?" asked Crystal.

Paula laughed. "What insurance?"

"Shit."

Paula put her hands on her hips and stretched her back, her spine shifting and popping in relief. "Where are we?"

"Indiana," said Crystal. "Pretty close to the Ohio border."

Paula laughed again. "I swear, it's like we're doomed. We spend last night in a storm cellar and tonight in a cornfield. It's like someone doesn't want us to get to Ohio."

Crystal thought of the girl stooped over in the center of the road. She had seen the porcelain of her skin, the satin locks of her full hair. Crystal had been tired, but not asleep. She was sure of that. She listened to the crickets chirp and the wind whispering through the corn, hoping to catch any sound of the girl retreating. The girl could have been no more than five. What would she be doing by herself in the middle of the road, well after midnight? Crystal thought again how easily she and Paula had eluded the security guards at the hospital in Los Angeles. One had scanned the car with a flashlight, completely oblivious to the substantial lump under the blanket which had been Crystal. The dream of Aunt Maude, rocking and shucking beans, replayed itself. *Soon there will be people coming.* Was the little girl one of these people? Crystal felt sure that Paula was. She felt like screaming in frustration, a helpless player pacing through a scenario scripted for her but without any direction. How would she know she was doing the right things? How does anyone know? Was she just imagining all of this, attaching significance to a dream which had only been that—a dream?

Paula popped the hatchback and retrieved a flashlight. "Do you know anything about cars?" she asked.

"Not really," said Crystal. "I know where the gas goes. That's about it."

"We are *so* screwed," said Paula.

Crystal nodded and wandered over to the car. "Well, let's see if we can get the hood up anyway. Maybe we'll luck out and whatever's wrong will be obvious."

Raising the hood, they finally had what might be construed as a small piece of luck. The top radiator hose was split and exhaling steam, though much less than when they had first come to a stop. Crystal knew that a hose couldn't be too expensive, but Paula didn't have tools in the back of her car, and Crystal wasn't sure that she could change the hose even if they had the proper equipment, not the least of which would be a replacement hose.

"We're screwed?" asked Paula.

"Screwed," agreed Crystal. "You don't happen to have a flare back there, do you?"

Paula shook her head.

"I don't think it will be much to get the car fixed, but we're going to have to wait until we can flag somebody down who's willing to give us a hand," said Crystal.

As if heaven sent, the sound of a siren emerged in the distance, gaining volume as it neared. Crystal and Paula struggled to get back through the corn and out to the road before it passed by. The corn gripped and pulled at their legs, and they had only just broken free of it before the sheriff's car roared past, its red bubble lights flashing, its siren wailing. It was traveling well in excess of the speed limit.

"*Shit!*" Paula screamed. "Shit! *Shit! SHIT!*"

"Someone else will be along eventually," said Crystal.

"It's so dark out here. They'll never see us. The car's too far off the road. We'd have to damn near stand in the middle of the highway to attract attention, and that's *if* anyone happens to drive by," said Paula, kicking dust clouds from the dirt at the side of the road.

Crystal thought of the little girl, stooping over to retrieve her stuffed animal. Had it been to attract Crystal's attention? For what?

"Let's get back in the car," said Crystal. "You're right. It's too dark out here. Without a flare or something, I'm afraid we'll get nailed by some drunk if we stay too close to the road."

"We're just going to give up and sleep there?"

"Unless you have a better plan," said Crystal. "We'll be more visible in the morning. There should be more traffic, too. I'm too tired to do anything else right now."

"Fine," said Paula. "You go ahead. I'm going to sit out here awhile and see if that sheriff comes back this way."

Crystal crawled back through the corn and got into the passenger seat of the car. Paula waited near the road for over an hour, but not another car passed. Certainly not the police car. It was far busier elsewhere.

175

III

Suze's eyes shone black and furious, spittle flying from her mouth as she barked the words out. *"You stupid shit!"*

Chad was confused. Suze had snapped the neck of a woman back in Pridemore and was now presuming to tell him what havoc he could and could not wreak? Unacceptable. "Don't call me that," he said, his voice a low snarl.

Suze erupted into tears, horrible wracking sobs which seemed to be wrenching her insides apart. She let go of the steering wheel and clutched at her temples while the car veered dangerously to the right. Her foot was still firmly planted on the gas pedal.

"Stop it, Suze," Chad whispered into her ear as he took the wheel of the car. "You're going to kill us if you don't stop it."

"You've already ruined everything!" she wailed.

"If you can't drive this car, pull over and let me do it," said Chad, his voice steady. "When we left Pridemore, you told me the only thing that was going to get us caught was my driving. You are all over the goddamned road. One of two things is going to happen. You're either going to kill us or get us caught. You told me to trust you, and I did. Now it's your turn to trust me. Pull over."

Suze's eyes cleared for a moment, examining Chad's earnest features. He had dreamed of the little girl, even if it had been crude and relatively uninformative. Maybe he *did* know what he was talking about. She eased her foot off the gas pedal slowly while Chad guided the steering wheel to the berm. As the car slowed, Chad spotted a dirt road which stretched off to the right.

"We're going to stop just a little ways down that road," he whispered. "Nice and easy. Everything's okay, babe. But we don't want to be sitting out in the open on the highway, you understand?"

Suze nodded, sniffling and dabbing at her nose. Her head pounded savagely, her pulse magnified in her temples. She could barely keep her eyes squinted open. Even the light from the dashboard was blindingly painful. Her stomach lurched and threatened to upset. The rocking motion of the car wasn't helping.

Once they had clumsily negotiated the turn and come to a stop, Chad jerked the gearshift into park and ripped the keys from the ignition. He brought his open hand up and slapped Suze sharply, snapping her head back from the blow. A guttural sound rose from within her, and she clawed at the soft flesh near Chad's throat. He slapped her again, and she hissed, raking her fingernails across his cheek.

Then she had the car door open, struggling to break free of Chad's grasp. He clamped one hand around her wrist, but she flailed like a slippery eel, using her free hand to strike Chad whenever the opportunity presented itself. She finally balled her hand into a fist and drove it down between Chad's legs. He grunted with surprise and relaxed his grip on Suze's wrist. She wrenched herself free and promptly fell out of the car and into the dirt. She was oblivious to the mewling noises that spilled from her throat, blinded by the headache which threatened to pull her into unconsciousness.

Chad was on top of her before she knew it, pinning her to the ground with his body, striking her repeatedly on the face. He was yelling at her, but she couldn't hear the words that were pouring out. Her ears were filled with the sounds of the ocean, louder than any beach on Earth. The abuse that Chad was piling on her was lost within the migraine. He was more annoying than anything else.

Chad's fury began to subside as his vision cleared, and he saw that Suze wasn't fighting anymore. She wasn't even trying to protect herself. Twin ribbons of blood trickled from her nose and mouth. Her left eye was already beginning to swell. Her mouth hung open and silent sobs hung frozen in her throat. He could feel her chest rising and falling below him, her breasts pressing against the fabric of her t-shirt. He traced lines down the length of her neck with his index fingers, continuing down until they rested on her erect nipples. He twisted them savagely, freeing the sounds trapped in Suze's voice box.

"Stop it," she cried, but she bucked her hips, grinding her pelvis against his swelling crotch.

He looked down at her and grinned, sliding his hands down her sides and around her buttocks. She wore gray, cotton sweatpants, and Chad could tell she wasn't wearing any underwear beneath. She shivered and cried, making a half-hearted attempt to push Chad away, but he had already relaxed the elastic tie, pulling her pants down around her ankles. Suze kept her eyes closed, avoiding the moonlight which caused searing agony in her temples. She gasped uncontrollably as Chad shoved three fingers roughly inside of her, stroking and teasing, brutal and sensual. She spread her legs further and rocked on her hips, her back arching and relaxing in cadence with his rough strokes. Soon, he had replaced his fingers with his throbbing penis, grunting and groaning like an animal as he abraded her bare buttocks on the pebbles littering the dirt below. They were completely exposed to anyone driving past, but the dirt road was even less traveled than the narrow highway from which they had come.

When it was over, Suze pushed Chad off of her and pulled her sweatpants back up, her breathing ragged and harsh. Her hands traveled back up to massage her temples, which still throbbed with white hot pain.

Chad studied her in the moonlight. The agony in her eyes was evident, but it didn't seem to be caused by anything he had done to her. He propped himself up on one elbow.

"What's the matter with you?" he asked.

Suze grimaced. "I saw one of the cups."

"The teacups?"

"Yes, the goddamn teacups," spat Suze. "That's what I was trying to tell you when you decided to blow the whole fucking place up. The other truck—the one that was parked in front of the gas truck—I saw a cup by the driver's door."

"So?"

"Goddamn, you're an idiot," said Suze, squinting her eyes to look at him. "Do you not remember a thing we talk about? I told you what happens if I don't follow directions. There was something I was supposed to see in that truck, but you blew it up before I got a chance to look. When I don't follow directions, I get migraines. Worse than that, I lose the thread."

"So, we'll find it again," said Chad, fastening the fly of his jeans.

"It's not that easy," said Suze. "Last time, I lost it for three whole months. Whatever's up with this little girl ain't gonna wait three whole months. We were supposed to do something very big, and I think you've fucked us over royally. *Goddamn* my head hurts." She doubled over and put her head between her knees.

"So, I'll fix it," said Chad. "If I wrecked it, I'll fix it."

"You're such a fucking idiot," said Suze from between her knees.

"You know," said Chad, "I've had about enough of that. You need to start trusting my instincts, too. I'm not stupid."

Suze lifted her head to look at him. It was useless. He was stubborn, compulsive, and young. He may not be stupid, but the combination of the other three made him dangerous. In essence, he was a tool, designed for a purpose that Suze didn't fully understand, although she did not question it. He was a proud man-boy, and it wasn't furthering their undisclosed cause for her to continually bash his ego.

"I'm sorry," she said, managing a faint smile. "It's the headache. I need something for it."

"We'll get you something right away, babe," said Chad, helping her to her feet. He carefully dusted the debris from her backside, just as a considerate lover might do. He was a different person from the infuriated beast who had beaten her senseless moments ago. "Just get in the car and let me do the thinking for a while."

"I don't know if we're safe anymore," said Suze. "It scares the hell out of me."

"It does me a little, too," Chad said, easing her into the passenger seat of the car and reclining it as far back as it would go. "I'm going to find us a place to stay tonight and get you some good medicine."

"The first night's always the worst," Suze said, covering her eyes with her palms. "I'll feel the headache until I find the thread again, but the first night's always the worst."

Chad went around to the driver's side and got behind the wheel. He started the car and rejoined Route 18, driving west. "You try and sleep, Suzy-Q."

She nodded and closed her eyes.

178

Chad didn't for a second doubt his own instincts. He had murdered his mother and framed his father, all without drawing even the slightest suspicion from Pridemore's finest. He knew that he was too important on a grand scale to be hampered in any serious way this early into his career. What he had accomplished to date had only whetted his appetite for bigger and better things.

The little girl and the teacups. Who could she be? Suze had said that they would kill her if they ever found her, and Chad found the proposition interesting. To still a young life seemed cruel beyond comprehension, and its appeal was not lost on him. He wondered if young flesh would yield to a knife more easily than that of an adult.

Chad found a Howard Johnson's in Fort Wayne and carried a sleeping Suze into the tidy room. She had fallen into a fitful sleep and was now reluctant to let go of it. She babbled gibberish while Chad tried to give her medication. He had stopped at an all-night grocer to buy Excedrin Migraine and a bottle of sleeping pills. He figured it would be best to keep Suze unconscious during the worst of her headache. It seemed ridiculous that he was trying to wake her in order to feed her sleeping pills, and eventually he gave up, allowing Suze to slump back against the pillows on one of the room's two double beds. He hadn't turned any of the lights on because he knew that they hurt her eyes.

The drive north had been uneventful. Where Chad had been paranoid about police pursuit when they had fled Pridemore, he was now relaxed and confident. He hadn't hesitated to present his very own driver's license to the clerk at the front counter, where he paid in cash for the room.

He sat in the dark and watched Suze as she struggled her way back to unconsciousness, occasionally moaning and whimpering. Her face looked like hell where he had hit her. He was glad that no one had seen him carry her into the room. There would've been questions. But as with everything else so far, gratuitous fortune had shone Chad's way. The terraced passageway that ran along the exterior of the building was quiet and empty. Suze now looked small and vulnerable, her arms hugging her face and covering her eyes. It would be so easy to kill her, cut her from sternum to pelvis, spread her insides around the room like a deranged child's finger painting.

Again, he couldn't. He knew that whatever purpose Suze served, it wasn't over yet. He sensed that they would find this elusive 'thread' again, and at the end of it would be the most delicious opportunity of all—the chance to kill the doe-eyed little girl.

◦————◦————◦

Chad sat at a small, round plastic table. It was pink and white, and his legs were too tall to fit under it, so he folded them awkwardly beside his squat pink plastic chair. There were four place settings, brightly colored plastic plates with shimmering eggs, sunny side up, twin strips of bacon, and golden-brown toast. Of course, the food was plastic too, frozen in a state of mass-produced perfection. Teacups rested beside each setting, resting on coasters made of newspaper. To his right, a green bear with a missing eye slumped against the table, stuffing erupting from the seam at its rear end. An oversized Raggedy Ann sat on his left, her hair restyled by a child's overzealous scissors. Straight ahead was the girl.

She smiled coyly and batted her innocent eyelashes at him. Dark curls surrounded her face, making it seem even smaller than it really was, and her clear brown eyes stared at him as she lifted the teacup to her lips and took a sip of the make-believe beverage. She looked at Chad expectantly, waiting for him to follow suit.

His hand reached down and touched the teacup, its smooth surface cool to the touch. His eyes remained fixed on the girl as he brought the rim of the cup to his mouth. As he lowered it, he lunged across the table, reaching for the girl.

She was gone.

Chad looked around, realizing he was outdoors. Raggedy Ann smirked from her chair, and Chad plucked the doll up and ripped its lollypop head off of its shoulders.

Chad was in a large, grassy yard beside a white Colonial style farmhouse. Its black shutters had recently been painted, reflecting sunlight in the gloss of the new finish.

From a second-story window, Chad saw the little girl watching him. She showed no horror at the mutilation of her doll, which still hung limply in Chad's hands.

Chad stood from the small chair and crossed the yard to the porch, his eyes leaving the girl only when he could no longer keep her in view. He trotted up the concrete steps to the wide wooden porch. Large picture windows faced out, sashes raised and screens in place. Through a screen door, he could see the interior of the house, done in all that modern country crap. It looked like an advertisement for *Martha Stewart Living*. The front door stood wide open behind it, as if beckoning him to enter. The little girl was just upstairs...

A hand on his elbow.

Chad turned to see Suze standing behind him. He could see over her shoulder that everything had changed. Night had fallen. The porch on which they stood

180

had narrowed and aged. The siding on the house was blanched and missing in a few places. A wooden porch swing was suspended on rust-infested chain, daring anyone to take a ride. The picture windows were gone, replaced by small squares which had been painted shut for decades.

"I told you," whispered Suze.

Chad looked at her curiously, unsure of her meaning. Suze had already stepped around him and approached one of the small windows. She peered inside and then nodded her head, tossing Chad a knowing look. He eased up behind her and peered inside.

The room was nearly empty. No lights burned within, just a small fire in the fireplace. A lone female figure sat on the floor in front of it, her back to them. This was no little girl. She wore a gauzy sundress that showed the sensual curve of her shoulders. Golden hair trailed down her back, catching the firelight and sending it back out in brilliant shades of gold. As if she could sense their presence, she slowly turned her head in their direction. She didn't seem the least frightened. In fact, Chad was pretty sure she was smiling.

She *was* smiling. Chad's smile was involuntary. He had seen this woman every night since he had entered puberty.

Crystal Bright winked and blew him a kiss.

Chad sat bolt upright in his chair. Suze was still tossing and turning fitfully while dawn seeped through the slats of the window blind. As incredible as it seemed, Suze had been right. Crystal Bright *was* involved in all of this. It was now a matter of finding her.

He shook Suze gently by her shoulder and she groaned, pulling the pillow over her head. He shook her again, and she emerged from sleep, her face colorless and drawn, speckled with bruises and dried, crusty blood.

"What in the hell do you want?" she croaked.

"I had a dream."

"Well, good for fuckin' you," said Suze, trying to burrow back into the bed sheets.

"An important one," he said.

She turned a curious albeit grumpy eye in his direction. "How so?"

"I saw the little girl again."

Suze sat upright and immediately winced. Her head still pounded, only minutely less than it had the night before. She groped for the bottle of Excedrin on the nightstand and washed down four capsules with the half-glass of water that remained from the night before.

"Could you tell where she was?" she asked.

Chad shook his head. "I think I may have seen her house, but it could have been anywhere."

Suze scowled. "That's not really very helpful."

"Hey, it's better than nothing," said Chad, pulling the sheets away from Suze. "There was someone else in the dream."

"Who?"

"Crystal Bright."

Suze smiled with satisfaction. "I *told* you that I saw her. I can't for the life of me figure out why, but she wants to kill you. I'm sure of it."

"I don't know about that," said Chad. "Looked to me like she wanted to fuck me."

Suze laughed. "Get over yourself. Why would someone like Crystal Bright want someone like you?"

Chad's face twisted with the sting of her words. "You think that only some average slut like you would have me?"

"I didn't mean it that way," said Suze. "I'm sorry. What I meant was, I can't figure out how our paths would ever cross Crystal Bright's. I can hardly see her slumming it. I know she's not on that television show anymore, but I would imagine she's still in California. Do you think we're supposed to go to California?"

Chad shook his head. "That's not the direction we were going the last time you saw one of those teacups."

"Yeah, but maybe they were only leading us to that gas station. Maybe I was supposed to find something in that truck and then I would understand why we were supposed to go to California."

Again, Chad shook his head. "I don't think so. You didn't see one of those teacups before we pulled into the parking lot, you saw it after we had come out, after that truck had arrived. Unless you're willing to accept divination by bladder as a new special skill—"

Suze thought about it and realized that Chad just may be right. "Did you see any teacups in the dream?"

"What's with all the teacups?" asked Chad.

"I have no idea. Did you see any?"

Chad nodded. "Four of them, at the little girl's play table."

"Just sitting there?"

"Uh-huh."

"Were they positioned like they were pointing at something?"

"Huh-unh. They were just sitting there by each place setting. I think you're trying to read too much into the teacups," said Chad.

Suze shook her head. "For me, they've always acted like pointers. I wish you'd paid more attention to them. I'll bet there's more to them."

Chad reflected on the dream. They had been the only real utensils on the child's small table. He tried to picture them in his mind, recall if the handles had perhaps been pointing to some clue on the landscape's periphery. If he recalled correctly, they had pointed to each other in a perpetual loop, positioned in the center of coasters made from newspapers.

Newspapers.

Chad closed his eyes and willed himself into the dream again, staring down at the arrangement on the table. The coaster closest to him bore the fragment of the paper's title page.

GAN GA

What the hell did *that* mean? Chad made a mental note and began collecting their scant possessions. They checked out and piled back into the Volvo, retracing the previous night's journey. They headed south on Route 1 toward Route 18. Chad was eager to see what the detonated service station looked like by the light of day.

IV

A sheriff's car squealed to a stop at the edge of the blazing inferno. Luke was oblivious, still on his hands and knees in the dirt across the blacktop, just outside the cornfield, staring at the small glossy photo in his hand. Virginia—Little Tater—Parnell stared back at him with dark, innocent eyes. Her mop of curly brown hair surrounded her head, making it seem larger than it actually was. She smiled impishly, unaware that her father had died this evening.

Luke closed his eyes tightly, feeling hot tears roll down his cheeks. He gasped and jumped when the police officer grabbed him by the elbow.

"What happened here?" he barked. He was a short, round man in his mid-fifties. His skin was cracked and leathery from years of overexposure to sun. Now it creased into deep furrows that conveyed agitation and urgency.

Luke opened his mouth and choked violently. Thick black smoke hung in the air, pushing the breathable stuff out of range.

The officer left Luke for a moment and walked halfway across the street, pacing right, then left. "Loretta!" he wailed repeatedly. When he returned to Luke, his face was flushed, and his own eyes were leaking salty tears. He was literally shaking with rage and helplessness.

"Where is everybody? *What in the hell happened here?*" he demanded.

Luke gasped for fresh air and managed to say, "They blew it up, oh *God!* They blew it up."

"Who did?" asked the officer, squatting down and getting within inches of Luke's face.

"I-I-I don't know who they were," said Luke. His coughing jag renewed, and he spat out a glob of tarry black mucous. "Red car. Went that way." He pointed west on Route 18. There were no other cars in sight, not from either direction.

"You stay right here," said the officer, knees popping as he rose. He crossed the blacktop to his patrol car and reached in through the driver's window. He pulled the transmitter for his radio out and began talking with his dispatcher. The fire roared angrily, and he was too far away for Luke to hear his words, but his face was flushed and contorted with grief.

The air was getting easier to breathe, and Luke managed to rise to his feet, still stooped at the waist, his hands on his knees. He realized he still held the photo of Bert's daughter between his fingers. He stood and slid the photo into his pocket. How could someone do a thing like this? Bert had needed to take a lousy fucking shit, that's all. Luke realized that the police officer had been crying out a name. Loretta. Maybe she had been his wife or sister or daughter. Luke was certain from the man's reaction that she, too, must be dead.

A cool breeze cut through the heavy air, tracing a line from the small of Luke's back to his scalp, causing his hair to prickle. He looked toward the officer who was sending and receiving instructions through his radio. The man's glare was pure hatred, and Luke was locked in it, feeling the accusation from clear across the street.

He thinks I'm responsible, thought Luke. It seemed absurd. Luke had never been in trouble any more serious than that of a misguided teenager. Paulie had taught him proper values since. He straightened his back and looked away from the officer's iron countenance, realizing he looked guilty even if he wasn't.

He's gonna haul your ass in, boy.

The words were Paulie's, floating through Luke's mind. He knew they were true. This pot-bellied lawman wanted swift revenge; he didn't appear preoccupied with finding the truth of the matter. Luke knew this as certainly as he knew that Bert's daughter had been the girl in his nightmare, running from something, terrified and screaming.

Go.

Luke felt helpless as his future was being decided out of earshot. He knew how the wheels of justice worked in rural areas, and he was scared for his own safety. The officer was twiddling with the butt of his gun, unfastening, and refastening the leather strap which held it in its holster, his eyes burning holes through Luke.

The little girl ain't gonna wait for the wheels of justice to turn.

Something inside the blazing food mart reached its point of endurance. Pressurized contents of unknown origin screamed shrilly before sending a fresh shower of sparks straight up into the sky. The officer jerked and dropped his mouthpiece, turning involuntarily to see the unexpected firework. When he stooped to pick up his CB mike, Luke ran.

He plunged headlong into the depths of the cornfield, running as if from the devil himself. Luke knew that there was no turning back. The moment he fled, he had sent the clear impression that he knew more about the fire than he had indicated. Still, the officer's eyes had glistened with contempt, having tried and convicted Luke before hearing more than a couple of sentences. Stay? Run? Neither option held much appeal.

The policeman's angry voice carried on the wind, his words unintelligible, but his intent crystal clear. Luke forced his way deeper into the corn, relying on his youth and fitness against the other man's age and girth. He hoped he was doing the right thing.

As the corn whipped across, stinging his face, Luke realized how much this was like part of his nightmare, too. He had heard the thrasher, sensed the girl's danger, and yet had been unable to find her. The helplessness of the dream threatened his resolve, but his legs continued to pump, pushing deeper and deeper into the field.

Deputy Sheriff David McElroy threw his hat into the dirt and kicked the cruiser's rear tire until his toe was numb.

"Goddamn it!" he shrieked. His puffy cheeks were crimson, his brow drenched in perspiration. His heart had been blown apart just as surely as the concrete convenience store. Loretta McElroy had taken this job eight months ago to assert her independence and earn mad cash. David had never wanted her to work the late shift, knowing she would be alone and susceptible to any nutball that drove down the highway. *When Loretta makes her mind up—*

When Loretta made *her mind up.*

David didn't know how he would tell their daughter. He didn't know how he would tell their friends. He didn't know how he would do anything anymore.

And now the goddamn suspect is gone.

David kicked the tire furiously with his other foot, his blood pressure soaring dangerously high. The bastard had been right across the street, staring at David like the cat who ate the canary. David had only looked away for a second. David hadn't seen any indication of which way he had gone. He obviously didn't run along the highway. It was a straight shot east to west, visible to the horizon in either direction. The man could have ducked back into the corn, but it seemed more likely that he would have crossed behind the burning building and—

Loretta is dead.

David McElroy dropped to his knees, his mouth forming a silent scream of anguish. He was helpless to do anything now. His wife was dead, and the bastard had gotten away.

185

For now.

———◆———

Luke's lungs burned as he continuously shifted directions, weaving diagonally from one cornfield to the next. His ears were filled with the sounds of his own heartbeat, silencing everything else around him. His peripheral vision was tinged with red. He had to stop soon.

He paused and knelt, listening for any sounds that might indicate a pursuit was in progress. He could hear nothing through the oceans swirling in his ears. There were no helicopters overhead, scanning the fields with spotlights, and Luke took that as a positive sign.

How had things gotten so far out of hand, and so very quickly? This was only Luke's second day out of Jasper, and he was now officially a wanted man. He had no idea what to do next. He knew that he had to sleep soon. He was exhausted and quite probably in shock. He had been pushing his body to the limits of its endurance, and he was beginning to feel unstable physically.

One thing for certain—he had to get to Borden, Ohio. Virginia Parnell needed protection as soon as possible. Luke intended to make sure that she got it.

The pressure in his ears receded as the muscles in his legs began to knot. He began walking again, moving in the same general direction as before.

He wished he had seen their faces. Luke felt sure that it was a man who had actually set the fire. He had no clue about the driver, only that he was ready to get the hell out of Dodge the moment the fuse had been lit. The car could have passed for any dark color by the light of the moon, but as it had zipped through the parking lot, the fluorescent tubes overhead had shown that it was burgundy. A square car—very, very square.

A Volvo. Of course. Luke was surprised it hadn't struck him earlier. He had occasionally worked on cars at Bud's Service in Jasper and was well informed with respect to automobile makes and models. Some cars he could identify by the sounds of their engines.

Suddenly the corn gave way, and Luke emerged on a narrow dirt lane which glowed phosphorescently in the silvery moonlight. The night was quiet, except for chirping crickets and other nocturnal creatures. Across the lane was a weather beaten and dilapidated wooden outbuilding with a rusting tin roof, standing sentry in front of an enclosed junkyard, encased behind tall wooden walls. Tire rims were strewn about the dirt at the side of the building, piled in teetering columns taller than Luke stood. Other discarded items littered the area with no semblance of order, save for the crude path to the gate of the junkyard's fence, wide enough for a single vehicle to pass through. The fence was too tall for Luke to see into the yard, but the hollowed-out corpses of ancient automobiles peeked over the walls randomly, as if to remind passersby that they were still there, waiting to be recycled by man or Mother Nature. The gate was secured by a padlock, and Luke heard the distant harrumph of the canine protector who lived within the walls. The outbuilding, no more than a one-room shanty, was dark, its sole window splintered and reinforced with plywood. At one time, there had been a door suspended on hinges at the entrance, but it was long gone, giving open access to anyone who wandered by.

Luke stepped inside, his hard-soled boots echoing hollowly against the walls. Moonlight spilled in around the window's plywood bandage, and Luke's eyes adjusted to the dismal light. The walls had accumulated calendars over the years, the common theme being cleavage. The only furniture in the room was a square card table with gritty, oxidized legs and four matching chairs covered in splitting green vinyl. A Styrofoam cooler leaned on its side against the wall, angled to let water run out and onto the wooden floor. Apparently, the junkman brought ice to work each day and used the cooler for a refrigerator.

Luke pulled one of the chairs back from the table, its legs screeching with an unnatural volume in the confined space. He plopped down in the chair and rested his elbows on the table, laying his forehead in his palms and massaging his head. From his position, he could see through the open doorway by simply raising his head, and he kept his ears attuned to the noises outside, ready to bolt if he heard anyone approaching.

Based on what Bert had told him, Luke must be relatively close to Borden, but he had never heard of the town, and had only a general idea of where in Ohio it was. He needed a roadmap. He needed transportation. He needed help.

He could acquire a roadmap at most gas stations. Transportation was going to be more problematic. Unlike when he had left Jasper, Luke knew it would be unwise to try and hitchhike from here. Every policeman from this and the neighboring counties would be looking for him. Even if he managed to find Borden and the farmhouse he knew belonged to the Parnells, he didn't know how he would approach them. It wasn't as if he could walk up to the front door and announce that little Virginia was in life-threatening danger just days after Bert had been blown to pieces in rural Indiana. The shock of it all would be too much for the family to absorb. Bert's wife, Greta, would probably phone the police once Luke had identified himself anyway, as he was now undoubtedly a suspect in the case.

Luke had never backed away from a challenge before. He had always prided himself on that. But this was more of a challenge than he knew how to handle. The consequences of his actions would have very serious repercussions for the little girl, therefore his participation in the unfolding drama was mandatory. He felt as if he had been drafted into a war that he knew nothing about, taking steps through a minefield and hoping to keep from blowing himself to kingdom come.

187

With his head still propped in his hands, his mind swirling with the magnitude of the last hour's events, Luke drifted off into a deep, dreamless sleep.

———◆———

It was the heat and humidity of the morning that brought Luke back to his senses. He jerked to his feet, surprised at how easily he had fallen asleep and how quickly the night had passed. If the policeman had stumbled across him during the night, Luke would have been a sitting duck. Luke glanced at his watch and realized that it was almost seven. The dog he had heard snuffling in the distance was now near the padlocked entrance to the junkyard, barking furiously and darting back and forth behind the closed gate. Luke couldn't see the animal at all, but pictured him as a black Rottweiler, the breed often used by Hollywood to elicit imagery of a hellhound.

The dog's keen ears had already picked up the sound which was only now registering with Luke. It was an engine, drawing steadily nearer.

Shit! thought Luke, scrambling out of the building and into the littered front yard of the place. The dog went wild at the sound of Luke's movement, throwing itself repeatedly against the wooden gate and causing it to pitch slightly forward with each strike. A dust cloud plumed on the right, near the horizon, tracing a line in the sky as the vehicle approached.

Luke hurried across the dirt lane and reentered the cornfield. The engine was loud, with pistons knocking and valves chattering audibly. Luke was fairly certain that the vehicle did not belong to the police. Under the cover of the corn, Luke watched an ancient Ford pickup jostle up the lane, rocking side to side and end to end on spent suspension. It groaned to a stop in front of the gray-walled shack, and an enormous man emerged from the driver's side. He wore faded bib overalls and no shirt, his flabby man-breasts and exposed sides darkened almost to the color of chocolate from the sun. The dog continued its angry barrage, its nails scraping on the wooden gate as it jumped against it time and again.

"Good Lord, Mook!" exclaimed the man, waddling lazily over to the fence. "What the hell's got in ya today?"

He was fumbling with his key ring, and Luke realized almost too late that the man was unfastening the padlock. The dog was anxious to have a piece of Luke and would be able to move through the corn much more freely than Luke could.

Luke felt like he was caught in an absurd loop. While the man continued to fumble with his keys, Luke plunged through the corn, putting as much distance as he could between himself and the junkyard.

"Hey!"

Luke heard the cry far in the distance, and he knew that the large man could hear him retreating, the cornstalks crunching under his feet. Luke wasn't afraid of dogs, but he had the good sense to steer clear of the ones with malicious temperaments. If he had to bet money, he knew that the beast inside the junkyard walls was a savage one, trained to protect the contents of the yard by whatever means necessary. Adrenaline coursed through his veins, pushing his tired muscles on.

Luke ran for fifteen minutes before he finally felt it was safe to slow his pace. He had expected the dog's vicious head to burst through the corn at any minute, its iron jaws snapping and spraying spittle, but he couldn't run any further. He paused to catch his breath, tuning his ears to the sounds around him. All he could hear was the sweet twitter of birds as they passed overhead and the whisper of the corn as it was coaxed by an unseen breeze. Luke was covered in perspiration, the humid air reluctant to cool him down. He had lost his sense of direction and now feared that he was too close to the food mart, where he might be intercepted and detained by the police. Indecision held him rooted to the spot, sure that any choice he made would be the wrong one.

Do *something*.

Luke wiped the sweat from his eyes and gazed at the sun, barely visible through the corn. He knew if he walked toward it, he would be heading toward Ohio, but as if they had minds of their own, his feet plotted a diagonal course westward. He pushed through row after row of the endless corn, trying to plot his next move.

His shin struck something solid, and he fell forward, yelping in pain. He landed face first on the shiny hood of a silver Honda which was embedded in the cornfield. Luke lifted his head and found himself staring through the windshield at two startled women, one blonde and one brunette, both of whom had been sleeping in the front seats of the car.

CHAPTER TEN

I

Lisa's heels clicked against the polished hospital corridor, and she felt rather than saw the appreciative glances which frequently found and lingered over her. Men and women alike, favorably assessing the new Lisa Mitchell. Most didn't know her, but those with whom she had worked did double-takes, and Lisa's self-confidence soared.

Helen was at the nurses' station, bifocals perched on the tip of her nose as she examined a clipboard. She smiled warmly as Lisa approached the desk.

"My, my," she said, scanning Lisa head to toe. "Don't you look lovely!"

Lisa could feel her cheeks warming. She had received more compliments on her appearance during this half-day than she had in the entirety of her existence on the planet.

"Thank you," she said.

"I assume you slept well, then," said Helen.

"Very," said Lisa, stretching lazily. "I was running my errands and thought I'd stop by to say hello."

Helen smiled. "That's very thoughtful of you, dear. Did you have a chance to call the telephone company?"

"Yes, I did," lied Lisa, smooth as spun silk. "It'll be a few days before they can come out."

"Oh, that's nonsense!" said Helen, reaching for her telephone. "A girl, just released from the hospital, without access to a telephone? I should think not!"

Lisa placed her hand on Helen's, keeping the receiver in its cradle. "It's not them, it's me," she said. "I'm going out of town for a few days, and we couldn't coordinate until after I get back."

"Out of town?"

Lisa nodded her head. "I had a job interview over in Borden before the accident. I called this morning, and the position hasn't been filled yet, so I rescheduled."

"Borden's only forty or so miles away," said Helen. "Why three days?"

"The old house is getting to me a little," said Lisa. "It seems so empty without Nanna Grace—"

"Or any furniture," said Helen before she had properly considered it, and regretted the words as she saw Lisa's face flush.

"It'll be delivered while I'm away," said Lisa, unable to hide a hint of defensiveness.

"Of course, dear, of course," said Helen. "I just meant that the house must seem *especially* empty without it."

"Anyway," continued Lisa. "I didn't want you to think I had disappeared, and since you wouldn't be able to phone, I was afraid you might waste a trip out to the house."

"I'm sure I would have done that very thing," said Helen. "I would've been afraid you were lying dead on the floor! I have to admit, I can be *such* a worrywart! Now what's this about a job?"

"At-home care for a shut-in," said Lisa, making it up as she went along. "Five days a week. The pay would be good."

"It sounds lovely, dear, and I wish you the best of luck. Did you say three days? What kind of interview lasts for three days?" Helen asked.

"They want to give me a test run, so to speak," said Lisa. "Since I haven't replaced my car yet, it would be easier for me to just stay. And, as I said, with Nanna Grace gone, it'll be nice to have a break from the house."

"Of course," said Helen. She pulled a small pink square of paper from a gummed pad and jotted a number down. "This is my phone. Call me when you're back in town. I'd love to do lunch and maybe sneak in some shopping." She winked conspiratorially.

Lisa took the note and tucked it into her pocketbook. "That sounds nice."

"Good luck!" Helen said with a wave as Lisa stepped away from the counter.

"Thanks," Lisa said with a smile. Good luck had already shone her way— Helen Martin wouldn't be dropping by for three whole, *glorious* days.

And why three days? She had no idea. It was the first thing that had popped into her mind, and she hadn't hesitated to say it out loud. It didn't really matter— she had gotten this far on intuition.

As she swung her hips from side to side, feeling the delicate material of the sundress slide against her flesh, she felt eyes watching her. She turned to look, and Leonard Barnes, the custodian who had always fascinated her, was standing just inside the stairwell to the lower level. His eyes were fixed on her, his expression unreadable. In all the time that Lisa had fantasized about him, he had never once looked at her. Now, here he was, but the expression was almost like— disgust. Lisa averted her eyes quickly and continued down the hallway and out into the street, feeling a little less full of herself than before.

⚬ ⎯⎯⎯◆⎯⎯⎯ ⚬

In blue jeans, a sleeveless white blouse and an oversized pair of yellow workman's gloves, Lisa helped Jack maneuver each piece of furniture out of the house and to the bed of his red Ford pickup. He had estimated three roundtrips, but it actually took four because of the oddly shaped joiner of the sectional.

Jack had been repellently chauvinistic at first, trying to offer advice on how to lift and bend, adding condescendingly to stop if anything got too heavy. As the afternoon went on, Lisa noticed with interest the mottled flesh of Jack's face, the perspiration that coated his entire body, the way his lungs frequently strained for air between hauls. She felt wonderful, a healthy burn coursing through her rejuvenated muscle tissue. Even her injured ribs felt normal. Her hair was damp, sure, but more from the heat and humidity of the sun than the physical exertion. Jack Lovell was in incredibly poor shape.

Lisa also noticed that Jack's eyes never strayed far, absorbing every detail of her with hunger. He watched her bend and lift, and the yearning in his eyes was nearly palpable, drying out his mouth and causing him to frequently lick his lips. Lisa knew that he wanted her desperately, even though she had never experienced such an unspoken feeling before. She had always faded into the background, invisible to men, but this one wanted her, whether he was married or not. He found reasons to brush up against her, lingering only a fraction of an instant longer than necessary. The effect was not lost on Lisa, and she found Jack Lovell interesting. He was unremarkable, but interesting. His overt hunger, his obvious desire—

Lisa was still a virgin.

She wasn't ignorant to the facts of life—it would be difficult to work in a hospital and not have some rudimentary knowledge—but she had never been moved by hormones to explore her sexuality. As she watched Jack huff and puff around, lifting, lugging, and leering, she felt the first curious heat in her loins, curiosity in capital letters, making her lean into him when he brushed against her, strategically placing herself where he would be required to make physical contact with her. His level of excitement was evident in the way that he walked.

When the last of the furniture was in place, Lisa took Jack to her bed. Her curiosity was overwhelming by then, not only encouraging but *requiring* that she investigate this basic physical act which was essential to human procreation. It was sloppy, awkward, and generally uncomfortable. Jack was overeager and clumsy, and Lisa was completely inexperienced—although she still suspected she was somehow better than him. He had been conditioned by his wife to make love like a machine, reliable but boring. When Lisa had bitten his shoulder, he actually yelped and looked a little frightened.

When it was over, Jack had rolled off to the side, his labored breathing reminding Lisa of how he had panted while they moved furniture. She had heard that the first time was painful to many women, but she had felt neither pain nor pleasure—Jack had been too small and quick for that. The whole experience frankly left Lisa wondering what all the fuss was about.

"You okay?" he asked, turning on his side and propping his head up on his hand.

"*Mmm-hmm*," said Lisa. "A little thirsty, though. How 'bout you?"

"Parched," he said, starting to toss the covers aside. "I'll go. What do you want?"

Lisa pulled him back to her and kissed him lightly. "Have to pee, too. I'll go. There's some iced tea in the fridge. Is that okay?"

"Beer would be better."

"Sorry."

"Iced tea it'll be, then," he said, stretching out on his back and folding his hands behind his head on the pillow.

Lisa slipped a long t-shirt over her head and padded across the hardwood floors on her bare feet. She stepped out into the hallway and pulled the bedroom door shut behind her. When they had come upstairs, daylight still spilled through the windows of the living room, but somewhere along the way, the sun had set, and the house was still and dark, shadows swallowing everything.

She passed the stairwell and continued into Nanna Grace's old bedroom. She could imagine the horror in the old woman's eyes, watching down from heaven and seeing Lisa commit adultery beneath the very roof under which she had been raised. There was a certain satisfaction in that.

The room was odd in its emptiness. Nanna Grace hadn't been much for rearranging furniture, and the room had been decorated in exactly the same fashion for as long as Lisa could remember. Now, with all of the furniture gone, it seemed much larger than before. Lisa walked around it in a slow circle, marveling at the emptiness. Nanna Grace was *gone*.

Lisa crossed to the small bathroom and stood at the small square mirror over the sink. Nanna kept her medications in the vanity, and Lisa hadn't yet emptied it out. She pulled the mirror by its lower corner, exposing the cabinet behind it. So many prescriptions...

The one in which Lisa was interested was an over-the-counter medication that Nanna Grace had used whenever she had been unable to find sleep because her joints ached, or her head whispered. Sominex Pain Relief. Nanna had always taken two on those occasions, so Lisa figured five should meet her requirements. She slipped them from the package and carried them in her palm, back through Nanna's empty room and out into the dark hallway. She turned left and descended the stairs into the gloom below, boards squeaking in protest the whole way. With age, a house attains its own audible voice, contributing comments as comfortable as a warm blanket. Lisa didn't fear the darkness of the waiting first floor. It belonged to her, and she was in complete control of it. There would be no more intruders like Chris Baylock, and even if there were, she would deal with them in the same manner. Swiftly.

When Lisa reached the foot of the stairs, she paused, her nose catching something faint but pungent and pervasive, rising like foul sewer gasses from the basement below. Chris Baylock needed to *go*.

She retrieved a pair of plastic drinking cups from the cupboard and went to the refrigerator from which she pulled a large glass pitcher of lemon-sweetened tea. She crushed the sleeping tablets between two spoons and dropped the powdery substance into the bottom of one of the cups. Afterward, she added ice cubes to both glasses, followed by the tea. With one of the spoons, she stirred a little extra sugar into the tainted brew, hoping to offset the bitterness of the medication.

Upstairs, Jack was propped up against his pillows, his clammy, shapeless chest looking sunken in the moonlight which peeked through the window. Lisa lowered her head impishly and smiled, offering the drugged tea to Jack. He took it without hesitation and put it to his lips, taking a long, deep drink. When he righted his head, he wiped the moisture from his lips and emitted a satisfied, "Ah!"

"You like?" asked Lisa, sitting on the edge of the bed.

"Me like," Jack said. "When can I see you again?"

The question threw Lisa. She hadn't even considered that Jack might want to see her again. After all, he was like a laboratory animal to her, borrowed for the sake of experimentation. Experiment over. The end. She looked into his eyes and smiled.

"You're married," she said.

"I don't have to be."

Lisa stood up and walked to the corner of the room, her hands on her hips, her back to the bed. "You need to slow down, Jackie-boy. This was fun, okay? But you can't decide to change your entire life after one night."

"It hasn't just been this one night," said Jack. "I haven't been happy with Janice for a long time now."

Good God, thought Lisa exasperatedly. She didn't have time to go into all this now. *Just drink the damn tea!*

And he did, as he continued to unburden his troubles on an unfeeling, unlistening audience. Lisa felt contempt for the man rising in her like bile, and she wanted to be away from him. Besides, it seemed that she could smell Chris Baylock wafting through the air. How could Jack not *smell* it?

After she had comfortably gotten her composure in order, Lisa turned and smiled. "Let's talk about it in the morning, okay? I'm tired, and you look tired, too."

Jack yawned. "We worked like dogs today. We did something else like dogs, too." He patted the bed beside him, and Lisa got back under the covers. His hands began to clumsily roam, but Lisa stopped them, pulling them close to her face.

"Just hold me," she whispered, and tucked up against him.

He nodded and fell in behind, curving his legs behind hers. In only minutes, he was fast asleep.

Chris's body was stiff and unyielding, and Lisa was pretty certain that she broke a bone or two of his while hauling him up the stairs. She had secured plastic trash bags over the mess that was his head, trying to avoid having to clean up again. Jack was snoring soundly by the time that Lisa had gotten up to fish the truck keys from his jeans pockets. He should never know that she was gone.

Lisa had little difficulty hoisting the plastic-wrapped package into the bed of the truck. Soon, she would be rid of this stinking pile of human waste. She started the truck and checked the clock on the dashboard. It was eleven forty-five. Her neighbors had retired for the evening, and the street was clear when she eased the truck out onto the pavement. She turned left and headed for Culvert Lane, which stretched lazily out into the countryside to the east of Morgan. McMillan Reservoir ran for three long miles along it, an openmouthed body of water that was fed by various tributaries and dammed for the use of the local population. A large section had been converted into a manmade beach, complete with sandy shores that covered its concrete basin. Fishing was allowed in another section and boating in another. The roadway crossed the dam, and the reservoir's deepest waters were visible from an observation deck which sat on its far side. A small picnic area was nestled on the tidy lawn beside the deck, and Lisa parked the truck along the curb beside it. At this time of evening, Lisa had the whole park to herself. Looking in the direction from which she had come, the road curved openly over the dam, its dark emptiness stretching for miles. Ahead, there was less visibility, but more than enough for Lisa to accomplish her purpose.

Quickly, Lisa exited the truck and went around to the tailgate. Chris Baylock's body looked like an obscenely large fish wrapped in butcher's paper. Lisa grabbed what she supposed was his ankle and roughly pulled the body toward her. She fumbled to get a grip around his shoulders and finally managed to lift him into her arms. He seemed weightless, as if his soul had also contained the majority of his mass. Lisa walked steadily forward, never off-balance from the extra load, looking eerily graceful as she carried her kill.

At the edge of the observation deck, Lisa lifted and pushed, sending Chris Baylock's body arcing toward the deep waters below. As his cocooned form splashed into the black depths, Lisa had the most peculiar sensation, like icicles melting down her neck, causing her skin to stand as gooseflesh.

She turned and examined the empty lot behind her. It was as if someone was watching her. She could feel eyes, hidden in some deep shadow, peering across the empty park, recording every detail of her activities. She took a few steps away from the observation deck, turning right then left, trying to pinpoint the source of her discomfort.

195

Darin Miller

The night was quiet, save for the gentle susurration of nocturnal creatures. The single streetlamp which stood at the corner of the park cast its paltry light in a narrow circle, obscuring more than it revealed.

"Hello?" called Lisa, taking a few more steps away from the deck. She strained her ears, listening for the crunch of breaking twigs or the rustle of shrubbery. Overhead, an owl hooted, startling Lisa into a gasp. She looked up and spotted the monstrous thing, perched on a tree branch, its enormous round eyes fixed on her.

A bird, she thought, goosebumps like Braille rippling across her bare flesh. Its eyes bore through her, its head cocking from one side to the other. Lisa stooped to the ground and retrieved a handful of quarter-sized rocks. One by one, she flung them at the owl, making contact with the fourth one. The bird ruffled its feathers angrily and cried in protest, then spread its wings and flew downward, directly toward Lisa. Her eyes widened as the bird approached, taking in its enormous size and wingspan. Instinctively, she covered her head and ducked, feeling the sharp talons of the birds claws as they grazed against her head.

Then the bird was gone, its obnoxious voice fading as it hunted a new place to roost.

"Shit," said Lisa aloud, as she let the rocks fall from her hand. She giggled and trotted back over to the observation deck. She peered over the railing and was satisfied that Chris Baylock was not bobbing like a buoy in the placid body of water. She saw no trace of him, not even the gentlest ripple in the surface.

She returned to the truck and climbed behind the wheel. She backed the tail end into the grassy picnic area and brought the nose around to face the direction from which she had come. The dashboard clock showed it was one o'clock. Good. Plenty of time to get home and slip back into bed.

No witnesses but an owl, thought Lisa satisfactorily as she accelerated down the road.

⸺⸺◆⸺⸺

As the twin red squares of the truck's taillights disappeared in the bend of the road, a tall, dark figure stepped out from where it had been hiding behind a row of shrubbery. Leonard Barnes' legs were stiff and tingling, asleep from being frozen in his squatted position for so long. In his sixty-two years on this planet, he had never seen anything so disturbing. As a young boy, his mother had told him stories of evil—men who lured innocent children to their doom and women who used their bodies in trade for men's souls. *Fairy tales, all of it!* he had thought. But when he had seen Lisa Mitchell in the hospital, that sweet young wisp of a girl who had always been so shy, so meek—when he saw her, he knew that the fingers of Satan had found a way to fold around her heart, guiding her with

196

catastrophic purpose. Leonard did not know what it was that the girl had tossed into the reservoir, but the shape had been vaguely human.

Yes. An evil had been unleashed in Morgan, and Leonard Barnes knew her name—and just where to find her.

II

The sound, metallic and heavy, combined with the sudden backward motion of the car lurched both Crystal and Paula into consciousness. Splayed across the hood was a wild-eyed man, his face covered in soot and grime, his clothes filthy, his sandy hair standing straight off his head—and he was staring at them, first Crystal, then Paula.

"What the fuck?" Crystal's eyes were still adjusting to the daylight.

"Oh, my GOD!" shrieked Paula, locking her door and fumbling across Crystal to lock hers. "Oh, *MY GOD! IS THE HATCHBACK LOCKED?*" She was hysterical, drawing her legs up underneath herself, straining to see if the toggle of the hatchback was in the correct position.

Crystal grabbed Paula's arm and hauled her back into the driver's seat. She shook her sharply until Paula's gaze froze on hers. "Stop it," she said. "Look." She turned Paula's face toward the windshield.

The man who had fallen across the hood had righted himself and stepped back to a comfortable distance. He raked his fingers through his hair, and now held a hand up as if in peace. He was young with an honest face underneath all of the dirt and muck.

"It's just some guy," said Crystal. "We scared him more than he scared us. *Look.*"

"But what's he *doing* here?" asked Paula.

"Let's ask," said Crystal, rolling down her window before Paula could protest. "Hey!"

"Hey!" he said, waving nervously.

"What're you doing out here, farm boy?" Crystal asked.

Luke's cheeks burned red at her condescension. "I could ask you the same," he shot back.

"I would think that's pretty obvious," she said. "We had a little accident. You think you could take us back to your farm or wherever and help us get out of here?"

"I'm not from around here," said Luke. "I had a little accident myself."

Crystal stared at the man curiously. Surely, he recognized her from television. He was certainly in the right demographic. But there was no recognition whatsoever in his eyes. Crystal jerked the side view mirror up to examine her reflection. Not great, but not bad. Not *unrecognizable*.

"Do you have any idea where we are?" asked Luke.

"Not really," said Crystal. "I got lost right before we wrecked."

"I'm surprised the police didn't stop," said Luke.

"What police?" asked Crystal. "You mean that sheriff last night? How'd you know about that?"

Luke hesitated. He had said more than he meant to. His natural progression of thought left him wondering how these girls could have been sitting here for very long without being observed. Surely the police were combing the surrounding fields for him, led by the officer who had seen him at the ruined service station.

His smile returned. "I heard it myself. Sometime last night. I slept in my car, too."

"Looks like you slept under the hood," mumbled Paula, her eyes still narrowed with suspicion.

"I've been walking a long time," said Luke. "Thought I'd take a shortcut through this field, but I've gotten all turned around."

Crystal regarded him warily. "I'm Crystal. This is Paula."

"Luke Leighton," he said, smiling and nodding his head. "So, what's wrong with your car?"

Crystal reached down and pulled the hood release. "We blew a radiator hose," she said, opening the door and wading out into the corn to meet Luke at the front of the car. She pointed to the gashed upper hose, its split running along the hose instead of across it, where it might have been cut back and reattached. It would need to be replaced.

"I think I might know where we can get one," said Luke.

It took some coaxing to get Paula out into the corn, but she eventually decided that she would rather take her chances with Luke and Crystal than stay behind in the car. They waded through, Luke trying his best to retrace his path to the junkyard. After twenty minutes, they emerged on the dirt lane, but the junkyard was nowhere to be seen.

"Great," said Crystal. "I thought you said you knew where we were going."

"I must've got a little mixed up," said Luke quietly.

"I'll say," said Crystal, pacing the quiet lane and kicking at the dirt with the toes of her shoes. "So, what now?"

Luke was frustrated. He didn't have to help them at all. It was taking time away from his own agenda—but all that was bullshit. He saw this as a golden opportunity, a way to get back on the road and headed toward Borden. Surely, they wouldn't refuse him a ride after he had helped them, would they? The blonde was impatient and bitchy, though, and if it suited her mood, he was sure she would leave him standing on the side of the road in the pouring rain. The other one, the brunette, was terrified of him, and he found it disquieting. She had no reason to fear him, yet she paced along quiet as a mouse, as alert to every movement he made as she was to her own. It was as if she expected him to suddenly whirl around and grab her.

Off to the right and far in the distance, the deep whoop of a large dog carried through the air. Luke smiled and turned to Crystal, indicating in that direction. "This way."

"You sure this time?" she asked.

"You can stay here if you want," he said, turning and heading down the lane without waiting for a response.

Crystal and Paula exchanged a quick glance. "C'mon," said Crystal, trotting off after Luke. "Let's go."

Paula hesitated. She didn't like this man. She sensed that he had some sort of ulterior motive, some unexplained reason for stumbling upon them not from the road, but from the thick of the cornfield. He was like a nightmare man, mysterious and full of ominous intent. Why Crystal was trusting him so easily was beyond her. This man might mean to take them to the center of nowhere and rape them until he'd finally had enough, carving what was left of their bodies like Thanksgiving turkeys.

Stay alert, thought Paula. *You have to stay with Crystal. You're* supposed *to.*

◦ ——— ◦ ——— ◦

Finally, the ramshackle wooden outbuilding appeared on the horizon. The dog was barking furiously now, aware of the approaching strangers long before his master could ever get a glimpse. The old junkman stood in the open doorway of the shack, his overweight belly hanging like a beach ball suspended in bib overalls. He strained his eyes and craned his neck, his slack jaw hanging open stupidly. The dog, who had sounded so brutally ferocious, was a squat bulldog, its jowls dripping slobber with each punctuated report. It hovered near its master's ankles, its courage at its height while standing in his master's ample shadow.

"Quiaaat, Mook!" the man barked through toothless gums. He scratched his ass languidly and watched as Luke, Crystal, and Paula approached through the piles of rusting automotive waste. "Hep ya?"

"You got car parts here?" Luke asked, shielding his eyes from the sun.

"Reckon I do," said the white-haired man. "What kinda part ya lookin' fer?"

199

"A hose," said Luke. "For a Honda."

The old man laughed and wheezed through his sunken lips. "Can't say you're gonna find much in the way of in-ports," he said. "If'n you want, you can dig round, find what you can that might do ye." He indicated the gate to the enclosed portion of the yard, which now stood unlocked and open.

Hollowed out corpses of cars were stacked in leaning columns throughout the littered area. Bolts, screws, and other unidentifiable hardware were strewn about, oxidizing from exposure to the elements. Crystal looked at Luke expectantly, and he strode purposefully into the enclosed area. The two women followed, Paula's eyes fixed to her own feet. The junkman didn't budge from his position in the doorway, though he did scratch his sagging backside again.

Once inside the rickety wooden fencing, Crystal eased up beside Luke. "Why are you wasting time here?" she asked. "That old guy *said* he didn't have any parts for an import."

"We might find a hose from another car that will work," said Luke.

"How will you know?"

"I'll try to find several that are about the right size—um, can you—" Luke indicated for Crystal to move to her left, and he lifted the hood of a crumpled Ford Escort. "This is only going to be a patch job. The hose'll need to be replaced at your first chance."

The Ford had been stripped clean; only a few burned-looking wires dangled into the empty shell of the engine compartment. Luke dropped the hood back into place and moved on to the next vehicle. Twenty minutes later, he had handed five various sized hoses as well as several rust-coated clamps to Crystal.

"One of these should do it," he said. "Do you have any tools in the car?"

Crystal shook her head. "Nope. What kind of tools do you need?"

"A flathead screwdriver should do it. Maybe the old guy at the shack has one," he said.

Paula trod along sullenly, watching Luke cautiously. He caught her unflinching glare from the corners of his eyes, and he felt the distrust dancing behind her eyes.

They passed the black-and-tan bulldog, who was now sleeping blissfully in the sun, and entered the wooden shack. The old man looked surprised to see them, as if he had completely forgotten they were even there. Luke saw him slipping a smoke-colored flask into the side pocket of his overalls. Luke laid the hoses and clamps across the square card table at which he had slept the previous night.

"How much?" he asked.

The junkman's eyes cleared at the prospect of profit. "Fifteen dollars," he said.

"I could almost buy them new for that," said Luke.

"I reckon you need 'em purty bad if you're standin' here in the middle of God's asshole," grinned the man.

Luke sighed and looked at Crystal. She handed the man a twenty. Paula watched the transaction disinterestedly from the quiet darkness of the corner.

"Don't got no change," the junkman said.

"You got a flathead screwdriver?" asked Luke.

The junkman turned and scanned the floor, kicking little bits of debris around in the dust. He finally spotted what he was looking for and plucked an ancient, wood-handled screwdriver from a pile of parts tucked in the corner. He handed it to Luke with a ghoulish, toothless smirk. Wordlessly, he went out the front door, waddling past. He walked around the side of the building and cranked a long metal handle that was positioned along the back of the shed. Rusty looking water sprung from a spigot as he pumped, and he eased an opaque plastic container he had retrieved somewhere along the way underneath the flow. When it was full, he returned to the shed, a proud smile on his face.

"You busted a hose, you'll need this," he beamed and added, "On the house."

"Thanks," said Luke, taking the heavy container. "What's the closest town to here? We'll need to get that car looked at right away."

The old man scratched the underside of his bulbous belly and squirreled his face into fierce concentration. "Reckon the closest might be up ta Morgan," he said.

Paula dropped the springed contraption she had been toying with. The color seemed to run like hot wax from her head to her toes, pooling on the gray dirt floor underneath her. She glanced at the others and saw them all watching her intently. She managed a weak grin and lightly said, "Whoops!"

Crystal shot her a curious glance before turning around.

"I never heard of Morgan," said Luke. "Is it east or west?"

"Just a li'l north," said the man. "Maybe thirty miles."

"I don't remember seeing Morgan on the map," said Luke.

"It's jus' a small little shitburg," said the junkman. "Just right across the state line a bit and over into Indiana."

Luke stopped and cocked his head. "We're not in Indiana?"

The old man wheezed with laughter. "Boy, you *are* lost. This is Ohio. Has always been s'long as I know."

Luke guessed that he and Bert had been closer to the state line than he had originally guessed when they had stopped at that damned gas station. Either that, or he had walked farther than he thought while he was in the cornfield.

Crystal struggled to digest the information, realizing the absolute *absurdity* of it. Sure, she had gotten turned around, but she hadn't been anywhere *near* Ohio. She was certain of it. She had gone the wrong direction on Route 1 and had only been on Route 18 a short while when—she had seen the little girl squatted down in the road, her lovely round eyes shining innocence, her nearly black hair gleaming blue in the beam of the headlights. She shivered involuntarily and wondered if maybe she was having some weird sort of drug-induced hallucinations. She had no idea what combination of pills she had taken back in California when she had tried to take her own life. She just knew that she had taken them *all*. It didn't matter now. She was standing in some Godforsaken hellhole with two complete strangers. She felt like she was trapped in some low-budget film in which the script was being written one page at a time before filming.

Paula was strangely silent, watching the room from a distance within herself. Her eyes were like glassy mirrors, offering no insight to the things which ran through her dark mind. Luke and Crystal were too busy with their own thoughts to notice the strangling silence that had fallen over her. Paula's breathing was short and shallow, and her face was the color of cottage cheese. She no longer watched Luke, was no longer interested in what it was that he was doing. She had folded in upon herself, taken prisoner by some inner demon that scared her far more than Luke ever could.

"Nice doin' bidness with ya!" the old man called after them as they took their junk and stepped back out into the sunshine, still quiet and reflecting over their own private thoughts.

The junkman absently scratched his backside again as he watched the three of them stagger off like zombies, across the dirt road and into the cornfield, as if it were the most natural thing in the world.

———————✦———————

"Are you telling me that I'm crazy?" Crystal asked, stopping suddenly in the middle of the dense rows of corn.

Luke turned and looked at her, rolling his eyes. "I'm not saying that you're crazy. *Jeez!* I'm just saying that you're wrong."

Paula stood frozen behind Crystal, her eyes still unfocused from her surroundings. She followed them wordlessly, stopping when they did, starting when they did.

Crystal glared at him. "What makes you so goddamned sure that you're right? I'm telling you, we weren't anywhere close to the Ohio border when our car went into the cornfield."

"You also said that you got lost right before that," reminded Luke. "You were tired, it was late—you must've gone farther than you thought."

Crystal shook her head emphatically. "Balls!"

"What difference does it even make?" asked Luke. "Didn't you say you were on your way to Ohio? I am, too. And whaddaya know? We're here."

"It's just—" Crystal struggled for words and became exasperated in the process. "Oh, never mind."

Luke looked at her a moment longer, studying the rebellious set to her jaw, wondering why she was having so much difficulty with the possibility that she might have gotten more lost than she originally thought. Initially, he too had been surprised to learn that they had crossed into Ohio, but it certainly was conceivable that Ohio was where they were.

"You still back there, Paula?" Crystal called over her shoulder.

Silence.

Crystal turned around and almost ran into the girl. She had been following on Crystal's heels like a subservient little terrier. Crystal put her hands on the girl's shoulders and shook her gently. "Hey!" she called.

Paula's eyes shifted into focus, and a quick inhalation whistled into her lungs. "What?" she asked.

"You okay?"

"Fine," said Paula, the corners of her mouth struggling upward in a faint smile before finally collapsing into a worried grimace. "Do we have to go?"

"What?"

"To Morgan." Her voice was nearly a whisper, as if she didn't want Luke to overhear her. "Please—let's not go there."

"We *have* to. The car needs to be fixed properly if we're going to make it the rest of the way home," said Crystal.

A little of the emptiness returned to Paula's eyes, and she nodded. Crystal turned and started forward, following Luke farther into the corn.

"You don't understand," Paula said weakly, the words barely audible to even herself. "Morgan *is* home."

III

The roof of the convenient mart had collapsed in on itself, and scorched cinderblocks spread in an outward circle around the jagged remains of the structure. A fire truck was still on the scene, pumping hundreds of gallons of water into the smoldering wreckage. Five police cars—some from the Sheriff's Department, others from the Indiana State Police—were positioned around the perimeter of the building, and yellow tape stretched across the entire crime scene, a flimsy barrier warning away curious onlookers. The canopy had collapsed onto the rows of pumps, flattening them like soda cans. The blistering heat of the fire had faded all of the gaily painted exterior, suggesting age which the building would never achieve.

Suze sat quietly in the passenger seat, observing the busy officers as they did their work. She didn't like being this close to the aftermath of Chad's handiwork, but he seemed unaffected by worry, his eager eyes drinking delightfully from the scene before him.

"My God!" he exclaimed, the corners of his mouth curling upward.

"Proud of yourself?" Suze asked.

"Oh, *yeah!*" said Chad, grinning widely.

"Let's go on," said Suze. "Before someone spots us."

Chad had slowed the car to gawk, and an old Chevy Camaro roared past them on the left. He wished that he had a camera. The aftermath of his fury should be preserved for posterity, a visual diary detailing the killing spree of Chad Collins. He knew that it was a foolish risk, but wouldn't it be *cool* to watch home video of Manson or Starkweather or Dahmer or Bundy, doing the things which came so naturally to all of them? Hollywood—in particular, Fox—would be all over the footage, airing it in carefully edited segments during sweeps. America's preoccupation with such things was not lost on Chad. He could be the hero to a whole new generation of psychopaths.

Suze would never go for it, though. Since her migraine had erupted, she lost whatever backbone she had earlier possessed. She looked like a frightened rabbit curled up in the passenger seat, her squinting eyes darting left and right, terrified that they might meet those of an investigating officer. One look, and the policeman would know they had done this awful thing. He would just *know*.

Reluctantly, Chad pushed the accelerator and coaxed the Volvo back up to cruising speed. "How's your head?" he asked.

Suze shrugged. "I'll live."

"You hungry?"

Suze soured her expression and shook her head. "I'd puke."

The corn finally gave way on the right-hand side of the road, replaced by contiguous fields of tall, rolling grass. Farmland, farmland, and more farmland. If it weren't for the overhead power lines trailing from pole to pole, it would be easy to imagine living hundreds of years in the past, before electricity and automobiles and other manmade conveniences, in the times when witches and warlocks were feared more than any human hunter—for surely any hunter as savage and brutal as Chad could not be human. It amused him to think of ancient peasants scattering away in horror as he traversed their cobblestone lanes, pulling their children near. They would run like frightened sheep into the foggy primeval night. Running from Chad. Running from the devil himself.

"What?" Suze was looking at him curiously through her pained countenance.

"Nothing," said Chad, his attention returning to the present. "Just daydreaming."

"So where are we going?" asked Suze. "Ohio?"

"I think so," said Chad.

"You *think* so?"

Chad shrugged his shoulders. "It *feels* right, doesn't it?" Her wounded look didn't escape him, and he realized the content of his last statement. It was like taking a blind man to a museum and asking him if he saw anything he liked. They drove in silence for several more miles.

"Does 'gan ga' mean anything to you?" Chad asked abruptly.

"What?"

"Gan ga," repeated Chad, feeling ridiculous for uttering what sounded like caveman gibberish, but those had been the words on the newspaper in his dream. The dreams were becoming more and more significant, and he doubted that the words were irrelevant.

"Isn't it that game with those wooden blocks that you stack? Remember that dumb ass commercial? All those neurotically happy partygoers chanting, 'Gan ga! Gan ga! Gan ga!' until some boob with clumsy elbows knocks the whole pile down," said Suze.

"That's Jenga," said Chad. He had played the game before, but not for years— Naomi sitting to his right, Peter sitting to his left, the pile of blocks growing taller and less sturdy with each round of play.

"Then what the hell is 'gan ga'?" she asked.

"I don't know," said Chad. "It's just something I saw in my dream."

Suze nodded and relaxed in her seat. If it was in his dream, it must be significant, and she stored the information away as something of which to be mindful. "Does the thought of killing a little girl excite you?" she asked.

Chad thought about it for a moment. He had never considered harming anyone at all until the last couple months, much less a child. He had been reborn the night that he had taken his mother's life, emerging as an entirely different version of the Chad Collins he had once been—studious, soft-spoken, *shy*, if he could imagine it. But even when the dark thing inside him had awakened, it wasn't without purpose. His mother, the faithless slut, had deserved the savage ending he had delivered. The smarmy bastard in the gas station had deserved the explosive preview of hell to which he had been treated. Although he hadn't necessarily intended to kill the red-headed cow behind the counter, he felt no remorse. She should have known better than to stand so close to a lowbrow, foulmouthed faggot like Earl. But to kill a child? Randomly, no, he felt no excitement at the thought. This *particular* child? *Yeeessssssss.* He wanted to feel clumps of her curly hair clenched in his fist, pulpy scalp still attached to the roots as it dripped blood onto the tops of his shoes. The delicious thrill of killing was powerfully addictive to Chad, and he wondered if there would come a day when he didn't care who or what he killed. It seemed like a natural progression.

"When we find her," he said, "we'll kill her."

Suze nodded mutely.

They passed a sign announcing the imminent approach of the Ohio state border in thirty miles, an imaginary vertical line demarcated years before by

205

cartography. Clouds were collecting overhead, suggesting an afternoon rain shower was imminent.

"You from around here?" Chad asked, his voice sounding startlingly loud in the quiet vacuum of the car's cabin. It sounded like a tired pickup line, uttered in the dark recesses of a tavern just before last call, but Chad realized that he really knew very little about Suzette Snyder, other than that she was a killer, like him. A killer with some kind of unusual metaphysical guidance system inside her head; a psychic eye that had, for the time being, been seared and left sightless in the aftermath of the explosion.

Suze nodded her head weakly. "I grew up in a little vomit trough called Morgan," she said. "We're going to pass through it pretty soon, but you better look fast. It'll be gone before you know it."

"What's it like?" Chad asked.

Suze sighed. "It's like any other backwards ass town, I suppose. A decade behind the rest of the world, resisting change, resisting *anything* new. Inbred fuckers running the whole goddamn show there. You had to keep your nose clean in Morgan. Everybody knows everybody else's business. It's no place to be conspicuous."

"Your family still live there?"

She nodded again. "My mother and her husband." The word 'husband' came out like curdled sick, regurgitated into the conversation.

"Doesn't sound like you care much for him," said Chad.

She shook her head and tears welled up in her eyes. "Nothing was ever the same after he came into the picture. Mom thought his shit didn't stink, but ours did twice as bad. I wanted to kill that fucker."

"So, why didn't you?"

"I was just a girl. Originally, I thought I wanted to do it on our way through. I wanted to do it in the dead of night. I wanted to do it when no one could see. I wanted to do it when my head told me it was time," she said.

"Oh." Chad realized that Suze had lost all of her earlier confidence. She relied too much on her unusual gift, and until it returned, she was going to require stern direction. Otherwise, she would wait frozen, her ambivalent sensibilities disabling her from making the simplest of decisions. Chad wished more than anything that she would see a teacup right about now. Her fear of the unknown was crippling both of them.

"Did you live there long?" asked Chad.

"Since I was a baby," she said. "In a town where the biggest occupation is unemployment, I didn't do too awfully bad. I've worked ever since I can remember. I delivered *The Gazette* on my bicycle until I was old enough to drive. I bought a little Chevette when I was waiting tables at Minnie's. I had to take a second job to be able to afford the payments, so I rang groceries at Morton's. I knew that the only way to get out of there was to work my ass off and figure shit out for myself."

"So, you made the 'big' move to Pridemore," said Chad, ridiculing her just a little.

"I came to Pridemore for you," she said. "I've been lots of places. I've seen both coasts. Anywhere the feeling took me, I went. I was surprised that it led me right back to my own backyard, so to speak."

"Don't you ever talk to your mother anymore?" he asked.

She shook her head, tight-lipped. "She isn't my family anymore. Hasn't been since she married that jackass."

Rain began to fall gently against the windshield, and Chad clicked on the Volvo's wipers and running lights. They drove for several more miles in silence, the wet tarmac adding its own voice underneath that of the tire treads.

"Who do you think this little girl is?" asked Chad.

Suze shook her head and popped another fistful of Excedrin into her mouth. "I don't know."

"How can she be dangerous? She's just a little girl," said Chad.

"I don't know," repeated Suze. "Maybe it's not what she is *now*, but what she'll be *then*."

"When?"

"When she grows up. I don't know. I never really thought about it much. I just know that I'll feel a whole hell of a lot better once she's dead. Her eyes— they burn right through me in those dreams. It's like she knows every little thing that runs through my mind. It's like she's mocking me, standing just far enough out of reach so I can't get to her," said Suze.

"But she's just a little girl," said Chad.

"You can't tell me you haven't seen enough in the last several weeks to wonder about that. How do we *know* that she's just a little girl? For all we know, she could be some horrible demon," said Suze.

Chad knew she wasn't right. If the girl was a demon, he wouldn't be nearly so afraid of her. It was the positively sticky feeling of goodness surrounding her that scared him stupid.

—◇—

They had only just entered Morgan when one of the front tires blew. The car wobbled sharply to the right, heading toward the concrete curb and several parked cars. Suze was wrenched from sleep as Chad wrestled with the wheel, stomping on the brake pedal. Time passed in slow, lazy loops. The Volvo missed the parked car by inches but rammed sideways into the curb with a distinct groan of metal.

207

"*Shit!*" screamed Chad, slamming both hands down on the steering wheel.

At least the rain had stopped.

"What happened?" asked Suze, groggily rubbing her eyes.

Chad got out of the car and crossed to the passenger side. The tire was shredded, the rim bent. The alignment had to be fucked. *Shit!*

"We're stuck," said Chad. "We'll have to have this fixed."

"Where are we?" she asked.

"Home, sweet home."

Suze sat upright abruptly, scanning the streets through strained eyes. It was a perfect little slice of Americana, laid out in pretty little squares with pretty little lawns and pretty little houses. The sidewalks, while not crowded, were not empty, either. A jogger, an impossibly young girl pushing a stroller, old crones catching up on gossip as they leisurely walked in their brightly colored running suits. No one she recognized. No one who would recognize her.

"Shit," she muttered.

"What?"

"I'm not exactly in love with this old place," she said. "How long do we have to be here?"

"I'm going to have to have the car towed. Get the rim fixed, new tire, alignment—it's gonna cost some bucks," said Chad.

"I've got money. How *long?*" She felt like a trapped animal and sunk down into the seat involuntarily. Her eyes flitted from sidewalk to sidewalk, scanning for something-someone-anyone she knew. Her tension permeated the car, and Chad realized that it was through sheer willpower that Suze was able to keep her composure.

"I'll know better after I find a place to tow it," he said. "Probably a few hours."

Suze nodded and fumbled with her seatbelt. They walked down the clean, wide sidewalk side-by-side, although Suze kept her head dipped, her eyes scanning, scanning—she wanted off of this sidewalk, off of this road, out of this *town!* She was bound to be seen. She didn't want to see them, and if they knew she was here, they would come. *He* would come.

Suze glanced at Chad and realized with a start how different he looked from when she had first met him. His stark jaw line throbbed as he involuntarily clenched and unclenched his teeth. His brow seemed hardened, more defined than before, as if he had aged years in days. His eyes were cool ice, detached and remote, insane and exciting. She would have never admitted it aloud, but she *was* a little afraid of Chad. His anger was unfocused and unpredictable. He had already beaten the shit out of her once. She remembered it in weird snapshots, not unlike her sensations of "empathy." The migraine had been at its apex, splitting her head in unimaginable ways. His fist raised, lowered, raised, lowered—all in a haze, as if Suze had been watching a movie and these things were happening to somebody else. She didn't remember *why* he was so angry, but for a moment, she had thought he would kill her. It startled her. She was *older* than this boy, *wiser* than this boy. He had more or less raped her on the side of the road. She should be furious with him. But she *needed* him. Her special gift had temporarily departed, but before it did, it had brought her to Chad. There had to be a purpose to it all.

She wanted her guardian angel back; she felt completely vulnerable.

Suze unconsciously guided them, walking along streets she knew too well. They had gone five blocks when she paused, taking Chad by the elbow. "About a block ahead on the right is a service station. Roy's BP. Go in and have them tow the car. I'll wait here."

Chad looked around. "Where?"

Suze indicated to their left. A small, square house sat back from the road, its overgrown yard and stacks of yellowed community newspapers testifying to its vacancy. Suze crossed the yard at a quick trot, keeping her eyes fixed firmly ahead. If she couldn't see the neighbors, then they couldn't see her, either—a ridiculous notion, but one that she refused to relinquish until she was underneath the awning of the porch. She tried the door. It was unlocked. She turned and looked back at Chad, who was staring at her dumbly from where she had stopped him on the sidewalk. His mouth hung slightly open. What a fucking moron. She clasped her thumb and fingers together before shooing him away with several flicks of her wrist.

Chad stood with his hands on his hips. Suze was completely crazy. How did she *know* this house was empty? There could be some poor elderly invalid nested within. What would she do then? Tear his or her head off, too? Probably. He sighed and continued down the sidewalk toward Roy's BP. He cast a glance over his shoulder to mark his position. He wasn't familiar with his surroundings like Suze was. One house looked like the next to him. He spotted a wooden plaque swinging on an old lamppost in the choked yard. *165, The Lovells.*

⌖

Roy's BP wasn't particularly cooperative. Sure, they would tow the car in, but it was late in the afternoon. They wouldn't be able to do anything about it until morning at the earliest. Chad made the arrangements and told a beefy mechanic named Steve where to find the car. Then he started back toward the house that Suze had entered. She wasn't going to be happy.

He stepped off the curb without thinking and was almost flattened by a silver Honda as it passed, its tiny horn crying out. He flipped his middle finger up and waved it like a flag after the car, then continued across the street.

He had traveled two blocks and was nearing the more residential blocks when it caught his eye. The coin-operated newspaper box was bolted to the concrete sidewalk, just beside a telephone pole. It was bright yellow, with the words *Get it in The Gazette!* emblazoned in bright black script on its side. It had a glass-fronted door which displayed the current edition of the paper. *The Morgan Gazette.*

the morGAN GAzette.

Chad fumbled change out of his pocket and thrust two quarters into the slot. He pulled the door down and extracted the paper. Its headline blared, "SUSPECTS SOUGHT IN FIREBOMBING." The blackened remains of the *Friendly's* gas station filled the top half of the page.

Chad tucked the paper under his arm and nearly ran the remaining blocks to the house. The dream had shown him this paper, even if it was only a portion exposed from underneath the edge of one of those damned teacups.

They were where they were supposed to be.

CHAPTER ELEVEN

I

The dreams were thick and syrupy, holding Lisa in bed far longer than she had intended.

In the one she remembered clearly, she had been creeping through the house like a predator, knowing that the bitchy little girl was roaming through the halls, sullying the air with her childish poison. Although she disliked all children, Lisa held a deep and burning hatred for this particular one. She hadn't seen the girl yet, but she could smell her essence like sickly sweet bubblegum, sticking to the walls, soaking into the furniture.

Lisa had just rounded the banister to creep up to the second floor when she had heard the familiar sound.

Thump! Thump! Thump!

Lisa had frozen on the first riser with her hand clutching the wooden knob at the end of the stair rail. The sound still echoed through the room, three distinct knocks chasing each other from one wall to the other as their volume lazily spiraled downward. She turned her eyes upward, and a scream died in her throat.

Nanna Grace stood at the head of the stairs, her ancient body a grotesque collection of gnarled branches poking out from her oversized nightgown. Even in the dream's murky darkness, Lisa could discern the network of purple veins bulging just below the surface of the old woman's tissue-thin skin. Her fingers were twisted and bent at bizarre angles, arthritis performing its slow torture on them. They were wrapped around the knobby head of her mahogany walking stick, and from where Lisa stood, it looked as if Nanna was being supported entirely by the point of that stick, her feet dangling freely below her.

"I can see your soul," the old woman croaked.

From behind her, Chris Baylock stepped out of the shadows. His face was spreading in two opposite directions, almost cartoonish in its monstrous display. His one remaining eye burned holes through Lisa, saying things his shattered mouth couldn't. Blood dripped from his chin like spaghetti sauce.

And then she felt it brush past her, so low to the ground that she had involuntarily taken a step closer to the things at the top of the stairs. Lisa pivoted her head in time to see the hem of a frilly blue dress disappear around the corner.

The girl.

Why couldn't she *see* the girl? Only little glimpses...

THUMP! THUMP! THUMP!

The sound boomed like thunder down the narrow stairwell. Lisa looked up the stairs, her head pivoting in slow motion. It was Nanna Grace from fifteen

211

years ago, sure and solid, fleshy and robust. She swung the cane with vengeance against the floor as she took an easy step down.

"The devil plays in your soul, girl," the woman said, her voice full of strength Lisa hadn't heard for so long—and had hoped to never hear again. This was the voice of the woman who had told her that television was bad, neighbors were bad, boys were *BAD*—but most of all, *LISA WAS BAD*. Nanna Grace had squeezed countless hours of empty prayer from Lisa over the years, hoping to salvage any good there might still be inside of her. The look in younger Nanna's eyes suggested she was apt to do it again now.

Lisa took a step backward and began to fall, the room tilting slowly as she drifted back, falling as if through cotton batting.

She awakened with a start, and the alarm clock read one-thirty in the afternoon.

Shit.

Jack Lovell was still sprawled on his belly across the other side of the mattress, one chicken white leg protruding from underneath the covers. He had the ugliest feet Lisa had ever seen, long feet with bright red toes. He had drooled a considerable puddle onto his pillow and was snoring loudly through his nose.

Lisa threw the sheet back and got to her feet, quietly crossing the room and collecting her clothes. She didn't want Jack to be here anymore. She *certainly* didn't want him to see her naked flesh again—he might get the wrong impression. Lisa had needed his help, and now she didn't. It was as simple as that, really. She hoped he would go away of his own volition. Chris Baylock had not and look what happened to *him*.

She was seated at her dresser, brushing her hair industriously with a wire brush when Jack finally stirred, lifting his tousled head from the pillow and farting long and low. He smiled sheepishly at her.

"Good morning," he said.

Lisa said nothing, turned back to the mirror and continued brushing.

Jack's smile faltered. "Something wrong?"

Lisa put the brush on the bureau and turned around to face Jack. Her head was cocked to the side, and her eyes shone pity. "Playtime's over, Jackie-boy," she said. "I've got things to do today. Do you think you could—?" She indicated the bedroom door with a shooing gesture.

"You want me to go?" asked Jack, his face frozen in humorous astonishment.

"Yes, please," Lisa said simply, turning back to the mirror.

"But I thought—"

"For heaven's sake, Jack, cheer up. You got yourself some last night. Way to go! Now why don't you go back home to Janice? You may not be able to find anyone else dumb enough to marry you," she said.

Jack got out of the bed oblivious to his white shriveled nakedness. He stood gaping at Lisa's backside, his mouth fumbling for words which would not come.

212

He had felt a connection with Lisa, had seen a lifeline, something to pull him from the disaster which life with Janice had become. Lisa had been so warm and gentle just hours ago. Now, she was like the evil doppelganger of the person he had met, cold, callous, and completely unfeeling. He had buddies who treated women just like Lisa was treating him now. It was an unusual juxtaposition, and certainly one he had never expected to experience firsthand.

He suddenly realized his nakedness and awkwardly fumbled for his clothes, tripping over his own shoes and toppling ass-up on the bed. When he had righted himself, he had found the leg holes and worked his pants up his pasty limbs. He was still fumbling with his shirt buttons as he slammed the front door.

Lisa sighed and watched from the living room window as his pickup truck blazed out of the driveway and down the quiet neighborhood street. Mrs. Varney craned her head from her stooped position in her rose garden, vainly trying to see what all the fuss was about.

Lisa turned and looked at her newly acquired furniture. The house still seemed empty by comparison to Nanna Grace's idea of decor—dark hues, ancient knick-knacks, heavy-handed paintings of Jesus and the Virgin Mary, their faces always painted in expressions of somber angst. Nanna Grace had always taken a hard line with regard to penance—all men are children of God, and all men are sinners. Restitution must be made in broad strokes.

Lisa wandered across the room, her eyes glued to the television she had purchased from the Lovell estate sale. It was a small 19" color portable, positioned on a rickety wire cart, its antenna bent into a lopsided V. It had to have been at least twenty years old; it had knobs to twist and buttons to push and pull—it didn't have a remote control. She stooped down and found the electrical cord, drew it out from the tangle in which it lay around the cart's feet, and plugged it into the wall.

The set blazed to life, its power switch already in the "ON" position. A grainy picture bloomed on the screen, frequent wavering lines flitting through and distorting the image. Her eyes were frozen in wonder as the images of people appeared and disappeared through patches of static. She reached overhead without rising from her stooped position and adjusted the rabbit ears. The picture, although never completely clear, stopped rolling and became viewable.

Lisa sat on the floor, leaning back on her elbows, watching the opening credits for *General Hospital*. It was like a blind man seeing the sunrise for the very first time. Nanna Grace's insistence that no television programming ever proliferate to defile Lisa's mind was so great that Lisa had never once been tempted to even sneak a peek in the waiting room at the hospital or in patients' rooms, as she wiped their fouled bottoms. She kept her head low, and her thoughts in her head so that she couldn't hear the assorted blasphemies which spewed forth from the electronic box. Nanna Grace promised punishment of the utmost severity if she should discover that Lisa had been watching television. Lisa had taken more than

213

one beating from the knobby head of the old woman's cane, and watching TV simply wasn't worth it.

But now, it didn't matter what Nanna Grace thought. The television was on, and Luke and Laura were arguing loudly about their son, Lucky, and there was nothing evil about it. It was intriguing and absorbing, and the saga that was unfolding in front of Lisa's eyes touched her mind like a sweet, addictive drug. She pulled a couple of pillows from the couch and eased back on the floor.

So, this was television.

Jack bit back angry tears. The bitch had used him. She had sensed his vulnerability and leached onto it, taking what she needed and then throwing him aside. It was humiliating. He had poured his soul out to her. He had exposed painful, personal secrets about his and Janice's private lives. He had truly felt as if Lisa wanted him, too.

God, I'm such a fool!

Lisa was amazing in bed. She had done things that Janice would never have done in a million years. When he had reached orgasm, he had thought all of his insides were going to come rushing out. He had never felt so much sensation in his entire life. Janice was like fucking a corpse by comparison. And then there was his impudent little asshole son, Cory. Red-headed like his mother. Had a screeching voice that sounded like it came from his nose instead of his mouth. Cory was the reason he had married Janice in the first place. Like so many idiot teenagers, Jack thought the laws of reproduction didn't apply to him, and he had forgone a condom one precocious college evening when things had drunkenly gone a little too far. When Janice told him she was pregnant, he locked himself inside his dormitory room for three days. His life was over.

And in many ways, it was. He finished college, although it took him twice the time. Janice's father, Horton Barley, installed him into a position of average pay with his legal firm, running papers and other oddball errands. He went to classes in the evening, after which he returned home to his and Janice's small house on Bickle Lane. She hated that house on Bickle Lane. The ceilings were low, the plaster was cracked, the carpets were threadbare and bore stains from previous tenants. She refused to meet her friends here, embarrassed by the depths of their poverty. It was Horton Barley's idea of punishment for both of them—his daughter for allowing herself to be touched, and Jack for doing the touching. As Janice's pregnancy progressed, her true temperament had reared its ugly head on frequent occasions, and in a slowly dawning horror, Jack realized to what kind of life he had committed himself.

The birth of their son had provided some blessed distraction. Janice had her hands filled with spoiling their son from his very first breath, providing him with the affirmation that yes, indeed, he *was* better than any of the other children in the neighborhood, playground, or school. The boy was a complete embarrassment to Jack, who loathed the whining tantrums, and he frequently had to fight back the urge to slap the little shit's mouth shut.

With Jack's graduation from college, he was promoted within the firm to the office's general business office, where he oversaw accounts payable and receivable, as well as overseeing the company's taxes. The pay increase had been substantial, as well as the title that accompanied the promotion. Although Janice could never possibly be satisfied, she did manage to hold her head a little higher. They finally were able to move from the house on Bickle Lane which she hated so much and into a sixth-floor apartment in Shaker Heights. She could have her friends over now without dying from the shame.

Oh, and she had her friends over, all right. They played cards and laughed and drank martinis and *laughed*. It irked Jack that he plodded off to work every day while Janice sat on her ever-widening ass and played with her friends, society matrons who spent their best moments emptying their husband's bank accounts.

What have I done to deserve all of this? Jack thought again, as he had so many times before. And now, he was going home to her and to all that shit. A lump formed deep in his throat, and his spirit sank entirely. He guided the Ford pickup toward his mother's house. He would collect his things and head back to Cleveland. It was only one-thirty. He could be home by six or so.

He turned onto Deerport and parked in the driveway of his mother's house. The last time he had been here, *she* had been with him, smiling that lopsided smile, brushing against him, winking coyly. Lisa had wanted him. She had *wanted* him. And now he wanted her so badly it hurt. He didn't want to go back to Janice. He didn't want to see that awful child who had been borne of his own seed. He didn't want to sit at that desk in Cleveland, under the watchful eye of Horton Barley. He wanted to go back into that lovely attic bedroom with the soft scent of rose petal in the air. He wanted—

He shook his head abruptly, as if to toss off the notion. It didn't matter what he wanted. She didn't want to see him. He walked through the overgrown lawn and past the yellowed newspapers piled on the porch. He unlocked the door with his key and went inside, quickly crossing the tiny living room and stepping into the small guest bedroom in which he had been sleeping. He collected his personal belongings in swift, jerky movements, reminiscent of a child who, in a fit of rage, has stormed to his room to pack his bags and run away. Only Jack wasn't running away. He was running home. Home to Janice. Janice and the boy.

Jack finished collecting his meager possessions and carried them out to the back of the pickup. He tossed them in and climbed into the cab. He backed the truck out onto the street and drove off, not realizing he had forgotten to lock the front door.

⚬————◇————⚬

Leonard Barnes swabbed the third-floor corridor of Morgan Township Hospital with slow and delicate swipes of his mop. He hadn't slept well, having gotten home well after two the previous morning. His back hurt from stooping behind that goddamned tree for so long.

Something wasn't right with the Mitchell girl.

He didn't want to believe it, not after all this time, but it had been apparent in her odd behavior the previous evening that something wasn't right. Not little Lisa Mitchell. He had worried about her for years, wondering what kind of perversity was happening to the little girl by warped and sanctimonious Grace Mitchell. He had met Grace shortly after she had settled in Morgan, which must have been at least twenty years. He tried to offer her assistance getting settled into that brooding old house, and she had treated him as if his intent was to rape her in a dark corner of the attic. He was stunned by her overall demeanor, but most of all the stern admonitions that would flow from her mouth at that quiet little girl. Most times when he had seen Lisa, she was cowering somewhere near the floor, as if afraid to be noticed at all. She had looked at him with such curiosity, he had wished he could take her home with him.

Then there was that bizarre evening almost two years ago when Grace had telephoned him out of the blue and asked him to come over. He was suspicious of her motives—maybe she had rigged an intervention for the sake of his immortal soul—but he had agreed to go, from curiosity as much as anything else. He had never been welcome in the house as a guest, only as cheap labor on infrequent maintenance situations like a burst pipe or a leaky faucet; he supplemented his wages from the hospital with such odd jobs—cash only, under the table, of course. For Grace to call and ask him to come over, no mention of any tools or of work to be done—well, it would have been impossible *not* to go.

When Leonard entered that dark house, he had felt his heartbeat accelerate and a chill swept over him. The cryptic religious portraits made him think of one of Stephen King's works, the one with the girl who got her period and then twisted everything to shreds with her mind. Her mother had been a religious fanatic. Grace had been waiting for him at the kitchen table, a steaming cup of tea in front of her; in those days, she wasn't confined to her bedroom.

"As you may know," she had begun. "The girl has taken a job with your hospital."

"Lisa?" he asked, sipping the bitter brew she had placed before him.

She nodded. "I didn't want her to, but I could hardly stop her, could I?"

216

Leonard shrugged. "I don't see why it's such a bad idea. It's an alright place to work."

Grace's eyes lit with what Leonard could only call lunacy. "The girl is evil, Leonard." He cringed when she said his name, as if it burned his eardrums. She leaned forward, her elbows on the table, her focused face looming forward. Her eyes were fixed on him, freezing him in his chair. "I want you to be my eyes at the hospital."

He blinked and sat back. "What?"

"I can watch her here, but I can't be there, too," she said. "I thought you might help me, not just from the goodness in your soul, but because our Lord and God would have it so."

He had looked at her eager face, his mind racing for a response. The woman needed professional counseling. He had never been more afraid for Lisa Mitchell than he was at that moment.

"Um," he finally managed, standing and backing away from the table. "I don't think I can help you, Mrs. Mitchell. I think you need to talk to your doctor or someone 'bout this, don't you? They could help you a lot more than I could. I mean, I'm only a janitor. What can I do?"

Grace looked at him with disappointment. "You think I'm crazy, don't you, Leonard Barnes?"

He stopped, involuntarily nodding his head just a bit.

She sighed and looked away from him. "One day you'll see, but it will be too late. I'm not crazy. The girl is evil. She needs to be watched—*always* watched."

"Whatever you say, Mrs. Mitchell," he said, working his way back through the front door. He had hurried home that evening with his hands in his pockets, his head hung low, his thoughts with Lisa Mitchell and the crazy woman who kept the girl under her roof.

But now, as he had seen Lisa in the hall just the previous day, swaying her hips from side to side, holding her head high and proud, he had felt the difference as if it had been a physical current which had leapt from her to him. For the first time since that crazy evening at Grace Mitchell's kitchen table, he considered the possibility that the old woman might have been right. Leonard had recognized nothing of Lisa in the woman he saw in the hospital corridor.

When he had left work that evening, he had driven by the Mitchell house, noting with interest the red truck in the driveway. It had been there all evening long, and Leonard's sense of dread had grown with each pass through the neighborhood. He hadn't even meant to drive by Lisa's house but found himself there time and again. When he saw her bring that large package out of the house, carrying it as easily as if it were a load of laundry, he had known where she was going, the knowledge as quick as a flash of light. He pulled away from the curb and drove to McMillan Reservoir on Culvert Lane, where he parked his dark blue Chevy behind a utility building, out of sight. He took cover in a dense thatch of

217

shrubbery and watched Lisa Mitchell bring the red truck to the picnic area and then toss her waste over the rail of the observation deck. For a moment, he thought that she had seen him, as she stopped to scan her surroundings intently. He held his breath until she had spotted an owl and moved on, back to the truck and down Culvert Lane.

The mop was heavy in Leonard's arms. The day was dragging, and Leonard was painfully aware of every second that passed. Although he felt uneasy leaving the girl unwatched, he couldn't afford to lose his job, and he knew no one who might believe his fantastic story enough to observe her in his absence. He couldn't believe that he had adapted to the idea so quickly; he himself had thought Grace Mitchell was a lunatic when she had told him on that afternoon so long ago.

Leonard sighed and trudged onward with his menial tasks. It would be a long day—and an even longer evening.

The credits rolled, and Lisa clapped merrily from her squatted position on the floor. Her legs and ass were numb from sitting so long. How long had she been there? Three hours? Four? Five? A rerun of *Three's Company* had just ended, but before that was *The Andy Griffith Show*, *Matlock*—which had confused Lisa because Andy Griffith starred in both shows but was so much older in the second—*The Mighty Morphin Power Rangers*, *General Hospital*, and *The Scooby-Doo Mysteries*.

Lisa found nothing inherently evil in any of the programming she had seen. Of course, *Three's Company* had that fellow who pretended to be gay, and Nanna Grace would have *surely* found that objectionable, but he was only *pretending*, so did it really even matter? And he was *so* funny! Lisa hadn't laughed so hard in her entire life.

She stood and stretched, realizing her bladder needed desperate relief. She walked clumsily to the restroom, her wobbly legs tingling and burning as blood resumed a normal course through her extremities. Lisa wondered what prime time might have in store for her. She looked forward to that most of all, because when her former co-workers talked about television, it was almost always prime time shows they discussed. Obviously, she never had anything to contribute, but she always listened. One show that was frequently discussed by her former co-workers was coming on shortly, frequent commercials advertising it between segments of the other programs, and she eagerly anticipated it.

It was a rebroadcast of the pilot for *Benny and the Girl*.

II

Gray clouds had sneaked across the sky, slowly devouring the bright blue morning. By the time Luke had replaced the split radiator hose with a suitable one, rain had begun to fall.

"Can you hurry up out there?" Crystal called from the driver's seat inside the relative comfort of the dry car.

Luke leveled a glare over the edge of the hood. He was soaked completely through, his wild hair now slicked down tightly against his skull, his shirt stuck to his back, his jeans impossibly heavy.

"What?" Crystal asked, mock innocence playing across her face.

Luke slammed the hood down and stepped around to the driver's window. Crystal looked at him through the open window. Paula was in the back seat of the car, curled up and asleep.

"Thanks," said Crystal, but the word sounded meaningless.

Luke looked at her expectantly. Crystal returned the gaze emptily, her eyebrows arched. How could this man not *recognize* her? It was unnatural. Her face had graced the cover of over a hundred magazines this year alone—and it was only August. More than anything, it really pissed her off.

"Christ," said Luke, shrugging his shoulders and turning into the rain. "Never mind."

"Oh, for heaven's sake!" said Crystal, rolling her eyes and opening the driver's door. "I was just kidding. Of course you can go with us to Morton."

"Morgan." The word floated up from the depths of the back seat.

"Whatever," said Crystal. "Only catch is, *you're* driving."

Luke looked at the mangled radiator hose in his hand and the car buried up to its nose in corn, and said, "I think I'd feel just fine about that."

Luke couldn't help but notice from the corner of his eye that Crystal had been staring at him. He could feel unbidden color begin to creep into his face. The effect wasn't lost on Crystal; she was smiling slightly.

"*What?*" Luke demanded.

Crystal narrowed her eyes but didn't avert her gaze. If anything, her focus became sharper, more scrutinizing. "Don't I look the least bit familiar to you?"

Luke glanced at her and then back at the road. The windshield wipers screeched across the glass, and Luke turned them off. The rain had stopped, at least for now.

"Not really," he said. "Should you?"

"C'mon," she urged, leaning toward him. *"Think* about it. Maybe you saw me in a supermarket—?"

He looked at her as if she was insane.

"Or on television—?"

"Are you like a weathergirl or something?" Luke asked, glancing at her quickly. "'Cause if you are, you coulda warned me about the rain."

Crystal slumped back in her seat. "Unbelievable," she muttered.

"What?" Luke asked. He glanced at her, studying her a little longer. Her jaw was again jutted out in that petulant, stubborn way. Her cheeks were tinted pink. She was actually *angry*.

"Don't you even *watch* television?" she asked.

"Sure," Luke said. "Some. Not too much."

"Ever heard of a smash show called *Benny and the Girl?"*

"Yeah, I guess so," said Luke. He remembered seeing the title listed in the *TV Guide*, but truthfully, he preferred reading the magazine to actually watching the programs. He would much rather his sparse television diet consist of news and sporting events. He preferred to read if he were looking for escape.

"Ever heard of Crystal Bright?" she asked, her angry eyes watching for a reaction, desperately needing *any* reaction.

Luke nodded unsurely. The name sounded somewhat familiar, but maybe that was the floor cleaner he had picked up the last time Paulie had run out—he couldn't be certain.

Then he realized that this woman's name was Crystal.

"Oh," he said.

She cupped her hands and dropped her face into them, laughing hysterically. *"Oh?"*

"Well, what do you want me to say?"

"You're an asshole," she said.

"What?"

"Never mind," she said, turning to stare through the droplets of water which still beaded on the window of her door. Life *sucked*.

They arrived in Morgan as the sun found a peephole in the gray clouds. The radiator had been gurgling suspiciously for the past several miles, and Luke would be glad once they had this thing safely to a shop.

"We're here," he said.

"So, we are," said Crystal, still sulking.

Paula said nothing, her posture suggesting sleep, but her eyes wide open.

The sign for Roy's BP loomed ahead on the right, and just as Luke was about to mention it, a lanky man with straggly black hair stepped in front of the car. Luke simultaneously hit the brake and horn, and the man jerked back to the curb, his black eyes willing their deaths as they passed. Luke knew before he actually saw it that the man's middle finger was coming next.

He pulled the Honda into the gas station's lot and turned the engine off. The radiator continued to roil away, and a small thread of steam issued from the front grille of the car. Luke took a deep breath and scanned the premises. The last fueling post at which he had stopped had blown into a billion bits, and he feared that the association might be too overpowering for him to handle. He was pleased to see that Roy's BP was an old-fashioned service station, the kind that checked your oil when you went through the full-service lane, topping off the pressure in your tires and washing your windshield while the pump dinged away in the background. It was the type of service station to which he was accustomed—the type found in Jasper. For a second, he was heart-wrenchingly homesick, but he forced the feeling aside—there was no time for it now.

Crystal said, "I'm staying in here. Handle it, farm boy."

Luke glared at her as he got out of the car, then turned to stride across the lot toward the office. Crystal couldn't help but grin. He was trying to look cool, adding a little swagger to his gait, but he was still pretty much soaked through, and his hair had been blown dry sideways from the window he had left inched down. His face was still streaked with dirt and grease.

After a few moments, he came back and sat in the driver's seat. "They can't look at it until tomorrow," he said.

"What?" said Paula, sitting up abruptly in the back seat. She glanced around furtively before ducking back down.

"You've *got* to be kidding me," said Crystal.

"I wish I was."

"Well, *great,*" she said. She turned to Paula. "I guess we're stuck here for the night."

"No," Paula said firmly.

"What is *with* you?" Crystal asked, twisting even further to face the girl. Luke tried to fade into the background, a difficult thing in a Honda Civic.

Paula looked from Crystal to Luke and back again. Her frightened eyes were pleading with Crystal, and tears threatened to drip from the corners. She glanced at Luke, then shook her head.

Crystal turned to Luke. "Give us a second, okay? Why don't you find out if there's a cheap motel somewhere around here?"

Luke nodded, got out of the car and walked to the service station office.

Crystal turned back to Paula. "Come on, talk to me. What's going on?"

Paula was shaking, her shoulders jerking involuntarily with each trembling breath. "Oh, God, Crystal. This is *it.* This is where I'm *from.*"

"Morton?"

"*Morgan*," she said through clenched teeth. "Oh, God, my mama could be here anywhere—*he* could be anywhere! Oh, *God*—"

"Hey, *hey*," soothed Crystal, reaching back and taking Paula's hand. "*Relax.* Nothing's going to happen. I'll make sure of that. You can just stay right where you are, down in the back seat—kinda like how you smuggled me out of the hospital, remember? We'll find a motel, and I'll check us in, get us a room that doesn't face the road. Then we'll get you inside. You won't have to come out again until after the car's fixed."

"What about Luke?" Paula asked.

Crystal hadn't considered the thought. "I guess he hits the road."

"Good," said Paula without hesitation.

"Good?" asked Crystal. "Why good?"

Paula shrugged. "There's something I don't like about him," she said.

Crystal considered. "Yeah, me neither."

Luke pulled into the parking lot of a nondescript motor lodge several blocks over from Roy's BP. He hoped that the radiator hose would hold for this little round trip. Why in the world they couldn't walk was beyond him.

"Would you mind getting us a room?" Crystal asked, her attention still with Paula, who had gone limp across the back seat. "I'm going to stay here with Paula. She isn't feeling well." She mouthed the words, *female trouble.*

Luke nodded and reached around to his rear pocket for his wallet. It was gone. He groaned and squeezed his eyes shut. His wallet had been in his duffel bag. His duffel bag had been in Bert's truck. Now, he had no clothes, no money, no identification. "I can't stay here," he said.

Crystal turned to look at him, her head cocked slightly to the right. "I didn't expect you to," she said.

"Oh."

One small word, and in just the right pitch. Crystal realized that Luke had somehow decided along the way they were some sort of Three Musketeers. *Oh, well*, she thought. *It's just as well that we get that thought out of his head right now.*

"What did they say about your car?" Crystal asked.

"What?" Luke's face was blank.

"Didn't you say you broke down last night? Are they towing it or what?"

"Um, yeah, but not until tomorrow," he said. The pause was a little too long.

"What's going on here?" asked Crystal.

"What are you talking about?" asked Luke, the tips of his ears reddening.

"You didn't have an accident back there. There's no car to tow. What's going on?"

For a moment, Luke didn't know what to say. He was afraid to tell her the truth. If the sheriff's deputy had thought that Luke was responsible for the explosion at Friendly's, Crystal could easily come to that same conclusion herself. But he wasn't a good liar. He hadn't even remembered mentioning a car before, and now it was biting him in the ass. To distort the truth any further would be reckless. He could also sense Paula's rapt attention from the back seat, hanging on his every word.

He sighed. "All right. I *don't* have a car back there. I was in an accident, though. I was hitching through Kentucky when I got a ride with a trucker named Bert Parnell. He was a real nice guy."

"Was?" asked Crystal.

Luke nodded. "We stopped at one of those gas station mini-marts, you know the kind? Twenty pumps and all the crap you can eat?"

Crystal nodded.

"While we were there, something happened," said Luke. His face darkened as the memories of the previous evening—*God*, had it only been one night?—replayed vividly in his mind. "There was an explosion, and the whole thing went up. It took Bert, too—gone just like that."

Crystal studied his face, prepared to respond skeptically. She had rejected scripts containing less bullshit. His countenance stopped her before the first word was out. The pain in his eyes, in the lines of his face—it was real.

"Oh, God," said Crystal. She sat back in her seat, digesting Luke's story.

"I'm surprised you didn't hear about it on the radio," said Luke.

"We weren't listening to the radio," said Crystal absently. "Why were you hitchhiking? Were you running from something?"

Luke laughed half-heartedly. "Not at all. It's complicated, and if I go into it now, you'll swear I'm nuts. Let's save that one for another time."

"So where were you going?" asked Crystal.

"Borden."

"Ohio?"

Luke nodded. "It's about thirty miles northeast of here. Um, I was really hoping you might be kind enough to drop me off there."

And there it was. Despite what Luke had just told Crystal, she still felt uneasy allowing him to tag along with her and Paula. The more unglued Paula had become, the more responsible Crystal felt for her. Crystal felt uneasy exposing Paula to someone they had picked up off of the street—out of a *cornfield*, for God's sake! What if Luke was psychotic? What if this was all part of an elaborate act to place Crystal and Paula at ease, to catch them off their guard? It sounded so paranoid that Crystal could barely believe the thought had passed through her mind. She remembered Paula screaming frantically when she had first seen Luke, struggling to lock him out of the car. Crystal thought Paula had gone around the bend. For Crystal to entertain such thoughts herself was entirely hypocritical.

"You just said that you can't stay here," reminded Crystal.

Luke flushed with embarrassment. Crystal decided that he would be a lousy poker player. His face was a veritable palate of color, tinting different shades of the spectrum as his moods changed. "My wallet was in my duffel bag. It was in Bert's truck when it—exploded," he said. "I don't have any cash on me."

He hurried to add, "But before you say anything, I'm not asking for money, I *promise*. I just need a ride to Borden, and then I'll be out of your hair. If you'll consider it, I could sleep out here in the car. I'll tell the guy at the BP to call the motel when he's ready to start working on the car."

Crystal cast a glance toward the back seat where Paula was anxiously shaking her head. She looked back to Luke and saw the desperation in his eyes. Normally, that would have made her decision much easier. She didn't trust anyone who was desperate. But this was a different kind of desperation. The kindness she had sensed in his face the first time she had seen him was still there. She didn't feel the least bit endangered by this man. His hair was still leaping diagonally from his head, and greasy tracks crossed his forehead and the sides of his nose. He looked like a very tall little boy. It was difficult to fear him. If Borden was only thirty miles northeast, what could it hurt?

"Okay," said Crystal. "You sleep here, but I'm taking the keys."

"Thanks," said Luke.

"And you still have to get the room for me while I stay here with Paula."

"All right," he said. "Can I use the shower?"

"Please."

<hr />

Crystal nearly gasped when Luke came out of the bathroom, his wet hair dripping onto the towel around his broad shoulders. Who would have ever thought he was so nice-looking underneath all the filth? He had rinsed his clothes out as best he could, wrung them in the tub, then had burned out the motel's courtesy hair dryer coaxing them into some semblance of dry.

"Thanks," he said.

"Don't mention it," she said from where she sprawled on one of the two double beds in the lime green room. Paula had curled up on the other one, looking small and frail in a huddle of blankets. Crystal hoped that they could get out of this town soon. Paula was sinking fast in this environment. She turned toward the television set. She had been casually flipping through the channels when she saw the ad for the rebroadcast of *Benny and the Girl*'s pilot episode. Now she stopped clicking, absorbed in herself on the screen, rolling her eyes and winking at Blake Jagger in what was to become a trademark expression for her during her run on the show.

Luke followed her glance, but the commercial had ended before he saw what it was. For a moment, he feared that she had caught a news story outlining the tragedy at Friendly's roadside stop, that the sheriff's deputy had provided some sort of composite of Luke and asked for viewers to call in if they had seen anyone matching his description. Although Luke had reluctantly divulged parts of the story, he had purposefully left out that he was, no doubt, wanted for questioning in connection with the crime. He figured Crystal was much less likely to extend the ride by even thirty miles if she thought she was traveling with a potentially violent criminal.

She turned with a wistful smile on her face. "That was me on the TV," she said.

"Oh," he responded. He hooked a finger through the towel and sponged out the insides of his ears.

"'Oh' the farm boy says," she sighed. "It really doesn't impress you at *all*, does it?"

Luke next buffed his head with the towel, again standing his hair on end. He shrugged. "It's a job. What's the big deal?"

Crystal looked at him in amazement. "What's the big deal? I'll tell you the big deal. It's a fucking bunch of money for staying pretty and trim. It's a cream crop of cash for being able to push all that bullshit dialogue through your lips and make it sound even halfway believable. But most of all, it's about charisma. And when you've got it, you're *in*. You're all over the place—magazines, talk shows, soda ads, awards ceremonies—you name it. If it's high profile, you're *there*. You don't drive yourself to these events in a tiny Honda Civic, either. Enormous limousines take you everywhere. Half of my goddamned high school *class* would fit in those limousines!"

"So, why are you here?" Luke asked, raking his hair into some semblance of order with his fingers.

"Because they're *done* with me!" Crystal ranted, her eyes wild and her voice rising steadily. "Sure, everyone *loves* you when things are going well, but when things start to take a turn for the worse, we're talking *landslide*. It's like you've suddenly gotten the plague. People you have lunched with for *years* are just *gone*. The magazines that wrote such glowing articles about you suddenly want you to fall flat on your big fat ass. Movie scripts that came daily suddenly just stop. About the only thing left to do is take your clothes off and sell the only goddamned part of you that the public hasn't seen."

"So, which is it?" asked Luke, studying her curiously.

"What do you mean?"

"Well, you either love the lifestyle or hate it, but I doubt you'll change it. It's up to you to pick which side you want to be on. Myself? I don't think I could ever put much faith in a career where life's over by the time I reach thirty. I think I've got more good years left in me than that." Luke crossed the room, paused to turn and look at Crystal. "And it surprises you that I'm not impressed?"

He stepped outside and closed the door behind him.

III

Chad hurried across the tangled yard and under the cover of the porch awning. Suze had been watching from a window and opened the door as soon as she saw Chad approach. He had a wicked smile on his face and was waggling a folded newspaper at her.

"What?" she asked, stepping back as he entered. The room was nearly empty. A braided rainbow area rug covered coffee colored carpeting. The wallpaper showed clean bright patches where pictures had once hung. The place had apparently been recently vacated.

Chad handed her the paper. "Remember when I asked about 'gan ga'? The Mor—*gan Ga*—zette. We're in the right place."

Suze took the paper and studied the headline detailing the explosion at Friendly's. "SUSPECTS SOUGHT IN FIREBOMBING" The article said nothing about Suze and Chad specifically, but it intimated that the police were closing in on unidentified suspects. Without her extrasensory tools, she couldn't tell if she and Chad were safe. Were the police busily surrounding the house as they spoke? Would a bullhorn suddenly demand their surrender? Would this be where newscasters would film their bullet-riddled bodies sprawled across the weedy front yard, because they *certainly* would not surrender. She realized she was unconsciously coaxing blood from her bottom lip with her teeth as she worried.

Chad looked at her in bewilderment. He thought she would be happy to see that he had made the connection. Instead, her eyes widened with fear as she read the article. He hadn't read it himself. It hadn't really seemed relevant. The longer Suze held the paper, the more he wondered what it was that he had missed. He eventually snatched it from her and scanned the story, finding nothing alarming in its content. "What's the big deal? All it says is there were three unidentified victims. Are you suddenly developing a conscience or something? I don't understand."

"It says the police are closing in on suspects," she said peeking out the front window at the empty street in front of them.

"That's just bullshit. They're counting on us reading that and getting nervous. When we fuck up, they catch us. Except that we're not going to fuck up, Suze. That's not what this newspaper is about. I'm telling you, I can *feel* it. I'm really sorry about your 'power outage' and all, but you're going to have to trust me."

Suze sighed and reluctantly turned from the window when she could no longer justify her paranoia. The police would have to be much stealthier than she knew the Morgan P.D. to be if they were actually observing the house. Chad was right. They were safe—at least for the time being.

"Okay," she said. "So, we're here. What now?"

"I guess we wait and see," said Chad. "The car won't be ready until tomorrow."

"What?" Suze paced the small room, massaging her throbbing temples. Her migraine had intensified ever since they had crossed the Morgan Township line. She could feel the muscles along her shoulders and neck knotting. She wanted to be free from this town as quickly as possible. She didn't like being this close to *them*, especially since she couldn't count on her foresight to steer her clear. If she were to actually see her mother and stepfather, she knew that she would kill them or die trying. Without her special instincts, Suze could almost guarantee that she would be captured by the police long before she ever found the little girl. She had to keep her head clear—this wasn't about her; it was about the little girl. Those bastards would get what was coming to them eventually.

"Unless you know of another service station in town, that's the best Roy's can do. As late as it is in the afternoon, I'd bet it's the best *anyone* could do," said Chad, sitting cross-legged against the wall. "Should we get a motel?"

Suze shook her head. "We'll stay right here."

"Do you think that's smart? What if someone comes by?"

"Then we'll hide," she said. "I don't want to be outside any more than necessary while it's still daylight. I don't want to see my mother or her husband. After dark, maybe we can wander around some."

"I think we should," said Chad. "My dream directed me to Morgan for a reason, don't you think? We need to get out there and find out what it is."

Suze looked at her watch. It was five-thirty. "What do you want to do until then?"

Chad smiled lewdly, already unbuckling his belt.

◆

Deputy Sheriff David McElroy eased his car onto Deerport and parked along the curb. He was driving his own vehicle, a powder blue Oldsmobile Cutlass like thousands of other powder blue Oldsmobile Cutlasses on the road. He was across the street and at an angle from *165*, but he could see both the front door and the side exit. He didn't want to appear too conspicuous to the vicious criminals inside.

Today, he wasn't acting as a deputy sheriff but rather as a vigilante. McElroy had two months of vacation time stored up from his many years on the force, and if necessary, he would use it all. The department had encouraged him to take time off to deal with Loretta's unexpected death, but he had nonetheless returned that morning to the burned-out shell of the service station wearing civilian clothes and in his own vehicle. His fellow officers on the scene had tried to get him to go home, but his need for vengeance was too great. He *wanted* to investigate what had happened, but without all the restrictions mandated by law. He firmly believed in an eye for an eye. McElroy's blood pressure rose when he thought about the smug son-of-a-bitch who had run from him the previous evening. When the man suggested that the perpetrators of the crime had driven a red car, McElroy had assumed that the man was only trying to divert his attention, but this morning, when the burgundy Volvo had driven by the wreckage slowly, *too* slowly, he had known these were the accomplices of the man who had escaped. Why the man had tried to betray his own gang was something McElroy had yet to figure out. He hadn't seen their faces clearly but could discern the distinct outlines of occupancy in the driver's and front passenger's seats, and neither one appeared to be the man whom McElroy had seen the night before. He had trailed the Volvo all afternoon, ending up in Morgan, Indiana, of all places. He had grown up in Morgan himself but hadn't lived there for over seven years. It was McElroy's home court advantage.

McElroy stared at the small house unblinkingly. It had been Shirley Lovell's house, but he heard that she had passed away recently. He had no doubt that these people were holing up, waiting to meet up with the man they had left behind. He wondered what they would think if they knew their comrade had so easily offered them up to the officer. He could go in now, led by the unmarked pistol he had filched from the evidence room years before. Shoot first, ask questions later. But he didn't want to risk losing the man who had eluded him. McElroy wanted him desperately, wanted to see the life ripped away from him the way he had ripped it away from Loretta. Perfect vengeance would be setting the man on fire and watching him burn slowly, much more slowly than poor Loretta had.

His eyes were clouding over, and he forced his thoughts away from his dead wife. He struggled to detach himself from his emotions, focusing his analytical mind on the case at hand. He had watched as they had lost a tire just inside the city's limits. He held his breath as the two emerged from the car. Although he got a good look at the man's straggly countenance, the woman who had been with him kept her head lowered, her straggly black hair falling forward to cover her features. One thing McElroy could confirm—neither of the car's occupants were the man he desperately wanted to kill. His intuition begged for patience; that son-of-a-bitch would be coming soon.

Jack Lovell had been driving for hours, crossing Ohio and nearing the town he had called home for the past eight years. The rolling countryside had slowly given way to small towns before he finally reached the outlying suburbs of southwestern Cleveland. He hadn't bothered to call Janice to let her know he was coming. The knot in his stomach had grown with each mile until he finally was forced to pull into a rest area just outside the city. He stumbled into a stall in the men's room just before the first stream of acrid vomit poured from his mouth. He retched repeatedly until he thought his stomach was turning inside out.

When he was done, he leaned against the cool gray wall of the stall, perspiration glistening across his forehead, his legs wobbly. He couldn't do it. He had driven all this way, but he couldn't go back to Janice. Not tonight, not ever. Every time he tried to picture Janice, he saw Lisa Mitchell.

Lisa Mitchell.

She was beautiful and intelligent. Jack's loins responded automatically at the fleeting memory of her in bed, but then his stomach threatened to turn over again, killing any autopilot his libido had been on. The connection he felt to her was so strong—*so strong!*

When he felt he could trust his legs again, he left the stall and stood at the sink, staring at his puffy eyes. He washed his hands and splashed cool water against his face. He was probably thirty minutes from home, but he wasn't going to go there ever again.

He went back to his truck and cranked the engine. He wouldn't give up this easily—he *couldn't.* There had to be something more behind Lisa's change in attitude, but like a coward, he had left without putting up a fight. He put the Ford in gear and began the long drive back to Morgan.

Chad awakened several hours later. The sun had mostly set, sending red-orange beams of light through the front window. Suze was squatted in a corner, holding her head between her knees and crying softly. God, she was getting on his nerves! He wished she'd take the whole damn bottle of Excedrin and go to sleep for a long, long time. He sighed and crossed the room on his knees, dropping down beside her.

"Head still hurts, huh?" he asked.

She nodded and leaned into him. "It's been getting worse ever since we got here. If you're so goddamned *right* about everything, why won't it go away? Why?"

Chad stared at the darkening yard through the window. This was getting old, yet he still couldn't bring himself to kill her and be done with it. Unknowingly, Suze was his anti-venom, containing and disabling his murderous desires.

"Then let's get this over with and take a look around town," he said. "Maybe you'll find one of those teacups."

"Do you think?" Suze's damp eyes glistened with hope.

Chad smiled and stood. "We can always hope."

By the time they had made themselves somewhat presentable, the sun had finished its descent below the line of the horizon. Streetlamps flickered on throughout the quiet neighborhood, bathing the corners in pale phosphorescence. As they crossed empty blocks, Suze found the darkness reassuring, and she didn't feel as paranoid as she had earlier that afternoon. Now she studied the neighborhoods in which she had grown up, noticing small changes, like Mrs. Birch's flower garden, as well as larger ones like the facelift to which Morton's Supermarket had been treated. She had spent countless hours at that store, ringing up an endless stream of groceries as they traversed the conveyor belt. When she quit her job, she hoped to never see the place again, but underneath the new siding and the new signage, Suze knew it was still the same old Morton's. She shivered and increased her pace.

Neither of them noticed the blue Oldsmobile trailing behind them at a discreet distance.

They had just crossed Rose Lane when Chad abruptly took hold of Suze's arm.

"What?" she asked.

"This is gonna sound crazy, but I swear I just saw Crystal Bright," he said.

Suze looked both directions. "Where?"

Chad was already pulling her forward. "She turned at the next corner. She was walking with some guy. Come on."

"I *told* you that she was involved," puffed Suze as they began to run.

Chad had fantasized about Crystal Bright for three years, beating off nightly underneath her approving smile from her place high on his bedroom wall. He was feeling weirdly ambivalent now, not sure how to react when they finally came face to face. *When.* Funny, but it seemed like a certainty that he *would* meet her now, despite how ridiculous the notion originally seemed. Why in the world would a superstar like Crystal Bright be in a place like Morgan? Furthermore, what possible danger could she present to him? Suze's visions had been eerily accurate up until now, and she had assured him that he'd best kill Crystal before she had a chance to kill him.

It seemed so *absurd*.

They rounded the corner and stopped, scanning the sidewalks. Crystal Bright and her male companion were nowhere to be seen. Chad pulled Suze's arm, dragging her along the sidewalk while he continued to search for Crystal. Maybe he would get an autograph and a kiss on the cheek. Or maybe he would kill her. It all depended on what his own instincts fed him at that pivotal moment.

"Are you sure it was her?" asked Suze, completely out of breath.

Chad stopped again, giving Suze a chance to breathe. He chuckled halfheartedly. "I guess not," he said.

"Don't be so quick to say that," said Suze. "I *told* you she was involved. Maybe the little girl belongs to her."

Chad shook his head. "Crystal Bright doesn't have any children."

"Maybe it's a niece or something."

"Crystal Bright doesn't have any brothers or sisters," he said. "Dammit, I'm sure it was your stupid story that made me see her in the first place. I mean, what in God's name would Crystal Bright be doing in Morgan?"

They continued walking along the sidewalk. Chad could've *sworn* that it was Crystal Bright. For God's sake, he had seen her face a thousand times. He'd know it anywhere.

He was deeply absorbed in thought as they turned onto Phelps Lane. It was darker than the other streets; its streetlamps were spaced further here, and some had burned out. When Chad's peripheral vision absorbed the difference in light, he stopped and looked around.

His breath caught in his throat.

Directly to his right was the house from his dream. In it, he had seen Crystal Bright through the porch window. She had been sitting on the floor, sitting as if she had been waiting for Chad to arrive.

"What?" asked Suze, observing the quiet street and finding nothing particularly notable.

Chad slowly turned and drifted toward the two-story house. Its dark siding was weatherworn and split, its masonry filthy with grime. Four windows faced the street, two on the first floor and two on the second, but flickering light spilled from only one of them. The others were so dark that the glass almost disappeared from perception. Compared to the houses which surrounded it on either side, the house was a dark canker sore on the face of the neighborhood. All the other houses boasted newer siding or fresh red or brown brick. This one was dark and foreboding and sinister. It had a feel to it that none of the others did, a living, breathing aura that enveloped the house so thickly that even Suze, without her psychic prowess, couldn't help but feel it.

She scurried up behind Chad and put her hand on his elbow, not wanting to be any farther away from him than arm's length. Something felt very wrong here.

The soles of Chad's shoes sounded abnormally loud as he ascended the three warped wooden stairs to the porch. The sense of déjà vu had heightened all of Chad's other senses, making him nearly giddy with anticipation. The wooden swing on its rusted chains winked knowingly at him from the side of the porch.

231

Suze couldn't stand the anticipation any longer. She stepped around Chad and peered into the window from which the flickering light came. Her mouth dropped open for a second, then she turned and looked at Chad.

"I told you," she whispered, startled as he said it with her in unison.

Chad stepped up to the window and peered inside. The room was sparsely furnished. A fire roared in the fireplace, despite the heat of the day. The woman in the sundress sat in the middle of the floor, her back facing him. Her long blonde hair spilled around her shoulders and down her back. Slowly, she turned, the smile already fixed on her face.

Crystal Bright winked and blew him a kiss.

PART THREE

CONFRONTATIONS

CHAPTER TWELVE

I

It *was* Crystal Bright, and yet it *wasn't*. Her blonde hair was long and straight, parted down the middle with dark roots visible near her scalp. Her eyebrows were too thick, something Chad would've never noticed if he hadn't spent so much time fantasizing over the poster in his bedroom. The face was the same in so many other ways, though. In his dream, he hadn't noticed the small television set in the corner. *Benny and the Girl* was on, and it was a rerun, for Crystal Bright was on the television screen too, conversing animatedly with Blake Jagger. It only helped to reinforce the differences between the Crystal Bright sitting before him and the one on the television. She was still smiling when she stood and crossed the room toward the front door.

"What's she doing?" Suze asked, straining to get another peek.

The door opened, and this almost-Crystal stood behind the screen, her eyes expectantly waiting.

"Do it," Suze whispered harshly, elbowing Chad forward.

But the moment of decision had come and gone for Chad. He wasn't going to kill this woman. She wasn't Crystal Bright. His own intuition told him this woman was not dangerous to them in the least.

"Can I help you?" she asked.

"I'm Chad Collins, and this is Suze Snyder," Chad said. Suze looked at him as if he were insane.

"Lisa Mitchell," the woman said, offering a hand. "You've come about the girl, haven't you? Come in." She stepped back and Chad and Suze exchanged a quick glance before entering the sweltering living room. The fire was dwindling, and Chad noticed fragments of blackened bric-a-brac spreading outward in a spiral from the center of the hearth.

Lisa followed his eyes. "I was just getting rid of some of my Nanna's things," she said.

"The girl," said Chad. "What about her?"

Lisa cocked her head to the side and smiled at Chad coyly. "That *is* why you're here, isn't it?"

Chad nodded numbly. "Do you know who she is?"

Lisa shook her head. "Don't you?"

Suze interrupted, "It's *amazing.*"

Lisa shifted her gaze to the dark-haired woman and the playfulness dropped from her face. "What?"

Suze was comparing the image on the television to the woman who stood before her. "You could be twins. I mean, the hair's all different, but—hasn't anyone ever told you how much you look like Crystal Bright?"

Lisa shrugged and shook her head. "No one ever mentioned it before. I really don't have too many friends, and until recently, I never watched television, myself."

Chad looked at her with disbelief. "No TV? Oh, come on!"

"Really," Lisa said. "My Nanna would never allow it."

Suze didn't trust this woman. Things still felt very wrong. Wasn't it possible that she had misinterpreted her own vision of Chad being killed by Crystal Bright and the killer had been this woman instead? Wasn't it possible that Crystal Bright had nothing to do with this whatsoever? Suze's head still pounded, and her mind stubbornly refused to process the possibilities. If she and Chad were indeed following the proper path to find the little girl, why hadn't the thread returned to her, glistening teacups marking her way and easing the piercing pain in her skull?

Lisa crossed the room and turned the television off. She was finding it difficult to concentrate on her visitors with the distraction of the set. Television was very interesting indeed. She had noticed the similarities between Crystal Bright and herself almost immediately. She had heard of people having doubles, but this was too much. With a new hair style and makeover, Lisa could easily pass for the other woman.

Lisa studied her new guests carefully, her face masking her studious deliberation. The woman was shrill and annoying. She smelled very poorly and needed a bath. The man—was he a man or just a boy?—was completely filthy too, but it lent him a raw, animal quality. Pleasing. His rugged jaw line rippled with tiny muscular movements, his straggly dark hair spilling over his dark eyes. For all the times that Nanna Grace had used the phrase, Lisa hadn't truly known what the old woman had meant. It was quite clear as she studied Chad's face.

She could see his soul.

It was primitive, powerful, dark, and boundless. His strength surged like an electric current racing along just underneath the surface of his skin. Together they would find this child, whoever she might be. They would find the child and silence her possibilities.

Helen Martin strolled through the humid evening air to the parking lot. She had just finished a ten-hour shift, and her feet were looking forward to an hour in warm water and Epsom salts.

She wondered how Lisa was doing in Borden with the invalid woman. She was sure that Lisa was doing a wonderful job, and the prospective employers were bound to fall in love with the dear, sweet girl. On a small, selfish level, Helen hoped that Lisa wouldn't get the position. If she did, she was bound to move to Borden, and that would be terrible.

Helen mentally chastised herself for even thinking such a thought. Lisa certainly needed a job. She shouldn't mean this much to Helen after such a short time. It was just that Lisa so reminded her of Evie...

Lisa had been gone two evenings now. She should be back the next night. Helen had already decided she would make a big pot of chicken and noodles and deliver it to Lisa just as soon as she got in. She couldn't wait to hear how the test run had gone.

Helen pulled out into traffic and slowly crossed the familiar streets which took her home. The sun was setting, its reds and oranges filtering through the flowering crowns of the majestic trees sprinkled throughout the neighborhoods. She was restless. She didn't want to go home, but where else was there to go? She had focused for so long on her career that she had let all of her social acquaintances go. They would have been too painful to maintain, anyway. Her girlfriends forcing conversation while their eyes said those same painful things, *How are you holding up dear? So sad about your sweet daughter. I don't think I could make it if my daughter were killed.* Only their daughters *hadn't* been killed. Just Evie.

Helen's empty house loomed ahead on the left, its dark windows serving as quick reminder of the loneliness inside. Helen sighed. Maybe she should get some ice cream. She always felt a little better after some butterscotch ripple. Of course, the seams of her uniforms were beginning to subtly protest her frequent indulgences. She must have gained fifty pounds since Evie had died.

She slowly cruised by her house, deciding she wasn't quite ready to go in just yet. Maybe she would drive by Lisa's house, just to make sure that the doors were locked, and everything was sound.

McElroy shifted uncomfortably behind the steering wheel. He had been in the car so long his haunches had drifted into a coma. He had thought that the man and woman were going to meet their accomplice, but it was a woman who had answered the door. The man and the woman had gone inside, where they had remained for the past forty-five minutes. He was parked across the street from the house in the shadow between two streetlamps. Despite his own years in Morgan, he wasn't familiar with this particular house. He had yet to get a really good look at either the man or the woman. He had nearly lost them when they started running along the sidewalks earlier. Fortunately, they had been completely engrossed in their own quest, for McElroy had allowed his surveillance to become sloppy, driving erratically to keep them in his sight. It was a rookie move, and he was embarrassed by it. One glance over their shoulders, and he would have been spotted.

Now he wondered if he should approach the house. There were three of them, and he wasn't entirely comfortable with his odds. He was in his late fifties, pudgy and undisciplined. Most of his strength came from brute force fueled by Irish temper. Still, he was plodding and slow when he fought, and while he might be able to take one of them down, he'd be hard pressed to handle two. He could shoot them, but that would be too easy. These people needed to suffer like Loretta had suffered, her skin carbonized by the searing heat, her blood boiling through her veins as her heart had burst in her chest. Shooting them would be *far* too easy.

Leonard Barnes clocked out and scurried out into the parking lot, his gait nearly at a trot. The longer he had been at work, the more certain he had become that something was happening with Lisa Mitchell. He needed to get over there right away.

Fortunately, he didn't have to worry about making excuses at home for his late-night excursions. He had lived by himself since his wife, Nell, died ten years ago. She had been quickly eaten up by a savage cancer that cheated them of the opportunity to gracefully age together. He wasn't a particularly bright nor motivated man, and while his custodian's position at the hospital suited him fine, it didn't seem to impress the ladies much, so he had never endeavored to find a replacement for Nell.

As if there could *be* a replacement.

Leonard was not at all sure of the source of his anxiety. He believed in God in the same convenient manner as so many others, turning for solace in times of need and using His name in vain most others. Once, when he was twelve, he could've sworn he had seen the ghost of his grandmother making cookies in the kitchen—but he had only been *twelve*. He didn't believe in the spiritual nor the supernatural. It was something best left to Boy Scouts around campfires, telling stories under moonlit skies.

Yet Leonard had known Lisa was taking that plastic-wrapped parcel to the McMillan Reservoir. She could have been taking it anywhere along the reservoir, but he had known the exact place she was going. He had no way of explaining that. It kept him awake for long hours after he had gotten home the night before, trying to find any rational explanation whatsoever. He came up empty.

All day, his anxiety had been building. He found the passage of time slow to the point of agony. His need to observe the Mitchell house was so powerful, he could barely keep himself from chucking his mop to the floor and dashing out the front entrance. Some tiny part of his rational mind had held him in place, knowing that he could not afford to lose his job.

Why was he so obsessed with the Mitchell girl? Why did he feel that she was staining the very fabric of decency around her?

It was a body in that bag, you half-wit.

The thought had come unbidden repeatedly throughout the previous night as he laid on his back and stared at his water-stained ceiling. He should've called the police the moment he had seen her throw the parcel over the edge of the observation deck. Somehow, he couldn't become the man that he saw in his head, standing nervously by as the police had divers comb the bottom of the reservoir, only to find a big bag of garbage. Sure, they could arrest Lisa for littering, but it hardly justified the expense of dragging the bottom of the reservoir. And Leonard Barnes would look like a gigantic jackass.

Of course *it was a body, you schmo! What else would it be? Morgan's got curbside pick-up. Someone tosses a big, black package over the edge of the reservoir in the dead of night, they're trying to hide something, and it ain't no big bag of garbage.*

Leonard's Chevy started with a groan, and he wrenched the transmission into reverse, backing out of his employee's parking spot, the one farthest from the door, and pointed his car toward the Mitchell house.

⋄

Jack Lovell was very tired. The roundtrip had been more exhausting than he had considered it would be. At last, he was nearing Morgan. The only thing that had kept him awake the last hour was the memory of Lisa's face above his as she expertly maneuvered her body overtop him. He knew there had to be some explanation for Lisa's odd behavior that morning. Maybe she was frightened by how strongly she was attracted to Jack. God knew *he* was frightened. He had wanted to be rid of Janice for so long but never had the courage to take that first step. Lisa was his courage.

But now, as he neared Morgan, he began to feel rancid butterflies dancing in his stomach. What if he had driven all this way only to be rejected again? The anticipation was agonizing, but he had to be absolutely certain that she hadn't simply been playing hard to get. He would never forgive himself for giving up so easily. Each time Janice bitched, or his runny-nosed son whined, he would kick himself for being such a chump.

He stopped for gas at a small service station twenty miles or so from Morgan, filling the tank of his pickup. As the gasoline coursed through the hose, Jack imagined what it must have been like for those poor people in Indiana he had heard about on the radio. What kind of sick bastard would do a thing like that? It made Jack shudder to think of all the daily activities which could be perverted into a scene of utter violence. It was in the news all of the time—hostile employees shooting up their co-workers over coffee and doughnuts, irate financiers deciding to take out their bad fortune at the stock market on hapless children who had the unfortunate luck of stopping at McDonald's that day for lunch. The world was off its axis, average people snapping and emerging as violent animals, and people were dying for no reason whatsoever.

Jack returned the nozzle to its holster and collected his receipt from the pump. The night was quiet around him, the humidity thick and oppressive. A slight breeze sporadically teased, moving the air like heavy velvet draperies. The coolness of the breeze suggested that rain might be on the way. Jack capped his tank and hopped back into the truck.

As he pulled back onto the highway, a light drizzle began to fall.

⚬ ———◇——— ⚬

Suze sat in the corner and watched. She wasn't amused. Chad had struck up quite an easy rapport with this Lisa Mitchell. He and Lisa had talked casually about their individual experiences regarding the little girl and the fervent desire with which they each wanted to eliminate her. Combined with Suze's own reluctantly volunteered information, all they really had was a whole lot of nothing; pieces of dreams that did nothing more than excite the part of themselves that needed the girl to die.

When Suze tried to explain about her visions, she had the distinct impression that Lisa didn't really believe her. Only when she had mentioned the teacups had she gotten Lisa's attention. It was only a momentary flicker, but Suze had seen it cross Lisa's face. Lisa had definitely seen the teacups before.

When it came to Chad, Lisa seemed to dote on his every word, absorbed in his stuttering stories as if the punk asshole was William Shakespeare himself. Suze couldn't shake the feeling of anxiety that had settled on her since they had entered this house. Suze didn't understand why she and Chad couldn't go on like they had before. Why did they need Lisa anyway?

Say what you want, you're jealous.

Their voices seemed distant, and the flickering light from the television made her vision blurry. Her head still ached, low and deep in her skull. She watched Lisa laugh at Chad's inane banter and cross her legs so that her ankle brushed against his as those eyelashes fluttered beneath her bushy eyebrows. And what's with the foot of brown root showing underneath her straw yellow hair—?

Suze closed her eyes and shut both of them out completely. This was ridiculous. They had only just met this woman, and she obviously had as much to contribute to finding the girl as either of them. She could be useful. If Suze could only shake the disquieting feeling that came over her when she looked at

239

Lisa. Lisa presented a façade that was perfectly calm and serene, but Suze knew that underneath that porcelain mask lay something much darker, much more malevolent. She felt no connection with Lisa. She felt like she was being summed up and discounted.

When she opened her eyes, she cleared her throat, and Chad and Lisa stopped mid-sentence to look at her. "I'm goin' out for a walk," she said. "I'll be back in a bit."

Chad stood up and crossed the room. "You okay?"

Suze nodded and managed a smile. "It's really hot in here, and I could use the air."

"You sure you'll be okay?" he asked.

Nice, you asshole, she thought. *Thanks for volunteering to come with me.*

"Yeah," she said. "Remember? This is my old hometown. I know my way around."

"You're from Morgan?" asked Lisa. "I don't remember you."

"You wouldn't," said Suze. "You're a lot older than me."

The corner of Lisa's mouth crooked upward in bemusement. "Stay out however long you like," she said.

The front door screeched on its hinges as Suze stepped out onto the porch. If she had to stay in that room with Lisa and Chad one more second, she would have vomited.

After the door closed, Lisa turned to Chad and asked, "How long have you been with her?"

"Not long," said Chad, leaning back in his chair and grinning. "Why?"

Lisa returned the smile. "She just doesn't seem to be your type."

Chad's grin grew. "And I suppose you are?"

She hesitated for just a suggestive second. "That's not what I mean, Chad. You seem to be fairly focused on finding this little girl. I am, too. That's not what I'm getting out of Suze at all. She's just sitting around and pouting. You damn near had to drag the words out of her anytime she spoke. What good is she?"

"You didn't see her *before*," Chad said. "That psychic shit she was telling you about is real. She's got some kind of high-level connection that most of us don't ever tap into. But it's gotten fucked up lately, and it's kind of my fault. She hasn't really been the same since it happened."

"And now you feel responsible for her?"

Chad hesitated, then nodded. "I suppose so. We seem to be so close to the trail of that damned girl that I can't help but think that Suze is going to find her mojo again. Then maybe you'll see how she can help us."

"So, we're working together now?" asked Lisa.

"I assumed we were," said Chad. "You know, the only thing I can't figure is, why the girl? I mean, what *is* it about her?"

Lisa shook her head. "I have no idea. Frankly, I don't even care why." She had told Chad about Chris Baylock and his inherited precognition courtesy of Nanna Grace. Chris had said a whole lot in a very short time that evening, but one thing had stuck with Lisa.

I can't let you hurt that li'l girl.

The sentence had come to her at odd times ever since, and slowly Lisa had begun to piece a few things together as Chad told her about his dreams as well as secondhand accounts of Suze's stories. Lisa remembered the little girl she had seen in the road the day Helen had brought her home from the hospital, the girl who had disappeared into thin air. She had dark curly hair, just like the little girl in Chad's dreams and Suze's visions. But who in the hell *was* she?

Suze.

How had she known about the teacups? *They* don't have anything to do with the little girl; they were just keepsakes from Nanna Grace's dead-and-buried ancestors. Even though Lisa had spotted them herself in moments of odd circumstance, she had always suspected they were from Nanna Grace, designed to drive Lisa crazy from beyond the grave. It seemed like a ridiculous notion, but no more so than having one of the damned things suddenly appear out of nowhere, and she had certainly been witness to that.

From what Chad told her, Lisa finally accepted that Suze had seen the girl, too. As such, Suze would have to reluctantly be accepted into Lisa's and Chad's new partnership. And that was how Lisa had already come to think of it. She and Chad were partners. She watched the muscles ripple in his wiry arms as he talked with his hands. He had long, thin fingers with rough, swollen knuckles.

"It's been a long night," she said, taking one of his hands into her own. "Why don't we get some sleep? Maybe one of us will wake up with some idea of what to do."

Chad smiled unsurely as she urged him up from his seated position. "Suze is still out," he said.

"We'll leave the door unlocked for her. C'mon," she smiled at him as she gently stroked his rough knuckles, pulling him to the bottom of the stairwell. "You have something I want you to show me."

⟵———◆———⟶

Suze stormed blindly through the neighborhoods, instinctively keeping her head low. Pissed off or not, she still didn't want to run into anyone in this shit-burg. Her headache had eased to a slow, steady throb, and she thought it might actually be relaxing its death grip on her consciousness. It always waned after the first day, making the rest of its duration seem mild by comparison. But until she picked up the thread, it would linger at the corners of her periphery, keeping cadence with her heartbeat, reminding her of the foolishness which had put her into this position in the first place.

That stupid bastard, she thought. *All this because he got a little pissed off.*

A light fog had enveloped the neighborhoods, making it look as though the night had been filmed through a Vaseline-coated lens. Suze relaxed, allowing herself to look around. The fog was by no means thick, but she doubted if anyone who happened by would recognize her under its cover.

God, the town was just like always. Pretty as a postcard—neat houses on checkerboard lawns, all lined up, side-by-side like a Fisher-Price play set. The neighbors smiled and waved and God-blessed you when you sneezed; on the surface, it was an idyllic town. It was the shit behind the scenes that turned Suze's blood to ice water. The political inbreeding that controlled this little patch of God's green earth was like a vise clamped tight around its boundaries. The police department most certainly knew who was up to no good in Morgan, because more often than not, it was one of their own who was growing pot, stealing automobiles, breaking into the bank—whatever the case may be. The boys on the force came from families who had lived in Morgan for generations. Their names alone carried a certain level of dignified clout, as if by virtue of birthright, they were entitled to anything they deemed worthy of having. They took care of each other when things got a little too personal, a little too ugly. The people of Morgan didn't take kindly to strangers, either. Sure, the occasional businessman on a layover is unavoidable, but after more than a few days' stay, people began to talk. Who? Why? When is he leaving? And those considering Morgan as a possible site to execute a grift should take heed—more than one dubious salesman had disappeared without a trace within the town's limits. Anyone who knew what was good for him would steer completely clear of Morgan.

Suze turned the next familiar corner and found herself on the street where she had lived. She stopped cold, realizing that her feet had traced the familiar path without her consent. She could see the little house, five down on the right, nestled in its patch of shrubbery and crabgrass. How many nights had she spent locked in there, forced to fend that son-of-a-bitch off as best she could? Suze's mother blamed her, saying that it was the way she dressed, the way she walked. It was all such bullshit.

A piercing shriek shattered the still of the night.

Suze's eyes darted around, trying to pinpoint the source. Then it came again, shrill and clear in its panic. It was coming from her former residence.

She ran down the sidewalk, no longer concerned with being seen by her mother or her stepfather. She recognized that scream, and if he was touching her, she would kill him where he stood.

II

Their room was on the second floor of the motor lodge, and Luke stood at the edge of the walkway which ran the length of the building, leaning against the safety rail and looking down into the secluded parking lot. He wanted to be in Borden. This forced delay worried him. What if Bert's daughter was in danger right now? He could try to hitchhike the remaining miles, but he was reluctant to take his chances, afraid that the police would be looking for him. He would be delayed a lot longer than one night if they picked him up for questioning.

He wandered down the open corridor, noticing the large number of vacancies as he went. Morgan wasn't exactly a vacation spot. There were only four other cars in the motor lodge's parking lot, and Luke suspected that one of them belonged to the motel manager. At the end of the corridor was a set of metal stairs leading down to the parking lot. As Luke rounded the landing at the midway point, he spotted a telephone booth in the corner of the lot. He didn't have any cash, but he hoped Morty King would accept his call collect.

Morty did, and after much operator-induced clicking on the line, he said, "Luke! I'm surprised to hear from you so soon. It's only been three days! Homesick already?"

Luke sighed. The story was so fantastic, but he relayed it to Paulie's lawyer, nonetheless. He felt completely alone in the world, and it helped to have someone else know what had happened to him.

"You *ran?*" asked Morty after an uncomfortably lengthy silence.

"I didn't know what else to do," said Luke. "You should've seen the look on this cop's face. I swear, I think if I'd stuck around, he would've shot me."

"I heard about that explosion on the news," Morty said. "There were three people killed in it. My God! I had no idea you were involved."

"I really wish you'd rephrase that," said Luke. "I wasn't *involved*. I just happened to be there. I saw a red Volvo driving away, but I didn't see much more than that."

"Did you tell the policeman?"

"Yeah, but I don't think he believed me," said Luke.

"That Parnell guy left quite a family behind. The evening news interviewed his wife and oldest daughter. They were understandably distraught."

"I know. Bert told me about his family."

"You need to turn yourself in," said Morty. "You've made yourself look bad by taking off."

"I can't do that, Morty," said Luke. "There's something going on here that I don't completely understand, but I have to find out before I talk to the police."

"Something's going on? What are you talking about?"

"I wish I knew. I think that Bert's youngest daughter is in some kind of danger."

"She's four years old! What kind of danger could she possibly be in?"

"I don't know," said Luke. "That's what I'm trying to find out. But I've got another problem, and I was hoping you might be able to help. My wallet and clothes were in Bert's truck when it blew up."

Morty sighed. "So, you have no money and no clothes. Shit, Luke."

"I know. I'm sorry to ask, but I wondered if you might be able to—"

"I'm going to have to think about it," said Morty abruptly. "Don't get me wrong, Luke, I'd love to help, but you're putting me in an awkward position. After what you've told me, I would be obstructing justice if I helped you. I still think you should go to the police. I'll go with you. How's that? Where are you now?"

Luke worried that he had made a grievous mistake. Morty King was Paulie's lawyer, not his. Luke hadn't retained the attorney's services before telling his story; attorney-client privilege didn't apply.

"I'm not sure of the town," said Luke, purposefully vague. "It's just some payphone on the side of the road. Listen, I'll call you in a few days after I know more of what's happening."

"That's craziness," said Morty. "The longer you stay out there, the guiltier you look. Surely you see that."

"I can see how it might look that way, but I'm going to have to take my chances. I have to make sure that little girl is safe."

"You're talking like a lunatic. Who could possibly want to harm a four-year-old girl?" asked Morty.

"Who could possibly want to blow up a gas station? The world's a wild place, man."

"Will you call me when you're ready to turn yourself in? I want to represent you if you need help."

"I don't have any money," said Luke.

"Don't worry about that," said Morty. "Let's just keep you out of jail."

"I didn't do anything, Morty."

"I know. Call me as soon as you know more. I'm going to be worried sick about you."

"Thanks."

Luke disconnected the call and rested his forehead against the shiny black receiver. He should've known better than to ask Morty for money at this point. Even if the lawyer had agreed, where would he have sent the money? Without identification, how could Luke have collected it? He hadn't even remotely thought it through in his haste to unburden himself on familiar ears.

What if Morty calls the police?

His inner voices were playing devil's advocate, suggesting things Luke consciously disregarded. Sure, Morty could report Luke's telephone call, have the telephone records searched and find out where Luke was, but he didn't think Morty would do that. Morty's concern sounded genuine. As a practicing attorney, he was completely cognizant of his role in the legal process and would never willingly do anything to compromise his ethics. When Luke had asked for assistance, he had indeed put the lawyer in an awkward position.

The sun was beginning to set, and shadows stretched longer with each passing minute. Luke hoped the Honda would be repaired early in the morning; he was filled with nervous energy and waiting around Morgan was only making things worse. He wondered again how Bert's family would receive him, if they would receive him at all. They already had so much to deal with; they weren't going to like what Luke had to tell them about the potential safety of their youngest. Bert's wife, Greta, might just call the police herself, but if she did, at least Luke would have the opportunity to warn her before he was taken away.

Lost in thought, Luke ascended the stairs, his feet clanging hollowly against the metal risers. As he stepped off the landing and into the open corridor, he saw Crystal leaning against the rail across from her room, standing in the position he had earlier occupied. When she watched him approach, she smiled weakly.

"Hey," she said.

"Hey," he replied, easing in beside her.

"I didn't see you down in the car," she said. "I thought you'd left."

Luke smiled. "Sorry to disappoint you. I'm still hoping for that ride in the morning."

"Of course," Crystal said. "I told you I would. I just thought—oh, never mind. I just wanted to tell you I was sorry."

"About what?"

"My little tantrum earlier," she said. "I must've sounded nuts."

"Maybe a little," said Luke, staring out into the failing daylight. "I imagine it's a big adjustment, being down here with all us little people."

Crystal sighed. "I wish you wouldn't talk like that. I know how I acted before, but I'm working myself into being embarrassed over it. Honestly, I know better than to think I'm any more special than anyone else."

They stood in silence for a moment longer, then Luke said, "How's Paula doing?"

"She's sleeping, the poor thing," said Crystal.

"Would you like to talk a walk?"

Crystal nodded. "Just let me leave a note for Paula in case she wakes up."

❦

They walked slowly through the sleepy neighborhoods of Morgan in silence, appreciating the serenity of the summer evening in small-town America. No one stopped to ask for an autograph, and Crystal was beginning to be humbled by all of the inattention.

"So, what's Paula's problem?" Luke asked abruptly.

"I told you," Crystal said. "Female stuff."

"She doesn't like me."

"Why would you say that? She doesn't know you," said Crystal. "She may be slow to trust, but that doesn't mean she doesn't like you."

"Morgan is her hometown?" Luke asked. He had inferred enough from Crystal's and Paula's conversations to make that extrapolation.

Crystal paused, then nodded. "She doesn't get along with her family, though."

"How come?"

"Why don't you ask Paula?" asked Crystal. "I really don't think I should be talking about Paula's business when she's not around."

"Then why don't we talk about you?"

Crystal shrugged. "I pretty much brought you up to speed at the hotel room. I was a big star. Now I'm not."

Luke shook his head. "I mean before that. Were you born in California?"

"Nope," said Crystal. "I was born in Ohio, little town called Lucasville. That's where Paula and I are headed. I was raised by my aunt, and she recently passed away. I want to see the old house."

"Are you and Paula related?"

"Nope," she said again. "She's a friend I met while working on the show in California, although I wasn't particularly friendly with her at the time. I threw a script at her head. I was kind of at the peak of my insolence then. It was before I got fired." It was the first time she had actually used the term 'fired.' Now that she said it aloud, it wasn't as mortifying as she had feared.

"Were you messed up in drugs or something?"

Crystal was shocked. "Drugs? *No!* Nothing like that. I almost wish it *were* drugs or booze, because then I could at least blame my behavior on that. No, I guess I just got too big for my britches, as Aunt Maude would have said."

"I'm sorry about your aunt."

"Thanks."

They walked in silence a few more moments as the sky deepened around them. A light fog had settled across the streets, refracting the pale light cast from the streetlamps overhead. Although it was only around nine, traffic had slowed to nearly nothing. Crystal could hear all of the sounds of nature, frogs croaking and crickets chirping—things she hadn't heard in such a long time. It was very peaceful and serene.

"Tell me something about yourself, farm boy," said Crystal.

"I wish you'd stop calling me that," he groused.

"Where'd you grow up?"

Luke shifted uncomfortably. "A farm."

Crystal giggled, and he looked at her crossly.

"I was adopted when I was a teenager by an old fella named Paulie Leighton. He didn't have any children of his own, but he seemed to like having me around, and I sure to God liked him better than Sister Margaret at the orphanage. He died recently. Left me the farm and the property, but on one condition," said Luke.

"What was that?"

"I had to leave Jasper for a year and sort of bum around the country. I had never been away from home, and he thought it was time."

"You're making this up."

"No, I'm not," said Luke.

"Jasper?" asked Crystal incredulously.

"It's in Kentucky, and if you don't believe me, you can check a map."

Crystal was skeptical. "I will."

Luke walked ahead, insult stinging his expression.

"Hey!" Crystal called after him, trotting to catch up. "I didn't mean it. Look, I'm sorry. That was pretty shitty of me to say, my own aunt having just passed away."

"Yeah, it *was* pretty shitty," muttered Luke.

"Really," said Crystal, stopping him by crossing in front to face him. "I'm sorry."

Luke shrugged helplessly. "What can I say? It's a crazy story, complete with an orphanage run by a mean-tempered nun. But it gets better. I've only been out of Jasper for three days. *Three days.* The first ride I get is from some nice guy named Bert Parnell, real gruff type with soft insides, you know? Proud to pieces about his family." He unconsciously checked his pocket for the crumbled Polaroid of little Virginia Parnell. It was still there.

"Bert was the guy who—" Crystal trailed off, not knowing a good way to finish the sentence.

Luke nodded. "He owned the truck that blew up. He was inside the station taking a shit—*OH!* Excuse me!" His hand clamped across his mouth and his cheeks reddened. Again, he looked like a very tall little boy.

Crystal laughed. "I've heard worse. Go on."

Luke cleared his throat, his face still red. "There isn't much more to tell. The place blew up."

"Do the police know who did it?" asked Crystal.

Luke shook his head. "I saw a red Volvo leave the lot, but I didn't get a good look at anyone."

They walked a few more blocks in silence. It was still humid, but the breeze that funneled through the treetops was cool. Amber porch lights winked from houses along the street and fluttering moths sought them out to haphazardly hover around.

"So, who's in Borden?" asked Crystal. "Girlfriend?"

Luke shook his head. "No, just some people I have to see."

"You're being cryptic, farm boy," she said.

"Bert Parnell lived in Borden. I'd like to pay my respects to his family," he said, leveling a steely gaze in her direction. "If that's all right with you."

Crystal had no choice but to shut up; her foot was wedged firmly in her mouth.

⁘

When Paula woke up in the dark motel room from her nightmare, she was already screaming as someone pounded on the door.

"Hey!" called a gruff male voice from the other side of the door. "If y'all don't quiet down, I'm calling the cops!"

Paula was disoriented, but she allowed the scream to trail away. She crossed the room and looked through the peephole. A disgruntled older man stood on the other side, his hands on his hips, his bald head cocked to the side, listening for further interruptions of his quiet evening.

"Sorry!" Paula called meekly through the door. "I was having a bad dream."

The man muttered something derogatory and unintelligible as he wandered back toward his own room two doors down. Paula realized that she must have been screaming pretty loudly for him to have heard her from such a distance.

The dream *had* been horrific. In it, she had been trapped in that little house on Briardown, every exit inexplicably leading back into the house. Joel waited in every room, alcohol floating in noxious clouds around him while his eyes gleamed with anticipation. She shivered involuntarily at the recollection. It had been months since she had seen the man, but it might take years before Paula could think of him without the familiar cold knot of fear twisting her stomach. It might never happen. Being in Morgan was shredding her nerves. Geographically, she was closer to the people and places of her past than she had ever hoped to be again. She did take a small amount of comfort in the knowledge that no one had seen her, no one could report to Joel that his little bitch was back in town.

When Paula was fourteen, Joel had given her crabs. When she had gone for treatment, he had blamed everything on Paula's loose morals and frequent boyfriends, telling Dr. Devereaux, the family physician, that the girl was spreading herself thin all over town with anyone who would have her. She had been subjected to a humiliating lecture from the doctor on the dangers of casual sex and unsafe sex, colored with enough religious overtones to let Paula know he thought she needed help on a spiritual level as well. Dr. Devereaux would have never believed her if she had told him that Joel had done this to her. As a boy, Joel had worked in Dr. Devereaux's stables, shoveling shit and doing whatever grunt work there was to be done. Joel must have had his venereal diseases treated in a different county, where everyone's eyes and ears weren't connected in a vicious sewing circle.

When Paula was fifteen, Joel had gotten her pregnant. Angel had already married and left home, and Joel threatened to kill Paula if she ever told Tammy, her mother. Although Joel could've blamed the baby on any one of the fictitious boyfriends he had created for Paula over the years, he knew that the possibility of a blood test someday might prove that Paula hadn't been lying. To eliminate that possibility, he had forced Paula into his old pickup and hauled her to a clinic in Dayton where they "took care" of such things. Paula had been scared and confused. She didn't *want* Joel's baby, but she couldn't stand the thought of abortion, either. Joel took her choice away. He knew precisely how to push Paula's buttons; he threatened to find Angel and cause her to have an "accident." Paula knew he was serious, and she made the journey in total silence. The pain during the return trip had been extraordinary, each bump in the road jostling her agitated insides, but she bit her lip and refused to make so much as a sound. She didn't want Joel to have the satisfaction of knowing that she was in pain.

Paula spotted Crystal's note on the dresser and scanned its contents. *Gone out for a walk. We'll be back soon. Crystal Bright.* The name was written with a practiced flourish borne of countless autograph sessions. The fan inside Paula folded the note into a tiny square and tucked the keepsake into her pocket.

She felt caged in the little room, and the more she paced the green shag carpeting, the more agitated she became. She was only sixteen years old, for God's sake! Would Joel keep her imprisoned for the rest of her life? Could she never pass through Morgan with her head held high? As Paula had done so many times before, she imagined a world without Joel, one in which her mother still loved and cared for her, and Angel was still a regular presence in her life. Although Angel had maintained infrequent contact with Paula since she had moved out, it wasn't the same as when she was just down the hall. Paula hadn't seen the darkest sides to Joel until after Angel had gone. She supposed that Angel had endured that burden up until then. Paula might have felt abandoned in the way that Angel had left, but she knew that Angel had seen an opportunity to get out, and who could blame her for taking it? Paula knew that she would have done the same thing if she were in Angel's place, though she probably would have tried to take Angel with her. But what could Angel have done? Paula was still underage, and Joel and Tammy would have called the police, cutting Angel's escape short. Paula couldn't blame Angel for getting out the only way she could.

The more Paula reflected, the more anxious she became. An idea suddenly came to her, and after a timid peek outside the door, she eased out onto the concrete balcony. She walked quickly to the metal stairs, descended them and crossed the lot to where the Honda was parked. She had assumed from the note that Luke had gone with Crystal and now saw that the car was, in fact, empty. She opened the driver's door and pulled the lever which caused the seat to drop forward and provide access to the back seat. Paula groped along the floorboards, her fingers finally finding what she was looking for.

It was the bottle of gin that Crystal had found in the dank storm cellar in Kansas. Paula had taken it as an afterthought and was now quite pleased with herself. She relocked the car and headed back to the room, the bottle tucked safely in the crook of her arm. Gin had calmed her down before; maybe it could help again.

———◇———

"Do you believe in ESP and stuff like that?" asked Luke, abruptly breaking the awkward silence in which they had walked for the last several blocks.

"You mean like those 1-900 numbers that will answer all of your questions for $4.99 per minute?" asked Crystal.

Luke shook his head. "Those are scams. Anyone dumb enough to fall for that crap deserves what he gets. No, I mean the kind of ESP you hear about on, say, *Unsolved Mysteries*. Like a psychic who helps the police solve cases."

"I thought you didn't watch TV," said Crystal.

"I said I didn't watch *much* TV," corrected Luke. "*Unsolved Mysteries* was one of Old Paulie's favorites. He never missed it."

Crystal considered it for a moment, then shrugged. "I've never really thought about it. I mean, psychic detectives aren't ripping people off in the same blatant way, but they certainly receive a lot of free advertising in the way of shows like *Unsolved Mysteries*. Why?"

"I don't know," said Luke. "I'd never really thought about it myself until the last few days. I've had a couple of wicked déjà vus."

Crystal grinned. "Aunt Maude used to call them wrinkles in time, like that book by Madeleine L'Engle, you know?"

Luke smiled and nodded. "I read that when I was a boy."

"So, you think you're suddenly psychic?"

Luke laughed, but it was without conviction. "I didn't say *that*. They were just so close together, and they played out exactly as I thought they would."

"That's the whole thing about a déjà vu. The sensation of familiarity coincides with the actual event, so how do you know you actually saw it before? I think it's something electrochemical in the brain, a misfire between synapses or something. Matter of fact, that's how I wrecked the Honda," said Crystal.

"What do you mean?"

Crystal laughed sheepishly. "It sounds dumb as hell now, and I was too embarrassed to even tell Paula about it, but I could've sworn I saw a little girl squatted down in the middle of the road. I ran off the road trying to avoid her, but it was all just an optical illusion. The road was completely clear when I checked."

Luke was staring at Crystal, unnerving her. "What?" she asked.

"You saw a little girl?" he asked. The serious look on his face made Crystal's smile fade.

"No, I *thought* I saw a little girl," she said. "That was my whole point."

"What did she look like?"

Crystal rolled her eyes. "What difference does it make? She wasn't *real*."

"Humor me."

Crystal sighed. "She was just a little thing, maybe around five or so, with big round eyes and—"

"Long, dark, curly hair," Luke finished. Crystal's mouth hung open for a few seconds before snapping shut.

"Are you telling me that I almost hit a little girl? Where did she go? Where did she—" Crystal's voice trailed off as Luke shook his head.

"Something's going on here," said Luke.

"What do you mean?"

He produced the crumpled photo from his pocket and showed it to Crystal. She gasped when she saw the familiar image that, although short-lived, had been burned into her memory.

"That's *her!*" exclaimed Crystal, taking the photo from Luke and looking at it closely. "Who is she?"

"That's Bert Parnell's daughter, Virginia. He and his wife call her Little Tater," said Luke.

"Did she run away from home or something?"

"I don't think so. She's only four. I doubt she'd get far."

"So, why was she standing in the middle of the road last night?"

Luke took the picture as Crystal handed it back, stuffing it into his pocket. "She wasn't. I think you had your own kind of déjà vu."

"That's ridiculous! That isn't how a déjà vu works!"

"Then where did she go?" challenged Luke. "Didn't you say you looked for her after you stopped the car?"

Crystal nodded. "She could have gone into the cornfield."

"*You* went into the cornfield," reminded Luke.

Crystal struggled for an explanation but couldn't readily find one. They had come full circle back to the motor lodge and were standing at the bottom of the stairs. Finally, she said, "I'm sure there's a logical explanation here."

Luke shook his head. "You're welcome to try to find one, but I'm out of ideas. Maybe I've been calling this déjà vu stuff by the wrong name. In both cases, they

251

were dreams I had. They didn't make a lick of sense when I had them, and by the time I recognized them, it was too late to change the outcome. In either case, the girl played a significant role in them. I have to tell you, I'm completely weirded-out by all this."

They reached the second-floor landing and walked down the corridor to Crystal's room. The door was standing open a crack, and when Crystal pushed it back on its hinges, Paula was nowhere to be found.

Paula's temper had peaked, unexpectedly fueled by the alcohol. It was only with great effort that she was able to maintain a somewhat steady gait. The neighborhoods passed by in a blur, like familiar images distorted through the subtle curves of carnival mirrors. She had walked this route so many times in the past, dreading the eventual destination. She would hide in her room and be as quiet as possible, hoping that Joel would forget that she was even there. Sometimes it worked, sometimes it didn't.

All of the humiliation that Joel had caused her over the years rose like bile in her throat. She was empowered by the notion that Joel would not expect her to suddenly show up; he wouldn't expect her to be so completely full of fury. Joel had completely dominated Paula in the time since he married Tammy. He had preyed on her insecurity, using violence and rape to make her fear him. Angel had been so strong. Angel had fought back occasionally, and for Paula, that somehow seemed worse. Worse because it was futile. Angel would bear the evidence of Joel's physical superiority for days. Once, Joel had cracked one of Angel's ribs, puncturing a lung. The look of terror that had been in her eyes had haunted Paula ever since. Angel thought she was going to die.

Paula didn't know how to feel about her own forced abortion. The whole experience seemed so unreal, as if it were happening to someone else. She hadn't formed a sentimental attachment to the fetus growing within her womb. She hadn't had *time*. Joel had taken the choice away from her. In that, she could be bitter and could allow the bitterness to quickly fester into something else. As she turned the corner of Briardown, Paula realized that she had come here to kill the son-of-a-bitch.

The house was set back from the road, nestled in a bed of light fog. The small outbuilding which housed Joel's neighborhood candy store was closed up tight, its hinged panel padlocked in place over the window which faced the road. Paula could see Joel clearly, leaning across the counter from behind that window while he sold hard candy to all of the neighbor kids, holding the little girls' hands longer than he should, leering down into their innocent round faces. She remembered Mary Jo Conrad, her best friend in first grade, who had abruptly called their friendship quits after a mysterious encounter with Joel inside the candy store had transpired. Mary Jo would never tell Paula *why* they couldn't be friends anymore, but Paula had a pretty good idea.

The house was in a constant state of disrepair. Loose siding drooped in places, and the windows were nearly opaque in layers of grime. The covered porch was home to an avocado green washer and matching dryer. A clothesline in the side yard had rows of sheets pinned in place, wafting lazily in the night air near an old tree stump where Joel split his firewood, the handle of an ax protruding from the stump. Joel's blue pickup was in the drive, a fifteen-year-old Dodge with rust proliferating like acne on a teenager's face. The front door stood open, a battered screen door pulled shut to keep the bugs out. As Paula approached, she could hear the TV blasting out into the darkness. She could picture Joel, bald and fat, wearing only a t-shirt and underpants, beer can in one hand, remote control in the other, chomping on one of those cheap, nasty cigars of his. She pictured the look of surprise when he saw her. She had taken the screwdriver from the back of the Honda, a long, thin flathead with a heavy wooden handle. While Paula would have preferred a knife, she figured she would have to make do. She would go for his eyes first.

Paula didn't expect her mother to be a problem. Tammy had become so passive she was almost non-existent. She would side with whomever was winning the battle. Paula had seen it a hundred times over. Tammy had no backbone whatsoever.

Paula crossed the grass carefully, easing her way to the porch. She could see the living room through the screen door now. Family portraits hung on the wall, pictures of smiling people whose eyes told other stories. Angel, Paula, Angel and Paula, Tammy and Joel, the whole group—smiling, smiling, smiling. In them, Tammy's eyes looked vacant, as if she had completely surrendered control of everything to Joel, including her soul. In turn, he smiled like the devil, his photographed eyes working their own magic on Paula's composure. A handmade sign from Joel's short-lived woodburning hobby was proudly displayed by the door.

714, McElroy.

She had almost reached the door when the voice came from behind her. The message was short, the tone vulgar. "Well, looky *here*."

Before Paula could even turn around, Joel had seized her right arm, forcing the screwdriver out of her grasp. He clamped another big hand around the base of Paula's skull as he twisted her captured arm behind her back. He began guiding her away from the house, toward the candy store.

For a moment, Paula was dumbstruck. Just mere seconds ago, she had been relishing the obvious beauty of her plan, only one outcome even remotely possible. She would walk into the living room and strike before Joel even knew what was happening. Somehow the tables had turned, and now it was too late. Joel had her again.

As he fumbled with the padlock on the back door of the structure, Paula finally found her voice and shattered the serenity of the night with the sound of her terrified screams.

CHAPTER THIRTEEN

I

"You son-of-a-bitch."

The words came from behind Joel a fraction of a second before Paula felt the man's weight abruptly thrust upon her back, his forehead snapping forward and cracking against the back of her head, forcing her face into the splintered wood of the candy shack. She stopped screaming as the muscles in her throat went numb with terror. Joel slid slowly down Paula's backside, holding her firmly in place against the wall.

Suddenly his weight was gone. He had slid all the way down and rolled aside, but Paula was too frightened to turn around and look. She covered her face with shaking hands, a pathetic mewling spilling through her lips.

"Pip?"

There were hands on her shoulders.

"Pip?"

The hands were trying to coax Paula to turn, but she struggled against them, trying to keep her face shielded. *Pip*—only one person called her that. When the nickname finally permeated Paula's alcoholic haze and raw terror, she relented and let the arms turn her around as tears poured down her cheeks.

"Angel?" Her voice was small and weak, like that of a small child. It was Suze's nickname since the two had been young girls. Though her vision was blurred, she could see Suze's face, the most welcome sight she had seen in months.

"Did he hurt you?" asked Suze, taking Paula's face in her hands and inspecting it maternally.

Paula shook her head and darted her eyes from side to side, trying to see what had happened to him.

"It's okay. I took care of him," said Suze.

Paula saw Joel a few feet to her left, lying face down in the crabgrass. The handle of his own ax protruded from a growing pool of blood between his shoulder blades. Angel had struck him more than once, judging from the telltale gashes riddling his backside.

"We have to get him out of here before any of the neighbors see," said Suze.

"Where?"

Suze finished removing the padlock from the outbuilding and opened the flimsy door on its creaking hinges.

"Get his feet," said Suze, taking Joel's lifeless arms and dragging him toward the opening.

"We can't leave him here," said Paula, obeying nonetheless. "Mama'll find him."

"Not for a while," said Suze. "Joel whored around all the time. If he doesn't come home tonight, Mama ain't gonna lose any sleep over it. Right now, we have to get him moved out of sight. Later, I'll worry about what to do with him."

"Is he d-d-dead?"

"If he isn't, he's not in any shape to give us shit. C'mon."

They finally maneuvered Joel's body into the building. As an afterthought, Suze put a foot on Joel's back and pulled the ax free from the flesh in which it rested. She moved her foot from Joel's back to the head of the ax, applying downward pressure while she pulled up on the handle. The wood splintered and broke, and Suze slid the ax handle into her pants leg, where it protruded suspiciously. Observing Paula's uncomprehending stare, she smiled at her younger sister and said, "Fingerprints."

Suze took Paula's hand and guided her out of the building, putting the padlock back in place before heading away from the property and away from Briardown Avenue. If her precognition was still functioning, she would have been operating calmly, assured of the safety of her actions. Tonight, she was flying solo and hoped to hell no one had seen her hacking away at Joel's fat back.

Paula had managed to regain some of her composure, although her senses were still dampened by the gin she had consumed earlier. She looked at Suze, barely able to believe that she was actually there.

"What are you doing here?" Suze asked. "What happened to California?"

"I did what you asked," said Paula. "I kept an eye on Crystal Bright after she was fired. I sprung her from the hospital before they could cart her off to the psych ward. I had no idea we'd end up in Morgan."

Suze nodded and smiled. "I *knew* she had something to do with all of this." It meant very little to Paula; she hadn't met Lisa Mitchell. She hadn't been forced to second guess her premonition, the one which told her that Crystal Bright was going to try to kill Chad.

"All of what, Angel?" asked Paula. "I don't understand what's going on. It all keeps getting weirder and weirder. What about Joel? His brother is bound to poke around when Joel turns up missing."

"David? He doesn't live in Morgan anymore. Took Loretta and moved," said Suze. "I'm surprised you didn't know that. All we need to do is buy ourselves a little time, and then we won't be anywhere near the scene when someone finally does find that asshole's body."

"You just gonna leave him in there?" asked Paula.

"Unless I can think of someplace better," said Suze. "Tell me about Crystal Bright. She's here in Morgan?"

Paula nodded. "We were heading toward her hometown when we had an accident. Some guy came along and helped us get back on the road, but the car needed more work. He gives me the creeps, but Crystal offered him a ride a little further along if he helped us with the car. I couldn't believe it when the damn thing ended up at Roy's!" Roy Snyder, Suze's ex-husband, had owned Morgan's only BP since his return from the Army.

Suze looked at her oddly. *"Roy's BP?* That's where Chad took our car. A little coincidental, don't you think? Where are you staying?"

"Louie's Motor Inn. I guess from here we're going through Borden to drop Luke off before we cross the state to Lucasville."

"That's Crystal's hometown?"

Paula nodded. "I'm scared, Angel. Of all the times we talked about killing Joel, I never thought it would actually happen."

Suze smiled. "I told you he'd get what was coming to him. Believe me, he had enough enemies that we won't even be close to the first people the police think of."

"David McElroy will."

"Fuck David McElroy."

"I've gotta get back," said Paula. "Crystal doesn't know I'm gone."

"Be careful, little Pip," said Suze, pausing to examine her sister's face one last time before kissing her on the forehead. "I'm still carrying the cell phone, so call me when you get to Lucasville or if your plans change."

"Why are we doing this, Angel?"

"I'll explain it all when we have more time," said Suze. "Now scoot."

Suze watched Paula's diminishing form until it was entirely enshrouded by the fog. She hated using her sister like this, but she knew that Paula was the perfect candidate to keep tabs on Crystal Bright. She had idolized the woman for years. Suze preferred not to think about the future and when she would inevitably kill her sister's idol. She hoped that by then Paula would understand her way of thinking. Thus far, Paula hadn't experienced any of the inner guidance with which Suze had been blessed. She was operating solely on blind faith in her older sister. Suze had never asked Paula to do anything violent because she didn't sense that capability in the girl. Suze hoped that this, too, would change with time.

Suze started back toward Lisa Mitchell's neighborhood, her footsteps slow and ambling. She wasn't in any hurry to return but didn't feel safe on the streets of Morgan any longer. After years of planning and plotting and daydreaming, Joel McElroy was finally dead. The aftermath wasn't nearly as rapturous as she had expected. It had all been too quick. Suze had wanted the man to suffer for all of the degradation and humiliation he had piled upon her and Paula throughout the years. Her ultimate fantasy involved tying the bastard up, sticking a curling iron up his ass, turning it on high and walking into the next room where she could enjoy his escalating discomfort from a comfortable distance. Somehow, she thought the smell of Joel's roasting anus might make her giggle.

As Suze approached the dark house, she noticed that only a single light burned from an upstairs window. That bitch had put the moves on Chad. Well, it wasn't like she hadn't seen it coming.

It was as she approached the porch that she saw the door was standing ajar.

<hr />

Chad and Lisa had been at it for some time. He pounded into her while she nibbled his shoulders and moaned in ecstasy. *He* didn't mind having his shoulder bitten. Chad was so much better at this than Jack Lovell that Lisa could hardly believe they were even doing the same thing.

Chad was so lost in the moment that he didn't hear the door creak open behind him. Lisa heard it, and a different sort of satisfaction crossed her face. She could imagine the look on Suze's face as she entered the room. She almost would've stopped to look.

"What in the hell are you doing?"

This time, Lisa did look and quickly. The voice was not what she expected at all. Instead of Suze's whiny timbre, it was booming and decidedly male. Lisa pushed Chad aside and raised up to see who was standing at the foot of her bed.

It was Jack Lovell. His sandy hair was whipped into wild tendrils dancing off his head. His complexion neared that of a ripe radish, and his hands were clutched into white-knuckled fists at his sides. His arms were actually *trembling* with fury.

"Jack?" Lisa smiled at him and let the sheet slide down to expose her right breast. "What are *you* doing here?"

Chad propped himself up on an elbow and watched the scene with disinterest. Lisa didn't seem to be alarmed by the man, so why should he be? Chad just wanted him to go away—he wasn't finished with Lisa yet.

Jack's voice caught somewhere between his lungs and voice box, struggling to find cohesive words to describe the way he was feeling. His eyes flooded with tears, and at that moment, Lisa saw him as the most pathetic creature she had ever laid eyes upon.

He looked at her, his whole face pleading. "I love you, Lisa. Please—"

Lisa was so caught off guard that she laughed out loud. What little composure Jack had drained away, and he began to sob pathetically.

"Who the fuck *is* this fag?" asked Chad, lighting a cigarette from his pack on the nightstand.

"No one," said Lisa.

"How can you *say* that?" asked Jack, his face contorted and glistening with tears. He dropped to his knees, leaning forward with his elbows propped at the foot of the bed. He almost looked as if he were praying. "I thought we had something *good*."

"Oh, Jack," said Lisa with such pitiful condescension that Jack buried his face in his hands. "You poor thing. We had one moment. Do you hear me? *One moment*. It didn't mean anything to me at all."

Jack looked up at her, begging with every line of his face. "But—"

Lisa shook her head. "No buts, Jack. Just get out."

For a moment, Lisa didn't think he was going to go. He lay defeated at the foot of the bed, sobbing into the blankets, his shoulders shuddering. Slowly, with a great spectacle of snuffling, he rose to his feet, casting Lisa one last pathetic glance. The smile on her face told him that she was *enjoying* this.

"Go on, man. You heard the lady," said Chad, grinning at him crookedly from where he was propped on his side of the bed. One of his naked legs poked out from under the sheet. He dragged it lazily from side to side, teasing Jack.

Jack was about to turn around when the bullet hit him from behind, burrowing in between his shoulder blades and piercing his shattered heart.

David McElroy watched as the red pickup truck pulled to the curb directly across from the house. McElroy had parked diagonally from the house, five cars down from where the truck had stopped. His lower extremities were still numb, so he rocked on his haunches to encourage blood to flow back into them. Things were starting to happen.

A sandy-haired man got out of the truck and stared at the house from across the street. McElroy's eyes narrowed. This was the man he had seen at *Friendly's* last night. He had washed the soot of the explosion from his face, but McElroy would recognize him anywhere. By the time his legs felt trustworthy, the man had already walked across to the house and trotted up the stairs to the porch. McElroy eased his car door open and slid out as quietly as he could.

The man disappeared across the threshold, leaving the door open behind him, as if inviting McElroy to enter. He approached the house cautiously, easing his stolen revolver from where it was holstered on his belt. He may have left his uniform at home, but he wasn't going anywhere without a gun.

He froze as the first porch step creaked under his weight, sucking his breath in and waiting. The first floor of the house was nothing but dark shadows where anyone could be hiding. A thin film of perspiration broke across McElroy's forehead. He was outnumbered and counted heavily on the element of surprise. What if they had seen him crossing the lawn? They could be lurking out of sight, waiting—

But the bastard had actually *come*. *He* was the one that McElroy wanted to kill. To think that he had actually stood face-to-face with this man as he tried to pass himself off as an innocent bystander.

His Loretta made the best orange sweet rolls, and McElroy would never eat them again.

His need for vengeance was like a quickly spreading poison, seizing control of his muscles and propelling him toward the door of the house. If they were waiting for him, it didn't matter—none of it mattered anymore.

As he stepped into the silent living room, he realized he should have brought his brother with him. Joel loved to shit-kick and didn't need a reason. It would have improved the odds. But as with all afterthoughts, it was irrelevant. He couldn't do anything about it now.

He stood in the dark room, listening for sounds. His eyes adjusted to the absence of light, and the outlines of furniture slowly began to form. He could hear voices coming from the second floor, indecipherable words trailing down the narrow staircase.

McElroy crossed the room and peered up to the darkened second floor. A rectangle of light spilled out from the right, casting a shadow around where the man stood in an upstairs doorway. Then he moved inside the room, and his shadow disappeared. McElroy could hear three distinct voices, two male and one female.

It was time to make them pay for what they had done to Loretta. The dark-haired girl may not be here, but he could get her later. The one who had made a fool of him was here, and McElroy wouldn't let him get away again.

He took a cautious step onto the first riser. He kept his feet toward the outer edges of the steps, hoping to prevent the betrayal of sound. It wouldn't matter. The people upstairs where completely preoccupied with themselves. McElroy could hear androgynous sobbing emanating from the room. He slowly made his way to the landing, creaking only occasionally. McElroy's hand was sweaty and hot against the cold metal of the gun, and his hand trembled slightly from the tension. He had to consciously relax his finger to keep from blowing a hole into the wall. As McElroy rounded the half wall which bordered the stairwell at the landing, he could see the young man standing at the foot of a bed, his back to him. He was saying something to the other two who were on the bed.

The advantage of surprise would be short. It was now or never.

McElroy raised his revolver and shot the man between the shoulder blades. The two under the sheets froze momentarily, and then began to slither in opposite directions across the bed. As Jack Lovell dropped to the floor, McElroy shifted his revolver to the right, sighting Chad's head down the short barrel of the gun.

His sweaty finger tightened on the trigger.

"Oh, fiddlesticks!" groaned Helen as handles of the plastic grocery sack slipped from her fingers and dropped to the pavement. The carton of eggs that had been carefully positioned at the top of the bag skittered off and came to a rest behind Helen's rear tire, forming a slowly expanding puddle of yellow goo.

Helen had remembered her notion of fixing chicken and noodles for Lisa's return the next day and realized she didn't have half of the ingredients that she needed. She pulled into Morton's Supermarket on the way across town.

Sighing, she unloaded the other two bags she was carrying into the Buick's trunk and ambled back toward the store gingerly holding the carton of shattered eggs in front of her while the yoke dribbled down her arm.

She could pick up another carton through the express lane and would be on her way shortly. She had all evening to make sure Lisa's house was secure; it wasn't like it was going anywhere.

Leonard Barnes eased his old Chevy behind the red Ford pickup at the curb in front of Lisa's. Apparently, the new man in Lisa's life was more than a passing ship in the night.

The house was dark, save for one lighted window on the second floor. Although he couldn't see anything that was out of place, he couldn't shake the feeling of dread that hung around his neck like a determined albatross since he had awakened that morning.

What was Lisa Mitchell up to?

He thought about creeping across the street and peeking in the windows, but this was a quiet neighborhood with as good a block watch as one might hope for. Leonard didn't want to have to explain to the police why he was trudging through Lisa's rose bushes for a quick peek inside. Anything he might say at that point would sound crazy.

Leonard rolled the window down and listened to the quiet nighttime sounds. As a whole, Morgan was a sleepy little town; this street was quieter than most. There were no teenagers blazing down the road in sports cars with stereos thumping, no loud conversation floating across from inconsiderate neighbors, no children screaming and laughing as they ran along the sidewalks. Even the cicadas were thoughtfully keeping their volume to a minimum. The overhead streetlights were the distinctive voices of the night, electric current humming while prompting pale illumination from their frosted globes.

A bright flash lit the upstairs window briefly, followed immediately by a sharp crack. For an instant, Leonard froze, his receptors not processing the events around him. Only a minute or so later, the strange sequence repeated, and Leonard knew what those sounds had been.

They were gunshots.

As Suze stepped into the darkened living room, she caught a blue-jeaned leg taking its final step upstairs. She heard the floorboards creak slightly as the footfalls progressed across the upstairs landing.

She didn't know why, but she was certain that the leg did not belong to Chad. The footfalls were too slow, too stealthy. Someone was trying to sneak up on Chad and Lisa. Part of Suze couldn't care less, figuring that the two of them might get what they deserved. An even bigger part reminded her that, for the time being, she needed Chad and Lisa to find that damned little girl. Suze hesitated only a second before she grabbed the heavy wooden cane of Nanna Grace from where it leaned against the wall and slowly ascended the stairs.

She was three-quarters of the way up when the explosive gunshot shattered the quiet of the house.

Suze hurried up the final few stairs and saw the backside of a very familiar figure standing just inside what she assumed was Lisa's bedroom.

David McElroy? How could he know about Joel already?

He was lifting the gun again, taking aim. Without allowing herself the luxury of thought, Suze took two long steps across the landing and brought Nanna Grace's mahogany cane crashing down on the back of McElroy's head.

He crumpled instantly, but not before the gun discharged one last time.

Leonard darted across the street, running up on the porch. As his hand reached for the knob of the screen door, he paused, experiencing the sudden quiet which followed the gunshots. Maybe he had simply imagined the sounds. He expected screaming, crying—*some* sort of commotion. Instead, he heard only the incessant hum of the streetlights.

As his fingers closed around the knob, headlights swept around the corner, approaching at a crawl. Leonard catapulted himself over the rickety rail which enclosed the porch, dropping painfully into a thorny bush on the other side. He watched as the dark green car pulled in front of Lisa's house at the curb, directly across from the red pickup truck. He recognized the Buick as belonging to Helen

Martin, and he cursed under his breath. He had seen Lisa hanging around the nurse at the hospital, but he didn't know that they were friends outside of that.

This wasn't good. The *last* thing he wanted was for Helen to see him prowling around the premises, especially after what had happened with Evie. Still, there had definitely been gunshots upstairs.

He hovered in a moment of indecision before pulling himself out of the bush and slipping away through the neighbor's side yard. Helen was still in her car, facing the other way and digging in her purse for something. She didn't see him as he disappeared into the night shadows.

Purdy's Convenient Mart was two blocks over. He would call the police and leave an anonymous tip. He prayed they would arrive before anything could happen to Helen. He hated himself for not meeting the woman and warning her off, but how could he face her now? If it hadn't been for him, Evie would probably still be alive.

Helen was surprised to see Lisa's front door standing open. She had stopped under the pretense of making sure that Lisa's property was locked up tight. She had never considered the possibility that something may actually be wrong. She dug in her handbag until she found her small canister of mace and got out of her car.

The fog which had developed over Morgan in the early evening was now a thickened mass of gray mist swaddling the neighborhood's checkerboard lawns in an ominous blanket.

Helen mentally scolded herself for being so skittish. She had lived in Morgan her entire life. There wasn't a safer place on the planet. There wasn't anything to fear.

With the exception of drunk drivers.

She crossed the porch and paused at the screen door. She could hear heavy footfalls coming from above, and her whole body seemed to seize up. The can of mace in her right hand seemed supremely inadequate, and Helen wished she had simply driven on and called the police.

The footfalls suddenly began an awkward descent down the stairs. Helen stood on the other side of the screen, her apprehension growing as she saw a pair of naked legs tromping down the stairs. She breathed a brief sigh of relief as she recognized Lisa's face emerging from the stairwell. Her hair was disheveled, and her cheeks were flushed. She was wearing a long t-shirt that would have barely covered her panty line had she been wearing panties.

Helen smiled and felt embarrassed color creeping into her cheeks. "I hope I'm not intruding. I didn't expect you to be home. I was just checking—" Her words trailed away as she saw the look on Lisa's face.

"Oh, thank God!" breathed Lisa. "Do you have a first aid kit in your car?"

Helen's expression changed to one of concern. "Of course. Is someone hurt?"

Lisa nodded and guided Helen back outside and to the trunk of her car. Helen fumbled with her keys until Lisa took them from her and opened the trunk. Lisa saw the industrial-looking kit tucked away neatly beside the spare tire. She grabbed it, slammed the trunk lid and led Helen back into the house.

"What's going on, dear?" asked Helen.

Lisa didn't answer, instead pulling her up the narrow stairs.

"Oh, my goodness!" exclaimed Helen as she entered Lisa's bedroom.

The grisly scene was too much to take in at once. Immediately she saw a dark-haired man sprawled out naked on the bed, a bloody wound high above his left nipple. Instinctively, Helen crossed the room and sat beside him, reaching for his wrist and checking for a pulse.

"I don't understand," said Helen. "What's going on, Lisa?"

She turned away from the boy when Lisa didn't answer, and that was when she saw the rest. Two other men were laying on the floor, pushed up against the wall in a tangled pile of extremities. One of the men had bled profusely from a sizeable hole between his shoulder blades. The other, although unconscious, suffered no visible damage. Attached to his belt, Helen could see his sheriff's badge glinting in the room's meager light. Lisa sat on the corner of the bed, her face betraying no emotion whatsoever.

"Oh, Lisa—" Helen began, then realized someone was standing in the shadows behind the door. It was a wild-eyed woman with straggly, jet-black hair. She held the policeman's gun in her right hand and was pointing it directly at Helen's face.

II

"Paula?"

Crystal searched the small room again, as if it were even possible to overlook Paula during her first pass. She saw the bottle of gin laying on its side on the dresser, a small puddle having leaked to the floor.

"Shit," she said.

"What?" asked Luke, peering in the door.

"Paula's gone," said Crystal. "And she's been drinking."

Luke grinned. "Does she mug old ladies when she's drunk?"

"It's not funny," said Crystal. She didn't want to divulge any of Paula's background to Luke without permission, but she was genuinely worried about Paula's safety. She might need Luke's help. Paula had practically been catatonic since they reached the corporation limit of Morgan. She was terrified that her stepfather might see her, might force himself on her again. Crystal couldn't imagine what it must be like to come home to that kind of life every day. It made her Hollywood crisis seem even more ridiculous than it had already started to become. Crystal had never been forced into a sexual experience against her consent. She had never been forced to fear for her life. She couldn't imagine the psychological impact on a young girl's mind and her perception of the world around her.

Yet, Paula had gotten tanked and hit the streets. It just didn't make sense. Unless Joel had found her...

"Hey, I think I found something," said Luke, kneeling beside one of the double beds. He produced the scrap of notebook paper upon which Crystal had left her note to Paula. It was rumpled from where it had slid to the carpeting and had then been stepped upon, but even from across the room Crystal could see Paula had made an addition to the bottom of the note.

In large, jagged letters, Paula had scrawled, "Went out." She used such pressure with the pen that the point had pierced the paper in several places.

Crystal took the note from Luke and looked at the backside of the paper. It was blank. There was a blotch of gin in the lower left corner of the page. "Shit," she repeated.

"What?"

"Look, I'm not real comfortable with this," said Crystal. "I told you before that I didn't want to talk about Paula while she wasn't around, but I guess I have no choice. Morgan is her hometown, and she was terrified of running into her stepfather."

"Why?" asked Luke.

Crystal stared at him blankly, waiting for him to catch the obvious.

"Oh," he finally said.

"I'm afraid she's gotten drunk and decided to do something stupid," said Crystal.

"Stupid like what?"

"Stupid like I don't know," she said.

"I'm sure she knows what she's doing," said Luke. "Like you say, this is her home turf."

"I don't know," said Crystal. "I really think we should try to find her."

Luke nodded, and they went back out into the night.

"So, what do you think is up with little Virginia Parnell?" asked Crystal. "I mean, why her?"

Luke shrugged. The street was even less traveled than it had been before, and the fog had thickened as the evening progressed. "I really wish I knew. I just have the most overwhelming feeling that she's in for some deep shit."

"Then why don't *I* feel anything?" asked Crystal. "I look at the picture, think 'cute kid,' and that's about it. How can you be so sure?"

"You saw her standing in the road. Do you think that was just coincidence?"

"All right," said Crystal. "For the moment, let's not focus on that."

"Just because it isn't logical doesn't mean it didn't happen."

They walked along, searching the sidewalks for any sign of Paula. They wandered through a picturesque city park, checking the wooden benches in case Paula might have passed out on one of them.

Nothing.

"I don't understand why you don't just pick up the phone and call Mrs. Parnell," said Crystal as they walked on.

"She doesn't know me from Adam," said Luke. "How would you react if someone called you out of the blue and told you that your child was in immediate danger?"

"I'd call the police," said Crystal.

"Right," said Luke. "But would you believe the person who called you was warning you or threatening you?"

"I see. And you think she'll react differently if she sees you in person?"

"I'm hoping," said Luke.

"Why don't you go to the police?"

"And tell them what? I'd come across like a complete crackpot. And they wouldn't have a personal stake in it. It's none of their daughters that I'm worried about. They would write me off before I finished telling my story. If I get the chance to talk to Bert's wife, it might at least raise her awareness, even if she doesn't believe me at first."

"And you're doing all this for a guy you only just met."

"It's the right thing to do," said Luke.

"What if you're wrong?"

"I hope I am. But I'd rather play it safe than sorry."

The stillness of the neighborhood was disrupted by a siren cutting a path through nearby streets. Luke tensed as he watched the illumination from the bubble lights sweep around the corner and the cruiser appeared at the far end of the street along which they walked. It was approaching quickly, and he looked down, obscuring his face with a heavy-handed attempt to wipe his nose. He straightened only after the cruiser had passed. His reaction wasn't lost on Crystal.

Before she had the opportunity to say anything, an older man appeared on the sidewalk from a cross street, his attention rooted to the receding taillights of the police car. He had silver hair that was parted crisply on the side and slicked back from his forehead in a sort of deflated pompadour. He wore an olive-green coverall with the name *Leonard* stitched over the right breast pocket in matching green letters. He was so oblivious to his surroundings that he almost walked directly into Crystal and Luke.

As he realized his clumsiness, Leonard Barnes shifted his focus to Crystal, the beginnings of a sheepish smile playing at the corners of his mouth. "I'm sorry, I—" His voice trailed away abruptly, and his eyes widened.

Finally, thought Crystal. *Someone who* recognizes *me.*

"How—?" Leonard began, but then stopped short and shook his head. He raised a quivering finger to hover in front of Crystal's face. "The devil's given you more power than I guessed! I won't let you hurt no one else!"

Crystal froze in her confusion, watching Leonard's pointing finger join the rest of his hand to form a fist, one that was being pulled back to strike.

Luke seized Leonard's arm before he could follow through. "What in the hell do you think you're doing, old man?" demanded Luke.

Leonard seemed surprised, as if he hadn't even seen Luke standing there. With more strength than he knew he had, he snapped his wrist free from Luke's grasp and backed away several paces. "You're in league with the devil!" he shouted at Luke as he continued to backpedal. His finger was pointing at them again. "She'll deliver you to Lucifer, young man! *Lucifer!*"

Leonard turned and ran, cutting through the nearest yard before turning down the street from which he had come. Luke and Crystal stood on the sidewalk, watching in stunned silence as he disappeared into the fog.

"What the hell was that?" asked Luke.

"I think he was going to *hit* me," said Crystal. "I've heard of crazy fans, but I've never had the firsthand pleasure of meeting one."

"You think that's what he was?"

"What else would he be? All that talk about the devil—he's probably a charter member of the Moral Majority. Some of their number are extreme. They see actors as being evil on general principle," said Crystal.

"Maybe we should get back to the motel," said Luke.

"What about Paula?" asked Crystal.

"If we haven't found her by now, I doubt we're going to. She's probably back at the motel wondering where we are. Besides, I think we should get off the street before you run into any more of your 'fans.'"

"Or before you run into the police," said Crystal.

Luke stiffened. "What do you mean?"

"I saw how you reacted when that police car went by. What is it that you're not telling me?"

267

Luke sighed. He was a miserable liar, probably because he detested being lied to. He considered the misinformation he had earlier supplied to Crystal as selectively necessary. He feared that her invitation for a ride to Borden would be revoked if she knew he was wanted in connection with the explosion at *Friendly's*. As he looked at her now, he knew that he was going to have to take that chance. Whether Crystal believed in ESP or not was irrelevant. She had seen Virginia Parnell in the middle of the road in a place where she could not have physically been. In Luke's mind, that indicated that Crystal played a more significant role in the unfolding events than he had earlier estimated. The vision of the girl acted as a stop sign, causing Crystal to wreck the car in a place where Luke was bound to come across them. He couldn't begin to guess whether her exclusive purpose was to provide him with a ride to Borden or whether fate had more in store for her. Either way, he decided it was safe to trust her with the truth.

"There was a sheriff's deputy that arrived on the scene right after the gas station exploded," said Luke. "He had already made up his mind that I was responsible before he even spoke to me."

Crystal slowly absorbed the implications. "What you're saying is that you're on the run from the police?"

Luke nodded, his eyes avoiding contact with Crystal's.

"Well, shit," said Crystal, walking purposefully back in the direction of the motel and away from Luke.

"Hey, wait!" called Luke. "At least let me finish."

"I can't believe this shit," said Crystal. "Paula and I could be arrested, you know. Aiding and abetting, I believe it's called. You asshole!"

"I didn't do it," protested Luke, keeping up with Crystal as best he could.

"That's not for me to decide," said Crystal. "That's up to the courts."

"So, you're going to turn me in?"

Crystal whirled around to face him, her eyes blazing. "You can bet your sweet ass I am! My life has already gotten complicated enough without having to worry about something like *this!* I'm trying to keep an eye out for Paula and what happens? I invite a criminal into the car with us. I should have my head examined. Road Rule 101—never pick up hitchhikers."

"I didn't do it," Luke repeated. "What would you have done in my place?"

"I sure the hell wouldn't have run! How do you think that looks? I'll tell you how it looks. It looks like you've got something to hide. It looks like you're *guilty*. Paula said that she didn't trust you. I guess I should have listened to her more carefully. I mean, what in the hell were you *thinking?*"

Luke retrieved the photo of Virginia Parnell from his pocket and held it up. "I was thinking about *her*. If I stayed, I have no doubt that deputy would have arrested me. Even if evidence had eventually come to light that proved I was innocent, it would have been too late for *her*."

Crystal turned and continued toward the motel in silence. Luke trailed along behind, fearing he had made a terrible mistake in trusting her. His legs felt strangely weak as he followed Crystal like a penitent child. He wanted to say more, but he felt like every time he opened his mouth, he was digging himself into a deeper hole.

They reached the motel, and Crystal ascended the stairs without a word, leaving Luke to stand alone in the fog-shrouded parking lot. When she reached the second-floor walkway, he called out, "What are you going to do?"

Crystal turned and looked over the balcony. "I don't know yet."

"Can I still get a ride to Borden?" Luke held his breath, afraid of Crystal's response.

"I don't know," said Crystal crossly. "I have to think about it, and it's not at the top of my list right at the moment. I need to make sure that Paula's okay, or have you forgotten about her already?"

"That's below the belt," said Luke. "I never once said I wasn't concerned about Paula."

"There are very few things in this world that *really* get under my skin, Luke, but lying is one of them," she said.

"I'm sorry. I thought you—"

"Another would be when people try to guess what I'm thinking, so if I were you, I'd quit before I lost any more ground."

Luke shuffled his feet and looked at the pavement below them. He hadn't felt so completely worthless since the time Sister Margaret had accused him of helping himself to the sacramental wine she stored in the cellar for communion. Of course, he *had* helped himself to the wine, so the feeling of guilt was justified. Despite all of his current rationalizing, he had damaged his credibility with Crystal by lying to her, possibly irreversibly.

"Can I still sleep in the car?" he asked meekly.

"I don't care. Do whatever you want," she said, walking the remaining few feet to her room and letting herself in.

Luke crossed the lot and settled into the passenger seat of the silver Honda. He doubted he would sleep a wink. The car was cramped and uncomfortable, but more than that, Luke was still unsure of whether Crystal would phone the police. He would need to stay alert. He had been wrong in lying, not running. If he had any indication that the police were coming to collect him, he would do it again.

⌖

Crystal opened the motel door and was relieved to see Paula perched on the corner of the bed. Her complexion was ashen, and she had dark circles underneath her eyes.

"Thank God you're back!" said Crystal, giving the girl a quick hug. "You had me scared half to death! Are you alright?"

Paula nodded and smiled weakly. "I just had to get out for a bit."

"I thought you didn't want anyone in Morgan to see you," said Crystal. "Especially Joel."

Paula flinched when she said the name. "No, no. I didn't. But I'm glad I went. I saw my sister."

"You went to your *house?*" Crystal asked incredulously.

Paula shook her head vehemently. "I wouldn't ever go there again," she said. "Angel was walking through the neighborhoods. It's actually kind of freaky that we ran into each other, you know?"

"This whole thing's freaky," mused Crystal.

"What do you mean?" Paula's voice trembled slightly. Did Crystal know what had happened to Joel that evening? Had the police already questioned her? Her paranoia was self-fueling, and her hands trembled in her lap.

"Luke's been lying to us," Crystal said.

Paula's eyes narrowed. "I knew he was up to something. I mean, what was he doing in that cornfield in the first place? That struck me as odd right away."

"He was hiding from the police, that's what," said Crystal. "He's wanted in connection with that gas station that blew up."

"You've got to be kidding me!"

Crystal shook her head. "Everything that's coming out of his mouth sounds like science fiction. He thinks he's supposed to protect a little girl from some unspeakable evil—the daughter of the trucker who was killed in the explosion."

Paula gaped at her. "He sounds like a psychopath. He probably killed the father to get him out of the way. I hope you told him to get lost."

"I didn't tell him anything yet," said Crystal.

"What? Are you *nuts?* He could be completely unbalanced. We could be his next two victims!"

Crystal sighed and shook her head again. "I don't know what to make of it. I don't think we're in any immediate danger from him."

"I think you should call the police. You don't want to get in trouble for helping him out," said Paula.

"I don't want to do anything without thinking about it," said Crystal. She glanced at the digital clock on the bedside table and saw that it was ten-thirty. "It's late. I'm going to take a shower then go to bed. Hopefully the car will be ready early, and we can get out of here."

Paula nodded, and Crystal went into the bathroom. As the water began to fall, Paula crossed the room and peered out from between the slats of the closed blind. She could vaguely discern Luke's outline in the passenger seat of the car below. She backed away from the window slowly, deliberating what she should do.

After a moment's consideration, she picked up the receiver of the telephone next to the bed, covered the mouthpiece with her hand and dialed 911. When the dispatcher answered, she said, "If you're looking for the man responsible for the gas station bomb in Indiana, he's sleeping in a silver Honda in the parking lot of Louie's Motor Inn."

Paula hung up the phone as the dispatcher asked her to identify herself. If Crystal wouldn't get rid of him, she would just have to take care of it herself.

CHAPTER FOURTEEN

I

"What's going on, Lisa?" repeated Helen, her eyes fixed to the gun clutched in Suze's hand.

Lisa looked vacantly over her shoulder at Suze. The understanding which passed between the two women was subtle to the point of invisibility. Suze pivoted and aimed the gun at Lisa.

"If you don't do exactly what I say," Suze said, her wild eyes burning holes through Helen. "I will blow this girl's head off. Are we clear?"

Helen nodded dumbly. She was still holding Chad's wrist in her hand, absently taking his pulse.

"Good," said Suze. "No screaming, no sudden moves. Okay? Good. Is Chad alive?"

Helen fumbled for a moment, blithering nonsense before finally nodding her head. "He's alive," she managed.

"How badly is he hurt?" Suze asked.

Helen was trembling visibly. She examined Chad's shoulder where the bullet had entered. As she began to turn him on his side, she abruptly broke into wailing sobs, her hysterics reverberating off the walls of the small bedroom. Suze marched across the room and grabbed the nurse roughly by her shoulder, thrusting the revolver in her face.

"If you don't get yourself under control, lady, I'm going to put a bullet right between your eyes," she hissed. Lisa shifted toward the door, and Suze swung her arm back around to point the gun at her. *"Stay where you are, princess."*

Lisa froze and raised her hands to cover her head. Suze watched the performance with fascination; Lisa's arms trembled, her cheeks flushed and tears dribbled down like rain. Her bottom lip quivered like that of a frightened child. "Please don't hurt me," Lisa whimpered. "Oh, *God*, Helen! Just do what she wants! Just do it!"

Helen turned Chad over and examined the messy exit wound. The bullet had passed completely through his shoulder. He groaned slightly as she rolled him on his side. "He's lost some blood, but it doesn't look like arterial damage. He needs a doctor."

Suze shook her head. "We can't do that. You're going to have to substitute."

Helen's eyes widened and she shook her head. "I-I can't—"

"You can and you will," said Suze, stepping over to where Lisa stood. She gestured toward Lisa with the muzzle of the gun. "If you want to keep everyone in one piece, that is."

Helen lost her composure for another quick second, more nonsense spilling from her lips. Lisa noted that all of the begging was on her behalf, and she felt strangely touched by the older woman's naiveté.

"Do you need anything else, or do you have what you need in your kit?" asked Suze.

"Towels," said Helen. "I could use some towels and warm water. I need to wash my hands."

Lisa guided Helen over to the small bathroom adjoining her bedroom. "The towels are in the hallway in the linen closet," she called to Suze. Suze backed out of the room slowly, keeping the gun steady in front of her. She quickly returned with several dark blue towels.

"Now you take care of my boy, there," said Suze, waving the gun in Chad's general direction. His eyes had opened to glistening slits now, but if he was aware of what was going on around him, he gave no indication. "Ms. Mitchell and I have a thing or two to discuss out in the hall. Now, don't get any wise ideas while I'm gone. One wrong move, and I'll be forced to execute your friend."

Again, Suze marveled at the thoroughly convincing act Lisa presented in front of the nurse. Tears streamed down her face, and her lips quivered with apparent apprehension. Suze motioned toward the hallway with the gun and Lisa preceded her out, her unsteady legs knocking knees as she passed. Helen turned toward Chad, and Suze's stomach clenched as she saw her begin a clinical palpation and cleansing of the wound site. She pulled the door shut, and she and Lisa stood in the darkness of the hallway.

"What in the hell is going on here?" asked Suze. "Were you expecting party guests that we didn't know about or something? Who are all these people?"

Lisa's terrified façade disintegrated, and she seemed slightly amused. "That was some swift thinking in there," she said. "I only met Helen Martin a few weeks ago, but she seems to have adopted me as a substitute for the daughter she lost to a drunk driver. I think she'll do whatever we want her to as long as she believes there's a danger to me if she doesn't. You manipulated her brilliantly."

Suze was caught off-guard by the sudden compliment. She wasn't used to flattery at all, much less from the woman she knew had been fucking Chad just before all this had unfolded. Still, a compliment was a compliment, and an involuntary smile flitted across her lips. "Thanks. We're not out of the fire yet, though. We've got to get rid of those two bodies in there."

"The one with the badge isn't dead," said Lisa.

"He will be soon enough," said Suze. "I know that guy. I'd just as soon he doesn't get a real good look at me."

They both froze as someone knocked sharply on the front door.

—————◇—————

273

Jessica Lybrook drove her Jeep Wrangler down the rutted country road. She had been on duty for long hours, manning the switchboard at the Jay County Sheriff's Department. It was a slow evening, a few domestic calls but that was all. She had spent much of the evening worrying about David McElroy. It was all such a shock. Jessica had seen Loretta that very afternoon when she had stopped to refuel her car. McElroy was a real piece of work at times, there was no doubt about it. But anyone who knew the man for long knew that Loretta was the center of his unique universe. Jessica had seen him only briefly before he had taken his abrupt leave of absence.

And why shouldn't he take a leave? He certainly had amassed the time. But there was something about the man's eyes that had stayed with Jessica long after he had clocked out and driven away. His eyes demanded revenge. While Jessica could certainly appreciate his angst, she was a firm believer in the wheels of justice. It would take extraordinary circumstances to cause her to act outside of the law. She worried that McElroy was going to torpedo his career and perhaps his entire future by exacting vigilante justice against the perpetrators of this heinous deed. She felt as if he knew something more than he had told his fellow officers, as if he were keeping a pertinent piece of information to himself so that he might have the personal pleasure of dealing with his wife's murderers.

McElroy lived in a newly built ranch house set far back from civilization on Horton Hollow. Bats dived lazily from the treetops, consuming small bugs innocently flitting through the night sky. A shiver crawled down Jessica's back as she drove the winding road back into the woods. There were no neighbors nearby, and after a few more miles of isolation, Jessica got the full-fledged creeps. She began to question the wisdom of her endeavor when the house suddenly emerged from the woods, its dark windows like eyes on the roadway. Jessica pulled her Jeep into the drive and cut the engine. McElroy's cruiser was in the drive, but his own car, a light blue Olds, was nowhere to be seen.

Jessica sighed and pulled some slack in her seatbelt. She was probably just imagining things. In times of grief, people turned to their families. McElroy had probably done exactly that. He had mentioned a brother in Morgan. She was reluctant to depart without leaving McElroy a note, just in case he was still hanging around, feeling lonely and alone. She wanted to let him know that he could call her anytime if he wanted to talk. After all, she knew what it was like to lose a spouse under extraordinary circumstances. She might be able to help ease his pain. They had been co-workers for over seven years. She considered McElroy a friend.

Jessica fumbled in her bag for a pen and piece of paper but came up empty-handed. Maybe she would check McElroy's door and see if he kept it locked. As security conscious as he was, it seemed natural that he would, but it seemed like such a waste of Jessica's effort to simply turn around and leave. Surely, he would have a pen and a piece of paper inside. Maybe he kept a key under the doormat or in a planter.

Jessica unbuckled her seatbelt and stepped out of the car, listening to the nocturnal creatures prowling the woods around her. The chill which had seized her earlier refused to let go, spreading down the base of her spine until her legs were shaky. She crossed the graveled driveway and ascended the pine stairs which led to a large porch. The entire house was free of stain or paint, its natural beauty preserved behind layers of protective sealant. The scent of pine tickled her nostrils.

Much to her surprise, the front door opened when she tried the knob. The dark living room still smelled of Loretta's perfume, and Jessica felt tears sneak into the corners of her eyes. She wasn't like other police officers; she spent her time in the dispatch room instead of out on the streets. She didn't have any experience with violent crime, and the cowardly murders of Loretta McElroy, Earl Bickner, and Bert Parnell hit far too close to home. They were being called thrill-kills, the most obscene and terrifying combination of words that Jessica was ever likely to hear.

Jessica crossed the braided rug covering the immaculate hardwood floor and sat down at McElroy's roll top desk. The brown leather chair had been with McElroy a long time and had conformed to the contours of his backside. Jessica felt fairly lost in the indentations. She noticed that the desk had been left open, and her eyes were drawn immediately to a stack of papers underneath a sealed business envelope. The envelope bore McElroy's spidery handwriting stating, "To Whom It May Concern." The sheets of paper below it were crude drawings of a vicious-looking, square-faced man with eyes like coal. McElroy had once functioned as a sketch artist in his early career, and while he may not still be as practiced as he had once been, his rudimentary talent remained. Jessica examined each of the pictures, noting the various angles from which McElroy had sketched the man's profile. With only a little imagination, she could easily apply horns and pointed ears to these devilish caricatures. The cold knot which had been in her stomach all day suddenly hardened into something closer to dread. It seemed clear that McElroy was, in fact, obsessed with avenging his wife's murder.

Jessica knew she should call her supervisor and explain what she had found. She knew it was the proper thing to do. Still, she hesitated, staring at the phone as if it might suddenly offer its own opinion on what she should do next. She picked up the sealed envelope and turned it over and over in her hands. She wanted to see its contents but knew she should surrender it to Sheriff Mahaney for inspection.

She worked a finely shaped fingernail underneath the corner of the flap and gently tinkered with the seal, hoping the damned thing would just pop open. It wasn't as if she was reading someone else's mail. It was addressed "To Whom It May Concern," for God's sake! She was certainly concerned...

275

She finally decided to open it, if for no other reason than to try and get a fix on McElroy's present location. He was obviously hunting for the murderer. If Jessica could find him, maybe she could prevent him from making a career-ending mistake.

She unfolded the letter and read it:

To Whom It May Concern:

Last night, my wife was murdered.
I have to make the bastard pay. I have to.
The law doesn't mean shit when a thing like this can happen.

David McElroy

Jessica refolded the letter and tucked it into her pocketbook. She didn't want anyone else to find it just yet. She realized she had been holding her breath and let the exhalation whistle out through her nose. She had to find McElroy immediately, before it was too late. As an afterthought, she scooped up the sketches McElroy had left behind and carried them to her car, examining the grizzled features of the suspect. She would certainly hate to run across *him* in a dark alley.

She hurried back out to her car, locking McElroy's door behind her. She didn't see the point in leaving his house open to vandals. She had the disturbing feeling that McElroy never expected to come home again.

—————◆—————

Leonard Barnes was winded, his ragged breath whistling through his nose and mouth as he rested his backside against a tree. He had assumed that Lisa Mitchell was in her house when he had been there earlier. He hadn't expected to see her on the street with her new boyfriend. If they weren't at the house, then who was? Where had the gunshots come from?

From where Leonard rested, he could see the Mitchell house nestled in the thickening fog. The front door was now closed, and Helen Martin's car was still parked at the curb. He felt cowardly for not warning the nurse away, but he knew that she would never take his word for anything ever again. Not since Evie had been killed.

Leonard sank to a squat and cupped his head in his hands, the immense weight of guilt pressing mercilessly down on him. In his lifetime, he had been dealt his fair share of misfortune, but he didn't think he would ever find a way to deal with his emotions regarding Evie Martin and her tragic death. She had been such a vivacious young woman, sure of herself and of what the future held for her. She had broken many a heart with her crooked grin and twinkling blue eyes, albeit unintentionally; the men who fell for her did so of their own volition. Evie Martin did not believe in playing those types of games. Helen had brought her up well.

Clinton McDermott.

The name was like acid on Leonard's tongue. If he could only have that night to do over again.

Leonard had been acting as a backup bartender at the Mixer, a small dance club on Fourteenth Street. Since his Nell had passed, he was consumed by loneliness during the empty evening hours. He had only taken the job to fill the time, not because of financial need.

Clinton McDermott was a fixture in the bar, arriving shortly after six and staying until at least midnight every evening. He was an obnoxious loudmouth who relentlessly milked an eternity's worth of wisdom from his forty-odd years on the planet. He had forceful opinions on every topic presented, whether it was politics, religion, or legalized gambling—he considered it every man's right to piss away his own hard-earned money. He was very grabby with female customers and had been warned on more than one occasion to keep his hands to himself or he would no longer be welcome at the Mixer. These were idle threats; Clinton McDermott was as much a part of the bar as the beer taps.

On that night five years ago, Clinton had just been laid off after twenty years at the lumberyard. He came into the bar in a foul mood, and drank twice as much as he usually did, which was a staggering lot of booze. Leonard had known as he served him those last few drinks that the man didn't need any more, and yet he had chosen to serve him rather than deal with his white-hot temper, which was inevitable once he had been refused.

When Leonard heard about the accident the next day, he was sick to his stomach. Clinton McDermott would never have to answer for what he had done. He had died in the crash. Unfortunately, so had Evie Martin, leaving behind devastation for her friends and family.

Helen Martin had been quick to file suit against Leonard, stating that he should have never knowingly sold drinks to a man who was clearly already intoxicated. The truth of the matter was, Leonard would have gladly given everything he owned and spent the remainder of his days in jail if it would bring Evie back, but nothing could do that. He understood Helen's need to assign blame and moreover, he willingly accepted the responsibility. His attorney, however, had operated with efficiency, and eventually the suit was dismissed for lack of evidence. No one would come forward to testify that Clinton was obviously drunk when Leonard had last served him. The whole litigious process took place between attorneys, and Leonard hadn't even had the opportunity to stand up and declare his guilt before the case was decided. He tried on numerous occasions to approach Helen, but the look of pain that stained her eyes whenever she saw him was more than he could bear.

If anything happened to Helen Martin now...

A City of Morgan police cruiser glided up to the curb, parking behind Helen's Buick. There were no bubble lights or sirens to announce its arrival, and two officers hopped out of the car and headed for the porch.

Leonard sighed with relief. The cavalry had come. Thank God.

◇

Lisa opened the door and smiled at the officers standing on the porch. She absently toggled the porch light on, bugs instantly gravitating toward it.

"Is there something I can help you with?" asked Lisa.

"We're sorry to disturb you so late, Ms. Mitchell," said the younger of the two. He was short and powerfully built, with a military haircut and an intense stare. The other officer, a tall Black man with spindly arms and legs, peered past Lisa at the empty living room beyond. "I'm Officer Charles, and this is Officer Woods. We've had a report of gunfire in the neighborhood. Is everything alright?"

Lisa laughed and her cheeks brightened a little. "Oh, gosh. I'm sorry. I just bought my first television set today. I must have gotten a little carried away with the volume."

"Your first TV?" asked Woods, his eyebrows arching. "Really?"

Lisa nodded. "I know it seems odd, but my Nanna Grace thought that television was bad. I'm sorry about the disturbance. I'll make sure and keep it down in the future. I was on my way to bed, anyway."

"Are you here alone?" asked Charles, his eyes searching the space beyond her frame.

Lisa hesitated. Jack Lovell's red Ford pickup was still in the driveway. Helen's car was at the curb, but many of Lisa's neighbors parked streetside. With Jack's stiffening corpse moldering upstairs, she didn't want to say anything which might make the officers take a closer look at the truck or, heaven forbid, the license plate number. Eventually Jack Lovell would be reported missing. Lisa didn't want his truck to be traced back to her.

"No," she said. "I have a girlfriend from Cleveland who came down to stay a few nights. I've only recently gotten out of the hospital myself after an automobile accident. Although I tried to convince her I didn't need the help, she absolutely insisted. Would you like to speak to her? I can wake her up—"

"Oh, no," said Woods, waving the suggestion away. "We wouldn't want to disturb her. I just noticed the truck's license plate was from Cuyahoga County, and—" He grinned crookedly and shifted the brim of his hat. "I guess I've just seen too *much* television. I wanted to make sure that you weren't being held here against your will or something like you'd see on *Unsolved Mysteries*. It isn't every day I see tags from that far away."

Lisa laughed again and stifled a yawn. "Dorie will get a real kick out of that when I tell her in the morning. Would you like to come in for some coffee? It would only take me a minute to put it together."

"Thank you, no," said Charles, smiling sheepishly. "We've already taken enough of your time this late in the evening. We're sorry to bother you."

"It's me who should apologize," said Lisa. "Both to you and to whichever neighbor I disturbed. You don't know who that would be, would you?"

Charles shook his head. "Sorry, ma'am. It was reported anonymously."

"Hmm," said Lisa. "That's too bad. Beyond apologizing, I'd like to thank whoever it was for being so concerned about me. It's hard to find good people nowadays, don't you think?"

"Oh, I don't know, Ms. Mitchell," said Woods. "Look here—there's three of us standing right here together."

Lisa smiled at the man's ignorance. "Well, I'm off to bed. Is there anything more I can do for you?"

"No, ma'am," said Charles. "Thank you. Have a nice evening."

The officers walked back toward their cruiser.

"So, what do you think?" asked Woods.

"I think anonymous is just another word for 'prank,'" said Charles, grinning knowingly.

⚬────◆────⚬

Leonard Barnes stood behind the old oak, staring in disbelief as the officers turned back to their car. Why didn't they go *inside?* And how in the world had Lisa Mitchell returned without him seeing her? The last time Leonard saw her, she had been walking with a young man several blocks over. There was no sign of the man now.

Leonard wanted to charge across the street to the police car and demand a satisfactory explanation. He wanted to tell them that Helen Martin was inside the house, and she must be in terrible danger. The problem was, he could offer no solid reason for feeling that way. The policemen would also know that Leonard had phoned the initial complaint in. If the Mitchell girl had somehow managed to satisfy their curiosity, they would be less likely to believe any future complaints.

Dammit!

Leonard had no idea what to do next.

———◇———

Suze hurried into the bedroom and closed the door behind her. Helen looked up from where she sat at Chad's side, doing her best to dress his wound with the supplies from her first aid kit. The boy was lucky, she thought. The bullet passed through without hitting any organs or major blood vessels. Although he should still be seen by a doctor, he would live.

The relief that Helen felt was enormous. She would hate to have to answer to Suze if something were to happen to Chad. The malevolent eyes which fixed on Helen terrified her. The gun was an extension of the woman's arm, trained on Helen's ample frame. Although Helen heard the knock at the door, she had wisely chosen to keep quiet. Frankly, she sensed that Suze was *looking* for a reason to shoot her.

"One word out of you, and you're dead," hissed Suze, as if reading her mind.

Helen wanted to ask where Lisa was. As fearful as she was for her own safety, she was more afraid for Lisa's. What if this woman had hurt Lisa? Helen's bottom lip started to quiver, so she focused on Chad to occupy her mind.

Suze's gaze shifted back and forth between Helen and David McElroy, who still lay slumped against the wall. She feared he would come to at any moment. She didn't like being this close to the man, even if he was unconscious. He shared a strong physical likeness to his brother, Joel, and that was enough to tie Suze's stomach into sick knots.

Suze wanted to get the hell out of this goddamned town.

———◇———

Leonard awoke with a start. He looked at the clock on his dashboard, and a sick feeling of dread came over him. He had lost an hour to sleep. He remembered going back to his car after the policemen had left so that he could resume his surveillance. Apparently, lack of sleep the previous evening combined with a long day at work had taken a bigger toll on him than he had suspected. He had nodded off without warning.

He looked across the street to the Mitchell residence. The red pickup truck was no longer in the driveway. Helen Martin's car was no longer in front of the house. The entire building was dark now. Leonard slammed his hands against the steering wheel in frustration.

He really didn't think he could live with himself if something had happened to Helen.

McElroy's tongue felt swollen and sticky inside his mouth. His head throbbed from near the base of his skull, and although he tried to reach back and massage it, he found that his hands were bound together behind him. As the fog continued to lift from his mind, he became aware of vibrations and noise coming from underneath him. He was in a vehicle.

Why couldn't he see anything? His vision was still as black as pitch, regardless of the direction in which he turned his head. It didn't feel as though he had anything covering his eyes.

Still, a satisfied smile played at his lips. He had shot that bastard dead, right between the shoulder blades. Whoever said it was cowardly to shoot a man in the back was never in a situation where the odds were so badly stacked against him. McElroy could have never handled all three of them. The look of surprise on the dark-haired boy's face as the gun swung toward him was worthy of another satisfied smile. But the next thing McElroy remembered was the floor racing up to meet him after something pelted him from behind. For a moment upon waking, he thought that he had been shot, but other than the headache, there didn't seem to be any permanent damage.

It must have been the dark-haired girl, he thought. *She must have come in behind me.*

The vehicle stopped, and the engine was suddenly cut. Above the normal sounds of nocturnal creatures croaking and chirping, McElroy could hear water in the distance. He struggled to pull his arms free, but they seemed to be drawn tightly together and bound by wire. The more he struggled, the more the wire bit into his wrists. His legs were bound at the ankles in a similar fashion.

McElroy felt as well as heard the vehicle's door open and slam shut. Soon, hands closed around his ankles and pulled. McElroy realized he had been in the back of a truck as he was pulled along the raised metal ridges of the truck bed. As his legs were pulled beyond the lowered tailgate, he was lifted at the waist from below. He was being carried over someone's shoulder. McElroy wondered who was doing the actual lifting; he was no small man.

The sound of water was closer, and McElroy was suddenly seized by a panicky impulse to try and escape. He wriggled side-to-side and kicked with his bound legs. His captor simply rammed McElroy's head into the side of the truck and continued forward. McElroy cried out but offered no more resistance—and suddenly he was falling. McElroy's stomach lurched up into his throat as if he were rapidly descending from a big rise on a roller coaster. He realized that he had been entirely covered with plastic as the material rippled against him in his descent.

For the first time that evening, David McElroy was truly frightened.

281

He felt a sickening crunch in his right leg, which broke in multiple places as he broke the surface of the cold, murky water. The plastic was not airtight. Water seeped in, soaking McElroy's clothes. He held his breath, but he couldn't hold it forever. Soon, he would see his dear, sweet Loretta again, with the satisfaction of knowing that he had avenged her death.

Of course, he didn't know that he had instead killed an innocent man named Jack Lovell.

Lisa walked down the dark sidewalk. It was very late. The fog from earlier in the evening had settled into dense pockets, shrouding visibility to a minimum. After disposing of Jack Lovell and David McElroy in the McMillan Reservoir, she decided it would be best to get rid of the extraneous vehicles parked near her house. She had driven Jack's truck over to his mother's little cottage and left it in the driveway. She didn't worry about fingerprints. Many of the neighbors had seen Jack helping her haul furniture, and they had taken turns driving, so there was no reason her fingerprints *shouldn't* be in the truck. She had taken Helen Martin's car to the parking lot of Morton's Supermarket and parked it amongst the employee vehicles. She knew she couldn't leave it there for too long, but it should be safe overnight.

As Lisa neared her house, she saw Leonard Barnes sitting in his car, staring toward her property. She smiled a little, pleased that Leonard was watching her. If he only knew how often she had watched him while he worked, his firm buttocks flexing as he walked along the corridors.

Suddenly, Leonard turned toward Lisa, his attention firmly rooted to her. Lisa smiled and waved, which seemed to fluster Leonard enormously. Within seconds, he had fired up the engine of his Chevy and pulled away from the curb, his red taillights disappearing into the fog. Lisa shrugged to herself and went inside the house.

Suze met her at the door. "What in the hell took you so long?" she demanded.

"I haven't been gone *that* long," said Lisa. "And I had to get rid of the cars, didn't I? How's Chad?"

"He's sleeping. That nurse is going to be a problem," said Suze. "You need to make an appearance or she's going to go bat-shit. She's beginning to think I've done something to you."

"Fine," said Lisa. "Is she still upstairs?"

Suze nodded. "Why don't we just get rid of her?"

Lisa pondered it for a moment. Although she had no real feeling one way or the other for Helen, she didn't think it was a good idea to kill her. She shook her head and said, "No, not just yet. We have a lot of work ahead of us, and we might need her medical expertise before it's all over."

"Yeah, maybe," said Suze doubtfully. "Isn't there somewhere else we can put her, though? I'm afraid she's going to break out the window and start screaming into the street."

"There's an old coal bin in the cellar. The outside chute has been sealed off for years, and there are no windows. We can also padlock the door."

"Sounds perfect," said Suze. "Let's do it."

———◆———

Chad languished in the murky waters of unconsciousness. He had surfaced into awareness on a handful of occasions, but everything his eyes took in was received by his brain as random photographs that meant nothing. His last clear memory was of the man in the doorway, round like Santa Claus, but not nearly so jolly. He had shot the man who Lisa had called Jack and then turned his gun on Chad.

After that, nothing.

Chad wondered if he had been shot by this man and was now dead, floating along in a state of semi-consciousness that was the beginning of the afterlife. Short, sharp twinges in his shoulder suggested something different. Dead men felt no pain. Or did they?

His dreams were constructed of nonsense, varied and colorful imagery dancing behind his eyelids with no sense of purpose. His final dream of the evening was the strangest of them all.

Chad sat in the kitchen of his father's Colonial in Pridemore. To his left sat his father and to his right, his mother. Suze sat across the table, smiling like she knew a secret. Peter looked pale and haggard, just as Chad had seen him when he last visited him in prison. Naomi's entrails were sliding out through jagged slits in her torso, her clothes dripping with blood. She smiled as if she felt no pain, but blood bubbled through the hole where Chad had savagely punctured her trachea.

Chad looked down at the table and saw the familiar wooden blocks of Jenga, stacked more than a foot high.

"GAN GA!" chanted Peter, looking expectantly at Chad.

Suze giggled and repeated, "GAN GA!"

Naomi vomited blood and as she wiped her mouth, added her own wet, "GAN GA!"

Chad looked from one to the other, perplexed. Was it his turn? Hesitantly, he reached toward the stack of blocks, deciding which one to extract from the teetering tower. Peter stopped Chad's hand before it made contact. When Chad looked at him, he merely looked puzzled, as if he had no idea what Chad was about to do. Peter whispered, "Gan ga."

Naomi nodded and blood sprayed from her throat. "Gan ga."

Suze reached out and swept the blocks from the table. "Gan ga," she said with satisfaction.

Chad's eyes fluttered open and registered the sunlight spilling in through the window. Lisa was sitting on the edge of the mattress, observing him closely.

"What happened?" he croaked. He felt as though he hadn't had anything to drink for days.

Lisa stroked his face gently. "You went and got yourself shot, stud puppy. You'll be fine. You just need rest."

"The girl—"

"We'll find her."

"Where's Suze?"

Lisa shrugged. "You were muttering in your sleep, and she suddenly took off. I'm not sure she's handling the pressure too well."

"Who was that guy who came in? Your boyfriend?"

Lisa grinned. "No. Just some guy named Jack. He thought more of me than I did of him."

"Is he dead?"

Lisa nodded. "Everything's fine now. Don't worry about a thing. You need to get some more sleep, though. You'll be back on your feet before you know it." She leaned across and kissed Chad softly on his lips.

Lisa backed out of the room as Chad faded out, gently closing the door behind her. She was on her way downstairs when the front door opened and Suze bounded in, her face flushed with excitement. In her hand, she carried the morning edition of *The Morgan Gazette*.

Suze thrust the paper toward Lisa and said, "I've found the girl!"

‖

Luke couldn't find a comfortable position in the passenger seat of the cramped car. He hadn't eaten in hours and was ravenous, his stomach gurgling with startling regularity. He didn't have any money and didn't want to press his luck by asking Crystal for food. He hadn't seen Paula but judging from how quickly the lights had been turned out, she must have already returned to the room. He didn't think Crystal could sleep soundly until the girl was safely accounted for.

Luke studied the motel. Most of the rooms were vacant, rows of dark windows like teeth that had been knocked out. He had been in the car for half an hour and hadn't seen a soul. Apparently, Louie's Motor Inn was in its off-season—provided it was ever *in* season. Morgan didn't seem like a particularly touristy place. Earlier, he had considered his parking spot a good one because it was beyond the scope of the lights in the lot. Now, as the fog continued to thicken, he was beginning to reconsider. It was spooky.

Luke wondered how badly he had damaged his credibility with Crystal. He wished he had told her the truth from the beginning, but it was too late to fix now. Luke wondered if Crystal would call the police, but he hoped she would think better of it. It was probably nothing more than dumb luck that allowed him to get away from the officer at *Friendly's*. He wasn't sure he could do it again.

He took the picture of Virginia Parnell out of his pocket and examined it under the faint light of the moon. She was a flawless little girl with big round eyes and the complexion of a porcelain doll. Her dark, naturally curly hair framed her innocent face. Why would anyone want to hurt her? What possible reason could there be? At this same time last night, Bert was telling him about what hell it was to have so many daughters. Of course, there was a twinkle in his eyes as he spoke, and Luke knew he wouldn't trade any one of them for anything. The memory was so vivid that Luke felt as though he should be able to take a step backward and be inside the semi's cab, able to tell Bert to forget about Friendly's, shit his goddamned pants if he had to, but keep *going*. It didn't seem possible that such a tiny thread of time could separate then from now. Luke tucked the picture away and tried again to find a suitable position in the car seat. Even with the seat all the way back, his knees were wedged against the dashboard. It was hopeless.

Out of the corner of his eye, Luke thought he saw movement in the shrubs near the motel office. He tensed, waiting for a uniformed officer to emerge, but it was only a large, yellow tabby prowling for a nighttime snack. Luke was so anxious about the possibility of Crystal calling the police that the muscles in his neck had worked themselves into knots. The only reason he stayed in the car was because he believed he had been guided at least this far by someone or something beyond his comprehension. God? Maybe. Surely, He wouldn't allow the police to capture Luke when he was this close to reaching Virginia Parnell.

Would He?

⌐———◇———⌐

Officers Woods and Charles had barely rounded the block from the crank call at the Mitchell place when the radio announced a potential suspect bunked in a car a few blocks over. Woods acknowledged the call and proceeded quietly to Louie's Motor Inn.

"What the hell's going on tonight?" asked Woods. "Shit like this don't happen in Morgan."

285

Charles smiled. "Feels like we're on *Cops,* doesn't it?"

He pulled the cruiser into the parking lot alongside the motel. It was an old two-story structure, shaped in a giant L. The second story rooms opened out onto a balcony with a wrought iron rail. The building had been gaily painted in soft pastels, but years of exposure to the sun had stripped away what color there once had been. The illumination in the parking lot was inadequate, to say the least. Of the four streetlamps guarding the perimeter of the lot, only two at the end closest to the street were operational. Of those two, only one worked well.

"Someone needs to talk to ole Louie about these lights," said Charles.

"I don't see it," said Woods, scanning the lot.

"The parking lot wraps around behind the building. It might be back there."

"So, what did this guy do?" asked Woods.

"I have no idea," said Charles. "You heard the call same as me."

"I hate this shit."

"I don't know anyone who likes it."

"David McElroy likes it."

"David McElroy's a fucking psycho," said Charles. "I thank God each and every day that he moved away. Let him practice his version of the law in another county."

Woods laughed appreciably. "Don't I know it? I was partners with him, too, remember?"

Woods certainly remembered. It had been seven long years since either of them had had to work with David McElroy, but the memory was forever etched in both of their minds. When Woods had been partners with McElroy, he was an unwilling participant in some questionable interrogation techniques which had resulted in the permanent paralysis of Willie Brighton, a seventeen-year-old boy who was wanted in connection with auto thefts in the area. Sure, the boy had done it, but McElroy had continued to beat the living shit out of him long after the truth had fallen from his busted lips. Woods stood helplessly by while his superior officer, his *trainer*, repeatedly kicked the boy until he was nearly dead. The most frightening aspect of all was that McElroy didn't think there was anything wrong with this perversion of power. Small town justice isn't held to the same level of accountability as it is in the big city. Corruption abounds in both places, but in a small town, it takes fewer corrupt officers to cover up the excesses of cops like McElroy. The boy's parents were poor and dumb. They never thought to hire an attorney.

After Woods had finished training and been assigned a permanent partner, Charles had been McElroy's next rookie. On Charles' second night, McElroy had shot and killed a dipshit punk named Ricky Glisko. Ricky was always beating up his wife, Teresa Ann, who was also McElroy's niece on his wife's side.

Nobody said Ricky Glisko was smart.

The exchange between the two had happened so quickly that Charles wasn't completely sure what had actually occurred. The only thing he knew for certain was that Ricky Glisko wasn't going to beat anyone ever again. McElroy had sworn that Glisko was pulling a gun when he had fired his own and sure enough, Glisko had a gun on him, but Charles was pretty certain that he had seen both of Glisko's hands in the instant before McElroy fired. Neither of them had been holding the gun. Charles hadn't known what to do. He had conferred with Captain Hemmingford who had quietly suggested that perhaps it was best to just leave well enough alone. Ricky Glisko was a bad seed—everybody knew that. He was going to end up killing little Teresa Ann, and then where would we be? Let's just let it go, shall we? And that's exactly what Charles had done, although he had never felt particularly right about it. It was the look on McElroy's face when he had fired the gun which stayed with him all these years. McElroy knew what he was doing that night. He knew it, and he *enjoyed* it.

"There it is," said Woods, pointing to the silver Honda parked at the far end of the parking lot. "Cut your lights."

Charles flipped the headlights off and cruised into the nearest empty parking space. He confirmed sighting the vehicle with dispatch. The Honda sat shrouded in fog, its shape barely discernible in the vague lighting. Both men unfastened their seatbelts and removed their guns from their holsters. In his left hand, Woods carried a long black flashlight which, for the moment, he kept switched off. The Honda was backed into its parking place with its rear bumper extended over the concrete stop. Charles branched off to the left, approaching the motel and its first-floor suites. He was briefly illuminated in dingy yellow light before vanishing around the side of the building. Woods counted to thirty to give Charles time to get around the building to the other side.

He began slowly approaching the Honda. The fog cut visibility in half, and Woods couldn't decide if he thought someone was in the car or not. He definitely saw *something*, but it could be the back of the seat just as easily as a person. Charles appeared in the distance from the far side of the motel, approaching the car slowly. He gave a quick shake of his head to indicate all was clear from his end.

Woods turned his flashlight on and shone it through the driver's side window.

⊶ ⸻ ◈ ⸻ ⊷

Crystal emerged from the bathroom in a long t-shirt she had borrowed from Paula. "You ready for bed?" she asked.

Paula nodded and slid beneath the covers. Crystal switched off the light on the nightstand and got into the other bed.

"Are you sure you're alright?" asked Crystal.

"Yeah," said Paula. "Sure. Why?"

287

"Why?" asked Crystal. "Because I care, that's why."

Paula was silent. No one other than Angel had ever given a good goddamn about her one way or the other. Everyone else had ulterior motives. But what motive could a big star like Crystal Bright have? Paula didn't have anything to offer that Crystal could possibly want. Paula was left with no choice but to assume that Crystal was being sincere. She felt awful for spying on Crystal, even if it was at Angel's direction. Angel had never led her astray before—Paula was just going to have to trust her now.

"I think we may end up spending a day or so in Morgan," said Crystal, her voice startling Paula out of her thoughts.

"Why?"

"Something weird is going on," said Crystal. "I'm sure it's nothing, but—"

"This has to do with that Luke guy, doesn't it?" asked Paula.

Crystal sighed. She didn't know what to do about Luke. He had misrepresented himself to her from the beginning, and it wasn't sitting well. Still, she couldn't deny that she had seen Virginia Parnell standing in the roadway the previous evening. How could Luke have a photograph of her? Unless of course the entire thing was an elaborate scam and "Virginia Parnell" was a fictional character created by Luke. For all Crystal knew, she could be Luke's daughter— she had seen *Paper Moon*. Trouble was, Crystal couldn't see what Luke had to gain by perpetuating the deception. If there was even the remotest chance that a four-year-old girl was in mortal danger, Crystal couldn't simply walk away.

"It's complicated," she finally said.

"You got the hots for him or something?"

"No! It's nothing like that. It's...it's complicated, that's all."

"Well, I've already uncomplicated things for you, and you can thank me later. That guy's bad news," said Paula.

"What do you mean, you've uncomplicated things?" asked Crystal, sitting up in bed.

"I called the police."

"You *what?"* Crystal was on her feet in an instant, struggling to pull her jeans on. *"Shit! Shit! Shit!"*

"What? You said the guy was a criminal," said Paula.

"No," said Crystal, unable to keep the annoyance from her voice. "I said I didn't want to do anything without *thinking* about it. I don't need you to do my thinking for me."

"Well, someone needed to," said Paula defensively. "Where are you going?"

"I'm going to warn him," said Crystal.

"Are you *crazy?"* demanded Paula, tossing her covers aside and standing. "What do you really *know* about this guy? I mean, for God's sake, what was all that he told you about saving this little girl? It doesn't even make sense. He's playing you."

Crystal looked through the slats of the blind. "Shit."

"What?" Paula stepped up behind Crystal and tried to peer over her shoulder. Crystal turned around to glare at her. "The police are already here."

The car was empty.

Woods panned his flashlight around the parking lot but found nothing more than a fat yellow cat nosing in the dumpster at the far corner.

"Nothing?" asked Charles, peering into the passenger side of the car.

"Nothing," said Woods. "You didn't see anyone on your way around?"

Charles shook his head and frowned. "Must've been another goddamned prank. Kids today have got too much free time on their hands."

Woods snorted. "Like you didn't get into some shit when you were younger."

"And you didn't?"

"I never said I didn't."

"Yeah, well," said Charles, walking back toward the cruiser. "Let's give Noreen a buzz, let her know it was a false alarm."

"Man, will she be pissed."

"She always is."

"I hear it's that asshole she married."

Charles grinned. He had been married to Noreen, the night shift dispatcher, for the past three years. "You got that right."

As they opened their doors, the radio squawked to life, Noreen's voice coming through. "We've got a three car on 40, south end of town. All available officers copy."

Woods snatched up the microphone. "Copy that, Noreen. We're on our way."

No longer concerned with stealth, they fired the engine up, turned on the bubble lights and sped out of the parking lot, sirens screaming.

Luke zipped his fly and stepped back from the bush, craning his neck to the right. When his straining bladder could no longer be ignored, he had ducked around the side of the building where dense evergreen shrubs provided cover as he relieved himself with an audible groan. He heard a car enter the parking lot. He couldn't see more than the mouth of the parking lot from where he stood. He slowly crept around the side of the building, stopping short when he saw the police car slide into a parking space. It was traveling without its lights—not a good sign. Luke took a couple of backward steps to his right, taking cover in the shadow of a sprawling maple tree. He looked up and into the network of branches thick with leaves, and without a second thought, hoisted himself up. He had climbed about fifteen feet when the doors to the cruiser opened, and two policemen stepped out. The driver was a tall, thin Black man. The other looked like a bulldog. He was broad-shouldered with a thick neck and a jaw line like a hatchet. He moved toward Luke, his feet not making a sound against the pavement. Luke clutched the limb he was straddling and held his breath. Although he was partially obscured by the foliage and the fog, he knew that all the officer had to do was look up and he'd be seen.

He couldn't believe that Crystal had actually *done* it. He had truly believed that she would come around. He had seen the look that flickered across her face when she had seen the photograph. She had been jolted far more than she was willing to admit. Three days ago, Luke wouldn't have bought into the story himself. So much had happened in the time between that he had been converted into a believer literally overnight.

A believer.

A believer in what? ESP? Predestination? Good? Evil?

God?

Luke wanted to go home. He wanted to sit his ass down on the big porch which wrapped around the old farmhouse and stare out into the empty night, smoking cigarettes and thinking about nothing. He wanted to see the constellations lining up in their familiar places alongside the Kentucky moon. He wanted to forget about Bert Parnell and all of the trouble he had caused.

He wanted to hear Paulie singing *Cotton-Eyed Joe* in his sweet, crackling old voice.

The policeman was passing directly underneath him now, and Luke had the peculiar sensation that he might laugh. He bit down on his bottom lip to squelch the hysterical reaction before it became a reality.

The officer passed by and soon rounded the building, going behind the motel and along the side away from the road. There was a small private courtyard bordered by trees and a small pool of murky water for those who dared to swim in it. There were no lights at all on that side of the building.

Luke felt as if he had been in the tree for hours. The rough bark bit at the skin around his wrists, and the branch he straddled pressed uncomfortably into his groin. From Luke's vantage point, he had seen the tall, Black officer head toward the Honda, but the building obscured his progress after walking only a few feet.

If he ever got out of the damned tree, he'd have to resort to hitchhiking again, a proposition that was now more dangerous than ever. If the police suspected the man responsible for the explosion at Friendly's was in the area, they would surely be alert to any transients passing through on the highways.

He should have never stopped to help these two. They would have been just fine on their own. It might have taken them a little longer, and they probably would have had to have the car towed, but they would have been on their way, and Luke would have been on his to save Virginia Parnell.

But Crystal had seen the girl, too. That couldn't have been for nothing. Nothing since Luke had left Jasper had been an accident.

"Nothing?"

"Nothing."

Luke could barely discern the words floating through the fog. There were more that followed, but they collapsed upon each other before becoming cohesive. He could barely feel the tips of his fingers from hugging the limb so tightly, but he relaxed ever so slightly. They hadn't spotted him. After a few minutes, the cruiser roared to life, the need for discretion apparently passed. Its siren wailed as it ramped out of the parking lot, taking a hard left and speeding off into the distance.

Luke stayed in the tree until the sound of the siren had faded entirely. When he dropped to the ground, his hands shook and his knees nearly buckled underneath him. It was time to get the hell out of Dodge. He hurried across the lot, stopping only briefly at the Honda before he realized he didn't have anything to retrieve from the car. All of his possessions had burned up in Bert Parnell's truck. He wanted a cigarette badly, but he was completely out and had no money to buy more. He considered scavenging the floorboards of the Honda, but he really didn't want to give Crystal any more reasons to believe that he was a criminal. He trotted off toward the row of hedges at the back of the lot.

He had nearly reached them when he heard a voice behind him.

"Luke?"

It was Crystal. She was hurrying down the stairs, the sound of her footsteps resounding against the metal steps. He pressed on, pushing through the bushes.

"Hey! Wait a minute!" called Crystal. She bridged the distance between them at a sprint and grabbed Luke's elbow.

Luke gently extracted his arm from Crystal's grip. "Look," he said. "I really don't mean you any harm. I intend to deal with the situation at Friendly's just as soon as I make sure Bert's daughter is safe. I didn't mean to put you in this position. If it's all the same to you, why don't you just forget you saw me and let me go?"

Crystal looked into Luke's eyes. If eyes are the windows to the soul, there wasn't a hint of deception anywhere in there. Just urgency. No matter how farfetched Luke's story might be, he believed he was doing the right thing. Crystal could not imagine Luke destroying a service station and everyone inside it. Something about him was both simple and pure.

"I didn't call the police," said Crystal. "Paula did. I'm sorry about that. If I had known, I wouldn't have let her."

A dispirited smile crossed Luke's face briefly. "She doesn't trust me."

"She doesn't know you," said Crystal.

"You don't know me either."

Crystal sighed. "I know. I don't know you any more than you know me. But I believe your concern for Bert's daughter is real. If I did something to delay you and then something happened to her, I could never live with myself."

"Well, what now?"

"I don't know," said Crystal. "If you're lying to me, I'll cut your balls off."

Luke was startled by her choice of words. He raised his hand like a Boy Scout. "Well, that's that. Nothing but the truth, so help me God. I might need my balls later on."

Crystal grinned. "So, after we get the car fixed, we go to Borden. What then?"

"I'll have to find Greta Parnell and try to convince her that I'm not crazy," said Luke.

"Good luck."

"Yeah, I'll need it."

"I'd like to go with you when you talk to her," said Crystal.

Luke raised an eyebrow. "Really? Why?"

"You might be more believable if you're not by yourself. Besides, I want to see Virginia Parnell. I want to know if she really is the little girl that I saw standing in the road last night."

"Did you tell Paula about that?" asked Luke.

Crystal shook her head. "When it happened, I thought I was seeing things. Now, I'm not sure what I believe. I don't really want to tell Paula about it until I have a better understanding of what's going on."

"I have the worst feeling about all of this," said Luke. "Like the shit's about to hit a high speed fan."

Crystal nodded. "That's the same way I feel, like something's eating away the lining of my stomach."

"I don't suppose you smoke."

"No. Why?"

"Oh, nothing," said Luke. "A non-smoker wouldn't understand."

Understanding, however, *did* dawn on Crystal. Luke had told her that his wallet had been in Bert's truck when it exploded. She dug into her pocket and retrieved a five-dollar bill. "There's a carry-out on the corner. Go get your smokes and then come back to the room. I don't think it's safe for you to sleep in the car tonight. The police might come back."

Luke stared at the money but made no move to take it. "I'm not taking your money. I'm not a bum."

"I didn't say you were. We'll call it a loan, okay?"

"Why are you doing this?" asked Luke.

"Doing what?"

"Being so nice."

Crystal laughed. "Well, thanks a lot! If you really want to know, it's selfish motivation. Do you think I want to put up with your crabby ass while you're going through nicotine withdrawal? I'd rather drive a nail into my own head."

"What about Paula?" asked Luke. "She won't want me to stay in the room."

"Right now, I'm not concerned with what Paula thinks," said Crystal. "I didn't appreciate her taking matters into her own hands and calling the cops while I was in the shower. She knew that I wasn't ready to do that yet, but she did it anyway. The girl's a real mess. She doesn't trust anyone. She's going to have to learn to start somewhere."

They walked slowly across the parking lot toward the stairs, and Crystal finally stuffed the five-dollar bill into Luke's closed hand.

"Take it," she said. "And hurry back. The police are probably still looking for you." Her smile was crooked and endearing, and Luke suddenly realized how truly beautiful she was. It was no wonder that Hollywood had welcomed her, even if only briefly.

CHAPTER FIFTEEN

I

Leonard Barnes awoke at seven o'clock, tangled in his yellowed bed sheet, his neck stiff and sore. He had barely slept at all, but on those few occasions when he had managed to drift off, his sleep was invaded by horrific nightmares. Clinton McDermott demanding, "Top me off, cornhead!" while the corpse of Evie Martin laughed and danced in the background. No matter what direction Leonard turned, he saw Lisa Mitchell, grinning wickedly and waving to him. He had awakened with an anguished cry on his lips, his pulse racing.

He sat up in bed and worked at the knots in his neck. He shouldn't have come home last night. He should've gone straight up to Lisa Mitchell's door and demanded to know where Helen Martin was. Now, it might be too late.

Slowly, he got to his feet and straightened his aching back. He was in good shape for his age, but lack of proper sleep made him feel every single one of his sixty-two years. He crossed the cold linoleum of the kitchen and picked up the handset from the wall phone beside the refrigerator. He quickly punched in the digits before he could change his mind.

"Morgan Township Hospital. How may I direct your call?" The nasally voice sounded almost computer-generated.

"Personnel," he said and was promptly placed on hold. In his entire twenty-year career with the hospital, he had never taken a sick day, but today was going to be his first. He couldn't allow another whole day to go by trapped at his job while Lisa perpetuated her evil unfettered. If there was any chance at all for Helen, Leonard was going to have to stick to Lisa like glue.

"What do you mean?" asked Lisa, taking the paper from Suze's hand. It was opened to the obituaries, and it only took a moment before Lisa understood.

BERT PARNELL

Bert Parnell, 54, of Borden passed unexpectedly Wednesday evening. He was an independent semi-truck owner-operator for over thirty years.

Bert is survived by his wife, Greta, and three daughters, Elizabeth, 18, Laurie, 16, and Virginia, 4.

A memorial service will be held on Sunday at Graham Whitaker Funeral Home...

As Lisa's eyes skimmed across Virginia's name, her equilibrium turned inside out, and she nearly dropped to her knees. She reached out for the stair rail to steady herself. The room seemed to pulse with electrical current. She realized that the corners of her mouth had pulled up in an involuntary smile. Yes. *Yes.* Suze *had* found the girl.

There were no pictures to accompany the small article, but she knew that if she could see Virginia Parnell, she would be looking at the child described by both Suze and Chad. Adrenaline coursed through her veins. She wanted to leave for Borden *immediately*.

"How long before the car's ready?" asked Lisa.

Suze looked at her blankly. "I don't know."

"Well, don't you think you better find out?"

Suze shook her head. "Not me. My ex-husband owns that service station. Nobody knows I'm in town. I want to keep it that way."

"Well, Chad sure the hell can't go down."

"I guess you're going to have to do it," said Suze.

"It isn't even my car!" said Lisa. "I didn't drop it off. Why should they release it to me?"

"Roy'll release it to whoever pays the goddamned bill," snapped Suze. "Besides, I should probably throw that old woman some food or something if you plan to keep her."

Lisa's eyes narrowed, but she went along, desperate to get underway. Virginia Parnell was waiting for her in Borden.

⸻◆⸻

Helen Martin was terrified.

Less than twelve hours ago, she had been on her way home from another in a seemingly endless series of night shifts. If she hadn't thought to check Lisa's house, she would be waking up in her own bed right now, and Lisa would probably be dead.

Like Evie.

Fresh tears streaked Helen's cheeks, but she forced her sobs to remain silent. She didn't want that strung-out freak with the gun to have the satisfaction of knowing how far gone she was. She had been locked into this small, square

295

concrete bin overnight, her arms bound together in front of her. There was a boarded-up section of wall where the coal chute had once been, but it opened to the rear of the house, into the enclosed backyard, where no one would hear her if she screamed. Even if Helen thought someone might hear, she didn't think it was the smartest move to make. She hadn't seen Lisa in hours. Suze might have already killed her.

Who were they?

She knew Lisa didn't run around with such people. She had done a little inquiring at the hospital, and for the most part, her co-workers seemed to share a collective amnesia with respect to Lisa Mitchell. They all remembered the name, could sort of remember her face—Helen found it deplorable. How could you work side-by-side with someone for any length of time and not know what they looked like? Still, the impression given was that Lisa had been a loner outside of work, caring for her elderly Nanna. Exactly as Lisa had told her.

What did these people want?

A malicious internal voice kept pestering, reminding Helen that she'd seen their faces. They would never let her go. They *couldn't*.

Her eyes darted around the room for anything she might use as a weapon, just as they had done a hundred times before. There was still nothing.

The frustration was maddening. Helen needed to see Lisa again, to make sure that she was still alive. She beat her bound hands against the metal door, shouting, *"SUZE!"*

Helen screamed until her throat was raw and was finally rewarded with footsteps descending into the basement. Quick, angry footsteps.

The metal door flew open, and Suze thrust her head in, her eyes wild with annoyance. *"What in the hell do you want?"* she screamed.

Helen flinched and backed away. She was relieved to see that Suze wasn't carrying her gun. "May I see Lisa, please?" she tried to sound steady and sure, but her voice cracked, morphing into a whiny sniffle.

"May I see Lisa, please," Suze mimicked. She leaned in toward Helen and sneered, "Chad's having his way with her right now before I put a bullet in her brain. Wanna watch?"

Helen fell apart completely. "Please don't hurt her, *please!* I'll do anything you want! I have some money—savings—it's not much, but it's yours! *Anything!* Oh, *please,* can't I see her?"

Suze shook her head, disgusted eyes fixed on the old woman's face. She wanted to smash it with her fist. She wanted to drive it to the ground, then stomp it with her foot. Her pulse accelerated.

So what if Lisa wanted to keep the nurse alive? Lisa wasn't in charge of anything. Lisa didn't call the shots. If Suze wanted Helen Martin to die, Helen Martin would die.

And Suze wanted Helen Martin to die.

Lisa entered the lobby of Roy's BP and approached the register. She rested her purse on the counter and smiled at Roy. He was tall and gangly, with greasy black hair and an oily complexion to match. He had several angry-looking zits peppered across his chin. She recognized him from high school, from the hallways and annuals, although she was pretty sure he had never noticed her before. He gave Lisa a quizzical look and glanced out toward the bay, then back at her again.

"Is there somethin' I can do for you?" he asked.

"If the Volvo's ready, I'm here to pick it up," she said.

He scratched his head and slowly got out of his chair. "You pullin' my leg?"

She arched an eyebrow at him. "How much?" She laid a stack of currency on the counter, and Roy's eyes were drawn to it like magnets.

"Ninety," he said and watched as she separated the bills into exact change. He slipped the key across the counter and handed Lisa a handwritten receipt. She folded it carefully and tucked it into her purse, alongside the rest of her cash. She snapped the clasp shut and took the key, glancing at Roy as she turned away. He was still staring like an idiot.

The car started easily, and Lisa took a moment to run her hands over the plush interior. Her old Toyota had seen its best days long before it had ever been hers. This car had been bought by someone with *money*. There wasn't a standard feature to be had, just option after glorious option. She was impressed with the fluidity of the transmission as she glided from the lot and pointed the car toward her house.

She could learn to appreciate such things.

Jessica Lybrook hadn't had a good night. After leaving David McElroy's cabin, she had proceeded to get her Jeep hung up on a log which had fallen across the road. She hadn't seen it on the way in, but she often got turned around in the woods and probably wasn't even on the right road. She knew she would never make it on patrol; she'd be a missing person herself half the time.

The Jeep was her personal vehicle, and it wasn't outfitted with a police radio. She was the dispatcher, for God's sake! Who would she call, herself? She wasn't married any longer, so no one was waiting for her at home. She wouldn't be missed until she didn't show for her next shift. She was off for the next two days. She spent the night folded uncomfortably in the back seat with the windows eased down a bit, listening to the sounds of the woods around her while the moon slowly crossed through the intertwined limbs above.

It gave her time to think. She hoped it wasn't too late for McElroy. Underneath it all, he was a good man. Bad things happen to good people all the time. He could persevere, if he chose to. Jessica knew what it was like to feel lost and alone. It had been so long ago. But she had confronted her demons and gotten help. She had been fine for a long time now. She could show McElroy, make him understand.

If she could find him.

When the first light of dawn crept through the morning sky, Jessica decided to rock the Jeep one last time before beginning the long walk back to civilization. Just as she was about to give up, the front wheel caught and hiccuped over the limb. Jessica sat speechless at the steering wheel, unable to believe that she had finally had a piece of good fortune. Laughter bubbled up from her gut and trickled unbidden through her lips.

After only a few wrong turns, she found her way back to the main road and headed toward Morgan. She remembered McElroy speaking fondly of his days on the police force there. He had been a real force to be reckoned with then, apparently.

Helen saw the look in Suze's eyes, and it was like nothing she had ever seen before. The raw hatred, the animal intensity...

Helen knew she was going to die. She braced herself as best she could and held her breath, watching Suze's fingers curl under into fists.

Through the rafters overhead came the sound of the front door opening.

Helen screamed as loudly as she could. Suze's attention had been momentarily averted by the sound above, but Helen's shrill cry snapped her back to attention.

"Shut the hell up!" Suze shrieked, swinging her arm around and backhanding Helen. Helen crumpled with the blow, dropping to her knees, then to her hands.

But she wouldn't stop screaming.

Just as Suze reared back to strike the nurse again, a hand seized Suze's wrist and held it back. It was Lisa, breathless from running to the basement.

"What's going on here?" she asked Suze. "The whole neighborhood had to have heard that!"

"Oh, *God!*" gasped Helen, struggling to her feet and crossing to Lisa. She threw her arms around Lisa and sobbed, "She was going to kill me, and all I wanted to do was to see you, and—"

Her words dried up, replaced by a look of utter confusion.

"Chad sent me down to see what all the racket was about," said Lisa, smoothing Helen's short, rumpled hair. "I didn't dare duck out the front door. They would have killed you."

Suze reached out and grabbed Lisa roughly by the hair, jerking her away from the confused nurse. Lisa shrieked and allowed herself to be led back to the door. "Count yourself lucky this time, old woman," she hissed. "I think I'll take out my frustrations on your little darling, here."

"NO!" Forceful as Helen's exclamation was, her eyes were still begging. Suze had no respect for beggars. She pushed Lisa out into the basement and slammed the door to the coal depository, snapping the padlock back into place.

She had no sooner gotten the lock in place when Lisa came alive in her grasp. Lisa pulled her arms free and swung her fist up to connect solidly with Suze's mouth. Blood exploded from Suze's bottom lip, and her wide eyes reflected her complete astonishment.

"Wha—?"

"Shhh!" Lisa grabbed Suze's arm and pulled her up the stairs to the first floor, out of hearing range for Helen. Once they were on the main floor, Lisa pushed Suze back against the wall, pinning her elbow against her throat. "Don't you ever touch me like that again, do you hear me? Not *ever!"*

Suze sputtered bloody saliva down her chin. "I thought you wanted things to be realistic so that nurse wouldn't catch on—"

"Bullshit," said Lisa. "You wanted the opportunity to yank around on me. Let me be clear—you touch me again, and I'll kill you. You got it?"

Suze bit back the profusion of smartass replies that threatened to bubble forth. Who in the hell did Lisa Mitchell think she was? Suze could twist her head right off of her shoulders, if she were so inclined. But it was a battle for another time. The only thing that mattered now was finding the little girl. As difficult as it was to do, Suze nodded her head slowly, knowing that if she said anything, her sarcastic tone would betray her. After the girl was eliminated, Suze would find a way to jettison the Mitchell woman.

"Good," said Lisa, relaxing her hold on Suze's throat. "The car's in the drive."

Suze dabbed at her lip with the hem of her t-shirt. "Let's go," she said, although her words were already distorting as the swelling began.

"We need a plan first," said Lisa.

"What's to plan? We know where we're going. We know what to do when we get there."

"And what do you suggest, that we drag Helen Martin along with us?" asked Lisa.

"We could kill her."

"Yes, we could," said Lisa. "But we might need her medical expertise again. There's no use being hasty."

"So, we're going to keep her around forever? You know that isn't practical. If she were to get away—"

"She won't," said Lisa. "Not as long as she fears for my safety. I think we should keep her at least until Chad is well enough to get around."

"Did someone call my name?" Chad stood at the top of the stairs, looking down to the first floor. His left arm was held by a makeshift sling. His complexion was sallow, and his eyes looked dark and sunken.

Lisa hurried up the stairs and took Chad by his good arm just as his knees buckled. She led him back to the bedroom and eased him back to the mattress. Suze followed, trying to jockey for position but finding nowhere to be that wasn't in the way.

"You shouldn't be out of bed," Lisa gently admonished. "Our boy needs to get his strength back if he's going to be any good at all. Right, Suze?"

Suze nodded and stroked Chad's cheek. Lisa's possessiveness was beginning to grate on her nerves, but she knew that Chad needed rest, not to be drawn into the middle as a referee to mediate their differences.

"What happened to you?" he asked, looking up at Suze's injured face.

"Nothing for you to worry about," she said, trying to smile through her split lips. "It looks worse than it is."

"You got the car?" Chad asked, turning his attention to Lisa.

Lisa nodded her head. "It's time to get going."

"To where?"

"Borden. It's the hometown of that trucker you blew to smithereens. It's his daughter that we're after," said Lisa.

Chad closed his eyes and smiled. Yes. It *was* the daughter. He could feel the truth of it, the nearness of his prey.

"I can't wait to get my hands on the little bitch," muttered Suze.

Chad shook his head. "It has to be Lisa."

"*What?* No way!" Suze began pacing the room, furious at the notion. "We don't even really *know* this bitch, Chad!"

Chad's eyes opened and fixed on Suze. "You're being stupid and selfish," he said evenly. "I'm too weak to go, and you need to stay to keep that nurse in line. Lisa's the best one for the job."

"Why can't I go and have her stay?"

"Because without you here, the nurse is bound to try something heroic. And why shouldn't Lisa help her? They're on the same side, remember?"

Suze didn't have an answer. Her frustration was skyrocketing, and the urge to break something was nearly undeniable. All this effort, and the new girl was going to get the kill. When Suze brought her eyes up to meet Lisa's, there was no way to hide the venom that bubbled just below the surface.

"Once you're back on your feet, we'll get rid of the nurse," said Lisa. "By then, she'll be one-hundred percent liability." As she said it, she glanced at Suze, and Suze felt a chill crawl down her back. Who was the liability, Helen Martin or herself?

Lisa bent over and kissed Chad tenderly on the mouth. She retrieved the gun from where it lay on the bedside table.

"It's time."

II

Greta Parnell listlessly wiped down the counter, staring vacantly through the large window over her double-basin stainless steel sink. Crumbs that fell to the floor escaped her attention, and after the counter was clean, she wiped it some more.

She hadn't slept since the deputy had come.

What had been a comfortable, predictable existence had dipped its toe into something awful, something contagious. She still expected to hear Bert come tromping through the door, crooning nonsense as if it were real lyrics, ambling up behind her to reach his arms around and—

A single tear rolled down Greta's cheek. She hadn't lost control yet. She knew she would eventually, but not right now. The whole thing wasn't *real*. How could Bert be dead? Who could do such an awful thing?

She had to be strong for the girls. Betty had completely fallen apart and wouldn't come out of her room. Laurie seemed to be in a state of shock. And Tater—well, Tater was Tater. She cried when everyone else did, but Greta hadn't found the courage to tell her about her father yet. She would have to do it today. Too many friends had already dropped by to express their condolences. Tater was smart. She already knew something was amiss, she just didn't know what.

Greta finally tossed the towel aside and crossed the kitchen to the large family room at the front of the house. Although it was July, her mind drifted to the previous Christmas, the full tree adorned in sparkling reds, blues and greens, the red felt stockings that hung over the mantle, the warm feeling of family and togetherness. Christmas was especially important for the Parnells because it was the one time a year that Bert would refuse work no matter the pay in order to be with his family. It was one of the few constants in their lives.

Now it was gone.

And somehow, Greta sensed that the nightmare which had begun when the deputy rang the doorbell wasn't over yet. She shivered as a nonexistent breeze tickled her shoulders and the nape of her neck. The girls were upstairs in their rooms. Betty was still undoubtedly crying, Laurie was probably staring at the ceiling, and Tater was probably removing Barbie's hair with Greta's good sewing shears.

Why did everything feel so *wrong?*

It was as if any possibility of the future had abruptly ceased to exist. She couldn't imagine being the leader of this family. And that's exactly what she had become. Both she and Bert had been only children. Both of their parents were dead. There were no cousins, uncles, or grandparents. Greta was all the girls had. Why did she feel like it wouldn't be nearly enough?

Greta was startled from her introspection by the soft padding of small feet on the wooden stairs. She turned to see Virginia pensively entering the room.

"Hey, Tater," she said, mustering the strength to speak cheerfully.

"Mom, we need to talk," Virginia said. Greta smiled. Virginia's language skills were far above average for her age. She didn't ramble nonsense. She always came straight to the point.

"What do you want to talk about, honey?"

"I know about Daddy."

"Oh, I'm sorry, sweetheart," said Greta, reaching out to pull the girl to her. Virginia placed her small hands gently on Greta's wrists, stopping her.

"It's not your fault. It's the way it is."

Greta pursed her lips and studied her daughter. Part of her wanted to scream that no, it was *not* the way it was. But the simplicity of the statement from the innocent face framed by dark curls—

"Mommy?" Her voice was small and apprehensive. She didn't often call Greta 'Mommy' anymore because she said she was too old for that. It was a word reserved for those insecure moments when Virginia realized she just might not know everything after all.

"Yes, sweetie?"

"What happens when you go?"

"When *I* go? Honey, I'm not going anywhere."

Virginia's dubious gaze said otherwise. "But what happens if you do?"

"I won't."

"But what if?"

"I won't."

Virginia looked as if she might burst into tears. Her bottom lip quivered, and her saucer eyes pooled. "I love you, Mommy."

"I love you, too, sweetheart."

"I think I should go upstairs now."

Greta smiled. "You don't have to be alone if you don't want to, Tater. You can come sit with Mommy on the sofa."

Virginia snuffled and wiped her nose with the back of her hand. "No. I think I should go upstairs now. Bye." She turned and trotted up the stairs, her tiny footfalls fading into nothingness.

Greta cocked her head quizzically. Was that normal behavior? Virginia was such a perceptive little girl. Maybe she needed to speak to a psychologist, someone outside the family who could help her sort out her feelings. She would have to ask her best friend, Judy, about it when she came over later.

Greta had been surrounded by her friends in the hours after she had found out about Bert. But finally, after she had taken all the support she could stand, she had politely asked them to give her some alone time. There were a few who didn't want to, like Todd and Cindy, who thought that being alone was terribly destructive. Eventually, Judy ran everyone off, but Greta knew it was only a matter of time before they started trickling back, one by one, to see how the Widow Parnell was holding up.

Greta went back to the kitchen, looking around for anything to busy herself. Anxiety hung in the clouds of the gray morning. Water, air, earth—everything felt flat and dead. It was as if someone had been walking over her grave all morning, and as time passed, the walk had turned into a jig.

The morning newspaper abruptly clattered against the storm door causing Greta to emit a startled gasp. She reached the front door in time to see the Hammond boy pedaling his way down the winding dirt road. She picked up the paper and went inside, tossing it to the sofa without a glance. Bert's obituary would be in this edition. She didn't think she could look at it quite yet.

Why was she so jumpy? Tommy Hammond had nailed her storm door every day for the past two years, and she had never once reacted like that. For a moment, it felt as if her heart had actually stopped beating. She needed sleep. Her body must be nearing the point of exhaustion. How could she take care of three girls when she couldn't even take care of herself?

There was a knock at the front door.

Crystal tossed and turned on the lumpy motel mattress all night long. Her dreams descended on her like hungry wolves, sneaking in from around the dark corners of her mind. She woke three times in the middle of the night, each time gasping for air. She could feel fingers locked around her throat, her scream unable to push past them.

The first time it happened, she was sure that it must have been Luke. Paula was correct, and Luke was every bit as homicidal as she had feared. But no, Luke was asleep in one of the uncomfortable vinyl chairs, his long legs draped over one armrest, his mouth hanging open as if he were waiting for someone to feed him.

After the third time, Crystal decided to forget about sleep. She was having the most extraordinary sense of déjà vu—if that's what it should be called. It was the dream. She had dreamt it before, but not for many years. She had been in high school—no, elementary school. The dream had plagued her for weeks. She remembered running to her Aunt Maude in the middle of the night, gasping for breath, pleading for protection.

Protection from a dream?

A glance at the bedside clock showed that it was only a little after four in the morning. It would be hours before she could even take the car over to the BP station.

She stared at the ceiling and reflected over the last few days. So much had changed so quickly. Stardom had been fleeting, and Crystal didn't think she'd want it again even if she could have it.

The only thing that mattered was the little girl.

Crystal longed for her Aunt Maude. She would know what to do. She *always* knew what to do. The dream that Crystal had while in the hospital replayed, Maude's voice instantly recognizable.

"Soon there will be people coming. Some of them want to help you, some want to hurt you. You need to be ready—and you need to be able to tell the difference."

People *had* come. First, there was Paula, then Luke. Was one of them planning to betray her? Were there others coming? What did any of it mean?

It always came back to the little girl, Virginia Parnell. Crystal had only gotten a fleeting glance of the image on the highway, but she could recall the face with complete clarity. She had originally attributed it to her actor's acuity, but now it seemed as if there was something more relevant.

Thinking about Virginia Parnell caused a cold knot to form in the pit of Crystal's stomach. Something was terribly wrong.

They needed to get to Borden as quickly as possible.

Paula hadn't slept at all. She turned her back to the room so no one would notice, but she couldn't make her mind power down enough to find sleep. As many times as she had dreamt it, as many times as she had *prayed* for it, Joel McElroy was dead. He could never force her to do anything again. Suze had killed him with her bare hands.

Suze was in a lot of trouble.

Modern forensics labs were amazingly competent. Surely, there must be some sort of trace evidence left behind, something that would tie Suze to the murder. Probably enough to tie Paula to the scene of the crime, as well.

Paula wished she understood why she was following Crystal Bright. Being such a big fan, she hadn't questioned Suze's motives originally. Hell, it was an opportunity to meet her idol. But there were things working in the background— Paula could sense them, and her intuition told her none of these things were good.

Luke suddenly snorted in the chair across the room before his breathing settled back to a steadier cadence. Paula still feared Luke. He had lied to them once, and he would lie to them again. He was a man. And now, he was in the room with them. For someone so accomplished, Crystal could be awfully naive. Luke could disembowel them in their sleep. The thought certainly contributed to Paula's insomnia.

Mostly, though, she thought about Suze.

What kind of people had Suze gotten herself involved with? What did they want with Crystal Bright? Would Suze let Paula stay with her when this was all over? She couldn't go home. Her mother would know that she knew something about Joel's death.

The room was dark and quiet, save for the occasional sleep sounds from Luke and the rustle of cotton sheets as Crystal tossed and turned in the other bed.

Paula sighed as the digits on the bedside clock slowly counted the minutes.

By seven o'clock, Crystal was dressed and trotting down the metal stairs to the parking lot. Her blonde mane was pulled back into a ponytail, and her eyes were hidden behind dark sunglasses. The morning light was dismal and gray with the possibility of showers hanging in the clouds overhead. Back in the room, Luke was still sawing logs in the guest chair, and Paula was babbling nonsense in what seemed to be a fitful sleep. Crystal left them alone, figuring they might need all the sleep they could get.

Daylight had done nothing to ease the anxiety gnawing at Crystal. The feeling had escalated into one of near panic, and she wanted to get the car to the service station as soon as it opened. Borden was only thirty miles away; maybe they should have taken a cab the night before.

Maybe it was already too late.

Roy was just opening the two large service bay doors when Crystal eased the Honda onto the lot. He nodded without changing his expression and directed her toward the mouth of the one on the left. In the other, a maroon sedan was suspended on a hydraulic lift, its passenger front tire pulled off and laying to the side.

"I only got one ahead of you, and she's nearly done," said Roy over his shoulder, not even bothering to make eye contact. "Your husband said you were in a hurry—"

"He's not my husband," said Crystal. "And yes, we're in a hurry. How soon can I pick the car up?"

"An hour—maybe two."

305

As Crystal walked back to the motel, she couldn't shake the horrible certainty that things were going sharply downhill.

⌐ ⎯⎯⎯⎯◆⎯⎯⎯ ⌐

Paula awakened with a start just as the water in the shower turned off. She didn't mean to fall asleep at all, but she had managed to lose the last hour in the blink of an eye. She glanced around and found herself alone in the room. Were Crystal and Luke showering together? *God!*

A moment later, Luke emerged from the bathroom wearing only a thin, terrycloth towel around his midsection. Paula's eyes danced over him before looking away in embarrassment.

"I'm sorry," said Luke with an awkward grin. "I thought you'd still be asleep."

"I wasn't sleeping," said Paula stubbornly. She didn't want Luke to think that she ever let down her guard.

"Hmm," he said, grabbing his dirty clothes from the floor and going back into the bathroom. As he closed the door, he said, "You snore pretty good for someone who ain't asleep."

Bastard.

As the bathroom door latched, Paula swung her feet out from underneath the covers and sat on the edge of the bed, stretching her back.

"Where's Crystal?" she called out.

"I think she took the car over," he said through the door. "She should be back soon."

Thank God. Paula didn't like the thought of being alone with Luke and was frankly surprised that Crystal had left her that way. She knew how Paula felt about Luke. Exactly why Crystal had determined this stranger was trustworthy was beyond Paula. He had that look in his eyes, the same malicious gleam that united men everywhere. He was big and broad-shouldered, able to take whatever wasn't given freely.

She glanced at the telephone on the nightstand and thought about calling Suze's cell phone. She wondered if Joel's body had been found yet, and if so, had Suze been arrested?

Luke reemerged from the bathroom wearing the same dirty clothes he had worn the previous day, his flannel shirt unbuttoned. He paused in front of the mirror above the dresser and began towel drying his hair. Paula couldn't help but notice the cut of his pecs, the ripple of his abdominals, the pungent masculinity that oozed from his every movement. Paula wished he would go away, fade back into the cornfield from which he had first emerged.

"What are you staring at?" asked Luke. He was watching her through the reflection in the mirror, noticing her keen scrutiny.

306

Paula squirmed uncomfortably. "Nothing."

Luke sighed and turned toward her, his fingers fastening the buttons of his shirt as he did so. "Why won't you trust me?"

"Why should I? I don't know you from Adam."

"I don't see that we have any choice," he said. "We're in this together now."

"Bullshit. I *always* have a choice, do you understand me?"

There was a clatter outside, and both of their heads turned in unison toward the door. A moment later, the flimsy lock released, and the door swung inward.

"Well, for God's sake, don't anyone help me or anything," muttered Crystal, her hands full with a greasy brown bag and cardboard drink container from McDonald's. "They were having a 2-for-1 sale on McMuffins, and I brought some ice water to drink. I hope that's okay with everyone. We can't really afford much more than that."

"Hey, that's great!" said Luke enthusiastically, his fingers already prying into the paper bag. "Thanks. I'm starved."

Crystal perched on the end of the mattress and absently watched while Luke and Paula pulled their breakfasts from the paper sack and spread them out on the small round table in the corner of the room.

"Ain't you hungry?" asked Luke between bites of half-chewed egg and English muffin.

Crystal shrugged. "I ought to be."

"What's the matter?" asked Paula.

"I wish I knew," said Crystal. She stood and began pacing the motel room, stopping to pull back the curtain to look out the window.

"Did someone follow you back to the motel?" Luke's voice immediately registered alarm. He pushed up from his chair and moved beside her, peering over her shoulder to the parking lot below.

Crystal shook her head. "It's nothing like that. I—I just woke up out of sorts. I'm sure everything's fine."

Everything's fine—what a stupid thing to say, thought Crystal. *Things couldn't be any further from fine. My career is over, Aunt Maude is dead, and the little Parnell girl—*

Her anxiety intensified just thinking about the girl. How could someone so small be at the center of something so volatile?

Luke settled back in his chair but remained watchful, his eyes studying the constant changes in Crystal's determined expression. Overloaded nerves jumped and twitched in her temples, and her hands flitted from one surface to the next, unwilling to remain still for any longer than a second or two. She was like a wire stretched taut to near the point of breaking.

"You said last night that you wanted to see Mrs. Parnell with me," said Luke. "You still up for it?"

"Mrs. Parnell?" asked Paula. "Who's that?"

307

Crystal shot Luke a warning glare, but he simply said, "C'mon—we're going to have to tell her sooner or later."

"Tell me what?" asked Paula suspiciously.

Crystal tried to be light and upbeat, but her laughter was forced and nervous. "I'm sure it's nothing—"

"Oh, c'mon!" said Luke. "If you're going to tell her anything, tell her the *truth*."

Crystal whirled on him. "And exactly what would that truth be? I don't know how much of this shit *I'm* buying into—"

"What shit?" asked Paula.

"You know what you saw," said Luke. "You know what I've told you."

"Like you're an authority on this kind of thing," said Crystal.

"An authority on *what* kind of thing?" asked Paula, her agitation growing.

"There *is* no authority on this kind of thing," said Luke. "All we've got to rely on are our own instincts. Mine are telling me that we're in some pretty deep shit, and it just keeps getting deeper. I don't think we're doing the girl any favors by keeping her in the dark."

"I don't think it's up to you to start calling all the shots," said Crystal, defiantly folding her arms across her chest.

"FOR GOD'S SAKE!" screamed Paula, glaring back and forth between them, their mouths frozen in mid-sentence, their attention finally on her. "I'm not a child," she said quietly. "If something's going on, I have a right to know."

Crystal sighed and sat at the small table across from Paula. "All right," she said. "But this is really weird, and you're going to think the two of us are completely crazy."

And Crystal told her story while Paula sat silent and still, absorbing the tale impassively. Occasionally, she glanced at Luke, as if she were looking for verification to Crystal's words, but neither he nor Crystal could tell how she was responding to the fantastic suppositions and concerns that they harbored for Bert Parnell's daughter, all based on dreams and psychic impressions. When Crystal finished, Paula sat back in her chair.

"Well," she said simply.

Crystal shrugged her shoulders. "That's it," she said. "Like I said before, it may be nothing at all, but if we're going to drop Luke off in Borden, it would make me feel better to see that Virginia Parnell is alright." She reached into the McDonald's bag and began picking at a cold McMuffin.

"Of course," said Paula.

"So, you're alright with this?" asked Crystal.

"What choice do I have?" asked Paula with a shrug. "If you're wrong, then we'll drop Captain Cowboy off and be on our way. If not, you might be able to help that little girl. I don't see what the big deal is."

Crystal and Luke exchanged a glance. They both realized that Paula wasn't experiencing any of the anxiety that had guided their own paths for the last few days. She was simply along for the ride.

———◇———

Traffic was thickening as morning commuters drifted into the small town to perform whatever jobs they did. Crystal kept her head down as she traversed the sidewalk, not wanting to draw any unexpected attention. She wondered why she even bothered. Initially, it had pissed her off when no one seemed to recognize her. Presently, it seemed a godsend. Still, now wasn't the time for a legion of fans to discover her. She needed to retrieve the car so they could *go*.

Roy's BP was filled to capacity when she arrived, not that it entailed too many customers. There was only a total of four pumps along the center aisle, the type of pumps that still required an attendant's assistance, and Roy was in the process of servicing four vehicles at them. He was currently leaning under the hood of a sky-blue Ford Pinto, pulling the bent dipstick out of its sheath. The other cars, all at least ten years old, were in the process of refueling, an annoying bell enumerating the gallons as they were dispensed. Crystal was relieved to see the little Honda outside of the service bay and pulled off to the side. She was afraid that Roy might've missed his time estimate, and the car wouldn't be ready. She hurried across the lot and into the small office to wait for Roy to finish up with his other customers.

She watched Roy wash windshields and make change, and then he finally headed toward the office. She hoped the bill wouldn't be too much. She was running out of money quickly. Once she got to Lucasville, she didn't know what she'd do.

Roy threw the door open and stopped cold when he saw her. He lowered his head and continued across the room to ease behind the cash register. "I suppose you're here for the other car now?"

Crystal's smile faltered, and she cocked her head curiously. "I'm here for the silver Honda," she said. "The one I dropped off this morning."

"Sure, sure," he said, smiling knowingly at her.

Crystal tentatively stepped up to the counter. "How much is it?"

Roy's gaze held for an uncomfortable moment before he turned and retrieved the work order from a bin on the wall. "Thirty-five," he grunted.

Crystal counted the money out of her wallet and was chagrined to see that she only had eight dollars left. At least there would be food at Aunt Maude's house. She kept enough dry goods on hand to weather a nuclear apocalypse. Crystal laid the cash on the counter, and when she started to retract her hand, Roy grabbed it.

"If you're trying to pull some kind of flimflam," he said, his menacing eyes boring holes through her. "You'll be sorry you messed with ol' Roy."

Crystal stared up at him openmouthed. What in the hell was wrong with him? She tried to pull her hand free, but he held tight. "Let go of me," she said. "I don't know what you're talking about."

"I ain't dealin' with hot cars," he hissed, and Crystal's breath caught in her throat. Paula hadn't made a payment on the Honda in months—she had said so herself. Was the car now considered stolen?

She finally managed to pull her hand free but stood frozen, not sure what to do next. She needed the keys but doubted Roy would give them up voluntarily. He would probably call the police, and it would be hours before they could get to Borden—if they could get there at all.

But to Crystal's astonishment, Roy reached underneath the counter and produced the small key ring, tossing it to her through the air. She fumbled the catch, and the keys clattered to the dingy yellow tile floor. She bent down and scooped them up, her eyes never leaving Roy. Closing her fingers tightly around the keys, she turned and hurried out the door.

She could feel his eyes on her back as she scurried across the lot to the Honda. In her haste, she nearly clipped the front fender of an Oldsmobile as she backed out of the parking slot and drove around the island of ancient pumps.

As Crystal pulled out onto the street, she looked into her rearview mirror and saw Roy framed in the doorway to his office, his eyes locked on her as she drove away.

⋯⋯◇⋯⋯

The engine purred softly as the Honda clipped along the highway, corn stretching as far as the eye could see. The gloom of the morning sky had steepened into heavy storm clouds, collecting overhead and hovering with menace. Paula hadn't said much since they had left but sat in the back seat immersed in her own thoughts. At least her anxiety seemed to have lessened since they had pulled away from Morgan.

Luke sat in the passenger seat, his long legs folded uncomfortably in the cramped floorboard. As Crystal stole a glance in his direction, she noticed how completely out of place he looked in the tiny compact. She wondered what he had driven when he was back on Paulie's farm. Probably an old Chrysler with bench seats wide enough to comfortably seat three in the front and three in the back. She noticed the steady throb of a vein coiled near his temple, the rhythmic flexing of his jaw muscles, his fingers clenched so tightly the knuckles were white. His anxiety had only heightened as the miles passed.

So had hers.

She wondered if death row inmates felt this way just before they were led to the gas chamber.

"There's the corporation limit," said Luke, noting the luminescent green sign on the side of the road. Thunder rumbled overhead, announcing their passage.

"Great," said Crystal, noting the heavy droplets that spattered against the windshield. "How are we even going to find the Parnells' house?"

Luke glanced around, taking in his surroundings. If it hadn't been for the roadside sign, he wouldn't have even known he was in a town. The speed limit had dropped to forty-five, but there were only a few poorly kept houses dotted along the highway.

"If there's actually a town up there, there should be a gas station. We'll stop, and I'll ask directions," said Luke. "A town like this, everyone knows everyone. I'm sure they'll be able to tell us how to get to the Parnells'."

Crystal slowed to forty as the rain suddenly broke loose in torrents, washing over the car and making the road very difficult to see. She flipped the switch that activated the headlights so any oncoming traffic could see her, but it was an empty gesture; there was no oncoming traffic. It was as if they had driven into a ghost town, devoid of any population other than themselves.

Luke suddenly sat upright and craned his neck to the left. He grabbed Crystal's arm and said, "Stop!"

Under normal circumstances, Crystal wasn't much for following barked orders, but these circumstances were anything but normal. She stomped on the brake, and the little car shuddered to a stop.

"What is it?" she asked, looking around.

Luke continued to stare through the driver's side window. "Over there," he said, his finger pointing in the same direction. "We passed a road just a minute ago. Turn around."

Crystal cut the steering wheel all the way to the left and eased the car through a U-turn. "What am I looking for?" she asked and suddenly didn't need the answer. She saw the gravel road a few yards ahead on the right, barely visible through a dense growth of weeds and gnarled undergrowth. Somehow, the sky seemed darkest just above it. Lightning ripped through the sky, and her nerve endings felt as if they were crackling with its electricity.

This was it.

Crystal turned right, and they soon heard the sound of the gravel road crunching underneath the tires. Paula leaned forward from the back seat, propping her elbows on the headrests of the front seats and peering through the windshield.

"You guys are nuts," she said, but her words sounded hollow in the car's cabin, muted against the steady pounding of rain against the roof. The heightened anxiety in the car was contagious, and Paula could feel the tiny hairs on her arms standing on end. Dammit, she wished Crystal hadn't offered Luke a ride. They could have been halfway to Lucasville by now.

The muscles along Luke's jaw line twitched as he intently studied the landscape. Woods that almost spilled out onto the road, thick tangles of underbrush nestled between the tree trunks, a small creek threading through the woods on the right. The geography was eerily familiar, like pieces of a jigsaw puzzle from outside its frame. The frame was his nightmare, the one in which he had met Bert Parnell's faceless family. He was almost there. He knew it with a certainty that stilled his mind.

Crystal continued slowly, not sure what they were looking for but sensing its proximity. If someone had told her two short months ago that she would buy into shit like this, she would have passed out from hysterical laughter. Now, as they drew nearer, she felt the horrible darkness ahead. It instilled such a sense of dread that she had to fight the urge to turn the car around. The little girl needed them, she didn't *have* anyone else—

How did Crystal know that?

"Oh, God," said Luke, his voice sounding queasy. "We're here."

Crystal saw the break in the woods on the right, marked by a mailbox built to look like a barn. "The Parnells" was emblazoned on the side, directly below the box number. She stopped the car and took a shuddery breath.

"I don't want to go," Paula said suddenly. "This is my car, and you can't take it down there."

"Are you alright?" Luke asked Crystal, noting her sudden pallor.

She nodded stiffly, slowly exhaling her deep breath. "I'm scared stupid."

"Me too." He smiled weakly at her and took her hand, giving it a gentle squeeze.

"Hey!" said Paula. "Isn't anyone listening to me? This car ain't going down there."

"Fine," said Crystal, slipping the gearshift into park. "We'll walk." She began unfastening her seatbelt.

Paula's eyes widened, and she struggled for something to say, some way to keep them from going down there. She didn't know when, but her feeling had somehow changed. It wasn't like group hysteria any longer. The danger felt *real*. And it was waiting, just at the end of that gravel drive. "Don't leave me here!" she finally managed, just as Luke and Crystal opened their doors.

Crystal stopped and looked back at her. "Make up your mind, Paula. You can't have it both ways. I've got to go in there."

"Come on," urged Luke. "We're wasting time."

Paula didn't know what to do. She was frustrated to the point of tears, which had begun to trickle down her cheeks.

"Oh, shit," Paula said. "Get in the car. Let's get this over with."

Luke glanced at Crystal, who turned to Paula. "Are you sure? I mean, this is it. No turning back."

Paula glanced from Luke to Crystal then nodded, wiping the tears from her eyes. "I'm scared," she whimpered.

Crystal nodded and slid behind the wheel. Luke didn't bother to fasten his seatbelt. They weren't going much farther.

When the farmhouse appeared around a bend in the driveway, Luke felt as if the air had been pushed from his lungs. It was exactly the same as in his dream with its clean white siding and black shuttered windows. Off to the left, he spotted the picnic table he had seen, the one the faceless Parnell family had gathered round to eat sandwiches and enjoy the summer sun as well as each other's company. But unlike the dream, its seats were empty, its wooden frame turning blood red under the falling rain.

It wasn't the only thing different from the dream.

The front door was standing wide open on its hinges.

CHAPTER SIXTEEN

As Crystal eased the Honda to a stop, she noticed the tail end of a maroon Volvo protruding from beyond the driveway, parked behind the house so as not to attract attention. Crystal's eyes were fixed on the car, recognition almost instantaneous.

"My God!" she said. "That car—it was at Roy's BP!"

"What?" Luke followed her gaze and said, "Are you sure?"

Crystal shifted the car into park and cut the engine. She turned to Paula, who was balled up in the back seat, and said, "I want you to stay here."

Paula glanced nervously at the house and then back to Crystal. She nodded shakily.

"I'm leaving the keys in the ignition," said Crystal. "Don't hesitate to use them if you have to."

Paula nodded again, her face pale and vacant. Thunder clapped overhead, and the ground rumbled beneath them. Crystal and Luke's eyes locked for a second, fear and adrenaline flooding the interior of the car. They opened their doors and stepped out into the torrential rain.

If anyone was watching from the windows, they would surely be seen. There was nowhere to take cover in the vast expanse of the Parnell front lawn. Luke instinctively pulled Crystal toward him and raced toward the wide front porch, where the open front door taunted them ominously, only darkness visible beyond its frame.

What in the hell were they doing?

They didn't have any weapons, nothing for protection. They could be walking into an ambush. *Shit!*

As they ascended the steps to the wooden porch, Luke pulled Crystal aside, staying out of sight of the yawning front door.

"Listen," he said softly. "We may well only have one thing goin' for us—surprise, and that's if we weren't spotted comin' up the drive. We need to be extra quiet. Get in, find out what in the fuck is goin' on—"

"And find Virginia." Crystal completed his thought, already on the same page. He nodded, and they moved silently toward the door. Luke paused at the frame and cautiously peered around its edge to see into the room beyond. It was a simple country living room, tidy but well lived-in, upholstered in a spectrum of beiges, shiny hardwood floors peeking out from underneath handsome braided rugs.

There was nobody lying in wait.

Luke eased into the room, urging Crystal to follow behind him. They paused just inside the door to acclimate their hearing to the confines of the house. The air inside was eerily still, as if all the acoustics in the room had gone completely flat. A ceiling fan with wicker blades swung lazily on its axis, suffusing the background with an innerving white noise. At one end of the living room, an open archway led to a shadowy hallway. Along the other side of the room was a spacious dining room with a passage that undoubtedly led to the kitchen. Crystal and Luke exchanged a glance before silently heading in opposite directions. Luke headed toward the dining room, each footstep measured and cautious, soundless. Crystal crossed the room to the archway, flattening herself against the wall before stealing a glance around the corner.

The hall was steeped in shadows, its single overhead lighting fixture switched off. The thunderstorm had stolen away any remnants of natural light that might have seeped through.

It, too, was empty.

Inside the hall, a stairway stretched up to the left, and what appeared to be a small study was off to the right. Its door stood open, but the room beyond was dark and empty. Crystal turned her attention to the wide staircase stretching up to the quiet gloom of the second floor.

She put her hand on the banister and slowly began to ascend.

The dining room table was made of heavy oak, its highly polished surface spotless. A squat silver vase graced the table's center, summer flowers skillfully arranged in a plume of color.

There was no sign of anyone.

Luke eased around the table toward the passageway to the kitchen, careful not to bump the enormous china hutch behind him. Rain pounded against the windows of the dining room, filling his ears and setting him even more on edge. An abrupt rumble of thunder nearly freed his bladder.

He was fighting the completely inappropriate urge to giggle when a brilliant flash of lightning flared behind the house, briefly illuminating the kitchen with the subtlety of a short circuit.

The floors were white ceramic tile, the walls papered in eggshell, the cabinets constructed from blond lumber.

The red spatters nearly leapt from the wall in contrast.

Luke's stomach tightened, and he felt his breakfast fighting to escape. He pressed himself to the wall and closed his eyes tightly, willing the nausea to pass. He took a shaky breath and inched toward the kitchen, trying to avoid looking at the worst of the mess, which was concentrated on the wall behind a small breakfast table. A bare foot extended from underneath the table, twisted to the side and unnaturally still.

Luke scanned the room and saw no one else. He slipped around the corner into the kitchen and extracted a butcher knife from the wooden block on the counter. He then crossed to the breakfast table, squatting down to see what lay beneath the tablecloth. His fingers hesitated as they caressed the fabric before pulling it straight up.

Greta Parnell lay underneath, her glassy eyes fixed to the ceiling. Luke recognized her from the photograph Bert had shown him. The bullet had entered through her forehead, leaving only the smallest dimple between her eyebrows. The back of her head would be in much worse condition. Mercifully, she was face up.

She wore a powder blue terrycloth dressing gown, its hemline fanning open to expose her scissored legs. A permanent look of surprise was etched onto her face, and Luke was overwhelmed by the horror of the moment frozen in her expression, the moment of recognition as the gun was drawn, a stab of sheer terror as she realized the inevitable—

Luke dropped the tablecloth back into place, but the image of Greta Parnell's body remained vivid, shaking his resolve and destroying his concentration. He fought the temptation to call out to Crystal. It was too dangerous. The killer was still somewhere in the house. It was with the sudden realization that he was a sitting duck, squatted down in the middle of the kitchen floor, that finally brought him to his senses. He stood quickly and went back into the shadows from where he had come.

At least he had a weapon now. Crystal, however, did not. She was exploring the other side of the house, hoping to find Virginia when she was just as likely to stumble across a killer.

⸻ ◇ ⸻

The stairs opened onto a landing halfway up, where a small writing table was positioned underneath a window looking out onto the backyard. Crystal could see the grille of the Volvo clearly, its boxy headlights jutting around the corner of the house.

She turned toward the second run of stairs leading to the upstairs hallway. Like the rest of the house, it was shrouded in shadow, a grandfather clock keeping count from somewhere along its length.

As she reached the top of the stairs, Crystal caught a suggestion of movement at the far end.

She dropped to her knees and held her breath, watching for another sign of motion.

Thunder rumbled and lightning flickered, providing a brief burst of erratic and insufficient light. Shadows leapt wildly across the corridor, but Crystal didn't

316

EQUILIBRIUM

see anyone else in the hall. She rose to a crouch and took a tentative step forward when another sudden burst of thunder rocked the walls, closer than the one before it, *different* somehow—

A gunshot?

She saw movement again, the farthest door on the left was being eased shut onto its latch, the twisting doorknob more apparent than the actual movement of the door.

A hand came from behind and closed on her wrist, another clamping across her mouth.

"*Shh,*" Luke whispered into her ear. "It's only me. I thought I heard a gunshot." He was pressed against Crystal's back and could feel her heartbeat hammering through her ribcage. He released his grip once he felt she would no longer scream.

"Me, too," she whispered.

"I found Greta downstairs. She's dead."

Crystal stared at him numbly, trying to absorb his simple statement. His eyes suddenly widened, and he pulled her backward, taking cover beside a small settee along the right wall. Crystal craned her neck over its arm to see.

A woman had emerged from the next door on the right and turned away from them, walking toward the rear of the hall. She wore a simple yellow sundress and white cloth tennis shoes, a mane of straw blonde hair flowing down her back. Gripped in her left hand was a gun, dangling casually at her side. She seemed unhurried and utterly unafraid.

She hadn't noticed them, or so it seemed. She didn't feel threatened by them in any event.

Crystal noticed the butcher knife in Luke's hand but took little comfort in it. What good was it against a gun? The woman's aura was like a foul odor, permanently staining everything it touched. Crystal was frozen to the spot, unable to move, unable to think.

As the woman continued down the hall on a direct path for the door Crystal had seen closing. She seemed to be on autopilot, internally guided to her next victim. As she drew near, Crystal realized with an inexplicable certainty that little Virginia's fragile presence was just beyond that door.

"Oh, God," Crystal said softly, her voice filled with helpless dread. She turned to Luke and discovered he wasn't beside her anymore. She frantically scanned the hallway and saw he had closed half the distance, stalking the armed woman from a crouched position. He kept the knife low and ready, moving stealthily forward.

The woman's hand brushed the doorknob and paused, her spine suddenly straightening. Luke froze where he was, still twenty feet away. Crystal could barely breathe.

The killer knew she wasn't alone.

317

She turned quickly, dropping into a crouch and raising the gun. Luke sprung through the air, his knife raised high above his head. Crystal watched in horror, seeing the trajectory, knowing he wasn't going to make it. The woman's gun swinging upward, upward—

Lightning flooded the hallway with a burst of illumination, and Crystal found herself staring into the eyes of the killer.

They were *her* eyes.

In a daze, Crystal stood and groped beside her for the wall plate she had seen earlier. She flipped the switch, and the shadows were abruptly driven from the hall just as Luke landed face first on the carpeting. He was too busy trying to protect himself to notice the woman. He covered his head and scrambled sideways, struggling to hold onto the knife.

A perfect silence settled over the house.

The woman stared at Crystal curiously, her grip loosening on the gun as her arm dropped to her side. The blonde of her poorly cut hair was achieved with a cheap rinse, unlike the golden tresses Crystal had found in Hollywood's salons, but the facial similarities were staggering. It was as if they were each looking into a mirror.

Crystal took a tentative step forward, her shock overriding her fear. How could this woman have her face? It wasn't possible!

It had all been so easy. The woman had even invited her in for coffee, prepared to receive condolences from another of Bert's friends with whom she wasn't acquainted. It was a purely magical moment when her eyes had focused on the gun, and she had realized Lisa's intent.

The single gunshot had ripped through the house, impossibly loud in Lisa's own ears. As Greta slid bonelessly to the floor, Lisa had remained in her chair at the breakfast table, sure that one or both of the teenaged daughters would come down to investigate. Maybe the little girl would make it easy for Lisa, wandering in and wondering where her Mommy had gone.

After a few silent moments, Lisa had gone upstairs.

In the first room to the left, Lisa had discovered one of the older daughters. She was asleep on a canopied bed, her disheveled hair piled upon a pillow. Her swollen cheeks were still damp from the tears that had flowed freely since her father's death.

This gunshot didn't seem as loud as the first one.

The girl's body gave a single, involuntary shudder before going limp. Again, Lisa paused, listening to the silence of the house around her.

Across the hall, she found the next daughter. Her back was to the door as she worked at her computer keyboard, fingers flying over the keys, headphones clamped firmly over her ears. An old Eagles tune overflowed the padded earpieces, easily identifiable from across the room. She was completely oblivious to what was going on around her.

The third shot was almost soundless.

Lisa turned and walked out into the hall, knowing she had only one more thing to do. She had to find the little one—root her out and put the gun's last three bullets into her head. She didn't want to take a chance on a single shot. Even if the girl survived in a vegetative state, she would still be dangerous. As ridiculous as it seemed, Lisa was sure of it.

She was drawn toward the end of the hall as if on a track, her destination already predetermined.

And then the short hairs along the nape of her neck had begun to prickle. As her hand brushed the doorknob, Lisa felt a presence behind her in the hallway. Curiously, she felt no fear, only a minor sense of inconvenience that she should have to dispose of anyone other than those she had come to kill.

She dropped to her knees, lifting the gun as she pivoted. She noticed the sandy-haired man immediately, crouched and preparing to pounce, a large butcher knife clutched in his right hand. He was too far away to be of any real consequence. With calm assuredness, Lisa adjusted her aim, aligning the gun's sight with the man's upper torso as he sailed through the air, calculating a point of intersection—

Lightning flared, chasing the shadows from the deepest recesses of the corridor, drawing Lisa's eyes to the woman standing near the head of the stairs. The resemblance was even more remarkable in person, as Lisa studied the nose that was her nose, the lips that were her lips. It was only in the eyes that a difference could be found. Oh, they were the same color and the same general shape, but there was a subtle warmth in the other woman's eyes that was completely absent from Lisa's, something intangible that somehow made her more—human.

Lisa barely noticed as Luke flopped onto the floor, shuffling sideways to avoid the bullet he undeniably expected next. Her attention had been disrupted by this unexpected intrusion. She had been prepared for a vigilant neighbor or even the police—but not this.

The woman flipped a nearby wall switch, washing away the afternoon shadows and squinting against the sudden burst of light. Lisa was entranced, transfixed by this other version of herself standing at the opposite end of the hallway. Her whole body had numbed, the weight of the gun pulling her arm down by her side. She wondered what other differences there were between herself and this other woman. Had she been raised by someone like Nanna Grace, someone who lorded over her every move, controlled her every thought?

Did she have friends, or was she an outcast, too? What was her interest in the girl? Had she come to kill her, too?

Lisa barely had time to formulate the thoughts before Luke suddenly pounced her from behind. The gun slipped through her fingers and clattered to the floor, as Lisa and Luke began wrestling for control of the knife he still gripped.

"Get the gun!" barked Luke, struggling to keep hold of his weapon. He was alarmed by the woman's raw strength. He had wrestled with other boys in Jasper that weren't nearly as strong. Her fingers were locked like a vice around his wrists, holding him back and trying to pry his fingers away from the knife's wooden handle.

After what seemed an eternity, Luke's words finally penetrated Crystal's stupor, and she regained control of her limbs. She hurried down the hall and stooped to retrieve the gun just as Lisa brought a knee up and into Luke's crotch. He doubled over and lost his grip on the knife.

Without the luxury of aiming, Crystal brought the gun up and fired two shots, both soaring over Lisa's head and embedding in the wall behind her. Lisa dropped the knife as she instinctively covered her head with her hands. There was a look of pure shock on her face as she realized what Crystal had done, and for a second, Lisa knew real fear.

From that fear came anger—as primitive and real as anything she had ever experienced. Adrenaline coursed through her veins, every muscle in her body tensed, her fingers hooked into claws. She launched herself at Crystal with explosive fury, a madwoman no longer concerned with the gun Crystal held in her shaking hand.

Crystal froze, her eyes wide with terror. The gun was as useless as the paralyzed hand holding it. Lisa collided with Crystal at full speed, knocking her down and sending the gun skittering across the hallway. Lisa stretched to retrieve it, but Luke was already there, kicking it aside, closer to his reach than hers.

Their eyes locked.

Lisa abruptly broke away, seizing Crystal by the collar of her shirt, hoisting her up as if she were made of rags. Crystal offered no resistance—she still hadn't recovered the air that had been expelled when they collided. A cry of pure frustration swelled in Lisa's throat, and she shoved Crystal headlong down the stairs, darting after her before Luke could make a move.

Luke stood stunned, watching as Crystal gracelessly disappeared into the stairwell, his stomach wrenching at the sounds of her body striking the risers and the wall panels followed by the sound of breaking glass. He ran to the head of the stairs and forced himself to look, afraid of what he was going to find. He had seen so *much* in the last few days—

Crystal lay in a crumpled heap in the landing, her arm twisted at an unnatural angle and resting against the writing desk, from which a glass urn had taken a fatal tumble. He couldn't see if she was breathing from where he stood.

He scanned the rest of the staircase. The woman who looked like Crystal had fled or disappeared into another part of the house. He didn't give her a second thought as he hurried down the stairs and knelt beside Crystal, pressing his fingers to her neck, fumbling to find a pulse.

He found what he was looking for, a strong and steady rhythm in the soft curve of her neck. He hadn't even realized he was holding his breath until it whistled out from between his teeth.

"Thank you, God," he whispered.

He heard the sound of an ignition, followed by the heady roar of an engine. He got the briefest glimpse of the Volvo as it did a U-turn in the backyard and launched itself from the drive, the crazed woman's fiery countenance barely visible through the falling rain.

Who is this woman? he thought. *And why does she have Crystal's face?*

Crystal moaned softly, her eyebrows knitting together as her eyelids fluttered. She tried to lift her ruined arm and shrieked, her eyes snapping open before filling with tears.

"Oh, shit!" she cried.

"It's broken," said Luke. "We'll have to get you to a hospital."

"Not that," she said through clenched teeth, her eyes locked on something at the head of the stairs. Luke reluctantly followed her gaze, turning slowly.

Standing on the top step was little Virginia Parnell, staring at them with her big round eyes.

PART FOUR

THE GIRL

CHAPTER SEVENTEEN

I

She just stood there, her tiny finger tucked into the corner of her mouth, her expression completely vacant, her eyes not focused on Luke or Crystal but beyond, someplace only she could see.

"I think she's in shock," whispered Luke.

"*Unh.*" Crystal nodded jerkily, adjusting her position, trying to find a way to hold her arm so it didn't feel like it was going to wrench free from her body. The agony of the fracture was white-hot.

"Virginia?" ventured Luke, his voice soft and soothing.

The girl didn't move. She stared at the same distant point, just over his shoulders, through the window that looked out onto the backyard.

"We're here to help you, honey," he said. "You've got to come with us now."

She stood stock-still, her little toes peeking over the edge of the step.

The sound of footfalls thundered downstairs, rapidly approaching.

Luke had left the gun where it lay in the hall. If that crazy bitch had brought another gun from the car, they were finished.

"Save her," urged Crystal, but when Luke turned, the girl was gone, retreating to wherever she had come from.

"*L-L-LUKE?*"

Luke breathed a sigh of relief as he recognized Paula's anxious voice bouncing off the downstairs walls. She appeared at the bottom of the stairwell, her face pale, her eyes frantically flickering from one direction to the next.

"It's alright, Paula," yelled Luke. "We're up here."

"W-w-who was that woman?" she asked, appearing at the bottom of the stairs. "She nearly plowed into the car on her way out of here—oh my God! *Crystal!*" She hurried up the stairs and knelt beside Crystal, easing her up into a seated position.

"I'm okay, Paula," Crystal said with a meek smile. "It's just a broken arm."

"*Just a broken arm?* My God! What happened? I thought I heard *gunshots*, and—" Paula's eyes went from Crystal to Luke, then to the top of the stairs. "Is that the little girl?"

This time, Luke could not contain the hysterical laughter that flowed from his lips. His quivering legs threatened to go out from underneath him, and he sat down roughly on one of the stairs. Out of the corner of his eye, he could see that Virginia had cautiously reemerged, her small oval face barely visible through the rungs of the banister.

"We have to go to the police," said Crystal, as Luke coaxed the Honda out of the driveway and back onto the rutted gravel road. She cradled her broken arm in her lap, wincing as the little car bumped and jostled.

Paula shared the back seat with the little girl, scrutinizing her intently as if she expected her to have eyes in the back of her head or wings underneath her terrycloth robe.

Luke chewed his bottom lip thoughtfully. "That might not be such a good idea."

"I don't think we have a choice," said Crystal. "There are three bod—" Her eyes flitted to the rearview mirror in which she could see the girl's eyes fixed on her own. "We can't just walk away from the situation back there."

"We should report it anonymously from a payphone," said Luke.

"Why? What difference does it make? We have to take the girl to the authorities."

Luke shook his head. "Not yet. We have to take care of you first."

"Forget about me," urged Crystal, ignoring the sharp complaints issuing from her fractured arm. "We need to take Virginia someplace where she will be safe."

"Absolutely," said Luke. "And at the moment, I think she's safer with us than with the police."

"You're being ridiculous," said Crystal. "You're only worried about your own ass! Well, don't worry, cowboy. I'll drop you off before I take her in."

He sighed with exasperation. "That car—the Volvo? I'm pretty sure it was the same one I saw leaving the gas station just before it blew."

"Yeah. I think it was the same one from Roy's BP, too. So?"

"There were two of them that night," he said. "A man and a woman. I think we just met her, so where's he?"

"What the hell *difference* does it make? We—"

"Dammit, use your head!" he barked. "Think about that little po-dunk town we just came through. I could piss from one end of it to the other. Exactly what kind of law enforcement do you think they're going to have?"

"What do you think these people are going to do?" she asked. "March right into the police station with guns blazing?" Her eyes guiltily returned to Virginia's, realizing that she and Luke were undoubtedly upsetting the girl with their bickering.

Virginia's face had drifted toward the window, gazing serenely at the rain-swept landscape as it raced by. Anyone passing would assume she was riding with her parents, daydreaming about any number of things that might occupy the minds of girls her age. Never would they dream that she had been witness to a scene of utter carnage. Never could they understand the indelible scars that would forever haunt her.

"Look," said Luke. "We've operated on instinct up 'til now, right? Well, I'm telling you that I haven't shaken that *feeling* yet. Everything I've got is telling me we should go and *quickly*. These people are really fu-fu—effed up!" He stumbled with his words, unsure if the girl was tuning in. "I don't think the local police would be ready for psychos like these. I don't think they'll give up this easy, either."

Crystal wanted to argue with him, but she realized the futility. He was right. The grievous anxiety had not lifted from her, either. What kind of animal would sequentially murder an entire family in order to get her hands on the most defenseless member? She didn't honestly believe the police would be able to help them, and despite her earlier assertion of Luke's selfishness, she really didn't want the police to arrest him for something he didn't do. It was frightening how clearly she could see that possibility, Luke sentenced to life in prison or worse for simply being in the wrong place at the wrong time.

"Where should we go?" she asked. "We have half a tank of gas and maybe three dollars left."

Luke drove in silence for a moment. "Do you think there might be some money tucked away inside your aunt's house?"

Crystal felt her blood pressure rising quickly, uncontrollably. "How *dare* you recommend that we ransack my aunt's home! It's the only thing I have left of her, and I'm not—" She broke away abruptly as her ears detected a new sound from the rear of the car. She glanced over her shoulder and saw that Virginia Parnell was no longer silent nor still.

She was crying.

Oh, Angel—

Paula occupied her own space in the cramped back seat, her mind turning inside out in a desperate attempt to make sense of the past hour or so. She desperately wanted to speak with her sister, ask for permission to cut and run on this little adventure. What had begun as a clandestine operation that ensured Paula would meet her TV idol was turning into something far too weird for her to handle. No one even mentioned the woman fleeing the farmhouse, despite her obvious physical similarity to Crystal. They could easily have been twins, but Paula knew that Crystal didn't have any siblings. *Entertainment Weekly* had kept her well-informed with respect to her idol's biography.

She glanced at the girl out of the corner of her eye, half-afraid that she'd be staring back at her. She wasn't. Virginia's round eyes stared languidly through the

325

wedge of glass to her right into the gray afternoon beyond, seeing absolutely nothing. Her chestnut mane of curls hung in limp bunches around her shoulders. She looked impossibly small and fragile.

Paula had seen the mother's body in the kitchen. The blood—and other stuff. What kind of monster could do that sort of thing? Even as Angel had struck Joel down, fulfilling a fantasy that had carried Paula through many dark and frightening nights, she had felt a sense of complicity, the sure sense that she was not entirely innocent in the murder of Joel McElroy, and someday, she would have to stand before God and answer for her part in the deed. It was unpardonable, and she was coming to believe that she was beyond redemption. She felt all of this because Angel had done this on her behalf. She couldn't imagine the weight of guilt that must rest on the shoulders of the person responsible for the slaughter back at that farmhouse.

Luke and Crystal were sniping at each other in the front seat, both of them stubbornly proposing opposing courses of action. Paula felt trapped in the tiny back seat, entirely too close to the eye of this storm. The girl was some kind of magnet to these insane psychopaths. As long as Virginia was with them, they were in grave danger.

Oh, God. Angel.

If Suze was following Crystal, and Crystal was looking for the little girl, and the murderers were *also* looking for the little girl—God, she needed a payphone! It was entirely possible that Suze had already crossed paths with the killers. She might even be—

Paula closed her eyes tightly, refusing to finish the thought. It simply wasn't possible. She had just *seen* Angel.

If only she could call her—just to be sure.

• ——— ✦ ——— •

"It's okay, honey," cooed Crystal, dabbing gently at Virginia's cheeks. *"Shh-shh-shh."*

They had pulled into a small rest area, parking behind the cinderblock outbuilding that squatted on a carpet of yellowing weeds and empty beer bottles. The rain had ebbed away, leaving behind a pungent dankness that pervaded and sullied what should have been sweet country air. They hadn't seen any sign of the Volvo, but it was too early to be cocky. Crystal had gotten out of the passenger seat and leaned into the back, favoring her broken arm. Luke had gone to take advantage of the facilities. Paula remained in the back seat, keeping a safe distance from the spooky little girl seemingly at the center of everything.

"I'm sorry," said Crystal, wincing slightly as she bumped her wounded arm against the edge of the seat. "We're just a little scared. Just like you're scared. But

326

we're here to help you. My name is Crystal, and beside you over there is Paula. Luke is the nice fellow driving the car. We're going to make sure that nothing bad happens to you, okay?"

To watch the girl cry was an excruciating experience. Her tiny frame shook with the intensity of her sobs, and Crystal wanted to scoop her into her arms and hold her, rocking her gently—but she knew the girl would resist, unable to allow contact with a stranger so soon after what she had just witnessed. Crystal felt a hard lump form in her throat as she realized her helplessness. She simply stroked the girl's hair and shushed intermittently, watching the waves of grief ebb and flow, radiating from the girl's small form.

After what seemed an eternity, Luke emerged from around the corner of the outbuilding clutching three stout sticks in each hand. He had a strange grimace on his face, and Crystal sensed immediately she wasn't going to like what he had in mind for those sticks.

He dropped them on the ground beside her and peered over her shoulder into the car. "How we doin'?"

Virginia looked at him with her big brown eyes, and the smile he had carefully presented faltered before falling away completely. The worst of her tears had subsided, leaving Virginia red-faced and exhausted. Her breath came in short little huffs, but they were slowly lengthening, returning to normal. She still hadn't spoken a word.

"What's the lumber for, cowboy?" asked Crystal, easing away from the car.

Luke grimaced again. "Do you trust me?"

"Goddamn it, I hate questions like that!" she said.

"Summers back in Jasper, I used to help Doc Jensen at the animal hospital. Not a lot of hours but over a few years, a hell of a lot of experience. I've splinted many a broken limb before."

"Oh, *uh-unh,* cowboy!" she said, pulling away from him. "I'm not a raccoon or a donkey."

"That would depend on who you ask," he said. *"C'mon,* Crystal. I don't like this any better than you do. But it's not like it's a compound fracture. There ain't no bone pokin' through—"

Crystal winced at the thought.

"—I can set this right up. If we take you to a hospital, there's a good chance you'll get mobbed by the press and an even better chance that those people will find us. You know this ain't over."

He looked into her eyes and saw that she felt it, too. The thickness of the air, the subtle darkness that had fallen over the afternoon, just one shade darker than that served up by nature. The people in the Volvo would be coming, and they would be coming soon.

"All right," hissed Crystal through clenched teeth. "Let's just get this over with. Paula? Any of that gin left?"

Paula stared mutely, then suddenly bobbed her head as the question penetrated. She fumbled around in the floorboard and came up with the nearly empty bottle.

Crystal drained the remaining liquid as Luke fashioned the sticks to an appropriate size using the knife he had held onto from the Parnells' kitchen. He rummaged through the floorboards of the Honda and found an old t-shirt wedged underneath the passenger seat. He was thankful for that, because otherwise he would have had to use his own shirt to tie the splint together. He tore the filthy garment into thin strips and laid them in a neat pile beside Crystal, who was just beginning to feel the effects of the gin coursing through her system.

He knelt in front of her and looked up into her eyes, his own conveying compassion and the promise that he would be as gentle as he possibly could. Without further warning, he grabbed her by the wrist, just below the break, and pulled down sharply, extending the jumbled bones inside. At first, Crystal felt nothing, but then her vision blurred, and she was nearly carried away by the need to purge the alcohol from her stomach. Pain traveled up her arm like a school of piranhas feasting on raw meat. Luke worked quickly, tethering the whittled twigs around the circumference of Crystal's arm with the remains of the old t-shirt. Hot tears streamed from the corners of her eyes, but with her bottom lip securely pinned between her teeth, she refused to give voice to the pain. They had already frightened little Virginia enough for one day.

"You okay?" Luke asked, tying the last of the cloth strips in place.

She nodded her head briskly, unable to speak for fear of screaming. Her arm felt hard and hot, the swelling already staining her skin with angry purple splotches. Her fingers looked like tiny sausages at the ends of her hands, and she wouldn't have dared moved them even if she could. Luke's handiwork was primitive but serviceable. The bone would probably have to be re-broken and set again at a later date, but that was a worry for another day. Right now, they needed to get back on the road and put some distance between themselves and the assassins.

Crystal turned to see Paula and Virginia watching silently from the back seat, their faces united in empathetic compassion. Anyone passing might think the two girls were sisters, a generation removed.

Crystal suddenly flashed upon the face of the killer, her *own* face. Why had she gone to such great lengths to resemble Crystal? The similarities between the two went way beyond coincidence, and Crystal figured it could only be the work of a first-rate plastic surgeon. Yet the woman had seemed as startled to see Crystal as Crystal was to see her. They say everyone's got a twin in the world, but *really*. The actual sight of this woman had frozen Crystal's breath in her lungs, stilled her heart for a fraction of a beat. It was the disjointed feeling of looking into a mirror with no barrier. Crystal Bright through Lewis Carroll's Looking-Glass.

By now, Crystal knew better than to doubt Luke's instincts. If he thought the killers would be in pursuit, then soon enough they would be. She was surprised at her own gumption, half-expecting herself to blame Luke for dragging her into this mess. But one look at the little girl dispelled any chance of that happening. She looked so lost and forlorn, tucked into the back seat of the compact car full of complete strangers whom she had no choice but to trust. Yet she had pulled herself back together and held her head a little higher than before. Crystal found it strangely reassuring.

She still had not been blessed with this sixth sense that came so easily to Luke on the reels of his dreams. She wished she could be more aware, more able to contribute, and perhaps that's what surprised her most—she knew she was in this for the long haul. Virginia Parnell needed someone to take care of her, see her to safety, and Crystal Bright was going to make sure it happened. It may well be the first selfless thing she had done since moving to California, but it wasn't about her own redemption. It was about Virginia Parnell. She had no one left, and now that Aunt Maude was dead, neither did Crystal. For the moment, they had each other, and it was a role Crystal wouldn't abandon—even if the cost was her life. She was almost overwhelmed with the child's instantaneous impact on her. Every maternal switch with which she had been equipped by God was suddenly flipped on. Even without Luke's extrasensory perception, she could see that Virginia Parnell was special, not just in the way that every child is special— and every child *is* special—but in a far rarer way. The girl hadn't even spoken, yet Crystal knew she possessed advanced intelligence. She somehow communicated it through her big, round, coffee-colored eyes. She had been born to this earth to serve a purpose, not be ground out like a spent butt in an ashtray at the tender age of *four*.

The pain had further receded, and Crystal struggled to her feet. The gin kept her equilibrium in the blender, and she nearly fell against the car before Luke caught her and propped her up against him.

"Steady there, cowgirl," he said. "You sure you're okay?"

She smiled at him weakly. "Cowgirl. I like that."

He grinned back at her. "Let's get you into the car and make tracks, whaddaya say?"

"You're the boss," she said, allowing him to ease her back into the Honda's passenger seat. He closed the door gently and crossed to the driver's side of the car, sliding behind the wheel and starting the engine.

"Lucasville?" he asked, hoping she wouldn't bite his head off at the mere suggestion.

She simply sighed. "Lucasville."

II

Lisa saw the afternoon through a haze of red vision, blurring the highway into barely discernible lines, yet she pressed the Volvo harder, faster. The latex gloves she wore crinkled against the leather steering wheel as she unconsciously flexed her knuckles nervously.

What in the hell had gone *wrong?*

Why was Crystal Bright here? Shouldn't she be in California, where all the TV shows are made? Of what possible consequence was that horrid little child to a star of her magnitude?

She wondered if Suze and Chad knew about Crystal Bright's involvement. She remembered Suze's initial suspicion, clearly sparked by the rerun of the *Benny and the Girl* that had been on television when they had arrived. Why hadn't they warned her about this? It was one thing to see the woman on television, but entirely another to run into her face-to-face. It had been like a quick jolt of electricity, short-circuiting her senses and allowing that bastard to get her gun away from her. She had been so taken by surprise that the only thing she could think to do was run. She had never been more disappointed in herself. What would Chad think? Who gave a good goddamn what Suze thought, but *Chad*— she didn't want him to think she was incompetent. Dammit, she *wasn't* incompetent. Inexperienced, perhaps. Despite her obvious natural talent for murder and mayhem, she was, by chronology alone, a rookie, but fulfilling her role, mistakes must be few and far between.

If she had it to do over again, she would've gone for Crystal's face, tearing loose those features they had been destined to share. Lisa felt drained by the link, as if she were being forced to share some part of herself with this stranger, valuable energy she could recover if only she could break the connection.

She was headed back to Morgan at warp speed. She didn't know what else to do. She wasn't intimately familiar with the biography of Crystal Bright. For God's sake, she'd only just seen her for the first time yesterday! Why she wasn't in California was a big enough mystery for Lisa, but to see her in a backwater like *Borden*—

There was simply no way to premeditate Crystal's path. All Lisa could do was push the Volvo as hard as she could back to Chad, hoping to hell he knew where they might find her. If they went to the police, it would cause complications, and it was too early in the game for complications.

Or was it?

Suze's constant headache had intensified, wrapping steely fingers around her skull and applying progressive pressure until she thought her brains might escape through her ears. She huddled in a dark corner of the upstairs bedroom while Chad rested on the bed.

The air smelled of sex and stale cigarettes. She curled her nose and breathed through her mouth. Chad's lean torso was visible above the sheet, and she watched the gentle rise and fall of his chest. She wanted to choke the bastard. Who the hell did this punk kid think he was, Mel Gibson? But what *really* got under her skin was the fact that it bothered her at all. Compared to him, she was mature and worldly. She didn't need to see a teenaged boy through his final tumultuous years of puberty. Yet there was undeniably something more between them. She had sensed it that very first night at Children's Services when she had spontaneously decided to give herself to him. There was something about their very nature that was unusually simpatico. Together, they could become history's most fearsome killing machine. The thought brought both elation and frustration, as she realized that this was no longer hers and Chad's future, but Lisa's as well.

She had quickly reached a saturation point where Lisa was concerned and would be just as happy to be rid of her. She couldn't believe that the bitch had actually *hit* her, all because of that stupid old nurse. Suze was so unprepared for the attack that she had been rendered utterly defenseless. If Lisa had wanted to kill her, she easily could have. It was a mistake that Suze wouldn't make again.

Still no teacups.

It had been so long since she had spotted one of the blessed little buggers, they almost seemed like a vague dream now. The throbbing of her headache had been slowly easing until this morning, when its grip had suddenly doubled, and then tripled, and she wondered if something had gone wrong with Lisa and the little vermin. She still couldn't believe they had sent this woman to do the work they had set out to accomplish together. Despite the logical constraints, it somehow seemed cowardly to have come all this way to send in a pinch hitter at the last moment.

Chad stirred and mumbled, communicating with people inside his dreams. Suze still wanted to choke him, but she knew she would get over it. Sex was only physical. He couldn't possibly connect with Lisa on the same level he connected with her, and of that, she was certain.

Chad mumbled again, and a lazy smile crossed his face. Suze frowned and strained her ears. She could have sworn he said Lisa's name.

Inside the comfort of sleep, Chad could feel himself recharging, regaining the strength that had been sapped from him by the errant bullet. Like Suze, he was profoundly disturbed at his own inability to be present for the girl's slaughter. The hunger within him had grown to a fevered pitch, and he required release. It was something that could not be achieved vicariously.

His dreams were riveting, exciting his pulse and feeding the hunger. He ran barefoot through a thickly wooded expanse, his feet impervious to the thorny underbrush. Ahead of him, the little girl darted along the path like a rat trapped in a maze. She was surprisingly speedy, but not enough to keep Chad more than a few paces behind, reaching out for the tendrils of curls that bobbed behind her with each piston-like footfall. He could *smell* her fear, and it was delightful.

And just as he was about to snare the girl's hair between his fingers, the scenery abruptly faltered, then shifted. He was in his father's bedroom, back in Pridemore. The photograph of his birth parents lay in the center of Peter's large cherry desk, their haunted faces seeming to gaze through the matte finish of the print and into Chad's eyes. He hated them instinctively, knowing that they would have purged him from the earth if given half a chance. Somehow, they had come to understand the truth of his nature, something his adoptive parents, the Collins, had never been able to do. Instead, they had stubbornly clung to the possibility that Chad was shy and unsociable, but otherwise entirely normal. After all, it wasn't as if he was entirely friendless. He and Ricky Whalen had been friends since kindergarten. Of course, Peter and Naomi never knew about the dogs—a veritable pet cemetery which littered the woods behind Peter's Colonial. Moldering bones slowly returned to the earth from which they had come— countless strays and runaways. Ricky was nearly as ruthless with a penknife as Chad and would have been an interesting addition to their little team. Unfortunately, he was also about as thick as a beer bottle and with stakes as high as these, good response time was critical.

The office lay in disarray, just as Chad had left it when he 'borrowed' his father's Volvo. The room had always been off limits to him, and he found a certain satisfaction in browsing its interior, even if it was only within a dream. A silent breeze wafted through the room, causing loose paperwork to lift from the floor as though charmed, rising and swirling into a gentle vortex that drifted toward the study's open rear door. Chad's eyes followed the maelstrom, now blowing out into the hallway.

The Parnell girl stood in the door frame, her glowing eyes fixed on him. Although they were flooded with terror, there was something else within them, something sickeningly powerful in its purity. He crossed the room in long strides, just as the hated girl stepped into the shadows of the hallway.

When he stepped through the doorway, he found himself somewhere other than his father's home. This was a place he had never before seen—a wide, hardwood corridor that stretched off in either direction. An oriental runner

332

graced the middle of the hallway, lending warmth to the confined space as well as protecting the highly polished surface of the floor. The girl had gone to the right, retreating behind a door at the rear of the hallway. He started to follow, then was suddenly transfixed by the sound of footsteps from the corridor's other end, rising from below on stairs he hadn't noticed. He turned to see Lisa floating up like an angel, the police-issued revolver clutched firmly in her hand. She had a look of determination on her face, her senses fine-tuned to her surroundings. She was hunting the girl.

He whispered her name, but she gave no indication that she was aware of him, gliding toward him without so much as a sideways glance. She was locked into her purpose, and her purpose was to exterminate the child. She paused at the first door on her right, taking the doorknob in hand and slowly turning it. She disappeared through the narrow opening with stealth, and there was soon a flash of light followed by a terrific clap of thunder.

Chad could smell the gunpowder hanging in the air.

Lisa reemerged, her expression unchanged, the gun still at the ready. She came toward Chad, pausing again to press her ear against the next door. After a moment, she reached for the doorknob and repeated her stealthy maneuver, sliding soundlessly into the room. Another flash of light followed by thunder.

Someone was on the stairs. No—two people. A man and a woman. Their faces were obscured by the shadows in the hallway, and Chad strained to see them clearly as they cautiously ascended. Lisa reappeared, unaware that she had company. Chad screamed with frustration, trying to warn her but unable to make her aware. He flailed his arms wildly and jumped up and down, but he was as invisible to Lisa as the air around her. Trancelike, she continued toward the door the little girl had just used.

In a final act of desperation, Chad reached out to seize Lisa, force her to acknowledge his presence. His stomach tightened as his hand merged seamlessly with the flesh of her shoulder, an electric sizzle passing between them. She suddenly froze, her head erect, her shoulders squared. She was *aware*. She turned to see what might be waiting behind her and—

Chad awoke with a start, crying out Lisa's name.

"Can you keep it down up there? I'm trying to have a cerebral hemorrhage over here," said Suze from the dark corner in which she sprawled.

"Something's wrong," he said, sliding the covers away.

Suze sat up, looking at him curiously. "What do you mean?"

"Lisa's not alone," he said, fumbling his legs into his jeans. He seemed oblivious to the injury of his shoulder, using both arms to boost the denims around his waist. "She's got visitors."

"What kind of visitors?" asked Suze.

"I don't know."

"Cops?"

"I DON'T KNOW!"

A thick silence settled over the room as Chad scrambled to find his socks. Once retrieved, he sat on the edge of the bed and began putting them on.

"Where are you going?" Suze finally asked.

"We need to be ready to move," he said. "Lisa should be back soon, and we'll need to hurry."

"I *knew* we shouldn't have sent her," grumbled Suze.

"Shut the fuck up," said Chad, glaring at her through darkening eyes. "It was the only choice we had. If Lisa wasn't able to get the girl, then we'll get her together. The thought of that should make you ecstatic."

And it should have. But despite Suze's deeply selfish nature, she understood the urgency of their mission and would have much preferred the satisfaction of knowing that the girl was already dead. For God's sake, she was only a four-year-old! How difficult could killing her be? Apparently more difficult than Lisa Mitchell had suspected, for she knew with equal certainty that Lisa had already failed. The increasing tension of her headache had all but shouted it into her ear.

Chad had mentioned visitors. Grieving friends of the family? They certainly would have come unarmed. Lisa should have been able to handle the situation with a few quick reports from the service revolver. No, these visitors were of a different nature. They were there because of the girl, too, but their motives were different. They wanted to protect her, nurture her, allow her to grow. They were the guardians of this being of light, and Suze and Chad would have to deal with them if they were to reach the girl. The game had suddenly gotten more interesting.

———◆———

Lisa sat in the car, drumming her gloved fingertips against the steering wheel. She had left the engine running, because she would need every assistance available in getting away. The last few weeks had brought sweeping changes to her life, heaping rich and unlikely experience after experience upon her. Fresh from killing five people, she was about to add armed robbery to her repertoire.

The gas station and food mart in front of her was not unlike the one Chad had described, the one that he had ignited like an oversized firework, killing the truck driver father of the odious cur. Its primary colors were red and yellow, and it squatted on a secluded patch of yellowed grass, far enough from the beaten path to make you wonder what in the hell the owner was thinking. A twin bank of self-service pumps huddled together in the center of the lot, protected from the tapering rain under cover of a metal framework canopy. Other than a snot green Chevy Nova left over from the seventies, there were no other cars on the lot. Through the plate glass of the storefront, she could see a frail-looking elderly woman manning the register behind a counter near the front. She was gazing out into the parking lot, watching the passing storm with the intense scrutiny of the simple-minded. She had barely noticed Lisa pulling into the parking lot, even though she was her one and only customer.

Lisa checked the interior of the car one last time, hoping to find a gun conveniently tucked into the armrest or a hunting knife in the floorboard, but no such luck. Taking a cue from her doppelganger, she would be forced to employ a touch of theatrics.

She shrugged out of her jacket leaving the latex gloves firmly in place. She wrapped the jacket around her right hand, forming a bulky appendage that she kept tucked to her side as she emerged from the Volvo. The storm's aftermath was cool against her bare shoulders, sending a tingle of anticipation down the length of her back. Apparently, the attendant still hadn't noticed Lisa.

Lisa strode purposefully across the parking lot, throwing the door wide and causing the bell that perched atop it to clang in protest. The birdlike woman's attention was drawn by the sound, and she squinted her eyes to observe her latest customer.

The smile Lisa offered was sweet poison, and she stepped up to the counter, placing her coat-wrapped hand on the surface.

"Kin I hep ya?" croaked the blue-haired zombie, looking from Lisa's face down to her covered hand.

"Why, yes, as a matter of fact, you can," said Lisa, her smile still firmly in place. "I'd very much appreciate it if you would load the contents of your cash register into one of your carryout bags and hand it over, please."

The old woman squinted, leaning forward across the counter. "Beg pardon?"

"I suggest you ease back, ma'am," said Lisa. "I have a gun pointed directly at you."

The deeply lined face of the cashier furrowed while she contemplated her options. Shrugging, she hit a button on the register that caused the drawer to spring forth. Gnarled fingers laced with thick blue veins forked the paper currency into a plastic bag. As she emptied out the last slot in the money tray, she paused, looking back up at Lisa.

"Is this on the peeky-boo camera?" she asked. "Am I going to be on the TV?"

Lisa's smile widened, pleased that the clerk had taken the bait. "Not this time, ma'am. This is the real thing."

"Pity," huffed the woman, handing the bag across the counter. "Jest had my hair set up to Myrtle's. If'n I'm-a gonna be on the TV, I couldn't do no better than to have my hair put on by ol' Myrtle. Still, at least, I got *you* on the peeky-boo."

She pointed an arthritic finger toward the ceiling, and Lisa followed her gaze. A small security camera was mounted in the corner, doing a slow side-to-side scan of the counter and its vicinity.

Lisa glanced at the wire rack of periodicals beside the register. She was amused to find a picture of Crystal Bright screaming from one of the front pages. She had been captured in a moment of pure fury—or perhaps a sneeze—but the effect was the same. The headline blared, "INSANE STAR BREAKS DOWN, FLEEING HOSPITAL BEFORE DOCTORS CAN EVALUATE HER MENTAL CONDITION!"

It was too good to be true.

Lisa pulled one of the copies from the stand, staring with delight at the newspaper. She turned toward the camera and held the gossip rag side-by-side to her own face. She smiled at the camera and then blew a kiss, tossing the paper over her shoulder and onto the counter in front of the befuddled cashier. She strolled from the store with the plastic bag of money slung over her shoulder. It couldn't have been much more than two hundred dollars or so, but the money was never the point. It had always been about the commission of the crime.

The old lady had never been in any physical danger from Lisa unless she had resisted giving her the money. Lisa actually *preferred* a live witness in this instance. She needed someone to call the police, report the crime. She needed the videotape of the crime to be seen, perhaps picked up by the wolverine media. She wanted all of America to see its sweetheart, Crystal Bright, holding up a gas station in rural Ohio.

III

"Can I help you, ma'am?"

Jessica Lybrook stepped up to the information desk and placed her handbag on the counter. She looked into the brown eyes of the officer and found herself at a loss for words. Her eyes drifted to his gold nameplate, upon which 'CHARLES' was stenciled.

"Ma'am?" He cocked his head inquiringly.

Jessica cleared her throat and found her voice. "Um, yes, I was wondering if you might help me. My name is Jessica Lybrook. I work for the Jay County Sheriff's Department."

"Yes, ma'am," said Charles, offering a smile of perfectly aligned, brilliant white teeth. "Let me get my sergeant—"

"Oh, no-no-no," she said, reaching out to take his hand. "I'm not here on any official capacity. There's no need to call your sergeant." She pushed her sandy hair behind an ear with a shaky hand.

Charles' eyes narrowed, and she could see suspicion creep into his eyes. "I'd like to see some identification, please, ma'am." There was none of the soft gentility she had heard when he had used the word before.

She forced a nervous smile and dug into her pocketbook for her ID. "I'm sorry. I'm probably making a bigger deal of this than it is. I'm looking for David McElroy. Do you know him?" She offered two pieces of identification to Charles, but his eyes were now locked onto hers. "I believe he used to work here."

Charles nodded slowly, his dislike for the man evident on his face. "That's right," he said. "Emphasize on *used* to. I haven't seen the man in blessed years."

Jessica was taken aback. Why would this policeman harbor such obvious resentment towards David? In her experience, his official performance had been nothing short of exemplary. Morgan was a small town, however, and bad blood could run deep. There was certainly no accounting for personal taste.

"What you want with him anyway?" asked Charles.

"Well, um—uh—I don't know how well you knew him—uh, or his wife—"

"Lo-retta!" he declared, pronouncing it *Low-retta*. His warm smile returned, easing the tense lines that had begun to build around his eyes and mouth. "Now *her* I've missed. Are you friends with Lo-retta? You'll have to tell her that Casey and Jason say hi and to stop by next time—"

"I'm afraid I can't," she interrupted. "Loretta's dead."

Jason Charles' mouth remained open, his words dead on arrival. "No," he finally managed. "How?"

"It's been all over the news," she said. "The gas station that was bombed in Indiana—"

"Oh, sweet Lord, it never connected," he said.

"Yes, well, David has taken a leave of absence from work, and—and I'm worried about him, Officer Charles. I fear for his state of mind. He was completely in love with Loretta, and to lose her like that—I don't know what he's going to do."

"What makes you think he'll come here?"

"I don't know. I guess because he's got nowhere else to go. I thought he might stop by to visit with old friends."

"Well, he ain't going to find many of 'em here."

"How can you say that?" she asked.

"Because it's true," he said. "A hot-headed bastard like that don't need to be walking around with a gun in his hand. I know our streets are safer with him gone."

Jessica looked at him blankly, her mouth slightly agape. Were they even talking about the same man? Sure, David had a temper, but she had never known it to interfere with his professional judgment. "Doesn't he have a brother who lives here in town?" she finally managed.

Charles pursed his lips and nodded. "That'd be Joel. Runs the candy store over on Briardown." He jotted down directions on a sheet of yellow legal pad and passed it across the counter to Jessica.

"Thank you," she said, folding the paper in half and tucking it into her pocket. She glanced around the small police department and tried to picture David McElroy working in this place. Under Officer Charles' steely gaze, it was impossible. She turned and walked to the door.

—◆—

Helen Martin's lips were parched, and her throat burned. She was hoarse from screaming and numb from fear and crazy with worry—

Where in the hell was Lisa? It had been *hours* since she had last seen her. Had that crazed woman and her doped-out boyfriend killed her? Acid roiled in her stomach, churning and bringing bile to the back of her throat, intensifying the burning sensation that already thrived.

For the millionth time, she wandered the cramped and musty cell, scanning the walls for weaknesses, the ceiling for faults. Her eyes came to rest on the small rectangular piece of plywood that was mounted near the ceiling at the far end of the room. Aged to an ashen gray, the plywood was held in place by dozens of rust-tipped nails. It appeared to be the former chute by which coal was deposited into this bin. If only she could pry the board loose—

She tugged at it with her bare hands, clumsily pulling and then pushing. She had been rewarded only with a three-inch splinter that found the soft spot between her finger and nail, planting itself deep within the tender flesh. She jerked her hands away and examined the damage, quickly extracting the splinter with her teeth and squeezing her fingers together to stop the droplets of blood from flowing. Her fingertips were of no use against the rusty nails. She needed to find something she could use to pry them away.

She scanned the blackened floors, searching for anything she might use as a crowbar, but it was an exercise in futility. She had been trying to find a weapon since she had first been deposited into this small corner of hell, but short of the brilliant arsenal she envisioned in her fantasies, she simply had nothing to choose from. There wasn't even a cot for her to sleep upon, just four walls, a floor, and a ceiling—all soot-saturated. Helen felt dirty beneath her skin, steeped so deeply in mildew and grime that it would take weeks for the scent to evaporate from her nostrils.

If she ever got out at all.

She slumped against the wall, sobbing soundlessly. Perhaps she was only delaying the inevitable, but she didn't wish to cause the dark-haired woman to return to the basement. Helen had seen the look in her eyes; she knew that the girl wanted to kill her.

I think I'll take out my frustrations on your little darling, here.

The dark-haired girl had smiled knowingly as she pulled Lisa from the room. Had she killed Lisa in Helen's place? She was sick with the thought. With no visible means of escape, her minutes were surely ticking by, as well. She buried her face in her knees and allowed hopeless anguish to sweep her away.

———◆———

Leonard knelt beneath the hood of his old Chevy, cursing everything except God and his own mother. He had followed the Mitchell girl all morning, watching her as she retrieved the Volvo from Roy's BP. He knew it wasn't the Mitchell girl's car. She had smashed up her junk heap in the accident that briefly landed her in the hospital. Besides, she could never have afforded wheels like these. Was she stealing automobiles now? Anything was possible.

She had returned to her house, either oblivious to or unthreatened by his surveillance. He had parked across the street, watching as she pulled into the driveway. She trotted up the stairs to the porch, not a care in the world. She was wearing another of those sundresses, the ones of flimsy fabric and low cleavage. She had never dressed like this before Grace Mitchell had died. The old woman would have forbidden it. Now it was as if she were a dark force of nature, answering to no one, spreading malignancy wherever she went.

She had gotten an early start. If Leonard had taken the time to eat breakfast, he might have missed her entirely. As it was, she was inside the house for only a short time before returning to the car. He had waited for what was an appropriate length of time before doing a U-turn in the street and following her.

Storm clouds had begun to collect overhead, draining the sun of its power to illuminate, sucking the color out of everything and replacing it with an oatmeal cast. He had stayed one car behind Lisa as she drifted east, transecting the wide blocks with the assurance of one who had lived in Morgan her entire life.

They had only just pulled onto the two-lane blacktop leading toward Borden when Leonard's engine suddenly shuddered before wheezing to a halt. He watched in frustration as the Volvo continued onward, leaving him stranded on the side of the road.

He had lost her. Whatever she was up to, whatever was next on her agenda, it would be accomplished without his witness.

He stared at the fused tangle of spark plug wires that lay across his engine block. Several had completely severed from an electrical overload. Maybe *she* had caused this, with her unholy aura and demonic affiliation. It wouldn't have surprised Leonard at all to learn the girl was a witch in direct allegiance with the Devil himself, capable of doing far worse than this.

For the moment, it was out of his hands. He was stranded.

339

———◇———

The directions should have been simple enough to follow, but Jessica had an inborn weakness for cartography and navigation, her internal compass in a constant spin cycle. She looped through the streets of Morgan, seeing the same houses, the same businesses, and yet still no sign of the road Officer Charles had called Briardown.

She stopped at a small BP to ask directions, but the attendant was busy, and his instruction only confused her more. Before long, she found herself on a two-lane blacktop, civilization receding quickly in her rearview mirror. She was pretty sure from Officer Charles' description that Briardown wasn't a rural route. She cut the wheel sharply to the right, swinging onto the berm before whipping it back to the left, bringing the car around in a U-turn. Just as the Jeep's nose swept across the pavement, Jessica spotted a car at the edge of the horizon, pulled off the side of the road, its hood raised. Its driver's lanky legs were visible, almost protruding out into the roadway. She stopped in the middle of her maneuver, then slipped the Jeep into reverse, correcting her angle and continuing up the road to where the other driver waited.

Jessica's father drove an old Chevy like this one, even down to the faded navy paint. It was roomy enough for the entire family to comfortably go anywhere, built in the days before fuel economy was a consideration. As she drew to a stop at its massive chrome bumper, the owner of the legs appeared from underneath the hood, his grizzled old face contorted into a question mark. He absently scratched his rear end through the heavy fabric of what appeared to be a work uniform. It was a one-piece drab gray number with a brassy zipper up the middle.

"Are you having trouble?" she called out the window.

He shuffled up to the car window, his expression a little too excited for Jessica's taste. "Can you help me?" he asked, his words running together. "I need parts. My damn car got zapped."

"Sure," she said, disengaging the power lock on the passenger door. "Hop in."

A million stories of highway psychopaths flooded Jessica's mind as the old man hobbled around the front of the car and opened the door. He smelled of stale perspiration and mothballs, and she tried to suppress her natural reflex to curl her nose.

"Actually," she said. "I was hoping you might help me, too. I think I'm lost."

After doing a comical double-take, he cocked his head and squinted at her. *"Lost?* How in tarnation can you be lost in a little pisshole like Morgan?"

She smiled. "I've got no sense of direction whatsoever. It's a wonder they'll even let me have a driver's license. I'm trying to find a street called Briardown. Ever heard of it?"

"Ain't no one in Morgan that hadn't. I'll tell you what. You take me to the BP, and I'll take you to Briardown."

———◆———

Helen heard the front door open and then close through the floorboards. Footsteps crossed above, then ascended the staircase. Which one of them was it? What difference did it make? Eventually, they would come down to kill her.

If there was any positive side to this ordeal whatsoever, it was the knowledge that she'd be seeing her Evie soon, reunited in an afterlife as wonderful and wondrous as Scripture had always promised. There would be no foul beasts like the ones upstairs, hunting like predators on the whole of humankind. There would only be creatures of pure light, sharing their earthly experiences over endless celestial tea parties. She clung to this belief fervently as a small mouse scurried from one corner of the coal bin to the other, its tiny feet propelling it like a small rocket.

She closed her eyes tightly and tried to distract herself with memories of her daughter's lovely face, her warm smile, her perfectly sculpted hands—

Footsteps descended from the second story. It was more than just one set. Two? More? Maybe Lisa was still alive after all. They abruptly parted in the upstairs hallway, two distinct patterns of footfalls traveling together toward the front of the house while a single set headed toward the door which led to the basement.

Through the thick metal door of the coal chute, she heard the door at the head of the basement stairs swing open on creaky hinges. There was a moment of silence before a single footfall descended a step. Then another pause.

Helen's senses went on alert. Something was wrong. Always before, when the dark-haired girl had been forced to tend to the nurse, she had descended like a hurricane, tossing down a pittance of watered-down soup while taunting Helen. Now, there was a slow deliberation about her approach, as if she were soaking up every detail of her crime.

Another footfall.

Adrenaline coursed through Helen, and she struggled against the chains that held her arms together. She struck up a symphony of chattering metal, but the chains held tight, refusing to allow even the smallest amount of slack to develop.

341

Helen's heart felt unnaturally high in her chest, hammering a steady flow of blood through her arteries. Despite the belief that Evie would be waiting for her, this didn't seem right, it didn't seem *fair*.

Helen Martin didn't want to die.

⟶ ◇ ⟶

They passed the rest of the journey in awkward silence. Jessica had learned that the man's name was Leonard Barnes and that he was a custodian at Morgan Township Hospital. He seemed edgy, eager to get what he needed and be on his way. She didn't press for details, not sure she wanted to know the types of things that might cause a man like this to hurry.

She hadn't asked him about McElroy, either. After gauging Officer Charles' reaction back at the police station, she was reluctant to inspire similar feelings in such close proximity to this stranger. She didn't want to lose his cooperation before she could find Joel McElroy's house.

With Leonard as a co-pilot, she found Morgan in no time and was soon pulling into the same BP that had dispensed her earlier directions.

Roy of Roy's BP informed Leonard that he had the spark plug wires in stock, but the distributor cap had to be picked up in Holling. He had a truck coming, but not until afternoon. Jessica watched Leonard's features drop, resignation settling over him like a thick wool blanket. He nodded his head in grim acceptance and turned to leave the station, completely bypassing Jessica.

"Hey, wait a minute!" she called, following him out into the parking lot.

He continued to walk, oblivious to her words.

"Leonard!" she spoke sharply, breaking his reverie. He turned toward her. "What about Briardown?"

He cast a sideways glance over his shoulder as if weighing his options, then lowered his head, shuffling back toward the passenger side of Jessica's Jeep. She hurried to the driver's side, sliding behind the wheel and starting the car before Leonard had a chance to reconsider. She had come too far to miss her destination now.

Briardown was only a few quick turns south of the BP, and Jessica wondered how she could have ever missed it. She coasted slowly, searching mailboxes for the correct name. It was the cinderblock structure of the candy store that she spotted, looking like a concession stand that had become detached from its ball field. A woman with bony shoulders and stringy hair hunched over a broom on the sidewalk, whisking away bits of leaves and dried grass. A crooked cigarette dangled out of the corner of her mouth, and she carried a sour expression that discouraged polite social interaction.

342

Nonetheless, Jessica parked along the curb in front of the house, switching the ignition off and hopping down from the cab. "Mrs. McElroy?" she called, walking around the front of the Jeep and stepping up onto the sidewalk.

The woman paused, leaning against the handle of her broom and studying Jessica from head to toe. She took a long drag from her cigarette and exhaled a plume of blue-gray smoke, which wafted upward to join the roiling storm clouds overhead.

"I don't believe I know you," she said, her voice like gravel.

Jessica smiled and offered a hand. "My name is Jessica Lybrook. I'm looking for David McElroy. Or Joel. Is either one at home?"

The woman ignored Jessica's hand in favor of another drag from the cigarette. "What business is it of yours?" she asked evenly, brushing a strand of her mousy brown hair behind an ear marred by legions of piercings.

Jessica reached into her handbag and produced her police identification. "I work with David," she said. "I've been trying to find him. Have you seen him?"

The woman stood silent for a moment before turning and wheezing, "That goddamn bastard."

Jessica arched an eyebrow. "I don't understand."

The woman whirled, her eyes wild. "Every time that goddamn *David* comes to town, him and Joel get into all kinds of shit. When Joel didn't come home last night, I thought, shit, he probably got thrown in jail for gettin' rowdy in town. It sure the hell wouldn't be the *first* time. But now you're here tellin' me his goddamn *brother* is in town? Christ *almighty!*"

Again, Jessica wondered if they were talking about the same David McElroy. "Do you know where they might have gone?" she asked.

"Hell, no!" she said, pacing the sidewalk nervously. "And wouldn't you know, Joel got his goddamn *check* last night! It'll be gone—just like that!" She snapped her fingers in time with a clap of thunder, and both women jumped in unison.

"What time did you see him last?" asked Jessica.

"He went out around nine or so," she said absently, still lost in seething deliberation. "Ain't that unusual."

"Can I look around?"

The woman sighed, tossing the broom aside and turning toward the house. "I don't give a good goddamn what you do." With a clatter of the screen door, she disappeared into the house.

A sudden bluster of wind, and small fat droplets of rain began to fall. Lightning forked across the darkened sky, followed by a rolling resonance that vibrated underfoot. Jessica scanned the property, unsure of what it was she was looking for. She started toward her right, then hesitated, turning around and going in the other direction. Toward the cinderblock cube that dispensed treats to the neighborhood children on summer afternoons. She wondered what kind of sweet man would devote his spare time to such a modestly lucrative enterprise. He must love children very much.

A well-worn path cut across the lawn and down to the shop. She followed it to the building, stepping around to the front and examining the façade. Hinged doors were battened down over the front, covering the counter from which Joel the Candyman dispensed his treats. She walked around the building slowly, as if David might be hiding around any corner. There was something about this place, something she couldn't put her finger on—

Lightning and thunder collided with a vengeance, a stray bolt striking the crown of one of the tall maples across the street. With a shudder and a crack, the electrocuted branches fell to the earth below, narrowly avoiding a carport that housed a new Chrysler minivan.

It was stupid to be out here. She should go back to her Jeep and find someplace to ride the storm out. She should—

She saw the padlock as soon as she rounded the final corner of the building. It was dangling loosely in its hasp, as effective in preventing intruders as a piece of Scotch tape. Jessica lifted the battered lock with her fingertips, examining the pocks that marred the casing. She pried it loose from the hasp and tossed it aside, placing her hand flat against the plywood door.

She pushed the door open and immediately covered her nose, gasping in horror.

The stench was overpowering.

CHAPTER EIGHTEEN

I

It was the unmistakable aroma of baking chocolate.

Crystal sat at the battle-scarred kitchen table watching her aunt move with practiced ease from one counter to the next, cracking eggs, sifting flour and measuring shortening, her slate gray hair frizzled and dancing on top of her head as her sagging arms blended the ingredients. A pan of brownies firmed in the avocado-green oven while Maude entered Phase Two of her bakeoff, dispensing cookie dough by the rounded spoonful onto twin non-stick baking sheets. They would be put into the wall-mounted oven as soon as the brownies came out.

"Can I help?" Crystal was shocked at the sound of her own voice, high-pitched and girlish, years-removed from the husky timbre that had become one of her Hollywood trademarks. She was suddenly aware of her swinging feet, uninhibited by the ground below.

Maude paused in mid-stroke, turning to smile at her niece. "You're already helping, dear," she said. "But you know, you might do me a favor and see what you can do about this." She placed one of her mixing bowls on the table in front of Crystal, remnants of cookie dough clinging to the sides.

Crystal dragged a finger through the sticky-sweet paste and touched it to her tongue. Cherry-chocolate chip with a touch of almond. "Linnie Bowles said I shouldn't eat raw cookie dough. She says it'll give me worms."

Maude scowled at the girl. "I'm seventy-three years old," she said. "I've eaten cookie dough since I was your age, and I ain't never had worms."

Seventy-three?

Crystal examined her aunt's features more carefully, realizing the absence of depth to the fine lines around her eyes and mouth. She looked down at herself and was startled to see straight through to her pink corduroys, no breasts whatsoever to obscure the view.

Crystal's finger absently found her mouth again, no longer concerned with Linnie Bowles' opinion. "How old am I?" she asked.

Maude turned toward her again, an eyebrow arched. "Excuse me?"

The kitchen door opened with a clatter, and Kathy Duncan bustled into the small room, her arms laden with paper bags of groceries, all of which would be used for the church bake sale. She was twenty years younger than Maude, but still ancient in Crystal's eyes. Kathy's once athletic body had thickened over the years, adding a disproportionate amount of width to her height. Her mousy brown hair was bowl cut with severe bangs framing her hazel eyes.

"Don't everyone rush to help me all at once," Kathy grumbled, losing her grip on one of the bags. Fortunately, it contained nothing breakable.

Crystal scooted off the edge of her chair, crossing the faded and cracked linoleum floor to help Kathy unload. She reached up, and Kathy smiled sweetly.

"Chrissy, honey, why don't you pick up those things on the floor before I step on them. These bags are much too heavy for your little arms," she said. "Maude's arms, however, would be very welcome right about now."

"All right, all right! I'm coming!" Maude tossed her fuzzy green oven mitts to the counter and began taking the grocery bags from her friend's overloaded arms.

Crystal stared at them, reliving the moment vividly, even though she now realized this was a dream. She knew Aunt Maude was gone; it was Kathy Duncan who had called her in California. Yet now, that phone call seemed more distant and vague than this memory of a young girl. She could actually *feel* the warmth of the oven, *smell* the cooling brownies, *taste* the sweet cookie dough.

She was only seven years old.

She remembered the pink corduroys she wore—her favorite pair because of the white bunny rabbits on the back pockets. She remembered how angry she had been with Aunt Maude when she wouldn't allow Crystal to wear them to school that fall; it didn't matter that Crystal had grown and the pants fitted her more like capris. They were still her favorite.

"Saw her again today," Kathy said absently as she unloaded one of the bags.

Maude looked up from her work and gave a brief shake of her head, her eyes darting toward Crystal. Kathy smiled apologetically and nodded, then began whistling as she finished unloading the groceries. She stacked the items by category on the turquoise countertop, the dry goods grouped at one end, canned goods in the middle, and fresh vegetables and fruit nearest the sink. There was no need to shelve or refrigerate anything; the two women would use it all in this day of marathon baking.

Maude heaped the last spoonful of dough onto the cookie sheet and slid it onto the top rack of the oven. As she did, she casually said, "Chrissy, honey, it's grown-up time now. Me and Kathy want to visit a spell, so you go on to your room for a while."

Grown-up time.

Even before the words fell from Maude's lips, Crystal knew what she was going to say; yet as familiar as the phrase was, its concept was completely foreign to her. Maude had been very forthright with Crystal from a very early age, as far back as Crystal could remember. Maude believed that worldly education was as valuable as academia. Many of life's lessons are hard and ugly, but Maude felt that sheltering a child from them was, in the long run, doing the child a great disservice.

Still, she was only a seven-year-old girl, and who was she to debate the point? She found herself nodding and walking—no, *skipping* out of the kitchen. It was the most unusual sensation. The adult Crystal was trapped inside this younger version, vicariously tasting history through her. She turned the corner and moved through the living room toward her bedroom.

And stopped.

The path was just as she remembered it. Orange shag carpeting—it always reminded her of Muppet fur—stretched back to the small bathroom, a bedroom on each side of the narrow corridor that crossed in front of it. Of course, Maude had the larger of the two rooms, the one on the right. It faced the rear of the house and, therefore, had the most privacy. Crystal's room was on the left, an old six-panel door with a glass doorknob and peeling paint. Pages from a coloring book were taped over its surface, some done with care and some with wild abandon. Many of them were bunny rabbits.

As she approached the door, her feet slowed, and her heartbeat quickened. She didn't want to go into her room. It was a ridiculous thought. Crystal not only had the memories of the girl, she had those she carried with her daily. Her room had been her refuge from the world. It wasn't that she didn't have friends, she certainly *did*, but sometimes she needed time to herself to think and dream. It was in this room that her dreams of stardom were born. She had been Princess Leia and Bonnie Parker, Cleopatra and Eleanor of Aquitaine, countless hours in a world of celluloid fantasy. But she never pretended to be a victim. It was one role she didn't think she could pull off.

Still, it was the overwhelming sensation that grabbed her now, a helplessness and futility that made Crystal want to turn and run, straight through the kitchen and out the back door. But the seven-year-old who possessed control of her legs wouldn't cooperate. She didn't seem to sense the malignancy of the moment and took another step toward the door.

There was something on the other side of that door, something that wanted to kill Crystal. She tried to focus all her energy on gaining control of those tiny little legs, but the task was insurmountable, and it really didn't come as a complete surprise. This was history that Crystal was experiencing. She had no more control over its outcome in her dreams as in her waking moments. As certain as she was of that, she couldn't seem to put her finger on this *exact* moment of her past. She had no idea what waited for her on the other side of the cheerfully deceptive door, but she knew it was horrible, something that would forever change her.

Her small fingers closed around the glass knob.

Out of the corner of his eye, Luke watched the slow rise and fall of Crystal's chest. She had fallen asleep almost as soon as they had rejoined the highway. He spied his handiwork on her arm and hoped to hell he hadn't permanently

347

disfigured her. She would probably sue him and take the only thing of value that he had—Paulie's farm.

He reached into his pocket and extracted a cigarette, pushing the lighter into the dashboard. His eyes caught Virginia's in the rearview mirror, and after a short deliberation, he reluctantly put the cigarette away. Virginia had been through enough today without the carcinogenic benefit of his secondhand smoke.

Paula's glassy eyes stared past him, through the windshield. She had become especially quiet since the scene at the farmhouse, and that was just as well with Luke. He had grown uncomfortable under her constant scrutiny, and he knew that she felt no better about him now than before.

Old Paulie had dictated one full year on the road.

Was this how it was going to be? One atrocity after another? He had barely met Bert Parnell before he had witnessed his violent death. Now Greta and the others were gone, too, victims of the same maniacs who had murdered her husband. It made Luke reconsider the whole episode at *Friendly's* gas and food mart. He wondered if Bert had been the intended target the entire time, eliminated before he could return to the farmhouse in Borden and act as a guardian for his family. But why? What possible threat could the Parnells pose to someone who would demand the systematic execution of the entire family? It was like gang warfare, but the players were all wrong. Of course, Bert may have used his rig to haul for less than legal purposes, getting himself in over his head with the wrong people, but Luke didn't think so. The Parnells were good, honest folks; he sensed it.

The fact that the killer was a dead ringer for Crystal was still sinking in. He honestly hadn't even noticed the resemblance at first. He was too caught up in his duty to protect the girl to notice such trivial things. All he had seen was the gun, and he knew he had to stop the woman before she found Virginia, even if it meant killing her. It was only after they had begun to tangle that his eyes absorbed the content of her face. For a brief, perplexing second, he had thought he was fighting with Crystal. The break in his concentration had allowed the woman to land that knee-shot to the groin. If Crystal hadn't fired the gun, her double would have probably killed him.

Luke turned the radio on and adjusted the volume to a comfortable level that was audible yet wouldn't disturb Crystal's sleep. He scanned the FM band until he found a country-western station with decent signal strength. The rain had stopped, but overcast skies continued to threaten. He used the wipers and the last of their windshield wiper solvent to clear the spattered front glass.

He had already decided that when they arrived in Lucasville, he was going to place another call to Morty King. Since he had last spoken with the lawyer, things had gone from bad to worse. He didn't want to see kidnapping added to the potential charges that were accruing against him. Despite the certainty that he would do whatever was necessary to ensure Virginia's safety—including kidnapping—Luke was not stupid. If there was a way to protect himself, surely Morty would help him find it.

Jasper seemed to be wedged a million years in the past, yet it had only been *days*.

Luke concentrated on the road, afraid to board that particular train of thought. If he focused on how long it would be before he could go home, he'd never make it—*never*.

The hypnotic thrum of tires against pavement was working its magic on Virginia. Her eyelids were beginning to droop, and her tiny lips suddenly parted in a wide yawn. Luke glanced back to the road, adjusting the steering wheel.

It would be another hour before they reached Lucasville. He wondered how far behind them the Volvo was. He was certain they were following. They hadn't invested this kind of involvement to a cause they would abandon so easily.

They wouldn't stop until Virginia Parnell was dead.

* * *

Paula pulled her knees up to her chest, curling into a ball and turning her back to the strange little girl beside her. She stared through the back glass and into the outside world.

Luke had stayed off the main thoroughfares, choosing narrow, winding two-lane roads that gradually wove across the state in a drunken line. Paula could see one eye and part of his nose through the rearview mirror. He was obviously in deep thought, guiding the car on autopilot.

She had decided it was time to bail out. This wasn't turning out anything like she had expected. When she had won the contest and the opportunity to appear on *Benny and the Girl*, she had naturally fantasized that her walk-on part would lead to something permanent, acting as a gateway from abused and troubled teen to fabulously adored and highly paid celebrity. When the shoot had gone so poorly—thanks to Crystal—Paula had shrugged it off as best she could, telling herself that she had never really believed it would happen in the first place. Resiliency from disappointment had become a tool of survival growing up in Joel McElroy's house. It bothered her enormously that Crystal should take such an immediate and extreme dislike to her, but she was a star and therefore entitled to act any way she wanted. It didn't dampen Paula's admiration for her hero but only helped to steepen her own lack of self-esteem. She had obviously done something to provoke Crystal's wrath. When Angel had offered Paula the opportunity to remain in California for a while longer, she had jumped at the chance. She couldn't imagine why Angel would have wanted her to keep an eye on Crystal, but it was an opportunity to redeem herself in the eyes of her idol. As it turned out, it was also extremely fortunate for Crystal. If Paula hadn't been watching, Crystal would currently be spending her days and nights in a padded room under the intense scrutiny of a team of psychiatric experts. Paula hoped to someday introduce Crystal to Angel. In Paula's opinion, Crystal owed her an enormous debt of gratitude. If it hadn't been for Angel's gift, Crystal's life would be in much worse shape than it already was. At least she still had her freedom.

And so did Paula. She would wait until the next time they stopped and find an excuse to use the payphone. She would call Angel and tell her that she was finished with this and needed a bus ticket. She didn't give a damn about the Honda anymore; she couldn't pay for it anyway. But if Crystal and Luke were going to keep the little girl with them, they needed the transportation far worse than she did. As a matter of fact, the woman who had fled the farmhouse had seen the car and would know what they were driving. If Paula were to ask Crystal and Luke to find another ride, she might inadvertently draw the attention of the assassins away by simply continuing to drive the damned thing.

Surely Angel would understand. Regardless of her motives for wanting Crystal followed, she couldn't have possibly foreseen the type of trouble Paula had encountered. She wouldn't want her little sister to be at the center of something so volatile and dangerous. She would come to Paula's rescue. She always did.

She found comfort in the thought, and that helped to combat the sense of betrayal she was feeling toward Luke and Crystal. She knew they didn't need her. As each subsequent mile had passed, her importance continued to diminish, and she had become more and more like extra cargo. She had served her purpose by springing Crystal from the hospital before she could be committed. Her work here was done.

Paula relaxed as much as she had done since before they had picked up Luke. She closed her eyes and listened to the soft country ballad that was playing on the radio. She knew that for her, it would all be over soon.

———◇———

Crystal awakened with a start, jerking her splinted arm against the seatbelt and issuing a short, sharp cry.

"What happened?" asked Luke, his eyes darting from the road to her and back again. "Are you okay?"

"Mmm," said Crystal, nodding. She waited for the stars to clear from her field of vision before attempting to speak again. "Where are we?"

"About seventy miles from Lucasville, if I'm figuring right."

She peered over her shoulder, noting that both Virginia and Paula had fallen asleep as well. She yawned and wiped her eyes with her usable hand. "How are you doing?" she asked Luke.

He smiled and shrugged. "Been better."

350

"Yeah."

She leaned back in her seat and stared out the window. The road they traveled was bordered by dense thickets and tall pines, curving sharply enough to require frequent use of the brake pedal. She could tell from the difference in terrain that they were in southern Ohio; the northern part of the state is flat as a pancake. As they crested the next hill, Crystal had the familiar sensation in the pit of her stomach of riding a rollercoaster.

"Did you get some rest?" Luke asked.

"Not really," she said. "I was having the weirdest dream."

"Hmm?" Luke's curiosity was instantly piqued. Some of his premonitions had been delivered in the form of a dream. Just because Crystal hadn't yet experienced anything extrasensory didn't mean she couldn't suddenly develop the talent.

Crystal frowned and shook her head. "It was a dream, but it was also like a memory, you know? Everything that happened in it really happened. I must've been about seven or something—I don't know. It's not like this was some special occasion or anything. It was just a regular afternoon in Aunt Maude's kitchen, just like a million others."

"Then how can you be sure it really happened?"

She shrugged. "I just know. Aunt Maude was making goodies for the church bake sale, and her best friend, Kathy Duncan, came by with some things from the store. They started working at the counter, then asked me to go to my room because they wanted some 'grown-up time.' It was when I went to my room that things started to get weird."

"Weird? Weird how?"

"I didn't want to go in there. Something was inside that room—waiting for me. And the damnedest thing is, I think I really went in there, you know, back when I was seven, but I have no idea at all what happened. I just know that I wanted to turn and run, get away from that room as quickly as possible."

Luke chewed his bottom lip. "Do you think it was something, you know—sexual?"

Crystal winced and shook her head. "No. In all my time there, there was never a man in the house. It's really the weirdest thing. I mean, I would think if something really horrible had happened to me back then, something that had made such an impression that I was terrified of whatever was on the other side of my own bedroom door—well, I don't think I would have freely spent so much time inside those same four walls during all the years that followed, do you?"

"It was probably just a dream," he said. "I'm sure you're still pumped up from—you know, before."

"Maybe."

She still hadn't told Luke about her dreams of Aunt Maude and her warning of those that would be chasing Crystal. Even though she had previously pondered its significance, current circumstances made it impossible to doubt the events Aunt Maude was foreshadowing. If she had tried to tell Crystal something in a dream before, she could have been trying again. What *was* it about that morning that she couldn't remember?

The Dixie Chicks were abruptly cut off in mid-sentence by the high-pitched tone of the Emergency Broadcast System screeching through the Honda's speakers.

"This is Scott Cramer with WCNW, and I've got a breaking news story for you folks out there in Preble, Butler, Montgomery, and Warren counties. We've just received a report that a gas station near Borden was held up at gunpoint by Crystal Bright, the troubled former star of ABC's hit sitcom, *Benny and the Girl*. As you may know, Ms. Bright is originally from Ohio. She left with the contents of the cash register, and no one was reportedly harmed. The entire bizarre incident was captured by a surveillance camera posted in the mini-mart, and there appears to be little doubt as to the identity of the robber. Ms. Bright has so far eluded police and should be considered armed and extremely dangerous. If anyone out there has any information, please call the Preble County sheriff's office at..."

II

Lisa threw open the door and hurried into the house. Every moment she spent in Morgan was time wasted in pursuing the girl. She needed to collect Chad and hit the road.

She was still buzzing from the adrenaline rush of robbing the gas station. It had gone perfectly. There was no way Crystal could run to the police without having herself arrested. Lisa doubted that Crystal would deposit the girl into protective custody either, at least not until she more fully understood the impending danger. An orphaned child would be shuttled off to a county facility to tearfully await adoption. Crystal would know that this facility wouldn't be prepared to protect this child from the inevitability of Lisa and Chad's agenda.

Lisa paused at the bottom of the stairs, wrinkling her nose distastefully. She had nearly forgotten about the other one—the sulking girl with the jet-black hair and piss-poor attitude. *Suze*. She could literally *smell* her, the unclean scent pervading the dankness that usually dominated. It was almost time for Lisa to persuade Chad that Suze's usefulness had run its course.

No time for that now. Every movement of the clock's second hand was distance they were gaining. Lisa hurried up the stairs and entered her bedroom. She expected to find Chad still on the bed, perhaps even asleep, but he had worked his way into clothing and was currently struggling with the laces of his

352

shoes. Suze squatted like a great fat turd on the corner of the mattress, massaging her temples in another pathetic cry for attention. *Poor, pitiful me. Me and my poor, pitiful, aching head.* Yeah, well, lop the damn thing off or shut the hell up.

They turned their heads in unison toward Lisa, their eyes posing the question their mouths were afraid to ask. Lisa's lips pressed together, and she shook her head.

"Goddammit, I *told* you—" began Suze.

"I thought I told you to shut the fuck up," interrupted Chad, shutting her down with a malevolent glare. His face softened when he turned back to Lisa. "What happened?"

"No time for details now," said Lisa. "Let's just say it's not over yet. Get your things and let's go."

"*Go?* Go where?" asked Suze. "I've about had it with—" Another glare from Chad effectively staunched her complaint. She flopped off the mattress and crossed to the window, finding a place where she could turn her back to them and shut them out for a few moments. It wasn't as if they were relying on her input anyway.

Lisa stooped and helped Chad finish tying his shoelaces. "Are you ready?" she asked.

He nodded. "Suze? You got your shit together?"

Suze nodded without facing him.

Lisa wished she could simply cross the room and push the petulant waste of skin straight through the window. Alas, no time for play.

"Let's go, then," said Lisa, turning toward the door.

"Wait a minute," said Suze, breaking her silence. "What about the nurse? We can't just leave her here."

"Shoot her," said Chad. "We'll meet you in the car."

"Gladly," said Suze. She approached Lisa with her hand out. "Give me the gun."

"I don't have it."

"*What?* Where the hell is it?" demanded Suze.

"Back at the farmhouse, I would imagine. Don't get your panties in a twist. I have another gun." Lisa had kept Chris Baylock's gun when she had disposed of his body. At the time, it had occurred to her that it might come in handy. Someday. "It's in the basement."

"Fine," she said stiffly. "*You* take care of the bitch down there, and *I'll* wait in the car with Chad." She didn't wait for a response, pushing past Lisa and Chad and out into the hallway. They exchanged a weary glance before following her closely.

As Lisa was driving back to Morgan, she had worried for a brief instant that Chad's disappointment in her would lead to anger, and their short-lived union might come to a bloody end. It wasn't that she feared Chad; actually, quite the

Darin Miller

opposite. Yet she sensed that if they were to ever really lock horns, only one of them would walk away from the altercation, and it was too soon to lose him quite yet. She had only just barely tasted him. His only word to her as they reached the bottom of the stairs and went their separate ways was, "Hurry."

As Chad and Suze exited through the front door, Lisa quickly made her way through the downstairs hallway to the door leading to the basement stairs. She paused, her hand on the knob, deliberating her next step. Part of her wanted to march down the stairs, throw open the door to the coal bin and strangle the hefty nurse with her bare hands. It was worth considering if for nothing more than shock value. Helen Martin would never see it coming and would never expect Lisa to turn against her. When she looked at Lisa, she saw only her deceased daughter, Evie, and the opportunity to collect those loose threads from her life, and bind them together into something positive, even if it was all illusory.

What made Lisa pause was a sensation she couldn't readily identify. She had known the nurse for no more than a few weeks and was reluctant to consider that she might have already formed an attachment to the nosy old bird. Yet after careful consideration, she realized that that might just be it. Helen Martin was a natural caregiver, maternal instinct dripping from every fiber of her being. A perfect stranger to Lisa, she had nonetheless made it her personal business to see Lisa through her recovery. She was the complete antithesis of Nanna Grace, whose iron hand and sharp tongue had controlled every facet of Lisa's development or lack thereof.

Nevertheless, Lisa opened the four-panel door and stepped down onto the landing. She couldn't just let her go; it was far too dangerous. Helen would make a beeline for the police, convinced that Lisa's life was imperiled. She really should just do it and get it over with.

She took a step down, and the riser creaked underneath her weight. Below her, the musty basement was completely still, immersed in darkness. There were no sounds from behind the heavy metal door which opened into the coal bin.

She took another step down.

You looked like a helpless little girl. Reminded me of my daughter, in fact.

Helen's words came unbidden, roaming the nearly empty chambers of Lisa's conscience. She shouldn't give a good goddamn about this woman. She should be *relieved* to be finished with her.

She took another step down.

"What in the hell's taking her so long?" groused Suze, craning her neck to peek over the headrest of the driver's seat. "She's probably fucking this up too."

354

Chad had crawled into the back seat where he could more easily favor his wounded shoulder. "Would you give her a break? I mean, *goddamn!* She can't do a thing right as far as you're concerned."

Suze looked at him incredulously. "You have got to be *kidding* me! She was supposed to take care of the girl. She didn't."

"We don't know what happened yet."

"It doesn't fucking *matter* what happened! She *blew* it, Chad!"

Chad said nothing more, but his eyes narrowed, darkening. It would surprise Suze to know he didn't understand his sudden forgiving nature any more than she did. But there was something different about Lisa Mitchell, a special quality that Suze could never understand, and Chad could only hope to. If things hadn't gone according to schedule, they would simply have to rewrite the schedule. That's the way life goes. He was sure that Lisa had done the best she could. Deep down inside, he knew they hadn't lost; the girl would ultimately be theirs.

The passenger door opened, startling Chad from his reverie, and Lisa slid into the seat.

"Is it done?" Suze's caustic tone drew a sharp sideways glance from Lisa.

"Everything's fine," she said, staring at Suze until Suze's eyes finally dropped away.

"Where are we going?" asked Chad.

"East," said Lisa. "Past Borden."

As they traveled, Lisa told them what had happened at the Parnell residence. Suze made frequent editorial comments by means of snorts and exasperated sighs, but Chad simply absorbed the details, realizing almost immediately that his sensation of being with Lisa in that house had been a real, tangible thing. She had been completely unaware of his presence yet had felt his hand on her shoulder at that crucial moment, the one in which she had turned to discover her pursuers.

"So Crystal Bright *is* here," said Chad. He shot a crooked grin at Suze. "I guess I'll have to watch my ass after all."

Lisa looked at Suze. "What's he talking about?"

"Never mind what he's talking about," snapped Suze. "You fucking let them get away! Do you not understand that? Goddamn it, Chad, if you don't shoot this bitch, I will."

"You won't shoot anybody," said Chad.

"Oh, yeah? Oh, *yeah?*" Suze craned to glare at him in the back seat, the Volvo weaving in and out of its lane.

"As a matter of fact, yeah," Lisa said simply, calmly reaching across to steady the steering wheel.

They fell silent, and Suze turned her burning eyes toward Lisa; her head was within easy striking distance.

Lisa looked up. "Are you going to drive this car?" she asked.

Suze's eyes narrowed, and her fingers tightened on the steering wheel. The smug look on Lisa's face was causing her blood to boil.

"You won't shoot me because you don't have a gun, remember?" said Lisa. "But I do."

"Hey, enough about the guns, already," said Chad.

"No, as a matter of fact, it's not enough," said Suze. She glared at Lisa. "She said she dropped the first gun at the farmhouse. Her prints will be all over it. We're liable to run into roadblocks any *goddamn* minute—"

"SHUT UP!"

Chad's voice ripped through the car's interior, leaving a thunderous silence in its wake. He leaned forward, resting his arms along the seatbacks. If he felt the injury to his shoulder, he gave no sign. He examined each of the women with curious intensity. They both fell silent. Lisa simply smiled at Chad while Suze felt rings of perspiration forming underneath her armpits. She felt like they were ganging up on her. Somehow, this had all gotten turned around. Lisa Mitchell was taking over, and it wasn't fair, it wasn't *fair!*

"Do you have any idea where they were going?" Chad asked Lisa.

"Well, I can pretty much assure you they won't be going to the police," said Lisa with a proud smile.

Her grin was infectious, spreading to Chad's face, reigniting Suze's rage like gasoline on embers. "And why's that?" he asked, resting his chin beside Lisa's headrest.

Lisa reached into the floorboards and extracted the plastic bag from the convenience mart she had burgled. She upended it, spilling the stolen currency into her lap. "I robbed a gas station—as Crystal Bright," she said. "The whole thing got caught on a surveillance camera. She won't be able to go anywhere without being recognized. Police everywhere will be looking for her—not for us. Eventually, they'll capture and arrest her for the robbery but surprise, surprise! She's got the little girl with her, the one whose whole family was murdered back in Borden."

She turned her attention toward Suze. "I left the gun at the farmhouse because Crystal Bright was the last one to handle it. *Her* prints are all over it, not mine. I'm not an idiot. I wore gloves."

A slow grin spread over Chad's face, followed by a slow chuckle, then uncontained laughter. He rocked back in his seat, nodding and applauding, laughing hysterically.

Suze narrowed her focus to the road ahead of her. She tried to block out the sound of Chad's approval, but it was everywhere, pounding at her eardrums, exacerbating her headache. Only one thought brought any form of relief at all.

Lisa Mitchell must die.

III

Jessica leaned against the bumper of her Jeep, her arms wrapped tightly around her midsection. She had been sick too many times to count. The local police were questioning the new widow, Tammy McElroy, in her living room while a crime scene photographer captured the gruesome spectacle inside the candy store.

"Are you alright?"

Jessica was startled to find Leonard Barnes looking down at her, concern filling his eyes. "I'll be fine," she said. "I thought you were in a hurry to get your car fixed."

"Yes, ma'am, I was," he said. "But it don't make no difference now. It's already too late."

"Oh, I'm sorry," she said. "I hope it wasn't too awfully important."

He nodded grimly. "So do I."

Officer Charles emerged from the huddle of policemen collecting on the McElroy's walk, nodding his head at Jessica as he purposefully strode toward her. "Good afternoon," he said. "Seems we have a little excitement here. You wanna tell me what you know?"

She stared at him blankly. "I don't understand what you mean. I was here looking for David McElroy. I understand that this is his brother Joel's house."

"Yes," he said, pinching his bottom lip and pacing. "It was. You said earlier that you were afraid of what David might do in his current state of mind. Do you have reason to believe that he might pose a threat to his family?"

She looked at him incredulously. "What? I didn't mean anything like that. I was just worried, that's all."

Charles studied her for a silent minute, and Jessica knew he was trying to decide if he believed her. It took a moment before she fully understood where his questions were leading.

"Surely you don't think *David* is responsible for this," she said.

"The timing's mighty coincidental, don't you think?"

"That's absurd! David McElroy is no killer," she said with certainty. Even if McElroy was hunting his wife's murderers, it wasn't the same as what had been done to Joel. She was certain McElroy wasn't capable of *that*.

The look in Charles' eyes wasn't reassuring. "How long you known David McElroy, Ms.—?"

"Lybrook. Jessica Lybrook," she said. "I've worked with him at the Jay County Sheriff's Department for a little over seven years."

357

He raised his eyebrows. "You knew him well?"

"Well, yeah, sure," she said. "I mean, Jay County isn't all that big. We all know each other."

He studied her again, his intelligent brown eyes alert to her every reaction. "Friends?" His tone fairly dripped innuendo.

"Of course," she retorted impatiently. "You told me that you knew Loretta. David would've never cheated on her. *Never.*"

Charles was silently skeptical.

"Oh, for heaven's sake, Officer Charles," said Jessica. "Exactly what are you implying? Why would David come here to kill his brother? It makes no sense. His wife had just been murdered—"

"Did McElroy ever talk to you about that brother of his?"

Jessica reflected. "Not much, I don't guess. What difference does it make?"

"Well frankly, ma'am, it makes a great big difference," said Charles, adjusting his hat. "Them boys had a real reputation up here, 'specially if they was together, and they was drinkin'. More'n once they been known to turn on each other. Had to stop David from stabbin' Joel once myself. It took everything I had."

"I can't remember the last time David even mentioned Joel's name," Jessica said, feeling restless and tired of this line of inquiry. "Really, Officer Charles, I only came here because I didn't know where else to look for David. So far, I haven't found anyone who even saw him, and in all likelihood, he's probably sitting in his own living room right now."

Charles looked at her skeptically. "I don't much believe in coincidence, and we seem to have a whole stinkin' pile of it right now."

"Can I go?" she asked.

"I'll want to know how to get hold of you," he said, retrieving a notepad from a clip on his belt. He took her home number and the number for the Jay County Sheriff's Department as well. She pushed herself away from the Jeep's bumper and was about to round the corner on the driver's side when Charles called after her, "You make sure and tell David McElroy we'd like to talk to him when you see him."

She paused briefly, nodded, then continued walking. She slid behind the wheel of her Jeep and was surprised to find Leonard Barnes waiting in the passenger seat.

"Hope you don't mind," he said.

She didn't know whether she minded or not. Her brain was reeling from the events of the last hour, and she needed to get away from there. Wordlessly, she started the engine and pulled away from the curb. Truthfully, she had again forgotten about the haggard old man in the navy jumpsuit, the image of Joel McElroy's brutalized body occupying the space behind her eyes.

"Something very wrong is happenin'," he added, nodding knowingly.

Jessica kept her eyes on the road, still saying nothing. She depressed the button on the door that caused her window to go down, and she inhaled the rain-scented air deeply, trying to clear her head. David couldn't have done this. It wasn't possible. She had worked with him for *seven years*.

She felt as if she had stepped into the *Twilight Zone*, a place where David McElroy had been an entirely different man than the one she had come to know. Of course, Officer Charles might have something personal against David. Maybe Charles had been passed over for a promotion because of him, who knew? She hated herself for even questioning David's integrity.

Finally, she turned to Leonard and said, "Your distributor cap should be in by now. How about I take you back to Roy's, then drop you off at your car?"

"Thank you," he said. "That'd be right nice of you." He shifted in his seat, and she was uncomfortably aware of his intense scrutiny. "You know you've been pulled into this, too," he nearly whispered.

She gave him a sidelong glance. "Excuse me?"

"Surely you feel it," he said. "Like the officer said, this ain't no coincidence. A murder like that—that is the work of something evil."

Jessica groaned inwardly. Great. The old man was a religious fanatic. She was about to be subjected to his sermon, and she had already volunteered to take him to the service station and then back to his car. Shit.

"There's been something evil in Morgan for some time now," he continued. "Dormant. Waiting. Woman named Grace Mitchell knew all about it. She tried to tell me, and I didn't believe her 'til it was too late. Now it's out."

Okay, not just a religious fanatic but a visionary. Jessica began working on an excuse to leave him behind at Roy's BP.

"It calls itself Lisa," he continued. "Grace raised Lisa from the time she was just a little girl. She was a shy, quiet little thing, but she had these big blue eyes that made your blood run cold. Grace died a few weeks back. Now there's no one to keep Lisa from doing as she pleases—"

"Wait a minute," interrupted Jessica. "You're losing me. Why would anyone have to keep a shy, quiet girl from doing as she pleases? I mean, what's she going to do? Stay up too late watching TV?"

"You don't understand," he said. "There is something going on inside Lisa Mitchell's head. She hasn't been the same since Grace died."

"I'm sure she's grieving."

"Not like that," he insisted urgently. "Grace tried her best to keep Lisa apart from the rest of the world. She knew what the girl was capable of. She didn't like it when Lisa got a job at the hospital, and she called upon me to see if I would keep an eye on her while she was working."

He saw the skeptical look on Jessica's face.

"Hey, I know this sounds crazy, lady—I thought it was, too. I didn't see any point to keeping an eye on the girl. She'd always been this quiet little mouse. But

359

after Grace died, she's been different. It's like something has been unleashed in her. I'm telling you, whatever happened back there to Joel McElroy, she had something to do with it."

How the hell much farther was that BP?

Leonard was still talking. "I've known the Mitchells for some time. Never once did they have any kind of get-together or party—nothing like that. Not even after Grace died, when you might have at least expected to see some extra cars from family or friends. But no. Not until that last night. A Volvo sedan and a red Ford truck in the drive, Helen Martin's Buick at the curb, and a blue Oldsmobile across the way. There were gunshots, I tell you! I heard them myself—"

"Wait a minute," said Jessica. Something in his spiel had penetrated her consciousness. "Did you say a blue Oldsmobile?"

"Yeah," he said. "It wasn't anything new. Maybe a Cutlass. One of them four-door deals with the dark blue cloth roofs. I never did see who belonged to it or the red truck. I-I'm ashamed to say I fell asleep while I was watching."

Jessica struggled to absorb what Leonard was telling her. He had apparently been conducting silent surveillance on this Mitchell girl's house, and Jessica didn't quite know how she felt about that. As she glanced at the grizzled old man, it seemed disgustingly voyeuristic, and her first instinct was to be repulsed. But David McElroy drove a blue Oldsmobile with a Brougham top. Why would he have been near Lisa Mitchell's house? Maybe there was some validity to Leonard Barnes' words after all. Looking at the man, it was hard to imagine.

"I think the girl might have put a spell on me," he suggested, the idea practically newborn. "Anyways, when I woke, all them cars were gone. I saw the Mitchell girl coming back to the house on foot, as if it was perfectly normal to take a stroll around the neighborhood in the dead of night."

"You said something about gunshots," said Jessica.

Leonard bobbed his head up and down. "Yes, ma'am. I heard two, maybe three. Scared the shit right out of me, if you'll pardon my French. I called the police, and they sent out a couple of officers, but that damned Mitchell girl must've cast a spell on them too. They weren't there no time at all before they turned right around and left."

"Who is Helen Martin?"

"She's a nurse at Morgan Township. I work there and so did Lisa until a few weeks ago."

"What happened?"

"She got fired. An older patient claimed she was really rough with her. Alma Baylock was her name."

"*Was?*"

Leonard nodded. "She died in her sleep a few days later. And that ain't all. The lady who fired Lisa—Ms. Kelsey? She was run over in the parking lot at

Morton's Supermarket. Had to scrape her off the pavement with a shovel. I'd say that's *all* pretty coincidental, wouldn't you?"

"All the cars were gone when you woke up," said Jessica, her mind spinning back to David. "You didn't see where any of them went?"

Leonard shook his head. "No, ma'am. I did drive by Mrs. Martin's this morning and saw that her car was in the driveway. I tried the doorbell, but she didn't answer. I'm very worried about her. She took a real shine to that girl after she had her car wreck."

Had David come back to Morgan and stumbled into something that he felt he should investigate? It seemed reckless and stupid, and Jessica didn't believe for a moment that David would ordinarily do something so dumb, but he wasn't acting like himself at the moment. His wife had been murdered in a senseless act of violence. She considered a scenario in which David McElroy acted as vigilante much more plausible than one in which he hacked his own brother to pieces with an ax.

Something inside Jessica's mind clicked. It was a feeling she hadn't had in many years, a tickling of her senses on the most fundamental level. It made the short hairs along the back of her neck stand erect.

"Where does this Mitchell girl live?" she asked.

The house looked empty. Its weathered façade drank from the gloom of the turbulent afternoon, casting the weed-choked yard in somber gray shadow. Dark windows stared out on the lawn from the house's square face. The driveway was empty, and there were no other cars besides Jessica's Jeep parked alongside the curb.

Jessica didn't need to ask Leonard if this was the Mitchell house. She could *feel* it. That peculiar sensation had returned, crawling along her arms and down the middle of her back, heightening her senses and filling her with dread. She hoped to God that David hadn't come to this place. Moments ago, she wouldn't have believed it possible that she could be the receptor of such negative and unnatural energy, and yet here she stood on the sidewalk, gaping stupidly at the front door, unable to bring life to her rooted feet.

Leonard eased up beside her. "Are you sure you want to do this, ma'am? I'm not so sure of the wisdom."

Jessica nodded and continued to stare. Had David gone into this house, having tracked Loretta's killers here? Had he come back out alive? What had *happened* here? What she wouldn't give to have been in Morgan a night earlier. She had the most horrible feeling that it was already too late; some very bad things had already come to pass.

361

Her feet finally responded to her brain's insistent request, and she found herself floating toward the porch in a daze. She had only the minimum required safety officer training and was unprepared to do battle with anyone who might wait behind those dark windows. She prayed the house was as empty as it looked.

She was on the porch now, Leonard one step behind her. He was busily surveying the windows of the second floor from around the eave of the porch roof. The wooden floorboards creaked underfoot, and Jessica felt a sudden shiver. She hurried across the porch to the front door and paused, wondering whether she should knock before entering. She hadn't even considered a surprise attack, and if anyone was inside the house, he or she would have already seen Jessica standing like a moron on the sidewalk while she tried to get her shit together.

Still, maybe they hadn't seen her.

She tested the doorknob, but it was locked.

"Dammit!" she whispered. "Let's try the back. Have you seen anyone?"

Leonard followed her off the porch. "No one. I don't think they're here. Why do you want to go inside?"

"If David McElroy was here last night, there might be some sign of what happened to him."

"And Mrs. Martin," added Leonard, as if the thought had only just occurred to him.

They followed the broken concrete of the drive along the side of the house, Leonard pausing at each window to peer inside. He was surprised to see how little of Grace Mitchell's furniture remained. The driveway led to a small garage that canted slightly to the left, as though it were wisely trying to escape the property. They continued to the rear of the house and paused by the gate of a tall wooden fence that enclosed the backyard. Its blanched exterior hadn't seen fresh paint in decades, and its walls swayed as if weary of standing. Jessica took one last look over her shoulder before lifting the rusty hasp and opening the creaking gate. She slipped through the opening and into the backyard, followed closely by Leonard.

Leonard was growing visibly agitated. A film of perspiration had formed across his forehead, and his breathing was rapid and shallow. He clearly didn't relish being this close to the place Lisa Mitchell called home.

"Are you alright?" asked Jessica.

He nodded his head, and they proceeded to the back door. Jessica stepped up on the narrow stoop and tried the doorknob. It, too, was locked.

"Dammit!" she said, more loudly this time. She eyed the thin wooden door with its six panes of glass looking into the kitchen. It would be so easy to do—but she couldn't. She worked for the Jay County Sheriff's Department, for God's sake! But she needed to see what was inside this house. She could almost feel David's presence.

Leonard sniffed the air and scowled. "Something's been burning," he said.

Jessica looked up and took a deep breath. The air in the backyard was tainted by the scent of charred wood and melted synthetics. She spotted the large burn barrel at the rear of the yard and nodded in its direction. "Is that normal?" she asked.

Leonard shrugged. "In Morgan, it is."

Jessica started across the yard, curious as to what Lisa had burned that had left such a residual stench. As she neared it, she was distracted by the sound of Leonard's voice.

"Well, looky here," he said.

She turned to find him squatted near the foundation close to the driveway. "What is it?" she called.

He scooted aside as Jessica approached so that she could see. Three wooden planks were affixed over a small square area, obviously an opening of some sort.

"Broken window?" she asked, but as she scanned the foundation, she saw that there were no other windows.

Leonard shook his head. "Coal chute. The original furnace in this house must have been a coal burner. It looks like it's been sealed up for some time. I'll bet we could pry these boards away easy enough."

Jessica didn't like it. It was still breaking and entering. But she had to know if David had been inside this house. She had to know if there was anything that might lead her to him. She couldn't be idle this time—she had to do *something*.

They worked together to pry away the top board. It had been fastened to a wooden frame with six-inch nails that had been driven deep. Just as Jessica thought she was going to have to return to the Jeep and rummage for an appropriate tool, the nails abruptly pulled loose. Jessica lost her balance and fell on her backside while Leonard leaned in for a closer look into the Mitchell basement.

"Oh, sweet Jesus."

When he turned back around, he was as white as a sheet.

CHAPTER NINETEEN

I

"Oh, God." Crystal's cheeks were ashen, her eyes wide. "What's going on?"

Luke glanced in the rearview mirror and saw that Paula and Virginia had slept through the news bulletin. The Dixie Chicks had returned to finish their song, but the infectious tune now seemed wholly inappropriate. He jabbed at the radio's power button, killing the sound. "I think your double from the Parnells has made a public appearance on your behalf."

Crystal's lips clamped together as her eyes danced furtively from side to side. Suddenly, she said, "Pull over."

"What?" asked Luke, shifting his attention toward her.

"I have to get off of this road," she said, her panicky voice rising. "I can't stay on this road, I—"

"Okay, we can do that," said Luke soothingly. "Stay calm. Everything will be fine."

He spotted a narrow dirt road ahead on the left. It may well have been a driveway, but Luke didn't care; it led into thick woods bordering the two-lane highway. If there was a residence tucked away somewhere back there, it wasn't visible through the thick clusters of foliage. He eased the Honda onto the narrow path and pulled forward until he was sure they couldn't be seen from the road. He switched the engine off.

"What's going on?" Paula's sleepy voice came from the rear. She had been wrenched from sleep by the Honda's jostling suspension on the unpaved lane. "Where are we?"

"What are we going to do?" asked Crystal, oblivious to the girl's question. "What are we going to *do?*"

"We'll have to keep a low profile," Luke said evenly, refusing to let panic take hold.

"*Keep a low profile?*" repeated Crystal incredulously. "I'm *Crystal Bright,* goddammit! *Everyone* knows me!" For once, the words were neither boastful nor arrogant. Crystal was terrified.

"What's going on?" repeated Paula, leaning forward between the headrests.

Luke glanced at her. "A gas station was robbed near Borden. The whole thing was caught on video. I guess Crystal's look-alike does more than just kill families."

"But we've seen this woman," said Paula. "We could tell the police that we've seen her."

"Yeah? And how do we explain Virginia?" asked Crystal. The little girl stirred at the sound of her name, her small jaws widening in a yawn before she shifted to her right and nodded off again. "They'll think we killed her family."

"But she can tell them it wasn't us," insisted Paula.

"She's four years old," said Luke. "No one's going to take the word of a little baby."

They sat in frustrated silence, phantom nooses tightening around their necks. The only sound in the Honda's small cabin was the rhythmic whistle of Virginia's soft snore.

"We need to find someplace to hide you," said Luke. "Somewhere no one would think of. We're near your hometown. You've got to know of *someplace*."

"Aunt Maude was my only family," said Crystal.

"Well, we can't go there," said Luke. "I'm sure the cops will be watching it closely. Can you think of anywhere else?"

Crystal's pale face reflected complete hopelessness. She slowly shook her head.

"C'mon," urged Luke. *"Think.* Surely, you've got an old girl friend or something."

Crystal shook her head more emphatically. "No. Everyone I knew there hates me. I made sure of that the last time I visited," she softly said.

Luke flexed his fingers on the steering wheel trying to contain his frustration.

"Can't we go back to wherever you're from?" Crystal's eyes flitted hopefully across Luke's face.

He shook his head. "In his will, Paulie said I couldn't go back for a year."

"Or what?"

"It doesn't matter," he said. "Point is, Jasper's small. Everybody knows everybody's business. If I were to show up in town, everybody'd know about it two minutes later. There ain't nowhere I can hide there."

"Oh, God," Crystal said weakly. "We're fucked."

"Don't say that," said Luke. "We're not fucked. We can figure this out. We can *do* this."

Crystal began to cry. The world had wobbled from its axis and thrown her entire life into unimaginable turmoil. She had no one to turn to for help. The strangers who sat around her were her only friends, and she didn't know if she could trust any of them. Soon, there would be a reward for her capture, and Luke didn't even have enough money for a pack of cigarettes, for God's sake!

And Virginia Parnell—

What was it about her that inspired such a calming effect? At first, Crystal had thought it was her imagination, but as her eyes found the sleeping angelic form in the mirror on the back of the sun visor, she felt warmth rush over her again. Protecting the child was of the utmost importance. Crystal couldn't afford to fall to pieces just yet.

She lowered her head and squeezed her eyes together tightly, inhaling deeply and forcing the panic away, one slow breath at a time.

Paula slumped back into her seat and pulled her knees up to hug them tightly. It was all too much. Everything was spinning out of control. Angel would have never gotten her involved with people like this. *Never.*

She needed to get to a phone. She needed to hear Angel's voice.

What kind of monster *was* this little girl? Paula's eyes shifted to covertly observe the tiny sleeping form. She looked like a porcelain doll, each feature painstakingly handcrafted. The texture of her hair was spun silk, framing her small head in a pillow of curls. Her lips were the color of cherries, softly moving with the sounds of sleep. In the aftermath of death and destruction, she was absolutely cherubic.

Paula wanted to be as far away from her as possible.

Luke watched as Crystal's whole body shuddered. He felt as if he should offer comfort, but he didn't know what he could say. He didn't have any ideas worth mentioning and figured it was only a matter of time before the police eventually caught up with them; Crystal's visibility was entirely too high. There wasn't a teenage girl who didn't idolize her. Hell, Paula was a testament to that fact.

The only thing he could think to do was to call Morty King again. Maybe the lawyer could arrange for them to go into protective custody in such a way that the media wouldn't find out about it—at least long enough for Crystal's double to make another public appearance. If she were to resurface while Crystal was in protective custody, there would at least be reasonable doubt as to the identity of the woman on the surveillance video. And Luke was sure that the woman *would* resurface. He doubted that the woman had robbed the convenience mart because she needed spending cash. She was aware of Crystal's celebrity and was willing to use their physical similarities to her advantage. The clerk at the gas station was lucky she hadn't been killed.

"We can't just sit here," he said softly.

Crystal nodded her head jerkily, dabbing at her eyes and snuffling. "I know."

"We'll just take this in little baby steps, okay?" he asked.

Again, she nodded.

"First, we need to make you a little less recognizable. How are you with makeup?"

Crystal shrugged. "I can get around with eyeliner, if that's what you mean, but nothing fancy."

"Any aversion to dyeing and cutting your hair?" asked Luke.

"At this point, I'd shave my head if I thought it would help."

Paula leaned forward. "I could help," she said. "Angel and I used to do each other's hair all the time. I've done perms and tints and makeovers—I'm not half-bad."

Crystal nodded numbly.

"Do we have any cash left?" asked Paula.

"A few dollars," said Crystal.

"We'll need that for gas," said Luke.

They sat in frustrated silence. Virginia shifted in the back seat and whimpered softly, her eyelids fluttering wildly. Luke instinctively reached out and placed his hand against her cheek, smoothing the creases in her forehead with his thumb. *She's so helpless.*

It wasn't the first time he had realized the extent of her vulnerability. Why anyone would want to hunt her down for extermination was unimaginable. He remembered the way Bert's face softened when he spoke of his daughter, unabashed pride stripping away years from his weathered countenance. Luke owed it to Bert to protect his daughter and protect her he would—even if it was the last thing he ever did.

Crystal was unraveling. Too much of the weight was being placed squarely upon her shoulders. Her eyes were those of a cornered animal.

Virginia's eyes opened suddenly, locking onto Luke's.

And he knew exactly what to do.

He cleared his throat. "I've got an idea. It's not much of one, but it's something." He turned to Crystal. "We need to find someplace here in the woods where you can stay for a little bit—maybe half an hour."

"Oh, no," said Crystal, shaking her head. "I'm not going to—"

"Listen to me, *listen* to me! We are *trapped* if we run out of gas. I'm going to have to go and—borrow some. I ain't never done nothing like this in my life, and I'm damned surprised at myself right now, but I don't see no other way. You and Paula and Virginia have to stay right here because, frankly, you don't need your name attached to no more crimes. Do you hear me?"

"I want to go with you," said Paula, suddenly leaning forward toward Luke.

Luke looked at her curiously. "With me? Why?"

"I—I just do," she said, realizing this may be her opportunity to break away from the group. She hastened to add, "If you're planning on stealing gas, it should be a two-man operation. You need someone to drive. The time it takes to get back into the car after filling up could be enough to get caught."

"That's ridiculous," said Luke. "It wouldn't take no time at all."

"No, she's right," said Crystal. "I know it sounds stupid, but we need every advantage we can get. In case you haven't noticed, we haven't caught too many breaks lately. And you should take Virginia with you. She shouldn't be outside in weather like this. It's liable to storm again."

Luke looked at Crystal incredulously. "You're actually suggesting that I take her along while I'm committing a crime?"

"Well—um, yeah," she said. She looked back toward Virginia who was now wide awake, silently observing the conversation around her. Crystal turned back toward Luke and lowered her voice. "If those people were to find us, I couldn't protect her. She should be with you."

Luke deliberated only briefly before realizing the validity of Crystal's point. With her broken arm and various scrapes and bruises, she would be no physical match for the woman who had murdered Virginia's entire family. He had tangled with her only briefly and had been astonished at her raw physical strength.

"Then let's find a place for you to hide," Luke said to Crystal, unfastening his seatbelt and opening his door.

Luke and Paula rode together in uncomfortable silence. It was the first time they had spent an extended amount of time together alone, and neither was particularly interested in exchanging banal chatter. Virginia was still awake but was behaving remarkably for a four-year-old, even more so considering she didn't know either of the people with whom she traveled.

Paula stared out the passenger window, gnawing on a knuckle of the fist pressed to her mouth. She didn't seem even remotely concerned that they were about to collaborate in the commission of a crime, so Luke wondered what it was that so raptly kept her attention.

"Crystal did say that there was a gas station down this way, didn't she?" Luke asked when he could tolerate the silence no longer.

Paula nodded slightly but continued to stare out the window.

Luke glanced at the needle of the gas gauge and grimaced. It lay flat on "E," and they could run out of fuel at any time. The narrow two-lane continued to wind through hilly, wooded terrain with little to no evidence of human occupation other than overhead power lines and the tarmac itself.

He glanced into the rearview mirror and found Virginia's eyes already focused on his reflection. There was a slight trace of a smile on her lips.

"Hey, is that it?" asked Paula, suddenly straightening in her seat and pointing ahead and to the right.

They had just crested a steep hill when the constant roadside canopy of hearty oaks and ancient elms abruptly dropped away. Below was a bowl-shaped valley of farmland divided along unseen property lines and belonging to the occupants of the four weathered farmhouses which were deposited near the outer edges of the valley. They were set back far enough to be invisible from the road that ran parallel with them, visible only from the current altitude. A gas station was visible about halfway through the clearing, its red, white and blue signage unmistakable.

It was another *Friendly's*.

Luke's stomach tightened as the sensation of déjà vu washed over him. He glanced into the rearview mirror to see if his feeling was contagious, but Virginia looked untroubled, her eyes busily scanning the countryside around her. She suddenly noticed that Luke was watching, and the suggestion of a smile returned to her lips. She reached out with her hand, fingers clenched together as if to offer something to Luke. He abandoned the mirror and glanced over his shoulder. She was definitely holding something.

"Whatcha got there, sweetheart?" he gently asked.

Paula glanced at Luke, then back at Virginia. She saw that the little girl was still offering her clenched fist, almost coyly. "What is it?" she asked redundantly before reaching back to cup the child's hands into her own. "It's okay, honey. Let me see."

Virginia looked warily from Paula to Luke, then decided it was alright to share with Paula since Luke was busy driving the car. Her fingers unfurled, and Paula gasped.

Although crumpled into a small, tight ball, the paper wadded in Virginia's hand was easily identifiable as currency.

———◇———

The minutes dragged like hours. Crystal perched on the blackened stump of a fallen tree, listening to the woods whisper around her. Droplets of water still cascaded down as the wind dislodged them from lofty branches, but the afternoon storm had finally passed. The sky, however, was still a malevolent gray, uniformly blotting out the sunlight and lending a chill to the air.

Her arm had begun to throb again, and she adjusted her position to try to find some relief. Two cars had passed on the main road since Luke had driven away, the volume of their engines steadily rising and cresting before slowly receding. Both times, Crystal's heart had nearly stopped with the certainty that the crazy woman in the Volvo was behind the wheel. Crystal couldn't see the road from where she sat, and instead of feeling safe, she felt even more vulnerable. When Luke returned, how would she know it was him and not her doppelganger? If her nerves were already shredding, she should be a basket case by the time Luke and the others arrived.

She wished there was another way. She didn't like the thought of Luke committing a crime, even if it seemed necessary. He had assured her that he would take careful notice of the gas station so that he could send reparations after they finally got themselves out of this mess. *If* they got themselves out of it.

Virginia had remained quiet while they planned, and Crystal was amazed that the four-year-old was capable of such remarkable restraint. She remembered some of the outings from *Benny and the Girl*, social events intended for cast members' entire families. Her experience with children of Virginia's age had indicated that they generally had short attention spans and were flurries of

369

hyperactivity, chirping little voices with an endless battery of questions and comments. Virginia wasn't anything like that. She didn't seem afraid of her new friends, although her eyes harbored the grief of losing her family. Although she hadn't spoken, Crystal assumed she was capable; she was certainly old enough. But the little girl seemed content in her position as crown jewel, tucked away safely in the back seat and guarded ferociously by her band of mismatched protectors.

Another car engine. This time, as the engine noise neared the turnoff where Luke had deposited Crystal, it began to noticeably slow down. Crystal could feel adrenaline resume its course through her veins, her heartbeat accelerating like a jackhammer. She strained to see through the thick branches of the trees around her, but she was too far from the trail to see anything.

This is ridiculous, she thought. *It's just Luke. He's back, and we're ready to go on.*

She forced herself to her feet and began trudging through the underbrush toward the trail. The sooner she reconnected with everyone, the sooner they could get underway, and she had gotten an idea of where they might find shelter.

"This is impossible," said Luke numbly, watching Paula as she flipped through the bills.

"There's three hundred dollars here," she said. She glanced into the back seat at Virginia, their proud, beaming benefactor.

"Where did it come from?" asked Luke.

"I guess she had it on her this whole time," said Paula.

"How many four-year-olds do you know that carry this kind of cash?"

"Who *cares* where it came from?" asked Paula. "Now you can buy gas and still have money left over for the things Crystal needs to disguise herself. Hell, we can afford to *eat!*"

Virginia giggled and began to hum softly.

They pulled into the parking lot of *Friendly's* and sidled up to the pumps. There were no other customers, no other cars. Apparently, whoever was working had been dropped off or arrived on foot. If it weren't for the florescent light spilling through the glass-fronted exterior, the station would have looked abandoned. New—but abandoned. Luke couldn't express how thankful he was that he wouldn't have to steal the gasoline. He had never stolen anything in his life, and he hadn't been looking forward to starting now. But he knew he would do whatever it took to protect Virginia, even if it meant stealing.

What if it meant killing?

370

The thought stopped Luke cold. It was almost a certainty if they were to be rid of the maniacs stalking the little girl. He absently got out of the car and went to its rear, snagging the nozzle of the pump as he passed.

"I need to use the restroom," said Paula, lifting herself from the passenger seat and stretching her legs. "Do you need anything?"

"Naw, I'm good," said Luke, deep in his own thoughts. Paula shrugged and jogged off toward the rectangular red, white, and blue building.

Luke unscrewed the cap from the tank and fed the nozzle into the opening. He squeezed the handle, and the pump began to wheeze as it slowly coaxed gasoline through its black rubber hose.

Why was all of this happening? He had asked himself the question a hundred times since Bert Parnell's truck had its unanticipated rocket launch to heaven. There had to be some *meaning*, some *reason* behind it. People did not behave like this for no apparent reason. And why did the killer look so much like Crystal? It *couldn't* be coincidental. If they could just discover the reason, maybe they could figure out a way to stop it—stop *them*.

Virginia peered through the side glass at Luke, her big brown eyes intently fixed on the mechanics of the refueling process. Luke grinned and hooked a finger in her direction, and she allowed the faintest trace of a smile to grace her lips before returning her attention to the pump and its animated display panel.

The pump's handle abruptly disengaged, and Luke returned the nozzle to its cradle. After recapping the tank, he reached into the car and extracted one of the twenties from the wad in the passenger seat. He crossed the parking lot with sure strides, wanting to get back to Crystal as soon as possible. He didn't like leaving her alone in the woods, but he didn't think it would be wise to make any unscheduled pit stops where she might be recognized. He briefly considered calling Morty King but decided it would be a call best placed later, after he had retrieved his missing passenger.

The twin glass doors parted with a *whoosh!* as Luke neared the entrance. The sounds of his heels on the tile reverberated in the empty store as he approached the counter. There wasn't even Muzak to break the odd silence.

"How-*dee!*"

The voice was high-pitched and sharp as a dart, coming from somewhere behind the counter. Luke craned his neck and peered over the cash register where he found an apple-cheeked, four-foot-tall woman with snow white hair and a wide smile that was undoubtedly stored overnight in a glass of effervescent cleanser.

"Hi," said Luke. "I had pump number three."

"That was some gulley washer, wudn't it?" she said, her expression coalescing into grim earnestness as she bobbed her head expectantly.

"Yes, ma'am," he agreed, smiling.

371

"God's way of giving His children a bath," she added, her head still bobbing up and down. "Fourteen fifty."

Luke placed the twenty on the counter and watched with amusement as she picked it up and examined it carefully against the overhead light.

"I can't stand these dang-fangled new bills," she groused. "They all look like Monopoly money to me."

Luke glanced around the store but saw no sign of Paula. "Are your restrooms outside?" he asked.

She paused from counting his change and looked up at him curiously. "I should hope not. This here's a brand-new building. They're in the far corner back there." She pointed a gnarled finger toward the rear of the store.

"Oh, I don't need them. I'm looking for—uh, my sister," he said. "She came in ahead of me. I would have thought she'd be done by now. Did you see her?"

Her curiosity deepened. "Honey, you're the first person to set foot through that door in the past couple of hours."

II

Suze's knuckles were practically cramping from the chokehold she had on the steering wheel. If she had to suffer through any more of Lisa and Chad's mindless banter, she was going to scream. She felt like their goddamned chauffer.

"I still can't believe you did it," said Chad admirably. "That was some quick thinking."

Lisa grinned impishly. "Thank you. I hoped you would be pleased."

Suze rolled her eyes. "Do you have any idea where we're going?" she asked with a touch of impatience.

"Just drive," said Lisa flatly. "I'll know when we're there."

Chad chuckled. "She sounds just like you used to, Suze. All vibes and sensations and bullshit."

Suze said nothing, keeping her steely gaze locked on the road ahead. The sensation of sinking hadn't abandoned her. She saw the bond growing between Lisa and Chad, and she felt completely cheated. Chad was *hers*, goddamn it! She bit her bottom lip to keep her tears from spilling. She wasn't going to go all *soft*. She wasn't that kind of woman. She was a fighter. She *took* the things she needed in life, and Chad was no exception. Why did the goddamn car have to break down in that little shithole, anyway? If it hadn't been for that, they would have never met Lisa Mitchell.

But somewhere inside, a small voice reminded her that everything happened for a reason. It was at the very crux of her most central belief system. It allowed her to catch glimpses of those stupid little teacups—*teacups* for God's sake!—but undeniably pointers towards things that had benefited Suze, sometimes simply, sometimes greatly. On many nights, they had kept her away from Joel McElroy. She felt satisfaction at what she had done to him, her only regret being that she couldn't prolong his agony. He had almost taken Paula *again!*

Paula.

Suze had always hoped that her younger sister would open her eyes to the cold, hard truths of the world. So many people waiting to take advantage of you, suck you dry, spit you out—she wanted to spare Paula the wasted frustration. Suze's way was so much simpler. Her wants and needs required no prioritization, she simply helped herself to it all, no matter who or what stood in the way. Admittedly, she had done a bit more killing in the last few days than was customary, but these weren't her first murders. It was the earlier ones—the vagrants, the runaways—that had made her realize her power. There was no fear in this hunter.

But Paula didn't think like Suze. She had a way of pulling into herself when things got ugly, a way in which Suze would have never allowed herself to be seen. She thought of it as weakness, a disgusting weakness. Holding out hope was futile; Paula would never be a warrior. In fact, she could easily be a victim.

But right now, Paula was with Crystal Bright, and the two mooning imbeciles in the car with Suze had no idea. Paula was Suze's trump card. Lisa may believe she could "sense" where the little girl was, but Suze could find out *exactly*. She wouldn't volunteer that information easily. It chilled her to realize that her trump card may be the only thing of value she had to offer. Three's a crowd, and the old idiom was beginning to feel like a personal threat.

And it had all started as a solo act. Suze had received her calling earlier than the others; she had, in fact, started the whole ball rolling. It was her dual visions of the little girl and Crystal Bright that had prompted her to go to California in the first place, taking a three-week leave of absence from her job with Children's Services. The little girl was a complete mystery, first appearing as a ghost then gaining substance as the months passed. At first, she had appeared faceless, a grotesque rendition of the human countenance that had jerked Suze into consciousness screaming on countless nights. And when the face finally appeared, with its nauseatingly sickly-sweet purity, she had been even more afraid. There was something in those soft round eyes that suggested the tide was turning, turning away from Suze and people like her. She may not have known who the little girl was, but she implicitly understood the underlying threat.

Crystal Bright was another story. She certainly had a high enough visibility. How difficult could it be to eliminate her? But Suze had been amazed at how well-protected the star was, a virtual army of bodyguards warding off her adolescent and not-so-adolescent legion of fans. Suze might have been able to knock her off at a public appearance, but the heavy security that surrounded Crystal would certainly ensure her capture. While Suze wasn't opposed to making the ultimate sacrifice for her cause, she just hadn't felt that her usefulness was completely spent. Not until she found the girl...

Suze wasn't known for methodical planning. She operated on a sharpened instinct that, to date, hadn't steered her wrong. It was such an integral part of her that it even punished her with crippling headaches when she hadn't heeded its advice. It was almost parental. For the first time, she had to examine what she knew, formulate an actual *plan*. She sensed that Crystal Bright could lead her to the little girl, even if she herself had no idea who the child was. But first, Crystal had to be separated from her iconic status.

The contest had been a godsend.

TV Guide and Pepsi-Cola had sponsored a mail-in contest where the grand prize was a walk-on part on *Benny and the Girl*. Paula had been so excited about it when she had spoken with her on the telephone. She often daydreamed of escaping Morgan and her abusive stepfather, Joel McElroy, and she had clearly seen this as her opportunity. Suze hadn't considered using her sister at that point. She had merely taken notice of the opportunity to get close to Crystal Bright. Suze discovered that the contest was being overseen by Talbot Information Systems, an independent group that specialized in the impartial selection process that such contests required.

She had seen teacups all over the fucking place the day she had visited Talbot's main office in downtown L.A. They had led her straight to the door of Howard Porter, a ghastly mistake of a man who worked in an enormous computer room that virtually pulsed with electricity. His build resembled a melting ice cream cone, and his head was the cherry on top, bald and perpetually red. His tiny eyes were hidden behind thick-lensed glasses framed in greasy black plastic. His lips were pulsing nightcrawlers, his breath a stagnant cesspool, his tongue a wedge of raw liver—but his mind was a thing of wonder. His understanding of Talbot's computer systems was complete. He could accomplish the thing that Suze needed done.

It hadn't taken much to convince him. He was an honest man, his life completely empty since the passing of his mother nearly three years before. He had always given himself completely to his work, but there was one thing he couldn't get from a computer, no matter how hard he tried. At forty-two, Howard Porter was still a virgin.

Sleeping with him had redefined repugnant. After he had drifted off to sleep, she had taken the world's hottest shower, scrubbing his layers of grease off of her. He had ejaculated prematurely, leaving his sickly seed to dry on her hip. She scrubbed at the area with a washcloth until her flesh was bright pink.

But it was worth it.

She had slowly suggested her plan to manipulate the contest over a period of overnight encounters, punctuating each suggestion by another invitation to her bed. Before long, Howard was hypnotized. He would have done any single thing that Suze had asked of him, the promise of intercourse as powerful a motivator as he'd ever experienced.

Suze had initially considered herself for the role Paula eventually played. She wanted someone to befriend the star, learn her secrets. Maybe one of them included the little girl. But then Howard had mentioned the star's volatile temperament, and she knew that she wasn't right for the part. The first time Crystal Bright raised her voice to Suze would also surely be the last. Suze wasn't known for her patience, either.

So, Paula had become the chosen one. Suze had known that there would be limitations to this arrangement. She certainly couldn't expect Paula to do much more than fawn over her idol, but that might still provide the insight Suze needed. She coaxed Howard into manipulating the outcome of the contest, and Paula had left for California, her bags already packed. She hadn't, of course, known that Suze was already there.

It was after Paula's tearful phone call describing Crystal's atrocious behavior on the set that Suze had realized that her plan was only part of a much greater scheme. There were other forces working to wrench Crystal out of her comfortable existence. Suze could sense the tautness of that fag, Marshall Dawson's nerves. As the producer of *Benny and the Girl*, he bore the weight of responsibility for the show's continued success, and Crystal Bright was rapidly becoming unmanageable.

It was the teacups again that had led her to Marshall Dawson's mother. Vida Leon was a washed-up has-been with a substantial taste for alcohol and an even more insatiable appetite for attention. Her pathetic need for the spotlight had made it so easy for Suze to gain entrance into the old woman's apartment. Killing her had been an act of mercy.

At the time, she hadn't clearly understood the impact of her actions. She hadn't killed in a while, and the physical act was certainly gratifying, but she failed to see the significance. Crystal Bright was already falling out of favor with the show, as those crazed photos of her chasing Marshall Dawson's SUV on the freeway had attested. She had walked off the set and refused to return, a last-ditch tactic of the artistically high-strung.

But what the murder of Vida Leon had done was create a permanent fault line between Crystal and Marshall. One of the last memories he would ever carry of his mother included Crystal's full-fledged tantrum after he had taken her to meet Vida. She was now a constant reminder of his mother who had been so cruelly murdered. Crystal's career was history.

"Slow down," said Lisa, breaking Suze's reflection. *"Slow down."*

"What?" asked Suze. She looked around but saw nothing more notable than a squirrel scampering through the underbrush that lined the sides of the two-lane highway. Nevertheless, she eased her foot off the gas and allowed the Volvo to slow.

375

"You getting something, babe?" asked Chad, leaning forward from the back seat and resting his chin on the back of Lisa's seat.

"*Shhh!*" urged Lisa, rolling her window down. She took a deep lungful of the rain-swept country air. "Can't you smell it?"

Suze looked at her crossly. This was a new one. Did Lisa Mitchell track her prey like a goddamn dog? She almost chuckled at the thought.

"I don't smell anything," said Chad after inhaling deeply. "How about you, Suze?"

Suze snorted. "I smell that scab's armpits."

"Pull over," said Lisa. "Shut the car off. There's something here."

"You think they're holed up in the woods?" asked Chad. "Why would—"

"*Shhh!*" Lisa stuck her head back through the open window and took another deep breath. When she turned back, her eyes were dancing, and a knowing smile played at her lips.

"They're here?" repeated Chad.

Lisa slowly nodded. She could smell the same sweet perfume that had clung to Crystal Bright in the farmhouse. Somehow, it overpowered the aromas nature had to offer and assaulted Lisa's nostrils. She would know it anywhere.

"Well, let's get them, let's—"

"Slow down, my boy," said Lisa, unbuckling her seatbelt. "You wait here. Suze and I will go out into the woods and circle around. We'll herd them your way."

"But I should go with you—"

"Hey," said Lisa, smiling sweetly as she placed her palm on Chad's cheek. "You're not Superman. Your shoulder is still healing. You'd make too much noise clomping through the woods, and you'd be at a disadvantage if they spotted you first. Let me and Suze do the dirty work." She shot a glance at Suze. "Do you think you can handle it?"

"I sure the hell won't let them get away," said Suze bitterly. She hated the way Lisa was taking control of everything. What right did she have? She had royally fucked things up back at the farmhouse. Why was Chad so ready to trust her? *Why?*

She unfastened her seatbelt and got out of the car. Lisa had already straightened and stretched. Wordlessly, she pointed to her right and nodded at Suze, then darted off to the left, slipping stealthily into the woods. Suze sighed, then followed Lisa's direction.

This is ridiculous, she thought. *All we're doing is allowing them to gain distance.*

But she continued to move quietly through the thick underbrush, working her way through thorny branches and tangled briar, her feet consistently finding soft earth instead of brittle twigs. She slid effortlessly, keeping her eyes peeled for any kind of movement in the woods. She hadn't bothered to take a weapon, and for a moment, she regretted it. But there were only two of them, after all. Paula didn't pose any threat to her, and according to Lisa, Crystal Bright was injured. That just left the man Lisa had mentioned. Who was *he?* What business was this of his?

As much as Suze would have enjoyed seeing Lisa be wrong about this, she was more afraid that Lisa was right. If she had actually sensed the presence of these people, Chad would no longer have any use for her. Even her trump card wouldn't make a damn bit of difference. The only way she could redeem herself was to find them first. There was no need to herd them like cattle. Suze would dispense with them herself—something Lisa hadn't been able to do with a *gun*. Chad would see the truth. He would remember why Suze had been so appealing in the first place.

And that's when she saw it. A tiny flicker of movement, branches rustling, twigs snapping. Suze dropped to the ground instinctively, her eyes wide and focused on the area of woods that had shifted before her eyes. The branches rustled again, and suddenly Lisa emerged through the bushes, looking a little disoriented as she favored her splinted arm.

Splinted arm?

This wasn't Lisa Mitchell—it was Crystal Bright! But where were the others? Why had the woods fallen silent behind her? Why was there no more *rustling? Where were the others?*

Crystal emerged from the brush and continued shuffling down the narrow path toward the road, completely unaware that she was walking directly toward Suze. She appeared skittish, but why wouldn't she be? If the scene at the farmhouse had played out as Lisa had suggested, Crystal had taken a bit of a beating. The makeshift apparatus on Crystal's arms silently verified Lisa's tale. Suze waited, crouched down and ready to spring, waiting for the others, the others, *where were the others?* Only a few more steps, and Crystal would be right in front of her...

Suze burst from her cover of brambles like a whole flock of birds taking flight. Crystal didn't even have time to utter a startled shriek before being knocked to the ground, her crippled arm pinned beneath her.

"You goddamn *BITCH!*" hissed Suze, her own arms pinwheeling, landing blows as quickly and as mindlessly as possible. Crystal tried to pull her knees up to protect her midsection, but not before Suze landed a solid kick to the abdomen which pushed all of Crystal's remaining air out in a loud *whoosh!* Suze grabbed Crystal's shirt collar and pulled her into a sitting position.

"Where are they?" demanded Suze, her face inches from Crystal's, her eyes blazing with murderous intensity.

"Th-they're gone," said Crystal, spitting a frothy glob of bloody saliva.

"Gone? Gone where?" Suze emphasized her question by kicking Crystal in her wounded arm.

Crystal saw stars just before the white-hot pain coursed through her nerve endings, and for a moment she thought she might pass out. She clung desperately to her consciousness, knowing that to lose it would also mean losing her life.

"Virginia's safe," Crystal managed. "You can't get to her now."

Suze's laughter was throaty poison. "I don't believe it."

"Look around," invited Crystal. "You won't find her here." As Suze processed the information, Crystal wondered how many of them there were. This certainly wasn't the same woman from the farmhouse. What if there was an entire dark army whose sole purpose was to find and destroy Virginia Parnell? A murderous cult with numbers unimaginable—

"Then you'll take us to them," said Suze, nodding her head slowly.

"I d-don't know where they went," said Crystal, hating the trembling sound of her own voice. Her fear was apparent, and the creature standing before her fed from it.

Suze knelt in again, taking the collar of Crystal's shirt back into clenched fists. "I'm about through fucking around with you," she said. "Either you tell me what I want to know, or I'll split you open right here, right now."

Crystal was no match for this woman. Her earlier struggles at the farmhouse had weakened her, and the pummeling she had just received had drained her of the last of her strength. She was defenseless, staring helplessly at the madwoman who towered above her. She could tell from the determination in the woman's eyes that there was no escaping this. Even if she offered Virginia up on a silver platter, the woman wouldn't be satisfied until she had finished Crystal off as well. The last few weeks had been a spiraling sort of madness. Was this where the ride ended?

"TELL ME!" Suze raged, thrusting Crystal's head against the ground hard enough to knock her teeth together and to split her field of vision into twin blurry regions that refused to coalesce.

And it was in this altered state of perception that Crystal saw something moving behind the woman. It was part shadow, part wind—but definitely a thing of substance.

She took a deep breath and bellowed as loudly as possible, *"LUKE! GET OUT OF HERE! THEY'RE HERE!"*

Even through her distorted vision, she could see the rage that darkened the woman's features. Her angry eyes had multiplied, and all sixteen of them glared with undisguised hatred at Crystal's swimming head. She saw the woman's arms—two, four, eight?—reaching out for her, a network of hands determined to settle around her throat. Crystal closed her eyes tightly and waited for the inevitable.

But there was nothing. No claw-like fingers around her throat, no kicks nor punches landed like rain. But there was a *scuffling...*

Crystal opened her eyes and was startled to find that the woman had been attacked from behind, a lean arm wrapped around her neck and pulling her away from Crystal. Crystal instinctively scooted backward, away from the ensuing fray. Her eyes had begun to clear, and her heart nearly stopped when they brought the scene before her into focus.

The person who held her attacker at bay was none other than her doppelganger from the farmhouse. She had a perverted smile on her face, her eyes drifting heavenward as she continued to apply subtle pressure to the other's woman's neck.

POP!

The dark-haired woman slid to the forest floor, her head lolling without resistance on her neck. Her maniacal eyes had lost their fire and now stared vacantly at the pearl gray of the afternoon sky.

Crystal had never been more terrified. As she again found herself face-to-face with this other version of herself, she felt icy fingers tracing simultaneous paths along her spine. Her skin stood up in rows of pea-sized gooseflesh, and she nearly lost control of her straining bladder.

The replica regarded her as a cat might a mouse, and just as Crystal was certain that she was going to spring forth to finish the job that the dark-haired woman had begun, she winked and disappeared into the underbrush.

III

"What is it?"

Jessica scrambled to get a better look while Leonard pulled away, covering his mouth and growing paler still.

Scant light managed to find its way through the small opening in the building's foundation, dimly illuminating a small, square room. Its years of service had long since expired, but the floor and the walls were permanently stained by the soot from the coal. It was like looking inside a black box. The figure huddled in the corner stood out like a sore thumb, her white uniform nearly gleaming against the filthy backdrop.

"Please help me."

The words were little more than a croak, spoken from the woman's downturned face. Her voice was raspy and raw, painful to hear.

"It's alright," said Jessica soothingly. "We'll get you out of there. Hang on." She turned to Leonard, who was distractedly pacing the backyard, his pallor now completely gray. "Is this the nurse?" she asked.

He nodded jerkily. "Uh-huh. Helen Martin."

Jessica peered back inside the chute and noticed the shackles on Helen's wrists. "She's tied up like an animal."

She straightened and made a beeline for the backdoor of the Mitchell house. She didn't even hesitate before kicking it in. It snapped as if it were made of balsa, its six panes of glass disintegrating as they slammed into the old workhouse refrigerator that squatted behind it.

Jessica stepped across the threshold, and her legs turned to jelly. She wobbled to the small kitchen table and leaned against one of the metal chairs for support. Her head was spinning, her stomach clenching, her eyes burning—

"Are you alright?"

She focused on Leonard standing in the doorway, leaning against the frame for support. His coloration was almost green now. She nodded and tried to concentrate on her breathing and find her normal rhythm. The air inside the house seemed as thick as syrup, running slowly down her trachea to collect at the bottom of her lungs. The ominous feeling that had teased her fears before now assaulted her from all directions. The Mitchell house was a very bad place, indeed.

Jessica nodded slowly after a delay that had begun to alarm Leonard. "Let's get her out of the basement."

She crossed the kitchen on unsteady feet and opened the door nearest her, revealing a five-shelf pantry loaded with canned goods and boxed groceries. There was enough food on those shelves for a full year's worth of dinners. She tried the next door and couldn't suppress the gasp that escaped her lips as the door swung open. She staggered backward and steadied herself against the wall.

"What is it?" asked Leonard, hurrying to her side. He put a calloused hand on her shoulder to steady her as she trembled violently. "Is there someone else down there?" he whispered.

"I-I-I—" stammered Jessica, closing her eyes and willing the panic to subside. "No. I'm just not feeling well. I don't know if I can manage the stairs."

Leonard guided her over to the kitchen table and pulled one of the metal chairs back. "Here. You sit down and rest. I'll get Mrs. Martin."

She didn't offer any resistance but simply dropped into the seat, leaning forward and cupping her forehead in her hands. "Thank you," she said. "Please hurry."

He nodded and returned to the top of the stairwell, peering down anxiously before beginning his descent. A single, bare bulb was suspended in the middle of the dank cellar, casting murky shadows everywhere beyond its scope. As he reached the cellar floor, he heard Helen in the coal bin, thumping her arms frantically against the door.

"Please don't go away!" she pleaded in her broken, jagged voice. *"Please!"*

He cleared his throat. "It's okay, Mrs. Martin. You're safe now."

He slid the bolt free from its hasp, and the door flew outward as Helen Martin pushed through. She tried to throw her arms around Leonard, but her wrists were still linked together by a pair of shiny silver handcuffs. Her face was swollen and wet with tears, her unabated sobbing like that of a wounded animal.

"Oh, thank God, thank *God!*" she said. "We have to get out of here. We have to—"

Her eyes came into focus upon Leonard's face, and she abruptly pulled away, her words drying up completely. Leonard didn't need for her to say anything; he had seen the expression before. Helen still held him responsible for the death of her daughter, and not even the sight of him rescuing her was enough to put it aside.

"P-please, Mrs. Martin," said Leonard. "We have to get out of here before they come back. I don't know when they'll be back."

Helen shook her head vehemently. "I'm not going anywhere with you."

———◆———

Jessica kept her head cupped in her hands as she sat at the table, sensations washing over her that she had forgotten so long ago. It was so painful to consider, and yet she seemed to have no voice in the matter. Those had been such dark times—

At the time, she didn't think they would ever pass. So many people telling her she was crazy, a *monster*. And she had been completely baffled by their response. How could they not have understood? How could they have overlooked the evil just below the skin, incubating into something more powerful with each passing day?

A powerful shudder passed over her as she hunched over the cheap Formica table, tears streaming down her cheeks.

———◆———

"Please, Mrs. Martin," implored Leonard. "I know you hate me for all that happened, but *please*. You've got to come with me now."

"Where's Lisa?" she asked, and her need to know possessed her. She suddenly realized that freedom was at the top of the cellar stairs, and she hurried toward them, her legs working like pistons as the aged wood creaked beneath her weight. Her shackled arms swung uselessly in front of her. *"LISA?"*

Leonard watched her pass in a daze. The Mitchell girl must have cast a spell on Helen, too. There was no other explanation. Despite her hatred for him, he knew that she was a good woman, certainly not one to take allegiance with a soul as stained as Lisa Mitchell's. But the panicked urgency with which she had thundered from the basement had been almost supernatural in its intensity. It was raw maternal energy.

Oh, God, he thought, hurrying up the stairs. *Don't let her hurt Jessica.*

They stared at each other, Jessica with her wet face and haunted eyes, peering up from where she sat at the table and Helen with her flushed cheeks and sputtering breath, standing frozen in the doorway at the head of the stairs, her fingers clenching and unclenching.

Helen alternated between relief and distrust, remembering how sweet this woman's face had looked when it had appeared in the opening which had once been the coal chute. The notion of a guardian angel had flitted through Helen's mind as she had realized she might actually survive this experience. But the first face she had seen upon rescue had been that of Leonard Barnes. *Leonard Barnes.* It was as if the Lord were testing her endurance, stretching her to the limits of what she could handle.

If it hadn't been for Leonard Barnes, Evie would still be alive. Grandchildren. There would be grandchildren!

The thought led back to Lisa Mitchell. The terrified look on her face as the woman called Suze had held the gun to her head. Lisa, who had already been through so much rapid change after the passing of her Nanna Grace. She hoped that the stringy fellow who had gotten shot hadn't touched her—hadn't raped her. But she had seen the madness in his eyes, had taken a long, hard look when she had been forced face-to-face with him, working on the nasty pulp of flesh that had been rendered by the bullet, fired by that policeman. He had been overwhelmed by the sheer number of them, beaten down before Helen had even stumbled into the room. She hoped that Chad's wound became infected. She hoped that his whole arm filled with gangrene.

And still she stared at the auburn-haired woman with the clear, green eyes, eyes that were swollen from crying, her elbows propped against the table and her hands knotted into fists. Was she one of them? Helen didn't think so.

"Who are you?" she asked, and Jessica made an attempt to dry her eyes.

"My name is Jessica Lybrook," she said, forcing composure back into her voice. "I really think we should get out of here."

And when Helen saw the genuine terror that tugged at Jessica's nervous movements, the way her eyes darted around the empty kitchen as if she were expecting a sudden ambush from the dark recesses of the house, she knew that Jessica could be trusted. What she didn't understand is why Leonard Barnes was involved. Hadn't he already caused enough damage?

But she had to trust them. She had no choice. Leonard was suddenly behind her, emerging from the stairwell, and she involuntarily started. It didn't go unnoticed by Leonard, and he demurred like someone deserving of a blow. Then, they were moving, out of the dingy kitchen with its cracked yellow surfaces and septic air, out of the house where Helen had thought she would die, out into the cool afternoon air, still clean in the aftermath of a thunderstorm. They moved as a unit, and Helen had the ridiculous notion that they were in a war movie, two men rescuing a third, scurrying across the pavement while everything exploded around them.

But today there were no explosions, just the revival of robins, peeking out from where they had taken cover during the storm to lend an inquisitive peep to the ambiance. They continued urgently to a large Jeep that was parked alongside the curb. Helen noted the license plate as she passed the front end on her way to the vehicle's back door. She wondered briefly if it was stolen.

And then she was inside the vehicle, seated in the spacious rear seat, her tired body almost breathing an audible sigh of relief as the cushions settled around her.

Jessica drove silently, her concentration locked on the road ahead. The dark feeling that had descended upon her in the kitchen of the Mitchell house had abated, but it still niggled at the corners of her periphery. It was amazing how successfully she had blocked it out, forgotten the way it could make her feel. The aftermath was much like coming out of an epileptic seizure; her limbs were shaky, her bowels were liquid, and her head seemed to float just a few inches above her shoulders. She cranked the temperature knob up and turned the fan on high. She was just so damned *cold*.

Helen Martin was a surprise. Jessica had expected Helen to be a quivering mess, perhaps unmanageable in her desperate need to reacquire freedom. Instead, she had been fully compliant, wordlessly getting into the Jeep and falling into her own silent introspection. Jessica was relieved. She didn't want to explain what had happened to her in the kitchen of the Mitchell house, and she certainly didn't want to talk about what had happened back then. She didn't even know if she remembered it all. She didn't think she wanted to.

Leonard sat frozen in the passenger seat. He would have been more comfortable in the rear, where he could remain silent and unnoticed, but Helen hadn't given him the opportunity. She had settled into the back seat and pulled the door shut behind her, refusing to even look at him as he straggled behind.

She would have found it impossible to understand the weight of guilt that he had carried with him since the night Evie Martin had died. In those days and in these parts, bartenders didn't carry the burden of responsibility for seeing their patrons safely home after a night of hard drinking. For Clinton McDermott, every night was a night of hard drinking. In retrospect, the accident with Evie or someone equally innocent had been inevitable. Leonard wasn't even the regular bartender, for God's sake, and it had to be upon one of those infrequent occasions that McDermott chose to drink his last drink. A drink poured from the trembling fingers of Leonard Barnes.

Top me off, cornhead!

Evie Martin's laughter, floating high above the noise of the bar crowd, rising and falling like gentle music.

Of course, Helen hated him. He hated himself. If he could take Evie Martin's place in the cold, hard ground, he wouldn't even hesitate. He was surprised Helen had gotten into the same vehicle with him. Her aversion to Leonard was always so obvious.

He wondered what the Mitchell girl had done to Helen. He worried what Helen might do for the Mitchell girl in return.

"We have to find her," Helen said finally, her voice still raspy and arid. "They'll kill her. I know they will."

Jessica glanced in the rearview mirror at the woman in her back seat. "Kill who?" she asked. "Who are they trying to kill?"

"Why, Lisa, of course," she said, and Leonard couldn't help but face her then, his disbelief showing in the whites of his eyes.

"What's she *done* to you, Mrs. Martin?" he gasped, his hand flying to his mouth. "How can you not see that the girl is—is—*wicked*, she—"

Helen's eyes locked onto his. "Lisa Mitchell—wicked? *Ridiculous!* You didn't see the way those others stormed in, taking control of her house like we were under siege in some third-world country! They threatened her life! Why would you say a thing like that, Leonard Barnes, unless—unless—" Her eyes were suddenly veiled, and the look she gave Leonard chilled his blood. "You thought my Evie was wicked, too, didn't you, Mr. Barnes? You believe she deserved what happened to her, don't you?"

Leonard gasped. "Oh, no! I certainly do *not!*" he insisted. "Your little Evie was just the sweetest little girl—"

"Don't mention her name," screamed Helen, and Leonard's voice dried up instantly. "You have no right to say her name, Mr. Barnes. Not after what you did."

Jessica was bewildered by the conversation. These two obviously shared a history, but it didn't seem appropriate to ask about it. The tension in the car was palpable, growing thicker with each passing second. She felt an enormous sense of relief when Leonard lowered his eyes, then his head and turned back in his seat to face the windshield. He looked utterly defeated. What could have possibly happened between them? Who was Evie?

"Where are we going?" asked Helen, snapping Jessica back to attention.

Jessica pondered the question. "I think we have to find them," she said.

"Shouldn't we go to the police?"

Again, Jessica pondered. She thought about Officer Charles and his stubborn insistence that David McElroy was responsible for the slaughter back at his brother's place. She didn't know how he would receive a tale like this, full of mysterious people with mysterious motives and mysterious plans. All she wanted was to know that David was *safe*. She didn't think the local police could provide her with that relief.

"I am the police," she said, surprising herself with the steadiness of her voice. She reached inside her open handbag and produced her wallet, flashing her Jay County Sheriff's Department ID. It looked official enough, and Jessica doubted the frumpy nurse would take the time to scrutinize it, thus discovering that Jessica was only a dispatcher.

"The police?" repeated Helen, surprised. "Were you partners with that other one?"

Jessica's head suddenly felt empty, Helen's words echoing off the shiny smooth inner walls. *Were you partners with that—WERE you partners—WERE—WERE—WERE*

"Were?" she repeated weakly. "You saw another officer inside the Mitchell house?"

Helen watched as Jessica's color faded. She leaned forward, clutching her bound wrists between her knees. "Yes, dear," she said solemnly. "I'm so sorry to have to tell you—"

"Oh, *no-o-o*—" wailed Jessica, jerking the steering wheel to the right and braking hard. The Jeep skidded to a halt near the guardrail, and an angry motorist blared his horn as he whipped around them, displaying his proudest, tallest digit in protest.

Leonard reached down and shifted the vehicle into park before Jessica's foot slipped away from the brake pedal. She was wracked with sobs, doubled over the steering wheel.

"They killed him for trying to stop them," said Helen, her voice still soothing and gentle. "Your partner was a very brave man—but they completely outnumbered him. There was nothing more he could have done. He did manage to shoot one of them, but unfortunately, he only hit the boy's shoulder." Helen was surprised at how easily she added that last bit. She was a woman committed to the continuing care of others, not one likely to wish pain and suffering and death upon someone. But these were not ordinary people. They were savage animals, predators stalking an unknown prey, determined to catch it regardless of who might stand in their way. They had to be stopped. They had to be stopped before they hurt Lisa.

After what seemed an eternity, Jessica pulled herself back together and straightened in her seat. Her expression had changed—hardened. Helen's words had only been a confirmation of what she had already known. As she sat alone in that musty kitchen, there had been no doubt in her mind that David had met his demise inside the Mitchell house. She knew it as surely as she knew her own name. Now, she turned the raw pain into anger and allowed it to replenish her diminished reserves. She suddenly realized that this must have been how David felt when he had heard about Loretta.

"So, what do we know about them?" Jessica asked, the steadiness back in her voice.

"There are two of them," said Helen, shifting awkwardly with her bound wrists to reposition herself.

Jessica reached into her pocket and retrieved a small ring of keys and handed them to Leonard with a key extended. "If those are David's handcuffs, that key should work," she said.

Helen pulled back at first when Leonard reached over the seat, but then she offered up her arms, the desire to be free overwhelming her disdain for him. The cuff snapped open, and soon she was rubbing the circulation back into her aching wrists.

"There's a dark-haired girl they called Suze," Helen continued. "I would guess she might be the leader. She was the one with the gun. She was the one who ordered everyone around. My Lord, you should have seen the way she looked at Lisa. She wanted to kill her. I *know* she wanted to kill her."

"What about the other one?" asked Jessica. She had already noted the discrepancy in Helen's perception of Lisa to Leonard's. She decided to stay neutral on the topic so that she might make up her own mind.

"The other one was a man—well, really not much more than a boy. He had gotten shot by your partner before I walked in, so I didn't see much of him. They made me dress his wounds." She shivered at the memory. "He was called Chad."

Jessica only had time for the briefest of gasps before her eyes fluttered, and she abruptly passed out.

CHAPTER TWENTY

I

Luke was dumbfounded. His glance wavered between the diminutive elderly woman with the small button eyes who stood behind the counter—her name tag read, 'Freida'—and the red neon sign proclaiming in cursive swirl, 'Restrooms.'

"I don't understand," he finally said. "Paula headed this way while I was pumping gas. She said she had to use the bathroom."

"Well, I surely don't know where she went, other than that she didn't come in here. Maybe she's usin' the phones around the side of the building."

Luke furrowed his brow. "She wouldn't have done that," he said, more to himself than to Freida.

She smiled nonetheless as she counted his change back to him. "Will that be all?"

Luke turned around in a daze, his eyes drinking in the interior of the convenience mart. All the new fixtures reeked of fresh paint, completely stocked with a varied selection of items that might appeal to the traveling consumer. But all of the aisles were empty, and Luke felt panic welling in his chest. He turned back to the clerk, whose cheery smile had diminished somewhat at his obvious distress.

"Would you mind checking?"

"Pardon me?" Freida's grandmotherly smile disappeared completely. The urgency of Luke's tone, the look in his eyes—it was beginning to unsettle her.

"In the bathroom," said Luke, his voice sharper than intended. He knew he was losing Freida, but he couldn't help it. People didn't just *disappear!*

Freida shook her head solemnly. "I'm sorry, mister. I'd like to help ya, but I can't leave my register." Her eyes darted nervously to the cashbox before returning to Luke's face.

"Fine," said Luke. "You said you haven't had a customer in hours, so it should be empty, right? *I'll* go see if she's in there."

"Now wait a minute, you can't—" began Freida, but Luke had already walked away, his long legs carrying him quickly past the gaily-colored rows of candy and the assorted sizes of foil-wrapped potato chips. He threw the door of the ladies' room back on its hinges and stepped inside as the last of Freida's words filtered through to him. "—callin' the *police!*"

"Hello?" he called out loudly.

The two syllables reverberated and faded away unanswered within the small cubicle with its twin stalls and wash basins. Luke was shocked at the sight of himself in the spotless mirror that was suspended above the sinks. He looked at least ten years older than he had the last time he had taken notice.

"Paula?"

Nothing.

He squatted low to the floor and peered underneath the stall dividers, but there was no sign of Paula's blue-jeaned legs. He pushed each of the stall doors back to make sure—make sure of what? That she wasn't levitating while taking a shit?

Where in the hell had Paula gone?

Crystal sat in stunned disbelief as her lungs finally began to return to a normal rate of respiration. Her look-alike had blended back into the woods, her diminishing footfalls against dry twigs now nothing more than a memory. In fact, if Crystal closed her eyes, she could almost believe that this entire ridiculous affair was just a nightmare; she wasn't in the middle of some godforsaken patch of woods in southern Ohio waiting for a band of maniacal killers to gut her like a fish. She was in Hollywood, asleep in her king-sized bed, tossing and turning restlessly as the nightmare progressed. Soon her alarm clock would sound, signaling four-thirty in the morning—time to head to the set.

But the dead woman who lay in a disheveled heap near Crystal's feet silently begged to disagree. Her face was frozen in a state of perpetual shock, her once wild eyes now strangely flat. Almost reptilian. A trickle of blood trailed away from the corner of her mouth, leaking slowly onto the bed of grass upon which her head rested. If this was a nightmare, it was a waking one.

Crystal struggled to her feet and surveyed the woods around her. Every nerve ending in her body tingled. For a brief moment, she was oblivious to the constant throb her arm had become. Her heightened senses were drunk on the woods, amplifying and distorting nature's soundtrack so that every sound took on a sinister undertone. She had the delirious urge to bolt, tossing caution completely to the wind as she bulldozed her way through the woods toward the highway.

Or deeper into the woods.

Oh, God, she thought. *Oh God, Oh God, Oh God—*

She looked up at the sky, trying to get some sense of direction from the position of the sun, but the gray afternoon effectively blotted it out entirely.

Crystal hugged herself tightly and turned in slow circles, scanning the sky, searching for a break in the cloud cover that might allow her to see, any break at *all—*

Panic was rapidly descending. In every sound Crystal heard them, and they were everywhere all at once. She clamped her hands to her ears, ignoring the shriek of pain from her arm and fought the desperate urge to scream.

◦———◦———◦

Alone in the car at last, little Virginia Parnell stretched her back and cracked her elbows, allowing a little of her unaffected façade to slip away. She tried to blot out the sounds from the farmhouse—the sharp, startled cry as her mother had been shot to death in her own kitchen, the two exclamation points that had followed shortly afterward, marking the ends of her sisters' lives—but they returned at irregular intervals, trying to claw through the iron mask that Virginia was determined to wear. At least in front of the others.

They were good people, and she sensed it intrinsically. She was surprised they hadn't demanded more of her, wanting to know exactly what had happened and how. They hadn't asked, and she hadn't offered. In fact, she hadn't uttered a single word. It wasn't that she couldn't speak; she had a remarkable vocabulary for a child of her age. It was just that she feared what would happen if she began to communicate. Luke, Crystal, and Paula would inevitably start asking questions, and she just couldn't face them right now.

Virginia was also glad they hadn't dropped her off as soon as they were clear of the murder scene. It would have been the easy way out for them, and Virginia appreciated it with as much conviction as a seasoned four-year-old could have. For some reason, she felt safer with them than she had in her own home for the past several days.

Ever since Daddy went to heaven.

Her eyes misted over, and she pressed her small fists against them to try and keep her tears in check. She didn't want Luke to find her crying in the back seat like some stupid baby. He would take the time to try and comfort her—he was simply that sort of man—but they really couldn't afford to be delayed. Crystal needed them. She could feel it.

She gave a startled cry as the passenger door was suddenly pulled open.

◦———◦———◦

"I'm not kiddin' you, mister, you get out of the ladies'!" shouted Freida. She carried a cleaning rag in one of her little biscuit fists and flapped it wildly as she ventured cautiously out from behind the counter. "We don't need your kind in here! Now *SHOO!*"

389

As Luke straightened, he saw the piece of paper folded and lying flat against the floor in the center of the first stall. He recognized it as a piece of letterhead from the motel where he, Crystal, and Paula had stayed in Morgan. He bent down and snagged it between his fingers, straightening to examine it curiously. Its creases were clumsy, and Luke could almost picture Paula's trembling fingers as she pressed them into place. He flipped the note open.

Crystal/Luke,

I'm so sorry to bail on you like this. I hope you understand. It's just too much. I got friends I can go to, so don't you worry about me. And you can keep the car, too. You need it worse than I do. Maybe I'll see you guys again someday.

Paula

Luke glanced around the empty facilities again, this time more thoroughly. He was puzzled, but not for the reasons he might have originally expected. The note really wasn't much of a surprise. He wouldn't have stopped Paula if she had flat out *told* them she planned to leave. He didn't think Crystal would have, either. At sixteen, Paula was little more than a child herself. She had been steadily unraveling ever since Luke had joined the team; she couldn't be expected to handle the kind of pressure they had been put under. Virginia Parnell didn't have a choice in the matter, but Paula Haversham did, and Luke could hardly blame her for exercising her options.

What puzzled Luke was how Paula had managed to get into the bathroom and out again without ever being noticed. Yes, Freida was shorter than the counter, but she wasn't deaf. The automatic door made a definitive *whoosh!* whenever it swept open, and if Luke wasn't mistaken, there had even been a soft, electronic chime that chirped as he crossed the threshold. The bathroom windows were mounted high off the ground, and there was no sign that they had been disturbed anytime recently.

It reminded Luke of his flight through the cornfield—only just a few nights ago and yet an eternity away—when he had suddenly found himself beyond the Indiana state line and several miles deep into Ohio. He had been running, but he wasn't the goddamned Flash! He didn't even know if he could cover that kind of distance as quickly in a *car.* He dismissed it at the time because there had been more pressing things to consider. But now, the memory raced back at him with a vengeance, and he found himself standing in the middle of the ladies' room, silently mulling questions to which he had no answers.

"That's it!" cried Freida. She had barely ventured out into the store at all, and now she turned and hurried behind the counter. "I'm callin' the sheriff. Don't say you ain't been warned." She snatched up the receiver of the telephone that rested beside the cash register and jabbed at the "0," her mouth set in a thin, determined line.

Virginia.

Luke suddenly realized how long it had been since he had left Virginia alone out in the car. When he had gone into *Friendly's*, he had known that he could keep an eye on her through the plate glass as he paid for his fuel. He had expected Paula to be waiting inside the building, and when she wasn't, he had almost completely forgotten about the girl who was waiting outside.

Alone.

His limbs were suddenly filled with anxious energy, trying to pull him into motion before his brain and equilibrium could agree upon a plan. He burst out of the bathroom in a frenzy, and Freida dropped the phone, her face a snapshot of surprise and fear. If Luke could have seen himself coming, the wild look in his eyes, the way his unkempt hair danced around his head with each sure movement, he would have realized that Friendly's Freida thought she was about to be murdered where she stood in her sensible brown Dr. Scholl's.

But Luke didn't see anything at all. His vision had tunneled, and at the far end was the gleaming rectangle of gray light which represented the automatic door at the front of the building. He was running, but it felt like his feet were mired in thick syrup, pulling him back one step for every two taken forward. The rush of blood thundered in his ears, and he couldn't hear the words Freida used as she frantically begged for help on the telephone, the receiver of which she had managed to recover. All he could focus on was getting through that door and out to the little Honda where Virginia waited in the back seat.

Defenseless.

◦———◦———◦

You can't lose it. Not now.

Crystal silently repeated this mantra to herself, forcing the panic back one inch at a time. She had to warn Luke and Paula. She had to reach them before these others did. How many of them were there? If they were the same people who had blown up the Friendly's gas mart in Indiana—and they almost certainly were—then there was a man to deal with as well; Luke had mentioned him when he had recounted that horrific night. Well, there was one less of them than there had originally been, that was for sure. Why had the Anti-Crystal—and that was surely how Crystal had come to think of her—stopped the dark-haired woman? If the dark-haired woman had known about Virginia Parnell, then she must have been in allegiance with the Anti-Crystal. Why turn on her then, why not let her kill Crystal? The surprised look on the face of the corpse suggested she hadn't a clue, either.

391

It's a trap.

Crystal looked around, wondering if the words had actually been spoken aloud. Despite her success in controlling her panic attack, her senses were still wholly unreliable. It was surely just the wind in the trees.

Trap.

Crystal's glance became more furtive, and for a brief moment, she thought the panic was going to consume her again. Take a deep breath. Swallow. Another breath...

trap-trap-trap-trap-trap—

Crystal's feet were suddenly in motion, operating under their own volition. She seemed to be along only for the ride. If it was a trap, she might be walking—no, *running* right toward it. But she had to try and reach Luke before he brought Virginia right to them.

She cut through the woods at an angle, leaving the shallow path behind and opting for something a little more unpredictable. She was suddenly no longer concerned about her sense of direction, for she realized she had never lost it; it had merely slipped from the conscious to the subconscious. Her feet certainly seemed to know where they were going. She was surprised at her own stealth as she soundlessly pushed aside thick scrub brush and worked her way through thorny briar patches.

All of this was on automatic pilot.

Crystal had surrendered herself entirely to instinct because she had nothing else left. If they caught her and killed her, so be it, but she had to try to reach Luke, she had to try to save Virginia.

It was funny how that whispering voice in the woods had sounded so *much* like Aunt Maude's.

Luke threw open the door, and Virginia emitted a startled gasp. When he realized that she was actually *there—alive—*all of the air rushed out of his lungs, and he sagged against the car's roof.

"Oh, thank God, Oh, thank God—" he repeated softly, over and over.

Virginia sat in the back seat, watching him curiously. She didn't understand what caused his fear, but she felt it nonetheless, and she was having a hard time keeping her careful composure intact.

Luke finally stopped chanting and squatted down on his knees, looking in through the open door and staring at Virginia. She looked back at him solemnly, her clear round eyes more anxious than he had seen since they had left the farmhouse.

"Crystal," she said softly.

And suddenly Luke understood.

⚬ ⎯⎯⎯⎯◇⎯⎯⎯⎯ ⚬

Crystal was drawing closer to the road; she could hear an occasional car or truck whizzing by. She had first traveled south, cutting her way through the woods as they thickened. The geography was hilly, but fortunately for Crystal, south was all downhill. She had crossed a thin stream and a not-so-thin stream, and her jeans were saturated from the knees down.

Her feet were still eerily soundless as they continually found solid purchase in a landscape that should have been full of loose pebbles and brittle twigs. When her feet had pulled her to the west, she had followed without question.

And now there were cars.

The first time she had heard an engine, her heart had leapt into her mouth because she was certain it would be Luke, and she was equally certain she couldn't reach the road before he passed. Then, she realized that the acoustics of the woods had been toying with her; the car wasn't coming from the direction in which she expected Luke. She was enormously relieved, but it only encouraged her to renew her efforts.

And then she could see it. The sun-bleached gray of the tarmac, the dirty steel rail that separated the highway from the woods. It was still a football field's length away, but it was *there*.

And so far, no sign of them.

Crystal pushed her way forward, watching the distance diminish slowly, then more rapidly, until she was finally standing at the guardrail, touching it with her good hand as if to make sure it was real. It was. As she threw a leg over the top, she heard another engine. It was coming from the right direction, and she suddenly knew it was them. She leaned against the guardrail, waiting for the front grill of the Honda to round the bend and come into view. She glanced around nervously but there was still no sign of the Anti-Crystal. It should have brought relief, but instead, Crystal's nerves only tightened.

When the Honda finally appeared, Crystal pushed away from the guardrail and ran right down the middle of the road, waving her usable arm high above her head. She almost called out before realizing she would also be alerting them, wherever they were.

Luke spotted Crystal and stomped on the accelerator. The car was light, and the engine was responsive, but it seemed an eternity before they finally reached her. He kept the car in gear as she rounded the front end to the passenger side.

She opened the door and leaned in. "Where's Paula?"

She slid into the passenger seat and pulled the door shut. She fiddled briefly with her seatbelt before giving up and slinging it aside.

"Didn't you hear me?" she asked. "Where's Paula?"

Her eyes traveled to Luke's face, which was frozen in place, staring at something ahead of them, something through the windshield. Crystal followed his gaze, and a strangled cry gurgled in her throat.

A maroon Volvo had just rounded the bend and was barreling down the highway directly toward them.

II

Chad sat behind the wheel of the Volvo and twiddled his thumbs. He was growing restless with his incapacitation, and he frankly didn't feel all that incapacitated anymore. When he had examined the wound on his shoulder that morning, he had been surprised at how much healing had already occurred. Granted, the bullet had passed clean through, and that fat nurse had swabbed the entire area with an antiseptic that felt like liquid fire, but even Chad knew that the wound should be worse than it was. As if to test his theory, he shifted his arm out of the sling that held it in place against his chest and extended it slowly. There was a little pain, but not much.

He was anxious to get back into the game, although frankly, it had been interesting to sit back and let the ladies do all of the dirty work. He was pleased with both of them, although in different ways.

Suze's usefulness had been immediate; if it hadn't been for her, he would probably still be in Pridemore, living in his father's abandoned house, amusing himself with the trial that would soon come, the conviction that would then follow, the execution that might come afterward. Peter Collins' self-image would be unsalvageable after incarceration, for he was a proud man incapable of suffering such an indignity. Chad wouldn't have been surprised to discover that his father had already, in fact, used his bedsheet as an escape mechanism, tying one end around the lighting fixture in the center of his holding cell while wrapping the other around his own neck. It wasn't just the loss of his own dignity—although that had certainly been enough—it was the constant image he carried with him as he lay on his hard bunk, staring sightlessly at the metal supports of the bed above him. It was a snapshot of Chad's face, that last day he had visited. It was the way Peter's blood had turned to icy slush as he realized that the monstrous thing that had been done to Naomi, his estranged wife—he refused to think of her as his ex; he was certain that reconciliation was an inevitability—had been done by her own son. Her own flesh and blood.

No. Not her own flesh and blood.

It was incomprehensible. Chad hadn't been that kind of boy growing up. If it were a category on the senior ballot, Chad most certainly would *not* have been voted Most Likely to Murder Indiscriminately. In school, he was quiet. He kept mostly to himself, turned in his assignments on time and always sat near the back of the class. The few friends he had were really only people with whom he passed time. They weren't the bad kids—the ones who smoked behind the school or sold drugs in the bathrooms. They were just a few boring kids who found that the days were a little less boring when they were with each other. Chad neither liked nor disliked them. He hadn't seen them in weeks, and this was the first time they had crossed his mind—even Ricky, with whom he had spent nearly every afternoon when they were between the ages of nine and seventeen. Julie had been alright, but Chad had only planned to use her for sex; she was too stupid and whiny for anything more. And yet, he had never gotten the chance. The thing inside him had awakened that stormy night, the night when he had served Naomi up like a sacrifice, and was it to God or the Devil? Did it even matter? He had surrendered easily to that inner beast, awakening from its long hibernation. It wasn't as if he were being possessed. Not at all—it was as if he were coming *alive*.

Suze was a gift. Twenty years to his eighteen, she was his first older woman. She was his first woman ever. She was not only a lover but a teacher as well. She clarified quite a few of the muddled viewpoints Chad had harbored in silence throughout adolescence. She understood that there was really no difference at all between people and animals, except that animals weren't capable of employing deceit. People, on the other hand, specialized in it. If there were things you wanted, you had to take them. If people got in your way, you pushed them down. If they didn't stay down, you killed them. Life is a one-way ticket, baby, and you have to get your kicks in before someone kicks you first. He had known all of this subconsciously but hadn't understood the freedom that would come with tapping into this primal reserve, not until after Suze had shown him. She made him feel invincible. Even without her psychic "snapshots"—which had since proven wholly unreliable; Chad was beginning to wonder if she had made them up for effect—Suzette Snyder was an integral part of this killing machine.

But Lisa Mitchell was The One.

He knew it the first time he saw her through the mesh of the screen covering her storm door. Lisa's comprehension of the nature of man was innate while Suze's was culled from personal experience. Anyone can learn to play a piano if he's willing to invest the time; very few are able to do it brilliantly. Even fewer are able to do it automatically, without any instruction whatsoever. But these people *do* exist. In that respect, Lisa Mitchell was a virtuoso. If she were asked to commit to paper a plan by which they would attempt to retrieve and assassinate the little girl, Chad knew that she couldn't do it. It wasn't the way her mind worked. She knew what to do and when, but only in that split second before the time was at hand. And in that respect, she was much more adaptable than Suze.

That was why Lisa's experience in the Parnell farmhouse hadn't infuriated him. Lisa Mitchell had taught him to roll with the punches, and that's all this really was—a minor delay. These people couldn't protect Virginia Parnell forever.

The girl.

The thought of her brought bile to the back of Chad's throat. He had never felt such focused hatred for anyone, not even his own mother as he had rammed the kitchen blade into her again and again. No, the girl was different. Although they never discussed it in detail, he sensed the same thing the others did. It wasn't what the girl was, it was what she would *become*.

He scanned the woods for any sign of movement, but he was utterly alone. If Suze had been the one who had told him to pull over, he would now be doubting her instinct, waiting for them to return to the car sheep-faced and empty-handed. But because it was Lisa's suggestion, he knew that something was going to happen; it was only a matter of when.

As if on cue, Lisa suddenly emerged from a cluster of bushes, plucking twigs from her hair as she crossed to the Volvo. She pulled open the passenger door and slid in.

"You want the good news first or the bad?"

Chad cocked his head. "Whichever."

"Good news is, I think we've got them. The bad news is, Suze is dead." She stared straight ahead, through the windshield and into the woods beyond.

Chad's head gave a short little jerk. He couldn't have possibly heard her correctly. "What did you say?"

When Lisa turned to face him, there were tears in the corners of her eyes, threatening to spill over. Her lips twitched as she tried to suppress her grief. Chad hadn't bothered to put his arm back into the sling and didn't even notice the absence of pain as he leaned across the seat and wrapped his arms around her. Her body was roiling with spasms as she spilled her tears onto Chad's shirt.

"What—happened?" he asked gently, kissing the top of her head.

"It was Crystal Bright," she said, and for the first time, Chad thought he saw fear in her eyes. How could someone as strong as Lisa Mitchell be intimidated by some Hollywood twat like Crystal Bright? But the expression on her face said it was so, and his heart ached for her. "She must have seen Suze from behind or something—I don't know. I had gone the other way and was circling toward them, but I was too far away. I didn't even see them until—until after I heard them struggling. I had just found them when that bitch broke Suze's neck. Just like that!" For a split second, a fire danced in her eyes, one that Chad easily mistook for outrage.

"Were the others—?"

"No. I don't know exactly where they are, but they're close," she said, straightening in her seat and drying her eyes. "They wouldn't just leave Crystal Bright alone in the woods like that. They'll be back to get her."

"How can you be so sure?"

"Because it doesn't make any sense. Why would they just drop her off in the middle of nowhere? They'll be back," she said. "I promise you."

"What do we do now?"

"We turn the car around and go about a half mile back," she said. "There was one of those scenic overlooks back there that looks right down on this valley. From there, we can see the other end of the road. We'll see them coming before they ever see us."

"We'll make them pay for what they did to Suze."

"After we kill the girl."

"Of course."

"Then we'll make the others pay."

A hint of a smile played at the corners of Lisa's mouth. "Yes. They'll all pay."

They only had to wait about twenty minutes.

The view couldn't have been more perfect if they had ordered its construction for their own express purpose. The two-lane blacktop lolled down the hill like a dog's droopy tongue, never straying far from the edge of a rolling drop-off, the kind that drunk drivers and teenagers always underestimated. On the opposite side of the road—the side where they had pulled off further down, the side where Suze had died—the hill continued upward and into various peaks and ridges. Somewhere among those trees, Crystal Bright was forging a path through the woods, but sooner or later, she would have to reemerge.

Chad spotted the Honda first, straightening in his seat and squinting his eyes. Lisa's pulse began to race as she saw it. The little girl was inside. She could feel her nearness. It would be over soon.

Chad started to shift the car into gear, but Lisa placed a hand over his, stopping him. "Not yet," she said. "We have to give Crystal time to come out of the woods. We want to get them all."

Chad's jagged smile would have given Virginia Parnell nightmares for years to come. "Yes. Get them all."

It was no more than a minute before the Honda had traveled the straight stretch that bisected the valley floor. It passed out of their range of vision as it began to ascend the hill.

"Now," said Lisa, releasing Chad's hand. *"Now."*

III

As she stood outside the house, staring up at its ugly, oblong façade, Jessica felt as if she were shrinking, puddling on the sidewalk. How many years had it been? Ten? Twenty?

No—not quite twenty.

She had hoped to never see it again. This was where it had all started. This was where everything had gone wrong. She saw the ten-speed bicycle, brick-red and rusted, leaning up against the stoop, a Day-Glo green security chain holding it to the porch.

Her heart was in her throat.

Jessica understood she wasn't *really* there. She could remember Helen Martin's look of concern as the world abruptly tilted, then folded away from her. This had happened to her before, but it had been so long ago.

The world was a sepia nightmare. All the colors of summer—the emerald rows of grass, the soft blue sky, the multi-colored flowerbeds—all of it had been stained with a horrible yellowish cast, like the entire world had been saturated with urine.

But the sidewalk felt solid underneath her feet, and as before when she had dreamt these dreams, her feet had their own agenda. She was moving toward the ugly little house even as her mind screamed in protest, trying to force herself to stop where she stood, turn and run before it was too late.

She was startled to discover a paper grocery sack nestled in the crook of her arm. Where had that come from?

Why, Goodwin's, of course. Goodwin's IGA. Freshest meat you'll love to eat, *wink-wink!*

And the skin of her arm was so smooth, so *young*—

It could have been nearly any day from back then. Jessica had gone to Goodwin's almost every day, picking up meat for dinner in the early afternoon so that she would have the rest of the day to put Bernie's meal together. He always liked his meat fresh. But it wasn't any of those indistinguishable afternoons. It was October 21, 1985. It wasn't a date she was likely to forget, even if some of the details eluded her.

And then her hand was on the gate, lifting the latch, letting herself into the small yard, carefully refastening the gate. The sidewalk seemed to move beneath her feet, drawing her effortlessly to the porch. She felt a tightness in her chest, but it wasn't the anxiety of the moment; it had been a constant companion in those days.

398

And yet, Jessica couldn't put her finger on exactly what waited inside those walls. She knew she was going to go inside—she didn't seem to have a choice. She knew that what was about to happen would permanently alter the course of her life. She knew, as her hand came to rest on the cool, brass doorknob, that in any second, the screaming would begin. She desperately wished she could seize control of her hands so that she could cover her ears.

Instead, she turned the knob.

———————◆———————

"Check the glove box for a pen," barked Helen, reaching over top of the headrest and gently easing Jessica back into her seat. When she had passed out, Jessica had slumped forward against the steering wheel, the Jeep's horn bleating in protest.

"Wha-wha—" Leonard started to question the order but decided it would be inappropriate. Helen Martin was a nurse. She knew what was needed.

He rummaged through the glove compartment and found a cheap blue Bic with its cap chewed to shreds. He offered it up doubtfully, but Helen snatched it almost without looking, inserting it carefully through Jessica's clenched teeth, holding her tongue in place with the pen's crystal body.

"Hold this," she said, directing his trembling hand toward the pen.

"Is she havin' a seizure?" asked Leonard, but his words were either unheard or ignored. Helen was too busy nursing, taking measurements of pulse and guestimates of body temperature. Her eyes fell automatically to Jessica's lap, checking to see if she had lost control of her bladder or bowels as many epileptics did while seizing. Jessica's jeans were still dry. In fact, by this point, Helen had pretty much ruled out a seizure. Jessica had only one violent reaction, just as she was passing out; no other convulsions followed.

"We need some water to cool her down," said Helen, glancing quickly around the car's interior, hoping to find one of the bottles of water that had lately become so fashionable. Unfortunately, Jessica didn't concern herself with what was fashionable. "Even a wet *rag*—"

Leonard fumbled with his door handle. "I'll see what I can find," he mumbled before tumbling out to the curb. Woods stretched off to the left, a steep drop-off on the right. He crossed the street like a rabbit, skittering across the two-lane blacktop and disappearing into the cluster of naked trees beyond.

Helen cupped Jessica's face in her hands and pried her eyelids up one at a time. Her irises had rolled back and now twitched wildly; maybe it was a seizure after all.

What in the hell are you doing here, Helen?

She had no idea. She was almost sick to her stomach worrying about Lisa Mitchell and what those people might be doing to her. Helen considered the burdens Lisa had faced as if they were almost biblical in proportion. Helen thought she could be the anchor this young woman needed in a world that was crumbling around her. After all, everyone needs an anchor, someone to keep them grounded and sane in an uncertain world. Without an anchor, tragedies like Evie's death would be unbearable. Helen's only hope these past five years since her husband had passed had been the intangible certainty that there was an anchor for her, too—somewhere. And when she had first laid eyes on Lisa, so small and fragile in her hospital bed, her eyes ringed with bruises—it was then she thought she might have found it. Lisa surely needed someone to take care of her. There were many things with which she would need help while recuperating.

Even when it became obvious that Lisa's recovery was going far better than expected, Helen still felt the urgent need to care for this lost child, only just out from under the wing of her overprotective Nanna. At twenty-two, Lisa had the life experience of a twelve-year-old. It would take some careful tutelage to bridge the gap between those two mindsets.

And yes, in Lisa Mitchell, she saw a little bit of her daughter, Evie. It wasn't a physical resemblance; Evie's hair had been chestnut to Lisa's dishwater blonde, her face perfectly oval while Lisa's was more defined. It wasn't even their personalities. Lisa was timid and shy and seemed to offer her opinion only when she was sure it was right. Evie had always been outgoing and vivacious, incredibly in tune with the world around her and what she wanted from it. No, it was more of the sensation of vitality that both wore like a second skin. It reminded Helen of a time when she had been in her mid-twenties, newly married and with her whole life in front of her. Those had been good times, the *best* times.

And now she was all alone. Except for Lisa Mitchell and these people who might help Helen rescue her.

Jessica held her breath as she pushed the door slowly inward. Her heart caught in her throat as the living room was slowly exposed. It, too, was cast in the same yellowish light, but the smells were all there, and they were all the same.

So far, no screaming—

She took an involuntary step inside, shouldering the door closed behind her. The familiar, musty smell of the small house assailed her as she crossed the threadbare carpeting of the living room, careful to avoid the toys that were scattered on the floor like land mines. The floor plan was simple and open, the living room spilling without boundary into the small kitchen, a narrow hallway stretching off to the right to two small bedrooms and one small bathroom that altogether comprised the house's interior. The toe of her shoe caught on the bent metal runner that marked the end of carpeting and the beginning of linoleum and Jessica suddenly remembered the time she had sliced her big toe on the same runner; it was a deep gash that had required six stitches. It was one of those things that Bernie was always going to fix but had never quite gotten around to.

Jessica was in the kitchen now, going around the chipped Formica table where they had shared their meals. The groceries were heavy on her arms, and she began to deposit them on the stained and gouged countertop.

Still no screaming—

She wanted so badly to leave, turn and run from that horrible afternoon. But if she had done that—

And that's when the screaming began, high-pitched and horrible from the far end of the hallway. With a sense of déjà vu like she had never known, Jessica watched in horror as a box of spaghetti, a can of corn, and a can of tomato paste slipped through her fingers, falling in slow motion toward the floor. She nearly pushed the table over in her haste to reach the hallway and locate the source of that awful, piercing wail. Her foot snagged the metal runner again but this time, it threw her off balance, and she slammed into the wall just inside the mouth of the hallway.

There was another sound inside the scream, a wet spongy sound that repeated at regular intervals, and then the scream itself was wet, as if it were coming from underwater. The two horrific sounds merged into one, and Jessica was almost certain she was going to vomit.

Oh, please let me go! I don't want to see this again!

Yet her feet were again in motion, moving her down the hallway and toward whatever waited at the other end. She was aware of her thought from that afternoon, culled from her memory and running through her like electric current.

What is it this *time? Dear God, what's happening* this *time?*

The hallway was short, with only two doors on each side. On the right was a small linen closet and the bedroom she shared with Bernie. On the left was the small bathroom and the smaller bedroom. It was from there that those sickly sounds came, spilling out into the hallway and causing Jessica's blood to run cold.

As she neared the doorway, she could already see it on the walls, spattered and trickling, running downward.

It was blood.

When Leonard returned to the Jeep, he saw that Helen had swapped positions with him, moving to the front where she could be closer to Jessica. He slid into the back seat and offered the damp piece of cloth he had torn from the bottom of his shirt. He had soaked it in a thin stream of crystal-clear water he had found only a few hundred yards deep into the woods. He hadn't been able to find anything to act as a suitable container for drinking water, and he wasn't entirely sure he would have felt safe feeding it to Jessica anyway, at least not without boiling it first. He knew that man's pollution of the earth ran deep, and just because the water looked safe didn't mean it was.

Helen's face was set with grim determination as she blotted the damp cloth against Jessica's forehead. Jessica had begun to thrash at irregular intervals, and Helen was about to suggest that Leonard take the wheel and drive them toward the nearest hospital when Jessica's eyes suddenly snapped open.

"I didn't kill him!" she gasped. "I wouldn't—I *couldn't*—"

"*Shh*," said Helen, gently stroking Jessica's forehead. "Don't try and speak. You're alright now. *Shh*."

Leonard could barely suppress his own anxiety as he watched Helen work. Jessica's lips were almost white, and a thin sheen of perspiration had erupted across her clammy complexion. She didn't look at all well. If something happened to her, Helen would probably blame him for that, too. And maybe it *was* his fault. Maybe if he hadn't accepted Jessica's ride, she wouldn't have been drawn any further into this mess—

"What happened?" asked Helen, her voice soft and soothing. She continued to apply the wet cloth to Jessica's upturned face.

Jessica reached out with her left hand and pressed the buttons that lowered the windows. She closed her eyes and took deep breaths as she tried to clear her head. She couldn't escape the imagery of the dream, however; it loomed fresh in her mind, pulled out of storage, dusted off and proudly displayed for all to see.

She felt the old guilt wash over her, a feeling she thought she had finally outrun. She should certainly have known better. Those feelings had been so *unnatural* and yet had become such a permanent part of her daily existence during those dark years. She could remember the awful, haunted look in Bernie's eyes as he had asked her if she had done it—as if she could have!

Jessica couldn't talk about it with these people. It wasn't the kind of story you shared with strangers; it wasn't the kind of story you shared at all. Jessica had spent the last fifteen years pushing it down, suppressing it all—

That wasn't entirely true.

She had spent the last thirteen or so years suppressing it all; the years before that were spent trying to convince everyone else she wasn't crazy. She knew it *sounded* crazy. Of course it sounded crazy! It wasn't as if she had awakened one morning with the curious urge to spread her gospel. It wasn't until after the accidents started—sometimes minor, sometimes not so minor—that she felt compelled, no *obligated* to convince them—Bernie, Jackie, her mother, her father, *anyone* who might listen. But none of them believed her. None of them could make the leap, face the horrid possibility that what she said might be true. Not even Bernie, with his haunted eyes full of unspoken accusation. How she had withered underneath that empty gaze...

Jessica's eyes opened and swam into focus. Helen's face loomed like the moon, full and round, anxious concern painting her features in a way that reminded Jessica of her own mother. Leonard's unshaven, angular face hovered just beyond the headrest, his eyes furtively glancing from side to side, only coming to rest upon hers for the briefest of instants, as if he was afraid to be caught staring.

He would understand.

Jessica bit her bottom lip as she heard the whisper of an inner voice she thought she had vanquished. It was the one that had encouraged her to tell the others, make them aware of the things she suspected. She had spent years learning to distrust that soft voice after the trouble it had caused; but here, in the quiet of the Jeep's cabin, flanked by strangers whose tangible concern for her was as deep and real as any she had ever felt, the voice's words held a sort of cool logic. Leonard Bates *would* understand. The things he had said about the Mitchell girl. He had said she was evil—

But that was also why Jessica couldn't tell Helen Martin. Helen espoused nothing but great concern for Lisa Mitchell. She was convinced that the girl was in real jeopardy, a hapless victim to these armed criminals who had besieged the Mitchell house for no apparent reason. Her protective nature for the girl precluded any open-mindedness. In Helen's features, Jessica saw the potential for that same look of open disgust that she had suffered at the hands of so many of her dearest friends.

Having never laid eyes on Lisa Mitchell, Jessica was forced to base her opinion strictly on what she had heard from Leonard and Helen as well as her own intuition. Her intuition was telling her that Leonard was the one to listen to, despite his odd appearance and almost frightening way of expressing himself. When he had told Jessica about the ones who had died in the supposed accidents, she had felt a cold finger on her spine, the dream trying to surface then but not quite able. Now, she remembered the way she had felt after those accidents, the way she had studied him carefully from across the room, distrustfully, certainty growing with each passing day that they weren't accidents at all.

If only Bernie had believed her. It would have all been so much more bearable.

Jessica shook her head as if shaking off cobwebs, smiling weakly at Helen. "I don't really know. I felt a little light-headed, and then—well, I guess you saw the rest. I'm so *thirsty*—"

"We should get you to a hospital," said Helen. "They should run tests to see—"

"No hospital," said Jessica firmly, shaking her head. Helen was surprised by the strength of Jessica's tone and flinched in response. Jessica tried to force the panic from her eyes and will a smile back onto her face. The result was almost grotesque. "No hospital," she repeated more softly.

Jessica saw Leonard studying her more intently from the back seat, his eyes daring to land for whole seconds before nervously pulling away. She wondered briefly if he already knew the truth, recognized her face from all of those vicious newspaper stories from so many years ago. His wizened eyes suggested it may be so. What surprised her was the total lack of contempt in his expression, a contempt that must surely be there if he knew the truth—

A truth that had begun in January of 1982, on a portentously stormy afternoon. She had gone for her annual gynecological exam and had learned something quite unexpected. She was three months pregnant. Her menstrual cycle had been uninterrupted the entire time, and Dr. Horwitz had indicated that sometimes happened in rare circumstances. He was, however, at a loss to explain her pregnancy in light of the operation she had undergone the previous year to have her tubes tied.

Three months pregnant.

Pregnant with the baby who, although christened Charles at birth, would more readily respond to the name of Chad.

CHAPTER TWENTY-ONE

I

"Oh, my God."

Crystal's voice was barely a croak. From the back seat, Virginia emitted the slightest of whimpers before falling eerily silent, wide-eyed and vigilant but utterly inside of herself.

The Volvo was blazing toward them, accelerating as it swooped down the hill. Crystal could see the outlines of their faces through the windshield, could feel their eyes bridging the distance, burning into her.

"I'm in! Go—go—GO!"

Luke's hand fumbled to the gearshift as his feet did a mad dance on the pedals. He had stopped the car while going uphill—not a good pole position with a manual transmission. He stomped the gas pedal and popped the clutch—and the engine abruptly died.

Crystal screamed in frustration, her eyes fixed on the front grille of the Volvo as it drew nearer and nearer. Virginia clapped her hands over her ears, wincing at the sound.

Luke fumbled with the keys as the Honda began to drift backward along the incline, and he realized he hadn't put his foot back on the brake pedal. The car was gaining momentum, but it was backwards momentum, the small car suddenly shuddering from side to side as the road's surface level shifted.

"Oh, *God!*" shrieked Crystal. "They're going to catch us! *They're right on top of us!*"

And they were. They had closed the distance to only about thirty feet. Crystal could see their faces clearly now—the anti-Crystal and her dark-haired accomplice who crouched behind the steering wheel—and the raw look of hatred that radiated from their faces. For a moment, she felt his eyes lock onto hers, and it was as if her soul was bleeding out, escaping through her eyes. She clapped her hands over them defensively.

"Oh, God, Luke! DO SOMETHING!"

Somehow, he did. His fingers danced a nervous jig along the steering wheel, abruptly grabbing and jerking it hard to the right. The Honda shuddered and leaned as its backward momentum was suddenly shifted, and the rear end jerked out and up to the right.

The front end of the Volvo missed them by inches. It whistled by at ninety miles per hour, the intention clear.

And then the Honda was suddenly facing the proper direction, its nose pointed down the hill instead of up. Luke popped the clutch again as the car began to roll forward, and the engine coughed and sputtered to life. Luke eased to the side of the road and shifted into neutral, his attention focused on the spectacle unfolding on the other side of the windshield. The Volvo was still rocketing forward, but now there were urgent brake lights, only slightly preceding the shrill squeal of rubber against pavement. The square car teetered along the highway's center line as its driver struggled to maintain control. For a blessed moment, it seemed to be a losing battle. First, the front end began to sway, then the rear began to fishtail as the driver overcompensated. Then the car was skidding sideways, plummeting toward the edge of the hill and the lip of a very nasty drop-off. The Volvo broadsided the guardrail a hundred yards downhill from where Luke, Crystal, and Virginia sat watching in a kind of transfixed horror. A moan of twisting metal carried back to their ears, and the Volvo's forward momentum pulled the car up onto two wheels, pressing the passenger side against the straining steel guardrail. Crystal held her breath as she watched the car hang in midair, the fate of its occupants still uncertain.

Then its driver's side dropped back to the ground, bouncing once before settling.

For a moment, no one said or did anything. A hazy plume of steam issued from the front of the Volvo, and no one seemed to be moving inside. Crystal glanced at Luke and saw how very white his knuckles were underneath his taut flesh. It was as if the tension was trying to forcibly expel his skeleton through his skin. His pulse throbbed at his temples, and his focus was absolute. Seeing the look of determination on his face made Crystal think that it might just be possible; maybe they could see this thing through after all.

"I say we go," he said, his voice low and gritty. "Get through before they come around."

"We should kill them," she said automatically. "Then it would all be over. We could—"

Luke silenced her with a sharp shake of his head. "Not while she's with us." His eyes flicked toward the back seat. "It would be a ridiculous risk. We have to get away."

Crystal nodded numbly, following his eyes into the back seat. "Where's Paula?"

"Shit."

"What?" Crystal turned around, and her eyes immediately found what Luke saw. Someone was moving inside the Volvo. The driver's door suddenly sprung open, and a blue-jeaned leg appeared, scrambling for purchase in the loose gravel that lined the berm. Then an arm slipped through the crack, reaching up to hook over the roof of the car.

Luke eased off of the clutch, and the Honda began its slow descent down the hill toward the place where the Volvo had come to its abrupt stop. As the speedometer crept steadily upward, Luke suddenly realized how easy it would be to finish it all right now. Turning the steering wheel toward one o'clock at precisely the right moment would slam the door on that blue-jeaned leg and groping arm, clipping them off as neatly as rotten toenails. The defenseless Volvo was already pressed against the guardrail. If Luke rammed it, it would topple effortlessly to the bottom of the valley below, surely killing whatever monsters lurked within.

Crystal looked at him suddenly—sharply. "Not while she's with us," she reminded, and it didn't even occur to Luke that he hadn't voiced the thought aloud.

Seventy yards.

Sixty.

Fifty.

The Honda continued to gain momentum as it glided down the hill, coming closer and closer to the resting place of the Volvo. Now, the dark-haired man's head appeared, popping up through the crack between the door and the car's roof. His lips pushed forth a tangle of expletives, and occasionally, his head would dart back into the car, barking something at the anti-Crystal, whose stirring form was now also vaguely distinguishable, struggling to free herself of her safety belt.

Luke's fingers trembled on the steering wheel, the impulse to cut the wheel toward them growing as the distance between them ebbed away.

Thirty-five yards.

Thirty.

Twenty-five.

Luke could only hear the pounding of his pulse against his eardrums, but he was vaguely aware of Crystal tugging at his arm.

"Police," she whispered, her eyes alternating between the red and blue flashing lights that had only just appeared in the rearview mirror and the wreckage that lay ahead of them. Crystal watched in horror as the anti-Crystal tossed a gun across the Volvo's front seat and into the waiting hand of the dark-haired man. His face was filled with murderous glee as he turned, preparing to sweep the gun around and fire its entire clip into the Honda and its hapless passengers. But then he spotted the cruiser, too, and his arm dipped back behind the cover of the car door.

For Luke, the spell was broken. Barely able to believe that he had almost pushed the Volvo and its evil occupants over the edge of the embankment, he automatically lifted his foot from the gas and shifted it to the brake pedal, slowing the Honda as it slipped past the Volvo and gliding to a stop about thirty yards beyond it.

"For God's sake, what are you *doing?*" screamed Crystal.

If Luke heard her, he gave no indication. He pressed his lips together and watched as the sheriff's cruiser thundered down the narrow blacktop, disappearing and reappearing from around short bends in the road, its strobe lights blinking urgently, its siren daring anyone to cross its path, its headlights drawing closer—closer.

"We can't let them catch us! *Either* of them!" Crystal urged frantically. "If they—"

"*Shh!*" The sound was a harsh hiss through Luke's lips.

Crystal fell into uncomfortable silence, waiting for the inevitable. The dark-haired man had stepped away from the car, his hands tucked into his back pockets, the gun left behind somewhere inside the Volvo with the anti-Crystal. He was shuffling toward the back bumper as the cruiser closed the distance, preparing to intercept the officer as he approached the car.

Crystal was filled with the sickening sensation that they were in a no-win situation. If the cruiser pulled off behind the Volvo, the anti-Crystal would have time to get a clear shot at the officer while he was being distracted by the dark-haired man. If he passed them and pulled in behind the Honda, he would find the subject of a statewide manhunt, along with her accomplice and four-year-old hostage. Panic closed in tight around her chest, squeezing her lungs and making it difficult to breathe.

And then the cruiser sailed by, its siren scream swelling to a crescendo before fading down the hill and into the distance.

The dark-haired man was already racing back to the Volvo when Luke popped the clutch and stomped on the gas. The Honda's tiny tires barked ferociously as they bit into pavement, loose gravel spraying out from underneath the car and hammering against the wheel wells. And then they were in motion, ramping down the hill in pursuit of the sheriff's cruiser, not trying to catch it but merely to stay within its protective shadow.

She sat in the back seat, straight and still, watching Crystal and Luke as they did their parts. The air in the Honda was almost crackling with an unbearable electricity, and the temptation to fidget was almost impossible to ignore. But she sat straight and still, just like her mommy had taught her to do in church. Straight and still like an angel, just like mommy's angel—

After only four years, Virginia Parnell already knew too much about this world. She would never experience the deceptively false sense of invulnerability that was the conceit of most children. Because at four years of age, Virginia understood one thing all too clearly.

No matter how many people awaken each morning, not all of them live to see the moon rise at night.

"Do you see them?"

Crystal twisted in her seat and craned her neck. "No," she said. "Not yet."

A strangled chortle worked its way up through her throat, tickling at her insides until she was giggling nervously. "I think we got away."

Luke wasn't ready to go *that* far. He had already witnessed too many coincidences to believe that was all they were. He was already wondering how they had been located. It wasn't as if there was only one road that cut through Ohio. They had purposely chosen an alternative route, not only to avoid the killers, but the police as well. What were the odds that these maniacs had randomly selected the same route?

As they passed the Friendly's where Luke had earlier stopped for gas, they noticed the sheriff's cruiser pulled to its door. Luke held his breath and hoped that tiny Freida was behind the cash register, too short to glimpse over the counter and see them pass. He watched the gas station recede in the rearview mirror and finally let out a relieved sigh when no bubble lights burst to life.

"We have to get off this road," he said.

"Where's Paula?"

"Gone. She ditched us at the gas station."

Crystal shook her head in disbelief. *"Gone?* Why would she—"

"It's been too much for her," said Luke. "Can't say as I blame her."

Crystal sat back, feeling the heat return to her broken arm. "But why *here?* I mean, this isn't exactly a hub of activity. Are you sure she's alright?"

"She left a note," he said, hooking a finger into his pocket and retrieving it. He tossed it to Crystal, and she read it slowly, eventually allowing it to fall to her lap.

"Well," she said simply. "I guess it's just us."

"I guess so."

She issued another nervous giggle. "I'm scared shitless," she whispered.

For the first time in hours, Luke grinned. "Me, too."

Crystal spotted the wadded-up currency wedged between the seats and scooped it up. She flipped through the bills, tabulating. "Where did *this* come from?" The color had drained from her face, and Luke suddenly realized what she feared.

"I didn't rob the place," he said, and her doubtful look was like a slap. *"Really."*

"Then where did it—"

"Virginia had it," he said, laughing as the ridiculous words spilled out. "She had it in her hands."

"There's two hundred dollars here!"

Luke's smile was bittersweet. Paula had helped herself to eighty dollars before bailing—a fair price for a used Honda, he supposed.

Crystal turned to stare at Virginia, wincing as she inadvertently pinned her splinted arm against the seatback. Virginia returned the stare, her brown eyes pure and innocent, the slight suggestion of a smile tickling the corners of her mouth.

"This is yours?" asked Crystal, holding the bills up.

For a moment, Virginia's eyes just fluttered shyly. Then her head began to bob slowly up and down, the corners of her mouth completing her bashful smile.

"Well, for heaven's sake!" said Crystal, her voice full of mock indignation. "You must be a very successful little businesswoman, then."

Virginia giggled and shook her head.

"We can't have Luke spending any more of your money, now can we?" she asked, offering the cluster of bills back to Virginia.

But Virginia wasn't interested in reclaiming the money. Instead, she just slowly nodded.

"What? You *want* Luke to spend your money?"

Again, Virginia nodded, the sly grin firmly in place.

"Well," said Crystal. "If I had known it would be *that* easy, *I* would've volunteered to be your personal shopper."

Another giggle.

"Show fur," said Virginia before collapsing into another fit of giggles.

For a moment, Crystal wasn't sure what the little girl meant. When realization dawned, she had to turn away from Virginia, her mind kicking into high gear. Virginia Parnell hadn't said *show fur* but instead *chauffeur.* What kind of four-year-old used the word *chauffeur?* Moreover, how many four-year-olds understood the concept of chauffeuring, or the fact that it was a paid profession?

When Crystal looked back at Virginia, the child was still grinning, perhaps even wider than before. It was as if she were privy to Crystal's reasoning, arriving at a conclusion that only deepened what she had already suspected. Virginia Parnell was neither ordinary nor extraordinary. She was somewhere beyond that, something that had never before been seen.

<hr />

Ducking in and out of the Friendly's had been a snap. The little old lady behind the counter hadn't even looked away from *As the World Turns,* playing on a small television suspended in the far corner. Paula slid past her to the bathrooms, dropping the note she had written in the car before hurrying back out. As she passed the counter the second time, she had the oddest sensation that if she were to speak, the lady at the cash register wouldn't hear her.

Luke's back had been turned toward her as she emerged from the building, but little Virginia Parnell's eyes had been staring right at her. Didn't matter. Paula had made up her mind.

She slid stealthily around the side of the oblong market, around to the back of the building. When she had planned this getaway, she had envisioned other motorists at the gas station, someone who might be willing to offer a ride to a 'young lady trying to get home to her parents.' That's what she would tell them. It sounded like it would work. But there hadn't been any other cars at Friendly's, no neighboring businesses or houses—in short, nowhere to hide. Still, Paula was determined to make a go of it. She might not get another chance before those crazed killers caught up to them.

As she was sure they would.

Behind the building she discovered a squat cinderblock enclosure surrounding a rust-riddled dumpster overflowing with trash. It had a chain link gate that was latched but not locked. Paula entered the enclosure without a backward glance, pulling the gate closed behind her before insinuating herself between the concrete wall and the dumpster. She worked her way around the dumpster's side stopping when she had gotten midway around its back. She slid to the sticky ground that smelled of something rotten, turned sideways and stretched out on the pavement, ignoring the impulse to recoil from the pulpy goo her fingers had stumbled into.

She only planned to stay there until Luke had gone. She hoped that her short explanation in the note would suffice, but even if not, she didn't think he would find her here. She didn't think he would spend much time trying, not with that girl in the car.

Paula placed her head on her arm and listened intently to the hypnotic silence of the country landscape surrounding her, chirping birds only then returning to the tree branches they had abandoned in the storm. The sun remained hidden behind clouds, and the air had been sullied by the pervasive refuse putrefying in the trash bin.

In a state of pure exhaustion, Paula slipped into sleep.

⌐————◆————⌐

"We really need to get off this road," repeated Luke. "They'll be coming soon."

Crystal snapped out of her moment of enlightenment. Suddenly, Virginia Parnell was just a little girl again, a little girl in dire need of protection. Crystal straightened in her seat and managed to bump her arm again.

411

"Shit!" she hissed, cradling the homemade splint.

"Are you okay?"

Her smile was tight, but she nodded sharply. "It's just this damn arm. Always in the way."

"Where should we go?" he asked.

Wandering through the woods, the idea had come to Crystal, and it still managed to fill her chest with the same bright hope. It was really the only place she *could* go.

"Take whatever roads you think best," she said, "but keep moving south. Try to find a phone booth we can use without being seen. I should probably make the call since Kathy doesn't know you."

"Kathy?"

"Kathy Duncan. She was my Aunt Maude's best friend for as far back as I can remember. She was the one who called me in California to let me know that Aunt Maude had—" She couldn't bring herself to say the word, 'died.' "She lived two houses down from us on Dale Street. She knows me about as well as anyone else on this planet. I don't think she'd turn us in."

"But if she lives two doors down from your Aunt Maude's, won't the police see us if we go there?" asked Luke. "I'm sure they'll be watching your old home, hoping to catch you there."

Crystal shook her head. "Kathy doesn't live on Dale Street anymore. She moved about ten years ago when her husband, Bill, built them a new ranch out on Otter Creek. They always wanted a little more privacy, and it's exactly what they carved out."

"Okay, so you think this Kathy person won't turn us in," said Luke. "What about Bill?"

"He died five or six years ago. Heart attack. I'm pretty sure Kathy lives alone, but I wouldn't want to go without calling first."

Slowly, Luke nodded. It was a plan.

II

"AAARRRGGGHHH!"

Chad slammed the tire iron against the front of the Volvo, and the right headlight splintered in a spider web of cracks.

"Stop it!" ordered Lisa, wrestling the tire iron out of his clutched fist. "This is the only goddamned transportation we've got!"

And a fat lot of good it did them, too. The impact after they had skidded down the steep hill had driven the Volvo's front bumper underneath the guardrail and then back up, locking the two together. Chad had tried prying, bouncing on the hood, and in a final act of desperation, had tried dismantling the guardrail. Now, he was seething with frustration, rage flowing through his network of veins like boiling lava.

He whipped his head around and scowled at Lisa, his jaw set. "They're getting away," he said, his voice low and menacing. "They are goddamned *getting away!*"

"Don't yell at me!" she snapped. "It wasn't *my* driving that got us into this!"

Chad turned around and took a deep breath. God, he wanted to hit her. He could barely believe it as the thought sneaked in; hadn't it only been moments ago that he had reflected upon her perfection?

And just as he felt the tension began to ease, her arms slid around him from behind, gently encompassing his tight midsection, fingers linking together in front of his belt buckle.

"I'm sorry," she whispered.

He nodded. "We can't let them get to us," he said. "We have to work together on this."

"I know."

"We'll still get them," he assured, turning around and cupping her face into his hands. She hugged him tightly.

"I know."

They turned back to the Volvo and stared at it for a long moment. For all of Chad's effort, the edge of the car's bumper was still firmly clamped onto the bottom of the guardrail. He had worked on it for over an hour, and daylight was now beginning to fade in the eastern hemisphere. The sheriff's cruiser, which had earlier thundered by, had not made its return via the same route. Only a few cars had come, none of them offering anything more than curious glances as they passed. Late afternoon was gray and still.

Lisa kept the radio on a local top forty station that cranked out one vanilla tune after the next, punctuated by frequent commercials and news every quarter hour. She slid sideways into the driver's seat and was about to switch the ignition off to preserve battery power when a male announcer's voice caught her attention.

"—where a grisly discovery was made late this afternoon. Greta Parnell and her two teenage daughters were found murdered in their country home by friends visiting for the funeral of Mrs. Parnell's husband. Bert Parnell was killed in an explosion at a rural Indiana gas station only three days ago. These friends, who wish to remain anonymous, have indicated that the Parnells also have a four-year-old daughter, Virginia, but so far, authorities have found no sign of the little girl, either dead or alive. There have been no arrests in the case, and citizens of Borden are urged to remain on high alert until the suspects are apprehended. Back to you, Tram."

"Thank you, Mike, for the update." The woman's voice reeked of the inappropriate cheerfulness that often plagued news reporters. She sounded almost elated at the news of the mass murder. Lisa liked her style. "My goodness! It's been a strange news day! In a recap of an earlier report, police are still on the lookout for Hollywood starlet, Crystal Bright, last seen robbing a convenience mart at gunpoint. The actress, best known for her volatile temperament on the set of *Benny and the Girl* and her subsequent release from the show, had been checked into the UCLA Medical Center following a massive overdose of sleeping pills but apparently escaped from the facility three days ago. The hospital has released a statement saying that Ms. Bright is a very confused young woman, and she checked herself out of the hospital without her doctor's knowledge or consent. Ms. Bright is a native Ohioan, and police are speculating that she might return to her hometown of Lucasville. Listeners should be alert and report any sightings to the Preble County sheriff's office—"

Lisa turned off the radio and smiled. She didn't know that the stupid little bitch had tried to kill herself. It was such an act of utter cowardice; as an adversary, it severely diminished Crystal in Lisa's eyes. The basest of all human instincts, the one for survival, was already weakened in Crystal Bright. Killing her wouldn't be much of a challenge.

She could have killed Crystal in the woods but had decided to wait. She didn't want to pick them off one by one. She wanted to kill them all together—one at a time, but all together. She wanted to kill the little girl first, of course. She wanted to watch the faces of Crystal and her square-headed cowboy as the little girl begged for mercy and shrieked in agony. She wanted to *bask* in it. She would kill the cowboy next, listening to the pathetic, mewling cries of Crystal Bright as she cowered in the corner. And finally, Lisa would end Crystal's suffering.

While at first it had seemed novel and had since proved useful, it was beginning to annoy Lisa that Crystal Bright was walking around with her face. More and more it felt like a violation, as if Crystal had purposefully violated the copyright of her features. When she finally caught up to Crystal, the first thing Lisa would do would be to slash that face beyond recognition, destroy those lines that taunted, teased, and stole from Lisa's individuality.

"They haven't connected the two stories yet," said Chad, leaning into the car and furrowing his brow.

"Give it time," said Lisa. "They'll have to take the gun back and have the fingerprints run. It'll take a little longer than this. But pretty soon, I'll bet we'll be hearing more about Crystal Bright than we can even imagine."

"We've got to do something about the way you look," he said.

It had never really occurred to Lisa that her resemblance to Crystal Bright could also have a downside. Now, she glanced at herself in the rearview mirror and tugged at her thick, shapeless hair. Chad was right. She required an impromptu makeover.

"We'll worry about that if we can ever get this piece of shit loose," she said, pulling herself back out of the car. Chad walked behind her as they rounded the front end and stared for what had to be the millionth time at the bound bumper.

"At least the engine's okay," muttered Chad. The steam that had been issuing from the front grille had been funneling up from the wheel wells and hot brake pads that had collected moisture from the road.

"Yeah, and we can idle here all day until we run out of gas." Exasperated, Lisa kicked the bumper.

And it fell off—well, most of the way. It still had a vague hold on the driver's side, but Chad was able to remedy that quickly enough with the tire iron. As the bumper fell to the ground, they began to laugh.

And then they were on their way.

Chad slowed the car as he pulled into yet another Friendly's, marveling in the sensation of déjà vu that washed over him. All of these gas stations were molded from cookie-cutter blueprints, and it was easy to imagine himself on that night in Indiana. Was it only a couple of nights ago? It felt like an eternity. He remembered the slobbering bastard in the bathroom and the rage that had engulfed him. He remembered the smell of gasoline and the small burst of heat as the flame from the lighter had merged with the bedsheet. He remembered the parking lot jolting below the wheels of the Volvo as they had rocketed away into the night.

Suze.

It was at that moment that she had lost her ability to foresee things. She had claimed that something in the explosion had severed her link. Now she lay dead in the woods, food for wild scavengers. Her death bothered Chad more than he cared to admit. For the most part, he had no real feeling toward anyone; he was the perfect picture of psychopathy. But he did develop fixations, and within these fixations, the people with whom he developed relationships were safe from the fallout of his mercurial temper. His had been a tight circle, comprised of first two, then three, and now back to two.

Chad missed Suze.

He didn't like leaving her body in the woods, but he knew that it would be impractical to bring it along. They would have no opportunity to provide a proper burial, and in his heart, Chad knew that Suze would have wanted them to go on, to catch the little girl and put an end to her. They were simply abiding her wishes.

He pulled up beside a pump and turned the ignition off. "You better stay here. You don't want anyone to see you."

415

Lisa reached into the floorboard and snagged the strap of her purse. She extracted a crumpled twenty and handed it to Chad.

"What's this for?" he asked. "This place is deserted. I can have the tank filled and be halfway across the state before they even know I'm gone."

"There's no sense lighting a fire everywhere we go," she said.

Chad smiled, reflecting again on the burning wreckage of that Friendly's in Indiana, three nights ago. He whistled as he rounded the trunk and popped open the fuel door, imagining the brightly painted building consumed by fire.

<hr/>

The last of the daylight had finally bled away, and Chad and Lisa traveled in companionable silence. They drove deeper into the rolling hills of the southern end of the state. There was no discussion as to where they were going; they had both heard the radio announcer mention Crystal Bright's hometown of Lucasville. Chad and Lisa knew that was their final destination.

When Chad went into the Friendly's to pay for the gas, he spotted a circular wire rack on the counter that held various state and local maps—your choice, five dollars. The obscenely short old woman behind the cash register regarded Chad warily as she completed her part in the transaction. She looked as if she might wet herself if Chad sneezed. He wondered what she'd look like if she were on fire.

Chad and Lisa had taken a few minutes in the parking lot to establish a course that would keep them off the main highways—they didn't want any passersby to mistake Lisa for Crystal—yet get them to their destination as quickly as possible. The Honda had gotten as much as an hour's head-start on them. Crystal and her crew should already be in the little shitburg by now.

The radio played softly in the background, but the occasional news reports were only updates, outlining what had to be the worst day in Borden's 113-year history. They still hadn't connected the gun left behind at the Parnell farmhouse to Crystal Bright, but they would. Eventually. They still hadn't captured Crystal, either, and the annoying reminder for all citizens to remain in a state of heightened vigilance was repeated with irritating frequency.

They braved a brief stretch near Peebles on the Appalachian Highway in order to reach SR73, another narrow two-lane blacktop that meandered in the general direction they wished to go. By then, Lisa had nodded off in the passenger seat, her head lolling back on the headrest.

Chad suddenly realized that his wounded arm hadn't given him any trouble since their earlier encounter with Crystal Bright and the bitch child. Since he had taken the helm of the Volvo, he had used his injured arm to steer without thought, an action that surely should have been painful. It only further imbued

416

Chad with a feeling of invulnerability, as if some powerful dark force was overseeing their actions and guiding them to a sure conclusion. Suze had fallen out of favor with It—whatever It was—and her prognosticating teacups had vanished in Its displeasure. It had ceased to protect her while It continued to guide Chad and Lisa, and that realization made Suze's death a little easier for Chad to bear. He would not disappoint It. He and Lisa were the Chosen Ones. Together, they would get the job done—and soon. Because every day that Virginia Parnell was allowed to exist also allowed her the opportunity to grow stronger, and although Chad would never say the words aloud, he *was* a little afraid of her.

Just a little.

<hr />

Lisa rarely remembered her dreams, and when she did, they were almost always nightmares about Nanna Grace. Nanna Grace yelling at her, belittling her—threatening her with her mahogany-tipped cane. In those dreams, Lisa was always much younger, probably no more than seven or eight years old. Nanna Grace was younger, too—younger and *stronger*, a malignant force towering over her that blotted out whatever light remained. Nanna's voice was always sharp, but in the dreams, it was almost *piercing*, an incessant barrage of sound that was like the continuous scrape of fingernails on slate.

As always, the dream started on the sidewalk in front of the Mitchell house, years before the creeping tangles of ivy and crabgrass would overtake the yard. As always, Lisa was alone, which was ridiculous considering that Nanna Grace had never let her go outside by herself, not without supervision.

Lisa looked down at her tiny feet, shod in ripped canvas tennis shoes that had once been white but were now heavily soiled with mud and what may have been spots of blood. She stared at her feet, waiting for the inevitable screech of the hinges on the screen door, the inevitable screech of Nanna Grace's voice.

The air was hot and humid, and Lisa could feel perspiration beading up along the back of her neck.

Still no Nanna.

Eventually, Lisa lifted her eyes and stared at the house. Her look was defiant, as if daring Nanna to charge out onto the porch now, daring her to come out and say *anything*.

It, too, was a ridiculous thought, because Lisa could never stand up to Nanna Grace. No matter how many horrible things Lisa had done and would continue to do, she had been utterly incapable of harming the old woman, no matter how many times she imagined it—*planned* it.

But now, Lisa really thought she could stand up to her—she *would* stand up to her—if only she were to lumber out onto the porch.

But the afternoon remained eerily calm. No sign of Nanna at all.

She climbed the wooden stairs and crossed the porch. She opened the screen door, only then hearing its familiar creak, and passed into the foyer. She paused just inside the doorway, listening for any sounds that might indicate where in the house Nanna Grace was.

Silence.

But the air inside the house was somehow different, somehow—*lighter?* The Mitchell house had always been without air conditioning, and Lisa had expected the house to be sweltering in the hot, humid afternoon. Instead, its coolness chilled the perspiration standing on the back of her neck, and she felt her skin draw up into tight rows of gooseflesh.

And then she spotted Nanna at the far end of the narrow hallway, laying in a heap half in and half out of the kitchen, her precious antique teacups scattered under and around her in a bed of jagged porcelain.

Slowly, Lisa began to move toward Nanna, and with each forward step, she felt herself growing taller, getting older, moving toward the person whom she had become. As if they were maintaining a grotesque dance of equilibrium, Nanna's appearance changed in time with Lisa's, and when Lisa reached Nanna's feet, she was the same frail creature she had become in the last years of her life.

She looked up at Lisa with pale, mournful eyes, her body trembling with weakness, fear, or both. For Lisa, it was an invigorating sight.

The old woman's lips parted, and her voice was little more than a croak. "I tried," she whispered. "I *tried.*"

And then she was gone, as shrunken and dead as she had appeared in her coffin. As Lisa watched the last flicker of life drain from Nanna's sunken eyes, she felt a startling rush of power that made her nerve endings pulse and tingle. And as she watched Nanna die, she understood that the old woman had finally relinquished her iron grasp on Lisa—the one she had managed to retain even after her physical passing. There would be no more nightmares featuring the fearsome Nanna Grace and her wickedly punitive mahogany-tipped cane.

Nanna Grace was dead, and Lisa had never felt more alive.

III

They had been driving aimlessly for some time now, drifting along the narrow country highways. Leonard sat behind the wheel, silently guiding the Jeep along. He occasionally stole a furtive glance in the rearview mirror, making sure Jessica was alright in the back seat. Helen had originally wanted to ride in the back with

418

her, almost desperate not to sit beside Leonard, but ultimately, she realized that Jessica could really use the extra room. Her color had still not returned to normal, although she remained responsive and insisted they not take her to a hospital.

If they hadn't been so absorbed in their concern for Jessica, they might have noticed they were drifting southeast, as if being pulled by an irresistible tidal force.

The gray of the afternoon had surrendered to dusky purple twilight, and there were few other cars on the road. As the outside temperature cooled, a fine mist shrouded the ground, and Leonard had to reduce his speed.

Finally, Jessica asked, "Where are we?"

Unprepared for the sudden break in silence, Leonard jolted in his seat. "Um— I can't rightly say. I just been drivin'."

Helen looked at him curiously. *"What?* I thought you knew where we were going. I thought we were trying to save Lisa."

Leonard paused to look at her briefly, considering the wisdom of his words but unable to stop them. "Lisa Mitchell isn't good, Mrs. Martin," he said. "She's one of them. She's one of the bad guys."

Helen looked as if she had been slapped, then her cheeks burned hot with indignation. "How dare you make such an accusation, Leonard Barnes! That girl is just the most helpless creature I have ever encountered! And talk about the pot calling the kettle *black*—"

"I wish it wasn't that way, Mrs. Martin, but it is. I've known the Mitchells for some time, and Grace Mitchell herself asked me—"

"Grace Mitchell? *Grace Mitchell?* She kept that poor little girl locked away from the entire world! She wouldn't even let her have friends! As far as I'm concerned, Grace Mitchell is the only 'bad guy' from the Mitchell household, and although I'm ashamed to say it, I'm glad she's dead."

"Grace Mitchell knew what that girl was capable of," Leonard persisted. "She tried to warn me, but I just didn't listen. And now I know she was right. I've seen it with my own eyes—"

"Exactly *what* have you seen?" demanded Helen. "I suppose you've caught Lisa robbing a bank—or maybe molesting a Cub Scout."

Leonard was withering under the intensity of Helen's onslaught, but he urgently needed her to understand. "It's not nothing *specific* that I've seen, but my gut instinct—"

"Your gut instinct?" Helen laughed contemptuously. "That's right. I forgot what a keen judge of character you are. It was your gut instinct that told you to feed another beer to Clinton McDermott so he could go out and kill my little girl!"

"Hey," said Jessica, mustering all the strength she had into her voice while struggling to sit up. "Apparently the two of you have a little backstory that I'm not privy to. That's fine. I don't know want to know about it. Not right now. But for

419

the time being, we're stuck with each other. What's more, we could use each other's help." She turned to Helen. "I'm not pronouncing judgment on Lisa Mitchell. I've never even met the girl. I promise you, I'll stay as open-minded as I can until we find out what's really going on. But the other two—we're all in agreement that they're up to no good. Right?"

Leonard nodded with gusto, and after a moment, Helen's head slowly bobbed, as well.

"I think we should keep going," said Jessica, staring through the windshield at the small arc of pavement that was illuminated by the headlights. "I think we can catch up with them."

"But how could you possibly know if we're even going in the right direction?" asked Helen.

A mother's instinct.

But Jessica wouldn't say that, although she still suspected Leonard might understand. Instead, she shrugged her shoulders and improvised. "One of the first things they teach you in the police academy is to trust your instincts. This is what my instincts are telling me. Helen, if you were to stay with us, would you be missing your duties at the hospital?" she asked, trying to change the subject.

"I'm off until Monday," Helen said. "Aren't we going back tonight?"

Jessica smiled weakly. "It's just—we've been on the road so long. You spent days in that tiny room with your arms shackled. Leonard told me earlier that he didn't sleep well. After my own little episode, I could use a little bit of rest myself. How about I put us up for the night on behalf of the Jay County Sheriff's Department? I think we'd be better ready to deal with those people if we were all rested up." Of course, the Jay County Sheriff's Department would never find out about this particular expenditure; Jessica planned to use her own personal MasterCard.

"But we'll never catch them if we stop," said Helen. "They could be halfway to Mexico by tomorrow morning."

Jessica shook her head. "I don't think so. I'm starting to get an idea of where they're going."

"Where? How could you possibly be certain?" Helen's questions were delivered with urgent hope, hope that she might actually find Lisa Mitchell before her abductors could do anything more horrible than the things they had already done.

Jessica was being stretched to the tips of her dramatic toes. She lowered her voice to a near-whisper, as if someone were listening to the private conversation that was occurring within the confines of the Jeep's cabin. "I can't really give you any details right now because it's classified. But let's just say I wasn't in Morgan on a whim."

Helen's eyes widened, and she emitted a startled gasp. But she swallowed the story completely—hook, line, and sinker, and Jessica was enormously relieved.

She wasn't an experienced liar and was uncomfortable with the act, but she knew that Helen wasn't ready to hear the truth. What's more, Jessica knew she wasn't ready to tell it—not all of it. At least not yet. Although the dream had been revelatory, she had managed to pull out of it before remembering everything. She believed these memories lurked just below the surface, separated from her consciousness by only the thinnest of membranes. She knew with equal certainty that these were dark memories, things she had struggled to forget and, for the most part, *had* forgotten.

But she clearly remembered Chad.

"I don't mind stopping," said Helen. "If you're absolutely certain you know where we're going. I'm awfully worried about Lisa. Those people were insane."

And although she had communicated with Leonard very little since she had passed out, Jessica noticed that he was driving a course she would have chosen. She *did* know where they were going—Lucasville. She had no idea why, but she was certain there were answers there.

Leonard kept his head lowered, staying completely out of the conversation. Helen's words had bitten him deeply, and he couldn't even look at her. If only she knew the guilt he carried with him—not that it should make a difference. He deserved her bitterness, her hatred. There hadn't been a day since that horrible accident that he hadn't reflected somberly on his own part in the deed, playing it over and over again in his mind. Helen Martin was single-mindedly focused on assigning the blame for Evie's death to him, and he was completely willing to accept it. His mere presence in the Jeep was an irritant upon Helen Martin's soul, and he promised himself he would not rile her again. If that meant he had to bite his tongue about Lisa Mitchell, that was exactly what he'd do.

He *was* able to meet Jessica's eyes, and something about the way she looked at him suggested that she might believe his warnings about Lisa. Something in her eyes had changed since emerging from her fugue state; she now seemed to carry a heavy burden of her own.

⋅⋅⋅⋅◊⋅⋅⋅⋅

They stopped at a Holiday Inn in Rosemount, ten miles south of Lucasville, and rented two adjoining rooms on the second floor; Leonard would have his own while the two women shared the other. There wasn't any luggage to carry, so check-in took very little time. If Helen or Leonard noticed that Jessica used her own credit card, they gave no indication.

They went to Room 210 first, and Jessica immediately stretched out on one of the beds. She still felt a little lightheaded from her earlier spell, and the bed's soft comfort almost cried out to her. Helen fussed along after, perching on the edge of the mattress and pressing the palm of her hand against Jessica's forehead to check her temperature. Leonard hovered near the door, willing himself invisible but unable to retreat into his own room until he was sure that Jessica was safely tucked in.

"Are you having another spell?" asked Helen, her fingers gently probing her wrist for her pulse.

Jessica shook her head. "I'm just tired. I need to get some sleep."

For a moment, Helen frowned, then pulled her hand away with a sigh. "You don't seem to be running a temperature. Your pulse isn't accelerated or irregular. Is there any history of diabetes in your family?"

"Not that I'm aware of."

"When did you eat last?"

Jessica suddenly realized it had been almost a whole day since her last meal. She smiled sheepishly. "I guess it was last night."

"Well, for heaven's sake!" Helen stood bolt upright and planted her fists on her ample hips in mock indignation. "In the absence of a doctor—which, by the way, I still think you should go to a hospital—I am forced to prescribe dinner, and you will eat every bite. It's no small wonder that you're weak. I saw a McDonald's just down the street. It's not exactly healthy, but it's convenient."

"Oh, no," protested Jessica. "I'm just planning to nod off, and—"

"I insist," said Helen, taking the keys to the Jeep from the nightstand. Leonard shrank away from her as she neared the door, but she paid no attention to him. As she opened the door, she turned, winking at Jessica. "Truth be known, I'm a tad peckish, myself. Anything special you want, dear?"

Jessica smiled. "Anything but fish."

Helen hesitated, then said, "Leonard?"

"No, ma'am. Thank you, ma'am."

"Nonsense," said Jessica. "Just get him whatever you're getting me."

Helen nodded stiffly, then left the room, pulling the door closed behind her. For a moment, Leonard hovered in the shadows near the exit, his hands in his back pockets and his eyes darting from place to place. Then he took a few slow steps towards Jessica's bed.

"Thank you," he said, his voice so low it was almost a whisper.

"You have to eat," said Jessica practically, if a little hypocritically.

"I'll just head on to my room now, if that's alright," said Leonard, easing toward the door.

"I wish you wouldn't," said Jessica, pulling herself upright against the headboard. With a sweeping gesture of her hand, she indicated the other twin bed. "Why don't you have a seat? Helen won't be gone long, and we can all eat together."

Leonard shook his head. "I don't think Mrs. Martin would much care for the notion of breaking bread with me."

"I suppose I noticed," said Jessica. "What's the story between the two of you?"

Leonard's bottom lip trembled as he shook his head again. "Please don't ask me about it," he managed, and Jessica could see the raw pain in his eyes.

"All right," she said. "Maybe some other time. Still, I'm glad we have this opportunity to talk, Leonard, while Helen's away—I've been thinking about what you told me—about the Mitchell girl—"

Oh boy, here it comes, thought Leonard. *She doesn't believe me. She's going to ask me to stop upsetting Helen. She's going to—*

"—about what she's capable of. What exactly do you mean when you say that? Do you think she's capable of murder?"

"Oh, yes, ma'am. Easy."

"Do you think she's already killed anybody?"

After only a brief pause, Leonard nodded. "But it ain't like I got any proof."

"That's okay," said Jessica. "I'm not asking in an official capacity, and I'm not trying to challenge you. I'm trying to understand the feeling that Lisa Mitchell causes in you."

He shuddered softly. "I don't know that I can rightly explain it. It's like—it's like—" He fumbled for words beyond his reach, faltering.

"Have you always felt this way about her?"

"No," he said. "For a little while now, but since Grace passed on, it's been much worse. I—I caught her staring at me. *Down there.*" His eyes flicked to his lap.

Jessica fought to keep a grin from surfacing. "Maybe she likes you."

He shook his head adamantly. "She only did it because she knew it bothered me. When she worked at the hospital, she had a reputation for being rough with the invalids. By that time, Grace was an invalid herself, and it was like Lisa was taking out all of her resentment on the older folk at the hospital. Eventually, they fired her. I saw her leave the hospital that day, Ms. Lybrook. The look on her face absolutely froze my heart. I'm not a crazy man, Ms. Lybrook. I know what I saw, and it was nothing short of evil. It was like the air around her had gone dead and anything she touched would be poisoned. Her eyes were black as coal."

Jessica bit her bottom lip and closed her eyes, pressing her head back against the headrest. She had forgotten that part. Those coal black eyes—slick and shiny like beetles—staring, *challenging.*

"Are you alright?" asked Leonard, easing forward.

Jessica nodded and took a deep breath. "I believe you," she said, gently touching his face. "And I'm not just humoring you."

"What do you mean?"

Jessica sighed as her eyes filled with tears. "I had a son once. His name was—is Chad."

Leonard's eyes widened. "The same Chad that Mrs. Martin—?"

Jessica nodded. "I think so. Don't ask me why. I suppose it's the same as how you feel about the Mitchell girl. I just *know* it's him. I haven't—*felt* him in a very long time."

"What happened?"

Jessica wanted so badly to tell him what she remembered, but she was afraid she would be met by that familiar expression, the one she had seen on the faces of every one of her friends back then. First amusement, then concern, then utter disbelief. In a few, she had actually seen fear.

Finally, she said, "I'll make you a deal. I'll tell you about Chad if you tell me why you and Helen don't get along."

Leonard mulled the proposal seriously. He didn't want to talk about Evie Martin, but he didn't think it was entirely fair to keep Jessica in the dark as to why there was a permanent wedge between her two traveling partners. And if Helen were to tell Jessica first, there was always the possibility that she would see him as a monster and leave him stranded, miles from home.

"All right," he said slowly.

Jessica took another deep breath before beginning. "I knew something was wrong with Chad from the moment I found out I was pregnant—*before*, actually. I had a tubal ligation, so I really never considered the possibility that I *was* pregnant. I hadn't been feeling well for weeks, but it wasn't like morning sickness or anything like that. It was like something was eating away at me from inside—"

She shuddered involuntarily.

"After he was born, I could barely stand to hold him. It gave me the sensation that I was holding an enormous, wriggling larvae. The way he *stared* at me—"

Another shudder.

"I went to a therapist for a while. They told me it was postpartum depression and all the usual bullshit." Jessica's voice had taken on a steely edge, trapped in a past she'd spent years trying to forget. "After a while, I started giving Dr. Hawthorne the responses he anticipated. Bernie and I were poor. We couldn't afford to keep sending me for treatments that I knew weren't working. And I knew that if I didn't start making *some* sort of positive response, Dr. Hawthorne was going to suggest that I be hospitalized."

She turned toward Leonard, her eyes sharp and focused. "I didn't dare allow them to hospitalize me," she said. "If they did, there wouldn't have been anybody to protect the others."

She choked on a broken laugh.

"He was barely three years old, you know," she said, giggling in the same grotesque manner. "And I was more afraid of him than I've ever been of anyone in my entire life. Nobody believed me. They thought I was crazy—hell, even *I* knew I sounded crazy! But I knew that little boy was unadulterated evil. I knew that death would follow him around like a murderous shadow. I was afraid for the lives of my friends and family!"

424

Her body trembled as she sobbed softly. Leonard shifted closer and made shushing noises. "Evie Martin was Helen's only child," he said softly, lowering his eyes. "She was killed in an automobile accident when a drunk driver—Clinton McDermott—ran a red light. I was subbing for the bartender at The Mixer the night it happened. I sold Clinton his last drink just five minutes before the accident. I shouldn't have sold him that drink. I shouldn't have let him leave the bar when I knew full well he was gettin' in his car and drivin' off. I shouldn't have—"

Now it was Jessica who was shushing. "There's no way you could have known what would happen."

"That doesn't make it any less my fault," he said. "And that's the one subject that me and Mrs. Martin agree on. I'm not proud of what happened, but I can no more change it than I can flap my arms and fly to the moon. I was scared of Clinton McDermott. He was big and loud and was always looking for a fight. *'Top me off, cornhead!'* That's what he called me all night long. He knew I wasn't the regular guy, and he was a mean drunk—a bully. I think he drank more than usual that night—challenging me to shut him down. He was rowdy the whole damn night. God help me, I just wanted to go home. It had been a long, hard shift, and I didn't like the thought of closing that bar down and then going out to the parking lot to find Clinton McDermott waiting with a ball bat to have a word with me. I topped him off every time, yessiree. And when he finally left, I was *relieved!* I made it through a night of his bullshit without aggravating him, and that's no small doing. I had no idea what would happen."

Reluctantly, Leonard looked back to Jessica's face, expecting to see his disgust and self-loathing reflected in her eyes. Instead, he was surprised to find heartfelt concern and empathy. She had stopped sobbing, but slow tears still ran from her eyes; Leonard wasn't certain if those tears were for herself or for him. She smiled and took his hand, squeezing it gently.

With a clatter, the door flew open, and Helen entered, her arms laden with tan sacks bearing the golden arches. "They were having a special, so I—"

She gasped when she saw them on the bed together, Leonard's hand resting in Jessica's.

PART FIVE

EQUILIBRIUM

CHAPTER TWENTY-TWO

I

It was with great trepidation that Crystal placed her phone call to Kathy Duncan. Her certainty that Kathy would be willing to take them in had waned considerably since she had first offered the suggestion; by the time she actually deposited her change into the payphone in the parking lot of a deserted service station, she had decided that Kathy Duncan would have to be crazy to offer them protection. Surely, she had seen the news by now.

It was to Crystal's great relief that Kathy responded graciously and without hesitation, offering shelter for as long as Crystal and her friends might need it. When Crystal tried to offer a vague explanation about the videotape that was currently circulating on the news, Kathy had dismissed it as outright nonsense and said they would discuss it later over a delicious, home-cooked meal.

As Crystal had replaced the receiver, she felt an intense pang of guilt. Kathy Duncan had been her Aunt Maude's best friend for as many years as she could remember. Crystal spent much of her childhood in Kathy's company, either at Aunt Maude's house or Kathy's own. It had been years since Crystal had taken the time to visit Kathy or to even send a quick note. Hollywood had been like poison for Crystal's soul, altering her values in ways that had allowed long-standing relationships to erode. She had dismissed these people from her life who would not have faded away as surely as the limelight always does.

They finally arrived at Otter Creek around eight o'clock. The journey was exhausting; Virginia had fallen asleep again in the back seat, and Luke was only blearily holding onto consciousness himself, guiding the car like an automaton. Crystal, however, was wide awake, keenly interested in the evolution of the landscape since she had last visited southern Ohio. Much logging had occurred along Otter Creek, and the thick foliage which had once offered almost jungle-like solitude along both sides of the narrow, two-lane road had been trimmed back to a fraction of its former glory. As the Honda bumped and jolted down the road, Crystal noticed that other new homes had been erected, mostly near the mouth of Otter Creek where it connected to SR 139. Despite the encroachment of modern progress, the Duncan property was still well secluded, hiding behind a line of ancient maples, oaks, and evergreens, the nearest neighbor at least two miles away. A lump formed in Crystal's throat as she spotted the mailbox that Bill Duncan had fashioned in his woodshop. Its colors had faded over the years, but in the Honda's headlights, she could still discern the multi-colored flowers that had been painted on its surface so many seasons ago.

The house was a long, one-story rectangle, fashioned from fragrant cedar lumber and stained with only a clear, protective coating so as to retain its natural beauty. It was really much too big for only one person, but Crystal could certainly understand why Kathy had remained after Bill died. This house had been their dream. To sell it would be like selling her last memory of her dear husband, something she would never do. They never had any children of their own to fill up all of those extra rooms, although they would have made wonderful parents. Now, the big empty house was all she had left.

As Luke and Crystal emerged from the Honda, Kathy appeared on the porch, wiping her hands on the apron she wore around her midsection. The smell of beef roast wafted through the clean air, and Crystal almost found herself drooling. She rushed across the lawn to meet Kathy at the foot of the porch stairs, throwing her arms around her old friend and hugging her tightly. She didn't even feel the warm tears as they flowed down her cheeks.

"Oh, my poor sweet Chrissy," said Kathy, stepping back to get a better look but unable to take her hands from Crystal's shoulders. "I'm so sorry about Maude."

Crystal nodded and blotted her wet eyes. "Thank you," she said.

Kathy had aged well since Crystal had last seen her—a little heavier, perhaps, a little more gray hair at the temples, but overall, she was much as Crystal remembered. There was a gentle kindness in her features that hinted at the quality of person within.

Crystal was suddenly aware of Luke standing behind her, holding the supine, slumbering form of Virginia Parnell in his arms. Crystal cleared her throat and said, "This is my friend Luke Leighton and his daughter, Virginia." She detested herself for lying, but the words slipped out effortlessly. She didn't want to overload Kathy with too much information all at once. Crystal was acutely aware of how ludicrous their story sounded, and she still wasn't entirely certain that Kathy wouldn't turn them away after hearing it.

Luke nodded. "Ma'am."

"Very nice to meet you, and *oh!* Isn't she just a *lovely* thing!" Kathy fawned over Virginia, leaning in for a closer look at the sleeping angel. Virginia lightly smacked her lips together, and her eyelids fluttered slightly. When Kathy turned back to Crystal, she was absolutely beaming. "I can't believe it's been so long! Our own little Hollywood starlet back home, and—*oh!* What happened to your arm?"

"I had a little spill," said Crystal.

"What's that on it? It looks like—*tree branches*? Haven't you been to a doctor?"

Crystal grinned sheepishly. "It's a little hard to do when you're on the lam."

"Well, let's get you all inside and put some food in your stomachs," she said, leading the way to the front door. "You can tell me about all of this nonsense while we eat."

The roast beef was more succulent than anything Luke had ever put into his mouth. It felt like it had been days since he had last eaten. On the side were homemade whipped potatoes—heavy with butter, green beans with bacon bits cooked in onion, and thick slabs of sweet cornbread. From a nutritionist's perspective, the meal was a one-way ticket to cardiac arrest, but this night, no one was protesting. The food could not have been more divine had it been prepared in the kitchens of heaven. Virginia had awakened at the mouth-watering aromas and now sat quietly at the far end of the table, diligently eating with much grace and aplomb.

"Thank you so much for everything, Kathy," said Crystal. "It's absolutely wonderful."

"Mmmphh." Luke nodded, his mouth full.

"You're absolutely welcome, sweetheart," she said. "I have to admit, I was kind of looking for you to call after I heard that nonsense on the television. You? Rob a store? *Really.*"

"I can hardly believe it myself," said Crystal. "But they say they have it on videotape, and although I haven't seen it myself, it must be awfully damning."

"Well, *I've* seen it," said Kathy, cutting through a slice of roast beef with her fork. "*I* could tell it wasn't you."

Crystal looked at her, startled. *"Really?"*

"Oh, sure, there were similarities, but I've known you since you were just a baby," she said warmly. "I'd know you anywhere."

"Unfortunately, the police don't seem to see it your way," said Crystal. "And we were on the road at the time that it happened, so we have no way of providing an alibi. I'm scared."

"I'm sure you are," said Kathy soberly. "But maybe it would be best to turn yourself in and cooperate with the authorities. It would save you a lot of trouble, and in the long run, everything would probably come out in the wash."

Crystal shook her head. "I know it sounds crazy, but I don't think that's the right thing to do. Not just yet. I think I need to wait until this woman who looks like me makes another appearance. I don't know what she's up to or why she's impersonating me, but I have to try and flush her out. That alone would provide reasonable doubt."

"You might be right. It's your call to make, dear. You can stay as long as you want. I won't tell anyone that you're here."

Crystal was embarrassed to find herself misting up again. "Thank you," she said, then returned her attention to her plate.

"You won't *believe* what a little heartbreaker Brian Knittle has turned into," said Kathy, changing the subject to something refreshingly light and banal while buttering a piece of cornbread.

Crystal recoiled in mock disgust. "That creepy little kid who always ate his own boogers?"

And the conversation shifted gears as easily as that. Luke watched with interest as the two women began mending the gap that time had brought between them. Kathy seemed perfectly content with Crystal's lightweight explanation of their outlaw status. She hadn't bothered clarifying Virginia's presence, so Luke did the best he could to play the doting father. He was relieved when the conversation turned nostalgic. Watching Crystal across the table, her eyes twinkling with the vivid memories that Kathy Duncan evoked, Luke was suddenly aware that the cold, bitter mask she had presented to him upon their earliest encounters had fallen away entirely. The woman he saw before him now was Crystal Williams, more sweet-natured and genuinely selfless than he had imagined possible. Despite her treacherous day, she was still beautiful in the soft glow of the overhead light.

For dessert, Kathy brought out a concoction entirely of her own creation. It was part chocolate, part caramel, part cream cheese—and all of it decadently delicious. It was a wonder Kathy didn't weigh four hundred pounds.

"I hope this isn't too awfully rude of me," said Kathy as she poured coffee for Crystal and Luke. Virginia was attacking her dessert with a little less than her usual diplomacy; her cheeks were liberally smudged with chocolate splotches. "I have to step out for a little bit after dinner. I have a regular meeting at the church, and I'm supposed to lead tonight. There's really no one to sub for me if—"

"Don't give it another thought," said Crystal. "I didn't expect you to drop everything to entertain me. The truth is, we wouldn't be very good company for you anyway. We're exhausted and will probably head right off to bed, if that's alright."

"Just as long as you don't try and take off before we have a chance to *really* catch up," said Kathy with a smile. "I've missed you something awful."

———◆———

Crystal and Luke helped Kathy clean up the dinner mess while Virginia exhausted herself running circuits around the house, entertained by imaginary friends and other things incomprehensible to adult minds. She hadn't once mentioned her murdered family since arriving. It was as if she understood that Crystal's oversimplification of the facts was, for whatever reason, necessary. By the time they finished the last of the dishes, Virginia had fallen asleep in Kathy's favorite recliner, an ugly overstuffed piece that was at least as old as Crystal.

Kathy brought a blanket from the hall closet to cover her, then showed the guest rooms to Luke and Crystal. Crystal was amused to note that Kathy had assumed she and Luke were romantically involved. She first showed them a single room, then flushed bright red as she realized her mistake from the look of discomfort that passed between them. After a quick recovery, Kathy had assigned them each their own room. She then collected her purse and a small book bag, heading out into the night and leaving them alone in the sprawling house. Despite their exhaustion, the incessant chatter of cricket calls from outside was hypnotic, and they soon found themselves drawn to the rear patio.

"You don't think she'll call the police, do you?" asked Luke, as they sat side-by-side on the porch swing, rocking languidly.

Crystal shook her head and inhaled deeply of the fresh country air. "No. Kathy would never do a thing like that."

"Do you think she knows who Virginia really is? I'm sure her picture's been in all of the newspapers."

"I don't know. Maybe. She asked about Virginia's robe, which isn't exactly normal traveling attire. I told her we had to leave in a hurry and didn't have time to grab a change of clothes for the poor thing. Kathy said she was laundering some clothing donations from the church and probably had something that would fit Virginia in the meanwhile. I plan to come clean with her just as soon as possible—probably tomorrow morning. I just thought it was too much to lay on her in one shot."

Luke nodded, lighting a cigarette and inhaling deeply.

Crystal stared out into the night, relishing the seclusion afforded by the natural boundary formed of two steep, tree-covered hills that came together directly behind and almost buttressing the rear of Kathy's house. There was a small, circular clearing of well-tended grass, but it was more decorative than functional. The *real* yard space was along the house's front and sides. This was more like a private garden.

"How do you think Virginia got that money?" asked Crystal. "I didn't see it in her hands when we took her from the house, and her robe doesn't have any pockets."

"I'm not sure," said Luke. "But it's not the first time something like that's happened."

Crystal turned toward him. "What do you mean?"

"When I was on the road with Bert, I found twenty dollars tucked inside a phonebook in a public booth."

"Okay, so it was your lucky day. I hardly think it's the same thing."

"Except that I dreamed about it first," he said. "It was one of those déjà vus that I told you about. It was the night before I left Jasper. I dreamt I was standing in one of those old-fashioned phone booths, the type that's all glass with a sliding door, you know?"

431

Crystal nodded.

"It was in some sort of parking lot with a lot of big rigs at the rear. The phonebook was swinging on one of those coiled chains that won't really let you lift the book far enough for it to be of any use. A twenty-dollar bill was just sticking out the end like a bookmark, so I grabbed it. Just as I did, a bright light flashed across the booth, and one of the semis roared to life. It was bearing down on me, and I woke up in a panic. Very next night, every single thing in that dream happened. Place was Fat Louie's BBQ just outside of Louisville, and being there was like the strongest sense of déjà vu I've ever had. The twenty-dollar bill was exactly as it had been in the dream, wedged between the yellow and white pages. The semi *was* coming toward me, but it was coming to pick me up. It belonged to Bert Parnell."

Crystal sighed. "I've had dreams of my own," she said softly. "I didn't mention them before because they seemed so personal. They were always about my Aunt Maude. I had the first one after I—took those pills in California." She laughed dryly. "She told me that she was disappointed in me."

"I'm sure that's not true—"

"Oh, but you see, the funny thing is, I'm sure it *is* true. In her eyes, the only thing worse I could do is kill someone else. But she told me other things in these dreams, things that were undoubtedly prophetic but part of me didn't want to believe. See, parts of this are challenging the things I know to be true about the world, the things I *accept* to be true. I feel like I'm trapped in an episode of *The X-Files*. And even though I don't want any of this to be happening, I can't go back to the way things were before. Everything that I had, everything that I was—it all seems so trivial when I consider what that little girl is going to have to go through."

"Odd, don't you think?" asked Luke.

"What?"

"Virginia seems to be handling the trauma of this morning unusually well. I expected her to blow your cover story at any moment over dinner, but she handled herself like a little trooper. It kind of worries me."

"I know what you mean," said Crystal. She glanced over her shoulder through the picture window and into the living room where she could see the steady rise and fall of Virginia's chest as she lay in the recliner. "So many horrible things have happened to her all at once—she might be in shock."

"She's an adorable child."

Crystal gave Luke a surprised smile. "I didn't even think you'd notice."

Luke could feel his cheeks flushing. "Well, I mean, aren't *all* children adorable?"

"No," said Crystal, her smile still firmly in place. "Some are fat, ugly, and awful."

Luke was grinning, too. "But she really *is* special."

"I feel it, too."

The dense cloud cover of the afternoon had finally given way to a crystal-clear night sky. The moon was full and bright, and stars twinkled in time to the chirping crickets. Before the moment could slip away, Crystal leaned across the swing and surprised Luke with the sweetest kiss he had ever known.

———◆———

I can't believe this shit.

Paula was slumped in the passenger seat of a Chrysler K-Car, the willing hostage of an insurance salesman who had happened by Friendly's shortly after she had awakened behind the dumpster. She knew traffic would only get thinner as the night progressed, so she had readily agreed to ride with him, despite his beady eyes and his distressing habit of frequently licking his fat, repulsive lips. Anything to get away from the insanity. It was only after they had gotten underway that she thought to ask him where he was headed. With cruel irony, she was informed they were heading to Portsmouth, a city only a handful of miles south of Lucasville. It seemed that no matter what she did to extract herself from the extraordinary circumstances of the past few weeks, it was useless. After witnessing the aftermath at the Parnell house, Paula could handle no more savage butchery. Why couldn't she get away?

She had tried to call Angel from a payphone at Friendly's. The cell phone had rung about ten times before forwarding Paula to voicemail. She considered leaving a message but decided against it at the last minute. She didn't want to forewarn Angel that she was ending her part of the plan. Paula was afraid her sister would try to talk her into staying, and she knew that ultimately, Angel's will would persevere. It always did. She was the strong one. She was the one who took care of Paula when Tammy was too busy, or Joel was too drunk. If Angel really insisted, Paula would have no choice but to try and find Luke and Crystal again and rejoin their damned circle. Paula owed Angel *everything*.

But she couldn't stay in the company of that little girl one more minute. Virginia Parnell was a lightning rod to trouble, and Paula had no desire to contribute to the body count that was collecting at the girl's feet. She didn't feel at all guilty leaving the child behind.

She had no trouble walking away from Luke, either. He seemed about as bright as a cinderblock and as trustworthy as a convict. She could still see the wild look on his face as he had burst through the corn and landed on the hood of their car. *Jesus!* How in the world Crystal could trust him was beyond her.

She *would* miss Crystal, though. It wasn't every day that you got the opportunity to meet your idol, much less travel cross-country with her. And even if recent events had gotten wildly out of hand, Paula would always treasure the time she had spent with Crystal Bright. She had been so sorely disappointed after their initial meeting on the set of *Benny and the Girl*—when Crystal had flung the hard copy of her script at Paula and accused her of trying to steal the spotlight. Subsequent events had given Paula a new perspective about the entertainment industry and the enormous pressure it places on its young performers, filling their heads with the notion that they are above everyone else and can do no wrong— as long as ratings are good, and revenue is high. It hadn't diminished her dream of someday becoming a star, but it hopefully would allow her to avoid some of the pratfalls so common to the young and naive once she arrived. And she *would* go back to Hollywood. Just as soon as she could get through to Angel and tell her that she was done with this whole crazy business, she would put her thumb out and begin her journey west.

Paula suddenly felt a weight on her knee and looked down to discover the fat pig with the earthworm lips had flopped one of his paws down to caress her kneecap. "Almost there, sweet thing," he said. "I got me a room at the Ett-Mar. We can get ourselves right comfortable."

Here we go, she thought.

His hand began to slowly slide up her blue-jeaned leg, moving toward her inner thigh. Her breath caught in her throat as she was flooded with memories of Joel and the things to which he had subjected her for so many horrible years.

She reached down and scooped his hand away as if it were a repugnant insect. "Don't touch me like that," she said, her voice sounding weak and pathetic in her own ears. Why couldn't she ever be forceful? Why couldn't she ever find the strength to fight back? She could feel panic welling as her control of the situation slipped away.

"Aw, *darlin'*," he protested, trying to work his hand back into her lap. "I just wanted a little squeeze—see if she's ripe."

If the past few days had taught Paula nothing, it had taught her that the unexpected sometimes happened. Suddenly, it was as if her body were operating independently of her mind. Her arm shot out and seized the knobby end of the column shift, jerking it upward into park. The transmission shrieked as its internal components were forced into positions that were never intended. The insurance salesman's eyes were as big as saucers as he snatched his hand away from Paula's leg and clamped onto the steering wheel, trying to keep the car under control while guiding it to the berm. It lurched to a halt in an obscene metallic squelch.

"You stupid bitch!" he screamed. "You could've *killed* us! You broke my goddamned *car!* Why, you—"

But Paula had already thrown open the passenger door and leapt out into the night. They were traveling east on US 52, and she remembered passing through a small section of civilization just a mile or so back. She ran as if she were being chased by the devil, determined not to let that sorry fuck get hold of her, because if he did, she knew she would lose her mind. Those earthworm lips would move, but the words would be Joel McElroy's. His smell would be Joel McElroy's. His *touch*—

She didn't bother pacing herself—she just *ran*.

II

Lisa stared at her reflection in the mirror.

Not bad.

Chad had bought scissors and a bottle of hair coloring at Big Bear in Rosemount before they checked into a motel a few doors down. He had cut her hair in a short bob that was remarkably straight and even considering he had never cut hair before. He had then opened the package of coloring, reading the instructions carefully before wedging his hands into the flimsy plastic protective gloves and changing Lisa's blonde tresses to fiery red.

The difference was startling. There was little chance that Lisa would be mistaken for Crystal Bright now. Her own Nanna would have had to look twice before recognizing her.

Afterward, they had made love with the ferocity of wild animals, working through the day's frustration with savage single-mindedness. Lisa had noticed that Chad was no longer favoring his wounded arm; in fact, at times he was rather creative with its use. Afterward, Chad had immediately fallen asleep, exhausted from their arduous day and more recent physical activity. Lisa had laid beside him for several minutes before sliding out from underneath the covers, returning to the bathroom mirror where she now re-inspected her new look.

Not bad, she thought again, rearranging her hair with her fingers.

She knew that Chad's remarkable recovery could only be attributed to the dark power that was guiding them through their journey. Nothing else could explain it. They had been chosen to perform this great task, this eradication of goodness, this *abomination*—

And that was what she had come to understand. There was something about the girl, something different, something that would someday change everything about the world as it existed. This new vision wasn't of a place in which Lisa wished to live. It would be a world without war or pain or suffering. It would be the most unimaginably boring theme park ever.

Lisa didn't believe in God or the Devil. Maybe it was because Nanna Grace had been so obsessed with her religion that Lisa found the notion ridiculous. While she understood the concepts of good and evil, she had never really applied them to herself. Presently, she did what was beneficial for herself, and if others interpreted those actions as evil—well, she'd kill them. But since Chad's

435

miraculous recovery and the dawning awareness that the girl's threat was a sort of global one, Lisa was beginning to rethink her theological conclusions. There was no doubt that a higher power of some sort was influencing things. Lately, she could feel the power flowing freely through her veins. It made her feel invincible. Seeing the speed with which Chad healed, she had become convinced of it. She would willingly be an emissary of this dark force so long as it continued to empower her in such an exhilarating way. Lisa was unable to imagine civilization in ruins as a direct result of the assassination of a four-year-old child, but she felt it was an important—no, *necessary* first step.

She was too wired to go to sleep. A glance at the bedside clock told her it was only a little before eleven, and it seemed like a waste of perfectly good time to lie on her back and stare at the ceiling. She slid into a pair of jeans and a t-shirt, jotted a quick note for Chad, then snatched the Volvo's keys off of the motel dresser.

The night was crisp and clean as Lisa emerged in the parking lot, shivering against the surprising coolness of the summer night. She whistled lightly as she crossed to the car, twirling the key ring on her fingertip. It certainly wouldn't hurt for her to drive around a bit, see if she felt compelled to head anywhere specific. She might just locate them tonight. She could still vividly recall the silver Honda in which they had been traveling. She might see it parked at a motel, or maybe even in someone's driveway. She smiled as she imagined herself leaving the little girl's head on the pillow beside Chad for him to see when he awakened.

As she opened the car door, she heard an odd tweeting sound from the rear of the car. She cocked her head and leaned in, listening to the curious, repetitious ululation. She unlocked the back door and slid inside, following her ears to the source of the sound. It was coming from Suze's shapeless black handbag, which the stupid bitch had left behind when she'd gone off into the woods.

Lisa fumbled with the clasp and produced a cell phone, its display panel flashing soft light in time with its ringing. She pressed the talk button and lifted the phone to her ear.

"Hello?"

"Oh, *Angel!* Thank *God!* I've been trying to reach you—"

Lisa remained silent, receiving the message meant for this person called Angel.

"—and this guy was chasing me, but I think I've lost him now." There was a moment of silence. "Angel? Are you there?"

Lisa cleared her throat. "You're looking for Suze, right?"

Another moment of silence, this one longer than the first. For a moment, Lisa thought the girl had hung up. But then, "Yes. Do you know where she is? I *really* need to talk to her."

"She's not here right now," said Lisa. "But she should be back in a little bit. Can I have her call you?"

More silence.

"Um, no, I'm at a payphone, and—and—"

The girl's voice was tremulous and faltering, and Lisa imagined her to be about fourteen years old.

"Are you alright?" asked Lisa, surprised at how easily she was able to lend warmth and caring to her voice.

The girl was crying now, trying to disguise it behind a series of soft snuffles. "It's just—it's just—I don't know exactly where I am, and I'm afraid that guy might find me again and if he does, I'm pretty sure he's gonna hurt me because I fucked his car all to pieces and I just don't know what to *do* and—"

"Why don't I come pick you up?" Lisa volunteered. "You can stay here until Suze—or Angel gets back." She chuckled. "Angel. I've never heard anyone call her that before."

"I don't guess anyone else would. I'm Suze's little sister, Paula. Angel's just always what I've called her."

"Can you find out where you're calling from? I'd be happy to come and get you."

"Hold on."

Lisa could hear muffled voices as Paula covered the mouthpiece and spoke with someone near her. After a moment, she returned. "I'm at a Duke and Duchess on 52 in West Portsmouth. Big yellow and black sign. You really can't miss it. It's almost the only thing around for miles. Listen, hey, I really appreciate this."

"Not a problem," said Lisa, emerging from the back seat and sliding behind the wheel. "Suze and I are really tight you know. I'd do almost anything for her, and I bet she'd break her neck trying to help me."

"I know," said Paula proudly. "I can't wait to see her again. I really need to talk to her."

"So, you've said," said Lisa, starting the Volvo. "Hold on just a minute."

She pulled out the map of Ohio that Chad had purchased from Friendly's and located West Portsmouth.

"Why, you're just down the road from here," said Lisa. "Give me fifteen minutes, and I'll be right there."

Paula was nervous.

She stood inside the Duke and Duchess, near the front glass of the carry-out, staring out into the small parking lot. Sodium vapor lamps cast circles of pale-yellow light underneath the canopy which housed a single bank of self-serve pumps. There weren't any customers at the moment, and US 52 was relatively untraveled at this hour. Every time a car passed, however, she held her breath, hoping it would turn in before that horny bastard with the earthworm lips stumbled onto the lot.

She was acutely aware of the way the man behind the counter watched her. He hadn't taken his eyes off of her since she had come into the building. After a moment, she realized how odd it must seem for her to come in out of the night and stand watch in his window. She belatedly considered the pretense of shopping and reached into her pocket, extracting one of the twenties she had taken from the pile of cash that the child had somehow produced. She ambled around the store, her fidgety hands lighting on items as if she were actually looking at them. Her attention continued to return to the front glass, and the clerk continued to openly stare.

Paula finally settled on a small bag of Funyuns and a bottle of Pepsi. She took them to the counter and tried to act inconspicuous as the clerk slowly shifted positions behind the cash register. He glanced at the items, then to Paula, then to the crumpled bill in her hand.

"You in some kind of trouble, miss?" He was middle-aged, fiftyish, with thinning hair and angular features. His eyes were bright behind wire-rimmed glasses, and if Paula hadn't been so afraid, she might have realized it was concern she was seeing in them.

Instead, when she looked at the man behind the counter, the man who made no move to process her order, take her cash and *quit staring at her*, she began to see traces of Joel McElroy in his features. The same square jawline, the same creases in his forehead, the same *earlobes*—

She had the sudden sensation that this man meant to do her great harm. She backed away from the counter, upsetting a display of Doritos as she bumped into it. The man was still staring at her, *staring* at her—coming out from behind the counter—nearly in front of her now, his arms reaching out—

Paula shrieked and ran for the door.

"Hey!" the man called, scrambling after her.

In Paula's mind, it was Joel McElroy who was chasing her, trying to pin her down again, trying to destroy everything that was ever pure about her. The man was making low, guttural noises—the *same* noises that Joel made when he—when he—

Running blindly through the door, she didn't notice the car that had just pulled into the lot. It had parked in the space nearest the doors, and Paula ran headlong into its grill, sprawling forward onto the hood in a move that was ironically reminiscent of Luke's dramatic entrance into hers and Crystal's lives. She heard the denim of her jeans rip as her legs raked over what she assumed was the license plate.

Paula glanced up quickly, certain that she would be looking into the infuriated eyes of the insurance salesman, who had somehow managed to get his car rolling again. She was relieved to discover that it was a red-headed woman who sat behind the wheel, her eyes wide with concern. She was gesturing for Paula to get into the car, so she slid across the hood and got in on the passenger side.

"You must be Paula," she said.

Paula nodded, watching as the clerk suddenly appeared at the entrance, waving his fist while his mouth flapped urgently. "Please—*hurry*," she said.

Without question, the red-headed stranger threw the car into reverse and backed away from the building. The front tires barked sharply as she shifted into drive and launched the car around the bank of pumps and out onto the highway. Neither of them noticed the startled attendant who stood behind, his fist still clutching the twenty-dollar bill that he had been trying to return to the girl before she fled.

"Oh, God," said Paula, leaning against the headrest and willing her heartbeat to slow down. "This has been the single worst day I have ever had in my life."

"Hmm."

"Thanks again for picking me up. Things were getting pretty weird out there. Has Suze come back yet?"

"Not yet. But it shouldn't be long. I'm Lisa Mitchell."

"Paula," said Paula, turning her gaze toward Lisa. "Paula Haver—" Her words froze as she focused on Lisa's face, so familiar underneath the sensible red hair. "—sham." She smiled crookedly as sweat trickled down the back of her neck.

"Suze didn't mention she had a sister," said Lisa, using a break in the median to perform an illegal U-turn, changing their direction from west to east. "She's never said much about her family at all."

Paula's eyes shifted to the door handle, tried to calculate the odds of throwing the door open as Lisa completed her U-turn and tumbling back out into the horrible night. Paula had been in such a hurry to escape from the convenience mart that she hadn't noticed that the car was a Volvo—*the* Volvo she had seen in the driveway of the Parnells. The red hair had thrown Paula, but she would have known those features anywhere; she had been living with a carbon copy of them for the past few days. But Lisa didn't seem to recognize her at all.

Paula replayed the scene over and over in her mind.

Lisa had emerged from the Parnell house in a hurry, focused only on reaching her car and getting away. She had cast one backward glance at the house, but Paula didn't think she had noticed her in the back seat of the Honda. She feared that Suze might have run afoul of these people. It had only been a feeling, but how else could she explain this Mitchell girl having Suze's cell phone?

Another thought crept into her mind. Could Suze actually be *working* with these people? No. It was unthinkable.

"Are you hungry?" asked Lisa.

Hesitantly, Paula nodded. She couldn't understand why this woman was being so kind. She didn't sense anything malevolent in her actions.

"How about Wendy's?" she asked. "I think they're open late."

439

"Sure," said Paula. "If you don't mind."

"Nope," said Lisa. "Matter of fact, I'm kind of hungry myself. It's been a long day."

Paula glanced at her quickly to see if there was any hidden meaning attached to those words. There didn't appear to be.

Lisa flipped on the radio and began humming along to an old Eagles song; the Eagles were one of the few bands that Nanna Grace found permissible. "What happened?" she asked.

"Huh?"

"Back there," said Lisa, nodding her head backward. "Sounded like you were in some trouble."

"This whole day's been trouble," Paula said, working diligently to keep her voice from quavering. "Some creep was trying to get into my pants back there."

"At the Duke and Duchess?"

"Well, no. Some guy I got a ride from. He started getting crazy with his hands, so I threw his car into park while we were flying down the highway."

Lisa threw her head back and laughed. "I wish I could've seen the surprise on his face!"

"Yeah, well, it wasn't so much surprise. He was pissed off. He wanted to—kill me." *Goddamn it!* she thought as her voice broke.

Lisa didn't seem to notice. "You shouldn't hitchhike," she said. "No way of knowing exactly who's out there. Why, you could be sitting right beside a psychopathic murderer. How could you know?"

Paula felt light-headed and rolled her window down a few inches.

"Are you alright?" asked Lisa. They had entered Portsmouth and were traveling north on US 23. Wendy smiled down from her pedestal on the right, and Lisa was slowing to turn into the lot.

Paula nodded, tilting her head toward the window where she could feel the breeze. Was Lisa toying with her? Every little thing she said was shredding Paula's nerves.

Where was Angel?

⸻◆⸻

"You'll have to forgive our cramped quarters," said Lisa as they crossed the parking lot of the Super 8. "This was an unexpected sort of pit stop."

She carried one of the sacks of food from Wendy's in her hand while Paula followed with the other bag and drink holder carrying four sodas. She had briefly considered trying to escape, but she needed to reach Angel, and this seemed like her best bet.

440

"You'll like Chad," Lisa was saying. "He's a little intense sometimes, but aren't we all? I *hope* you like him." She paused at the door to the motel room, turning to smile. "He's Suze's fiancé."

Paula tilted her head curiously. *"Really?* She didn't tell me—" She let her words trail away as she considered how very little she really knew about her big sister's life. When Suze lived in Morgan and they had shared a room, she had known Suze's boyfriends by name and was usually the subject of their gentle ribbing. After Suze divorced Roy, she started traveling, taking to the road for months at a time before spontaneously calling Paula from somewhere halfway across the country or showing up unannounced for a few quick minutes of catch-up before she darted off again. On these rare occasions, Suze's concern for her sister was evident, and they always spent their time talking about Paula's life and how things were going for her. They never talked about Suze or the things that were happening in her life. Perhaps it wasn't so unusual that Paula didn't know about Chad.

"He's a real looker, too," said Lisa. "But you better keep your hands off of him," she warned playfully. "Suze would kill you both if she ever caught you messing around."

Lisa unlocked the door and opened it, turning on the lights as she entered. "Yo, Chaddie-boy, up and at 'em," she said, slapping Chad's feet as she passed the bed. "We got food—and company, too."

Chad stirred on the bed, grumbling as he struggled up onto one elbow. He was about to complain about being interrupted from his slumber when his eyes caught Lisa's, and he fell silent. He sat up and adjusted his position, pulling the sheet up and folding his arms across his lap.

"This is Paula," she said, placing the bag of burgers on the dresser. "You be real nice to her. You'll be related soon enough. She's Suze's sister. I told her that she was welcome to stay with us until Suze got back from her little errand. I hope you don't mind."

"Not at all," said Chad, suddenly aware that he was completely naked beneath the sheet.

"I told her Suze shouldn't be long," she said, opening the bag and distributing its contents. "I got you chicken. I hope that's okay."

Chad nodded as he took the sandwich from her, tossing her a questioning look.

Lisa shook her head slightly. "If you'd rather have a cheeseburger, I got one for Suze, so I suppose you could trade her."

"This is fine," said Chad, unwrapping the foil.

Lisa arranged her own food on the small table by the door, just beside Paula. As she passed, she flicked on the television set that was bolted to the counter.

"—and new evidence suggests that Crystal Bright's earlier holdup of a local carryout may be connected with the gruesome murders discovered in Borden. A new warrant has been issued for Crystal Bright, and although she has not been formally charged with the crimes, she *is* wanted for questioning in the execution-style murders of Greta Parnell and her two daughters, Elizabeth and Laurie. Police are remaining tight-lipped, but an unnamed source has suggested that officials are able to place Crystal Bright at the crime scene. The Indiana State Police are showing an active interest in these events as they continue to investigate a terrorist-style bombing of a Friendly's gas station which claimed the life of Bert Parnell, husband to Greta and father of the two slain teens. Still missing is four-year-old Virginia Parnell, last seen in the company of her mother and sisters by friends who had been visiting to offer condolences. We will provide updates on this strange case as it continues to unfold—"

III

Helen turned her back to Leonard and Jessica as she arranged the food on the top of the dresser.

"I didn't mean to interrupt," she said stiffly.

Leonard snatched his hand away from Jessica's as if it had been resting on a hot plate.

"You weren't interrupting," said Jessica. "This is your room, too."

Helen made an unintelligible sound in the back of her throat as she continued to sort the food. The air in the room thickened as the seconds passed, and Leonard looked as if he might just bolt for the door.

"I have to admit," said Jessica, doing her best to dispel the growing tension. "I didn't think I could eat a single bite, but that smells awfully good. What did you get?"

"Quarter pounders," Helen said, then added glumly, "With cheese."

"Will you stay and eat with us, Leonard?" asked Jessica, self-consciously noting the false cheer in her own voice.

"Um, no—no," said Leonard, scooping up a sandwich, a container of fries and plucking a cup of Coke from the cardboard drink carrier. "Please let me know what I owe so I—"

"Nonsense," said Jessica. "This will all be billed to the Jay County Sheriff's Department anyway."

Leonard nodded and smiled nervously. "Then if it's all the same to you, I'll just head over to my room. I'm sure you ladies have lots to discuss."

"Fine," said Helen flatly, keeping her back to him as she crossed the room toward the small table tucked against the far wall.

Jessica offered Leonard a meek smile and shrugged her shoulders. He eased the door open and slipped out into the corridor, leaving the two women alone.

The tension didn't dissipate with Leonard's departure. Helen sat at the small table, taking slow, steady bites of her sandwich, pointedly ignoring Jessica.

Jessica pushed her covers aside and slid out of bed. "Helen? Are you alright?"

Helen's shoulders slumped, but she nodded.

Jessica retrieved her food from the mattress and carried it over to the table, sitting across from Helen and forcing the nurse to look at her. Helen's complexion was an angry, mottled red, and the swelling around her eyes threatened tears at any moment.

"What's going on here?" asked Jessica. "Surely, you don't think that Leonard and I—"

His name was the key to her floodgates. Helen began sobbing with deep, wracking coughs that began to frighten Jessica. She wondered if the woman had a heart condition she was about to demonstrate. But eventually the tide ebbed, and Helen was merely snuffling to regain her composure.

"I'm sorry, dear," she said, blowing her nose on one of the flimsy brown napkins. "I'm just having a terrible time being this close to—that man."

Jessica didn't know how to respond. Ever since Leonard had shared his sad story with her, she had been mulling it over. She understood guilt like that which Leonard carried around as a second skin; she knew his feelings were genuine. In a world of ifs, Leonard had once chosen the wrong path, and the consequences of his actions or lack thereof had inevitably cost Evie Martin her life. Selfish and cowardly, perhaps, but in no way premeditated. Leonard Barnes suffered the same folly as every other person on the planet. He had made a mistake. It was the tragic consequences of that mistake that differentiated it from all the other, normal sins that are committed every single day. And as penance for his sin, Leonard Barnes was condemned to live with the knowledge that he might have averted Helen Martin's loss if only he had been a stronger man who had been able to stand up to Clinton McDermott. Did his actions put him beyond redemption? Jessica would never be so presumptuous as to speculate; she who lives in glass houses...

No amount of grieving could ever recover what was lost to Helen, however. The years of mourning had etched fine lines into the nurse's round face, and her features fell too easily into despair. Helen needed someone to blame for what had happened to her daughter, and if Clinton McDermott couldn't pay for his deeds, then she would simply look for the next in line. Unfortunately for Leonard, that would be him. If Clinton had chosen to drink himself stupid at home on a case of beer he had bought from 7-Eleven, Helen would likely have gone after them, as well. She was a woman who constantly struggled with patience. Her need for retribution on behalf of her murdered daughter was a constant, insatiable presence. Helen would never be able to look at Leonard without seeing him as the man who had murdered her daughter, and there was nothing Jessica could do to make her reconsider her position—Jessica understood retribution, too.

Traveling with these two was going to be pure hell.

Jessica wasn't even sure what they were doing yet, but she knew that solidarity was a prerequisite to success. If Chad were involved in this—as she was sure he was—there would be injuries, some of them severe. Helen's medical expertise might make the difference between life and death to someone. Leonard had actually seen the vehicle in which these people traveled and was the only hope they had of spotting it on the road. Moreover, he understood that what they were facing was more than just two or three rotten apples. He knew that these people formed a collective force of evil fueled by a power so primal that most men refused to even acknowledge its existence. Neither Helen nor Leonard were dispensable in this mission, and Jessica had to find a way to keep Helen from tearing Leonard apart before they ran into *real* trouble, as she knew they inevitably would.

Her years on the switchboard had made her an unwitting witness to countless exchanges by policemen of various rank as they had passed through the sheriff's office. She again found herself relying on this subliminal knowledge to present herself convincingly.

"Helen," she began, her voice soft but firm. "I know what happened with Evie."

"He told you?"

Jessica nodded. "And believe me, my heart goes out to you. But that was then, and this is now. Leonard is the only one who has seen their car. I need him. *You* need him. If you want to find Lisa, he's your best bet."

Helen's tears returned, but softly. "I never wanted her to stay in that house by herself. She was just out of the hospital, much too weak to be responsible for her own care. She was an easy target."

"For what?"

"A home invasion," said Helen, not without a touch of exasperation. "You hear about them on the news all the time. Burglars who don't even bother picking your locks or breaking a window—they just come right through the front door! Lisa wouldn't have stood a chance, alone in that house by herself. I tried to stop by as often as I could, b-but—"

"Don't do that to yourself," said Jessica. "It's not doing anyone any good."

"But you don't understand the kind of misfortune that has stalked that poor girl! First, she loses her nanna—I may not have cared much for Grace Mitchell, but she was the only family that Lisa ever knew. Next, she's broadsided by a delivery truck, and it's nothing short of a miracle that she even survived. She had only just returned home when all of this happened."

Jessica cocked her head. "How long was she in the hospital?"

"Not nearly as long as we expected considering the severity of her injuries," said Helen, finding renewed interest in her lukewarm sandwich. "Why?"

"Nothing," mumbled Jessica, leaning back in her chair and sipping her Coke. Something about Lisa's rapid recovery niggled at her memory.

Helen finished her sandwich and sat back with a sigh. "I don't have to like it, but if you say we need Leonard Barnes, I suppose we do."

Jessica smiled and placed a hand on her arm. "We do. And I want you to believe me when I tell you that I'm remaining as objective as possible as far as Lisa is concerned."

Helen looked at her sharply. "He was filling your head with poison about her, wasn't he? I should've never left the room!"

Jessica was surprised at how quickly Helen's anger resurfaced, her cheeks again infused with deep, crimson splotches.

"Listen to me, Helen," she said, her voice commanding attention. "I need to be aware of all possibilities, no matter how remote they may be. If there is any potential that Lisa Mitchell is dangerous, then *yes*, I have to proceed as if she is. I understand that you don't believe it or like it, but what possible harm can come from being cautious?"

Helen studied her with narrowed eyes. "If only you had *met* her, we wouldn't be having this ridiculous conversation."

"But I didn't have that luxury, so you'll just have to forgive me if I follow procedure," said Jessica. She had no idea what procedure might have been in such a circumstance, but she was pretty sure it didn't involve dragging two civilians into a case that might easily cost them their lives. "I will tell you only one more time that I will form my own opinion about Lisa. I need you to respect that, Helen, and if you can't, then maybe we better figure out a way to get you back to Morgan."

Jessica held her breath, expecting Helen to call her bluff. The splotches on her face had turned from deep crimson to purple, and her fingers were linked together to keep her hands from shaking.

"Fine," said Helen, finally, her voice tight.

"No," said Jessica. "We're not going to play that way, Helen. I will not tolerate your grudging cooperation. If you're staying, I have to be able to depend on you without question. If you can't do that, then we should go ahead and drop you at the local Greyhound."

"Please, no," said Helen, her face crumbling. "I can't go back to Morgan when I know that Lisa still needs me. *Please*."

Jessica stared at Helen until the nurse averted her eyes.

"I'll behave," Helen pleaded. "I promise."

Jessica slowly nodded. "As long as we are clear on that. I could certainly use your help. And I will do everything I can to respect your feelings about Leonard whenever possible."

445

Helen nodded amicably, having been successfully put into her place.

Jessica allowed the silence between them to stretch while she finished the rest of her food. "Thank you for picking up dinner," she said, wiping the corners of her mouth. "I feel a lot better."

"I knew you would," said Helen, trying to regain some of the bedside manner she had earlier demonstrated. "Your body needs *something* to keep itself going."

Jessica glanced at her. "Are we okay here?" she asked.

Helen nodded.

"Good," said Jessica. "It's almost midnight. You should get some rest. After your ordeal in Morgan, I imagine you need all that you can get."

"What about you?"

"I'll be along shortly," said Jessica. "I'm going to take a shower first."

"Jessica?"

"Yes?"

"Do you think we'll find them?"

Jessica nodded without hesitation. She knew that by tomorrow they would have either found the killers—or the killers would have found them.

———◇———

Leonard sat on the floor of the motel balcony, just outside his door. His legs poked through the security rail and dangled like pendulums over the parking lot below. His stomach was so upset that he had barely touched his food. Helen Martin frequently had that effect on him.

He wondered what Helen was saying to Jessica over dinner. He wondered if Helen could convince Jessica that Leonard had no place in their little group. Normally, he would have considered any excuse to remove himself from Helen's company a blessing, but not this time. When his car had broken down just outside of Morgan, he nearly surrendered to defeat. Jessica Lybrook had arrived at precisely the right moment, offering a ride and more importantly, a chance to stop that evil creature and her allies before they were able to fully implement their plan—whatever it may be. His stomach was tied in knots worrying about this unknown plan, but he fervently held onto the hope that it wasn't too late to stop them. He wanted *so much* to do something positive for this world, something that might partially redeem him for his past transgressions.

He was surprised when the door to Helen and Jessica's room opened, and Jessica emerged. She was wearing the same clothes she had worn all day, but her hair was swept up on top of her head, wrapped in a damp towel. She pulled the door shut gently and motioned for Leonard to remain quiet. She sat down and dangled her legs out over the edge of the balcony beside him.

"Helen's asleep," said Jessica, her voice little more than a whisper.

"Look, Ms. Lybrook—"

"Jessica."

He smiled, and for a moment he looked like a little boy. "Jessica. I know that Mrs. Martin wants me to leave, but I hope you understand why it is that I can't just walk away. It's a chance for redemption. It can't make up for what I done, but I hope it's a step in the right direction."

Her tired smile was melancholy. "I know. I made it plain to Helen that we needed to work as a team, whether she liked it or not."

"I'm sure that went over well."

"Like a ton of bricks. But I told her that I am reserving judgment about Lisa Mitchell until I have the opportunity to decide for myself. That seemed to calm her down a bit."

"But you've already decided."

Jessica cast a guilty look over her shoulder. "Yes."

Leonard was almost elated. He had never expected anyone to believe his theories about Lisa Mitchell, much less a police officer. For the first time since these strange events had begun, he didn't feel alone. His hope faded almost as quickly as it came. He remembered Jessica's partial tale of the boy to whom she had given birth. His blood ran cold thinking of *two* adversaries sharing Lisa's goals and working toward them. Helen had mentioned another one, a girl. Who was to say that she wasn't equally cold-blooded? Hell, they could be part of a small army for all Leonard knew, closing in on an unsuspecting population from the shadows.

"I told Helen that she needed to lay off of you," said Jessica. "I can certainly understand the friction, but we can't let it get in the way."

"And she *agreed?*"

"She didn't want to, but I didn't really give her a choice. And it goes two ways."

Leonard looked at her quizzically. "How so?"

"You need to keep your feelings about Lisa Mitchell to yourself. Helen doesn't need any additional reason to dislike you."

"But she'll find out eventually—"

"And I imagine that it will be a lot easier to accept if she sees it with her own eyes. I haven't mentioned anything about Chad, either. I—I don't think she'd understand," said Jessica, looking down at her feet.

"You haven't seen him since he was two?"

Jessica's mouth drew together in a tight line, but she kept her eyes on her feet. "Three. I've spent years trying to forget the whole mess, and you know, I almost did. How someone can forget anything so devastating is beyond me. Now that I've remembered part of it, I'm afraid to remember the rest. The only thing I know for certain is that it was the most horribly painful period of time I have ever been through. In the beginning, I had lots of friends to turn to, people I

447

thought would provide the support I needed when I feared there was something wrong with my son. It didn't happen all at once, but one by one, they turned away from me. These were people I had known for *years*—hell, I went to high school with most of them! But the looks on their faces were all the same. They thought the problem was with me, not Chad.

"My pregnancy was rough. I was sick all the time, but not just morning sickness. I developed toxemia and was hospitalized for a while. I had some of the scariest dreams I've ever had then—a woman stabbed, buildings burning, mobs in the streets, people on *fire*—"

She shuddered.

"I wasn't a particularly religious woman," she said. "I guess I'm not now, either—at least not by conventional means. But the things I saw in my dreams were absolutely apocalyptic—end of the world kind of bullshit. I was scared out of my mind—literally, according to most people."

She swallowed hard. The story was so hard to tell; it was still coming a piece at a time, but with each recollection came the cold stark remembrance of what it had been like to be Jessie Lybrook in 1985. She couldn't believe it was happening again.

Please God, don't let it happen again.

"The accidents started when Chad was about a year old. A neighbor was electrocuted in her own yard while using electric hedge trimmers. The water came from our garden hose, which had apparently been left on. Neither Bernie nor I had used it in weeks. If we had left it on, the whole side yard would've washed away. But there were other children in the neighborhood, and I chalked it up to one of them. It wasn't beyond one of those little rascals to steal a drink from a hose and forget to turn it back off. Even I didn't suspect Chad at first. For God's sake, he was only a year old! Later, I noticed that the window in his room overlooked the spot—you know, where she died. He was down for his nap when it happened, but he wasn't asleep. I'm sure of it now. Don't ask me how he managed it, but I—"

Jessica's voice trailed away as she slowly raised her head, staring blankly out into the night.

She could see Chad's crib in the corner; soon he would need his own bed, and the very thought made her uneasy. She liked to think of the crib as a sort of cage where she could contain him. She remembered the way he looked at her that afternoon, from within his small cell. In the shadows of the afternoon, his eyes appeared to be all pupil. She had looked over his head and peered out the window, a startled sound freezing in her throat as she watched Elena Mingus dance the electric slide with her hedge trimmer held high above her head. She had turned at once, running toward the telephone in the hall. As her vision swept across the room, she saw the other bed, the one on the other side of the room.

The Spiderman sheets. The stacks of comic books on the floor at the head of the bed.

Jessica gasped. "Oh, my God!"

Leonard reached out to steady her. "What's wrong, Ms.—Jessica? You're not havin' another of your spells, are you? Do you want me to get Mrs. Martin?"

Jessica shook her head and held Leonard in place. She couldn't face the nurse right now. She didn't even know if she could face Leonard anymore.

She *remembered.*

CHAPTER TWENTY-THREE

I

The hands were around her throat again, squeezing, *squeezing*—

She gasped and tried to look around, but all she could see were splashes of white light dancing across her field of vision.

A burst of stars, then everything went black.

She didn't know how long she'd been asleep, but in her dream, she was in a car, lying in the back seat with her damp head in Kathy Duncan's lap. Kathy was cooing nonsense but avoided touching her any more than necessary. Kathy had never before seemed so frightened, and it was contagious. Crystal didn't know what was going on, but it wasn't good. Aunt Maude was driving—*driving?* Maude hadn't driven in years. It had begun to wreak havoc on her nerves, so she had retired herself. But she was driving because Kathy had never learned how—

Crystal sat up, a thin sheen of perspiration crawling across her skin as she tried to cling to the last vestiges of her nightmare. She was disoriented, and her eyes adjusted slowly to the moonlight that spilled through the windows. Kathy's house. That's right. She shoved her covers aside and got to her feet, shuffling toward the door. Her heart was still thumping in tempo with the dream, and she could still picture Kathy in the back seat, afraid to comfort her, afraid to *touch* her.

What in the hell had happened?

She remembered that Kathy Duncan had gotten her driver's license around that time, as if she never again wanted to be stuck without transportation, especially in an emergency.

Crystal paused at Luke's door and considered peeking in at Virginia. They had decided that it made more sense for the girl to stay in Luke's room. Not only was he supposedly her father, he offered more protection than Crystal if those people were to suddenly arrive. She knew they were nearby—she *sensed* it. But they couldn't possibly be traced to Kathy Duncan this quickly. Could they?

She left the lights off as she walked barefoot down the hardwood hallway. She didn't want to disturb anyone's sleep, but she needed a glass of water. She had come out of her dream on an adrenaline buzz that had left her with cottonmouth.

Outside, a breeze stirred in the trees, quieting the sounds of night creatures with its irregularity, leaving behind a heavy silence that was broken only by the rhythmic ticking of the grandfather clock in the living room. It was going to storm again. As if in confirmation, a wicked bolt of lightning forked across the sky, igniting the heavens and briefly exposing the bloated bands of dark clouds that hung overhead.

Crystal shivered. It was cold in the house. At the end of the hallway, she turned right and went into the kitchen. She pulled a glass from the cupboard and filled it at the tap, drinking the water in one long gulp. She refilled it and repeated the process.

"Bad dreams?"

Crystal nearly dropped her water glass. She whirled to find Kathy leaning in the doorway, her ratty blue bathrobe drawn tightly around her.

"I didn't mean to scare you," said Kathy, crossing the room to stand beside Crystal at the counter. "I heard you tossing around in there. I thought you might want to talk."

Crystal smiled. "I didn't hear you come back from your meeting."

Kathy went to the refrigerator and poured herself a glass of milk. "Yes—well, it ran late. I haven't been home long." She turned on the light over the sink, casting a fragile glow into the center of the room.

Crystal was surprised to see that it was only a little after one in the morning. It felt so much later. She and Luke had transported Virginia to Luke's room and had themselves retired around ten.

Kathy produced a bag of chocolate graham cracker cookies and plopped it in the middle of the small breakfast table that was against the far wall. She sat down and waited expectantly for Crystal to join her.

"So?" she finally asked.

Crystal blinked. "What?"

"Do you want to tell me about your dreams?"

Crystal studied her friend's face in the curious lighting. Kathy seemed almost *eager* for Crystal to share with her, like she already knew what Crystal had dreamt and only needed confirmation. Her eyes were brightly inquisitive behind her round spectacles. Despite her attire, she didn't look like she had even considered going to bed yet.

Crystal plucked a cookie from the plastic tray and nibbled at its corners. "What happened to me?" she asked. "Back then?"

Kathy inhaled sharply and sat bolt upright.

"What?" asked Crystal, alarmed.

"Then it's true," murmured Kathy, turning sideways in her chair. "I always told Maude that it wasn't over. A child like that can't just be isolated. Time is *always* on its side."

"What are you talking about? What child? Are you talking about Virginia?"

Kathy looked at her blankly before she remembered Luke's supposed daughter.

"No, not Virginia."

Kathy had known from the moment she had heard about Grace Mitchell's passing; the child was free—and she was coming home. Kathy's eyes flitted to the back door involuntarily to ensure it was locked.

451

"What *is* it?" asked Crystal, pushing away from the table. "You're scaring me."

Kathy patted Crystal's hand and tried to smile, but it was unconvincingly halfhearted. She looked away quickly. "I'm sorry, dear," she said. "It's just—half of me already knew it when I saw her in that surveillance video, but the other half didn't want to accept it."

"Saw her? You know who this woman *is?*"

Kathy nodded slowly. "You really don't remember her at all, do you?" She shook her head in wonder. "It's really amazing how the human body can react to trauma. Selective memory loss as a defense mechanism. *Hmm.*"

"I don't understand," said Crystal. "Can't you just speak English?"

Kathy hesitated. "You have to understand," she began. "Maude made me swear I would never discuss this with you. I didn't agree with her even then because part of me knew this day would come. Grace wasn't all that trustworthy to begin with, and to entrust the care of that—*child* to her was only an invitation to trouble. Maude's defense was to pretend it never happened. I mean, it wasn't exactly a love lost between her and Grace."

Crystal shook her head in confusion. "Grace? Grace Mitchell? The woman who you just said had died? Who is she?"

Kathy's gaze settled upon Crystal's face. "Grace Mitchell was Maude's sister. They were identical twins." She hesitated again. "Twins are all throughout the generations of your family."

"Twins?" Crystal laughed, picturing two of Maude in their small, avocado green kitchen, working side by side at the counter. The deeper implication only then pierced through, and Crystal suddenly slumped back in her chair. The other woman—the Anti-Crystal—was her own twin. But she had never *had* a twin! Neither had Aunt Maude. It wasn't the kind of thing one would easily forget. She tried to place herself at that time, at any one of those moments from when she was a child. Crystal barely remembered her own parents. They had died in an automobile accident when she was only five. She had lived with Maude ever since. Every now and then, Aunt Syl would hobble over from her own house across the street and babysit Crystal while Maude went out with Kathy; Crystal recalled those times in vivid snapshots. Syl was Maude's oldest sister, eighteen years her senior. Peggy, Crystal's grandmother, had come next and was five years older than Maude. Peggy had died of pancreatic cancer long before Crystal was even conceived. Syl died peacefully in her own bed when Crystal was fifteen. Crystal had been the unfortunate soul who had discovered Syl's body while delivering one of Maude's daily lunch trays. By that time, Syl was no longer trustworthy in the kitchen, and Maude had begun sending all of her sister's meals over with Crystal. But in none of these memories had there been any mention of Maude's twin Grace or another version of herself running around. There had never been any twins.

"That's ridiculous," said Crystal. "There were no twins. Someone—sometime would have mentioned it. It isn't the kind of thing you can keep quiet."

Kathy pressed her lips together. "It is if you really work at it," she said. "Grace and Maude hadn't spoken in over forty years. People who knew Maude weren't likely to mention Grace—or Lisa."

Lisa. Crystal remembered the way the woman had looked at her in the upstairs hallway of the Parnell house. There had been a brief flicker of something in her dead eyes—was it recognition?

"I can't accept this," said Crystal, pushing out of her seat.

Kathy held her gently but firmly by her wrist, urging her back into her chair. "You need to hear the rest of this. If Lisa's back, she won't stop until she finishes what she started—back then. She won't stop until she's killed you."

Crystal shook her head. "She's not after me. She's after Virginia."

"Virginia Parnell."

Crystal looked up in surprise. "You *know?*"

Kathy nodded. "It's been all over the news."

"I didn't even turn the television on," said Crystal. "Virginia was already asleep, but I didn't want her to wake up to a recap of her morning."

"You were there, then," said Kathy. "When it happened."

Crystal slowly nodded. "It was horrible."

"The police are now looking for you in connection with the crimes at that house."

Crystal looked at her blankly. "But we've been so careful to stay out of sight! Other than you, no one's seen Virginia with me!"

"The news report was vague, but it indicated that the police had reason to believe that you had been inside the house."

Crystal felt panic welling in her chest. Fingerprints. It had to be fingerprints. She and Luke had entered the Parnell house worried about Virginia's safety, not the implications of leaving fingerprints behind.

Or was it Paula?

Would Paula have phoned the police and relayed the events of the morning? She knew the girl had come unglued in the aftermath of the violent confrontation, but she didn't think she would have done something so utterly stupid. After all, she had seen Lisa fleeing from the Parnell house with her own eyes. She *knew* that Crystal and Luke had only come to help the girl.

"I went there because I knew Virginia was in danger. Luke sensed it, too. When we arrived, Lisa was already there. She had killed Mrs. Parnell and the two older daughters."

"Oh, my Lord." Kathy's hand trembled as she lifted her glass to her lips.

"Tell me what you know," said Crystal. "Start at the beginning."

Kathy took a moment to steady herself. "You know that Maude always did her best with you. You know that she would never have intentionally done anything to harm you—"

"Of course, of course!"

Kathy sighed. "It began in 1985. You and Lisa were seven at the time—"

"That's impossible!" said Crystal, her voice rising sharply before she remembered the others trying to sleep down the hall. She whispered, "I *remember* being seven years old! I don't remember Lisa at all!"

Kathy held up a hand. "This story is hard enough to follow without you interrupting me every five seconds. Now, I know you'll have questions, and I'll do my best to answer them, but you've got to let me finish."

Crystal nodded and closed her mouth.

"1985 was when it began," said Kathy.

"In February, Kate and Bill—your parents—were in their accident. They were on their way to Hocking Hills near Lancaster when a semi jumped the median. They never knew what hit them. They were taking a vacation, and you would have had to have known your parents to understand what an odd statement that is. Bill was a plant manager at Royal Crown, a real workaholic. He tried to provide everything he could for you and your mother—and Lisa. He never suspected the things about your sister that would ultimately cause your mother to act so erratically those last few months. You see, that's why they were going to Hocking Hills. Kate had worked herself into a near panic over Lisa, and Bill thought that some time away would solve everything. Bless your father's heart, he *tried*, but he couldn't understand that Kate was being plagued by something a little more serious than cabin fever.

"You girls were staying with Maude when it happened. There was never a question that she would take you in. Despite the tragedy, I know she was thrilled at the opportunity she'd been given, the opportunity to finally be a mother since she could never have children of her own. She had always been fond of both of you girls, but she was especially close to you. Lisa was always more of a loner."

Crystal massaged her temples. "I'm sorry," she said. "I'm trying not to interrupt, but I wasn't seven when I moved in with Aunt Maude. I was five."

Kathy cocked her head. "Are you going to let me finish?"

Crystal lowered her eyes. "Sorry."

Kathy sighed. "The accidents started shortly after you moved in. Dusty Parkes took that bad spill on her bicycle, nearly split her head open on a rock. There were a number of girls there when it happened. Lisa was one of them. One of the others, I don't remember which, had to get twenty-seven stitches after cutting herself on a broken soda bottle. She and Lisa had been throwing rocks at the empties when one of the broken pieces flew backward."

"Sheila," said Crystal, her lips numb. "It was Sheila."

Kathy nodded. "Yes. Sheila Boldman. I remember now."

454

Crystal closed her eyes tightly. She was very close to remembering it all herself, but it wasn't something she desired. She felt her reality slipping away like hot candle wax, exposing a truth so ugly that Crystal had actually managed to edit her own internal timeline.

"Other accidents followed, each one a little scarier than the one before it. There was only one common denominator, and it was Lisa. By summertime, most of the other parents on the block had realized it, too. They forbade their children from playing with Lisa. Some of them wouldn't allow their children to play with you, either."

"In my dream," said Crystal. "I remember you and Aunt Maude at the counter, making cookies and treats for the church bake sale. She asked me to go to my room so that the two of you could talk, but when I went, something happened to me in there. The next thing I remember, I'm in the back seat of the car. You're holding my head in your lap, and Aunt Maude is driving, but I have no idea what's going on."

Moisture formed at the corners of Kathy's eyes as she relived the moment. She had never been more scared in her life. She had been certain that Crystal wouldn't survive.

"Lisa tried to kill you that afternoon," she finally said. "She had filled the tub and waited for you in the room you two shared. We were so busy with the bake sale and hadn't seen Lisa for hours. It wasn't unusual. Like I said, she was a loner. The only time she sought companionship was apparently when she felt the need to make one of those little accidents happen. She waited in there for I don't know how long, waiting for you to come back to your room for something, *anything*. She met you at the door, pushing you back into the bathroom. We heard the commotion, but by the time we got there, she had already shoved you into the tub. You must have hit your head on the way down—there was so much blood. She was straddling your chest in the water and squeezing your throat. We didn't think you would—" Her voice crumbled away. After a moment, she continued, "Maude arranged for Grace to take charge of Lisa. Believe me, that set tongues wagging. Maude hadn't spoken to Grace since they were just out of high school, but out of the blue, she calls and tells her that she's sending Lisa."

"Why don't I remember Lisa?" asked Crystal. "I can remember bits and pieces of what you tell me, but I can never actually picture Lisa being there."

Kathy shrugged. "You were in a coma for two weeks. The doctors weren't sure how permanent your head injuries were. You fractured your skull when you fell. If you had hit any harder—" Her eyes flitted nervously away. "Maude had only hoped that if you came out of the coma, you wouldn't remember the moment of the attack, the pain of seeing your own flesh and blood launch upon you with the idea of seeing you dead. She got her wish, but a little more, too. When you awakened, you didn't seem to have any recollection of Lisa whatsoever. Maude had already sent her to live with Grace, so she simply removed all signs of Lisa's existence from her house and allowed you to return believing that you had been an only child. I still remember when she went around the neighborhood, carefully explaining to each of the neighbors that doctors thought it best to allow you to put the horrible event behind you, and if they would be so kind as to refrain from mentioning Lisa's name. And of course we would! Why wouldn't we do such a thing for our dear friend, Maude? Except that the doctors would have never proposed such a thing. I had my own difficulties being sworn to silence. It wasn't that I thought we should torture you with a graphic rehashing of that afternoon. I just thought it was wrong of us to intentionally suppress your memories even more than you were already doing yourself. Still, in the long run, I did as Maude asked."

Crystal's head was positively swimming, and she tried diligently to find flaws in the logic of this new piece of history, something that would allow her to identify it as merely fiction, therefore making it dispensable. But after a few moments of turning the story around, holding it up to the light, pulling at the corners for loose threads to unravel, she closed her eyes and surrendered to its apparent accuracy. How could she have successfully blocked seven years of her life? *How?*

"Why wasn't Lisa sent to a doctor?" asked Crystal.

"Grace had worked as a child psychologist, and the courts approved her custodianship. I really don't know much else about her. I never actually met her, and Maude certainly didn't elaborate. The only reason I know about Grace at all is because Maude had to contact her when all of this happened. There was a very dark history between Maude and Grace, but I have no idea what it might have been."

Kathy's face was serious as she took Crystal's hand. "But I've always worried about this moment," she said. "I mean, eventually Grace would pass away, and Lisa would be free to do as she pleased. I remember that girl, Crystal. I remember the look in her eyes, the way her pupils were dilated almost so large as to swallow the whites. She was *overjoyed* at what she had caused. She was corrupted all the way to her soul. I always worried that when Grace eventually passed, she would explode like a volcano, spewing years' worth of pent-up destruction. And I thought if Lisa ever again had the opportunity, she would go for you in a minute. I tried to convince Maude that it was doing you a great disservice not to let you know about Lisa, about the things she had done and the things she might yet do. Maude told me I was being melodramatic, and eventually I let it drop. I take no pleasure in having been right."

"But she's not after me," repeated Crystal. "She's after Virginia. She's always been after Virginia. I just stumbled into this."

Kathy's smile was melancholy. "Maude would say that there are no such things as accidents. Tell me, Crystal, how did you hurt your arm?"

Crystal looked away. "She knocked me down a flight of stairs."

"No matter what her original agenda was, do you think she's going to dismiss another opportunity to kill you?"

Crystal remembered the smile that had tugged at the corners of Lisa's mouth after she had broken the neck of her dark-haired accomplice. She remembered the mischievous twinkle in her eyes, the amusement of a gamesman. Although Lisa might have killed her then, she had instead elected to let Crystal go free, to lead her and her greasy thug straight to Virginia and Luke where they could kill everyone all at once. Only by the grace of God had they survived the experience, and Crystal had no doubt that Lisa would be out for revenge. Her stomach felt hollow when she considered she would be facing an enemy who had once cracked her head open before resorting to strangulation. Her hands involuntarily fluttered to her throat, lightly touching those places where she could almost feel the squeezing fingers of her dreams. Lisa's fingers.

Kathy sighed and leaned back in her chair. "I'm just a simple Methodist woman, Crystal," she said. "I go to church on Sunday mornings and evenings and Wednesday nights, too. I volunteer for all the charity work they throw my way, and it fills my days, makes me feel good. Makes me feel *useful.*" She smiled. "Maude was like a sister to me, and I was especially thankful of that because I didn't have any brothers or sisters of my own. I'm sure you remember we were over at each other's houses all the time, for whatever reason. Maude was equally respectful of the Lord and went to church with me Sunday mornings and most Wednesdays. She volunteered for her fair share of the charity work, and we found ourselves working together frequently. Still, there were things about Maude I can't say I ever understood. She had this whole idea about the universe being like a pendulum or some such, and I'll admit, my first reaction was that she was being blasphemous. We had been friends for years before she first offered up her theory, right after she had sent Lisa to live with Grace. I thought it sounded like a bunch of New Age nonsense, and you know me—I told her so. She clammed up and never mentioned it again. We continued to go to church like always, and soon enough, it was as if it had never happened. I was relieved. I didn't want to believe any of the things Maude said because they conflicted with the values I have held dear for so long. Now I'm sorry I don't remember more of what she said."

Kathy stood and took her empty glass to the sink where she rinsed it out and set it in the basin.

"I'm afraid I told a bit of a fib earlier," she said casually. "And much as I understand your reasoning for introducing Virginia as Luke's daughter, I hope you'll understand mine. I didn't have a meeting at the church this evening. I needed to visit an old friend, someone from our neighborhood—back when all of this happened. I spoke with her about your situation—"

"Oh, Kathy—*no!*"

457

Kathy shushed her and pointed toward the rear of the house. "Do you want to wake them? I'm not *stupid*, for heaven's sake! I spoke with one little old lady whom I believe you knew when you were a girl—Enid Bowles. She's ninety-six years old and isn't likely to turn you over to the police because—she just wouldn't."

"How can you be sure?"

"Enid *Bowles*, Crystal."

Crystal reflected on that for a moment, and she suddenly remembered the withered old woman from down the street, ancient even then. Enid Bowles was her friend, Linnie's grandmother, and a good friend of Maude's, as well. But unlike Maude's friendship with Kathy, Crystal wasn't privy to much of the conversation that passed between Maude and Enid. She remembered Enid's strong presence in the house just after she had been released from the hospital and returned to Maude's house. She had always smelled of plums.

"Why would you need to speak to Enid?" asked Crystal, momentarily appeased. "What could she know about all of this?"

Kathy chuckled. "You underestimate the importance of longevity. Enid may look frail on the outside, but there's not a thing wrong with her mind. She's lived on that same property for so long that she knows all of the local history, inside and out. She was there at the time that Maude had her falling out with Grace. Just like Maude made me swear I wouldn't talk about Lisa, she swore Enid to a similar oath about Grace."

Kathy looked away. "I'll admit, I didn't ask her to explain to me what was going on. I'm still not sure I want to know. But I thought she might be able to explain something to you about it. She and Maude shared a similar viewpoint on this whole 'New Age' thing." She smiled weakly when she said it and forked her fingers in airborne quotation marks. It was painfully evident that she still found this viewpoint generally inaccessible, although she was willing to set aside her own beliefs if it might help Crystal stop Lisa before she killed anyone else, especially that poor little girl.

"She wants me to come tonight?" asked Crystal.

"In the morning," said Kathy. "The police are keeping watch on your Aunt Maude's house much as you might expect, and since Enid lives just down the street, you'd stand out like a sore thumb if you went at this hour. I'll smuggle you over in the morning when all the moms are taking their kids to the pool. We'll blend right in, and since we aren't actually going to Maude's house, they probably won't give us a second glance. It's much safer that way. Besides, Enid's ninety-six, dear. She needs her beauty rest."

Crystal crossed the room and hugged her old friend tightly, thankful for the support of someone she had long ago dismissed but who had nonetheless managed to remember her.

II

Paula's eyes slid away from the television screen and froze upon Lisa's face. Her breath caught in her throat, and she felt time slow to a crawl, trickles of icy perspiration running down the back of her neck.

Lisa turned the television off and sat down on the corner of the bed, clasping her hands in front of her knees and staring at Paula. "My God," she said. "So, it's true. You *are* the girl who was in their car."

Paula swallowed hard, unable to speak even if she had anything to say. Chad observed from his position on the bed, his attention momentarily drawn away from his food.

"It's okay," Lisa said softly, smiling crookedly. "It's *okay*. It's just taking me a minute here to connect the dots. Suze told us that she had someone on the inside, but she never mentioned that it was you." Her smile broadened, then faltered. "But wait a minute. If you're here, then where are they?" She stood abruptly. "We have to go find them immediately!"

Paula cowered in her chair, squeezing cleanly through her sandwich and oblivious to the warm condiments that oozed through her fingers. She didn't understand what was going on. Lisa was obviously agitated, but she didn't seem interested in hurting Paula. What had Angel gotten herself into with these people?

Lisa looked at her and saw raw fear radiating from the girl's eyes. She was shivering and holding that stupid sandwich in front of her like some kind of shield. It was nearly impossible not to laugh. Instead, Lisa leaned into the girl and placed her hands on Paula's knees, causing her to jolt in her seat as if receiving live current. Lisa tried an easy smile.

"Look," she said, her voice gentle and soothing. "I know you want to see your big sister. I'm sorry she's not here to explain things, but she's out trying to track Crystal and that man. Didn't she tell you anything about what is going on?"

Paula shook her head as fresh tears trailed down her cheeks. "She just told me to watch Crystal Bright, keep track of where she was, and—and I was supposed to call her with updates, which I did." She looked up at Lisa, her eyes pleading. "I just want to get out of here," she mewed, meekly sniffling.

She stiffened as Lisa gently enfolded her in her arms, rocking her slightly. "*Shh.* It's going to be fine. You'll be able to go wherever you want soon enough. But for now, you've got to help us find them. Don't you understand? Virginia Parnell's life is in great danger as long as she is with them. I was *inside* the farmhouse, don't you remember? I saw the whole thing happen. That man who you've been traveling with, he—he shot that poor woman right in the *face*, and—" Her voice trailed away, and she stared vacantly over Paula's shoulder.

459

Paula's head was reeling. This couldn't be the truth. She didn't care much for Luke, but she couldn't imagine Crystal standing idly by as he murdered an entire family.

Lisa looked at her oddly. "You've been riding with them this entire time. Surely, you know what they want to do."

Paula shook her head. "Crystal wouldn't do a thing like that. I'm sure of it."

Lisa shrugged. "Well, I know the man would. I saw him do it with my own two eyes." Her voice lowered. "I didn't think I was going to get out of there alive."

Paula's head was still shaking. "But why did you rob that convenience store?" she asked. "It *was* you, wasn't it?"

Lisa hesitated, then nodded. "I admit, that wasn't the smartest move on my part," she said. "But they managed to get the little girl away before I could save her. I thought it might be a good idea if I recruited a little unwitting help in finding them. It seemed natural considering how much she looks like me. But I promise you, I would've never hurt that old lady behind the counter. I didn't even have a gun." She laughed. "Finger in the pocket."

Paula stood abruptly and pushed back from the table. "I think I'm going to be sick," she mumbled, stumbling toward the bathroom. She went inside and latched the door, flipping a switch so the vent fan whirred to life.

Chad slid out from beneath the covers and pulled his jeans up over his bare ass. "You don't think she'll try to sneak out a window, do you?" he asked.

Lisa smiled. "No windows. She can't go anywhere."

"What's with all the playacting? Why don't you just tell her that her sister got killed by that stupid bitch. That might convince her that Crystal Bright ain't exactly her friend."

"I think it's safer this way," said Lisa, stretching out on the bed. "I mean, *God,* Chad! Did you see the look on her face? She's stretched *tight.* I think she'd completely blow apart if she found out about Suze right now. We'll have more luck if we just convince her to do things our way, make her believe that it's how Suze would've wanted it."

"And exactly what *is* our way?"

Lisa pursed her lips together. "First things first, we have to locate them."

Chad groaned. "Pretty much exactly like before."

"But we *will* find them," she said, and her tone of voice allowed no room for argument. "And think how easy it will be. We'll convince Paula that the girl isn't safe around them, that the square-headed hayseed is little more than a Charles Manson wannabe and won't stop until he kills her. They *trust* Paula. If she were to stumble back into their lives, they'd welcome her with great big bumpkin arms. She could walk right in, grab the girl, and deliver her to our door like a fresh, hot pizza. We wouldn't even have to get near them."

Paula sat on the closed cover of the commode, clasping her hands tightly around her midsection. Why was this happening to her? Why was she being forced to consider things of such obvious importance when she herself was little more than a child? She wished Angel would return. Her mere presence would soothe Paula's shattered nerves as they had on so many prior occasions.

Paula's first instinct had been to fiercely doubt Lisa's version of the events in Borden. She had spent long hours on the road with Crystal and couldn't make herself believe that the same woman who had calmed her shattered nerves with a bottle of gin while a tornado raged just outside the storm cellar where they had taken refuge could be responsible for something so insidious. True, Crystal was an actress, but Paula frankly didn't think she was *that* good at her craft.

But if this Lisa woman was lying, if she was the one who had done these horrific things as Luke had suggested, then why was Angel part of her team? Angel would never do anything to hurt an innocent child, not even one as creepy as that little Parnell girl. Angel was tough, sure, but she wasn't *mean*. She wasn't *vindictive*.

She wasn't *evil*.

Paula cradled her face in the palms of her hands. Her forehead was slick with perspiration, and she felt a wave of anxious nausea pass over her. She didn't know what to do. Every time she tried to focus on the events of the past few days, she began to see the plausibility of Lisa's story—with one notable exception—Paula didn't believe for a minute that Crystal knew what Luke was doing. She couldn't see the woman she idolized for the better part of three years being involved in something so completely monstrous. Crystal hadn't explained in detail what happened back at the Parnell residence. With Virginia strapped into the back seat, it would have been wholly inappropriate. But it was a large house. They had both entered through the front door, but it stood to reason that they might have split up once they had entered. It was *possible* that Luke had killed these people without Crystal's knowledge. And Crystal's presence might be the only reason that Virginia Parnell was still alive. But no—when Paula had decided to hit the road and take her chances, she had left the little girl alone with him.

Oh, God—

She was suddenly lightheaded, her heart heavy with uncertain mix of guilt and utter confusion. The little girl may have been spooky, but she didn't deserve to be murdered. For all she knew, Virginia Parnell had already rejoined her family in heaven, failed by her only earthly protection, a complete coward named Paula Haversham who had ducked and run at the first opportunity and allowed Luke to finish the slaughter he had begun back at the Parnell house.

461

She tucked her head between her knees, but it was too little, too late. She fainted, slipping quietly to the cold tile floor.

⚬————◇————⚬

"She's been in there a long time, don't you think?" observed Chad as he flipped through the television channels with the remote.

"Oh, leave her be," said Lisa from where she lounged on the bed. She tousled her new hairstyle and pulled a strand forward to examine the color. "Does this remind you of Ronald McDonald?"

Chad laughed. "Not even close. You look—hot."

"Ah," she said, ticking a finger at him. "Remember, you're Suze's fiancé. I think we'd blow our cover if little sister walked in and caught us fucking."

Chad sighed and pulled a sour face. "I don't know why you had to go and do that," he said. "It's not right to use Suze like this."

Lisa laughed. "What are you *talking* about? This is exactly what Suze would *want*. I promise you, we'll find them. That girl is going to be an incredible asset, just you wait."

Chad frowned, searching for better objections before admitting, "It's hard for me. I suppose I sort of loved her."

Lisa managed to keep the smile on her face. "Then do what you can to make sure this succeeds! We'll break it easy to the girl about Suze after this is all over. She's Suze's sister, and out of respect, I don't plan to harm one little hair on her head. She's already too valuable to us. I can't believe Suze actually planted someone in the same car with that girl! Why do you suppose she kept it to herself?"

Chad shrugged.

"Don't you think she trusted us?"

"Probably not completely."

"Still, it was a good plan to get Paula in there, even if the girl obviously has no idea what she was doing there. Suze was resourceful like that."

Chad's frown turned into a scowl. "You're laying it on a bit thick, don't you think?"

Lisa's eyebrows arched. "How so?"

"You and Suze didn't exactly—co-exist well."

Lisa bit her tongue as the silence stretched. She wouldn't volunteer anything more until she knew what Chad was implying. Did he already suspect that it had been she and not Crystal Bright who had killed Suze?

"I suppose in some ways, that Bright bitch did you a big favor by killing her," he finally said, and she realized his momentary pause was caused by an inexplicable wave of emotion. He cleared his throat. "But Suze meant a lot to

462

me. I feel sort of robbed and cheated that I won't be seeing her again, you know? And because of that, there's one thing I want you to promise me. Can you do that?"

"What's that?"

"I want to be the one who kills Crystal Bright. I want to be the one who extracts her pain as slowly and as brutally as I can. And then I want to step on her throat until I can feel the floor beneath my foot. I want this for Suze." His gaze was steely and unwavering.

What harm would it do to indulge his fantasy? Lisa simply smiled and nodded.

Paula's legs were wobbly as she pulled herself up by the rim of the sink. She stared at her sallow countenance in the sparkling mirror, noting the dark circles that clung to the underside of each eye. She looked frighteningly like her own mother.

She splashed cold water on her face and filled one of the complimentary plastic tumblers from the tap. She perched on the edge of the toilet and took slow sips, willing the feeling back into her legs. She had to make a decision and quickly. She couldn't stay in the bathroom forever.

As if on cue, a light rapping sounded against the door. "Are you alright?" asked Lisa.

Paula took a deep breath to steady her voice before answering. "My stomach's upset, but I'll be okay." She hesitated. "Has Angel made it back yet?"

"Sorry," said Lisa. "She's liable to be out for a while, you know. She's desperate to find that little girl before it's too late."

Paula wondered again if it was already too late. She wondered again if her departure at Friendly's had been the signature on little Virginia's death warrant. She pushed those thoughts away as she ran her fingers through her tangled hair, trying to coax it back into some semblance of presentability. She didn't know if she was making the correct choice, but it was time to make one, nonetheless. She ran the facts as she knew them through her mind again, looking for things to tip the scale's balance. There were four significant things that helped her reach a decision. First, she was still convinced that Crystal Bright was in no way directly involved with the murder of the Parnell family. Second, Luke had come into their lives suspiciously and had done little-to-nothing to earn their trust in the time since. He could simply have been using them to get to the girl. It was not only plausible, but in Paula's opinion, probable. After all, he *was* a man. Third, if Lisa and Chad were mad killers as Luke had suggested, why hadn't they so much as threatened Paula? Lisa had been almost maternal in her desire to ensure that Paula received a proper meal that evening. When she spoke about the incidents at the farmhouse, she looked truly haunted by the things she had seen. It didn't make any sense. But the single most important factor was that Angel had elected to align herself with these people, and Paula couldn't accept the image of her older sister as nothing more than a rabid, mindless huntress.

She quieted the overhead vent and opened the bathroom door.

Chad and Lisa had already finished their meals and were companionably watching television. They both seemed completely at ease with Paula's presence, and it helped to reinforce that Paula had made the correct decision.

She crossed the room and reclaimed her seat at the small table underneath the window. She fought the temptation to pry the slats of the blinds apart and peek out into the dark parking lot to see if her sister may be on her way up. This would all be so much easier if Angel were here.

"Feeling better?" asked Chad, trying his own hand at compassionate chatter. He offered what he believed to be a warm smile but presented more as a threatening grimace. He allowed it to fall away as he saw the girl's eyes widen.

Paula cleared her throat. "Just a stomach bug, I guess. I'll be okay."

Lisa slid off the bed and reclaimed her seat at the table. She leaned in toward Paula, her hands clasped together and her eyes anxious. "Look," she began. "I know this is weird—you don't really know us, and Suze isn't here to confirm what I'm saying, but—"

"I believe you."

Lisa worked hard to keep the corners of her mouth from curling upward. "You do?"

Paula hesitated only an instant before nodding. "Suze wouldn't be involved in trying to murder an innocent child."

"Of course not," said Lisa. "And neither would we."

"What I *don't* understand is why Luke would want the girl and her whole family dead. Believe me, after all of the strange shit I've seen in the past few days, I wish I'd never laid eyes on the child. But I can't imagine someone wanting to kill her. Why would they? *Why?*"

Lisa sighed and shrugged her shoulders. "I wish I could tell you. Suze understands this kind of thing better than I do. She was blessed with second sight, as I'm sure you already know."

Paula blinked. She most certainly did *not* know.

Although Suze had relied heavily upon her visions, she didn't share them with many. She always feared that others would be envious and wouldn't understand, and she wouldn't have wanted Paula to become one of those narrow-minded people.

"Second sight?" repeated Paula, rolling the notion around. She had honestly never given the idea much consideration. She had always liked scary movies and was fascinated by gothic mysteries, many of which featured elements of the supernatural, but these were only pieces of fiction, and the idea that a person

464

could actually see things not physically present seemed farfetched, to say the least. And yet, how else could Angel have known that Paula needed her help just as Joel McElroy was plotting another foray into his stepdaughter's underpants? Paula hadn't spoken with her on the cell phone since the night she had helped Crystal escape from the hospital. There was no way that Angel could have known that Paula would be in Morgan. Second sight?

Hmmm.

Lisa nodded earnestly. "I wasn't sure I believed in it myself until I saw her in action. I mean, *wow!*"

"You mean like visions of the future?"

"I guess," said Lisa.

"It was the teacups," interjected Chad, realizing a moment too late that he had used the past tense. Paula didn't seem to notice, but Lisa straightened in her chair. "She says they're like beacons pointing in the right direction. I guess it isn't a family trait—?"

Paula giggled nervously and shook her head. "No. I can't do anything special."

"That's where you're wrong," said Lisa. "We believe they were headed to Lucasville because that's where Crystal is from. If Suze doesn't find her tonight, we'll go out in the morning and see what we can turn up. If we can find them, you could get back inside, get to the little girl and save her."

Paula shook her head again. "Oh, no. I don't want any part of this anymore. I just want to go—"

"But Paula," said Lisa, kneeling in front of Paula and taking her hands into her own. Her eyes were serious. "If Virginia Parnell is going to stay alive, she *needs* you."

III

"You're scarin' the bejesus out of me," said Leonard. He had pulled his legs in from where they dangled over the edge of the balcony, and he hovered above Jessica as she continued to deflate in front of him. "Are you *sure* you don't want me to get Mrs. Martin?"

Jessica squeezed his arm with cold fingers but refused to look up. "No. Please. I'm fine. Just—I just need a minute."

Leonard relaxed his posture, but he continued to keenly observe Jessica. She was pale and shivering, clutching her arms around her midsection as she stared vacantly out into the motel parking lot. Her head was lowered as if the damp towel which still perched atop it was too heavy to hold up.

Jessica didn't see a thing. She wasn't aware that her mouth was hanging slightly open. She didn't feel the loose strands of wet auburn hair that tickled the back of her neck as the night wind stirred. She was only peripherally aware of Leonard Barnes standing nearby, but she was thankful for his presence. She felt as if she might be swept away, sucked over the edge of the balcony and tossed into her past. As the memories broke through, her circuits were overloaded with all the intense emotions that had defined those days. She remembered the fear, the shame, the *abandonment*—

And she remembered Lucas.

Just the thought of his name made her throat constrict and her heart ache. She and Bernie had produced him in record time, causing people's heads to spin from all of the mental mathematics. He was the reason why Jessica had been so sure of Chad's true poisonous nature—because Lucas's was anything but. The boys, born three years apart, were as different as night and day, both physically and spiritually. Lucas had been the light of Jessica's life. She remembered that later doctors had intimated she had an unnatural attachment to her firstborn and had treated Chad poorly as a direct result. And as untrue as she knew the assessment to be, she could understand its validity when presented to a panel of experts, selected by the courts to determine her viability as a fit parent. She presented like a complete monster before these experts, most of whom were parents themselves. There was no one who would believe her, not even Bernie. His spirit had died as those final months passed, his family disintegrating around him. The last time she saw him was just before she had been admitted to the hospital. What she saw in his eyes was something that she never expected to see. His love for her had completely died. In his eyes, she was the reason he was losing his children. He, like all the others, believed that she was the one who had caused all of this. He couldn't believe that a three-year-old child was capable of doing such a thing to his six-year-old brother.

There was blood everywhere—splattered on the wall, soaking into the Spiderman sheets. Her beautiful son laying in a pool of his own blood as Chad struck him repeatedly with one of Bernie's hammers. If Chad had turned the hammer around and struck just *once* with its claw—

She ran into the room screaming, but Chad was not to be deterred. Lucas's face was unrecognizably lumpy and swollen, and he was bleeding from every orifice in his head. She had grabbed Chad by his free arm and yanked him up, feeling as well as hearing the soft bone in her young son's arm give. He had looked at her with wild, surprised eyes, pupils dilated to the size of quarters.

And then he tried to use the hammer on her. Almost as if he had read her mind, he suddenly figured out the clawed end was more destructive and adjusted his grip accordingly. He even managed to get a few shots in before she had lashed out, striking his face with her closed fist and knocking him unconscious.

Bernie appeared in the doorway just in time to see it happen. She had already pulled the bloody hammer from Chad's fingers and was hurrying back to Lucas, hurrying to make sure that he was still *breathing*. She got the surprise of her life when she was abruptly tackled from behind, Bernie misinterpreting his wife's intentions as she approached Lucas with the hammer in her outstretched arm.

Jessica cleared her throat and sat up straight, pulling her legs back from where they had dangled over the edge of the balcony. She turned toward Leonard. "We should get some rest," she said, avoiding his eyes. "Tomorrow's going to be a busy day."

"Are you sure you're alright? You don't look good."

I don't feel good, either.

She smiled weakly and forced herself to look up. "I'll be alright. I'm just tired."

He looked at her dubiously but headed for his own room. "If you're absolutely *sure*—"

"I am," she said, hugging herself tightly and shivering.

"If you need anything at all, don't you hesitate to knock."

"I won't."

"Ms. Jessica?"

She paused at her own door and turned to find him nervously staring at her. "Yes?"

"I don't know what's going on inside your head, but I want you to know, for what it's worth, that I don't think that it's your fault that your son turned out this way. I don't think that a thing like that can come from bad parenting. Encouraged, maybe, but somehow, I can't see you as a bad mother."

She felt her throat catch, but she managed a smile before quietly slipping back into the room she shared with Helen.

⟡

Helen lay flat on her back staring at the ceiling. She knew they were out on the balcony, and she couldn't for the life of her understand what Jessica saw in Leonard Barnes. He was old enough to be her father, but maybe she went for that sort of thing. Helen had worked the emergency room at Morgan Township long enough to see all sorts of things. Having a father fixation was rather tame by comparison to some predilections.

But *Leonard Barnes?*

Every moment near him was going to be an exercise in self-restraint, but she would do her level best because she had promised Jessica she would try. Helen wasn't entirely sure she believed Jessica when she said she was reserving judgment on Lisa. If that were true, then what was the point of all the clandestine meetings that had been happening this evening? What was so private that they could only discuss it when Helen was gone or playing possum? She almost *hoped* it was a bizarre sex thing, because the alternative was that they were conspiring against Lisa behind Helen's back.

467

She had a hard time picturing Jessica as a traitor, though. She seemed strong, seasoned. Her words felt honest and sincere, and Helen believed that Jessica genuinely wanted to do the right thing, even if Leonard Barnes had temporarily poisoned her opinion of Lisa Mitchell. Surely, she would come around after meeting Lisa. Jessica was intelligent and intuitive. She couldn't *help* but sense Lisa's innocence.

Helen wondered if she should creep over and press her ear against the door. She was almost dizzy worrying about what Leonard might be telling Jessica. She was debating the likelihood that she might get caught when Jessica suddenly entered the dark room, sliding through a narrow crack in the door and easing it closed behind herself. Helen's eyes snapped shut, and she feigned a soft rumble, but after a moment, she allowed one eye to peek.

Jessica stripped to her undergarments and was adjusting her bed sheets. The vague moonlight that seeped through the blinds suggested she might have been crying; her cheeks appeared damp and swollen. What had Leonard Barnes *done* to her? Helen crackled with hatred for the man. She wanted to say something to Jessica, but something in the other woman's face made her hold her tongue. Jessica looked very tired, and what she needed was sleep, not another lengthy conversation. Tomorrow was another day.

But they *would* have that conversation tomorrow. She had agreed to take it easy on Leonard, and she intended to keep her word. But she would be *damned* if he was going to go around spreading filthy lies about Lisa Mitchell and causing grief for the one woman who might be able to help Helen save her before it was too late. The very thought of him lying on his bed, just on the other side of the wall made her *nauseous*.

<hr>

Sleep was a long time coming to Jessica. Shortly after she had returned to her bed, thunder had resumed its rumbling in the distance, and flickers of lightning were visible through the narrow slats of the blinds. She turned her back toward Helen in case the nurse awakened during the approaching storm. She didn't feel like chatting anymore.

Lucas.

She could still hear him screaming as they had pried him out of her arms. His face was still testimony to the savage beating he had endured. The fact that he had survived at all was a miracle. For them to think that *she* had been responsible for such a thing—for *Bernie* to think such a thing...

David McElroy's face floated through her mind, and her heart ached all over again. It was strange. She had never considered how very much like Bernie David was. As a matter of fact, she and Loretta were similar in many ways. Although

468

she had always found David attractive, there was never any consideration that she might try and act upon her feelings. She understood the way he felt about his wife, and maybe that was part of the attraction, too. Though a decade older, David and Loretta were what Bernie and Jessica should have been. She was able to live vicariously through them by remaining close to David. It really wasn't a physical attraction at all; it was the opportunity to observe what might have been. And David and Loretta were without children as well, just as Bernie and Jessica would have been. After that horrific summer, she had known that she could never again be a mother. She could never give herself so completely to something that could be taken away by some heartless government agency.

She had been in the hospital when she found out about Bernie's accident. A mean-spirited nurse had delivered her morning pills and orange juice and said, "By the way, your husband's funeral will be next Tuesday. He ran his car into a tree."

Jessica didn't speak or eat for three weeks, and they eventually had to feed her intravenously to stave off starvation. It wasn't that she had ever expected a reconciliation with Bernie; he had made his feelings clear on the matter. He blamed her for everything. Jessica hadn't been the only one to suffer greatly during these times. In the court's opinion, Bernie had been lax in his parental duty as well, allowing such a volatile situation to develop right underneath his nose. A hawk-like woman from Children's Services, Penny Spears, unleashed a lethal character assassination of both Jessica and Bernie, and by the time she left the witness stand, there wasn't a soul in the world who would have returned custody of the children to either one of their parents. As a small concession, the court had allowed the youngest son to be taken by family friends, Peter and Naomi Collins. Both Jessica and Bernie were forced to sign away visitation rights, which meant they could only see their friends when Chad was not present. It didn't much matter. As it turned out, they would never see their friends again anyway. Jessica was institutionalized and Bernie had already begun a drinking binge that would eventually cost him his life in the automobile accident that had decapitated him.

She wondered what Chad would be like now. At David McElroy's insistence, she kept a handgun locked in the back of the Jeep and was quite proficient with it after weekly outings with David to the shooting range. He firmly believed that a single woman should always be prepared to defend herself, and while she had readily gone through the motions, she wasn't at all certain she could pull the trigger in the heat of the moment. There was a world of difference between a paper target and a human being, but she suspected it would come to that. She shuddered as she imagined what he must now be like, eighteen years old, wiry and muscular, dark and brooding. She didn't understand how she could have given birth to such a thing. There was nothing of either Bernie or herself in that child. There *couldn't* have been.

He would be so much *stronger* now.

And Lisa Mitchell. The things Leonard had described had set off warning bells in her head. This girl was cut of the same horrific fabric as Chad, and there was every reason to believe that the third girl was equally capable. As Jessica considered her own sad troop—a middle-aged switchboard operator, a heavyset nurse, and an ancient janitor—she felt nothing but despair. What was she doing here? Did she really think she could change *anything?* She hadn't been able to make a damn bit of difference back then. What made her think she could now? Was she leading Helen and Leonard to a slaughter? Considering her personal history of tragedy, it seemed all too likely.

Four years in the hospital had given her the time to distance herself from her past and excise the parts of her memory that were the most painful. It was an odd phenomenon; she would still respond properly to questions regarding these individuals and events, consistently saying the things she knew the doctors wished to hear, but she no longer had a true sensation of who they were or how they had figured into her life. It had happened around the time that Enid Bowles had visited her out of the clear, blue nowhere.

She hadn't thought about Enid Bowles in over a decade.

Jessica's hospitalization had been an exercise in solitary confinement. Friends and family have a way of disappearing when they believe you are capable of murdering your own children. No one came to visit Jessica other than the elderly volunteers from the Methodist church on Charles Street, but even they began to avoid her after the truth of her circumstances began to circulate. But one day, Enid Bowles had signed the visitor's log and entered her room, a complete stranger with more than a passing resemblance to one of the not-so-friendly witches from *The Wizard of Oz*. She was a shriveled, bony thing even then, hobbling along in an unwise choice of footwear and dressed in deep plum. She had taken Jessica's hand into her own and smiled in such an engaging, genuine way that Jessica thought there must be some mistake. This tired old woman was senile, and she had come to the wrong room. That must be it. But when she had spoken, Jessica's world had begun to change. She now remembered those words clearly.

I can't stand seeing someone punished for something she didn't do. I think it's time you rejoined the tea party. I've brought a little something for you.

She had produced an antique teacup from behind her back, filled with a vaguely green liquid. The whole thing was impossible. Hospital security would have never allowed this woman to enter a patient's room with a piece of ceramic crockery. It could be broken too easily and used as a weapon. They would never have allowed this old woman to bring in food or beverage from the outside world, either. It was strictly against hospital policy. Why, the woman could be a self-proclaimed vigilante, delivering poison to those who she felt deserved the death penalty.

And it was poison that Jessica truly believed the concoction was when she drank it down. She didn't care about living anymore. She had lost everything that had ever meant anything to her. The oatmeal walls that surrounded her were like an eternity in purgatory, and she was more than ready to get on with judgment. She was weary of life and everything it had shoved down her throat.

But it wasn't poison. It was very light and minty and left her teeth feeling slick and clean. Enid hadn't stayed for long, and Jessica could remember nothing of what she might have said in that brief time. Afterward, she had only visited a few times more, and Jessica couldn't remember the details of those visits either, only that Enid had always brought the strange tea, and Jessica had willingly imbibed each time. As the weeks had passed, the weight of her burden shifted, never completely lifting but lightening to a level she could bear.

It was a gradual improvement. She began by combing her hair. It occurred to her one morning as she had been shuttled through the shower room and caught sight of her tangled hair in the mirror. It was suddenly urgent that it be tamed. After an inconsiderate male nurse had grudgingly helped, she was stunned to see the hollowed corpse that stared back at her from inside the mirror. She had lost an enormous amount of weight, and her bones threatened to protrude through her skin in places. Her neck and shoulders looked particularly bad. Dark circles stained the fragile flesh beneath her eyes, and she looked more like a ghost than a human being. From that point, intravenous feeding was no longer necessary for Jessica. It had been a long, steady healing, but eventually, she had been returned to society as restored to sanity.

She had been returned to a world in which she had nothing.

Jessica floundered through a series of jobs before finally landing her current position with the Jay County Sheriff's Department, and at first, she lived with the fear that every day would be the day they wouldn't let her clock in because of her past instability. She was surprised they hadn't done a more thorough background check when they hired her, but perhaps it was because her job was almost clerical in nature, and they hadn't felt it necessary. Dispatching calls didn't require carrying a firearm, although as it turned out, the laws regarding who can legally carry one were surprisingly lax. As the years passed, she had slowly found a sense of security and had eventually stopped fearing discovery. She wanted nothing more than to live the remainder of her life quietly, imposing upon no one and enjoying the freedom that had been returned to her, even if it was a terribly lonely freedom. She had allowed herself to hope that she was free of Chad and free of the terrible things he could do. Despite the many things she had forgotten, not the least of which was her oldest son, the memory of Chad had remained, even if the specifics of his misdeeds did not. The peace of mind that Enid had somehow given her seemed cruel in retrospect. It had allowed Jessica to become soft and unprepared. It had allowed Chad time to grow older and stronger. Like sublimating in drugs or alcohol, it had only been a way to avoid reality, and the reality was that Chad was back, staining everything he touched with the malignancy of his soul. She had brought him into this world, and she was going to have to take him out of it. It didn't matter if she landed in a hospital—or even on death row. Either way, it was better than living with the guilt that gnawed at her insides. And if Lisa Mitchell and the dark-haired girl were like Chad, then Jessica would kill them, too. She simply couldn't allow it to go on any longer.

She thought of Lucas and wondered where he was. It occurred to her that he might not still be alive, but she thought he might be. When she thought about him, his sandy, tousled hair and boyish grin, she felt the only warmth she had experienced in days. She could feel her muscles relax as she remembered the soft sound of his voice calling for her, and the way he was prone to giggle himself into hiccups.

Thinking of Lucas and smiling, she finally found sleep.

CHAPTER TWENTY-FOUR

I

Morning arrived without a residual trace of the storm that had rumbled all throughout the night. The sky was a cloudless blue, stretching from horizon to horizon. It was warm but not humid, and the air was redolent with the sweet fragrance of wildflowers and freshly mowed grass.

Over a quick breakfast, Crystal explained to Luke her morning plans. He, of course, objected, worrying about the wisdom of placing herself within easy grasp of the local police, but he knew that she had to go. They needed to find out why Virginia Parnell was so important as to prompt an almost fanatical pursuit, and Enid Bowles was the only person left to consult. Although he couldn't imagine them coming from the same mold, Luke wasn't altogether surprised to learn that Lisa and Crystal were twins. Only nature could physically reproduce someone so flawlessly. What he couldn't understand was the shroud of secrecy that Crystal's Aunt Maude had created around the girls. Enid Bowles was the only person who might be able to lift the veil.

Virginia was sullen as she ate a bowl of Fruit Loops. Crystal watched her nervously, afraid that her brave façade was almost at its breaking point. She was surprised to learn that the little girl simply wasn't a morning person. After she had finished her cereal, her energy began to return and soon, she wanted Luke to take her outside where she could play in the large front yard. Luke and Crystal exchanged anxious glances before Luke suggested they go to the back yard instead. It wasn't as large but was completely invisible from the road. Some children would have protested, maybe even pouted, but Virginia's face lit up at the suggestion, and before Luke could set his coffee cup back on the kitchen table, she was dragging him toward the back door. Kathy had managed to find a bright yellow dress that fit her well amongst the donations she had been laundering, and she looked like any other little girl enthusiastically tugging her father along to play.

"She really likes him, you know," said Kathy. "You wouldn't have much trouble passing her off as his daughter."

Crystal smiled as she watched Luke being pulled from the room by one arm. He made a spectacle of being off-balance, much to Virginia's delight, and then they were through the door and into the yard. "He's a nice guy," she said.

"*Hmm*," Kathy knowingly remarked.

Crystal let it pass as she carried breakfast dishes from the table to the sink. "Are you about ready to go?"

Kathy finished her coffee, blotted the corners of her mouth with a napkin, then nodded. "Just let me get my pocketbook."

⟳————◇————⟲

It was an odd sensation driving back into the old neighborhood. As Kathy turned onto Nile Run, Crystal noticed that some things had changed but most remained the same. She rode in the back seat of the Explorer amongst sacks of groceries that Kathy had picked up at Big Bear. One of the many things Kathy did for the church was deliver groceries to elderly shut-ins, and this morning, she had a rather large delivery for Enid Bowles. As they neared Dale Street, Crystal slid into the floorboard and pulled several of the bags down to cover herself, trying to avoid pinning her splinted arm, which was itching like crazy underneath the makeshift cast. She desperately wanted to see her former home, the place where this had all begun, but she resisted the temptation to peek. She would do her part according to plan; there was no sense in being reckless. Besides, she might be able to see it from inside Enid's house.

"Busy day in the neighborhood," said Kathy, slowing to allow a couple of children racing Big Wheels to thunder past on their plastic chariots, laughing madly as their little feet frantically worked the pedals.

"Are they still watching Aunt Maude's?" asked Crystal from where she crouched.

"Mmm-hmm. We're just passing now."

They were quiet for a moment as the Explorer coasted onward. Kathy tried not to look directly at the sheriff's deputy parked in a Chevy patrol car at the mouth of Maude's driveway and then wondered if she had been too conspicuous in avoiding his gaze—if he was even looking at her in the first place. How could she tell? She hadn't been looking.

After a moment, when no sirens or bullhorns had sounded, Kathy breathed a shaky sigh of relief. "I'm not cut out for this," she muttered. "Almost peed myself."

"Are we there?"

"Almost," said Kathy. "We're just turning into the drive."

⟳————◇————⟲

Luke was deep in his own thoughts as Virginia diligently pursued a butterfly across the backyard. He sat in the same spot he had occupied the night before,

474

when Crystal had leaned forward and kissed him. He could still feel her soft lips against his. She made him feel something he had never experienced before, and he was terrified that it might end before it even had the chance to begin.

Virginia had caught up with the butterfly, coaxing it to the end of her finger and was discussing something of utmost importance with it.

Okay, so let's assume we can save her, thought Luke. *What then? Where does she go? Who's going to take care of her?*

She was looking at him now, showing him the butterfly and smiling so sweetly. Why would anyone want to hurt her?

<hr/>

Crystal hadn't been inside Enid Bowles' house since she was a teenager. The Bowles were of old money, and the three-story Gothic house with its multitude of spires and staggered elevations had always before intimidated Crystal. As an imaginative child, it had been easy to imagine the house as haunted, and she had never ventured near it on Halloween just in case. But Enid's granddaughter, Linnie, had been a close friend, and Crystal had occasionally found herself within those walls, awed by the spacious rooms and high ceilings. Maude's house could have easily fit inside four times over.

Enid's master bedroom was paneled in rich mahogany with tall windows that overlooked the neighborhood below. Portraits of dour-faced ancestors peered down from gilded frames, suspicious eyes following Crystal's every move. She stood nervously at the foot of the bed, fidgeting and shuffling, feeling as if she were seven years old again.

"My goodness, child, you've grown up nicely!" said Enid from where she nestled in her four-poster bed, her voice a rusty nail. "I had hoped I would feel like being up in my chair today, but my hip's been flaring from all the rain last night."

Crystal smiled. "Don't you worry. I'm just as happy to visit you in here. I'm only sorry it's been so long."

It was bittersweet looking at the old woman. Her silvery hair had turned white and thinned, patches of pink scalp peeking through. Her cheeks were sunken, and the skin was like onion paper in those delicate areas around the eyes. Her eyes, however, still twinkled with the same, familiar intensity, and she still carried the vague scent of plums. After a moment, the shock of her natural physical decline began to fade.

"I suppose Kathy's gone?" asked Enid, her eyes twinkling mischievously.

Crystal nodded. "She's taking some food trays and groceries around to the shut-ins and will be back around noon with some KFC for lunch."

Enid smacked her lips in a dry laugh. "Bet she couldn't get out of here fast enough."

"What do you mean?"

Enid arched a thin eyebrow. "I think you already know."

"Well—yes, I suppose I do. She doesn't want to hear the answers to the questions I have for you."

"She wants to keep her head buried in the sand is what she wants. I never could understand why she finds the whole notion blasphemous. It's really quite the opposite."

"And we're talking about this 'New Age' concept that Kathy mentioned?"

Enid rolled her eyes and groaned. "She *would* call it that. There's nothing 'New Age' about it. It's as old as time."

Crystal perched on the edge of the bed, staring at the old woman intently. "This isn't some kind of witchcraft or anything—"

Enid's cackle startled Crystal with its strength. When she had recovered enough to continue, she said, "No, it's not witchcraft. It's nothing so organized."

Crystal nodded.

"Kathy Duncan isn't the only one who buries her head in the sand. I'm sorry to say your Aunt Maude did, too—on the day she decided to send Lisa to live with her sister in Indiana. Out of sight, out of mind. Well, I always knew this day was coming. For heaven's sake, even Kathy Duncan understood the inevitability. The forces of equilibrium demanded it."

"Equilibrium?"

Enid smiled. "It's our more eloquent way of describing this 'New Age' thing."

"Oh. Our? And who would 'we' be?"

Enid shrugged. "You'd be disappointed, dear. It's not like we get together for regular meetings or anything, although the internet has been a real boon for us. Don't look so surprised, dear. Occasionally, you *can* teach an old dog new tricks."

Crystal smiled, only just noticing the nondescript laptop that was in the center of the antique mahogany desk along the far wall.

Enid sighed and shifted positions, propping herself straighter against her pillows and trying to ease the throbbing in her hip that was a constant source of discomfort. "I really don't know where to begin," she said. "For years and years, I've honored Maude's wishes, even though I tried to convince her she was being hard-headed. I don't think she ever fully recovered from what happened when she and Grace were girls—younger than you are now, in fact. It was after that when Maude first accepted the reality of equilibrium, and although she firmly believed, she could never see the business between her and Grace as anything but over. Unfortunately, equilibrium tends to be a little more cyclical than that."

Crystal's smile became puzzled. "I'm not following."

"Simply put, equilibrium simply means balance, and its concept in this context is no different. The universe is full of more mysteries than the human mind could ever hope to address, and that's why we have religion. It's easier to face the coming days if you have a sort of user's guide to life—does that make sense? Christianity, the mysteries of the Koran, the Jewish Old Testament, all of those little aboriginal tribal religions that vary from village to village in South America and Africa—hasn't it ever struck you as odd that so much time is spent battling over which religion is the 'correct' one? Holy wars, they've been called by history—and I want to know any one thing that could possibly be holy about war. And when you take each religion down to its finest points, get to the real *heart* of its teachings, they are all nearly the same! According to the Christian doctrine, if you haven't accepted Jesus Christ as your personal savior, you've got a one-way ticket to hell along with I don't know how many Jews, Hindus, and other so-called heathens who happened to be so unfortunate as to be born in a part of the world where Christianity isn't the accepted religion. Isn't it rather unappealing to think that God—by whichever name you wish to call Him— would operate in a fashion so inconsistent with His own teachings?"

Crystal slowly shook her head. "I've never really thought about it."

"Most people don't. They inherit their belief systems from their parents or other family members and continue to pass them along to their own children, never once questioning anything. I've often wondered if the passages in the Bible which praised blind faith were actually penned by one of the many men who revised the original text over the years. I'm sure religious scholars everywhere would gasp at my assertion but think about the temptation. The men who ordered the scriptures to be reinterpreted were kings. Why not slant a passage here or there to support the current political agenda?"

Crystal shifted uneasily on the corner of the bed, trying to scratch her itchy arm beneath her splint. "I'm starting to understand why some people might find your viewpoint blasphemous."

Enid cackled again, her voice dry and brittle. "Oh, sweetie, there's nothing blasphemous about it at all. I still believe in God and the Devil. And for most people, that's enough."

"What about this equilibrium thing?"

"It's all about balancing the scales. For the greatest good, there must be the foulest evil. Without one, the other doesn't have any meaning. I believe that the world and the universe around us are nothing but a testing ground for souls who haven't become enlightened enough to move on to the next higher plane—and yes, I believe there is something waiting for us after we pass on. I don't know if it's heaven, hell, or some other place—maybe another series of tests designed to strengthen our souls so that we can, yet again, ascend. In the meanwhile, the world remains in a constant pendulous state, evil surfacing and good overcoming—or at least hopefully overcoming. It doesn't always work out that way, but it does more often than not. There are dark forces working around us constantly, wreaking havoc wherever they can take hold. Some people are born with diseased souls, and rather than try to find redemption, they cling to this awful energy and draw strength from it. These forces are wildly unpredictable and are surprisingly adaptable, able to corrupt those who straddle the borderline in their own ideas of right and wrong. Sometimes, these people aren't even aware of the repercussions of their actions. Sometimes, however, their actions are more significant. Fortunately for the rest of us, the good folk—the positive forces— are constantly in motion, too, sending emissaries both willing and unwitting into battle. Tell me, Crystal, how many people do you think walk this planet?"

Crystal shook her head. "I have no idea. Billions."

Enid nodded. "And when you think back on your history lessons from school, wouldn't you say it's amazing that only a comparative handful of names rise above the general populace? These were the people who shaped nations and guided civilizations. The odds of winning the lottery are better than being born one of their number."

Crystal stared at her blankly.

Enid reached out and took Crystal's hands into her own. "These were very special people. They understood things that most couldn't even begin to contemplate. Not all of them were good—Adolf Hitler, I believe, was the poster boy for evil six years running. But then you have Mother Teresa, Mahatma Ghandi, Abraham Lincoln, Albert Einstein—so many others whose work made a profoundly positive difference on the world and its people. If you think of it as a sort of high school, these were the valedictorians of classes past, the scholarship winners—beacons in a sea of light. Without them, our history would surely read differently. But do you suppose that maybe some of them never achieve their potential?"

"Well, if they're born to greatness, I don't see why—" Crystal's voice trailed away as Enid's true meaning sank in.

Enid slowly nodded. "It's a constant battle," she said. *"Constant.* Each of us has our own energy to contribute, and we do it every day, mostly without conscious effort. Whether we choose to pass along goodwill or something a little less useful—either way, it's a chain reaction. Some battles, however, are more important than others. Some are literally for the sake of keeping the scales from tipping too far out of balance."

"What would happen if—?"

Enid smiled. "I can't answer that. I can only imagine—but I'd prefer not. Thankfully, there are others—although they are rare, too, I believe there are more of them than the people they protect—more of *you.*"

"More of me?" asked Crystal, her eyebrows knitting together. Her arm was still itching like crazy, and she was beginning to get a headache. "I don't understand."

Enid gingerly shifted positions again and leaned forward. "Let me see your arm," she said, her eyes twinkling brightly.

478

Crystal looked at her warily but complied, figuring that the old woman didn't have enough tensile strength to do any real damage to her wounded arm. Enid surveyed Luke's handiwork with a dubious eye, slowly turning Crystal's arm this way and that, examining each side.

"What is this?" she asked. *"Plywood?"*

"Maybe."

Enid suddenly smiled. "Itches like the dickens, doesn't it?"

"Lord, yes," said Crystal. "I think it's infected or something."

Enid's eyes absolutely sparkled. "It's healing."

Crystal cocked her head dubiously.

Enid nodded. *"Healing.* You could probably take off this ridiculous contraption."

Crystal pulled her arm back and cradled it in her lap. "That's impossible," she said. "It was a bad break, Enid. It wasn't like the bone cracked—it *snapped*. This was *yesterday*. It can't heal that fast!"

"It can if you're one of them," she said, her eyes still bright. "The others of whom I spoke, they are the ones who protect those shining examples of humanity and try to ensure that they live to achieve their goals."

Crystal laughed, a high-pitched, hysterical noise that rose from her chest before erupting. "You know, I can buy the first part of all of this," she said. "I'm not saying that I agree with it, but as a concept, I admit it's plausible—and maybe even a little intriguing. But this last bit—I'm no one's protector. That doesn't even make sense! In my entire life, I've never even been in a fistfight! I'd hate to be the person relying on *me* for protection."

"Go ahead," urged Enid, eyeing the splint. "Take it off."

Crystal looked at the bulky thing and was beset by a fresh wave of itchy tingling. It *had* to be an infection. What else could it be? It hadn't been set properly, and she was probably now disfigured for life. Maybe it would be better to look at it, assess the damage—before gangrene set in, and the whole damn thing had to be amputated. Wouldn't that be the perfect way to round out the week? She began to pick at the tights knots in the cotton strips that held the wooden pieces together, and after several attempts, they came loose, one by one.

"If this is really gross, I'm liable to faint," warned Crystal, already feeling a little nauseous.

Enid's eyes still twinkled, a knowing smile playing on her lips.

Crystal closed her eyes tightly as the last of the pieces of wood dropped away. She waited for the searing agony that she knew would follow, the feeling of her bones sliding apart again, the jagged ends digging into tendons and muscle tissue. Her stomach roiled in anticipation, and her head began to feel very light.

There was no pain.

She slowly opened her eyes and looked at her bruised and battered arm. It was so purple it was nearly black at the swollen elbow; her forearm was mottled

479

with greenish-yellow bruises, and the remainder of the exposed flesh was a deep, angry crimson.

But it was whole.

▌▌

"I can't believe she's fucking *gone!*" screamed Lisa, ripping the sheets from the bed and tossing them aside. She wanted desperately to break everything that was breakable in the small motel room, but she wouldn't draw attention to herself and Chad. Not when they were this close. She lowered her voice to an angry snarl. "How could you let her get out of here?"

"Hey!" barked Chad. "Don't blame me—I needed sleep. I'm the one who's recovering from a gunshot wound, remember?"

"Keep your voice down," she hissed. "Do you want someone to call the police?"

Chad sat down heavily on the corner of the bed. "We fell asleep," he said. "We *both* needed sleep. So, she's gone. So what?"

Lisa sighed and flopped belly first onto the mattress. "It just sucks, that's all," she said. "She could have gotten back in there so *easily*—"

"I don't think so," said Chad, shaking his head. "I mean, I was watching her last night. She wasn't too together. She probably would've blown it all to hell."

"You think?"

"Yeah, I do. She was too much of a wildcard," he said, settling onto his back beside Lisa and staring at the ceiling. "We've already let them get away from us two too many times. I'm not for putting all our eggs in that basket case."

Lisa pursed her lips. "Maybe you're right."

"Besides, I was sure I was going to let it spill about Suze being dead," he said. "I didn't like that. It's hard enough knowing she's gone, let alone having to pretend she's just out cruising around."

"I know, baby," she said, stroking his cheek lightly. "I know. But soon enough, this will all be over."

She pushed herself off of the mattress and crossed to the window, twisting the blinds open to the sunny morning. She stretched lazily in the beam of sunlight that spilled into the room.

"It feels like a good day," she said with a smile.

So, this was Lucasville, a mile-long stretch along US 23 with shallow neighborhoods spilling off in either direction, as well as the birthplace of Crystal Williams, better known as Crystal Bright. It was entirely unremarkable. A local grocer, a few gas stations, Wendy's, Star Bank—that was about it. Paula wandered along the cracked and uneven sidewalk, the heat of the morning sun beginning to collect along her neck and shoulders. Her skin burned easily, and she could already feel it drinking in the rays. She tripped along like a zombie through the ethereal morning, feeling as though she had drifted into an alternate universe that was undeniably different, even if that difference couldn't exactly be pinpointed. Her feet were sluggish, and she stumbled several times over breaks in the sidewalk. Where was Angel? Didn't Lisa say she was trying to find Crystal in Lucasville? Paula didn't know what she hoped to accomplish. Was she just going to stand on the sidewalk and wait for Angel—or perhaps Crystal, herself— to come driving along? Even if Crystal *was* coming to Lucasville, she wouldn't be using the main roads. Paula had already seen several state troopers and a sheriff's car pass. She knew they were keeping an eye open for their infamous hometown outlaw. Crystal would know it. Angel would know it, too.

Please let Virginia be alive.

The thought had haunted her, taunting since the moment she realized that Luke might have already accomplished his mission, thanks to her. She could only hope that there had been others at Friendly's, too many witnesses for him to dispose of the child without endangering himself. Oh, why couldn't she escape this?

She hadn't slept at all.

It had been long hours before Chad had finally drifted off, and Paula had nearly burst out of her skin waiting. He was watching her. He didn't think she noticed, but she saw. Despite Lisa's protests, Paula had slept in the uncomfortable bucket chair that squatted at the foot of one of the double beds. Lisa had stretched out on the one nearest her while Chad took the other. Paula narrowed her eyes to slits, sure that they couldn't be seen in the darkness of the room. At first, he had just ventured peeks. After he was convinced she was asleep, he had stared more openly.

Lying in the quiet darkness, Paula had become convinced he was going to rape her. She had listened as the tripping hammer of her heartbeat curved up-tempo and cold sweat blossomed across her neck. She was so tired, and yet she couldn't fall asleep—she *couldn't!* She was afraid to blink, afraid to lose even that tiny sliver of vision for fear that he would be right there when she relaxed her eyelids, right there in her face, his hands reaching out for her—

And then he began to snore. It was the most godawful racket Paula had ever heard. Joel always had a distinctive rhythm to his night breathing, a reassuring buzz that confirmed he was too drunk to do any more damage until morning. Chad's sounded more like an obstruction in his throat, causing him to wheeze and burble like he was drowning in his own mucus. For a moment, Paula was certain that Lisa would wake up. How could she sleep through that roar?

But she didn't wait long. Paula was afraid her window of opportunity would close before it had even fully opened. Despite the fact she believed Lisa, she couldn't trust Chad. Something about him wasn't right. Something about him made her afraid.

Paula shielded her eyes from the sun and looked both ways along the busy highway, waiting for a break in traffic to cross to the Speedway on the other side. She needed to get a cup of coffee—maybe two. She was lightheaded from exhaustion and didn't have a clue where to go from here. She pushed open the heavy glass door and entered the small food mart. She helped herself to a self-serve 20-ounce cup of black coffee, barely aware of the transaction as she tossed the cashier a twenty and nearly forgot her change.

"Are you alright, miss?" A woman with owl-like glasses suddenly appeared at her elbow, a concerned look on her face.

Paula smiled weakly. "I've had a bug."

"Well, you need to get some rest, young lady," she said firmly but with a warm smile. "I hope you're not driving."

Paula shook her head and moved toward the door.

"So how are you, Mrs. Duncan?" asked the pimply-faced cashier, turning his attention to the woman who had just spoken to Paula. "Making the rounds?"

"You know it, George," she said. "If you don't mind, I'm going to leave my car here while I drop off a couple of my food trays around the corner."

"Not a problem, Mrs. D."

Paula continued outside, but her mind wouldn't let go of the exchange she had just overheard. Mrs. Duncan. Didn't Crystal have a friend in Lucasville named Duncan—Kate, maybe? There were three picnic tables standing empty along the rear of the parking lot, and Paula crossed over to sit at one of them. She pried the plastic lid from her foam cup and sipped at the searing coffee, aware that her taste buds were being singed but unable to stop herself from sipping. She needed full access to her faculties. This felt like an opportunity presenting itself, and she was afraid that she was too scattered to realize it.

She watched as the stocky woman hustled out of the Speedway and crossed to a large Ford Explorer that was parked at one of the gas pumps. She opened the driver's door and tossed in whatever it was she had just purchased, then went to the rear of the vehicle, releasing its tailgate and extracting two foil-covered platters. She noticed Paula watching her and nodded, smiling as she passed, trotting along with the trays in hand and heading off on foot across the parking lot and into the neighborhood that was directly behind the gas station.

Paula continued to sip and scald as she watched Mrs. Duncan trot up a steep flight of stairs to the porch of a weather-beaten shotgun house that cowered behind a row of sickly elms. She could hear the staccato burst of knuckles against storm door, and soon Mrs. Duncan was invited inside.

Paula finished her coffee and went back inside the gas station. She refilled her cup at the coffeemaker, then waited patiently at the counter as an older gentleman dug through his pockets for correct change.

"Back so soon?"

"Huh?" Paula was startled to attention by the acne-riddled cashier's words. She pushed the Styrofoam cup toward him along with a dollar and smiled. "Just a refill."

"Twenty-five cents is all for a refill," he informed her. "You gonna stick around for your change this time?"

Paula could feel her cheeks flushing as she nodded. "I was wondering if maybe you could help me," she said, glancing around to make sure she wasn't holding up the line. When she looked back at the cashier, her embarrassment was even greater; she suspected from the look on his face that he thought she was about to produce a gun and rob him. She forced herself to relax and offer the same steady smile she had used in all her school pictures, the one that made all the boys look twice.

"I used to live in Lucasville when I was little," she continued. "I've been trying to place the woman who was in line behind me earlier. She seems so familiar, and it's driving me crazy."

"Mrs. D?" asked the cashier, loosening up a bit. After all, any friend of Mrs. D's couldn't be *all* bad. "Kathy Duncan. She does so much volunteer work for her church you can't hardly help but know her if you spend very much time at all in these parts."

"*Kathy!* Oh, that's right!" exclaimed Paula, scooping her change from the counter and tucking it into her pocket. She remembered Crystal telling her that Kathy had lived several doors away when she was growing up. "I used to live a few houses down from the Duncans on Dale."

"She ain't lived there in years," said the cashier, adjusting the ball cap which covered his greasy red hair. "Her and her old man built this huge-ass house way out on Otter Creek, past all that new crap they're throwing up on the 139 end. He up and died on her a while back, but I guess she likes it out there in the middle of nowhere. I'm surprised she didn't recognize you. She's got one hell of a memory for details."

"I was pretty young last time I saw her," said Paula. "I didn't want to say anything to her in case I was mistaken. Thanks."

Paula smiled again as another customer approached, a harried looking housewife with rollers in her hair and a Camel hanging crookedly from the corner of her mouth. She flopped a copy of *The Columbus Dispatch* onto the counter and pointedly looked at her wristwatch before leveling her gaze at the cashier. Paula took the hint, taking her freshly refilled cup back outside where she returned to the picnic table, trying to decide the best way to Otter Creek.

———◇———

Chad wasn't happy.

The pugnacious teenager at McDonald's had screwed his order beyond recognition and had then tried to shortchange him by five dollars. When Chad pointed this out, the fat little turd had the audacity to be insulted that Chad had questioned his integrity. Chad wanted to leap across the counter and shove the sniveling shit's face into one of the deep fryers—really give him something to cry about, as Naomi Collins had been fond of saying when Chad, as a boy, had become petulant or sulky. This was, of course, before he had plunged a knife into her trachea, forever silencing her. But instead, he waited patiently until a manager had confirmed the error and returned his change, remaking his order personally. It was a little better, but not much.

He needed to kill someone.

Not just anyone—someone very specific. His internal rage had been festering since Lisa stumbled out of those woods, telling him that Crystal Bright had killed Suze. She would pay dearly for that. For him, the little girl was practically incidental. He imagined they would kill her, too, since she'd be right there and all—but it was the thought of wrapping his fingers around Crystal Bright's throat and squeezing until her eyes bugged out of her skull that allowed him to keep his cool. He couldn't afford to lose control now, not when he was so close.

He had taken his food and left, heading back to the motel where Lisa was showering.

A quick bite to eat and then on to Lucasville.

———◇———

Although she detested the thought of it, Paula went to the side of the highway and stuck her thumb out. Had it only been the previous evening that she permanently swore off hitchhiking? Today, it couldn't be helped.

Today was a better day. Paula couldn't believe her luck when a station wagon pulled off almost immediately, a middle-aged housewife-type behind the wheel. She leaned across the cavernous interior and yelled through the passenger window, "You need a lift, hon?"

Her name was Rita Underwood. She was a newly divorced mother of three and was expecting her first grandchild. She chattered non-stop as they sailed south on US 23 in the big Chevy Caprice wagon.

"Where you headin', sweetie?"

"I don't suppose you'd be going anywhere near Otter Creek?" asked Paula.

"As a matter of fact, I'm on my way to Beaver Run. Otter's only a little farther down. I don't mind taking you. Your family from out that way? Now, isn't that something! I know the Blevinses on the corner—Gordon and Dorothy—and I believe it's a family named Parker that's building a few doors down. I spoke with her once when I was over at Dot's. Oh, and, um, it's the Duncans who own that beautiful ranch farther down the hollow..."

And she chattered on and on, asking questions but never waiting for answers. This was all fine with Paula. Other than an occasional perfunctory grunt, this conversation required no participation at all.

Chad's mood was dark as he guided the Volvo north on US 23.

He hadn't slept well the previous evening because he found his attention constantly drifting back to Paula as she slept fitfully in the motel chair. Under the shadow of night, the family resemblance between Paula and her older sister was unmistakable. As he continued to stare, he had decided that Paula would look very much like Suze in just a few short years. For a moment, he entertained the fantasy of performing an obscene sort of *Pygmalion* on the girl. Surely, she would be attracted to him once she understood the things he had to offer.

"You're being awfully quiet," said Lisa, slurping the last of her Coke through a straw. She crumpled the empty container and tossed it into the floorboard. "You're *not* still pissed off about the mix-up at McDonald's, are you? Let it *go*."

Chad shook his head. "It's not that. I—I just didn't sleep very well last night."

"I'm surprised I slept so well," said Lisa. "I would've thought a stranger in the room would have been rather distracting."

Chad nodded. "It was."

"Look," said Lisa, straightening in the passenger seat and pointing through the windshield. "There it is."

A green metal rectangle announced the corporation limit of Lucasville. Lisa somehow expected the event to be more momentous, but the Volvo glided into the small area of population without any fanfare. Oh, well. It wasn't a very big town. If it were necessary to go door-to-door, it shouldn't take longer than an afternoon.

"I've gotta pee," Lisa announced. "Pull over."

Chad nudged the car into the left lane and turned into Speedway's parking lot, feeling insignificant in the shadow of an SUV that was pulling out onto the road and turning south. The round-faced woman behind the windshield looked lost in the monster truck, holding onto the steering wheel for dear life as she clumsily rolled over the curb before finding her lane.

"Some people shouldn't drive," he muttered, sliding the car into an empty slot between a canary yellow Chevette and a navy-blue Jeep Cherokee. Lisa hurried into the building while Chad stood outside, smoking a cigarette. He watched the people of Lucasville as they pulled up to the various pumps underneath the canopy, fueling their cars and never knowing how very close they stood to a ruthless, cold-blooded killer. Some may have suspected, though, judging from a few of the looks he received.

He smoked his cigarette to the filter and wondered how in the hell long it took to piss. He cast an annoyed glance through the glass storefront but didn't see Lisa anywhere inside. He was about to return his attention to the banks of wonderfully flammable gas pumps when something inside the store caught his eye. There was a red-haired woman near the back wall, as far away from his position as she could possibly be. She was speaking with a grizzled old man, but he couldn't see either one of them very clearly because of the glare from the sun. Something about her was very familiar. She didn't seem to be aware of him.

He decided it was time for a better look.

Paula remained as still as possible, careful to keep her weight evenly distributed between her feet so as not to cause the ground to shift and betray her presence. She was in the thick cover afforded by the woods of Otter Creek, crouching low and hoping Luke wouldn't spot her.

She couldn't believe her dumb luck.

She had nearly cried when she spotted Virginia, laughing and running in the landlocked backyard. She hadn't been too late after all. Thank God! She didn't think she could live with the guilt of knowing that she had been responsible for leaving the child in the hands of her killer.

But her feelings of joy quickly diminished when she realized that Luke was sitting on the back porch, staring vacantly into the distance, rocking slowly as the rusty chain creaked under his pendulous motion. Where was Crystal? She must be inside the house, too close for Luke to kill the girl now. Paula stared at him with pure loathing as he kept a disinterested eye on a child he later planned to murder. She wished she could go right in and speak to Crystal, try to convince her that Luke was using her, but she was afraid Crystal wouldn't listen. More to the point, it might prompt Luke to action, forcing him to accelerate his plan despite whatever witnesses there may be. He might simply choose to dispatch them as well. He certainly hadn't had any trouble taking care of the Parnell family.

From somewhere inside the house, the telephone rang.

Paula crouched lower to the ground as Luke suddenly straightened and craned his neck around. His eyes caught up with Virginia, and he smiled at her knowingly. "You stay right there, sweet pea," he said. "Phone's ringin'."

And with that, he turned and went into the house, leaving Virginia Parnell to fend for herself. Paula couldn't believe her good fortune. She eased forward, shifting a branch of evergreen that had been acting as the biggest part of her shield. Virginia was only about fifteen feet away, her back to Paula as she crawled along in the grass, speaking urgently to a honeybee.

"Hey," Paula called softly. *"Hey*. Remember me?"

Virginia turned, the smile freezing on her lips as the bee flew away.

III

Helen remained distant as she and Jessica took turns in the bathroom, showering before slipping back into their worn clothes. Jessica began to suspect that the nurse had eavesdropped on hers and Leonard's conversation the previous evening. She was growing weary of Helen's petulance and was beginning to suspect it had been a mistake to allow the nurse the option of staying with them.

Leonard was ready by the time the women had dressed and emerged from their room. They met in the motel lobby, surrendering their room keys and checking out. Jessica didn't think they would be staying another night.

The day was deceptive in its beauty with a warm sun suspended in a cloudless blue sky over emerald carpets of freshly mowed lawn that were still damp from the overnight thunderstorm. They piled into Jessica's Jeep, surprised at the warmth that had already collected as the sunlight poured through the windshield. Jessica turned the ignition and set the air conditioner on high before backing out of her parking space.

"Where are we going?" asked Helen.

"North," said Jessica, pulling out onto US 23. She now remembered why Lucasville had earlier come to mind. She seemed to recall that Enid Bowles was from somewhere around there. She couldn't possibly still be alive after all these years, could she? She had helped Jessica before, maybe she could help her again.

"I couldn't get my mind off of Lisa all night long," muttered Helen from the passenger seat. "Every time I nodded off, I saw Chad and Suze, their faces so close I could almost feel their breath. Suze would have killed me if it hadn't been for Lisa, you know. She came down to the basement and stopped her—"

"They let her wander around the house?" asked Jessica in amazement. It didn't sound like the type of thing an intelligent captor would do and only helped to confirm in her mind that Lisa was one of them.

Helen hesitated. "It wasn't as if she could go outside. They told her that they would kill me if she tried anything. I-I really don't know how she got downstairs in time, but it really doesn't matter. What matters is that she saved my life. Don't you see, Jessica? She can't be the monster Leonard is trying to make her into."

Jessica shot her a warning glance. "I thought we came to an understanding last night."

"We did, we did," said Helen hastily. "But I'm still entitled to my opinion just as much as I suppose he's entitled to his. Eventually you'll see which one of us is right, and I can't help it if I might point out the obvious here and there."

She shot Leonard a brief, victorious glare as Jessica returned her attention to the road, electing not to pursue the conversation any further. Helen was entirely blinded by this girl. She hoped that it wouldn't become more of a problem than it already was. Helen was a hostage waiting to happen. Jessica knew Chad wouldn't stop at anything to achieve his end goal, and Helen could blunder right into the line of fire, all in the name of blind devotion to a girl who didn't give a damn about her. If she were the type to believe in it, Jessica might have suspected that Lisa had put Helen under some type of spell.

She glanced in the rearview mirror at Leonard and was pleased to see that he had taken Helen's comments in stride. There was no use in being offended. It would only add fuel to Helen's fire. He was staring out the window at the railroad tracks that ran parallel to the right lane of traffic, about twenty yards away from the road, watching as they slowly overtook a train that was also traveling north. For a moment, she could see him as a much younger man, one whose face was unlined by worry and the burden of guilt. It was an odd sensation, but it passed quickly, and she returned her attention to the road.

"Lucasville," muttered Helen as they passed the sign at the corporation limit. "Are we just going to drive around Ohio until we bump across them?"

"I had a friend who lived in Lucasville once," said Jessica. "I thought I might look her up. She might be able to help."

"Oh, is she police, too?" asked Helen.

Jessica laughed at the thought of the spindly old woman, armed and in uniform. "Oh, no. She's more of an information source than anything else."

"How could she possibly know anything about Lisa? This doesn't make any sense," said Helen. "Why would those people drag her all over God's creation? What could they possibly want with her?"

Jessica was finding it harder to evade Helen's questions, questions that were increasingly ridiculous. Helen should have been able to figure out Lisa's participation all on her own.

"I've never been to her house," said Jessica, "and I'm not exactly sure where it is. I think I'll check the phonebook over at that Speedway, and we can go ahead and fill up while we're there."

She eased into the left lane and guided her Jeep into the parking lot of the gas station, sidling up to a pump behind a Ford Explorer. There were a couple of pole-mounted payphones at the rear of the lot, near a grouping of picnic tables where a dark-haired girl sat, staring vacantly ahead while she sipped from a Styrofoam cup. *Probably on drugs,* thought Jessica as she switched off the engine.

"Leonard, would you mind filling up the tank while I try and get the address?" asked Jessica, opening her door.

"Not at all, ma'am," he said, opening his door and sliding out of his seat. "Any particular grade?"

"Regular unleaded is fine," she said, digging into her purse for her notepad and a pen. She nearly walked into the path of a Camaro as it rumbled onto the lot at warp speed, skirting the bank of pumps and skidding to a halt in front of the store. She smiled sheepishly at the girl, who had noticed her clumsiness, and then crossed to the first payphone. Its phonebook had been snipped from the security chain and lay in a pile of shreds on the ground below. She went to the second payphone where she had better luck. She flipped to the B's and traced her finger down the short column for Bowles. Sure enough, Enid Bowles was listed. 57 Dale Street. 555-6555. She started to rummage for coins, then decided she'd rather just stop by. It had been fifteen years since she had last seen this woman. Enid Bowles might be bedridden and on life-support for all Jessica knew. For the first time since all of this had begun, she felt the vaguest glimmer of hope that things might actually work out. The need to speak with Enid had become overwhelming ever since Jessica had realized that Enid's unusual herbal tea had been responsible for allowing her to forget her painful past. Enid must have understood what Chad was. She *must* have. Maybe she would know how to stop him, too. A phone call simply wouldn't do—Jessica needed to *see* her. Something about the woman was immensely comforting. She jotted the address into her notepad and tucked it back into her purse.

As she returned to the Jeep, she noticed that the dark-haired girl had crossed the lot toward the highway and was now climbing into a station wagon she had managed to flag down. Jessica hoped that a ride was all the girl was after, and not someone from whom she could steal money for her next fix; it was all too common anymore. Why people continued to pick up hitchhikers was beyond her, despite the fact she had recently done the same for Leonard.

She looked up and noticed Helen was no longer in the passenger seat of the Jeep. She walked around the front of the vehicle and saw that Leonard had returned the nozzle to the pump and was replacing the fuel cap. "Where did Helen go?" she asked.

"Said she had to go to the ladies' room," he whispered, and as his face flushed with the words, Jessica again pictured him as a much younger man. She thought he was oddly and utterly charming.

Jessica noticed that the owner of the Ford SUV had returned to her vehicle and was having one hell of a time trying to maneuver it away from the pump. The Camaro that had ramped into the lot had taken the spot directly in front of the SUV, making it impossible for the woman behind the wheel to pull forward without clipping the other car. She couldn't back up without hitting Jessica's Jeep. After a few awkward attempts at trying to work her nose out of the bind, Jessica walked over and pecked on her window.

"We're all done," she told the grateful woman as she rolled down her window. "I can move my Jeep out of your way."

"Oh, thanks, dear," said the woman with a smile, pushing her round glasses up the bridge of her nose. "I'm doing meals-on-wheels, and I don't want the Salisbury steak to coagulate, if you know what I mean," she said with a wink.

Leonard had just finished using a squeegee on the Jeep's windshield as Jessica approached. "I'm going to pull into one of the parking spots by the store and let this woman out," she said. "That asshole in the Camaro has her completely blocked in. Why don't you go on inside and see if they have a street map for Lucasville. I've got Enid's address, but I don't have any idea where Dale Street is."

"All right."

"I'll meet you inside," said Jessica, climbing behind the wheel and starting the engine. She rounded the bank of pumps and took a spot near the door of the building. The lady in the Ford tooted her horn and waved her appreciation as she began maneuvering herself away from the pump.

There was quite a crowd inside the building. Morning travelers digging through aisles of chips and candy, pouring coffee from the self-serve dispensers, scratching off lottery tickets, and waiting in a line that was several people deep for the cashier to process their various fuel and food purchases. A heavyset woman in a blue Speedway smock was ambling around the endcaps, affixing signs which displayed special pricing on Pepsi 2-liters for 99¢ each. She looked particularly befuddled by the cheap, plastic tape dispenser that refused to surrender its pieces in any length shorter than a foot, so she eventually pulled a pair of scissors from the pocket of her smock to use instead of the ineffectual trimmer on the plastic dispenser. Jessica worked her way toward the rear of the building where she spotted signage for the restrooms, smiling as she passed the clerk and recognizing the tune she hummed as the theme from *I Dream of Jeannie*.

Helen was just emerging as Jessica neared the door. "It's filthy in there," she said, shooting a disgusted look at the Speedway employee who chose to ignore her. "I wouldn't actually sit on the toilet if you can help it," she said from the corner of her mouth.

Jessica smiled and nodded, entering the bathroom and locking the door behind her. It was a small room—a one-seater—and not nearly as dirty as Helen had indicated. The floor tiles had yellowed with age, and there was a ring of rust around the faucet, but the mirrors were clean, and the toilet itself suffered nothing more than a bit of dark grunge around the bolt covers near the floor. What the hell did Helen expect? A paid attendant? As she settled herself onto the cold porcelain, she decided that Helen Martin was the most difficult woman she had met in a very long time.

* * *

Leonard found a stand of maps near the checkout at the front of the store. His choices were Portsmouth, Scioto County, or the entire State of Ohio. He selected the one for Scioto County and used the legend on the back to locate Dale Street. He was surprised to note how close it was to where they were. He could probably see the roof of Jessica's friend's house from the parking lot, if he knew which one he was looking for. He glanced at the line which was now five persons deep and decided to wait for Jessica. If she was buying anything for herself, there wasn't any sense in waiting through the line twice.

Helen appeared at the rear of the store shortly after Jessica went into the restroom alcove. Her accusing eyes locked onto Leonard's, and he turned back toward the rack of maps, unable to face her even briefly. Something in her eyes was different this morning—worse somehow. Had she been listening to his and Jessica's conversation on the balcony last night? That was probably it. She probably realized that Jessica understood about Lisa and what she truly was. He had noticed Helen acting differently toward Jessica as well, and it made him nervous. Jessica was their leader. What if Helen decided she no longer wished to be led? He quickly pushed the thought away; it was too much to consider on top of everything else.

He hadn't slept well the night before. He passed the time staring at the motel ceiling, his heart aching for Jessica and the pain her own flesh and blood had caused her. He knew there was more to Jessica's story than she had shared, but he hadn't wanted to push her. He saw the heartbreak in her eyes as she told him about Chad and some of the things he had done. As a parent, she felt responsible for his actions, both good and bad. It sounded as if Chad had never done anything good in his entire life, and if he were the same greasy-haired boy Leonard had seen skulking around the Mitchell place, he didn't look as if he were about to start any time soon.

* * *

To the casual observer, Helen Martin appeared to be deeply engrossed in the selection of baby food offered by the fine folks at Gerber, but she had merely chosen her position because it allowed her to keep an eye on Leonard Barnes as he hovered near the map rack. She didn't understand how the man could have Jessica so completely fooled. If Helen had even the remotest idea of where Lisa might be, she would have tried to find her on her own. The clandestine meetings of the previous evening had begun to make her distrust Jessica, and she knew she wouldn't be able to hide it for much longer.

She was suddenly aware of a young mother standing near her, trying to edge closer to the baby food but unable to reach it because Helen was in her way. Helen smiled apologetically and shifted positions to the next aisle, which contained cookies and other packaged snacks. Her view of Leonard wasn't quite as good, but she could still keep him in her sights. *If only he weren't here*, thought Helen bitterly. *Jessica could be such a great help if he wasn't poisoning her mind. I wish he'd just go away.*

But she knew there was little chance of that. Leonard wouldn't be dissuaded as long as he had Jessica's attention. It was positively nauseating how he had begun mooning over her whenever she entered a room. She was young enough to be his daughter, for heaven's sake!

<hr />

Jessica spotted Leonard as she exited the restroom alcove, her hands still damp because there weren't any paper towels in the dispenser. She excused herself as she struggled around the heavyset woman who was still hanging signage and worked her way around to where Leonard stood at the map rack.

"Any luck?" she asked.

He nodded. "I don't think we're very far away at all. Dale Street looks like it's only a few streets over from where we're standing."

"Good," said Jessica, following Leonard's finger as it traced a line on the map of Scioto County. "I'm still a little groggy from last night. I think I'll grab a cup of coffee. Do you want one?"

"Thanks, that'd be great."

"Where did Helen go?"

Leonard shifted his eyes covertly toward where Helen lurked at the far end of the building. "She's been over there since you went into—the ladies'. She thinks I don't see her staring at me, but she hasn't looked away for longer than a few seconds. I'm sorry about all of this."

"About what?" asked Jessica. "I promise you, this is Helen's problem, not yours."

Looking at his new friend, he wanted desperately to believe her, but there was no way Jessica could fully understand the guilt he carried over Evie's death, and no way that her simple words could provide absolution for his soul. Nonetheless, he smiled weakly and nodded.

Jessica returned his smile and headed across to where Helen was lurking. As she attempted to navigate the busy aisles, she bumped into a red-headed woman who snapped, "Bitch!" as she continued on. Jessica watched in amazement as she disappeared into the alcove leading to the bathrooms, never once looking back. She would have expected that type of attitude in Indianapolis or Cincinnati, but she had believed manners were better in rural areas. Apparently not.

"We're getting coffee," said Jessica as she neared Helen. "Do you want anything?"

Helen shook her head stiffly. "I'm fine, thank you."

Jessica sighed and stared at Helen with disappointment. This wasn't going to work. It just wasn't. Jessica needed the full support of her entire ragtag team if she had any hope of defeating Chad, Lisa, and Suze. Any dissention amongst themselves would only weaken them to the point of ineffectuality. It might even cost them their lives. Helen's attitude exceeded Jessica's tolerance, and she had only just opened her mouth to tell her so when all hell broke loose.

Leonard poured himself a tall cup of strong, black coffee and secured the contents with a plastic lid. He took a few packets of sugar and creamer and stuffed them into his pocket, more out of habit than necessity. In years past, whenever Leonard traveled with his wife, Nell, she was consistently forgetting these things for herself, and he had been pleased to find a way around the problem. "That's my thoughtful guy," she would say any time she had to dip into the collection of condiments that Leonard had amassed in his glove compartment.

When he turned around, he nearly ran into a tall, red-headed woman who was emerging from the restrooms. He only looked at her peripherally, but something about her features caught his attention, and he turned for another glance.

"Leonard Barnes?" she said in disbelief, and it shocked him that she might know his name.

And suddenly she was in motion, pushing the heavyset clerk away from the endcap she was marking and into a large display of corn chips, which collapsed upon impact. In a move almost too smooth to follow, the redhead grabbed the scissors whose handle protruded from the clerk's smock and pulled them out as the surprised woman toppled over. It was only as she plunged the scissors deep into Leonard's throat that he realized the hostile face belonged to Lisa Mitchell.

CHAPTER TWENTY-FIVE

I

"Tell me about Aunt Maude and her sister," said Crystal, tucking her injured arm self-consciously against her midsection. "What could have happened that would make them completely sever their relationship? Was Grace like Lisa?"

Enid's smile was melancholy. "Oh, no. Grace certainly had her issues, but she wasn't evil. They didn't have an easy childhood. They were barely out of diapers when your great-grandmother, Sallie, caught the consumption and passed. Your great-grandfather, Lawrence, was a hardworking man with a good heart and the best of intentions, but he wasn't cut out to raise little girls by his lonesome. Syl had already married and was expecting her own child. That left your grandmother, Peggy, to raise them as best she could, but considering she was only five years older than they were, it was asking an awful lot of someone so young. In fact, Peggy dropped out of school after the eighth grade to run the household. She married your grandfather later than most girls her age, and she had already raised one family by the time she had her own—but we're not here to talk about Peg, God rest her soul. This is about Maude and Grace."

Enid patted Crystal's hand, her cloudy eyes reminiscing of a distant past.

"They were both beautiful—blonde hair that flowed like silk down to their waists, and although they were just as different as night and day, they got along quite well. But all of that changed once they were seniors in high school."

"What happened?"

"What *usually* comes between two women?" Enid answered Crystal's question with one of her own and didn't wait for a response. "A man, of course. That was the year the Leightons moved to town."

Crystal's smile was uncertain as a chill passed through her. Luke's last name was Leighton, and that couldn't possibly be a coincidence. "Aunt Maude never mentioned anyone named Leighton."

"And why would she?" asked Enid, her thin eyebrows pushing her forehead into a sea of wrinkles. "It was the heartbreak of a lifetime, and she swore to never trust another man again, but I'm getting ahead of myself."

She reached for the glass of water on her bedside table and took a sip, clearing her raspy throat.

"Maurice Leighton and his family relocated from Columbus when he was promoted to president of the local branch of First Federal Savings and Loan in Portsmouth. They built a house just two streets over on Bickle Lane—biggest house this little town has ever seen! I could see it just as plain as day through my window over there until it burned in '73, but that's neither here nor there," she said, indicating the tall window to the right of her nightstand.

"Grace had her sights set on Paulie from the moment she saw him with his shirt off, playing football with the other boys from school, and I can't rightly say I blame her." Enid's cheeks brightened as she fanned herself with a bony hand, and Crystal couldn't help but laugh.

"Nice to look at, was he?" she asked, grinning.

"Oh, all the girls thought so," said Enid. "Except for Maude, that is."

"Really?"

"I don't think she was so much put off by his looks as his attitude. He was a bit of a showboat in those days. He knew the effect he had on folks. All the boys wanted to be him, and all the girls wanted to be with him. His family had money, and he wasn't above flaunting it. Maude thought he was vulgar."

Crystal smiled. "Sounds like her. She couldn't stand people *'putting on airs.'*" She flew a pair of air quotes while approximating her aunt's Southern Ohio accent.

"And life just has the funniest way of turning the screw, don't you find? The *only* girl Paulie had eyes for was Maude from Day One. He was determined to wear her down, no matter what it took."

"Uh-oh," said Crystal, wincing. It didn't take much imagination to see where this was going.

"Grace was furious," said Enid. "It was the first real trouble those girls ever had between them. I mean, sure, they had little spats about this and that, but envy is such an ugly thing, and I think we were all surprised by the lengths Grace would go to get what she wanted—and Maude wasn't even interested in the boy!"

Enid paused for another sip of water.

"Well—at least, not initially."

Crystal leaned in, riveted. "What happened?"

"The Great Depression—that's what happened. Ruined lives near and far, but around these parts, it was folks like the Leightons who were hit the hardest. Piece by piece, they lost everything. First Federal was one of the first banks to fail, and Maurice Leighton found himself out of work and without any prospects. It wasn't long before they foreclosed on the house, and it was all just too much for Maurice to take. He sent his wife, Regina, and son to stay with relatives in Franklin County while he stayed behind under the pretense of liquidating all their worldly possessions and vacating the premises. They had no sooner hit the road when Maurice swallowed the business end of his Colt .45 and pulled the trigger, taking the coward's way out and leaving Regina and Paulie to fend for themselves."

"That's awful," said Crystal.

Enid nodded. "Sadly, it wasn't uncommon. Suicide rates skyrocketed during those dark times, and alcoholism soared, despite the fact that Prohibition was still in effect. Lots of folks made ends meet by peddling bathtub gin, and Regina made some of the finest in the county, but none of that could replace the man of the house, and Paulie may have taken it hardest of all. Your Aunt Maude couldn't help but feel sorry for the boy as she watched his friends turn on him one by one. Her perception had started to change, and she began to enjoy his company upon occasion, surprised by his wit and intelligence. He was determined to rise above the tragedy his family had endured, and Maude finally understood his appeal. She was beginning to fall in love, and that drove Grace absolutely wild. Every single effort she had made to get Paulie's attention fell flat, and she couldn't understand it. Physically, they were virtually identical. What made Maude so much more appealing than her?"

Crystal harrumphed. "Having never met Grace, I can't say with any real certainty, but Aunt Maude was one-of-a-kind."

Enid placed the tip of her forefinger to her nose and winked. "Exactly. It wasn't Maude's physical attributes that had attracted Paulie, enviable though they were. It was her fire and the way she carried herself. By comparison, Grace was just a pale imitation. She was bawdy and loud and far more apt to find herself in trouble than her twin. But she was also determined, and giving up was simply not an option. She began to observe her sister almost like a school science project, noting their many likenesses, but more importantly, their differences. As little girls, they had occasionally attempted to fool people by swapping places with one another. In fact, I would imagine it's a gimmick many twins try at least once, but Grace had decided to give it another go, albeit without her sister's consent this time. The Fourth of July holiday was approaching, and for the first time since Sallie had passed, Lawrence had agreed to take his two youngest daughters to spend the holiday with cousins over in Meigs County. I remember how excited both girls were, although it was for completely different reasons. Maude hadn't been away from Scioto County in years, while Grace saw this as her opportunity to finally get her hooks into Paulie. The night before they were due to leave, Grace started complaining about not feeling well, and by morning, she was begging off, claiming female problems—something her father would never begin to question. She insisted they go without her and extend her condolences to the cousins while she spent the weekend in bed—*recovering*."

Crystal refilled Enid's water glass without being asked. The elderly woman's voice was like sandpaper at this point, and she accepted the glass with a nod, drinking nearly half of it in one gulp.

"They hadn't been gone more than a half hour before Grace was raiding Maude's closet and dressing in one of her favorite outfits. She found Paulie tossing a football around with a few of his buddies, and he was startled to see her. Maude had already told him of their holiday plans, and when he asked what had happened to change things, he called her by the name she hoped to hear."

496

"He thought she was Maude," said Crystal, and Enid's forefinger once again flew to her nose.

"Exactly. She told him that she hadn't felt well enough to go earlier but was feeling much better now. And now that she had the whole house to herself for the long weekend, maybe he could join her for a little picnic that evening, even suggesting that he try and sneak some of his mother's infamous dandelion wine. What was the harm in being a little naughty? I think you can see where this is going without me going into all the sordid details."

Crystal slowly nodded. "Grace stole Paulie away from Aunt Maude."

"Well—not exactly, but she certainly did seduce him. Somewhere over the course of that weekend, Paulie figured out what was going on, but it was too late. He was a teenaged boy with raging hormones, and he could no more have walked away than he could have flapped his arms and flown. After Maude returned, he could barely face her. There was certainly nothing wrong with his sense of guilt," said Enid, scowling as if it had happened just yesterday.

"That's awful," said Crystal, and she suddenly understood why her aunt always avoided discussions about their family history. It wasn't a pleasant road to travel.

"If only that was the end of it," said Enid.

"Oh, no."

"Oh, yes," Enid continued. "When you live in a town as small as this one, it's difficult to avoid the folks you don't want to see, so Paulie decided his best choice was to enlist in the Army. Without a word to anyone, he was gone. He was in basic training by the time Grace found out she was expecting. Your great-grandfather was furious. Things like this could ruin an entire family's reputation, so he shuttled Grace off to Indiana where she could have the baby and give it up for adoption, far enough away to avoid the local grapevine, but your poor Aunt Maude didn't need for anyone to fill in the details for her. Paulie's erratic behavior and sudden departure coincided too neatly, and one look at Grace's eyes was all the confirmation she needed. She was absolutely crushed. She swore she'd never trust another man again."

"And she didn't," said Crystal, her heart breaking for her aunt. "So, Grace gave her baby up?"

Enid was already shaking her head. "No. The baby didn't quite make it to full term. Grace developed large ovarian cysts over the course of her pregnancy, and they ruptured. Doctors were able to save Grace, but not her infant daughter, and it was something she never fully recovered from. Once she decided that it was God's way of punishing her for her earlier transgressions, there was no bringing her back. She refused to return to Ohio, not that her father or Maude were in any real hurry to see her, although I believe with time, they would have forgiven her. She just couldn't forgive herself.

497

"I guess in the long run, it worked out just as well. Maude and Grace were exactly where they needed to be when your parents were killed in that horrible car crash. Selfishly, I'm grateful for their relationship with Paulie. After he was discharged from the Army, Paulie settled down in Kentucky. He had inherited a farm from a relative he didn't even know he had. He wasn't the bad guy Maude convinced herself he was, and he suffered the consequences of his poor choices just as much as anyone else. I kept in touch with him through the years. Letters first and then e-mail—until he passed away a few weeks ago, poor soul. I'll miss him terribly. I tell you, it's hard to take when everyone around you dies, and you're left behind with nothing but memories. I've buried my husband, my children, and one of my grandchildren. I've outlived the entire Classes of 1924 through 1929. It's just so *difficult*." She shook her head sadly as her eyes threatened to cloud over. "After ninety-six years on this planet, I have stopped asking *why*. Sometimes it is irrelevant. Things are the way they are, and we can only deal with them, doing our level best to influence their direction in our favor whenever possible. It just isn't always possible."

They sat in companionable silence for a moment as ghosts from the past sifted like sand through their memories.

"Do you think that someone born bad is capable of redemption?" asked Crystal, her mind serving up a replay of the look on Lisa's face as she had taken Suze's life.

"Well, of course, dear. It would all be rather pointless if our actions were scripted, wouldn't it? I think it's *harder* for some people to get themselves turned around. Their natural instinct will always be the incorrect one. I would imagine that every decision is a very difficult process. That's why Grace stayed in Indiana. She wanted a fresh start, and no one really tried to stop her. She plotted her own course to redemption and spent the rest of her life adhering to that path."

"Did they ever speak again? Aunt Maude and Paulie, I mean."

Enid shook her head. "Not a word, although he frequently asked about her in his letters to me. In fact, Maude only contacted Grace when she had no other choice. Lisa had tried to kill you, and she couldn't have you both under her roof. Grace accepted the responsibility of Lisa as a penance for her past sins. There would be no contact between you girls, no need for any. Maude believed it was safest that way."

Crystal was silent for a moment, drinking it all in. "There's still so much I don't understand," she finally said. "How is my arm healing so quickly? I broke my ankle when I was a little girl, and I seem to recall that it took quite some time to heal."

"It isn't the gift of invincibility, dear," said Enid. "But right now, things are very—turbulent. Gifted people like yourself can occasionally manipulate your environment, causing the things you need to simply happen. Both Maude and Grace were gifted. Grace read tea leaves and had some sense of things to come.

Of course, the way she did it, it seemed very vaudevillian, so no one paid much attention, but I personally witnessed more than one occasion where she got things exactly right. Maude's gifts were more internal. She seemed to sense things that others didn't."

"So, what is your gift?" asked Crystal.

Enid chuckled. "Oh, I don't have anything to offer. Except that I have spent the greater portion of my life exploring the possibility of this concept, finding others who believe because they have known of people like yourselves. I have learned how to make a few useful 'potions', for lack of a better word. One of them has been known to ease the strain of painful memories."

The green tea. Crystal remembered it now. It had been the *tea* that had smelled of plums, not Enid herself. It had been thick and syrupy, sliding down her throat like molasses.

"Kathy told me that you believe there is a man traveling with Lisa," said Enid.

"Yes," said Crystal. "Why?"

Enid pursed her lips. "That worries me a great deal. You see, very shortly after Grace took Lisa away, I received a call from Paulie Leighton. He asked me if I had been following the news over in Indiana. I told him I had no idea what he was talking about, and he told me about this family, the Lybrooks. They had two boys; one was six and the other was three. The oldest one was savagely beaten one afternoon, allegedly by the mother in a fit of psychotic depression. When Paulie saw the boys on the news, he said that there was something about the youngest one, and he had the overwhelming sensation that it was the child who had clubbed his older brother, not the mother. Jessie Lybrook was nearly catatonic when they arrested her. By then, I had already told Paulie about what Lisa had done to you, and he thought the story in Indiana had some fascinating parallels. I admit, I wanted to investigate it further, and so I met that poor woman, institutionalized for something she didn't do. I learned all about her son, Chad, and I believe that he may be the young man who is riding with Lisa now. If he is, God help us all."

"But why would you think that he's with her?" asked Crystal. "Precognition? I thought you said you didn't have any special talents like that."

"I don't," said Enid. "But it only stands to reason. Jessie's older son would be the fellow you call Luke. If this equation is to truly balance itself, I would imagine that Chad is somewhere in the formula."

Crystal stared at Enid dumbly. It was entirely too much to swallow. How could four strangers crawl across the country, unwittingly seeking each other out like guided missiles on a collision course? She bit her bottom lip as she remembered Luke mentioning his father, Paulie, and realized that the pieces, however ridiculous, were falling into place.

"What do they want with Virginia?" asked Crystal. "She's the one they're after. Lisa was on her way to kill the girl. She didn't even expect me. I just happened to be there in time to help stop her."

Enid nodded, smiling. "As I would fully expect. You *are* the little girl's protectors. You and Lucas. I don't know what they want with the girl, dear, but I suspect she must be someone of great importance."

The grandfather clock in the hallway chimed, and Crystal was surprised to note that it was already eleven. Kathy should be returning shortly with a bucket of chicken and assorted sides, but Crystal wasn't even remotely hungry. Too many thoughts bounced around in her head. She hoped that conversing with Enid would make her feel better, but it had quite the opposite effect. It was as if everything Crystal had ever believed was hidden in lies, and the world she thought she knew was actually the set of a sci-fi movie in which she starred. She was suddenly very worried about Virginia.

"May I use your phone?" asked Crystal. "I'd like to check in with Luke to make sure everything's alright."

"Certainly, dear," said Enid, reclining a bit in the bed. "I have a cordless here, but there's an extension out in the hallway, if you'd care for a little privacy."

Crystal stepped out into the dusky foyer and found the phone about halfway down the hall. She punched in Kathy's telephone number and waited as the rings sounded.

"'Lo?"

"I didn't know if you'd answer," said Crystal. "It's me."

"Caller ID," said Luke. "I recognized Mrs. Bowles name."

"Everything okay?"

"Yeah, great," said Luke. "I'm still not sure if that should make me feel better or worse. I keep expecting Virginia to break down or something, but she's in the backyard, chasing butterflies and having a good ol' time. Did you find out anything useful?"

"Yes. No." Crystal sighed. "Maybe. I know a lot more than I did before I came, I'm just not sure what it means. I don't know. Anyway, Kathy should be here soon, and after we eat, we'll be right back. Keep a close eye on her, Luke. They're out there somewhere."

"I know," said Luke. "I won't let her out of my sight."

———◇———

Luke replaced the receiver in the cradle and was surprised at how buoyed he felt simply by hearing her voice. He whistled as he crossed through the kitchen and into the dining room, stepping around the oak table and pushing the sliding glass door open onto the backyard.

"It was Crystal," he called out to Virginia. "Just checking in. She should be back soon."

Silence.

The smile on Luke's face abruptly dropped away as the stillness of the late morning descended upon him. There was no soft laughter, no sing-song melody, no sound whatsoever. He hurried out into the backyard, calling her name with increasing urgency, running from one end of the lot to the other, his stomach brewing acid.

Virginia was gone.

II

"*Shh*," whispered Paula, leading Virginia by the hand along the narrow trail. "I bet they'll never catch us."

Virginia looked over her shoulder, staring back toward the place from which they had come. She couldn't see Kathy's house anymore, but she could hear Luke screaming her name. Paula's pace quickened at the sound of his voice, and at times Virginia was fairly certain that her arm was going to wrench free from its socket. She started to protest, but Paula shushed her again.

"Remember?" said Paula with a nervous smile. "Crystal said we have to be especially quiet. It's our turn to hide and Luke's turn to seek."

Paula's mind was racing as she tugged Virginia along. Her relief at finding the child unharmed had quickly turned into fear for her own safety should Luke catch her before she could get far enough away. She decided the best escape route would be straight through the woods, avoiding roads whenever possible. Truthfully, she hadn't planned this far ahead. Now that she had found the girl, she had no idea what to do with her. She thought about taking her to the Super 8 where Lisa and Chad were. Surely, Angel would have returned by now. She wasn't entirely comfortable giving the little girl to them without Angel being present. Paula wished she could leave a note for Crystal, something to let her know that Virginia was safe, but there was no way of doing that without Luke seeing it first, and he would never allow Crystal the peace of mind.

So, for the time being, she walked on, pushing through thick brambles and thorny branches and hoping that the next time she called her sister's cell phone, Angel would answer.

Lisa entered the Speedway at a brisk march, heading straight toward the sign which pointed out the restrooms. Her bladder was absolutely straining for release, and she was frustrated with the amount of customer traffic inside the small building. There were more people inside than might have been indicated by the cars in the lot. They clogged the narrow little aisles, selecting snacks and beverages at a crawl before moseying to the counter. An auburn-haired woman abruptly dug her elbow into Lisa's side as she passed. Under other circumstances, Lisa would have probably returned the jab, but her bladder urged her to reconsider, and she settled for growling, "Bitch!" as she continued into the dingy alcove.

The restroom was apparently a single-seater, and Lisa had to wait in the hallway behind a scrawny teenage girl who smelled of stale perspiration and alcohol. Lisa noticed the distinct trail of track marks that crawled along the girl's inner arm, and a quick glance at her bleary, bloodshot eyes confirmed the diagnosis. Lisa had little tolerance for those who relied on chemical substances. She wasn't against their occasional recreational use, but it was obvious that this hollow-faced little prostitute had been abusing for years. She was oblivious to Lisa's open stare, apparently fascinated with something about her tennis shoes.

The restroom door finally opened, and a bewildered woman with a puff of cotton-candy hair emerged, shaking excess water from her fingertips with a look of disgust. "No paper towels," she muttered, as if an explanation were necessary.

The teenage junkie hadn't made a move toward the restroom, so Lisa stepped around her and went inside. Just as she engaged the lock on the door handle, she heard the girl utter a disoriented, "What the——?"

She took care of her business quickly and washed her hands at the sink, surveying her new hairstyle in the mirror. Under the bright overhead lighting, her new hair color was brassier and seemed more unnatural than before; she still wasn't sure if she liked it. But it wasn't enough to spoil her mood, which was unusually upbeat this morning. She could feel the nearness of the others and believed they would find them before the day was over. It would be good to be done with this. She and Chad might just take a vacation afterward, travel the globe and see what was out there. She couldn't recall ever being out of Indiana, much less out of the country. And yet, something about this little town was familiar, although she couldn't for the life of her imagine what it might be. Maybe all little towns looked the same.

The junkie had given up waiting by the time Lisa reemerged, drying her hands on her jeans. As she wandered out into the store, she saw through the plate glass that Chad had apparently grown impatient for her return and was moving toward the building's entrance. She started to sidestep an old man who was about to bump into her when all of her senses suddenly went on alert. He straightened and started to apologize, but Lisa couldn't hear anything over the pounding of her own heart.

"Leonard Barnes?" she asked, dazed. It couldn't *possibly* be him, could it? Why would he be this far from Morgan? Unless, of course, he was following her...

Like lightning, Lisa sprang into action, pushing over a heavyset woman who was hanging signs along the store's endcaps. Florescent light glinted against metal, and Lisa's hand snaked out to hook the handles of the metal scissors that were protruding from the clerk's smock. As the woman tumbled into a display of corn chips, Lisa whirled and planted the scissors all the way to the hilt into Leonard's neck.

His eyes widened as his arms flailed jerkily, his fingers trying to find whatever it was she had stuck into him. Bright jets of arterial blood spurted from the wound in time with Leonard's accelerated heartbeat. Someone behind Lisa started screaming and was soon accompanied by others, horrified at the gruesome scene unfolding before them. None of them seemed to realize that Lisa was the one responsible except for the downed clerk, who was still trying to find her feet in a sea of yellow and red potato chip bags. The fall had knocked the breath from her, and she was unable to say anything. All she could do was gasp for her breath and continue to point at Lisa as pandemonium enveloped the room.

Lisa didn't intend to stick around. The police would soon arrive, and who knew if one of these hayseeds might attempt to detain her until then? She pushed her way through the gathering crowd, aware that someone was screaming, "I'm a nurse! I'm a nurse!" Chad had only just stepped into the building when Lisa grabbed him by the elbow and jerked him back outside.

"Hey!" he protested. "What the hell is going on? I thought I saw—"

"Leonard Barnes," she said, guiding him toward the Volvo before hurrying to the passenger side of the vehicle. "I don't know what the hell he was doing here, but it can't be good."

"You killed him?"

Lisa nodded jerkily. "I think so. He was bleeding all over the place. *Dammit!* I wish I'd had more time to react. I think I just fucked us over. There were surveillance cameras everywhere."

Chad already had the car in gear, rocketing out of the parking lot. "We'll worry about that later. Let's just get the hell out of here."

———◆———

"I'm tired," said Virginia.

They were the first words she had spoken since Paula had lured her from Kathy Duncan's backyard, and Paula was so unprepared for them that she nearly pissed herself at the sudden sound.

Paula glanced around, looking for any movement in the thick woods around them, but she saw nothing that hadn't been placed by nature's haphazard design. A fallen tree was off to the left, beyond the trail and partially obstructed by wild shrubbery. Paula led Virginia to the thickest end of the trunk, and side-by-side, they rested their bottoms against it.

"Are you alright?" asked Paula.

Virginia nodded and offered a vague smile. Her attention had already been captured by a squirrel that was leaping spectacularly from treetop to treetop.

"We'll just take a minute, and then we should go on," said Paula. "We don't want Luke to catch us now, do we?" She tried a laugh, but it come out high-pitched and tinny. Virginia's eyes continued to follow the squirrel, and Paula wasn't even sure if the girl was listening to her. Oh, well. It didn't matter. The important thing was that they had gotten away from Luke before he had spotted them.

She glanced upward, trying to gain some sense of direction from the position of the sun, but it was too high in the sky to be of much use. Paula had a sudden vision of herself lost in the woods, leading the girl to a death of starvation just as surely as if she had left her in Luke's murderous hands. She wasn't familiar with this area, and for all she knew, she was taking them farther and farther from civilization. She swallowed hard and refused to allow panic to overtake her. She didn't want Virginia to sense that anything was wrong. So far, the little girl had been completely compliant, but Paula didn't figure the charade could last much longer. Eventually, Virginia would suspect this was no game. Paula didn't know how to communicate with children and didn't know if she could make Virginia understand that she had only done what she thought was best for her.

As if Paula was in any position to determine such a thing. She was little more than a runaway herself, and now responsible for the life of a child whose entire family had been slaughtered.

She decided that it would be prudent at this juncture to try and find her way back to a road. Her need to speak with Angel was overwhelming, and she certainly wasn't going to find a payphone out in the middle of the woods.

Surely Angel had returned by now.

Paula wanted desperately to turn the care of this child over to her sister. She would know what to do. She always did.

With renewed determination, Paula forced herself to smile. She stood and held out a hand to Virginia. "Are you ready? We'd better get going before they catch us."

Virginia nodded, placing her tiny hand inside Paula's and pulling herself to her feet. She giggled abruptly. "They're *never* gonna find us," Virginia said with a certainty that sent a chill down Paula's spine.

In a space of no more than ten minutes, Lisa's mood had tanked. They had gotten away from the gas station before the first policemen arrived but even so, she feared their license plate had been captured by surveillance cameras, and now Crystal Bright wouldn't be the only one running from the law.

Chad seemed relatively unaffected. As a matter of fact, he was more disturbed about being pulled out of the building prematurely than anything else. Who was that auburn-haired woman, and why did she inspire such a complete sense of revulsion in him? He hadn't been able to get a close look at her before all hell had broken loose. He sulked as he guided the Volvo along country roads, trying to keep a low profile. They could no longer leisurely explore Lucasville as originally planned.

"So, what now?" he finally asked.

"We need a different car," she said.

The residences along the desolate stretch of pavement were few and far between. It was an ideal place for a quick carjacking with no close neighbors to act as witness. Of course, country folk were a bit unpredictable. It was more than likely that some kept a shotgun by the back door for just such an emergency. Chad almost hoped it would be the case; it had been too long since he had been able to express his rage against someone, and the release would be nearly orgasmic.

He cut the steering wheel hard to the right, turning sharply into a narrow drive which meandered back through a field of tall grass to a farmhouse that stood well away from the road. There was a small silver sedan parked beside the house, perfect for their needs.

Paula was almost giddy with laughter when she heard the sound of a car engine ahead. It passed and faded away to the right, but Paula wasn't discouraged. Where there was a car, there had to be a road. She no longer worried that Luke would be waiting on the other side. She and Virginia had traveled quite a distance since leaving the Duncan ranch. Virginia had completely worn out some time ago, and Paula was struggling to keep her perched atop her shoulders. The little girl was bleary-eyed and exhausted, ready for a nap, but there was no time for sleep yet. Paula needed to find a telephone.

Please, God, let Angel be back.

505

When they finally reached the roadway, Paula was disappointed to see that it was little more than a broken asphalt ribbon, winding drunkenly through the hilly landscape. She hadn't heard another car since the one that had drawn her attention, and from the look of it, it might be hours before she saw another. She hadn't expected to find a convenient payphone along the side of the road, but she *had* hoped for a residence or two, somewhere she might be able to borrow the use of a telephone. From where she stood, all she could see were woods, weeds, and broken asphalt. She sighed and eased Virginia from her shoulders. They both plopped down into a squat beside the road, and Paula struggled to fight back tears. She didn't want to fall apart now, but she was quickly running out of ideas.

"I've gotta pee," said Virginia, looking embarrassed by the admission. "I don't want Luke to see me pee."

"No problem," said Paula, forcing her voice to be steady. "I have to go, too. We'll just go into the woods a little ways."

Paula struggled back to her feet, but Virginia had already trotted back to the path from which they had come. She paused at the edge of the woods and waited for Paula to catch up. They reentered the woods and went in far enough so that they wouldn't be spotted from the road before veering off into a patch of tall grass.

Just don't let it be poison ivy, thought Paula as she unfastened her jeans and slid them along with her underpants down around her ankles. She squatted low to the ground and had only just begun to relieve herself when she heard the sound of another car on the road, this time approaching from the right.

"Shit," she muttered, struggling to pull her pants up. "Stay right here. I'm going to see who that is."

"Luke and Crystal?" asked Virginia, her eyes twinkling merrily.

"Maybe," said Paula, fumbling with the clasp of her jeans. She stumbled back toward the path and then ran to the road, breaking free of the woods just in time to see the taillights of a compact silver Toyota disappear to her left, the sound of its busy little engine trailing away. This time, Paula couldn't hold the frustration in. She burst into tears and dropped to her knees, sobbing uncontrollably. She just wanted her sister—that was all. If only Angel was here, everything would be alright.

"Paula?" Virginia was suddenly beside Paula, placing a small hand on her shoulder.

Paula snuffled but didn't attempt to speak. She had wanted so badly to spare Virginia any concern, but she wasn't like Angel or Crystal or even Lisa. They were all born survivors, and Paula could never feel that kind of strength. It had been foolish to think that she could offer protection to this little girl.

"Come on," said Virginia, offering Paula a hand. Paula looked at the girl through tear-blurred vision, amazed by what she saw. There was no fear whatsoever in Virginia's face, despite Paula's obvious distress. Paula took Virginia's hand and pulled herself to her feet, ashamed of her own weakness. Virginia only smiled, her face angelic underneath a mop of dark, bouncy curls.

They brushed themselves off and started walking hand-in-hand. They turned right, following the berm of the road in the direction from which the car had come. Surely there was a house around here *somewhere*.

The Toyota was a rust bucket, but it ran, and that was all that was important. Chad wasn't accustomed to a stick shift and ground away at the transmission as they traveled back toward Lucasville.

"That was good," he said, and he could have easily been talking about a fine meal or an entertaining movie. He wasn't.

Lisa scrutinized her hands. "I've got blood underneath my fingernails," she said with a frown.

"Whose?"

Lisa thought about it for a moment. "I'm not sure."

With each passing step, Paula felt a little better. She continued to hold Virginia's hand as they walked, and anyone passing might have thought they were sisters. However, it was Virginia's hand that seemed to offer protection and reassurance, and Paula couldn't help but notice the calming influence of her touch. Originally, she had been frightened by the girl, but now there was a growing sense of awe. What kind of person could watch her whole family be destroyed and still manage to find the strength to deal with a silly little git like Paula? Virginia was not like other little girls her age. Even though Virginia had said very little, Paula could tell that she was intelligent. More than that—she was *special*.

Paula felt a renewed sense of hatred for Luke—as well as a growing sense of dread for Crystal. How much longer would he pretend to be a benevolent companion before showing his true self? She didn't think that Crystal would live through the experience.

When Paula saw the rusting mailbox perched at the end of a long dirt driveway, she almost laughed with relief. She saw power lines forking back across a field to what must surely be a house. Hopefully, some of those lines were for telephone, too. She scooped Virginia into her arms and hurried down the drive.

507

Her enthusiasm was contagious; Virginia started to giggle as if she were enjoying the ride.

And then they were standing before a small, square two-story house. It had weatherworn gray siding and black shutters. There were no vehicles in the driveway, but Paula wouldn't even allow herself to feel discouraged. If there was a telephone inside, she was going to get to it one way or another—even if she had to break in. It was only as they reached the bottom of the porch steps that she realized the front door was standing open behind a wooden storm door.

Paula climbed the half-dozen steps to an elevated porch. It was a small rectangle of concrete that sat under cover of a corrugated tin roof, its edges guarded by black wrought iron rails. She eased Virginia down, placing her on her own feet, before straightening. She was about to knock when something caught her eye through the glass of the storm door. Her hand hung in midair as the moisture in her mouth seemed to simply evaporate.

"What's the matter?" asked Virginia, tugging at Paula's jeans.

Paula's tongue was frozen, her knees beginning to buckle. She gently pushed Virginia away from the door, back toward the porch steps. "Don't look inside," she finally managed.

Virginia looked at her warily but crossed to the top step and sat down. Paula returned her attention to what she saw through the door. There was a telephone on an end table, its pushbutton face almost taunting her with its proximity. And while she *would* go inside—she had to try and reach Angel—she didn't want to go anywhere near that particular phone. Beside it, sprawled out in a recliner with a newspaper across her lap, were the bloodied remains of its rightful owner.

III

Even as Jessica pushed her way through the screaming crowd, she knew somehow it was Leonard who was in trouble. A horrible tingling had seized her entire body, and her stomach roiled. People were shoving from all directions, some trying to get a closer look, most trying to get away. As Jessica neared the center of the melee, she saw the first traces of blood, droplets spattered in wide arcs staining the glass doors of the soda coolers. A strangled cry escaped her lips as she knelt at Leonard's side, completely unaware of the red spray that intermittently stained her clothing. He was fumbling for the handle of the scissors that still protruded from his neck, blood gushing out around the horrible wound, his eyes wide and bulging.

"I'm a nurse! I'm a nurse!"

Jessica heard the distinctive boom of Helen's voice and anxiously searched the room for her. She was overwhelmed by the sea of faces gathered around,

508

transfixed by their own morbid curiosity. She felt Leonard's hand tugging at her sleeve, and she returned her attention to him, afraid of what she might see. He was mouthing something so urgently it was difficult to decipher, but just as Helen finally broke through the crowd, Jessica understood.

Lisa.

Helen froze where she stood, every limb locked in place. She stared down at Leonard with a gaze so cold and empty it sent a shiver down Jessica's spine.

"Do something," said Jessica. "Oh, *God*, Helen! *Do something!*"

Helen cocked her head to the side, watching Leonard's desperation grow as his lifeblood leaked away. She slowly began to shake her head. "There's nothing I can do," she said simply.

Jessica was on her feet instantly. "What in the hell do you *mean?*" she shrieked. "I don't give a good golly god*damn* what the problem is between the two of you! *Do something!*"

Helen continued to shake her head. "It's too late," she said. "There's nothing I can do to save him. Surely you can tell that just by looking at him."

Jessica's gaze wavered between Helen and Leonard, whose struggling had weakened, the tension in his face beginning to abate. *Oh, God*, she thought. *He's going to die.*

"There's nothing I can do," Helen repeated, folding her arms across her ample bosom.

Jessica had never been more enraged. Leonard was watching them, *listening* to them, and this was all the cold comfort that vengeful bitch could offer?

And then his eyes were still.

The macabre shower of blood was exhausted, and it was no wonder. Jessica realized that she was almost entirely covered in Leonard's blood. Gruesome spatters streaked the walls and displays, some of it as far as twelve feet away.

"Oh, God, *no-o-o-o*—"

Jessica's hand was shaking as she closed Leonard's vacant eyes. Helen's expression remained cool and unaffected as she drifted back into the crowd, leaving Jessica alone to deal with the curious onlookers.

Jessica sat at one of the picnic tables in the parking lot of the Speedway, a Virginia Slim held between shaky fingers. She took long drags from the cigarette, finding no consolation whatsoever in its warm flow of nicotine.

Leonard was gone.

She had expected to find danger in Lucasville, but nothing so swift in presentation. If only she hadn't recommended that they stop at the gas station. Why had she thought it necessary to involve the others anyway? This was her battle. It had been handed to her one fateful summer morning eighteen years ago when she had unleashed that devil-child onto the world. And now, she was responsible for the death of an innocent person.

What happened immediately after Leonard died was still a blur. The police had arrived in a hail of sirens, followed shortly by an ambulance that had no need for its own. Jessica answered a seemingly endless battery of questions.

Jessica Lybrook. I work for the Jay County Sheriff's Department. No, I'm on the switchboard. Leonard Barnes. I hadn't known him long. Yes, a friend. A good friend. I didn't actually see it happen. I don't have any idea why anyone would do such a thing.

The answers had been mechanical. She hadn't told the officer what Leonard had mouthed just before dying, and she wasn't entirely sure why. Maybe it was because she knew Helen would staunchly defend Lisa once she heard Jessica's statement. It would only complicate matters, and she was afraid that the police would want to detain her and Helen until they had sorted things out. With Chad, Lisa, and Suze still on the loose, she couldn't afford to lose the time, and she didn't think that the police, operating under conventional methods, would be fully prepared for the things those three were capable of. She didn't care if Helen heard her admission about being a switchboard operator. It no longer seemed to matter.

The manager of the gas station had closed the Speedway until further notice, unsure how to proceed in such an event. He had contacted his corporate office and was nervously awaiting word in his own small cubicle. His employees had gone home, and the other patrons had dispersed as quickly as the police could finish questioning them. Jessica had given numbers where she could be reached if there were any more questions, and after a photographer had sufficiently captured the crime scene, the police had left, too.

The manager had been gracious enough to allow Jessica to clean up in the restroom before turning her out. He even found an extra uniform shirt that he gave her so that she wouldn't have to wear her own blood-saturated blouse. There wasn't much he could do about her jeans, though.

Helen waited in the passenger seat, wisely steering clear of Jessica. Jessica needed some time to collect her thoughts before she attempted to speak to Helen. She was still reeling from the nurse's icy demeanor as Leonard lay dying before her. It was unconscionable, regardless of the circumstances of their shared history. The look on Helen's face had almost been one of satisfaction, and the realization made Jessica sick to her stomach. She simply couldn't travel with Helen any longer.

As if on cue, the door of the Jeep opened, and Helen emerged from the vehicle. If Jessica wasn't misinterpreting, the look on her face was impatience. Her hands were planted firmly on her rotund hips, and her head was cocked slightly to the side. Jessica took a defiantly slow pull from her cigarette and made no effort to acknowledge Helen. After a moment, the nurse sighed and waddled across the parking lot, resuming her stance beside the table at which Jessica sat.

"So, what now?" she asked with a hint of exasperation. "Are we just going to sit here all day?"

Jessica leveled a steely gaze at her and took another hit from her cigarette.

"I didn't know you smoked, dear. It isn't good for you," chided Helen, oblivious to the anger brewing behind Jessica's smoldering eyes.

Jessica shifted positions, offering the nurse her back while she struggled to keep her mouth in check.

Helen sighed again. "Look," she began. "I know that you and Leonard were close, for whatever reason I can't imagine—"

Jessica whirled around. "Don't even *start*, Helen," she said. "Even now, he's not quite dead enough for you, is he?"

Helen's mouth flapped emptily for a moment before she again found her voice. "I didn't mean to upset you, dear. But what's done is done. We still have to find them. For *Lisa*."

Jessica shook her head absently, recalling the abstract lip sync that Leonard had offered just before dying. *Lisa*.

"I'm going to give you bus fare, and I want you to go home," said Jessica with a note of finality.

"What?" screeched Helen. "I'm not leaving now! You can't *make* me go—"

"I'm sick and tired of your bullshit, Helen," said Jessica, surprised at the evenness of her voice. "I can't make you do anything you don't want to do, but I can assure you one thing, you won't be doing it with me."

"You're *stranding* me here?" Helen demanded incredulously.

Jessica took a deep breath, forcing back the lump that was threatening to close off her throat. "Leonard Barnes did not kill your daughter, Helen. Clinton McDermott did. There's no point in trying to pin the blame any farther back than him, and you know why? Because in the end, Evie is still *dead*. As Leonard laid on that floor, a goddamn pair of *scissors* sticking out of his neck, I knew he was a dead man, just as surely as you did. The difference is, I didn't stand there and *tell* him that he was a dead man. What in the hell is the matter with you? I've never seen anyone so coldhearted in my entire life!"

Helen stood there with her mouth dangling open, dumbstruck by Jessica's onslaught. She didn't know how to react, but eventually settled for indignation.

"I'm not the one who lied and said that I was a police officer," said Helen. "I wasn't going to dwell on that because I thought you meant well, but I wouldn't be casting stones—"

"Shut up, Helen," said Jessica, getting to her feet. "I'm not particularly interested in playing this game. I told a fib—big fucking deal. You ensured that a man's last few living moments were as filled with fear and anxiety as possible. Which one of us is the monster?"

511

She didn't look back as she crossed to the Jeep. She slid behind the steering wheel and stretched across the passenger seat to open the door. Helen, mistaking it for a sign that Jessica had reconsidered, began to shuffle across the lot, but Jessica had only opened the door to shove the nurse's handbag out to the pavement. She reached into her own purse and extracted three twenties from her wallet, flinging them out after Helen's things. She pulled the door shut and started the engine, backing up without looking and turning south on US 23.

Jessica drove blindly. She held onto her composure only until she could no longer see the sign for the gas station in her rearview mirror, and then the grief was simply too much. She could still smell Leonard's blood and feel its stickiness on her hands. She pulled off the road and sobbed like she hadn't done in years.

Of all the unmitigated gall.

Helen sat at one of the picnic tables and rearranged the contents of her purse, which had gotten all jumbled in the spill from the Jeep. She still couldn't believe that Jessica had abandoned her in the middle of God's armpit with nothing more than the clothes on her back and a few dollars in her purse. If Jessica thought Helen would abandon Lisa this easily, she had another think coming.

Lisa.

It seemed like months since she had seen her. Helen hoped she wasn't suffering too much. Soon, the nurse would make Lisa's captors pay just as Leonard Barnes had finally gotten exactly what was coming to him.

It hadn't crossed Helen's mind to question what had prompted the attack on Leonard. She hadn't even feigned polite curiosity about the identity of the perpetrator. It didn't matter who had done it; it was a job well done. Evie could finally rest in peace, her murder completely avenged, and for the first time, Helen felt the smallest sense of closure in the matter. How ironic that it should coincide with Lisa's kidnapping. She didn't think she could take it if she were forced to lose another daughter.

And that was how she had come to see Lisa. Lisa needed guidance. She was all alone in this world since her Nanna Grace had died, and no one deserved that kind of solitude at such a tender, formative age.

A dark brown sedan pulled into the parking lot and sidled up to the pumps, seemingly oblivious to the store's current status. Helen started to point to the sign on the door, then decided to approach the car. Maybe whoever it was would offer her a lift into Portsmouth where she could rent a car. She still had her credit cards in her purse; she had checked.

A balding man with a narrow face and long chin sat behind the wheel. He smiled congenially as Helen approached. "Good afternoon," he said. "I guess I'm too late."

Helen looked at him questioningly. "Too late? Too late for what?"

He chuckled sheepishly. "Barney Fenton, *Daily Times*. I was supposed to cover this story, but I got caught in traffic up by Waverly. Tractor-trailer overturned, and they had the whole stinking road closed down. I don't suppose you saw anything?"

It was Helen's turn to smile. "I'll tell you what," she said. "You give me a ride into Portsmouth, and I'll tell you about the whole damn thing."

Jessica wiped the tears from her eyes and inhaled shakily. Helen had been right about one thing; she couldn't just sit there. Lisa Mitchell had been in that Speedway. It was almost a certainty that Chad had been there, too. The sensation of vulnerability was nearly overwhelming. Jessica had expected to *feel* him if he were near. She had fled the parking lot in blind anger, forgetting the entire reason she had stopped there in the first place.

Enid Bowles.

Leonard had located Dale Street on a map. She glanced to the passenger seat and was surprised to find the crumpled and bloodied map lying there; she had no recollection whatsoever of bringing it with her. She carefully unfolded it and retraced the coordinates with a shaky finger. Leonard had been right. Enid's house was within walking distance of the gas station.

With a resigned sigh, she started the engine of the Jeep and pulled back out onto the highway. She made an illegal U-turn through a break in the grassy median and headed back toward the place where this had suddenly gone so wrong. She only hoped that Helen was no longer there. She didn't ever want to see her face again.

Helen stared at the headline of the newspaper she had found in Barney Fenton's passenger seat. She answered his questions mechanically but kept her attention firmly affixed to the paper. It wasn't the headline that caught her eye, it was the picture.

Darin Miller

It was Lisa—or at least it could have been. The picture was captioned, "Crystal Bright at the 2000 Primetime Emmys." Crystal Bright. Helen had heard of her, of course, but had never actually *seen* her. *Bennie and the Girl* and its type of show were a little too progressive for Helen. She liked the old shows on Nick-at-Nite, like *The Andy Griffith Show* and *The Brady Bunch*.

The front-page story detailed the all-points bulletin that was out for Crystal Bright and an unnamed male companion. They were wanted in connection with the kidnapping of a young girl and the murder of her entire family. There was a grainy sketch of the male accomplice that bore a striking resemblance to Sasquatch. It was now being considered a rampage of sorts, because the girl's father had been killed a few days before the rest of the family. No one could even speculate on Crystal's motivation for these crimes, but there was evidence of her presence everywhere. The FBI was now involved as the crimes spanned two states. A sheriff's deputy from Jay County had gone missing and was believed to have been investigating the crimes on his own. Helen was startled to see the town of Borden listed. That was where Lisa's job interview had been. It all felt so long ago. She had gone to stay with some family—why, it could have even been the same family! Lisa might have been killed if she had been there. It seemed ironic that Helen should find relief when Lisa's alternative course of fate was still so very uncertain. But it all made sense to her now. Leonard Barnes had been a simple and foolish man. Despite her feelings against him, she was admittedly disturbed by his dogged persistence that Lisa had done things, things that he had witnessed. Although she didn't believe him, he probably did see *something*, and it occurred to Helen that it might have been Crystal Bright. She was apparently in Morgan at the same time that Leonard claimed to have seen these supposed crimes. It was obviously Crystal Bright who was behind them.

The striking similarity between Lisa and Crystal couldn't be coincidental, could it? If Helen had learned anything during this ordeal, it was that nothing happened by chance. It suddenly occurred to her that Lisa's life was not only in danger from her captors, but now also from the police. What if a trigger-happy rookie spotted Lisa and fired without verifying her identity first? The notion brought a fresh wave of butterflies into Helen's stomach.

———◇———

Jessica was pleased to see that Helen had gone by the time she returned to the area. The parking lot of the Speedway was now completely deserted, and Jessica turned back in, sidling up beside one of the telephones that was mounted to a pole. Originally, she had planned to just drop in on Enid. Part of her feared that the name Jessica Lybrook wouldn't mean anything to the old woman anymore, and if Enid was unable or unwilling to help, she didn't know what she was going

514

to do next. She hadn't felt so completely alone since her time in the hospital. She dug change from the bottom of her purse and got out of the Jeep, reading Enid's phone number from the crumpled note she had made earlier.

The phone rang five times before it was finally picked up.

"Hello?"

"Mrs. Bowles?" asked Jessica, her voice suddenly quivering. "Mrs. Enid Bowles?"

"Yes, dear," confirmed the concerned voice on the other end. "Oh, my. Is something wrong?"

Jessica took a shaky breath to steady herself as she realized she was unduly alarming the old woman. "I don't suppose you remember me," she said. "My name is—"

"Jessie Lybrook," said Enid, delighted. "It's been—oh my goodness, it's been too long! Of course, I shouldn't be surprised—"

"Then you know," said Jessica.

There was a brief pause at the other end. "Perhaps you should come over, dear. We should really speak face-to-face."

Jessica found herself unable to speak, overwhelmed by relief. Enid remembered. She *remembered*.

"Are you still there?"

"Yes, yes," said Jessica. "I'm sorry. I'd like that very much. I'm at the Speedway around the corner. I can be there in just a few minutes."

"I'll look forward to it. Please let yourself in," she said. "I'm a bit of a convalescent these days, but I keep a spare key under the big flowerpot on my porch for just such occasions."

Jessica's hand lingered as she replaced the receiver. Enid's voice was as familiar as if she had heard it only yesterday. The sound of it had served to lighten the oppressive burden that Jessica carried, and for a moment, she allowed herself to look beyond hopelessness.

But only for a moment.

Her reverie was broken by the sudden snarl of a small engine followed by tires squealing in protest to the actions of the car's driver. Jessica's eyes widened at the odd, 3-D spectacle, but her feet were rooted to the spot. The wild-eyed man behind the wheel was guiding his light silver sedan like a missile—with Jessica as its target.

CHAPTER TWENTY-SIX

I

Crystal felt as if her heart had stopped in her chest. She held the cold plastic receiver to her ear and suddenly felt faint.

"What do you mean, 'she's gone?'" she asked in a voice that was dead with fear.

Luke was nearly hysterical. "I was only gone a *second*, Crystal, I *swear*. I was on the phone with *you*, for Christ's sake! We didn't talk long, did we? Oh, God—*did we?*"

Crystal leaned against the telephone table, steadying herself while clenching the receiver with white knuckles.

Oh, God, no—not Virginia.

"Kathy's not back yet," she said. "You have to come get me. There's a police officer camped out by Aunt Maude's house, so you'll have to be careful when you pass. Are you absolutely *sure* you're not overlooking her?"

"I'm sure, I'm sure," said Luke impatiently. "If anything happens to her, it's all my goddamn fault."

Crystal wanted to tell him that it wasn't true, but she couldn't find any conviction for the words. It was too easy to picture Virginia's tiny lifeless body. Had all of this been for nothing? *Nothing?*

"Just get here," she said tightly and hung up.

⟶————◇————⟵

Enid looked on from deep within her pillows, scowling as Crystal told her what had happened. Crystal hoped her old friend might have words of wisdom and encouragement to offer. Instead, she watched concern spread across her face like a rash.

"She's probably already dead," said Crystal, the words mechanical.

Enid pursed her lips. "She might be," she said quietly. "But then again, maybe not."

Crystal choked back a sob. "I can't take this," she said. "I'm not capable of protecting this little girl from these—these *monsters*. I feel so *helpless*."

"You told me that you all dreamed about this girl, as if you were being called to her," said Enid.

Crystal nodded.

"Tell me, don't you think you would feel—*something* if the girl were dead?"

516

Crystal snuffled and considered Enid's words. It was small comfort, but it was something. Maybe Virginia had wandered into the woods on her own. Since her family's brutal murder, she had been entirely too calm. For heaven's sake, she was only four years old! She had probably been in shock ever since. She might not have seen Luke as he went in for the phone call, becoming frightened and disoriented when she found herself alone in Kathy's backyard. She might have gone looking for Luke or Crystal, and the only way out would have been through the woods. It wasn't much—hell, it was barely plausible—but it was *something*.

Crystal leaned over the bed and kissed Enid on the forehead. "I'm sorry that we had to see each other again under these circumstances but thank you so much for everything."

"I only wish I knew more," said Enid. "I don't know of a way to stop any of this from happening."

Crystal shook her head and smiled. "It's better than nothing. At least now I know who Lisa is and how we are connected. I wonder if she's figured it out yet."

"It's only a matter of time, I'm sure," said Enid. "Everyone has converged."

Crystal shuddered. "I don't like the sound of that."

"I'll let Kathy know what's happened when she turns up," said Enid. She gripped Crystal's hand tightly. "Be brave, dear. Light has its way of shining through the darkness—and good luck!"

Luke turned onto Dale Street, forcing himself to obey the speed limit of twenty-five. He didn't want to appear suspicious to the officer watching Maude's house, but it was everything he could do to keep from stomping the pedal to the floor. He felt absolutely hollow inside. How could they have gotten this far only to lose her now? It wasn't fair.

Crystal was waiting outside, tucked behind an ancient maple tree at the end of the long drive and near the garage. She ducked out and dipped into the Honda, pulling the door shut quickly behind her. She didn't think the policeman could see this far into Enid's driveway, but she wouldn't take the chance.

"I'm so sorry—" began Luke, but Crystal waved his words away.

"Don't," she said. "It doesn't help anything. Let's get back to Kathy's house and search the woods. Virginia may have wandered back there and gotten lost."

"She would have heard me," said Luke with stubborn futility. "I hollered until my voice was raw."

Crystal shot him a warning look. She wasn't about to give up yet. He put the car in gear and whipped its nose around in the wide area near Enid's double garage doors, turning to face the street. The radio was on with its volume very low, and it took Crystal a minute to realize that the high-pitched tone she had just heard was the beginning of a news bulletin. She reluctantly turned the volume up.

"—leaves one man dead and two unidentified suspects on the run. The victim, Leonard Barnes, was traveling with two female companions when they stopped at a Speedway on US 23 in Lucasville. Eyewitnesses claim that a red-headed woman in her mid-twenties stabbed Mr. Barnes with a pair of scissors taken from one of the store's employees. Police are advising Lucasville residents to be on alert for—what's that? Hold on a second, folks, I'm getting an update from the newsroom—let me see—oh—can we substantiate this?"

Crystal waited anxiously while the rural newsman consulted with others at his station.

"It would appear that the red-headed woman wanted in connection with Mr. Barnes' murder has been identified as none other than troubled starlet, Crystal Bright. Several eyewitnesses commented upon the perpetrator's facial resemblance to the actress, but there has apparently been confirmation from the store's surveillance videos. Cameras mounted outside the building captured images of Ms. Bright and an unknown male accomplice leaving the scene in a maroon, four-door Volvo sedan. The owner of that vehicle has not been named, but police have indicated they are following up on all leads—"

Crystal snapped the radio off. She looked at Luke, and a wide smile crept across her face. He returned her gaze with empty puzzlement.

"Don't you see?" she asked, but Luke only shook his head. "Lisa was *there*. Her 'unknown male accomplice' was *there*."

Luke still looked baffled.

"They couldn't have been in two places at once," said Crystal. "They *can't* be responsible for Virginia's disappearance."

Luke wanted desperately to believe her, but he couldn't force any enthusiasm. Until Virginia was standing in front of him, he wouldn't assume her safety. And if he was lucky enough to be given another chance, he wouldn't let that little girl out of his sight until Lisa and Chad were safely behind bars. Or dead.

Crystal sighed. "Oh, Luke, don't you *see*? She *must* be in the woods behind Kathy's place, and those woods go on for miles. It's not even *unlikely* that she may have gotten lost."

Luke began the slow journey down Enid's long driveway. "All I know is that she isn't with us," he said softly. "There's no one to protect her if Lisa and Chad find her first."

"They won't," insisted Crystal.

"How can you be so sure?"

"Because we're her protectors," said Crystal with a conviction she did not entirely believe herself. She began explaining the finer points of equilibrium as they pulled away.

518

———◆———

Enid shifted uncomfortably in her bed and stretched for the cordless handset that rested behind her alarm clock on the nightstand. It had begun ringing just as she heard Luke's car drive off. She had hoped to see Luke; it had been years since she had seen the child who Jessie was accused of abusing, and her curiosity was inevitable. Her twisted fingers finally closed around the handset, and she lifted it to her ear.

"Hello?"

"Mrs. Bowles?" The trepidation in the female caller's voice was palpable. "Mrs. Enid Bowles?"

"Yes, dear," Enid confirmed, nodding her head involuntarily. "Oh, my. Is something wrong?"

———◆———

"I don't know if I buy all that," said Luke, easing to a stop at the end of Nile Run.

Crystal unfolded herself from the squatted position she had assumed in the floorboard of the Honda's front seat. "It's too much for me to absorb, too," she admitted. "But at least now we know who Lisa and Chad are."

Luke pressed his lips together tightly and turned south on US 23. His mind was reeling from all of the information Crystal had summarized. He had known that Paulie was originally from Ohio, but he had no idea that he had been raised near Lucasville. Paulie had never mentioned Lucasville, Grace, Enid, or Maude—in fact, he had spoken very little about his own past. Luke's own recollections only went as far back as his time at Sister Margaret's orphanage in Jasper and in retrospect, Luke's complete apathy toward personal history seemed incongruous with his generally curious nature. Somehow, he had mentally blocked the people who had brought him into this world, as well as Chad—the brother who had tried to murder him when he was only six. Luke was swallowed by the emptiness, checking his reflection in the rearview mirror as if he might suddenly notice long-faded battle scars from a time he could not remember.

"There's the Speedway up ahead that they were talking about on the radio," said Crystal, pointing to the blue and red sign on the right. Even under the ample rays of sunshine that warmed the afternoon, there was an aura of cool darkness around the empty building, as if it were permanently stained by the violence that had so recently transpired within its walls.

519

Luke's hands suddenly tightened on the steering wheel. "It's her," he hissed.

Crystal followed his gaze to the only person remaining in the parking lot, a redhead using one of the payphones, her back turned to them.

"How can you be sure?" asked Crystal, as Luke's gaze steeled. *"Luke!* How can you be sure? Her back's to us."

"It's her," he repeated through clenched teeth. "It's time to stop this thing once and for all."

He stomped on the accelerator, and the car's frame bumped over the curb. He pulled the steering wheel sharply to the right and launched into the parking lot, a murderous glint in his eye.

———◇———

Enid's fingers were trembling as she disconnected the call.

Jessie Lybrook—after all these years. And while it shouldn't have surprised her, somehow it still did. Enid carried the most overwhelming sense of foreboding, as if the sound of Jessica's voice had been the last tumbler falling into place. Jessie's children were both within easy reach, and it was certainly no coincidence. Enid thought back to the tortured soul she had met behind those institution walls, the hollowed eyes and gaunt skin that stretched across her beautiful bone structure like translucent tissue paper. Jessica had either forgotten how to eat or was punishing herself through starvation, and Enid supposed it was the latter. Jessica's pain had been a dark beacon as Enid had ridden the Greyhound across the Indiana state line, reassuring the old woman that she was doing the right thing. All of her research through the years—it was about to come in handy. If she could do something to ease this tortured woman's pain, it would certainly be worthwhile. Paulie had volunteered to accompany Enid, but she had declined his invitation. She felt it was important to make this journey alone. If pressed on the issue, Enid would reluctantly admit that she, too, had a gift, meager though she felt it was. Her ability was to provide absolution from, if nothing else, one's own mind. Crystal, Lisa, Lucas, Chad—she had visited each of these four when they were children, administering her special green tea concocted from recipes compiled centuries before.

Even then, she had known it wouldn't be the end of it.

She still remembered the way Chad had looked at her as she had offered the tea, the look of utter defiance that sullied his otherwise angelic face. She had thought he would refuse, and what would she have done then? She had slipped past security under the ruse of being his great-aunt and didn't wish to draw attention to herself. She certainly couldn't ask the staff nurse for assistance in administering the tea. But at last, he had sipped it, tasting it pensively before gulping it down. And then he had flung the antique teacup as far and as hard as

520

he could, shattering it against the concrete wall of his makeshift room at the Indiana Department of Child Services. He was scheduled to leave the next day with his new parents, the Collinses, and the special remedy would have plenty of time to do its magic before they arrived.

But still, she had known it wasn't over.

She remembered the look of pure hatred that emanated from the little boy's coal black eyes. He had looked as if he wanted to kill Enid with his tiny little hands—and she believed he would have attempted it, too, if he'd had the chance.

From downstairs, Enid heard the sound of the key in the lock, followed by the creaking of the door on its hinges. The sound grated on her nerves, reminding her of a Halloween record her grandson, Rusty, had loved as a child. She'd have to get him to oil the hinges next time he stopped over to mow her lawn.

Enid adjusted her sheets and fluffed the pillow she rested against, unconsciously tinkering with the thin strands of white hair that clung determinedly to her pink scalp. She detested taking visitors this way, but time had left her little choice in the matter. It was either this way or none at all.

"Jessie, dear?" she called. "I'm upstairs. Just come straight down the hallway. I'm at the big room on the end."

Her hands were shaking in her lap as she heard the soft footsteps ascending the stairs. As she thought of little Virginia Parnell, she simply couldn't shake the feeling that something was terribly wrong.

———◇———

Jessica stood dumbly with her mouth hanging slightly open and her hand frozen to the receiver of the payphone. She watched the Honda thump over the curb, its nose pointed directly at her, its small engine growling like an angry poodle. She knew that if she didn't get out of the way, it was going to knock her into the side yard of the house that neighbored the service station—yet her feet refused to respond. She watched as the Honda bumped across the lot, its driver guiding the steering wheel with white knuckled determination.

And then there were other hands on the wheel, pushing it to the left.

Jessica blinked, trying to focus on the event as it unfolded in slow-motion before her eyes. She hadn't noticed the woman in the front seat, and now she was a blur of action, struggling with the man behind the wheel for control. He was trying to shake her off, but she doggedly persisted, finally derailing the car from its present course.

It whisked by within a foot of where Jessica stood. It leapt the curb at the rear of the parking lot and bulldozed through one of the twin picnic tables in an explosion of wood and plastic bumper. The brake lights flared on, but the car seemed intent on pushing forward, its little tires digging trenches through the lawn that separated the service station from its neighbor. It stopped just short of the neighbor's driveway.

Jessica's feet were still frozen to the pavement, her mouth still hanging open. She knew she should run, take advantage of this respite, no matter how brief, to put some distance between her and this madman before he had time to emerge from the car. Surely the woman who had saved her life was being killed right now for her insubordination.

But still, she didn't move.

She watched as the man threw open his door and extended one long leg out into the grass. The blonde woman who had, for whatever reason, saved her life, was also emerging from the car, hurrying around its front and trying to restrain the man as he pulled himself to his feet.

"It's not her!" the woman screamed into his angry face, and Jessica watched the scene with almost detached curiosity, as if she weren't the one to whom they referred.

And then her eyes focused on the man's features.

"Oh my God," she whispered, her hands fluttering to her throat.

Something in his expression changed almost simultaneously, his thick brows knitting together in confusion as he suddenly lost the desire to pound her senseless. The blonde was familiar, too, and Jessica suddenly recognized her as Crystal Bright.

But it was the man who captivated her attention.

Enid's words washed over her, and she felt a sudden tingle of anxiety that made her afraid to blink for fear he wouldn't still be there when she reopened her eyes.

Yet there he stood—broad-shouldered and tall with sandy hair. They were his father's rugged good looks with just enough of Jessica's thrown in to soften the rough edges.

He had cautiously stepped closer, stopping every few feet as if to reassess the situation. When they were finally no more than ten feet apart, he suddenly blinked and opened his mouth, struggling to find his voice.

"Mom?" he croaked.

Jessica's throat tightened and her eyes filled with tears. Like a thunderstorm breaking, she began to sob.

||

Paula paused at the doorway and looked back to where Virginia sat on the edge of the porch. "You stay right there," she said. "If you see anyone coming, call for me. Do you understand?"

Virginia nodded her head and smiled, then turned her attention to the large expanse of yard that had been hidden from view behind the tall grass which bordered the road. She was delighted by the odd assortment of carved wooden figures that were sprinkled throughout the lawn, and Paula could tell it was taking every bit of resolve the girl could muster to keep herself in place on the porch.

That's fine, thought Paula. *She can stare at the yard all damn day. Just as long as she doesn't look inside.*

Paula used the tail of her shirt to open the storm door, not wanting to leave her fingerprints anywhere near the grisly scene. The air inside the small house was tepid, and Paula could feel her heart pounding in her chest as she crossed the threshold. She took a few cautious steps into the living room and stopped abruptly. What if the killer was still here? What if she had inadvertently led Virginia to a place every bit as dangerous as her own home had been just the day before?

Paula forced herself to calm down and listen to the sounds of the house. If anyone was waiting inside, surely she would hear some sign, some *movement*. A small tabletop fan whirred noisily from a desk in the corner, and Paula could hear the refrigerator humming in the kitchen, but otherwise, all was quiet. The woman in the recliner stared vacantly at a blank television screen, her mouth slightly open and a small trickle of blood escaping from its corner. Her hands still clutched the sides of her newspaper tightly, as if she were determined to take it with her while awaiting God's judgment. She had been shot twice in the chest, and her terrycloth bathrobe had acted as a towel, absorbing the blood as it leaked out and spread into wide, circular blossoms that grotesquely approximated her breasts. There was a cup of coffee on the end table beside the telephone, its contents half consumed, as well as a half-eaten donut. It didn't look as if she'd had time to react much less defend herself from her murderer. Paula hoped that meant she hadn't suffered.

Still no sounds.

Paula took a few more cautious steps into the room, noting with distaste the similarities between the furnishings in this small house and the decor of her own. She could almost picture Joel sprawled out on the couch in his underpants, his bulbous belly protruding from underneath his t-shirt while he slept off another drunken stupor.

But Joel was dead.

The remembrance hit Paula like a thunderclap. She could *hear* the sound of the ax blade biting into Joel's flesh. She remembered the gleam in Angel's eyes as she swung it a second time, then a third. It was the only time Angel had even remotely frightened her. Paula had never seen such a look of grim determination, and she hoped to never see it focused on her. Of course, Angel had as long a history with Joel as Paula, so her rage was at least partially understandable. And what would have happened if she hadn't shown up?

I would've gotten myself raped again, that's what, thought Paula.

An unhealthy amount of her childhood fantasy time had been devoted to destroying the monster her mother had married, and most of those fantasies had been constructed with autopsy-like precision. But when it came time to act, Paula knew that she would have remained frozen, just as she had done all of those other times when Joel had put his hands all over her.

She peered through the storm door and saw that Virginia was still in place at the head of the steps. She was singing softly to herself, but Paula couldn't pick out the words.

Paula cut a wide path around the corpse, trying not to look directly at her. She had the most peculiar feeling that the middle-aged woman might suddenly ask her if she wanted breakfast.

Beyond the living room was a small, tidy kitchen. The walls were lemon yellow with a wallpaper border featuring groupings of various fruits. The compact counter gleamed in the sunlight that poured through the kitchen window, and the air was redolent with the scent of disinfectant cleaner. The linoleum floor was worn in places, but there wasn't a speck of dirt to be found. The amber light on the coffeepot still glowed softly, and Paula could detect the beginnings of burnt coffee wafting into the air. She flipped off the power switch as she passed. A square breakfast table occupied the center of the room with a small vase of fresh flowers in its center. Plastic placemats featuring waddling ducks marked each of the four place settings. Beside the sink, a few breakfast dishes were stacked in a strainer, water still standing in small puddles on the drip tray.

Paula had the overwhelming urge to turn and run. There was no reason whatsoever to stay in this house where a thing so heinous had only just transpired. This tidy little woman had gotten up this morning thinking what a grand day it was. The sun was shining, and the humidity had not gotten too awfully overwhelming as it was wont to do in Southern Ohio. She had come downstairs and prepared breakfast—for herself alone, judging from the number of dishes. She had put her morning coffee on to brew while she collected the newspaper from the front yard, casually skimming the headlines as she returned to the house. When she was finished with breakfast, she had quickly washed the dishes and wiped down the surfaces, just as she had done every other morning for so many years. She had then taken the paper to her recliner to take in the day's news. At what point had the intruder interrupted her routine? Or maybe it wasn't an intruder at all. Maybe it was a domestic disturbance. Maybe this was the work of this poor woman's husband. It didn't matter. The conclusion was the same. She wouldn't be washing any more breakfast dishes.

Telephone, Paula reminded herself. *Got to find another telephone.*

She scanned the four walls for the customary wall-mounted model, but there was no phone to be found. She backed out of the kitchen and returned to the living room, carefully avoiding the murder scene. She craned her neck and peered through the front door.

Virginia was dutifully in place at the top of the stairs, her dark, curly hair glinting in the sun.

Paula stood at the foot of stairs leading up to the dark shadows of the second floor. She paused, straining her ears to filter out the normal sounds of the house. There was only silence. She didn't want to go upstairs, but there wasn't another extension on the first floor. What if there wasn't another phone in the house? There was simply no way Paula could use the phone by the dead woman—no *way*. She would have to go to the next house, however many miles down the road.

Paula took a cautious step up, pausing as the wooden riser creaked beneath her foot. Nothing rushed out of the darkness to attack, so Paula slowly proceeded. Was it her imagination, or could she actually *smell* the dead woman in the living room? The air inside the house was pervasively hot, and Paula could feel perspiration accumulating around the collar of her shirt. Claustrophobia was beginning to overtake her, but she wouldn't leave the house without searching the second floor for a phone.

And if I find one, Angel, thought Paula, *please be there to answer my call.*

⟵ ⟶ ◆ ⟵ ⟶

The rental car was a bright yellow Ford Focus. Helen stuffed herself uncomfortably behind the steering wheel and began identifying the various controls of the instrument cluster, all of which were so very different from the ones in her Buick. She thought the car's simple design was stark and unappealing, but at least the engine ran smoothly, and the air conditioner was powerful. It was definitely warmer and more humid in Southern Ohio than in her part of Indiana. She hoped she would be going home soon. She could certainly use an uninterrupted night's sleep.

But not before finding Lisa.

After seeing Crystal Bright's picture in the newspaper, it seemed only logical that Helen should return to Lucasville. Her stomach knotted at the thought of crossing paths with Jessica so soon, but Lucasville was Crystal Bright's hometown. It seemed unlikely that Crystal's high-profile escapades were independent of Lisa's current plight.

Helen straightened in her seat.

That was it! This whole madness was being orchestrated by that spoiled renegade actress who probably had so goddamn much money that she could get away with anything. Look at O.J. Simpson, for God's sake! Helen was both enraged and suddenly sure of her convictions. There was a certain perverse logic that made all of the tumblers in Helen's head fall into place. Crystal Bright was

525

trying to frame Lisa Mitchell for all of these things that she had done. So far, the outcome was still uncertain.

"Okay," muttered Helen. "I might not know where to find Lisa, but in a town this size, it sure as hell shouldn't be hard to get a line on Crystal Bright."

She slackened her seatbelt and rocked on her ample backside, trying to force the seat to more generously accept her girth. Without any further consideration, she pointed the little car north toward Lucasville.

It was where Leonard Barnes had died.

She considered it a good sign.

Paula struggled to contain her tears as she stepped back out onto the porch. The only phone in the entire goddamn house was within inches of the dead woman's fingers. She didn't want to do it—oh *God*, she didn't want to do it!—but she had forced herself to pick up the handset—only to find that the line had been cut. The corpse had Mona Lisa's eyes, vacantly following Paula's every movement.

Virginia's sing-song humming stopped when she heard Paula step through the doorway. When she turned around, she wore a decidedly adult look of expectation. "Are we going now?" she asked.

Paula nodded jerkily, forcing a fractured smile onto her face.

"We're not lost."

Paula looked at the girl curiously. It was a statement of fact, not a question, and Paula was ashamed that this little girl seemed to have her shit so much more together than she did. She turned away so that Virginia wouldn't see her bottom lip quivering and took a few deep breaths to steady herself.

"We should go," said Paula. "Surely there's another house down the road, and maybe we could call—"

"Why do you think Luke is bad?"

Paula pivoted, her mouth hanging open. "I-I didn't say that," she stammered. She started to construct another whimsical story, but something about Virginia's solemn expression suggested it wasn't worth the effort. Paula's mouth snapped shut before anything more could tumble out.

"Luke's my bud," said Virginia, affecting Luke's lazy Kentucky drawl and causing Paula to smile for the first time since she had stepped inside the house.

"He is, is he?" she asked with a shaky voice while Virginia's brunette curls bobbed enthusiastically. The girl's naiveté was touching. Paula wouldn't tell her how mistaken she was about her bud; let someone else burst her bubble. No. The top priority was to distance themselves from the grisly scene inside before somebody else came a-callin'.

526

Paula took Virginia's hand into her own and pulled the girl to her feet. "Okay, kiddo," she said. "Let's move on. We can't just—"

Paula's voice trailed away as her eyes caught a glint of sunlight in her peripheral vision, where tall grass rushed up to meet the backside of the detached and dilapidated garage. She grabbed Virginia and instinctively pulled her close, taking a few steps backward until her back was pressed against the wall and the garage was out of sight.

Sunlight on metal.

A gun?

◆

Helen eyed the customers of the IGA. There were only a handful, maybe eight, and all of them were well past retirement age. Some walked, some wheeled, and some hobbled along, aided by walkers or canes. Any one of these old-timers should know of their hometown star, Crystal Bright.

"Oh, she's just the *sweetest* girl," said the first old woman Helen approached. Her face was shrunken like a rotted apple core, and fine tendrils of jet-black hair clung to her skull. "What I remember most about her—oh, and it's too bad— was her lovely singing voice. I say it's too bad because they never let her sing on that show of hers. Her and my little granddaughter, Amber, used to spend afternoons playing." She nodded proudly as if Helen should be impressed with her famous connection.

"But what about all of this in the news?" asked Helen, stepping away from the open-faced meat cooler she had been leaning against. She shivered as her forearms turned to gooseflesh.

"Oh, that's rubbish!" the old woman snapped. "Anyone who ever met Crystal would know better. And I hope that's not why you're bothering me. If you're some shady reporter from one of those trash rags—"

Helen forced a smile and shook her head. "No, not me. I guess I'm just concerned."

"Well, we're *all* concerned!" said the woman, still perturbed. "Anyone who would spread that kind of nonsense is just asking to get his."

"Of course, of course," said Helen. She cleared her throat and decided to try a different tactic. "How close to here did she grow up? Crystal, I mean."

"Why, just around the corner. She was raised by her aunt, Maude Williams. I suppose you didn't know that her name was really Crystal Williams, either."

"No, I didn't," admitted Helen. She didn't bother to mention that before that morning, she had never even heard of Crystal Bright or Crystal Williams or whatever else you wanted to call her.

527

The old woman abruptly snuffled and dabbled at her nose. "It's been a rough few months for that poor girl," she said. "Maude was the only blood family she had left, you know. I was so relieved to see Kathy Duncan and hear that she had spoken with Crystal a few days back on the telephone. She said that Crystal seemed fine."

"Kathy Duncan?"

"An old family friend. She's probably the closest thing to kin that poor child's got." A momentary shadow flickered across the woman's shriveled features but passed almost as quickly as it came.

Helen smiled. "I'll let you get on with your shopping. It's been nice talking with you, Mrs.—?"

"Parker. Anita Parker. Maude was one of my very best friends, you know." Another of those purposeful nods.

Helen turned, heading toward the front of the store. There was only one more piece of information she needed before leaving. She hovered near the bank of two old-fashioned cash registers, only one of which was operational, and waited until the densely freckled redhead finished ringing up her customer.

"Can I help you find something, ma'am?" asked the girl whose nametag read, CHLOE.

Helen approached the counter and affected what she thought was her most charming smile. "I hope so, dear," she said. "Although it's not anything that's in the store. I was hoping you might be able to tell me where I could find Kathy Duncan."

The girl's face brightened. "Mrs. Duncan? Oh, she was just here maybe an hour ago. She was doing her meals-on-wheels run, but she usually goes home after that."

Helen's smile broadened. "Home? And where would that be, dear?"

Paula's lungs seized up. The heat of the summer sun was stifling even in the shade, and fresh droplets of perspiration trickled down from her armpits. Her stomach felt hollow and queasy.

"What's wrong?" whispered Virginia.

"*Shhh.*"

Sunlight on metal.

Once Paula had ascertained that the killer was no longer inside the house, it had simply not occurred to her that he might still be lurking around somewhere outside. She shuddered at the thought of leaving Virginia alone and defenseless on the front porch while she meandered about indoors.

"Wait right here," whispered Paula as she positioned the little girl against the front wall of the house. "Don't move until I come back, okay?"

Virginia tried a smile, but for the first time, she looked a little uncertain. Paula stepped cautiously to the edge of the porch and peeked around the corner at the detached garage. She cupped her hand over her brow, shielding her eyes as she scanned the structure. The garage door was open, revealing a narrow, empty bay. An assortment of tools and other odd junk cluttered the inside, barely leaving room for the vehicle that, judging from the oil spots on the concrete floor, was normally parked inside. The lawn had been trimmed along the side of the garage which faced the house, but behind and beyond, tall grass waved languidly in the mild afternoon breeze. The glimmer of light had come from behind the building, and as Paula's eyes tried to find it again, she saw that the grass had been driven down in twin rows, spaced several feet apart.

Tire tracks? Of course.

Overhead, the clouds shifted, and Paula saw the same metallic glint. This time, she realized what she was seeing. It was the rear bumper of a car that had been pulled behind the building.

Paula turned back toward Virginia. "Wait right here," she repeated.

She descended the porch steps and slowly eased herself around the house, her eyes alert for any movement in the tall grass that wasn't caused by an occasional lazy breeze.

There was nothing to see.

As Paula stepped away from the house and toward the garage, she suddenly realized she was completely vulnerable. If the killer was hiding behind the garage or in the backyard, he would see Paula long before she saw him. Her feet felt like they were steeped in molasses as she crossed the expanse of tidy grass that stretched between the two buildings.

She reached the garage and pressed her back flat against the side wall, exhaling deeply. She wasn't aware that she had been holding her breath since she had stepped away from the porch, and her lungs burned for the effort.

She could see that the backyard was empty.

Paula inched along the side of the building, feeling its rough exterior scrape at her skin and pick at the fabric of her blouse. The garage seemed to be a mile long. The tall grass waved tauntingly from behind the building, as if motioning for Paula to hurry.

When she reached the end of the wall, she involuntarily took another deep breath and stepped around the corner, fully expecting to be assaulted by whomever had murdered the woman inside the house. What she didn't expect was to see the very car she had ridden in only the previous evening.

Lisa Mitchell's Volvo, nestled deep within the tall grass.

Helen could feel every jolt and jostle as the little car tooled over the ancient road. Chloe had insisted this was the quickest way to Otter Run, but Helen felt more as though she were driving straight into the bowels of hell. The tar and gravel that comprised this narrow ribbon of roadway had been tamped down into the ground and broken apart after years of enduring local traffic. Morgan was no metropolitan area, but it certainly wasn't riddled with the type of poverty that Helen was seeing now. The few houses that speckled the landscape were little more than shacks, some of them leaning unsteadily on their foundations. It wasn't uncommon to see garbage strewn carelessly through overgrown lawns or laundry machines squatting on sagging porches. Helen's lips curled involuntarily with distaste.

"Cleanliness is free," muttered Helen as she thudded into another pothole.

The road jutted over a sharp rise and veered to the left, woods suddenly appearing on the right. The houses were less frequent this far back, and the relative isolation gave Helen the creeps. If someone were to get run off the road back here—why, they might never be heard from again. Helen had seen enough horror movies in her day to know this was exactly the kind of place where things like that happened. Helen had never cared for those kinds of movies. The heroines were always doing the very thing they shouldn't—and any self-respecting woman should be offended by the depiction. But Evie was always partial to the genre, and if nothing else, Helen had enjoyed seeing that her little girl was being entertained. There was a time when Helen had worried that maybe there was something psychologically wrong with Evie. Why else would she want to watch such rubbish? One of the staff psychologists at Morgan Township had assured her that it was only a normal form of escapism—not for everyone, for sure, but she should only worry if the neighborhood pets started disappearing. But still, some of those films were really disturbing. Especially the ones about cannibals. Being eaten by another human being was a concept so revolting to Helen that she had nearly been unable to watch *Silence of the Lambs*. And this was exactly the kind of place where cannibals—nested?—waiting for their next victims. In Texas, they cook you up and turn you into barbecue. She'd learned that from *The Texas Chainsaw Massacre*.

Helen's heart stuttered as two young girls suddenly darted out into the road. For a wild moment, she considered turning the wheel and stepping on the accelerator, flattening these inbred cannibals in one shot, but instinct took over, and she stomped hard on the brake, cutting the wheel sharply to the left. The nose of the Focus dipped low, and the car came to a screeching halt in what may have been the deepest pothole yet—Helen's teeth clacked together from the impact, cracking one of her molars.

"Dammit!" she screamed as the tooth sent a fresh burst of pain along its nerve ending.

The girls stood frozen in the middle of the road, clinging fiercely to one another. *Sisters*, thought Helen. *They must be sisters.* She rolled down her window and stuck her head through, sizing them up across the shallow expanse of the Focus's bright yellow hood. "Are you girls alright?" she asked.

The older one—she looked about sixteen—nervously stroked the younger one's cheek before answering, whispering something gently to the child. She straightened and faced Helen. "Can you please get us to a phone?" the girl asked, her voice trembling. "I need to get to a phone. I—"

"What's the matter?" Helen considered setting the automatic locks.

The girl drew a shaky breath while her younger sister glanced around nervously behind them. *"Please.* I don't know what else to do. I have to call Angel. *Please."*

Helen's hand hovered briefly over the lock switch before dropping away. She sighed and motioned to the girls. "Come on," she said. "I think I know where there's a payphone a way's back."

III

Kathy glanced nervously over her shoulder from where she stood at Enid's door. The sheriff's deputy was still parked at Maude's, and she couldn't tell if he was looking this way. Where in the hell was Crystal? She glanced at her watch, noting that it was almost one o'clock, no later than she had told Crystal she would be. She pressed the button on the intercom again. Why wasn't Enid answering the intercom? Terry had installed a bedside handset that she could use without much effort, and there was another in the bathroom just off the master suite. What if Enid had slipped and fallen while going to the bathroom? What if she was laying on the floor in a pool of her own blood, unable to answer the persistent ring of the damned intercom?

Kathy glanced over her shoulder again. Something wasn't right here. She needed to make a decision quickly, though, or she *would* begin to look suspicious to the officer in Maude's driveway. She squatted, her knees popping in protest, and scooted the large clay flowerpot that held Enid's rose bush.

The key wasn't there.

But the key was *always* there. Anyone who would have known about that key would have also known to return it after using it. Her friends had talked her into this system when it became apparent that Enid's legs were growing less and less reliable. They could sometimes carry her upstairs but not back down, and she'd had one of those motorized stair lifts installed to help on those occasions. But the key wasn't where it belonged now.

Kathy slid the pot back into place and straightened, dusting herself off. She tested the doorknob again only to find the door was still locked, and then took a final jab at the intercom button in the futile hope that Enid's voice might suddenly appear.

Silence.

Kathy returned to her SUV and started the engine. She scanned the face of Enid's house, examining each window for signs of movement. There was nothing. She shifted into reverse and cut the wheel sharply, turning around in the wide section of driveway just in front of the garage. She sat with her foot on the brake, trying to decide what to do next. She was desperately worried about Enid, and her first instinct was to run to the officer who waited only a few doors down. But if Crystal was still inside, Kathy would be handing her to them—and while little Virginia was still in so much danger. She didn't know what to do.

She shifted the car into gear and rolled down the driveway.

CHAPTER TWENTY-SEVEN

I

Crystal leaned against the Honda, her arms folded across her chest. She knew she should be inside the vehicle, moving it out of Mr. Hildeman's yard, *staying* inside before someone spotted her and phoned the police, but she couldn't take her eyes from the scene before her.

Jessica had seized Luke in a mama bear hug, pulling back every few seconds to reexamine his face. Her fingers fluttered up to dab at the tears that flowed from his puffy eyes before pulling him back into a tight embrace. She couldn't believe that after all this time, she was holding her baby again. It wasn't anything she had ever expected. In fact, it was something that had been forbidden by the courts. At that moment, she didn't give a good goddamn what the courts or anyone else said. Amidst all of the horror of the past few days, she had found her son, and she would never give him up again.

Luke was surprised at his own intense reaction to Jessica, a woman who should have been a stranger to him. Until that moment, he had carried no recollection of his mother's face, had known nothing about her at all. Yet it was her very face which shattered the memory block that had become so comprehensive he had literally come to think of himself as a man without a past. He instinctively *knew* this woman was his mother. He remembered the gentle curves of her face, the funny way she crinkled her nose when she was about to sneeze—things you simply can't know about a stranger. He remembered the sound of her laughter as his father—was it Bennie? No, *Bernie*—tried to teach him to ride a bicycle. He couldn't picture his father's face, but he could almost feel his sturdy arms bracing the small bike, ensuring it wouldn't topple.

And he remembered Chad. He remembered the nightmares that had plagued him for *years* as that monstrosity grew in the crib across the room from him. He remembered Chad's eyes and how black they glistened when he was angry, and this was often…

Mercifully, he remembered almost nothing about that horrible afternoon— the day that Chad had tried to loosen Luke's brain from his skull. He remembered being in their bedroom, playing with Matchbox cars near the foot of his bed. He thought he may have been humming—what was the tune? It was irrelevant. One moment he was there, squatted over his network of imaginary roadways, and the next he was in a hospital bed, his head and neck held still by a cumbersome apparatus around his small shoulders. He could barely see anything through his bruised and swollen eyes, only tendrils of light that managed to filter through his eyelashes. His mouth was so *dry*—he could barely swallow. And then there was

533

a soft hand on his chin, tilting his head ever-so-slightly backward so that the cool liquid offered wouldn't escape his lips.

Then nothing.

Then Sister Margaret.

Then Paulie.

Was this possible? Another look at Jessica assured him that it was.

"Lucas," she croaked, cupping his face in her hands. "I have missed you *so* much, I—"

Luke held a finger to her mouth. "I know," he said. "Me, too—I think. I've got some holes in my recollections."

Jessica snuffled and nodded. "Enid Bowles," she said. "She helped us deal with the aftermath of what Chad had done. She lives right here in Lucasville. I was on my way to see her. I thought maybe she could help me again."

Luke smiled. "We just came from there," he said. His smile dropped away abruptly as a minivan pulled to a stop at the traffic light on the corner. Through the rear glass, he could see two little girls squabbling in the rear seat, one of whom had hair very much like Virginia's. "Oh, God."

He bolted toward the road, leaving Jessica and Crystal to stare at each other in confusion. He had to reach that van before the light changed! Flushed and tear-stained, his eyes bulging wildly in their sockets—he had no idea how frightening he looked. He had no time for stealth, and his shoes slapped the pavement loudly with each step. A dark-haired woman was driving the minivan, and she abruptly saw Luke in her side view mirror. Her eyes widened at the sight of the lunatic who was running across the southbound lanes of US 23, heedless to any oncoming traffic, single-mindedly advancing toward her vehicle. She glanced around quickly, and when she saw that there were no cars approaching the intersection on the cross street, she stomped on the gas, causing her tires to squeal as the minivan shot forward.

"No!" screamed Luke, the cords of his neck standing out.

The two little girls in the back seat turned to see what was chasing them, their faces lowered against the bench seat so all that showed were eyes, foreheads and hair. Luke stopped on a dime and suddenly laughed, causing the girls to dive for deeper cover as the van sailed away.

The little girl wasn't Virginia.

The resemblance wasn't even close. This little girl's forehead was too high, her eyes too narrow. Her hair didn't have that same sheen. It wasn't her.

It was a cruel slap, but useful, nonetheless. Luke suddenly realized they were wasting valuable time. He also realized he was standing in the middle of a four-lane highway as a passing motorist laid on his horn and tossed out a colorful phrase in passing. Luke turned and crossed back to the Speedway's parking lot where Crystal and his mother waited.

"What were you doing?" asked Jessica. "You ran right out into traffic—"

"We have to go," he said, taking his mother's arm.

"I told Enid that I was coming—" protested Jessica as Luke dragged her along toward the Honda.

"She'll understand," said Luke. "A little girl's life depends on us right now."

Kathy Duncan paced the hardwood floor of her living room. Her stomach had soured a half hour ago. Where *was* everyone? Was it possible that Crystal had taken Enid somewhere in Howard's old Studebaker? Enid hadn't driven in years, but she had insisted that her grandson, Rusty, keep the car maintained. Rusty didn't mind so much; he had enjoyed taking the car out for an occasional spin ever since he was old enough to drive.

But where would they have gone? It hardly seemed likely that Crystal would have left without leaving some kind of note for Kathy. She would have *known* how worried Kathy would be.

But now that she was home and could see that Luke and Virginia were gone as well, the credibility of the idea gained momentum. Maybe something had happened at this end. Maybe Luke had seen the maroon Volvo driving along Otter Creek. He might have called Crystal at Enid's—the phone number was on the refrigerator—and told her that he and Virginia needed to get out of there immediately. There wouldn't have been time to bother with leaving a note for Kathy.

Kathy paused at the picture window that looked out into the front yard. The tall pine trees that acted as a barrier from the road obstructed any real view of it. Luke couldn't have spotted the Volvo from here. Maybe the bad people had come through the woods and stormed the house from the rear.

Kathy folded her arms across her chest and shivered as the house creaked and settled. She had a sudden, paranoid suspicion that she wasn't alone.

"Wow." Jessica slumped back in the back seat and cradled her forehead in her hands. She shook her head dazedly. "She's only four?"

"I know it sounds crazy," said Crystal, guiding the Honda onto Otter Creek. "But you don't know what Lisa's capable of."

Jessica's head snapped up, her eyes locking on Crystal's. "She stabbed my friend in the throat with a pair of scissors. I'm pretty sure I know what she's capable of."

Crystal offered an apologetic smile. "I'm sorry. We heard about it on the radio."

"Leonard knew what she was before I did," said Jessica. "He had worked with her at Morgan Township Hospital for some time. He knew her Nanna Grace."

Nanna Grace. Maude's sister.

Crystal felt lightheaded as confirmation of Enid's story came from another direction. She could feel pieces of her past falling into place, pieces that she hadn't even known were missing. It was a sensation not unlike vertigo.

"But what could she want with Virginia?" asked Jessica. "Why is she so fixated on *her?*"

Luke shrugged. "We haven't figured it out. The only thing we know for sure is that Lisa, Chad, and a girl named Suze have killed her entire family. They are determined to stop at nothing to get to her."

"There are three of them to worry about?" asked Jessica, struggling to keep up.

"Two," said Crystal. "Suze is dead. Lisa killed her."

Jessica knitted her brows in confusion. "I thought you said that—"

Crystal shrugged. "I don't understand it either. Maybe there was some infighting going on—I don't know. But I saw Lisa snap Suze's neck with my own two eyes. I have no doubt about the monstrous things she could do to Virginia. I can only pray that she hasn't found her yet."

Had she checked the back door? Kathy couldn't remember. She had been so distraught when she realized the Honda was missing from the driveway that she remembered little of her entrance into the house. She had tossed her purse into the recliner by the door and done a quick sweep of the premises, looking more for a note than for Luke or Virginia. If the car wasn't there, odds were good they weren't either.

But had she checked the back door?

Kathy's feet were frozen to the floor, and she felt gooseflesh crawl up her arms. She was tempted to call the police, but again, she remembered she couldn't involve them. She had never been afraid in her own house—*never*. Until now. Now, she felt disconnected from the entire world, the solitude of her vast ranch house closing in from all sides.

If you scream, no one will hear you.

The thought came unbidden, and Kathy swallowed hard. Thank goodness it was still the middle of the afternoon. Under the shadow of night, her paranoia would have been totally debilitating. Even now, it was only with great effort that

536

she managed to force herself, one foot in front of the other, toward the hallway which led to the kitchen.

She needed to check that damn door.

She paused beside the archway leading to the kitchen and took a deep breath. The only thing she could think of that might be useful as a weapon was a knife from the butcher's block—which wouldn't be much help if an intruder was already inside the kitchen.

She counted to three and stepped quickly through the archway, her eyes darting left, right, then back again. The kitchen was empty. The backdoor was locked and bolted. Kathy exhaled slowly and twittered, her forehead damp with nervous sweat. Her knees were still wobbly from the adrenaline rush when her front door suddenly slammed open. She shrieked and ran for the butcher's block, snagging the biggest, sharpest knife she could find.

"Kathy?"

Crystal's voice took a moment to register, and it wasn't until Kathy actually saw her face that she loosened her grip on the knife handle.

"Where have you been?" demanded Kathy as she crossed back into the living room. Luke and Jessica were filing into the house behind Crystal. "Oh my God. Where's Virginia?" Her eyes shifted to the redheaded stranger in her living room. "And who's this?"

"Come with me," said Crystal, pulling her friend back toward the kitchen. Kathy started to drop the knife on the countertop, but Crystal shook her head. "Keep it."

Luke and Jessica followed them. Kathy didn't like the looks on their collective faces. "Where are we going?" she asked.

"Into the woods," said Crystal. "We'll split into two teams. Luke, you go with your mother. Kathy, come with me. I'll catch you up."

"Your *mother?*" asked Kathy incredulously. There was a slight family resemblance, but had she not been told, she never would have guessed. "And where in the world is that little girl?" she repeated. Why wouldn't they just *answer* her?

They emerged in the backyard and stopped abruptly as Crystal and Luke pulled forward and put their heads together. Jessica smiled pensively and extended a hand. "Jessie Lybrook," she said by way of introduction.

"Kathy Duncan. Won't you please tell me what's going on?"

"The child is missing."

Kathy gasped, a hand fluttering to her chest. "But how could that be? She was just here! Was she kidnapped? Where in the world could she have gone?"

Jessica's only response was to stare out toward the seemingly endless line of trees that surrounded Kathy's backyard.

II

Paula nearly burst into tears as she replaced the receiver of the payphone. *Where in the world are you, Angel?*

Helen had driven them to a small BP in Lucasville, one of those rare, rural posts where full service was still offered. A grease-covered old man squinted at them from behind the murky plate glass window, disappointed that they were only using the phone. Virginia was unwilling to remain alone in the car with Helen, so Paula allowed her to tag along. She was standing so close to Paula that she nearly trampled the girl as she paced nervously.

They had ridden almost entirely in silence. When Helen had asked their names, Paula had lied immediately, calling herself Julia and introducing Virginia as Claudia—she pulled the names straight from *Party of Five*. She didn't know how much of her story had leaked to the press; it was possible she was wanted in Indiana for questioning in the murder of her stepfather. The last thing she needed was for Helen to recognize her civic duty and haul the girls to the nearest police station. Helen had been so preoccupied with her own concerns that she hadn't thought to ask any more questions. After all, she'd never laid eyes on these girls before, and it wasn't likely she would again. That had been absolutely fine with Paula. She wasn't about to offer any information voluntarily.

Helen stuck her head through the driver's side window. "What's the matter? Isn't your sister answering?" She sounded impatient.

Paula found herself looking to Virginia for guidance, but the little girl's earlier reassurances were no longer evident on her face. For the first time since Paula had met her, Virginia looked her age—small and defenseless. This time, Paula *did* burst into tears.

Helen turned off the car and with an irritated shake of her head, got out. "Oh, now, now," she chided. "Don't go all to pieces."

"You don't understand!" sobbed Paula. "I don't know what to do!" Virginia took a step backward, partially hiding behind Paula.

Helen planted her hands on her hips and studied the girls, sighing. "Why don't you start by telling me what's going on? Maybe I can help."

Paula chewed on her bottom lip as she considered her options. She could simply have Helen leave them there. She could try calling Angel every half hour or so until she finally got through. A glance at the old man behind the plate glass made her shrug off the consideration. There was a 'No Loitering' sign posted on the door, and Paula had no doubt that the attendant would enforce the rule. She knew she should simply call the police and turn Virginia over. They would be able to protect her from Luke. Still, she was reluctant to make the call. Some niggling internal voice warned her against it. Paula was certain that any contact

538

with the police whatsoever would eventually lead to hers and Angel's arrests for the murder of their stepfather. It was a completely selfish notion, but one she couldn't ignore. She looked up at Helen through a veil of tears. Should she trust this stranger? Should she tell her about the dead woman who waited out eternity in her countryside recliner? Should she invite her into this nightmare world that had become Paula's day-to-day reality?

Runaways, thought Helen as she watched the older girl frantically deliberate over her options. "Just exactly what kind of trouble are the two of you in?"

Paula's eyes darted to Helen's. *"No!* We're not in trouble at all." *No police, no police...* "We're just worried about our sister, that's all. She was supposed to pick us up a while ago." She locked a protective arm around Virginia, whose back was already firmly pressed against Paula's legs.

"What's the big emergency?" asked Helen impatiently. She could feel Lisa's presence so close that it made the surface of her skin prickle. What had *possessed* her to waste time with these two? Lisa *needed* her. "Why don't you just call your parents?"

Paula shook her head quickly. "No. I don't want to worry them. Suze is supposed to be taking care of us," she said, unconsciously using her sister's real name. "I don't want to get her into trouble."

Helen blinked. Did the girl who called herself Julia just utter that name, that unusual name? Were these two somehow connected to the maniacal bitch who, miles and miles away, had forced her down into a coal cellar where Helen had every reason to believe that she was going to die? Was it possible? She opened her mouth to question the coincidence, but the girls' furtive demeanors encouraged her to play it cool. As repugnant as it had seemed a few short moments ago, the objective was to get the girls back into the car. If Lisa were still being held by Suze and Chad, possession of these girls could prove invaluable. "Well, listen, I don't think it's a good idea for the two of you to be wandering around like this in the hot summer sun. You'll dehydrate, and poor little Claudia's getting sunburned—just look at her arms! Are you hungry? There's a Wendy's across the street. Afterward, you could try your sister again."

Paula was surprised to note that her stomach was grumbling. She thought she'd never find her appetite again after seeing the dead woman in her recliner, but somehow, there it was. She didn't know when Virginia had last eaten, but they had walked a long way, and she was bound to be hungry, too. "I don't know," she said at last. "I don't have any money."

"It's on me," said Helen, a wide smile creeping across her face. Her sudden change in demeanor should have been jolting, but Paula didn't seem to notice. *"Please.* It's my Christian duty."

The old man in the service station had moved from the window to hover in the doorframe, blatantly staring at them with eyes both suspicious and inquisitive.

Paula glanced at Virginia, but again, there was nothing to guide her decision. She took Virginia's hand and followed Helen back to the Focus.

"Have you lived here all your life?" asked Helen as she casually twisted a French fry in a puddle of ketchup.

"Yes," Paula said immediately, quickly taking another bite of her Junior Bacon Cheeseburger so she wouldn't feel compelled to say more.

"How did you get separated from your sister?" asked Helen.

Paula took her time chewing and swallowing to give herself time to formulate a story. "She has a boyfriend," she said. "Mom and Dad aren't crazy about him, so she sneaks to see him."

Helen's face registered distaste automatically. "What kind of boy is he if she has to sneak around to see him?" In her mind, she clearly saw Chad's menacing visage.

"Oh, he's alright," said Paula, taking another bite of her sandwich. "Mom and Dad are a little overprotective, that's all."

"How overprotective can they be? They let you and your little sister run around with her."

"She's not a monster, Mrs. Martin," said Paula. She found her composure was returning as her belly filled. Her hands had almost entirely stopped shaking now.

"Well, she's irresponsible," said Helen gruffly. "What kind of girl would leave her little sisters off so she could do God-only-knows what with her boyfriend? And what were you doing out there anyway? You were in the middle of hell's half acre?"

"My friend Judy," said Paula automatically, the strings drawing together almost seamlessly now. "We were invited to spend the morning, but Judy's mother had things to do at noon. Angel was supposed to pick us up before then."

"So, this mother of Judy just put you out? *Hmmph.* I thought these parts were supposed to be hospitable. I guarantee no such thing would happen back home. You've *always* lived here?" Helen struggled to remain casual. She wanted to *interrogate* this girl. She wanted to know where she was from. She wondered what she would see in this girl's eyes if she mentioned Morgan Township. She suspected she'd see *something.* Why had she called her sister 'Suze' and later referred to her as 'Angel?' 'Suze' had been a slip. Helen was sure of it, and what's more, the longer she was in the company of this girl, this girl called Julia, she could see a resemblance, albeit slight. There was none of the anger, none of the malignancy that had stained the other girl's face. This girl was too young to be that jaded. Still, the hair was almost the same color, and the lips were the same fullness and general shape. The resemblance was growing with the passage of time, and Helen felt an odd twinge. A coincidence like this was too great to be ignored. How in the hell many 'Suzes' could there be out there anyway?

"We've been here all our lives," said Paula. She took a sip of Coke. "Where are you from?"

"Indiana," said Helen, deciding to back away from the big gun. What if she mentioned Morgan Township and this girl ran? She might never find Lisa if she lost the girls now. She watched for a reaction, but one wasn't forthcoming.

Paula finished her sandwich and checked Virginia's progress. The little girl had nervously picked at her food but eaten little. Her eyes still telegraphed a nervousness that was unsettling. It reminded Paula of a documentary she had seen on the Discovery Channel that postulated over how some animals seem capable of detecting a tornado or earthquake just before it occurs.

She cleared her throat. "Thank you very much for the food, Mrs. Martin. If you'd like to leave your address with me, I'll make sure that you get repaid."

"What's your hurry?" asked Helen, almost going on point. She knew that subtlety wasn't her strong suit, and it was only with great effort that she managed to stand down. "It's terribly hot out there and look at poor Claudia's shoulders. They're already blistering a little. It's no wonder the poor dear doesn't have any appetite. Why don't you try calling your sister again? I'd feel a lot better if I knew that you girls had reconnected with her before I take off."

Paula paused in wiping her mouth, then shrugged. "Sure. I mean, if you don't mind waiting."

"I don't mind at all. Go on. Make your call. I'll watch this little angel. Maybe I can coax her to take a bite or two more."

Paula glanced at Virginia, half-expecting her to leach on, refusing to be separated, but she seemed content with the arrangement—or at least she wasn't voicing any complaints. Paula slid off the bench seat and retrieved the last of the change she had in her pocket. It was barely enough for a minute or two, but that would be enough. She remained aloof as she strode from the restaurant, oblivious to the storm clouds collecting overhead. In her mind, she was already silently repeating a prayer for Angel to answer this time. *Please answer.*

She fed the coins into the slot one at a time and took a deep breath before pecking out the familiar number.

One ring.

C'mon, c'mon, c'mon.

Two.

Paula glanced into the restaurant through the plate glass to her right. Helen was attempting to draw Virginia to her food, but the girl was staring dreamily over Helen's shoulder, oblivious to the other woman's animated ministrations.

She's cracked, thought Paula. *It's all finally been too much, and she's cracked.*

Three rings.

541

C'mon, Angel! Answer the damn phone! I don't know how much longer I should stay with this woman, and I don't know where to go if she leaves! Please help me!

On the fourth ring, her call for help was finally answered.

CHAPTER TWENTY-EIGHT

I

"Virginia!"

The name echoed through the woods time and again, four separate voices chanting the same mantra. They had entered the woods as a unit, synchronizing their position with an ancient silver maple that stood high above its neighbors at the back of Kathy's yard before splitting into teams. Crystal and Kathy followed a tangled footpath that wound around to the right, Luke and Jessica wove left. They agreed to reconvene at the silver maple in an hour. Hopefully by then, one of the groups would have found the girl and would have her in tow.

Crystal glanced at her watch and saw that they had already been in the woods for almost forty minutes, screaming themselves hoarse. Every moment that passed brought a fresh wave of despair, the sinking certainty that Virginia was already dead. Crystal pushed the thought away yet again and found herself praying that everything would be alright. She had never been particularly religious and wasn't even sure to whom she was praying, but after her discussion with Enid, she believed there was *something* out there governing these events. She could only hope that this all-powerful force might show mercy to a four-year-old orphan.

"We should head back," said Kathy, noticing the time on her own watch. "We'll have to haul ass to meet them on time."

"We can't just give up!"

"We're not giving up. Luke and Jessie may have already found her."

"May? That's not good enough, Kathy. If these people find her first, she'll be dead. You know that."

"You act as if these people are—I don't know, superhuman." She tittered nervously as a flock of blackbirds burst from the crown of a towering oak. "They can't find her any easier than we can."

"I don't know about that. They've been on our tail pretty much since we left that house in Borden. And after talking to Enid—"

"I told you, I don't want to know what Enid said," interrupted Kathy.

"You're not the least bit curious?"

"No," said Kathy, smiling almost apologetically. "I know that may seem narrow-minded and maybe it is, but I just can't deal with all that nonsense. It just seems—blasphemous."

"How can it seem blasphemous when you don't even know what she's talking about?"

543

Kathy shifted on her feet, her eyes glued to the leather uppers of her tennis shoes. She reminded Crystal of a stubborn schoolgirl, and it made Crystal want to put her hands on her friend's shoulders and shake her—*hard*. The past few weeks had been a series of tightly interlocking events that couldn't possibly be chalked up to mere coincidence. To completely discount an ideology without first examining it was more than foolish; it could prove deadly.

Kathy sought to change the subject. "Just beyond that line of trees is Carver's Run. If Virginia made it this far—and I can't see her little legs carrying her all this way—we'd be better off searching for her in a car. Besides, we should check the radio to see if there have been any new developments. If someone found Virginia wandering around, they surely would have turned her in to the police, and after all the news bulletins about her family's murders and your alleged involvement, you better believe that we'd hear about it before long."

"That's the *last* thing I want to hear. How can we get to Virginia if she's with the police? Their focus would be on arresting me, not protecting her. Lisa and Chad could walk right in there and blow her away before the police even knew what was happening. I can't believe Luke was so careless with her. What in the hell was he *thinking?*"

"Hey, take it easy on him. I'm sure he's kicking himself all to pieces over this. And what makes you think that Lisa and Chad would do that? They surely wouldn't make it out of the police station alive."

Crystal laughed bitterly. "I'm not sure they care about that. All they want is to see that little girl die, no matter the cost. You're the one who told me about Lisa. Don't you think she's capable of doing such a thing?"

Kathy was silent. Crystal's point was certainly valid. They had started moving back toward the majestic oak, passing through the lengthening shadows of the surrounding foliage that provided, if nothing else, brief respites from the accumulating heat of late afternoon.

"Virginia!"

Jessica's voice carried on the gentle breeze and dissipated into the summer air. After the first fifteen minutes or so of constant bellowing, she and Luke had begun alternating their calls in an effort to spare a little vocal power. A fat lot of good it would do them to be calling out Virginia's name if their voices gave out under the strain.

"I still can't believe I was so stupid," muttered Luke, kicking through tangled undergrowth that all but obscured the abandoned footpath they traveled. "I should have kept her with me every single minute."

"Please, Lucas, don't," said Jessica, barely able to take her eyes from her precious son's handsome face. She still expected to awaken at any moment, this reunion only the cruel byproduct of a dream. "I can't tell you how many times I said the same thing about you. Why did I leave you in that room with him? Why didn't I recognize the evil underneath his skin? Do you realize how many people's lives have been horrifically impacted simply because I gave birth to that—that *thing?* We're human, that's all. Sometimes we make mistakes. There's no way that you could have anticipated what would happen in those few moments while you were on the phone."

They walked in companionable silence for a few moments, and Luke was surprised at how comfortable he was around Jessica. He sensed a purity about her as polar and yet definitive as the feeling of dread he had experienced when exposed to Chad. As much as he loved Paulie, he resented the years lost in which he might have better known this woman who was his mother.

"I'm glad you're here," he finally said, and Jessica beamed. "Ever since I left Jasper, things have been happening to me that I can't explain. Some good, some not so good. This is definitely a good thing. I have a feeling that you've always been part of the solution here."

Jessica slowly nodded. "I feel the same. My life hasn't been the same since— well, you know. I mean, I moved on. I had to, didn't I? Your father was gone, and I had nothing when I was released from the hospital. All I could do was start over. I've tried for years to distance myself from everything that happened back then, and I've actually been sort of successful. I'm the best damn police dispatcher in all of Jay County, Indiana. I've got a few girlfriends back home that I run with here and there. But I've always felt that something was missing. A woman cannot become a mother and then simply eradicate the memories, no matter what some stupid court says about her maternal fitness. I've always secretly prayed that this day might come. Of course, I didn't know that it would be under such horrible circumstances. It must have been awful finding Virginia's family like that."

Luke's face was grim. "I'll learn to deal with it. I can't help but wonder what it's done to Virginia. She hasn't really acknowledged what happened that morning."

"Children are amazingly resilient," said Jessica. She glanced at her son. "I should know."

Luke's smile was melancholy. "It's easy to rebound from something you don't remember happening."

"Maybe so, but I didn't know that. I can't tell you how many nights' sleep I lost wondering what had become of you."

"What about Chad?"

She pressed her lips together tightly. "I *knew* what would become of him."

Luke fell silent for a moment before quietly asking, "Do you think you could kill him? If you had to, I mean."

Jessica considered the question long and hard. It wasn't as if she hadn't considered it before. "I don't know," she finally said. "I don't know if I could kill *anybody*. Why?"

"Because I really think it's going to come to that," said Luke grimly. "I can't see where either Chad or Lisa will stop at anything short of death."

Jessica slowly nodded. "I suppose you're right, but I still can't say that I could be the one to do it. Killing is an unnatural concept to me. What about you?"

Luke nodded. "I could do it," he said automatically, and Jessica was startled by his lack of hesitation. "After the things I've seen, the things he's done—hell, I had enough incentive without even knowing what he did to me personally. But I know what he wants to do to that girl, Mom—is it okay if I call you Mom?"

Jessica felt warm pride flowing through her, and she almost began to cry again. "I've been waiting to hear it for years, honey. You bet your sweet ass you can."

Luke glanced at his watch. "We need to go back. Maybe Crystal and Kathy have found her."

"You like her, don't you? Crystal, I mean."

"I barely know her," said Luke. "But yeah, I think I do."

"I suspect she likes you, too," said Jessica. She reached out and stopped Luke with a hand on his arm. She sought his eyes with her own and held them. "No matter what happens from here, you need to understand that this isn't your fault. If you and Crystal start playing the blame-game, it will rip you apart before you get a chance to know each other better, just like it did with me and your father, and that would truly be a shame. It can be awfully lonely wandering this big old world by yourself, and believe me, I know."

Luke said nothing, just nodded briefly before resuming his course, and Jessica knew that her words on the subject were meaningless at this point. If something terrible happened to Virginia Parnell, it would become a permanent stain on Luke's soul, an anchor around his neck.

It was another thing that she knew all too well.

⚬———◇———⚬

Crystal, Luke, and Jessica clustered around Kathy's kitchen table, the radio tuned to WPAY as they waited in frustration for the next news bulletin. It was close to four-thirty when they had reconvened empty-handed under the silver maple. They had decided to take a restroom break at Kathy's before piling into Kathy's SUV and scouring the country roads, but it seemed prudent to see if there had been any new developments of which they were unaware.

Kathy was just returning from the bathroom when the country-tinged newscaster said, "Police are still on the lookout for local celebrity, Crystal Bright. Eyewitness reports and surveillance videos place her at the scene of a homicide in Lucasville earlier this morning, in which Leonard Barnes of Morgan Township, Indiana, was fatally stabbed. You may recall Ms. Bright from her starring role in the hit sitcom, *Bennie and the Girl,* or from multiple tabloid accounts of her rampant misbehavior, which culminated in her release from that series. Citizens are advised that Ms. Bright may be traveling with one or more accomplices and is considered armed and extremely dangerous. In sports—"

Crystal snapped the radio off. *"May recall.* Jesus."

Luke looked at her with surprise. "With everything that's going on, you're hung up on the announcer's poor choice of words?"

Crystal flushed guiltily. Old habits were hard to break. "I'm sorry. You're right. It's just hard to hear yourself labeled as a has-been when you've worked so hard to make a name for yourself."

"A has-been? What about the murderer part?" asked Luke sarcastically.

"Well, they didn't mention Virginia at all," said Jessica, trying to bring everyone back to the point. "So apparently, the police haven't found her yet."

"I just hope Lisa hasn't," said Kathy with a shudder.

"Or Chad," added Luke.

"I feel so damned *helpless,*" said Crystal as she began to pace the kitchen. "I wish that Enid could have given me something more concrete, something that might help me figure out where Lisa and Chad were hiding."

"That's likely," said Luke dryly. "You're talking about that old woman like she's got superpowers."

"I really don't want to hear about this," said Kathy, pacing nervously.

"Jumping in the car and rambling around doesn't strike me as a particularly good plan," said Crystal.

"But what else is there?" asked Kathy.

"Tell me about your visit with Enid," said Jessica. "Maybe there's something more than you realize in what she said."

"Oh, no," said Kathy, covering her ears. "I *really* don't want to hear about it."

"For God's sake, Kathy! A little girl's life is at stake here!" said Crystal, her patience nearing its end.

"What's the big deal?" asked Jessica, looking from Kathy to Crystal and back again.

"Enid's religious beliefs apparently offend Kathy," said Luke.

"It's ridiculous!" said Crystal, her frustration transforming into full-blown anger. "So, you don't believe what she says—fine! You have the right to your own opinion. But to close your ears without even *listening*—"

"I believe that Jesus Christ is Lord and Savior. I believe that there is but one merciful God in heaven looking down on us. It's how I was raised, and how I

547

would have raised my own children, had I been blessed. The things that Enid suggests border on *witchcraft*." Kathy shook her head vehemently. "Lord knows I love that woman dearly as a friend, and I include her in my prayers every night, but I will not subscribe to her deviation from Scripture."

"I think you're afraid," said Crystal. "I think you're afraid that if you listen to her, you might actually agree with what she says, or some of what she says. I think you're afraid—"

"And I think you are showing me an inordinate amount of disrespect in my own home!"

"Ladies!" snapped Luke, his voice commanding. Crystal and Kathy froze in mid-sentence, their mouths hanging open. "This isn't productive. We need to decide what we're doing here."

"Why don't you call Enid and see what her crystal ball says?" suggested Kathy snidely, before her face abruptly changed expressions. "Oh."

Crystal was about to unleash a response of her own when she saw her friend's focus shift. "What? What is it?"

"We've been so concerned about Virginia that it completely slipped my mind," said Kathy. "Was Enid going somewhere after you left?"

Crystal blinked. "Going somewhere? That's not very likely, I wouldn't think. She couldn't even get out of bed when I was there. Why?"

Kathy shook her head. "I stopped at Enid's to pick you up after my last meals-on-wheels delivery. You had apparently already left with Luke, but she didn't answer the intercom when I buzzed. The spare key wasn't under the flowerpot either, so I couldn't let myself in to check on her."

"*Shit*," said Crystal, and Luke and Jessica were already on their feet.

II

Lisa perched on the plum cushions of the window seat, staring through gauzy curtains at the property below. She could see the lone sheriff's deputy guarding Maude's property, and she was nearly overcome with a sensation that bordered on nostalgia. She *knew* this place. She had lived here once. She didn't think that the old neighborhood would have been capable of generating such a punch, but here it was, and she didn't quite know how to deal with it. She clasped her arms around her knees and rocked slowly, hypnotically. She remembered some of the children—mostly faces, occasionally names. She remembered a girl named Jenny White, who had lived with her grandmother at the end of the block. She was blonde and pasty and about as big a pantywaist as you'd likely meet. Lisa had taken great pleasure in providing glorious afternoons of terror for this girl, delighting in her frightened screams and occasional yelps of pain. It had been a good summer.

Chad paced the rooms, using his father's gun as a pointer. "Who the fuck would think a place could *smell* like this," he groaned. "Can't we open a goddamn window or something? It smells like this woman's been dead for years."

Lisa shook her head, only half-listening. "Don't want to draw any unwanted attention. There's a policeman right across the street."

"It ain't like she's gonna scream."

"No. Breathe through your mouth."

"What the Sam Fuck are we doing here anyway?"

Lisa shifted her attention to him disgustedly. A marvelous physical specimen, perhaps. Einstein? Not even close. "We wait."

"Wait? Wait for *what?* I say we—"

"I say you shut the fuck up. I mean, how fucking stupid are you, anyway?"

Chad's brows furrowed, and he stormed across the room, the pistol pointed at Lisa's head. "I think you'd better watch your fucking mouth, bitch."

Lisa cocked her head, looking at the gun with amusement. She ducked under the gun and jabbed Chad where he had been shot. Despite his rapid healing, the area was still bruised and sore, and he dropped the gun immediately, wincing. "They're *coming.* Can't you feel it? This is where it all started, and this is where it all ends. Can't you *feel* it?"

Chad rubbed his shoulder, seething with contempt. "Don't you *ever* call me stupid. *Ever.* Do you understand?"

Lisa smiled sweetly. She didn't love this boy. She didn't even *like* him. But she understood that he somehow complemented her in a way that was, at least for the moment, essential. Suze had been excess baggage, an irritant. Her disposal was inevitable. She needed to keep Chad happy for just a little while longer.

"I'm sorry," she said. "I'm just impatient. I just want to see this thing through."

"What is it about this fucking little girl, anyway?" said Chad, still massaging his shoulder. Lisa had used considerable force. "I mean, shit. You know what I think we should do? I think we should wait 'til dark and go to that drive-in, the one I saw when we drove into this hellhole. Go from car to car, snappin' necks the whole fucking way. Now *that,* to me, sounds like a fucking good time."

Lisa's jaws clenched as she struggled to contain herself. Chad had lost sight of everything, completely caught up in bloodlust. She concentrated on her breathing—in and out, in and out. "We need to get the girl, Chad. You know that. You *know* that. Think about it. Picture her face. Picture her perfect little vomitous face. We can't let her continue. We can't. The older she gets, the more powerful she is. This is *our* time. We can finish her now. Can't you *feel* how important this is?"

549

Chad paced a moment longer, his bottom lip sullenly jutting forward. He knew she was right. When he thought of the little girl, even so much as *pictured* her face, the intensity of his hatred magnified a thousandfold. No simple murder spree at a drive-in could replace the feeling of satisfaction that would be his if he could squash the life from that child. It would be the ultimate supernova for him, and he damn well knew it. His eyes flicked to Lisa's, and he cleared his throat. "Whatever."

Lisa continued to stare. "Are you in this with me or not?"

He returned her stare.

"Because if you're not," she continued, "I've gotta know. I *need* you, Chad. There's going to be a lot of them. We've got to stay together on this." Her eyes softened, and she applied the subtle charm she considered necessary to accomplish her task.

Chad's eyes darted around the room, avoiding Lisa at all costs. He hated this. He hated being played, and he knew that was exactly what Lisa was doing. Still, she was right. Virginia Parnell had to be eliminated and now, before it was too late. "Yeah—I guess so."

"No. You don't *guess* so. You have to tell me—"

"Yes," he spat. *"Yes.* I'm *here.* We do what we have to *do."*

Lisa studied him a moment longer, feeling his wounded pride and feeding upon it. Chad was nothing to her. When this was all over, she would dispatch him as easily as she had done with Suze. She returned her attention to the window, feeling the pull of the neighborhood that had once been her own. "Take the first floor," she said absently. "They'll be coming soon."

Chad stared at her and ground his teeth. He couldn't remember what he had so recently seen in this woman. It had to have been infatuation due to her uncanny resemblance to Crystal Bright, the woman of his fantasies since early adolescence. He shook his head in disgust and headed for the door, retrieving his gun as he passed the bed. He wished that Suze were here to share this with him. He was surprised at how much he missed her, but the feeling was undeniable. They had been a good fit. They would have been a force to be reckoned with, and if Chad were forced to, he would have to admit that he was as interested in punishing Suze's killers as he was in killing the little girl. The bitterness he felt was the same, whether picturing the fetid little girl or his poor, dead lover. Before this was over, vengeance would be his, and of that, he had no doubt. He tucked the gun into the front of his jeans, continuing through the doorway and down the hall, toward the staircase.

Clouds thickened as afternoon shadows lengthened, first as great patchworks of billowy cotton floating across a vibrant blue backdrop before gathering the steely gray bulk of impending rain. The old house was eerily silent, amplifying the gusting wind that was gaining momentum outside.

Lisa continued to watch the street below perched in Enid's window seat. In anticipation of the weather, the children of Dale Street had abandoned their bicycles, skateboards, and jump ropes in favor of various indoor activities. Wind-shorn leaves tangled and swirled along the narrow road before depositing themselves in storm drains and ditches. Lisa hugged her knees to her chest, exhilarating in the gloom. Enid's bedroom was rapidly darkening, but Lisa wasn't inclined to switch on any of the antique table lamps. She could feel things coming to a head, and the murky dimness added a desirable ambiance to the proceedings. Lightning forked in the distance, bringing the trace of a smile to the corners of Lisa's mouth. The fine hairs on her arms stood on end in the ozone-charged air, and she finally stood, stretching, continuing to stare through the window at the house in which she used to live. It was such a curious sensation, as if she could only remember those times in snapshots. She wanted a tour of the old homestead, but she didn't want to risk getting caught when she was this close to her objective. She walked up to the glass and pressed her palm flat against it, wishing the officer would just get in his car and go.

And suddenly, he moved toward the driver's side door.

Lisa watched in amazement as he slid behind the wheel of the patrol car and started the engine, shifted the car into gear, and pulled out onto Dale Street. It was as if he was heeding her silent command, and a thrill of adrenaline coursed through Lisa's veins.

Things are *coming to a head*, she thought.

She watched the Chevy's taillights flick on at the end of the road before winking off and disappearing around the corner. She found herself counting to sixty. No—one hundred twenty. If he didn't come back by the time she got to one twenty, she would cross the street and see what remained inside Maude's house. The idea appealed to her on an almost unreasonable level, maybe because she hoped that the house might unlock her past and piece together the fractured images that flitted through her mind.

One.

Two.

Three...

Lisa's count was interrupted by the shrill chirp of the cell phone in her pocket—Suze's cell phone. She had nearly forgotten she was carrying it. She fished it out of her pocket and frowned as she studied the small display.

Unknown caller.

She almost ignored the call, but after several rings, curiosity got the better of her, and she answered.

551

"Hello?"

A slow smile spread across Lisa's face as she recognized the simpering voice on the other end of the line.

———◆———

Chad slung his legs over the arm of the stiff-backed plum chair in which he sat in the downstairs library. He scanned the room with distaste, wondering what would ever possess someone to decorate a room in her house like a funeral parlor. There wasn't a piece of comfortable furniture in the entire room, and the place smelled vaguely of musky flowers and mothballs. Yellowed volumes of classical literature lined the mahogany shelves, their spines in varying degrees of decomposition. Chad pulled himself to his feet and crossed the room, running his fingers along the shelf. *Moby Dick. The Catcher in the Rye. Wuthering Heights.* The same old shit he never read in high school.

He sighed and slowly paced the room, his eyes running from floor to ceiling and back again. He was quickly becoming bored with this whole thing. And he was especially tired of taking orders from Lisa. This old woman was no fun at all. Hell, she was probably looking forward to death, having long since passed her prime in life. He wanted to see that stark look of surprise that could only be found in the young and unsuspecting. Perhaps the little girl wouldn't be such a bad choice after all.

Chad wandered out into the foyer, suddenly aware that the sky had changed, and the house was growing dark. Automatically, he reached for a light switch, but his hand hovered in place just before flicking it upward. He could already hear Lisa, chastising him for drawing unwanted attention to them, and the *imagined* sound of her voice set his nerves on end. His fingers curled into a tight fist, and his hand dropped to his side.

This is ridiculous, he thought. *What are we waiting for? Does she really think that they'll just drive right up and ring the doorbell?*

He took a left through a paneled door into the foyer and found himself in a narrow hallway that lead to the kitchen. This was obviously some sort of servant's passage, and Chad tried to imagine living in a home that required actual *servants*.

This old bitch must be loaded, he thought, wandering the aged tile of the spacious kitchen. Lightning flared through the window, illuminating an industrial refrigerator and a stove that sat in place of the typical household models, and Chad tried to guess the size of meal this galley could generate. He shook his head and passed through the room, noting a door at the far end. Another hallway, this one not quite so narrow. Halfway down on the right was a laundry alcove, with machines that were respectable counterparts to the kitchen appliances. At the far end was another set of stairs leading to the second floor, a nearly hidden passage that would allow maids to replenish fresh laundry to the upstairs bedrooms and baths without ever having to be seen. Another door was at the foot of the stairs, behind which was a room that Chad assumed was the maid's sleeping quarters. His hand closed around the knob, twisting it and pushing the door inward on creaky hinges. There were either heavy draperies on the windows or no windows at all, because the room was swallowed in complete and total darkness. He could hear rain hammering on the roof above, a slow roll of thunder thrumming through the floor beneath his feet.

Chad groped along the inside wall for a light switch, confident he could turn the light on without drawing any attention whatsoever; after all, if it was this dark *inside*, how much light could actually escape?

His fingers finally brushed the switch, but they froze, along with his breath.

Someone else was in the room.

***

Mickey Tapscott wanted a do-over.

Every single choice he had made since graduating high school had been wrong, not the least of which was his decision to join local law enforcement. Unpopular and teased all throughout his teenage years, he thought the uniform would make him more interesting to the ladies—it hadn't—but might, at the very least, command the respect he so sorely craved. Folks might not be so quick to rib a guy carrying a gun on his belt.

It didn't take long to realize he had only traded one set of tormentors for another. Every other officer on Sheriff Dutton's force was more proficient than Mickey, and in every way imaginable. Even scrawny Ida Longbottom had eclipsed him on the shooting range, and she didn't even patrol! She was the head dispatcher and had immediately tagged him with the nickname 'Pudge,' which spread like wildfire amongst their fellow officers. He'd been relegated to a desk for most of the past year, a year in which he'd watched his midsection grow and his hair thin.

At twenty-three, he looked every bit of forty, and if his uncle wasn't the sheriff, he'd likely be flipping burgers in some fast-food joint.

His stomach gurgled at the thought.

Mickey made another sullen pass around the old Williams house for lack of anything better to do while he wondered what in the hell was holding Jethro Evans up. Evans was supposed to spot him for lunch over an hour ago, but he was tied up in some nonsense over at the Speedway, and when Mickey complained about it to Longbottom, she only reminded him of how thin the department's resources were stretched, but not before reminding him it wouldn't exactly hurt to skip a meal.

Thin-necked, bony, *emaciated* scag.

Storm clouds were collecting above as perspiration soaked through Mickey's tan uniform shirt. Time had never moved so slowly as he waited for something—*anything*, to happen. Mickey knew that he had been given this particular assignment based on the likelihood that whatever happened, it wouldn't happen here. Whatever business the Bright woman and her accomplice had in the area, they were undoubtedly too smart to stage a homecoming, and to what end? Maude Williams was dead. The property had been vacant for weeks now, and with Mickey's patrol car parked in the drive, no one in his right mind would trespass now.

Just as Mickey was contemplating another pass around the cinderblock structure, he felt a sharp prick at the base of his neck. He reached back, slapping at the pain, and pulled his hand away to find a stunned bee squirming in his palm.

He gasped, his pulse quickening as he tossed the injured wasp to the gravel and stomped it repeatedly. He was severely allergic to bees, and he could already feel his throat beginning to constrict. He fought the urge to panic, knowing from past experience that keeping a cool head and a steady pulse would buy time to react. He went to his patrol car and slid behind the wheel, his mouth turning to dust as a wave of pent-up heat enveloped him. He leaned over the passenger seat and opened the glove compartment, looking for the EpiPen he kept inside for emergencies, oblivious to the fact that the extreme heat would have likely rendered the auto-injector useless. He was never particularly good at following directions.

It didn't really matter. The EpiPen was gone. No amount of frantic rummaging through the glovebox's contents could cure that.

Mickey could feel his heart racing in his chest, and he fumbled with the keys, turning on the engine only to receive another furnace blast of air directly to his face. Perspiration stung the corners of his eyes as he focused on his breathing and tried to determine his next best step. He lived with his mother just a few blocks away, and she always kept pens in her refrigerator.

As the air conditioning finally surrendered a hint of coolness, he shifted the car into gear, easing out of the driveway and turning right, focusing on his breathing and keeping his patrol car in its proper lane. He barely noticed the Explorer he passed as it slowed near Dale Street.

Maybe he'd have time to swing through Wendy's drive-thru on his way back.

⎯⎯◆⎯⎯

Paula was breathless by the time she returned to the table where Virginia continued to push her chicken nuggets listlessly around the table. Helen stared openly as Paula began loading their refuse onto the plastic tray on which it had been served, oblivious to the rumble of thunder in the distance.

"Did she answer?" Helen asked, aiming for nonchalance but falling far short of the mark. She couldn't seem to suppress the anxiousness in her voice.

"Yes," said Paula, taking the container of nuggets from Virginia and adding them to the pile of trash on the tray. She was too excited to sit. "I mean, *no.*"

"Well, good Lord, child!" exclaimed Helen, sitting back in her seat. "Yes—no—which one *is* it?"

"She's *there*," answered Paula, excitement plastered across her face. She turned her attention to Virginia. "C'mon, sweetheart. It's time to go meet sis." She reached for the little girl, but Virginia pulled away, for the first time showing dismay.

"What do you mean, *'she's there?'*" asked Helen, confused. She absently added her own wrapper and napkins to the tray. "Did you speak to her?"

Paula sighed, flummoxed by Virginia's sudden reticence and tired of being interrogated by Helen. "No, Lisa said she was in the bathroom, but she was really upset when she heard I'd been there and left."

Helen's eyes widened. *Lisa.*

Virginia continued to pull away, whimpering softly.

"She offered to pick me up, but when she asked where I was—well, it turns out they're just a few blocks away," said Paula, reaching for the little girl as she continued to shrink away. Her excitement was tempered by the girl's sudden, inexplicable non-compliance. "Can you believe the luck? *Virginia!* You stop that this very minute and come here!"

Helen practically choked when she heard the little girl's real name, dots connecting so quickly she was almost dizzy. This *was* the girl who was all over the news, the lone survivor of a mass murder that had taken the lives of her whole family. Helen's gaze hardened as she watched Paula roughly seize the child's arm and pull her closer. The similarities between Paula and Suze had never been more obvious, and Paula's mention of Lisa couldn't be coincidental. She was so near that Helen could practically feel her presence.

"Let me drive you," offered Helen, pushing up from her seat and grabbing her pocketbook from where she had laid it on the seat.

"That's not necessary," said Paula, shaking her head as she continued to struggle with Virginia to get her out of the seat. Other patrons were beginning to take notice, an incoming tide of disapproving scowls. "It's not far."

"But it looks like it's about to storm," said Helen. As if on cue, a jagged burst of lightning flared through the plate glass, followed by a low roll of thunder they felt through the floor. "You don't want to be caught out in this. And really, it's no bother. I'd feel so much better if I knew I had delivered you both into the safety of your sister's care."

Paula looked at Helen uncertainly as Virginia continued to struggle against her grip.

"Please?" implored Helen, doing her very best not to lay it on too thick.

And that's precisely when Virginia began to scream, keening in a pitch only available to girls her age. She clawed at Paula's arms with desperation, trying to pull away before her pupils suddenly rolled upward, leaving only the whites of her eyes exposed. Paula watched in open-mouthed horror, releasing her grip as Virginia fell backwards on the hard plastic seat, her limbs thrashing wildly.

"She's seizing," said Helen, pushing Paula aside to carefully ease the little girl to the floor. She used her pocketbook as a pillow to keep the convulsing girl's head from striking the floor as she continued to jerk sporadically. Spectators were beginning to form a claustrophobic circle around the scene as both employees and customers couldn't resist satisfying their morbid curiosity. Helen surveyed the scene in disgust, effortlessly slipping into the role she knew best.

"Everybody—stand back! I'm a nurse!"

CHAPTER TWENTY-NINE

I

They had already circled the block twice, so focused on spotting the maroon Volvo which was Lisa and Chad's last known transportation, that Kathy nearly clipped the front end of the patrol car lurching across the center line as it turned from Dale Street, ramping away in the opposite direction.

"Wasn't that car parked in Aunt Maude's driveway?" Crystal asked from where she crouched beside Luke in the spacious floorboard in the back of Kathy's vehicle. A shotgun belonging to Kathy's late husband lay across the seat behind them, a nearly full box of ammunition beside it. It was a 12-gauge, the same kind Paulie used to hunt ducks and wild turkeys, and Luke felt comfortable, if a tad conspicuous, handling it.

"I believe so," said Kathy, slowing to watch the patrol car fade in her rearview mirror, marveling at its reckless speed in a residential neighborhood. She adjusted her mirror, only just noticing the dark clouds rolling in from the west.

"Do you think he saw us?"

"*Pffft*. I'm pretty sure that was the Tapscott boy. He wouldn't know his own reflection in a mirror. I didn't realize he was the one watching your Aunt Maude's property earlier. I was too afraid to look. That certainly makes things easier."

She started to turn onto Dale Street, but Jessica reached across from the passenger seat for the steering wheel, pulling it back.

"Hey! What are you doing?" Kathy protested as the car teetered drunkenly back into its lane. She cast a sideways glance at a woman she wasn't sure she trusted entirely.

"Not here," Jessica said. "Go down one street. We can cut across the yards on foot. If anyone is in there with Enid, they're sure to be keeping an eye out for us."

Kathy grudgingly complied, silently acknowledging the other woman's point. Her concern for Virginia's safety was challenging her patience, threatening to make her careless. They had already lost enough time pulling into the Speedway's lot on the way over, but Jessica had needed something from her Jeep, and it wasn't anything Kathy could question.

Clutched tightly in her right hand, Jessica held a Sig Sauer 9mm pistol, and its presence was oddly comforting. Other than for target practice, it was the first time she had removed it from the lockbox in her Jeep, but David McElroy had always insisted she go nowhere without it. The world was a dark and dangerous place, and a single, attractive woman like Jessica needed to be able to protect herself.

557

It was almost like her old friend was still watching out for her.

Kathy eased the car to the curb on Valley Street under the shade of an ancient maple. Maude's house was no longer visible, hidden behind a modest split-level and its uninviting rectangular lawn that was cordoned off by chain link fencing. The adjacent lot was occupied by an oblong trailer that had seen better days, and Enid's house loomed large behind it. Its yard was littered with abandoned children's toys and a plastic kiddie pool filled as much with leaves as murky water, but there were no cars in the drive, and the yard was completely open.

"We can cut through there," noted Jessica, absently pointing to the yard with the muzzle of her handgun.

Kathy nudged the gun below dash level with one finger, pointedly glaring at the other woman. "Can you be any more conspicuous? If one of these neighbors sees you flashing that thing around, they're bound to call 9-1-1."

Jessica smiled sheepishly. "I'm sorry. You're right. I'm not thinking straight." She checked for what seemed like the thousandth time to make sure the gun was loaded before tucking it into her jeans at the small of her back, letting her shirt fall over top of it. "There."

"All right, then," said Kathy. "What now?"

Crystal sat upright in the back seat. "We're going in," she said, as a lone, fat droplet of rain hit the windshield. "You stay here and keep the engine running. We might need to leave in a hurry."

Kathy's sigh of relief was audible. As concerned as she was about Enid, her stomach was in knots at the prospect of tagging along with this ragtag cavalry. She wasn't equipped to engage in any sort of conflict with Lisa and Chad, both of whom had proven themselves to be ruthless and violent. It had taken all of her resolve to accompany them this far.

"Okay, fine," she said. "And if I see anyone coming, whether it's police or that Volvo you described, I'll head your way and lay on the horn all the way around the block."

Luke lined his pockets with as many additional cartridges from the box of ammunition as they could hold. He opened the door and stepped down onto the street with Crystal following right behind. He held the shotgun against his profile so it wouldn't be so obvious to any of the neighbors who might happen to look his way. Jessica joined them, and for a long second, they looked at one another, gathering what courage they could muster.

Jessica was the first to look away, glancing at the darkening sky as nervous laughter erupted from her throat. "I don't know what in the hell I'm supposed to do," she said, absently patting the small of her back to ensure the gun was still there.

Crystal smiled sympathetically. "Like any of us do. We've been making this up as we go the whole goddamn way."

Luke scanned the neighborhood across the Explorer's hood. Residents had seemingly abandoned all outdoor activity, taking refuge ahead of the impending storm. "You any good with that thing?" he asked his mother, indicating the pistol she couldn't seem to leave alone.

"Rated sharpshooter on the range," she said with a hint of pride. "Not bad for a dispatcher. Never thought I'd have to use it, though. How about you?" She pointed to the shotgun tucked against Luke's side.

"Been hunting with Old Paulie since I was knee high to a grasshopper," he said. "I bagged my fair share of birds over the years."

Crystal looked nervously between the two. "What about me? I've got nothing."

"Stay behind me. I've got you covered," said Jessica, sounding far more confident than she felt.

"Give me a ten second head start," said Luke. "I'll go in through the rear, and the two of you go up the front. I'll try and clear the place before you ever get too far inside. Watch your backs and stay alert. We ain't no good at all to that little girl if we get ourselves killed."

<hr />

Luke cut around the right side of the trailer, keeping the shotgun against his profile and his head down. He held his breath as another clap of thunder sounded, this one closer than the last. Fat droplets of rain began to fall as he darted through swirling bed sheets that had been left pinned to a clothesline in the backyard. He was glad for the cover, expecting to be ordered off the property at any moment.

He approached Enid's house from the southwest corner of her lawn. A detached garage sat at the end of the drive on the opposite side with a small outbuilding at the rear of the postage-stamped sized yard. The house loomed ominously against a backdrop of threatening clouds, its Victorian structure overpowering the tiny plot of land upon which it was situated. No light shone through any of the rear-facing windows, and if Luke didn't know better, he would have thought the house was empty.

He stepped up onto a narrow, oblong porch just as a blinding bolt of lightning illuminated the block, unleashing a torrential rain that aggressively pounded the roof above Luke's head. He said a quick prayer as he reached for the knob on the back door and turned, but it was locked.

Shit!

The back porch was virtually devoid of furnishings, plants, or other bric-a-brac where a spare key might be hidden. The clean expanse has only home to an old wooden rocker and a small table that squatted beside it. Luke brushed across the top of the doorframe, cursing as he picked up a splinter for his troubles.

He examined the door, dismayed to find it was of solid construction with a sturdy deadbolt. He'd dislocate his shoulder before forcing his way through, but the nine-panes of tempered glass offered a glimmer of hope, even if the grills were made of unyielding metal. Without giving it a second thought, he brought the shotgun up and swung its stock into the pane nearest the lock, shattering its glass and sending it into the house. He flipped the gun around and used its barrel to remove any jagged pieces that remained before reaching his hand inside.

Please, oh please, oh please, he thought as he nudged aside the heavy blind covering the windows from the inside. *Let it have a thumb-turn release on the inside— not another key lock.*

He was almost euphoric when his fingers fumbled across the latch, and he twisted it, unlocking the door. He slipped into the darkness beyond, allowing the door to remain open long enough to get a feel for what appeared to be a mud room. Narrow and long, it had a low bench running along the exterior wall, above which a line of peg hooks provided ample storage for outerwear. Currently, the hooks were empty, and the floor was spotless—not a single pair of shoes in sight. A door on the far side of the room led into the house, and it was closed.

He prayed it wasn't locked, too.

As Luke eased the back door shut, the room was plunged into blackness, the heavy blind effectively squelching the dim light of the stormy day.

He had only taken a few steps into the room when the sound of the knob turning in the door across the room somehow broke through the cacophony of rain battering the siding. Pressing himself flush against the interior wall, Luke held his breath, watching as the door slowly swung into the house, revealing a lanky silhouette standing in its frame. His grip tightened on the shotgun as the figure reached into the room, feeling for a light switch.

The soft click of a switch, and ancient, yellowing fluorescents came to life overhead.

Luke's mouth turned to sand, his tongue sticking to the roof of his mouth as he recognized the dark-haired, lanky boy who stood in the doorway sneering as his hands were already fumbling for the pistol he had tucked into the sagging front of his baggy jeans.

<hr />

Jessica paused on the sidewalk, taking a moment to look up at the monstrosity that Enid called home. She shuddered with the realization the house bore more than a passing resemblance to the house made famous in Alfred Hitchcock's *Psycho*—minus the elevated view and shotgun motel, of course.

Crystal fidgeted behind Jessica, worried about being recognized by her former neighbors. This was the neighborhood where she had grown up, riding bikes and climbing trees. She had given her first kiss to Victor Nolan behind old man Pritchett's garage just across the way. She felt incredibly conspicuous and vulnerable.

"Are we just going to stand here?" she asked, urging Jessica forward.

"No, of course not," said Jessica, steeling her nerves and climbing the stairs. A bright flash of lightning lit up the sky, followed almost immediately by a ground-shaking peal of thunder, heralding a downpour that caused the women to scamper up the remaining stairs to take cover on the porch.

"I don't like this one bit," muttered Crystal, looking back out onto Dale Street where rain fell in sheets across the pavement. Gusts of wind shook the neighborhood trees like pom-poms, cooling the outside temperature by degrees almost instantaneously. "The last time I saw weather like this, Paula and I spent the night in a storm cellar, worrying we were gonna get blown to Oz."

"Paula?"

Crystal nodded absently. "She's been with us most of the way, but it all got to be a little too much for her. I hope she's okay now." Jessica inhaled sharply, and Crystal turned back towards the house. "What's wrong?"

Jessica indicated the front door.

It was open.

The gust of wind had blown it inward, and Crystal could see the familiar carpet runner just inside, but the lack of interior lighting and the storm's gloom made it impossible to see much more beyond that.

"Didn't Kathy say the door was locked, and the key was gone?" Jessica asked, thinking she might have misunderstood.

"Uh-huh," nodded Crystal, quickly killing that hope.

Jessica fished the pistol out from the small of her back. She took a tentative step inside, sweeping the gun left and then right as her eyes became acclimated to the gloom.

Nothing moved inside the foyer, not even air.

As Crystal followed Jessica into the house, she eased the front door closed, effectively cutting much of the storm's angry volume. Another bolt of lightning flared through the windows, pushing back the shadows if only for an instant, but it was mildly reassuring. Nothing came lunging from the shadows at them.

"Where to now?" Jessica asked, her voice barely more than a whisper. She followed Crystal's gaze to the grand staircase that led to the second floor, the carpet runner acting as a guide to the gloom at the very top. As before, a high-backed wheelchair remained parked at the bottom of the stairs, and a motorized chair sat empty at the top of its rail, waiting to safely convey its elderly owner to the first floor upon command.

"Her bedroom's up there," said Crystal. "That's where she was when I spoke to her earlier."

Jessica took the lead, continuing to shield Crystal as she began ascending the stairs, staying close to the outer edges in the hopes of minimizing any squeaks or loose boards that might betray their presence. The air inside the house was stifling, and both women were bathed in nervous perspiration as they climbed the steps one at a time, the sound of the grandfather clock disproportionately loud in their ears.

Once they reached the top of the stairs, Jessica looked back to Crystal for guidance. A hallway cut to the right with two closed doors along either side, but Crystal nodded straight ahead, where Enid's master suite occupied the northwest corner.

It stood open.

Jessica inched forward with Crystal right behind. She suddenly stopped and pulled back, grimacing. "What's that smell?"

Crystal took a tenuous whiff, trying to pinpoint the difference from when she had been here earlier. She always thought that Enid's house had a certain redolent aroma that was fairly common for women of her generation, a heady blend of lavender, furniture polish, and mothballs, but lurking within this olfactory profile was something acrid and sickly sweet. She frowned, shaking her head. "I don't think I want to know."

Luke crossed the narrow room in three long strides, swinging the stock of his shotgun like a baseball bat as Chad brought the pistol up, disengaging its safety. Luke connected with the back of Chad's hand solidly, sending the gun flying from his grasp.

"Mother*fucker*, that *hurt!*" Chad howled, massaging his reddening knuckles with his other hand, while glaring at Luke with raw hatred even before recognition dawned. *"Hey*—you're the asshole from the highway—in the car with Crystal Bright," he sputtered, before adding, "And the girl."

Luke flipped the shotgun around, raising it to his shoulder and sighting Chad down the long barrel. He steadied his aim and nodded sharply, muscles tightening along his square jawline as he clenched his teeth and tried to ignore the perspiration stinging the corners of his eyes. His finger rested on the trigger.

"That's right," he said. "Now, you just stay where you are."

The corners of Chad's mouth twitched in amusement, and Luke found it exceedingly difficult to hold his gaze, unsettled by the extreme dilation of Chad's pupils.

"Just tell us where she is," said Chad. He furtively licked his lips in a serpentine manner as he took a small step forward. "We might just let you and your girlfriend live."

Luke remained stoic, holding the shotgun steady as relief coursed through him.

Just tell us where she is…

They hadn't gotten to Virginia, at least not yet.

"I'm warnin' you, fella, *stay where you are*," Luke barked, his voice cracking from his parched throat. His finger fidgeted against the trigger as Chad's crooked smile widened.

"Are you going to *shoot me*, big guy?" asked Chad, his voice taunting as he threw his arms up in mock surrender.

"I will if I have to," said Luke, projecting a certainty he wasn't entirely sure he felt. It was one thing to imagine a lethal ending to their nightmare scenario, but here in the moment, the trigger seemed immutable. This wasn't anything like shooting a deer. The ramification of taking another human life was proving a greater obstacle than he had imagined—it wasn't a position in which he had ever expected to find himself.

Almost as if he could read Luke's mind, Chad's smile twisted into a smirk. "Will you?" he asked, cocking his head curiously and taking another small step forward. "This is coming from the same guy who didn't have *the balls* to finish this back there, out on the highway. Why, you had us *dead to rights,* fucker! You could have squashed me like a bug between the front of your car and the side of ours, but *no-o-o-o.* Pulled out at the last minute, afraid to get your hands dirty, running off like the little pussy you are."

"I'm warning you, *friend,*" Luke said, adjusting his sight and involuntarily taking a step backward. "One more step, and I will blow your motherfucking head off."

Chad pursed his lips and scratched his chin, narrowing his eyes in scrutiny. *"Will you, now?"*

In one fluid motion, he seized the barrel of the shotgun and twisted, wrenching it from Luke's grip. He reared back and immediately thrusted forward, attempting to coldcock Luke in the face with its wooden stock, but Luke stumbled backward and out of range. He barely managed to keep his feet underneath himself, watching in horror as Chad flipped the gun around, preparing to use it as intended.

"No," Luke growled, throwing himself at Chad before he could take aim. He seized the younger man by both of his thin, sinewy arms.

The instant Luke's hands made contact with Chad's skin, both men's heads snapped back as if struck by any one of the frequent bolts of lightning haphazardly punctuating the storm raging outside.

Luke's vision faded to white while the world fell away.

‖

Virginia's spasms stopped as suddenly as they had started.

"Should I call an ambulance? I should call an ambulance. Let me call an ambulance," fussed a horse-faced girl who purported to be the manager on duty but didn't look old enough to drive a car. Her nametag read, 'Marge,' and she hovered alongside customers and crew in handwringing indecision as Helen tended to the girl's episode.

Paula's face had drained of all color as she chewed a knuckle, watching in horror from the other side of the table and wondering when they might ever catch a single, solitary break. If an ambulance came, they'd be followed by the police, and Paula would be stuck here for who knows how long—probably taken away for questioning as she was currently in the company of a little girl who was the subject of a tri-state AMBER alert. Suze was just a few short blocks away, and Paula couldn't get out of this goddamned Wendy's!

"No," said Helen, her mind working quickly. "Please don't call—I don't think that's necessary."

It didn't behoove her any more than it did Paula to have the authorities involved at this juncture, and it was more than a little ironic that both women were thinking of Suze. Helen was prepared to offer Paula and this little girl up to Suze in exchange for Lisa's safe release. For the first time since crossing Suze's path, she felt like she actually had some leverage with the raven-haired killer and her psychotic boyfriend.

Marge seemed less sure, her handwringing reaching new heights as she struggled with protocol. "Are you sure? I'm sorry, I've never had this happen to a customer before. I'm not sure what the procedure is. I think maybe I should file an incident report? I really don't want to get written up."

Helen summoned her best soothing smile. "It's alright, dear. I'm a nurse, remember? I'll take the young lady to the emergency room straightaway so she can be checked out, but I'm sure the worst of it has passed."

Customers were already beginning to drift back to their own tables, sensing the show was over.

"Are you sure?" Marge asked, her eagerness evident. She was only too happy to let someone else take responsibility for the situation at hand.

"I am," said Helen, absently patting Virginia's bare leg as the little girl stared vacantly at the ceiling.

Virginia's skin was beyond pale, and Paula would have worried she wasn't breathing if it weren't for the occasional flutter of her eyelids. Paula felt her own anxiety subside as the threat of sirens diminished. If the old nurse insisted on taking Virginia to the hospital, fine, but she could surely drop Paula off first. And if she wasn't willing to do that, Paula would simply dash across the street and into the neighborhoods. She felt confident she could find her way. Even though she'd never visited Lucasville before, Dale Street was vaguely familiar, but her mind was beyond its capacity for connecting any more dots.

"Are you ready, dear?" Helen asked, and it took Paula a few long seconds to realize she was addressing her.

She nodded, getting up from the table and easing around it.

"Julia, can you carry little Claudia to the car?" asked Helen, invoking the aliases Paula had adopted for them as she gathered her things. "Your back has got to be stronger than mine."

"Um, sure," said Paula, squatting down and working her arms underneath the prone girl's body.

"Make sure and support her head," urged Helen, moving toward the door. "Yes, just like that."

She held the door open while Paula carried Virginia out to the parking lot, startled when a fat droplet of cold rain landed on her head. She used the key fob to unlock the doors of her bright yellow rental car.

"Hurry and lay her down in the back," said Helen, bustling across to the driver's door. "It looks like the heavens are about to open up."

Paula followed her instructions, easing Virginia into the back where she stared like a mannequin at the car's charcoal ceiling. She shut the door and paused, contemplating her own next move. She wasn't sure if she should risk getting trapped in the passenger seat without knowing for certain she could trust Helen to drop her off a few blocks over.

Helen looked across the top of the car at her and sighed. "What are you waiting for, Julia? Let's go! We're about to get soaked!"

As if by invitation, more fat raindrops fell from the heavens, multiplying at an alarming rate. Paula hesitated for only an instant before ducking into the passenger seat and pulling the door closed behind her.

"Heavens to Betsy, look just look at it come down!" marveled Helen, starting the car as the sky brightened beneath a webwork of lightning. The engine was indiscernible beneath the rain pelting off the car's surface, and visibility was greatly reduced, even once Helen had activated the windshield wipers on their highest setting.

"Hey, listen," said Paula tentatively, hating herself for the lie she was about to tell. "You really don't have to take Claudia to the hospital. It's not like this is the first time this ever happened."

"Really?" asked Helen, shifting the car into reverse before craning her neck to peer through the rear glass. "You sure seemed unsettled by it."

"Well—" Paula hedged as her mind raced through plausibilities. "I'm not usually the one who has to deal with it. Angel is so much better than me in a crisis."

"And Angel is the sister you just spoke to?"

"Yes, ma'am, she is. And she's just around the corner from here. You could just drop us off and be on your way." Paula tried not to sound overly eager, but the look Helen gave her was dubious.

Helen shifted the car into drive and nosed to the edge of the parking lot. Traffic had evaporated as the rain swept US 23 in sheets.

"Well?" the nurse asked expectantly.

Paula blinked. "Well, what?"

"You'll have to give me directions if we're ever going to get there."

⚬————◆————⚬

Lisa crossed the street quickly, her left hand shielding her eyes against bits of debris carried by the sudden gusts of wind that forewarned of the imminent storm. She kept her right hand tucked against her side, clutching a bloody butcher knife so tightly her knuckles were practically numb.

She hurried up the short gravel driveway, passing through its open chain link gate and hurried to the door along the end of what had originally been a breezeway but had since been enclosed. She expected the door to be locked and was fully prepared to batter her way in, but she was pleasantly surprised when the knob turned easily in her hand. The door swung inward, and weeks' worth of hot, pent-up air washed over Lisa. She allowed the house its moment to exhale before stepping inside and closing the door behind her.

She paused just inside the breezeway, taking a moment to examine the organized piles of clutter that lined both sides of a room that was likely a carport at one time. Gauzy, moth-eaten curtains permitted just enough ambient light that Lisa could see her way around without the need for additional illumination. It was just as well. Judging from the unsettling absence of white noise, the electricity had been turned off for some time.

To Lisa's left, boxes of fading fabric were stacked beside teetering columns of newspapers. Other boxes were labeled in black marker, spindly block letters proclaiming RECORDS, SWEATERS, NICKETY NACKITYS—things that had long since served their purpose only to be packed away and forgotten. Along the right wall was a mismatched holy trinity of outdated appliances—an avocado green stove, a burnt sienna washing machine, and a harvest gold dryer.

None of it was even remotely familiar to Lisa, and yet something about the room itself was. It was an incongruity that made her a little light-headed, or maybe that was just the extreme heat—she couldn't be sure. With the back of her hand, she swept away droplets of perspiration that threatened to breach the natural defense of her eyebrows and run down into her eyes.

A yellowing plastic runner separated the room into equal halves, leading to a short set of cinderblock stairs that stepped up into the main part of the house, its interior hidden behind yet another closed door.

Lisa climbed the stairs and turned the knob, not quite so surprised this time when the door was unlocked.

It was like the house was waiting *for her.*

She backed down a step before pushing the door inward, removing herself from the direct path of stagnant exhaust that seized its first opportunity to escape. Lisa ascended into a dark-paneled living room, almost every square inch of its walls covered with fading portraits of unsmiling relatives, most of whom were undoubtedly deceased. Thick, goldenrod carpeting covered the floor with well-worn patterns of traffic crisscrossing the room. An overstuffed recliner sat between the main entrance and a picture window looking out through more gauzy curtains into the front yard, and it was catercorner to a matching sofa. Both ancient pieces were encased in protective plastic and aimed toward a console television in the corner. Behind the television was a half-wall separating the living room from a small kitchen, its turquoise appliances in stark contrast to the walnut cabinetry.

Lisa closed her eyes and inhaled deeply as something within her subconscious slowly stirred. Whispers of voices from the past teased from the corners of her perception before racing back from where they came.

I've been here before, she thought to herself, slowly circling to survey the room. *But how? And when?*

Her gaze landed on a school picture of Crystal Bright—then Williams— hanging on the wall amongst the others. She looked to be maybe thirteen, her eyes looking unfocused between bottle-bottomed glasses. Her lopsided dark brown hair suggested a style achieved at home versus a salon, but even then, her smile was captivating. Lisa tried to remember herself at that age, but it was so very long ago. Upon further inspection, she found other pictures of Crystal scattered around the room, a photographic chronology presented in no particular order. Lisa studied the pictures earnestly, searching for some sense of self behind those eyes but finding nothing. Despite their obvious physical similarities, this girl was a complete stranger.

As Lisa turned toward the kitchen, her attention was drawn to another smaller collection of framed photographs standing on top of the television. A row of five gangly-limbed girls stood side-by-side with their arms linked in front of a dilapidated farmhouse. One was smiling, another scowling, and one was caught with her mouth open, frozen mid-sentence. But the two on the leftmost end were looking at one another, identical bemused expressions captured for all eternity in sepia tones.

Lisa lifted the picture from where it rested, leaving its footprint in dust on the top of the console television. She looked from one woman to the other, barely able to believe what she was seeing.

One of these women was Nanna Grace.

Chad stumbled out into the raging storm, missing a step on his way off the low porch and sprawling headlong into the muddying yard. He was oblivious to the various grunts and groans that fell from his own lips. His useless eyes were adrift in a sea of stars, and blistering pain cycled through his head, making it impossible to focus beyond his panic.

What in the hell did that bastard do to me? he thought, digging at his eyes with his knuckles.

The kaleidoscope of stars obscuring his vision allowed a small pinpoint of focus through, and when Chad saw the blood covering his hands, his heart lurched in his chest, certain he must have once again been shot. What else could explain the searing pain cleaving his head in two? He frantically used his fingers to palpate his own skull, expecting to discover a pulpy mass of leaking brains at any moment.

It wasn't until the coppery taste invaded his mouth that the sensation of a runny nose registered. He dabbed at his nose tentatively, fresh blood coating his fingertips as he pulled them away to examine through his extraordinarily narrow field of vision. He barely had time to register relief before another wave of agony ripped through his head, turning his stomach inside out. With a horrific hork, he emptied its contents all over Enid's lawn, his muscles continuing to spasm long after it was completely empty. He felt light-headed as the dry heaves passed, and he wasn't sure how much longer he could cling to consciousness. He began a slow, steady crawl toward the garage, where he hoped he might take shelter until the storm passed and he felt better. As it was, the torrential rain had saturated his clothing, weighing him down more than he would have ever imagined in his weakened state.

Three feet shy of his destination, another bolt of pain exploded through his brain, and he clutched at both sides of his head, howling like a wounded animal before dropping face-first into a muddy puddle of rainwater and going still.

CHAPTER THIRTY

Luke floated weightlessly on a sea of pure light.

Was this death? He couldn't be sure.

He looked down, examining what he could see of himself, and nothing looked out of sorts. He felt like he was supposed to be doing something, but he couldn't quite put his finger on it.

Oh, well. It must not be too important.

He closed his eyes and laid his back against the softest pillow of nothingness, feeling relaxed and utterly at peace.

Softly at first but slowly gaining volume, a familiar tune wormed its way into his consciousness. The corners of his mouth drifted upwards as recognition dawned.

Cotton-Eyed Joe.

He opened his eyes to a cloudless blue sky. The world tilted as his perception shifted, and he found himself standing in a field of tall bluegrass, a soft breeze gently stirring.

Luke's smile widened as he recognized the thick copse of trees at the far end of the field where he used to sneak cigarettes as a boy. To his left, dense woods separated this property from the neighbors, and to his right was fenced-off pastureland shared by three cows, two horses, and a handful of goats.

The song was getting louder, and Luke turned to find himself in the last place he ever expected.

He was home.

Paulie's cabin was off in the distance, and the old man himself was on the rickety back porch, putting everything he had into the jig his spindly legs performed. He seemed oblivious to Luke's presence, even as Luke began to gleefully wave his arms above his head.

"Paulie!" he shouted, his voice muted and flat in his own ears. He flexed his jaw, trying to unclog them, but to no avail.

He began jogging towards the house, eager to have another conversation with the man who raised him. His feet moved faster as he closed the distance, giving him the peculiar sensation of floating just above the ground.

Luke had nearly reached the base of the weathered and warped stairs leading to the back porch when Paulie finally noticed him. The smile dropped from Paulie's face as his rhythmic stomping faltered before stopping altogether. The volume of the music diminished as if remotely quieted by some unseen hand.

"Boy?" he asked, clearly dismayed to find Luke standing before him.

Luke couldn't keep the grin from spreading across his face as he bounded up the steps, his arms wide and ready to embrace the old man. "Paulie! I've never been so glad to see your ugly old face. I—"

He stopped short as Paulie pulled away, recoiling from Luke's outstretched arms. "What in the Sam Hill are you *doing* here?" Paulie demanded, scowling at his protégé. "I told you not to come back for a year. What's the matter with you? Can't you follow simple instructions?"

Luke stared at the old man, confused by his reaction. Never in all of their time together had Paulie been put out by Luke's mere presence, and the look of disappointment on the old man's face was a dagger to his heart. He couldn't imagine what he'd done to receive such a frosty reception now.

"But, Paulie," he stammered, barely able to meet the other man's disapproving glare. "I just need to rest up for a minute. I ain't never been so tired before in all my life. I'll just lay down in my room for a minute, if that's okay."

Luke shifted toward the door, but Paulie was quicker, stepping nimbly into his path and blocking the entrance.

"You'll do no such thing, boy," he said, crossing his arms in front of him. "You don't belong here."

Luke stared up at him in wounded astonishment. "But Paulie—"

"Now, *stop it*," Paulie commanded, his tone harsher than any Luke had ever heard the old man use. "You've got important work to do, and you can't very well be doing it from here. Go on, now. *Scat!*"

He shooed with both hands for Luke to get off the porch, but Luke's feet were frozen in place. He couldn't believe what he was hearing. Tiny pinpricks of pain blossomed inside his head as a vague memory sharpened at the periphery of his consciousness—Paulie's prostrate form lying peacefully in the only casket Luke could afford, his eyes closed for all eternity with his gnarled fingers interlocked across his chest. Luke acknowledged the memory with a gasp, his eyes locked on Paulie's.

"You're—" He couldn't bring himself to say the word as yet another possibility landed like an anvil. "Am I dead, too?" he managed to ask, desperately afraid of the answer.

He didn't think it possible, but the look of utter disappointment on Paulie's face deepened. "I ain't got time to be answering stupid questions, boy. Now, get on out of here. Don't make me get my shotgun an' chase you off."

With that, he reached out to turn Luke around, and the moment his calloused hands brushed Luke's arm, the pinpricks of pain in Luke's head detonated into agony, snapping the younger man's head back as his eyes rolled towards the heavens. He was assaulted by a slideshow of relentless images, and with each one, pieces of his memory fell into place before launching into a sequence of coming attractions. Paula lay at the foot of a short run of stairs, her pale face in stark contrast to the crimson blood covering her arm and staining her clothing. Crystal tangling with her doppelganger in the tight confines of a bathroom while little Virginia Parnell fidgeted nearby, all alone and unable to look away. Jessica sprawled across a cracked and yellowing plastic carpet runner, bleeding profusely as the young man named Chad stood over her, his fingers flexing in anticipation of what he might do next. Crystal's lifeless eyes stared up from the bottom of the bathtub as her vindictive twin seized Virginia's head with both hands, lifting her off the ground as her little legs pinwheeled helplessly in the air…

Luke cried out as the images raggedly cut to black, a reel of film unexpectedly cut short before the climax could completely unfold. It was soon replaced by images somehow even more disturbing. Armed troops of unknown origin storming suburban neighborhoods, individual faces protected by tactical masks that gave the soldiers a decidedly insectile appearance. Civilian bodies abandoned in the streets, bleeding and mutilated, sightless eyes frozen in horror at the escalating carnage. Thick, black smoke billowed into the air as houses were torched without regard as to who or what may still be inside. Helicopters peppered the hazy skyline, unleashing a mixture of toxic fumes and live rounds of ammunition into a community utterly unprepared for this type of aggression. Years of fighting its wars strictly on foreign soil, the United States had grown complacent, lulled into a sense of false security that such things could ever happen on its home turf.

The pain behind Luke's eyes intensified, blotting out the horrific sampling of devastation as he placed his hands over his temples and screamed at the top of his lungs.

⚬———◆———⚬

Jessica stumbled sideways against the doorframe, practically knocking Crystal down as she brought the back of her hand to her mouth, fighting desperately to keep the contents of her stomach. She brought her pistol up and swept the room from left-to-right, alert for any sudden or unexpected movement from the shadowy recesses of the room or its attached master bath, but there was nothing nor no one else to see.

Eager to see what sparked such a reaction, Crystal ducked beneath Jessica's arm but only managed a single step into the room before grinding to a halt, transfixed by the grotesque spectacle on display.

Enid's face was forever frozen in a mask of horrific agony, her widened eyes bulging from their sockets. Her wrists were bound by sheets to the tall bedposts behind her while her ankles were bound together, approximating a pose of crucifixion. Her fragile frame was splayed open from throat to pubis with her blood-soaked nightgown spread about her perversely like a crimson angel's

571

wings. Her violated entrails were scattered willy-nilly about her corpse, the hideous aftermath of an amateurish and careless autopsy.

"But—I was just *here*. How could this—this—" Crystal managed before a strangled sob stole her voice away. She staggered out into the hallway only to retch all over the landing's immaculate antique rug.

Jessica backed out of the room, shifting her focus to the hallway that bisected the upper floor, feeling extremely vulnerable. The monsters responsible for slaughtering Enid could wait behind any one of those four closed doors, and even with the cold steel gripped tightly in her hands, Jessica felt entirely ill-equipped to face opponents capable of unleashing such monstrous evil on someone so elderly and frail.

"Should we clear the rest of the house or wait for Luke?" Jessica asked, looking for any sort of reinforcement. She didn't feel qualified to be making decisions that were essentially life or death.

Crystal wasn't thinking any more clearly than Jessica.

Dizzy from retching herself into dry heaves and the sweltering heat trapped inside the house, she allowed herself to drift to the bay window across the landing and perch on the edge of its upholstered window seat, leaning her forehead against the cool pane of glass that looked down into the neighborhood below, the view partially obscured by torrential rain falling in relentless sheets.

She blinked, pulling her face back and staring down into the street.

"What?" asked Jessica, moving closer while keeping an eye on the shadowy corridor to their left.

"I—I'm not sure," said Crystal. "There's a car pulling into my old driveway."

Jessica leaned in, peering over Crystal's shoulder. Sure enough, a bright yellow Ford Focus had nosed through the open chain link gate, its brake lights bright as the car idled in place.

"Well, that's certainly not a police car," Jessica observed, and Crystal nodded absently.

Crystal watched as the passenger door opened, and a young girl ducked out into the rain, shielding herself futilely against the wind-driven precipitation. She scurried to the rear door and opened it, leaning in to retrieve something. There was something about her and the way that she moved that was vaguely familiar, but she wouldn't stand still long enough for Crystal to get a good look at her.

Lightning seared the air followed immediately by a tremendous boom that shook the entire house. Crystal flinched, involuntarily pulling away from the window with the realization that the storm must be right over top of them now. Her vision was marred by the phantom image of the lightning strike, and it took a few seconds to clear, but once it did, she gasped.

"Oh, my God," she said, slowly standing up.

"*What is it?*" hissed Jessica, keeping her voice low. She couldn't shake the feeling they weren't alone in the house.

"It's Virginia," said Crystal, her hand fluttering to her heart. "And I'm pretty sure that's Paula who's carrying her."

Jessica followed Crystal's gaze just in time to see the rain-drenched figures take shelter through the open door at the side of the house. She looked to Crystal for confirmation. "Are you sure?"

Crystal couldn't contain the relieved laughter that burbled up through her throat. She nodded, feeling real hope for the first time since the little girl had disappeared. "And Virginia's alive!"

Jessica grabbed Crystal's hand and pulled her toward the top of the stairs. "Let's keep her that way."

———◇———

Helen slowed in front of the address Paula had given her, squinting at the block house through foggy windows the compact car's defroster failed to clear.

"It looks awfully dark," she said dubiously, unaware that Paula was no longer paying attention. The young girl's eyes were locked on the house with an expression just short of astonishment.

This was Crystal Bright's house.

No wonder the address seemed familiar to Paula. It had been featured in countless fanzines that Paula devoured when she lived at home, dreaming of someday meeting her idol. She could almost see the caption now—*The Humble Beginnings of an American Sweetheart.* Despite having spent the last several days with the woman herself, Paula couldn't help but get a little lost in the surreality of it all. A picture of this very house was tacked on her bedroom wall back in Morgan, the starting point of Crystal's career chronology as seen through the eyes of her Number One Fan—and yet here she was, parked directly in front of it.

"Pull in," Paula said absently, and when that brought a sharp look from Helen, she added, "Please."

With a sigh, Helen pulled the car into the driveway and through its open chain link gate. "I really don't like the looks of this," she muttered, shifting the car into park. "I mean, look. The door's just standing wide open."

Paula was already unfastening her seatbelt. "Angel's waiting for me," she said.

"But—it's *pouring* out there," protested Helen. "You might as well sit a spell and wait for the worst of this to blow over."

But Paula wasn't listening. She had already opened the passenger door, the rain blowing in as she stepped out. Instantly drenched, she pivoted to the back door and pulled it open, leaning in to where Virginia lay, staring vacantly at the car's ceiling.

"Oh, *no*," Helen said, reaching between the seats to pry Paula's hands away from the girl. "Don't tell me you're hauling poor little Claudia out into all this

573

after everything she's just been through! That's just *foolish*, Julia! Leave her here with me. There's no need to—*oh!*"

Helen's eyes widened in shock as Paula smacked her hand away and pulled Virginia's prostrate form toward her, a look of grim determination on her face. A steady stream of nearly unintelligible pleas fell from Paula's lips, begging for the girl's cooperation, if only just a little, but to no avail. Virginia was as stiff as a board. The term *rigor mortis* came unbidden, and Helen couldn't stifle a shiver as Paula finally succeeded in freeing the girl from the back seat and tucking her rigid body against her own. She bumped the door closed with her hip before hustling around the front of the car and disappearing through the open doorway without even a second's hesitation.

Helen fiddled with the gearshift for a moment, unsure of what to do next. If Suze was inside waiting for her sister—whatever her name might be—odds were fair that Lisa might be in there, too. But after being locked in the cellar of Lisa's house by that violent psychopath, Helen was hesitant to follow the girls inside. She was certainly no physical match for the dark-haired woman whose utter contempt for the nurse had been palpable. It would probably be best for her to find a payphone and call the authorities. They would certainly be better equipped to rescue Lisa from her demented captors.

Helen stared at the dark windows along the front of the house, unable to shake the feeling that she was being watched. The dark-haired boy hadn't been any less menacing than Suze, even after being shot in the chest. Everything about the two of them set Helen's nerves on edge, and with a resolute nod, she shifted the car in reverse, her decision made.

A blinding flash of strobing light tore through the neighborhood followed by a deafening crack of thunder, prompting a startled cry from Helen's mouth. From the corner of her eye, she saw sudden movement to her left, but it wasn't until the heavy branch fell across the rear glass, causing the compact car to bounce on its suspension that she realized lightning had struck the towering silver maple in the front yard, shearing a limb and sending it crashing down onto the back of her rental. The back glass splintered but held, a webwork of cracks radiating outward from the point of impact.

Adrenaline raced through Helen's veins as she breathed deeply from the ionized air that lifted the tiny hairs at the base of her neck. She shifted the car back into park and slapped the steering wheel with both hands, almost whimpering in frustration. The car was pinned in place, removing Helen's safest and smartest option. She cast her eyes around the interior, looking for something—*anything* she might use as a weapon, but the only thought that came to mind was the rental car's ignition key. She switched the engine off and extracted the key, palming its black fob. Squinting through the downpour that battered the car's hood, she looked for something in the yard that might serve her needs better, finally landing on a rusty hoe that lay on the ground near the door.

A car key and a gardening implement—cold comfort as protection, but better than nothing, she supposed.

Helen sighed before closing her eyes and pressing her hands together, her lips moving soundlessly in prayer as she steeled herself for whatever was to come. She unfastened her seatbelt and opened the door, stepping out into the driving rain.

In the gloom of the tiny kitchen, Lisa stood before the sink with her hand hovering near a window that looked out into a surprisingly large backyard. Giant puddles had sprung up where the lawn was saturated, but Lisa wasn't focused on any of that. Her eyes were fixed on the four teacups lining the windowsill, each turned exactly so. The pattern was unmistakable; she'd only seen it every single day when serving Nanna Grace her afternoon tea. Discovering more of the teacups here felt like synchronicity as ghosts from her past niggled at the corners of her consciousness, teasing recognition while withholding revelation. She eyed the cabinets, certain she would find eight more teacups if she bothered to look, but she didn't require any more confirmation of the undeniable connection.

She went back into the living room and turned right, passing into a smaller sitting room that looked out onto the concrete slab porch that fronted the house. The glass in its picture window was unobstructed by curtains, yet little light found its way in due to the tangled shrubbery that crowded the porch from all sides.

Lisa's fingers trailed along the dust-covered top of a vintage stereo console centered along the wall to her right, and hints of Elvis Presley crooning hymns through the lattice-fronted speakers pierced the veil suppressing her memories.

Yes, she had most definitely been here before.

Straight ahead was a claustrophobic bathroom, its dated Pepto-Bismol pink fixtures barely leaving room to turn around. She kneeled by the tub, placing the bloody butcher knife on its rim before turning on the faucet. She dipped her fingers into its murky flow until the water ran clear and began to warm. She slid the stopper into the drain and watched as the tub slowly began to fill.

575

Luke sat upright with a start, completely disoriented in a narrow room he didn't recognize. Gusts of wind carried rain through a door that stood open, and Luke quickly surveyed his surroundings, only to find himself alone. His head throbbed with every accelerated beat of his heart, prompted by an inexplicable dread that he was running out of time.

But running out of time for what?

His thoughts stubbornly refused to coalesce. He dug at his eyes with his knuckles, breathing deeply to calm the panic that threatened to overtake him.

When he spotted a shotgun discarded against the wall, he suddenly remembered the other man—his brother, Chad. He whipped his head around, giving the room a more thorough inspection, but there was no one else to see.

An interior door leading into the house stood open, and Luke abruptly remembered where he was.

Enid Bowles' house.

They had come to check on the elderly shut-in when Kathy Duncan was unable to reach her just after Crystal had visited. Crystal and Jessica had given Luke a head start to approach the house from the rear while they would approach from the front, but it felt like hours had passed.

How long had he been out?

Driven by the certainty that he was already too late, he grabbed the gun and proceeded into the house, his senses heightened as he moved through the empty and eerily silent kitchen. It took a second to recognize the total absence of white noise and ambient light from the industrial appliances. The storm had knocked the power out at some point, and Luke stepped out into the shadows of a darkened corridor that led to the front of the house.

Once in the foyer, Luke paused, hopeful for any indication that the ladies were safely upstairs, awaiting his arrival. Rain lashed at the windows and siding as he peered hopefully up the long flight of stairs.

There was nothing to see.

The stagnant air carried a trace of something acrid, and Luke grimaced as he placed his hand on the banister, beginning his ascent to the second floor.

"Angel?"

Lisa stiffened at the timid voice drifting in from the shadows of the living room. A slow smile spread across her face as she turned the water off, palming the handle of the knife and shielding it from view with her body. Suze's idiotic sister had returned, a willing worm ready to be hooked and dangled like bait to lure Crystal and her farmhand in, and wherever they went, the little girl was sure to be nearby. This wasn't just a matter of dumb luck—it was fate. Lisa could feel the stars aligning with a near gravitational pull. Keeping the knife hidden, she stood and turned to face her new arrival.

She froze, unable to suppress the short, sharp bark of laughter that escaped her lips.

Just two rooms away, Virginia Parnell peeked out from behind Paula's legs, her pensive eyes wide as saucers as she absently sucked on a tiny forefinger. They stood just inside the living room, briefly illuminated by another flash of lightning.

"Oh—it's you," said Paula, clearly disappointed. "Where's my sister? You said she came back."

"She did," said Lisa, fighting to keep from smirking. "She's eager to see you, too. She's in the other room lying down. All this shifting barometric pressure gave her a whopper of a headache."

She stepped out of the bathroom and nodded to a closed door to her right, suddenly certain that it was a tiny bedroom she had seen before. A fleeting image of Crystal as a chestnut-haired girl came and went, followed by a surge of hatred unlike anything she had ever felt before. Her fingers tightened on the grip of the knife she held behind her back.

Paula took a hesitant step forward before stopping again. "What are you doing in Crystal Bright's house? Isn't this trespassing?"

"Technically, I guess it is, but I could ask the same of you." Lisa took a step closer, her eyes glued to the little girl hiding behind Paula. Virginia's fear practically radiated in waves from her trembling frame as she clutched Paula's jeans.

"I'm the president of the Crystal Bright Fan Club," Paula said, as if the position gave her an all-access backstage pass to Crystal's entire life. "Where's your friend—Chad?"

Lisa pursed her lips. "He's—around." It was getting harder to fight the smirk.

"Oh, my goodness—*Lisa?*"

The familiar voice was like nails on a chalkboard as something stirred in the darkness from the breezeway. Helen Martin rested the garden hoe she clutched in one hand just inside the door as she nudged her way past Paula and Virginia to stand dripping on the living room carpet. Her short hair was plastered to her head as she stared at Lisa in stunned silence.

"I almost didn't recognize you," the nurse said. "You changed your hair."

Lisa absently touched an auburn strand, nearly having forgotten that she had colored it and struck dumb for a response that made any sense. Helen's ample frame was now between Lisa and the little girl, and she craned her neck to keep sight of the child, but Helen seemed to match her every move, determined to be the focus of Lisa's attention.

Grimacing with impatience, Lisa was startled when Helen burst into tears of joy, holding her arms wide as she crossed to where Lisa stood. "I was so afraid they'd hurt you," she blubbered, pulling Lisa's rigid form against her ample bosom and hugging her tightly. "Now, let's get out of here before the others get back. I told you I'd keep watch over you, didn't I? Now, let's—*unnnh*."

A sharp pain registered at Helen's side. As she slowly stepped backwards, she felt the blade of the knife as it retraced its path, exiting her abdomen. Lisa's knuckles were stark white on the wooden handle as she held it out, curiously observing Helen's face as it first registered surprise followed almost immediately by confusion.

"Lisa? I don't—" Helen's voice trailed away as she brought her hand to her face, struggling to make sense of the blood-covered spectacle.

Lisa sighed. "You probably won't believe this, Helen, but I'm really sorry it had to come to this. This isn't even your fight, but you never could take a hint and just mind your own fucking business."

She drew the knife back and plunged it into the startled nurse's torso repeatedly, each blow more savage than the last.

From only fifteen feet away, Virginia Parnell began to scream.

———◆———

Crystal and Jessica paused near the trunk of the little yellow car, startled to see that it was now pinned beneath a massive tree limb.

"I guess we know what that last round of lightning struck," said Jessica, peering through the passenger glass to see if anyone remained in the car. "It's empty. Whoever it was must have gone inside the house. Are you ready?"

Crystal nodded, trying to project confidence but feeling like a drowned rat. Jessica didn't look much better. Her grip on the pistol was noticeably shaky, and the pair didn't look the part of formidable opponents.

A piercing shriek cut through the bluster of the storm. The women looked at each other and then the house, hesitating only a second before charging forward and entering through the darkened doorway that taunted them with its open invitation.

Jessica paused just inside the doorway, giving her eyes a chance to adjust to the cluttered, gloomy space while Crystal charged forward, drawn by the girl's distress and undeterred by the familiar, claustrophobic stacks that lined the breezeway walls. Nothing much had changed in the time since she'd called this place home.

She bounded up the trio of cinderblock stairs into the living room, placing her hands protectively on Virginia's shoulder and prompting an even higher-pitched noise from the child. Virginia's head whipped around, panicked by the possibilities of who or what may have grabbed her from behind, but when her eyes focused on Crystal's face, relief flooded her features followed by hysterical tears. She clung to Crystal's legs with all her might, nearly knocking Crystal back down the stairs and into the breezeway. Crystal's every instinct told her to scoop the child into her arms and run, but there was something about the expression of terror frozen on Paula's features that held her in place.

She followed Paula's wide-eyed stare to where Helen was deflating like a balloon, punctured time and again by a knife-wielding lunatic version of herself. Her likeness was covered in the spatter of her victim and grunted like a wild animal as she hacked away with wild abandon. It was only after Helen's lifeless corpse hit the ground that she realized Crystal had entered the room.

"*You*," Lisa hissed, pointing the gore-covered knife like an extension of her finger.

"Take Virginia and get out of here. Jessica will keep you safe," Crystal said, her voice low in Paula's ear. She tried to turn Paula around, but the girl was rooted to the spot, her head reeling from the shock of what she'd just witnessed.

"B-b-but—Suze," she stammered. "I can't leave without my sister."

Crystal grabbed Paula by both shoulders, shaking her hard. "Suze is dead, Paula. I saw this woman kill her with my own two eyes."

Paula struggled to process this new information, Crystal's devastating words landing like blows. "She's—*what?*"

"How about I arrange a little reunion?"

Crystal was startled at the proximity of Lisa's husky suggestion, instinctively pushing Virginia out into the breezeway once she realized Lisa had moved within striking distance, her arm nothing more than a blur as she lunged at Paula with the knife. Paula threw her arm into its path, diverting its lethal trajectory while sustaining a long slice that cut through muscle and glanced off bone. Her jaw worked soundlessly as the color drained from her face, and she grabbed the gaping wound with her other hand, trying to hold the sides together as warm blood oozed through her clenched fingers.

"*Jessica!* Take the girls and get the hell out of here!" Crystal yelled, roughly shoving Paula through the door to the breezeway and out of harm's way. She was afraid to take her eyes off the knife as Lisa pulled it back, preparing to strike again. From the corner of her eye, Crystal spotted the rusty garden implement that Helen had foolishly abandoned. She took the handle of the hoe in both hands and used its business end like a battering ram, shattering Lisa's nose while knocking her backwards and to the ground. The knife flew from Lisa's hand, swallowed by shadows as it slid through the shaggy orange carpeting and underneath the recliner.

Crystal took the opportunity to glance quickly over her shoulder, praying that Jessica and the girls would be gone. She cried out in frustration when she spotted Paula slumped at the bottom of the stairs, unconscious and bleeding onto her jeans while Virginia stood in the middle of the room, paralyzed by fear and indecision. Jessica knelt by the door, calling the girl's name and urging her to come, but all the little girl saw was another stranger holding a gun. For a frightening second, Crystal thought Virginia was going to come running back to her.

"*Virginia!* Go with Jessica *right now!*" Crystal ordered, summoning more conviction into her voice than she thought possible. "She'll take you to Luke—I promise. Now, *go!*"

At the mention of Luke's name, something flickered in Virginia's eyes, and she began to move toward Jessica. Crystal barely had time to register relief when a flicker of movement caught her eye, and she whirled around, gripping the handle of the hoe with both hands while holding it in front of herself. Lisa was already on her feet, grinning ghoulishly as blood from her ruined nose ran over her lips, smearing her teeth. She held her hands out to her sides like a gunslinger without a weapon, flexing her fingers in eager anticipation of the inevitable conflict that was unfurling.

Crystal thrust the handle forward with both hands, driving Lisa back first one step and then another. Another volley of lightning strobed through the windows as they crossed the center of the living room, and Crystal shifted her grip on the handle, bringing it around to where she could swing it while she still had the clearance to do so. She reared back, aiming to plant the hoe's blade directly between Lisa's eyes, but as she brought the implement around, Lisa grabbed its rusty head and leaned in, using the momentum to pull Crystal off balance. She stumbled into the sitting room where she collided with the console stereo with a grunt, losing her grip on the handle as well as her breath, and she dropped to the floor. Dazed and seeing stars, Crystal instinctively rolled aside as the hoe's blade bit into the flooring where her head had just rested. She struggled to her knees as Lisa tugged on the wooden handle, trying in vain to free the blade from where her rage had buried it deep into the subflooring. As Crystal rose to her feet, Lisa suddenly let go of the handle, her feverish gaze locked on the woman who had taken so much from her. If it hadn't been for Crystal, Lisa would have never been sentenced to live like a prisoner with Nanna Grace for all those years, denied even the most basic of conveniences other girls her age had. What was so fucking *special* about this bitch that had entitled her to a life that could have been—*should have been* hers?

White-hot rage coursed through Lisa's veins as she stared at her sister, crouching in the bathroom doorway like frightened prey. With a guttural cry, Lisa charged forward, driving Crystal into the pale pink bathroom where she slipped on a puddle of water that had escaped the tub. She fell backwards, cracking her head against the tile wall before landing in the tub with an enormous splash. Lisa dropped to her knees, crab-walking through the displaced water to the edge of the tub where she leaned over the edge, placing both hands around Crystal's neck and pinning her to the bottom. She was rocked by a sensation so much stronger than déjà vu as she realized this wasn't their first time here—only this time, the stakes were so much higher. It was like coming full circle to right a tremendous wrong, and Lisa felt an extraordinary amount of satisfaction as she clamped down with renewed determination. Tiny bubbles of air escaped through Crystal's nostrils as her eyes bulged beneath the water's surface. She clawed at the flesh of Lisa's wrists and hands, but Lisa was fanatically committed to her purpose and impervious to the pain, even as Crystal's nails drew blood.

Stars multiplied and darkened, and Crystal's vision tunneled to focus on her sister's determined face, hovering just above. As the first traces of water entered her lungs, she prayed that Jessica had managed to get the girls to safety. Crystal had tried but failed. Her arms were growing heavier by the second, and she felt the fight draining out of her as the ripples in the water distorted the savage mirror image staring down at her until sweet darkness mercifully blotted it out.

Jessica watched in horror as Crystal engaged in battle against this other version of herself. She was relieved that Virginia was finally moving in her direction, and she continued to urge her forward, even as her attention kept drifting back to the two women duking it out inside the house. As much as she wanted to get the little girl to safety, she felt like she should help Crystal, too. After all, she was the one with a gun in her hand. The look on the other woman's face sent chills through Jessica, but there was no way she could safely take a shot without possibly hitting Crystal. Their struggle was too frenetic and unpredictable.

And then there was Paula.

Unconscious and defenseless at the bottom of the cinderblock stairs, she continued to lose a frightening amount of blood from the gash on the underside of her forearm. She needed urgent medical attention, and it felt wrong to just abandon her, too. Jessica felt the encroaching fingers of panic as she tried to prioritize her responsibilities.

She looked down, surprised to see that Virginia's progress had faltered, and the little girl was simply staring at her. Seeing the utter despair on her tiny face snapped Jessica's priorities into order, and she stood, reaching out towards the girl.

"It's all right, honey," she said, her voice surprisingly calm and steady. "Let's go find Luke. We'll come back for the others."

Virginia didn't budge. Her wide eyes continued to stare, and Jessica's heart sank as she realized she wasn't the focus of the child's gaze. She turned to find herself face-to-face with a gangly, dark-haired boy whose eyes positively radiated hatred. Saturated from the storm, he dripped in the doorway, his filthy t-shirt clinging to his wiry frame.

"Hello, *Mother*," he spat, sneering.

Startled, she raised her gun, but it was too late. Searing pain ripped through her left shoulder as another thunderous clap sounded, closer than ever. She stumbled back into the room, staring in disbelief at the stain spreading across her shoulder before her eyes focused on the gun Chad gripped in his own hand. Her knees went wobbly and weak, and she dropped her own gun before collapsing at Virginia's feet. She could taste something coppery in the back of her throat.

Virginia shrank away from Chad as he took a menacing step towards her, pointing the gun in her general direction. She tripped over Paula's extended foot, landing beside her on the stairs. Chad drew a lazy circle around her with the muzzle of the gun, thoroughly aroused by the heightened terror he elicited from the hysterical girl who was already screaming.

Luke choked back bile as he hurried across the street, images of Enid's gruesome remains still flashing through his mind. Rain mixed with perspiration and salty tears to sting his eyes, doubling his vision. He carried the shotgun openly, long past caring if the neighbors saw him. Let the police come—*all* of them.

He felt like he was chasing his tail as he rounded the tiny car that blocked the drive to Crystal's house, pushing his way past the severed branch that had fallen across its trunk. None of this had been here moments ago, and as Luke wondered what else he may have missed, a flash of light and a sharp crack sounded from within the house, followed by a child's high-pitched scream.

He raced around the front of the car and through the open doorway only to stumble across more carnage waiting for him in the breezeway. Paula's face was completely devoid of color as she leaned against a cinderblock step with all the grace of a rag doll that had been carelessly cast aside. Her eyes were closed, and it was too dark to see if there was any rise or fall to her chest. On the ground beside her, Jessica laid in an expanding pool of her own blood, her eyes focused on the ceiling and blinking rapidly.

Oh, Mom, no.

His eyes adjusted to the gloom, following the sound of Virginia's screams to where they originated, past where Paula sprawled on the stairs and up into the living room of the main house.

Lisa emerged from the bathroom, her soggy, wrinkled fingers dripping on the carpet. She watched as Chad whipped the little girl into hysterics, taunting her

582

with his gun. The child was so distraught she'd completely lost her bearings, screaming her fool head off and oblivious to the fact that Lisa had entered the room from behind, continuing to back away from Chad while inching closer and closer to where Lisa stood watching.

Waiting…

Slowly, Lisa held up a forefinger, catching Chad's attention as she waggled it from side-to-side and an unspoken understanding passed between them. No guns—it would be too easy. After all the trouble she'd caused along the way, dismembering this awful child was an experience that should be relished.

Lisa's hands were poised to latch on to the girl's head from behind when another pair of thunderous blasts rocked the acoustics, startling Virginia's scream to silence as Chad's eyes widened, and he staggered slightly forward, his mouth a perfect circle of surprise. The pistol slipped from his fingers and fell to the floor seconds before he dropped to his knees and planted himself face-first in the shaggy carpet, his sightless eyes frozen in perpetual shock. The back of his head had been rendered into goo by the double-shotgun blast that had also ripped into his shoulders and back. Free flowing blood rapidly soaked into his grungy t-shirt, turning it bright red as his arm flopped involuntarily beside him.

Luke stepped into the entrance, already ejecting the spent shells and reloading the rifle with an easy fluidity gleaned from years of hunting with Paulie.

The smile faltered on Lisa's lips for a fraction of a second—just long enough for a glimmer of hope to flicker in Virginia's eyes—before Lisa stepped forward and clamped her hands on either side of the child's head, lifting her like a shield. Virginia's tiny hands clamped over top of Lisa's in an effort to support some of the weight her neck was never intended to carry as her feet left the ground, pinwheeling in the air as Luke watched in horror, his previous vision rapidly coalescing into reality. He lifted the shotgun to his shoulder, sighting down the barrel, but Lisa only laughed.

"Go ahead," she dared. "Do it. You can't take me down without hitting the girl too. I mean—look at the mess you made of Chad, there. *Holy shit!* But I'll tell you a little secret—" Her sickening smile shook Luke to his very core as her fingers tightened on Virginia's head, pulling her even higher into the air. "I'm willing to die as long as this little bitch gets what's coming to her too."

"Yeah? Well, I can help you with the first part of that."

The weary voice came from behind Luke and just over his shoulder, followed immediately by an explosion that set both his ears ringing.

Lisa's smile abruptly dropped as a circular hole appeared on her forehead, nearly dead center. Her fingers tightened before releasing their grip on Virginia, and the girl was already scrambling towards Luke when she dropped to the floor.

Jessica rested against her son's broad shoulders as he leaned down to scoop Virginia into his arms, unable to hold herself upright any longer. She let the gun slip from her fingers as she eased herself to the floor, laboring to catch her breath.

Her fear that she wouldn't be able to shoot another person turned out to be baseless. Shooting a monster was a whole different matter.

Luke suddenly stiffened. "Oh, God. *Crystal.*"

He transferred a much more compliant Virginia into Jessica's care and hurried to the bathroom, his stomach in knots. Crystal stared up at him from the bottom of the tub, her hair floating in the pink-tinged bathwater, her expression perfectly tranquil.

"*No,*" he said, refusing to acknowledge what his eyes were telling him. He scooped her limp body from the tub and carried her out into the sitting room, leaving a trail of bathwater in their wake. He laid her on her back just beyond Helen's bloody corpse, alternating between patting her cheeks and listening for a heart that refused to beat. "Oh, *no-no-no-no-no—*"

"What in the—?" The startled query came from the breezeway, and Luke looked up through tear-stained eyes to find Officer Mickey Tapscott dropping the better part of a Wendy's double as he surveyed the assorted carnage, fumbling for the gun on his belt. *"Everybody freeze!"*

"You're a little late, junior," Jessica managed weakly as she tried to keep Virginia from staring at Crystal's supine form. "You've got an officer down and civilians in need of immediate medical attention. Call it in."

Tapscott's look of indecision would have been comical under less urgent circumstances. "But I—uh—"

"*Now,*" Jessie ordered, summoning the last of her energy as her eyelids fluttered and closed. Tapscott backtracked into the diminishing rain and hurried to his car, mentally tabulating the number of bodies he'd seen while realizing this was very likely the end of his career in law enforcement.

Luke continued to work over Crystal, gently at first but more urgently as time passed. He had never learned CPR although he had seen the basics, and he alternated between blowing air into Crystal's lungs and compressing her chest, afraid of cracking a rib and desperately alert for any sign of life.

She remained unresponsive.

His throat hitched, threatening to close as he renewed his efforts, thrusting his palms flat against her chest and pushing once, twice—over and over again. Hot tears fell freely from his eyes, and he nearly snarled when he felt a hand on his shoulder, pulling him back.

"Hey, fella, let me have a try." It was Officer Tapscott, kneeling beside him. "It's the one part of training I actually did pretty good at."

Luke backed up just enough to give the man access, clasping his fingers together beneath his nose and sending up a steady stream of prayers. He watched as Tapscott initiated the repetitive tasks, stopping occasionally to check progress and feeling the officer's frustration mount as nothing seemed to help. Finally, Tapscott sat back on his heels and sighed.

"I'm so sorry, sir," he said. "But she's gone."

His knees cracked as he stood, and he wandered back to the living room to watch for reinforcements through the picture window.

Luke's breath caught in his constricted throat before erupting in a wail of sorrow that filled the entire house. He pressed his face into his open palms, sobbing for a woman he had only just met but who had felt like his destiny.

A small hand rested on his forearm, and he looked up to find Virginia at his side, doing what little she could to comfort him. He was surprised that Jessica would have let the little girl wander so close, and his heart lurched again when he saw his mother's head lolling against her chest. She had either passed out or passed away, and Luke was afraid to find out which. Either way, she was beyond caring for the girl who stood by his side.

"Don't look, honey," he said, putting an arm around Virginia's shoulders. "She wouldn't want you to see her this way."

But Virginia's curiosity wasn't that easily satiated.

She ducked out from underneath his arm and crossed to where Crystal lay on the floor. She knelt down beside her, adjusting wet tendrils of hair that partially obscured her face before leaning in to very gently kiss her forehead, and Luke's heart broke all over again.

He stood, prepared to pick Virginia up and carry her outside when Crystal suddenly spasmed, her limbs twitching as her eyelids fluttered. She rolled onto her side, coughing up what seemed like endless gallons of bathwater.

Luke stood speechless over her, his mouth hanging open as Officer Tapscott raced back into the room. "What in the—?" he sputtered. He dropped to his knees beside Crystal. "Oh, my Lord! I just made a miracle. I—I—*Miss?* Are you alright? Can you speak to me? *Miss?*"

Virginia stood, easing her hand into Luke's as she smiled up at him.

Sirens approached in the distance.

585

EPILOGUE

The afternoon sky was painted in near-perfect cerulean hues with a bank of cumulus clouds collecting along the western horizon. It was hot and humid, and Crystal fanned herself under the cover of the newly constructed deck that spanned the back of the house, still redolent of freshly cut lumber. A pitcher of lemonade sweated beads of perspiration on an ancient picnic table that squatted incongruously in its new home, a trio of plastic tumblers stacked beside it.

"You're not getting too hot out there, are you?" Crystal called, her voice carrying across the enormous grassy expanse that comprised their rear acreage. "I've got some lemonade whenever you're ready!"

Virginia's giggles carried back to her as the little girl responded, "Watch this!" She sprinted for several feet through grass that needed mowing before launching herself through a chain of cartwheels culminating in a dramatic backflip that always caused Crystal to hold her breath, afraid the child might misjudge her rotation and land on her perfect little head.

Virginia *always* stuck the landing—not even a trace of bounce once her feet met solid ground. She struck a pose while Crystal applauded, and then she was off again, fueled by endless energy that is reserved strictly for the young.

Phoebe, their Miniature Australian Shepherd, trailed along behind, nearly lost in the tallish grass, yapping enthusiastically before rolling on the lawn herself, albeit a lot less gracefully. Virginia dropped down beside the dog to lavish her with attention, and before long, they were up and off, zigzagging through the yard and playing tag amongst the wild dandelions.

Just as Crystal felt the vague stirrings of a breeze nudging the stagnant air, a pair of strong arms embraced her from behind, latching fingers in front of her growing midsection.

"Hey, you," she said, laying her head back against Luke's chest and smiling. "I didn't hear your truck."

Luke kissed her neck. "Can't stay but a minute. Darby's supposed to have the rest of my lumber ready, and that includes those fancy French double doors you picked out."

Crystal turned into his arms, straining to return his hug. She was just entering her third trimester and felt as big as a house. "Hallelujah," she said. "I'm tired of dealing with that thing."

She indicated the heavy-duty tarp Luke had tacked up over the gaping hole in the back of Old Paulie's house that would eventually serve as the rear entrance from the deck. On windy days, its flapping was a noisy nuisance, and on more than one occasion, it had provided access to critters best left outside, most memorably a startled skunk. It was all part of the process of building their dream home with Paulie's cabin serving as the structural foundation. It was the perfect blend of things old and new.

There was a time when the inability to secure the premises would have kept Crystal awake at night, but those days were quickly fading into distant memories. That wasn't to say that they had abandoned due diligence. Every room had a weapon stashed and ammunition at the ready should darkness dare to show its ugly face, and Luke and Crystal made target practice a regular activity to ensure they remained sharp and on point. They had fought hard for this family, and they would protect it at any cost.

It had been a little over a year since the events that brought them all together.

They stood with their arms around each other watching Virginia cavort with her faithful dog, her melodious laughter carrying back to the deck as they romped and rolled about.

"School's going to be starting soon," said Crystal. "They're telling me she's testing way above her age. They're talking about her going straight into first grade."

"I can't say I'm surprised," said Luke. "Are you?"

Crystal shrugged. "Not really. I just can't help but wonder if it's all too much—too fast."

"She's not having the nightmares again, is she?"

Crystal shook her head. "No more than usual. In fact, I'd probably say less."

Luke slowly nodded his head, remembering all too well those rare occasions when Virginia would erupt from a deep sleep, screaming as if her very life depended on it, memories of her family's murder emerging unexpectedly and seemingly out of nowhere. Luke could certainly empathize.

His night terrors were much more frequent.

He tried his best to hide it from Crystal, and while she humored his valiant attempts at bravado, it was hard to keep that kind of secret in their marital bed. He would likely be embarrassed to know how many nights she watched over him, waiting for his quickened pulse to return to some semblance of normal so he might slip back into a tenuous sleep before a new day began.

"Paula should be home this evening," said Crystal. Paula had spent the earlier part of the week touring the University of Kentucky with her friend, Chelsea. The two girls hit it off while working at the Dollar store in town over the summer and were planning to room together in the fall. "It always feels better when both our girls are home."

Luke nodded his head, fulfilled in a way he had never imagined. He had gone from complete loner to family patriarch in the short space of a year. "Do you think Mom is happy down here?" he asked absently.

Crystal snorted. "I don't think she's ever been happier, and I'm not gonna lie, I'm thrilled she's agreed to help when the baby comes along. I don't know that I could handle all this without her."

They leaned into each other comfortably, watching as Virginia investigated a thatch of wild honeysuckle. A family of butterflies seemed drawn to her across the meadow, and she was delighted to make their acquaintance once she spotted them.

"What do you—" Luke cleared his throat, his voice trailing away.

Crystal looked up at her husband. "What do I what?"

Luke was sheepish, his cheeks brightening. "What do you think she—you know," he said, fumbling for the right word. *"Is?"*

Crystal's smile was immediate. "She's just a little girl, silly."

Luke's gaze was serious when he met her eyes. "You know that's not *all* she is," he said.

Crystal tightened her grip around his waist, pondering his words while struggling for her own. Finally, she sighed. "The only thing I know for sure is the world is a better place with her in it. She may find the cure for cancer, AIDS—end poverty—who knows? At this point, her potential is unlimited. I guess we'll just have to wait and see."

Almost as if she heard them discussing her, Virginia turned a bright smile in their direction and waved. Luke and Crystal returned the wave just as a low rumble of thunder sounded in the distance. Shielding her eyes, Crystal realized the bank of clouds along the western horizon had grown heavy and dark, drifting lazily toward them on the first real vestiges of a breeze she'd felt all afternoon. She extracted herself from Luke's embrace.

"Better go get that lumber, Mister," she said, beckoning for Virginia to return to the deck. "There's a storm brewin'."

Meanwhile
Just outside Bayou La Batre, Alabama

Rain lashed the walls and windows of the old cabin relentlessly as the storm raged overhead. Howard had placed an assortment of buckets, pots, and pans to collect the water dripping and, in some cases, pouring, through a roof that had seen better days. The power had long since failed, and the only illumination was provided by lanterns and handheld flashlights.

Maggie held the swaddled newborn against her chest, her hammering heartbeat lost amidst the screams of Vera Newton, who lay on blood-drenched bed sheets in the tiny back bedroom of the three-room shack. Maggie was a trained midwife, but nothing had prepared her for anything quite like this. Just when she thought Mrs. Newton's screams couldn't get any louder, her agony pushed her into a new range of decibels.

Maggie had gladly left the room as soon as Howard Newton returned with Dr. Taymor, both men drenched to the bone. They were forced to abandon their vehicle on the other side of the culvert, braving the footbridge as the only access to the islet for vehicles had been swept away by the violent storm. With heavy lightning and tornadoes threatening the entire tri-county area, it was a miracle they had arrived at all.

Maggie found herself humming absently as she rocked the child, trying in vain to drown out the urgency of Mr. Newton's pleas interspersed with Dr. Taymor's increasingly grim directives.

"You've got to help her, Doc—"

"Steady your hand with that light, Howard! I can't see where all this goddamn blood is coming from—"

"I can't do this without her—"

"More towels, dammit! Get me some more towels!"

As Maggie's mind struggled to process her sensory overload, it suddenly occurred to her the one sound she *wasn't* hearing.

The baby wasn't crying.

Oh, God, no, she thought, taking the child back to the small kitchen where a kerosene lantern glowed from the counter. She moved the lantern over to the small table where the Newtons normally ate their meals and laid the baby down, fumbling with his blanket and carefully unwrapping him.

The boy was still, his eyes closed.

Maggie's throat constricted as a fresh wave of grief seized control. How could she possibly deliver this news to Mr. Newton? Judging from the commotion in the other room, the fight to save Vera was already a losing battle.

Maggie gasped.

The child stirred, and out of the corner of her teary eye, she saw it. She placed her hands on the boy's tiny bare chest and gave him the smallest of nudges, desperate to see the movement repeated. He was just so *still*.

Didn't most newborns cry?

Maggie's heart began to sink as she decided it must have been a trick of the flickering lantern, but then the little boy's eyelids flickered and opened. Hysterical laughter broke through the grief holding her throat hostage.

Maggie's sense of elation was cut short as she looked into the tiny eyes that studied her, eyes that were nothing but pupil. An icy finger traced its way down Maggie's spine as Vera Newton rent the air with one final, agonized shriek.

The boy smiled.

THE END

acknowledgements

I've always loved a good thriller.

When I was a child, my parents refused to let me read or watch anything even remotely scary because I was prone to nightmares—and when I say nightmares, I'm not talking about the type that startle you from sleep only to settle back in once you've gotten your bearings. I mean the ones that send you screaming into your parents' room with boogeymen hot on your heels. I must've shaved years off their lives. In fact, they both passed in their early seventies. *Hmmm…*

It only made me more determined to immerse myself in the material. Something about the surge of adrenaline, the heightened tension, the primal *fear*—it drew me in every time. After reading countless books by Stephen King, Dean Koontz, Peter Straub, John Saul, and so many others, it was really only a matter of time before I tried my hand at something a little darker. While I will always love Dwayne, Melanie, and that whole gang, it was refreshing to shift gears and try something new.

My editing team was a little different this go-round, as Lynne Hobstetter simply doesn't care much for horror or stories with this sort of length, and that's perfectly alright. I'll still be having lunch with her on Saturday. Teri Lott and Traci Steele were willing to give it a go, as were a group of beta readers who surprised me with the level of high-quality feedback they provided. Great big shout-outs to Rob Neto, Amanda Collier, Dawn Weast, and Arlyse DeLoyola. This book is undeniably better for all of their input, and any mistakes that still remain belong solely to me. Thank you for putting in the community service. It's a hefty read.

Special thanks go to my niece, Crystal Helms, and her husband, Chad. The two of you had been dating for all of ten minutes when I stole your names and used them in this story. It's like I knew even then we'd be laughing about it all these years later. The real Chad is just the nicest guy. Here's hoping his sense of humor is as good as I think it is…

Last but never least, the biggest thanks go to each and every one of you who has given this book a chance. It's miles removed from Dwayne's world, but I'm getting a little too old to worry about taking risks. I hope you enjoyed reading it as much as I enjoyed writing it.

I've already shifted gears and am working on completing the seventh Dwayne Morrow book, *Deception,* but I suspect I have a bit more darkness to share, too.

Stay tuned.

Until next time,
Darin Miller
Grove City, Ohio – August 2024

ALSO AVAILABLE

REUNION
Dwayne Morrow Mystery #1

CIRCUMVENTION
Dwayne Morrow Mystery #2

RETRIBUTION
Dwayne Morrow Mystery #3

DIVERSION
Dwayne Morrow Mystery #4

ISOLATION
Dwayne Morrow Mystery #5

ABDUCTION
Dwayne Morrow Mystery #6

DECEPTION
Dwayne Morrow Mystery #7

DELUSION
Dwayne Morrow Mystery #8

OVER CONSUMPTION
*A Dwayne Morrow and Jane Bond
Novella
(Co-written with V.R. Tapscott)*

OTHER WORK

BROKEN BITS AND BOBS
*A Collection of What Ifs, What Was,
and What Never Should Be*

HOUSE OF SECRETS
*Every Room Holds a Story
(Contributor, "Redemption")*

THE LIBRARY
CENTENNIAL
ANTHOLOGY
*Celebrating the Lives and People of the
SPL Community
(Contributor, "Meredith's Bad Day")*

DID YOU LIKE ME?

☐ YES! ☐ NO ☐ MAYBE?

May I ask a favor?

If you enjoyed reading this book as much as I enjoyed writing it, won't you please consider leaving a rating and/or review on Amazon, Goodreads, Barnes & Noble, BookBub, or anywhere else you might see fit? It only takes a moment to leave a rating and a maybe a couple more for a short review—even a simple 'I would recommend this book!' will do nicely.

Word of mouth is the single most powerful tool in an Indie author's toolkit, and ratings and reviews help more than you may realize in growing our audience. Think of it as a gratuity you might leave a server after an evening of fine dining, but this gratuity doesn't cost a thing—only a few moments of your time.

Thank you for your kind consideration.

Darin

Amazon   Goodreads   Barnes & Noble   BookBub

ABOUT THE AUTHOR

Darin Miller was born in Portsmouth but currently resides in Grove City, both of which are located in Ohio. While he has worked in Information Technology for three decades, he has *not* solved a single, solitary crime to date. He is the BookFest award-winning author of the Ohio-based *Dwayne Morrow Mystery* series, as well as an unrelated short story collection, *Broken Bits and Bobs,* and a standalone psychological horror thriller, *Equilibrium.* With equal parts action, humor, suspense and mystery, the *Dwayne Morrow* series features characters you're sure to love—and in some cases, loathe.

Stay current with updates, short stories, and other special promotions at www.darin-miller.com.

www.ingramcontent.com/pod-product-compliance
Lightning Source LLC
Chambersburg PA
CBHW050838030726
47503CB00007BA/2218

* 9 7 8 1 9 6 3 3 2 5 0 4 1 *